SECRETS

OF THE

MAGICKAL

GRIMOIRES

About the Author

Aaron Leitch has been a scholar and spiritual seeker for over a decade. His explorations have taken him into many fascinating areas of human spirituality, their history and their modern practice. His writings (both in print and on the web) cover such varied fields as Middle Eastern religion and mythology, shamanism, Neoplatonism, Hermeticism and alchemy, traditional Wicca and Neopaganism, the Hermetic Order of the Golden Dawn, Thelema, angelology, Qabalah, Enochiana, psychology and consciousness expansion, cyberspace, modern social commentary, and several student resources. His most recent project is *Secrets of the Magickal Grimoires*, released by Llewllyn Worldwide in August 2005.

To Write to the Author

If you wish to contact the author or would like more information about this book, please write to the author in care of Llewellyn Worldwide and we will forward your request. Both the author and publisher appreciate hearing from you and learning of your enjoyment of this book and how it has helped you. Llewellyn Worldwide cannot guarantee that every letter written to the author can be answered, but all will be forwarded. Please write to:

Aaron Leitch
℅ Llewellyn Worldwide
2143 Wooddale Drive
Woodbury, MN 55125-2989

Please enclose a self-addressed stamped envelope for reply,
or $1.00 to cover costs. If outside U.S.A., enclose
international postal reply coupon.

Many of Llewellyn's authors have websites with additional information and resources.

For more information, please visit our website at

http://www.llewellyn.com

SECRETS

OF THE

MAGICKAL

GRIMOIRES

The Classical Texts
of Magick Deciphered

AARON LEITCH

Llewellyn Publications
Woodbury, Minnesota

First Edition
Fifth Printing, 2015

Cover design by Lisa Novak
Editing by Tom Bilstad
Interior art provided by the author

Llewellyn is a registered trademark of Llewellyn Worldwide Ltd.

Library of Congress Cataloging-in-Publication Data

Leitch, Aaron, 1974–
Secrets of the magickal grimoires: the classical texts of magick decyphered / Aaron Leitch. -- 1st ed.
P. cm.
Includes bibliographical references.
ISBN 978-0-7387-0303-9
 1 Magic. 2. Solomon, King of Israel. 3. Mysticism—History. I. Title.
 2 BF1611.L44   2005
 3 133.4'3'09—dc22

Llewellyn Publications
A Division of Llewellyn Worldwide Ltd.
2143 Wooddale Drive
Woodbury, MN 55125-2989
www.llewellyn.com

Printed in the United States of America

Grimoire

('Grim war') From the French; translated into English as "Grammar."

Merriam-Webster's Dictionary:

Grammar: n. . . . 3 a : a grammar textbook . . . 4 : the principals or rules of an art, science, or technique . . .

Etymology: Middle English *gramere*, from Middle French *gramaire*, modification of Latin *grammatica*, from Greek *grammatikE*, from feminine of *grammatikos* of letters, from *grammat-,gramma* . . . Date: 14th century.

In popular modern usage, the word *grimoire* refers specifically to a set of medieval European magickal texts (notebooks, journals, and teaching aids) that record that culture's form of practical magick. Their main focus is the summoning of spiritual entities (celestial and infernal) for various shamanic purposes.

Contents

Acknowledgments

First and foremost, I wish to thank the many people who have taken an inconceivable interest in my efforts. Many of them have been my teachers, some have offered me wonderful opportunities, and most of them have done both: Chic and Sandra Tabatha Cicero, Steve Kinney, Stuart Myers, John Pilato, AJ Rose, Tony Hutchins, Philip Farber, and Brendan Tripp. And such dedicated authors as Donald Michael Kraig, Janet and Stewart Farrar, Robert Anton Wilson, Robert Heinlein, and the many others who have changed my life without knowing it.

Special thanks in regards to this book, as well as many other projects, must go to: Carrie Mikell and Ocha'ni Lele for their invaluable input on the subjects of African-descended spirituality, Carrie Mikell again for the contribution of her artwork, Steve Kinney for helping me slay the Illustration Dragon, as well as Mitch Hensen, Bick Thomas, and most of the great folks listed above.

And, finally, to the fond memory and legacy of Matthew Sparks.
"The Entertainer."

Preface

It is often difficult for people living in the twenty-first century to appreciate the intelligence, beliefs, and nobility of those who lived in medieval Europe from roughly 476 to 1453 C.E. This period, sandwiched between antiquity and the beginning of the Renaissance, is often described contemptuously as the "Dark Ages," even by a good many of today's magicians, priests, and priestesses. And yet the methods and esoteric knowledge of medieval magic, which was itself drawn from ancient sources, formed the ancestral backbone of what would later come to be known as modern ceremonial magic. The magical worldview of the medieval mages was largely carried over into the Renaissance, where it continued to fascinate the leading scholars of the day. Renaissance academics and magicians, such as Marsilio Ficino, Pico della Mirandola, and Henry Cornelius Agrippa, came to see magic not as some left-over relic of a superstitious age, but rather as an enlightened philosophy, a sublime science, and a part of the natural order of the world.

In order to comprehend medieval magic, it is necessary to examine the primary repositories of this knowledge—the grimoires, or magical texts containing spells, incantations, and ritual instructions for working with angels and conjuring spirits. This is not an easy task for modern readers who are often bewildered and sometimes put off by the antiquated language of these texts, not to mention the fact that many grimoires seem incomplete or are written in a manner which assumes that the reader is already familiar with grimoiric techniques.

To understand the grimoires within their own context, we must not look at them through the eyes of twenty-first century readers with modern sensibilities. We must examine them with the eyes of the medieval magician, who lived in a world much harsher than our own: famine, epidemic illness, religious persecution, and warfare often meant that human life was cheap. As a result, the magic employed by medieval mages to protect home and hearth was a very serious business and not for the faint of heart.

A better understanding of the grimoires can be arrived at by delving into the life and times of the magicians who wrote them. This involves an evaluation of the historical perspectives, the social and cultural realities, and the religious mindset of the world these magicians lived in, as well as a detailed exploration of magical practices outlined in the grimoires themselves. It also involves an examination of the more archaic magical practices of Babylonia, the ancient Hebrews, and the Hellenistic world, for these ancient cultures had an enormous influence on European magicians and on their magical writings.

Aaron Leitch's *Secrets of the Magical Grimoires* provides a tremendous amount of new insight into the world of the medieval mage. By clarifying the objectives and procedures covered in these texts and spell-books, Leitch sheds light upon a subject which has been greatly misunderstood for far too long. In addition, he provides a valuable comparison between many of the magical practices described in the grimoires and various shamanic methods of working with the spirit world.

It is refreshing to hear the historical and anthropological facts about *goety*, or working with lower or infernal spirits—one area of magic that is covered in the grimoires. Leitch reveals that the roots of goetic magic can be found in ancient shamanic practices which dealt with the exorcism expulsion, or binding of evil spirits, which were often associated with illness, disease, and other forms of misfortune. The shamanic exorcist had to be a mage of the highest spiritual purity and training in order to carry out this dangerous duty and protect his community from harmful spirits. Compare this to the flippant attitude of some modern magical dabblers and psychobabblers who contend that no spirit could ever hurt anyone, or that such spirits only exist in the mind. The fact that exorcism of harmful spirits is the origin of goetic magic is certainly lost on the throngs of ill-trained people who wish to evoke goetic spirits for fun and profit, or invoke them as part of some sexual exercise.

One of the greatest assets of this present work is the meticulous attention paid to the subject of theurgy or "god working," which Leitch describes as "the heart of our work." Theurgy is designed to elevate the magician's soul toward the celestial realms by invoking and communicating with angels, archangels, and various levels of deity. The detailed regimen of magical work, purity, humility, and self-control required of a medieval theurgist should leave the reader with little doubt that the spiritual path of the adept magician is a high caliber discipline that takes work, perseverance, and dedication.

This book is also invaluable for the manner in which it helps to explain and clarify the work of Agrippa, the influential sixteenth-century mage whose magnum opus, *Three Books of Occult Philosophy*, was a primary source book for later Hermetic magicians. Other important and well-known grimoires, such as the *Key of Solomon* and the *Book of the Sacred Magic of Abramelin the Mage* are also covered at length. Rarely have these works been examined with such thoroughness.

With the publication of *Secrets of the Magical Grimoires*, the magic of our medieval predecessors has finally been removed from the "Dark Ages" of modern misconception to the light of day.

Chic Cicero
Sandra Tabatha Cicero
Metatron House
Autumnal Equinox, 2001

Introduction

The magick of the medieval "grimoiric" texts has long mystified and fascinated the people of our culture. Especially in the 1980s, we saw the rise of knights-in-armor role-playing games and fantasy literature, even a fad for "choose your own adventure" books, literally overflowing with wizards and natural magick. Even today—on television, film, and print—we are presented with images of white linen robes, arcane sigils, and the utterance of names in long-dead tongues. We see magickal circles, tools crafted in tribal fashion, mysterious rites, and daring sorcerers summoning forth demonic princes from the mists. Very often obscure books are credited for the magick, even said to be alive themselves, and given names such as *The Key of Solomon* or the *Grand Grimoire*.

Such is the manifestation of classical occultism in modern pop culture, especially that of my own early years. When I began my studies of the magickal arts, I found I possessed a natural inclination toward the romanticism of renaissance and medieval literature and philosophy—especially in the realm of magickal practice. However, I quickly learned that such information was difficult to acquire. I had discovered enough information to be on the lookout for various names:[1] *Key of Solomon the King, Goetia, Three Books of Occult Philosophy, The Magus, Book of the Sacred Magic of Abramelin the Mage*, etc. Over the next few years I gathered these very titles, attempting to gain a view of the realities behind the cultural legends. The problem I then faced was a difficulty in understanding them; they were presented in such a befuddled and obscure fashion as to seem impossible on a practical level.

Advice from others was no help at all. My neopagan peers only warned me away from the texts—reciting the same old, and rather stale, stories of *Necronomicon* and Ouija board infamy. They also spoke cryptically about the Judeo-Christian nature of the texts (a big negative in those times), and the horrible manner in which innocent spirits were browbeaten into servitude by the Solomonic practitioner. My colleagues in the ceremonial communities merely chuckled at my interest and suggested I not get myself mired within the superstitious prattle of uneducated men from the past. In many cases, it was strongly implied that any magick from before the early twentieth century was useless today. So the classical grimoires languished on my bookshelf, existing as historical curiosities more than anything else. In the meantime, I pursued interests in the Qabalah and Hermetic magick as well as studies of the ancient Middle East (especially Egypt, Canaan, and Mesopotamia). All of these areas of study proved useful later, as we shall see in this book.

Still, the older texts called to me, even if their medieval language was incomprehensible. It was after many years of off-and-on searching that the breakthroughs began to occur. I attribute these breakthroughs to a few specific events:

First, I took a serious interest in the art of summoning (or evocation), especially the angels from the Qabalistic Tree of Life. It is perhaps needless to state that this interest was born directly from my romance with the classical grimoires. While I could not yet use the older texts properly, I was lucky to have access to the study and practice of modern techniques, such as the methods taught in *Modern Magick*, or the evocation rite buried deep within Israel Regardie's *The Golden Dawn*. With these sources at hand, I set out to become proficient in the rites. I moved forward slowly, by trial and error, and it eventually became impressively effective.

Although these techniques differ in many ways from the medieval traditions I wished to experience, they still succeeded in grounding me in "the basics" of spirit work. That is, those specific points of practical technique that are universal to all forms of magick. By doing this (i.e., by actively experiencing the process of evocation), I learned much about the nature of spirits and how to interact with them from a practical standpoint. To an extent, I was even able to begin making heads and tails of the grimoires themselves. I began to recognize the procedures that the two traditions held in common; eventually, I began to draw from the *Key of Solomon the King* and the *Goetia*, making use of their prayers and conjurations where I could in my own ceremonies.

The angels and earthbound spirits slowly emerged as living beings, with existences and agendas distinct from my own. Angels, especially, tended to come and go as they wished; and when I petitioned an angel for help with a problem, my environment reacted strongly. At times the ceremonies were not even necessary on my part. In general, the angels called upon me with lessons, guidance, and information much more often than I used the ceremonies to call upon them. I found that I had developed a very recognizable relationship with the intelligences of my natural environment, and they have exerted their will upon my life as much as I have done toward them.

This was entirely different from what I had been taught to expect. Modern descriptions of evocation are most often based upon a "summon-question-banish" formula, while the classical texts describe a system of ongoing relationships with individual spirits. The more I understood of this, the more sense I was able to make of the *Keys*. My performances of modern rituals such as the Pentagram and Hexagram in conjunction with the grimoiric invocations became uncomfortable "breaks" to the flow of the rites. The grimoiric methods struck me as something akin to tribal shamanism, rather than the ceremonial magick of today. The two systems of modern and medieval magick are from different times and are ultimately based upon entirely different principles.

The next piece of the puzzle fell into place when I entered communication with other experienced mages via the Internet, especially through an e-mail list dedicated to "Enochian" magick. I had long felt drawn toward this magickal system: a form of angelic summoning that promised to make the more common Qabalistic methods pale in comparison. I had a number of books that focused upon the Golden Dawn and Thelemic versions of the magick, and only two that addressed the original system as recorded by the Renaissance magus Dr. John Dee and his skryer Edward Kelley.[2] The only problem was that these men lived in the late 1500s, which placed their work with the other classical grimoires, and made them just as incomprehensible.

Through the mailing list, however, I found myself connected to the top minds in the field, true scholars who knew the material and its history, and practical occultists who had put their knowledge to use. Most importantly, they studied the system in its Renaissance origins. They knew the meanings behind the obscure Elizabethan language of Dee and his angels, and they were happy to teach me all I would learn. Eventually, I became much more familiar with medieval and Renaissance culture and literature. I could comprehend the texts, and even take part in the studies and scholarship of the others on the list. A veil had finally been lifted from the obscure English (somewhat akin to grasping the language of Shakespeare or the King James' Bible), and I could progress to study all of the classical texts.

At last, I felt a call to put one of the grimoires to practical use. The grimoire of choice was a heavily involved angelic summoning ceremony, which included several months of ritual purification and invocation. One of the first instructions in the procedure was to enter a half year study of the grimoire itself before attempting the rites. Doing so allowed me to organize the instructions and practical secrets hidden throughout the book into workable notes; as well as to gather and assemble the various tools necessary for the magick. Directly experiencing the process in this manner, and being forced to delve so deeply into the writing itself, taught me much about how such magick works and how the authors of the classical texts were thinking.

As luck would have it, two final events occurred in my favor within that study period. These experiences completely altered my magickal worldview and ultimately made my performance of a purely grimoiric rite possible. The first event in question was my introduction to the Afro-Cuban faiths of Santeria and Palo Mayombe. The second was my study of Agrippa's the *Three Books of Occult Philosophy*. I feel that these were the most significant factors in my eventual understanding of the classical grimoires.

I will save the results of that research for chapter 2, which is itself concerned with the subject of a magickal worldview and the relationship between the magick of the grimoires and tribal shamanism. Before we continue, however, I would like to outline the factual history of the classical grimoires to counterbalance the romantic mythologies described above.

---

1. A book titled *A Dictionary of Angels*, by Gustav Davidson, offered me much information in the form of provocative looks at many grimoiric texts. Don Kraig's *Modern Magick* also offers glimpses of two texts, along with an introductory course on summoning spirits, or "evocation," from a modern standpoint.

2. These were *The Enochian Magick of Dr. John Dee* by Geoffrey James and *The Complete Enochian Dictionary* by Donald Laycock. A third book, *Enochian Magick for Beginners* by Donald Tyson, was not yet published.

PART ONE

Oculta Philosophia

Medieval Magick

The Medieval and Renaissance Eras[1]

The "classical age" of the grimoiric texts is roughly equivalent to the span of the Middle (or medieval) and Renaissance ages. The Middle Ages began roughly in the fifth century CE, when the western empire of Rome was both infiltrated and violently overrun by Germanic tribes. This is when the famous sacking of Rome took place at the hands of the Vandals, in the year 455 CE. The established government was slowly inched out of power, and Italy became little more than an extension of a German kingdom. The vast western Roman Empire faded away, and was replaced by a wholly agricultural society.

The eastern Roman government, however, was not willing to simply vanish into the pages of history. It quickly shifted from its past political structure and focused upon a theocracy instead. Much of the groundwork for this was set as early as the mid-300s, when the Roman emperor Constantine decided to take action against the fragmentation of his empire. He saw his chance within the various religious cults of Christianity (which had steadily gained popularity with the people regardless of attempts to exterminate it), and the already widespread worship of Mithras (a rather Christ-like solar god). If the people could be united under one religious structure, then the entire land would finally be controllable again.

In 325 CE, Constantine called together the famous Council of Nice—where four hundred bishops gathered to establish a unified and government-controlled religion. Constantine built churches across the land and enforced the observance of the new faith. Highly adept at persuading his people, he combined the most popular elements of Christianity with those of other cults such as Mithraism in order to make the new doctrine as attractive as possible. His maneuvering paid off; as this was the foundation of what would become the "Holy Roman Empire." (A few hundred years later, it would take on that very name under the rule of Charlemagne.)

The decisions of the Council of Nice—recorded as the Nicene Creed—became something of a holy scripture itself. It contained the specific outline of what *made* one a Christian, in the form of theological beliefs. For example, one line of the Creed reads as follows:

> We believe in the Holy Spirit,
>
> The Lord and Giver of Life,
>
> Who proceedeth from the Father.

The Nicene Council is often considered the birth of Catholicism, but this is not entirely the case. Originally, the Christian religion was quite decentralized,[2] and any given church had its own way of doing things. When issues arose that concerned the religion as a whole, large gatherings of bishops and religious leaders were called together so the issues could be debated and ruled upon. The Council of Nice itself is an example of this process.

It was not until three hundred years later that a major schism took place within the organization, creating two distinct branches of the faith: Orthodox and Catholic. Though it may be hard to believe, the division was created by the inclusion of a single Latin word into a song. This was done by a French priest who was working on setting the Nicene Creed (in Latin) to the music of Gregorian chant. Apparently, he had trouble with the line quoted above,[3] as the meter of the song left a few notes of the chant without lyrics. In order to "flesh out" the words to fit the music, the priest added the four-syllable word *filioque* onto the line—changing it to:

> We believe in the Holy Spirit,
>
> The Lord and Giver of Life,
>
> Who proceedeth from the Father, *and from the Son.*

As the song became popular, it brought the theological implications of the lyrical addition into the spotlight. One camp saw little problem with the inclusion, while others felt it inappropriate to alter the Creed—especially where it concerned the natures of both the Holy Spirit and Jesus Christ. In 589 CE, the Third Council of Toledo officially accepted the new word into the Creed, and effectively divided the faith in two. Those who refused to accept the new Creed separated into the Eastern Orthodox faith (centralized in Constantinople under the guidance of the "ecumenical patriarch"), and those who remained became the Catholic Church (centralized in Rome under the "pope").

Such was the state of Europe at the beginning of the medieval era, ruled by its Germanic kings and Catholic clergy. The people gathered together upon "manors," which consisted of the landlord's castle, the church, a village, and the farmlands that surrounded them. These manors were actually land grants given by the king to powerful noblemen. In return, the noblemen had to declare loyalty, and promise tribute and access to military troops to the king. The noblemen then divided their land amongst various lesser nobles called "vassals," or land barons. Finally, the land barons contracted peasants ("serfs") to tend and cultivate the farmland in return for military protection. This was the basic structure of the feudal economic system. The serfs were uneducated, traveled very little, and were heavily taxed by their landlords. The rulers themselves were constantly embattled in petty political and military intrigue.

By the seventh century, the religion of Islam arose upon the Arabian peninsula, and swept through the middle east. Its armies defeated the Byzantine and Persian kingdoms that ruled there, and took control of the Holy Land by the year 638 CE. Over the next three centuries, the Arabians pushed northwestward onto the continent of Europe—engaging in a holy war against the empire of the Christians.

In the eleventh century, the Christians were experiencing more difficulty at home. The East/West schism that had begun nearly half a century before finally came to a boil in 1054 CE. In an effort to mend the dissolving relationship between the Churches, emissaries from Rome[4] journeyed to Constantinople and visited the ecumenical patriarch. Unfortunately, the discussions failed, and ultimately ended with both sides casting anathemas of excommunication at each other. The schism was complete, and the Eastern Orthodox Church had no involvement in the later actions of the Roman Catholic Church.[5]

Meanwhile, the Turks displaced the Arabians as the rulers of Islam. Where Arabian rulers had often been tolerant of the Christians' interest in the Holy Land, the Turks were not so kind. Christian pilgrims to the Middle East soon found themselves traveling in armed bands for protection against Turkish attackers. In the year 1095 CE, the Byzantine emperor, Alexios I Komnenos, sent an urgent plea for help to Pope Urban II. The sympathetic pope addressed a council of leaders in Clermont, and the Crusades were created in answer. The Holy Land thus became a place of bitter religious war.

There were several Crusades that took place over the next few hundred years, all directed against non-Christian peoples. The warrior class of Europe had become a religious order in its own right, fighting one holy war after another in the name of God and king. Military conquest continued even after the loss of the Holy Land to the Turks in 1291 CE, though this date is often considered the "official" end of the Crusades.

The Knights Templar arose in the environment of the Crusades in 1118 CE. They were a mystery cult of warrior-monks who protected the merchant lanes of the Holy Land and practiced the rites of ancient Gnostic Christianity. They were established at the site of the Temple of Solomon in Jerusalem by the French king Baldwin II. By 1128 they had been confirmed by Pope Honorius II at the Council of Troyes. As the Holy Land fell to Islam, the Templars slowly withdrew toward Paris, and finally established their headquarters at the Temple Monastery there.

The Knights Templar had grown in wealth and power over the years, and eventually excited the greed of the king of France, Phillipe le Bel. Declaring that the mystery rites of the order were heresy to the Church, he began to systematically destroy the order one member at a time. All of the treasure of the Templars was to go directly to his coffers, but none of its members could be coerced or tortured into revealing its whereabouts. Phillipe had wasted his efforts. In a final maneuver, he attempted to demand judgment against the Templars from the pope. When the holy leader refused to be manipulated, the king dismissed him and instated his own man, the Bishop of Bordeaux, as Pope Clement V. This pope gladly issued a papal bull suppressing the Templar order in 1312 CE.

This was the basis of the dreaded Inquisitions. Their stated objective was to discover heresy within the Church, and thus rid the world of all rival Christian (i.e., non-Catholic) groups. The Templars were merely the first to fall, with their Grand Master Jaques de Molay burned at the stake with several others in March of 1314. The order went underground, and its history becomes shaded from that point forward.

The "Holy Inquisition" had been growing since the twelfth century, though it had not become institutionalized (under the governance of Dominican monks) until the thirteenth century. In 1231 Pope Gregory IX declared life imprisonment for heretics who confessed and repented, and death for those who refused. Once rival Christian sects had been obliterated, the Church turned its attentions toward others. Two Dominican monks—Heinrich Kramer and James Sprenger—penned the *Malleus Maleficarum* (Witches' Hammer) in 1468 CE; a text of hatred, lies, and methods of torture dedicated to the eradication of Pagan practices.[6] It is in this book that we find the stereotypical images of medieval witches, midnight sabbaths, black witchcraft, and pacts with Satan. It also happened to give exceedingly graphic instructions for torture, and outlined some of the ludicrous "tests" for witchcraft with which many of us are familiar today. Needless to say, this was the textbook upon every Inquisitor's desk. As late as 1492, the queen of Spain established the Spanish Inquisition—aimed at the conversion, expulsion, or eradication of its Jewish and Moslem people. This latter was by far the bloodiest chapter of the Inquisitorial period.

This entire episode of human history in medieval Europe is where we find very little beyond bloodshed and ignorance. There was little cultural advancement, much ancient knowledge was lost forever, and the world existed under the iron fist of a Church gone mad.

However, there was some light during these dark times. The 1200s saw great gatherings of scholars and philosophers in Spain and other areas of Europe. This class of people did not harbor the all-too-common religious bigotry of the day, and they met Christian, Muslim, Jew, and Pagan alike. It was here that the Qabalah as we know it was created, marked especially by the publication of *The Sepher haZohar* (Book of Splendor)—a mystical commentary on biblical literature—by Moses de Leon.

This was also the time of the famed Magna Carta, a human rights contract that the English land barons of 1215 forced King John to sign at peril of his life. It changed little for the serfs, but it greatly restricted the king's right of taxation and required trials before punishment. In many ways, it is the historical forerunner to the American Bill of Rights.

Finally, the domination of the medieval Church was dealt its greatest blow, in the fourteenth century, by the spread of the bubonic plague from China. The spread of the disease continued until the seventeenth century, and wiped out a large portion of the population of Europe. For centuries the people had paid heed to the Church's doctrines of the end of the world and to the armies of angels who would come to the aid of the faithful in those times. When the Black Death struck, the Church lost no time in proclaiming the final rapture, and insisted that only the sinners of the world would suffer.

This was a political disaster. The plague swept through the known world, and paid no attention to the piety of its victims. Worse than this, the one segment of society least affected by the plague were the Jewish peoples, due to their strict religious laws regarding cleanliness.[7] These were the people whom the Church had promised would first fall. Now, if the plague were truly the Armageddon, then it was the Jewish people who were proving themselves the "Chosen." The Church could do nothing, and its armies of angels languished with sheathed swords. This ultimately broke the spell the Church held over Europe. These sixteenth century people felt that, when the chips had been on the table, their spirituality had failed them. Thus, they slowly began to seek for alternative answers. This ended the stranglehold of the Catholic Church, and began the age of the Renaissance.

The invention of the printing press by Johann Gutenburg in 1450 revolutionized communication and scholarship in a manner comparable to our own development of the Internet. Columbus explored the New World in 1492. On October 31, 1517, Martin Luther nailed a copy of his "95 Theses" to the doors of Castle Church in Wittenberg; leading to the separation of the Roman Church into Catholic and Protestant sects. King Henry VIII created his protestant Church of England, and his daughter Elizabeth established it during her reign from 1558–1602.

Johannes Kepler, Galileo, John Dee, and a host of others came to the forefront of the scientific world in the late sixteenth and early seventeenth centuries; many times such men were in direct opposition to the Catholic Church. This was also the time of the most famous wizards of history, such as Johannes Trithemius (1462–1516), Dr. John Dee (1527–1608), Giordano Bruno (1548–1600), and others. It isn't taught in our modern schools, but the very men who originally fashioned the basic scientific assumptions about our world had copies of the grimoires upon their shelves, and/or claimed membership to various mystery orders.

One thing for which the Renaissance is particularly known is the shifting of thought from the medieval philosophy based on Aristotle to the more pantheistic Neoplatonic views. In the late 1400s, Marsilio Ficino translated the *Corpus Hermeticum*—believing it was a true reflection of ancient Egyptian religion and the source for the philosophy of Plato and the Greeks. Of course, today we know that the Hermetic arts arose in the early Common Era, and that it was they who were affected by Plato. However, this was not understood in the fifteenth century, and Ficino's work created something of an Egyptian craze among mystics and occultists.[8]

At the same time that Ficino was disseminating the Hermetic teachings, Pico della Mirandola was doing the same for the Qabalah. Both of these traditions (Hermetic and Qabalistic) had been in vogue centuries earlier, but had been largely lost due to Church suppression. The efforts of men such as Ficino and Mirandola re-created the mystical movements that gave rise to the spiritual values of the Renaissance mystics. This Neoplatonic Hermetic-Qabalistic philosophy is the very one described in detail by Henry Agrippa in his *Three Books of Occult Philosophy* (an extremely important book in relation to the grimoiric literature—see below).

This philosophy endured until the 1600s, where it would culminate in a German mystical movement known as the "Brotherhood of the Rosy Cross." In 1614 and 15, two manifestos (generally known as the *Fama* and *Confessio*) were anonymously published in the name of this Brotherhood. Each of them took a very strong antipapal stance, and insisted on religious tolerance, the advancement of science as a spiritual art, and the reform of education, religion, and ethics. These "Rosicrucians" were deeply Hermetic (holding alchemy as the most sacred of sciences) and they drew much from the philosophy outlined by Dr. John Dee in his *Hieroglyphic Monad* of 1564 CE.

It is most likely that the Brotherhood did not exist in any tangible sense. The Rosicrucians claimed to meet only at an "Invisible College"—and there are many subtle hints to suggest that this was meant as an allegory. The Rosicrucian manifestos were addressed to all freethinkers and spiritual seekers in the world; especially those who yearned for the dawning of a new age, the advancement of learning, and freedom from the oppressive Roman Church. The Invisible College was the common ground within the hearts of all who sought such goals.[9] There is no known historical philosopher or Hermetic mystic, whom we would call "Rosicrucian" today, who ever claimed membership to such an order. Instead, it is the results of their "Work" that make them Rosicrucian thinkers.

This represents the end of the classical period upon which this book focuses. The Rosicrucian movement initiated a new magickal current—much less shamanic in nature than the grimoiric material (see chapter 2). After the initial furor caused by the publication of the manifestos, the Thirty Years War broke out in Europe, driving the freethought movement underground. There it continued until it finally found expression in the Age of Enlightenment and within Freemasonry. It is from Freemasonry that so many of our modern magickal systems descend. Rosicrucianism, therefore, stands as a midpoint between the authors of the grimoires, and the Masonic founders of our own post-Victorian magickal systems.

The Classical Grimoires[10]

Though the time of the grimoires rests mainly in the late medieval era, the legacy upon which they were founded extends much further into the past. The methods of magick they utilize are as ancient as the tribal magicks of prehistory. Their forms, however, seem to have been set during the first four centuries of our Common Era; specifically within the Greek magickal papyri.[11] These Greek spells drew from such sources as ancient Christianity (Gnosticism), Judaism, and Egyptian magick. Their focus was much the same as the later medieval texts—healing, obtaining visions, exorcism, the destruction of enemies, the gaining of beauty, etc. They incorporated mystical names and words into their prayers—the so-called "barbarous names of invocation" that have no earthly meaning, but indicate magickal formulas of vibration.[12] They insist upon ritual cleansing and purity, and the donning of priestly linen garments.

The list of similarities between the Greek and later European literature could continue, though an example would serve as well. Perhaps the most famous Greek ritual today is an invocation performed before attempting an exorcism, known as the Rite of the Headless[13] One:

> Write the names upon a piece of new paper, and having extended it over your forehead from one temple to the other, address yourself turning towards the north to the six names, saying . . . [14]

Compare this, then, with a quotation from the *Key of Solomon the King*, Book I, Chapter 13:

> . . . write upon a slip of virgin parchment . . . this Character and Name; . . . thou shalt hold with thy right hand the aforesaid strip of parchment against thy forehead, and thou shalt say the following words:

At the same time, another influence played a primary role in the formation of the classical grimoires: the apocryphal biblical text known as the *Testament of Solomon*. Elizabeth Butler considers this work "The turning point between ancient and medieval magic . . ."[15] The *Testament* outlines the mythology of King Solomon, from his subjugation of the spirits for building the temple to his eventual entry into worship of foreign gods. Most important for our consideration, however, is the fact that the text describes a sophisticated demonology wherein the king summons, questions, and binds several spirits. Each spirit revealed to Solomon his functions, an (often hideous) composite appearance, and the name of the angel who directly opposes him. For example, one of the demonic princes interrogated by King Solomon was known as Beelzeboul:

> I Solomon said unto him: "Beelzeboul, what is thy employment?" And he answered me: "I destroy kings. I ally myself with foreign tyrants. And my own demons I set on to men, in order that the latter may believe in them and be lost. And the chosen servants of God, priests and faithful men, I excite unto desires for wicked sins, and evil heresies, and lawless deeds; and they obey me, and I bear them on to destruction. And I inspire men with envy, and murder, and for wars and sodomy, and other evil things. And I will destroy the world."

Many of the lesser spirits in the book were associated with physical ailments rather than social taboos, and the angelic names given are regarded as curative formulas. This links the entire tradition to older rites of exorcism:

> The third said: "I am called Arotosael. I do harm to the eyes, and grievously injure them. Only let me hear the words, 'Uriel, imprison Aratosael', at once I retreat."

> The sixth said: "I am called Sphendonael. I cause tumours of the parotid gland, and inflammations of the tonsils, and tetanic recurvation. If I hear, 'Sabrael, imprison Sphendonael', at once I retreat.'

The *Testament* even lists four demonic rulers of the cardinal points of the compass, who were later echoed by a great number of medieval grimoires: Oriens (of the east), Amemon (of the south), Eltzen (of the north), and Boul (of the west).[16]

It would seem that the direct inheritor of this material among the medieval grimoires is the *Goetia*—or *Lesser Key*—which lists seventy-two such spirits, along with their characters, functions, appearances, and information on how to bind them to the will of the magician. The four "cardinal princes" even make an appearance, called here Amaymon, Corson, Zimimay, and Goap. The *Goetia*, in turn, had a major influence on the texts that followed. Therefore, the demonology of the *Testament of Solomon* became the grimoiric standard.

This occurred along with another trend that ran throughout the European texts—the assimilation of Jewish mysticism into the primarily Christian material. Even before the rise of the Qabalah in the thirteenth century, there existed a form of Jewish shamanic magick known as *Mahaseh Merkavah*, or the "Work of the Chariot." This was a practice of astral travel through the seven palaces of heaven (i.e., the planetary spheres), where the ultimate goal was the vision of the throne of God.

This practice does not seem to have originated with the *Merkavah*. The oldest examples of such literature we have found to date are the *Egyptian Book of the Dead* and the *Tibetan Book of the Dead*, which both deal with the ascension of the soul through the heavens after death. Apparently, the Chaldean or Babylonian priests of later times made this after-death journey while still alive—creating a kind of controlled near-death experience. The practice was then adopted by both Gnostic and Jewish mystical schools, which have each had a large influence upon medieval European magick.

The *Ethiopian Book of Enoch*, the *Hebrew Book of Enoch*, the *Pirkei Heichaloht*, and even such canonical biblical texts as Ezekiel and the Revelation of St. John are all centered upon—or connected to—the *Merkavah* tradition. The *Merkavah*'s use of ritual drugs, its focus upon talismans and seals, the summoning forth of angelic gatekeepers, and the gaining of mystical visions are elements that run throughout the grimoiric spells.

The fascination of the medieval mages for the *Merkavah*, and the reputation of its Jewish practitioners as extremely powerful wizards, led to the adoption of quite a bit of Judaic material into the grimoires. Richard Kieckhefer lists several examples in relation to the *Sworn Book of Honorius*,[17] though the ideas extend to many texts. Meanwhile, he explains that Jewish tradition was likely a main source for the grimoires' insistence upon "moral purity" along with the usual ritual purity. Also, the texts' use of prayers with linguistic variations on similar words[18] is probably derived from the Jewish Qabalah. Even the instructions to bury the grimoires if their owners could not find suitable successors[19] may be a reflection of the Jewish custom of burying (rather than destroying) prayer books containing the name of God.

Professor Kieckhefer suggests that the grimoiric manuscripts, drawing as they do from Judaic magick, are examples of a primitive form of medieval Christian mysticism that preceded the Christian Qabalah of the thirteenth century. He points out that medieval society had a surplus of clergy, and thus the spawning of an underemployed, largely unsupervised, and frankly mischievous "clerical underworld" was the inevitable result.

It is obvious enough that the grimoires are clerical in nature, beside the borrowings from Judaism. The rites of the Church are mirrored in the texts, such as techniques of exorcism, recitation of Psalms, the Litany of Saints, and other established Catholic prayers and sacraments. In many cases, access to an actual church is necessary: such as placing a grimoire on the altar during a service to consecrate it, the use of the elements of the Eucharist, or the necessity of holy oil used in a church. All of these presuppose that the mage either has close connections inside, or is perhaps employed in the Church itself. Other grimoires instruct the use of Christian observances without describing them, or fully explaining their use in the spell, which indicates that the authors of the texts considered them "given" and felt no need to write them out in full.

Another Christian trend that runs through the texts is the use of pseudepigrapha, or the attribution of a text by its author to someone other than himself. In many cases the supposed author may be a purely legendary figure, and in some cases it might be a historical personage. Most of the books of the Bible fall into this category, starting with the Gospels (at least Matthew, Luke, and John), and continuing into the Apocrypha such as the *Book of Enoch*, or the *Testament of Solomon*. Where it comes to the grimoires—such as the *Key of Solomon*, *Sworn Book of Honorius*, etc.—it might be said that tradition was simply followed.

Yet, there were other factors involved as well. Books of "ancient wisdom" tend to sell better when attributed to someone great from the past. Besides this, the books were illegal, and it was a rare mage who could enjoy seeing his name on the title page of such a work. (It may even be true that this is why a tradition of pseudepigrapha arose among the early Christians, as they were also persecuted heavily in their day.)

The existence of the grimoires on the shelves of medieval clergy strikes me as a perfectly natural occurrence. By this, I am not merely indicating the dynamic of a group of mystics caught in a land where magick was illegal, and thus producing a body of underground mystical material. I am also indicating the very nature of Christianity as a written tradition. From the original circulation in Palestine of anti-Roman war literature, known today as the four canonical Gospels, the Christian religion has been dedicated to the written word. From Bibles to prayerbooks to litanies, Christian magick is very often centered upon its sacred writ. This is no less true of the Judaic tradition, which may have adopted this aspect from Babylonian and Egyptian sources.

The medieval era itself saw the advent of paper, a medium much cheaper and convenient than parchment. An explosion of written material and bound books resulted; even if it was a specifically limited explosion. Most of the world remained illiterate, and it was the clergy who were charged with producing and reading written material. Those in Kieckhefer's "clerical underground" were the same monks who took on jobs of transcribing and translating texts on a regular basis. If a literature arose that circulated amongst a reading audience, these men would have been both the audience and the authors. The grimoires were such literature.

It may be true that much of the grimoiric material was originally transmitted orally. Oral transmission might also help explain some of the more blatant corruptions of Hebrew, Greek, Arabic, and Chaldean words in the invocations. It was during the middle to late medieval era that the tradition began to surface on paper thanks to the pen-happy and ambitious monks. Not only this, but the Christian mysticism of the written word had woven itself into the tradition, and the books surfaced as living magickal objects. They were often regarded as alive, or as possessed of spirits. When they were burned, witnesses actually reported hearing screams coming from within the pages. Even the cleric-mages themselves warned against the opening of the books by those unpracticed in magickal lore.[20]

When the Inquisitions did come, it was indeed the clergy who made up the majority on the prosecution's list. Remember, after all, that it was to ferret out heresy within the Church that the Inquisition was founded, and those who possessed grimoiric texts were highly suspect. Pope John XXII, in 1318, had the Bishop of Frejus investigate a group composed of clerics and laymen accused of necromancy, geomancy, and similar magickal practices. In 1406, a conspiracy was uncovered in which another group of clerics was accused of working magick against the king of France and Pope Benedict XIII. By 1409, Benedict himself was charged with both using necromancy and employing necromancers. In 1500, a monk from the Sulby monastery named Thomas Wryght was caught with a book of magickal experiments and was fortunate to escape with light punishment.

So the grimoires arose in a world of drastic political and religious change. They draw from several sources of mysticism and magick, which we have only begun to cover in this chapter. They were born from the hands of a clerical underground, perhaps even from mystical groups associated in some way with the Knights Templar. They represent a community of mages existing within the confines of its contemporary religious doctrine, experiencing mysteries that lay far outside of that doctrine. This is perhaps the most romantic trait of the grimoires. They embody a rebellion of the human spirit, and a refusal to let go of the light even in the darkest of ages.

At this point, I feel it will be helpful to offer a list of the most popular and influential of the European grimoires. I will explain what the books contain, when they were published, and how they have transmitted their subtle influences to our modern systems of magick.

The Picatrix (Ghâyat al-Hakîm fi'l-sihr)

Recent scholarship on this Arabic text indicates that it may in fact be a major sourcebook for many of the later grimoires (listed below). According to Joseph Peterson,[21] the Latin translation most familiar to scholars of the West dates to 1256 CE, from the court of King Alphonso the Wise, of Castille. Copies also exist in Arabic, German, French, and Latin. (At the time of this writing, there are at least two English translations underway, and at least one of them will likely be completed by the time of publication.)

According to Martin Plessner, the text is extremely erratic while covering a surprisingly wide range of occult topics. The philosophical doctrines that form the basis of the talismanic art (the theory of magick, astronomy, astrology and love, extensive instructions on practical magick, and anecdotes concerning the employment of the magick) are jumbled together throughout the book without apparent rhyme or reason.[22]

The work is divided into four books. The first contains a preface with "autobiographical" information about the author, his reasons for writing the book (i.e., to make available the secrets of magick as guarded by the "ancient philosophers"), and a summary of the material found in the four books. The chapters of book one contain large portions of occult philosophy according to its author (largely Neoplatonic and "pseudo-Aristotelian" according to Plessner), a definition of magick (into theoretical and practical), as well as preliminary information on astrology and the mansions of the moon. The latter is given as vital information for the formation of talismans.

Book Two continues the discussions of philosophy above, the correspondences between earthly creatures and celestial archetypes, and gets further into the mysteries of astrology—the triplicities, degrees, conjunctions, the fixed stars, etc.—along with (in Chapter Three) some long and in-depth information about the occult virtues of the moon. Yet another definition of magick follows in Chapter Five—dividing it this time between the talismanic art, worship of the planets, and incantations. These three, it is suggested, were divided among the human race so that different cultures became the masters of different arts. In the same chapter, material concerning the art of prophecy and divination is related. Chapters Six and Seven (as well as several following chapters) then go into depth upon the philosophy of talismans, explaining even that "Man makes talismans unawares as soon as he begins to manipulate nature in such processes as dyeing cloth, breeding animals or compounding drugs, as well as in the manufacture of objects of everyday use from the products of nature, as in cooking, spinning and the like."[23] Beyond this, such subjects as the natures of the four Elements (which Agrippa seems to have adopted—see below) and further astrological information are related.

Book Three continues its lessons in astrology—this time treating the planets and signs "more individually, with their specific qualities. The planets are personified to such a degree that they are virtually conjured and worshipped."[24] The chapters include information on images, inks, perfumes, colors, robes, metals, etc.,—all used in the worship/invocation of the planets. The dominions (i.e., jurisdiction) of the planets and signs are all outlined, along with magickal hours and the like. From here, about Chapter Four (which discusses Islam and astrology), the book returns to philosophy, the nature of man, the spiritual essence of the wise man, etc. From there, beginning at Chapter Seven, the text shifts to more practical concerns. Initiation into the worship of the seven planets is given, along with prayers and adorations, and the gifts to be gained from each. Full ceremonies for each planet are outlined in Chapter Nine. From Chapter Ten onward, practical talismans and other information are given for various effects common to the grimoires (love, honor, protection, etc.). The final chapter (Twelve) returns to philosophical concerns (the absolute need for practical magickal operation, the love of God, etc.) that run almost directly into the first chapter of Book Four.

Finally, Book Four continues the philosophical discussion, outlining various substances of nature and the theory (history) of creation. It continues outlining the threefold nature of the world that began in an earlier book—dividing creation into substance, intellect, and soul (once again, this seems to have been a probable source for Agrippa—see below). From here, prayers, ceremonies, and information are given for the twelve signs of the zodiac—along with stories to illustrate the possible effects of these rites. Plessner states that each ceremony is preceded by a seven-day fast, and magickal characters are used in the ceremonies (pp. 319–22). Some aspects of this may be found in various Hermetic manuscripts.[25] I find this suggestive of the *Ars Notaria* (see below). Chapter Four returns to the subject of astrology and talismans (etc.), and Chapter Five outlines the ten disciplines considered necessary *before* one can become a master in the magickal arts. Oddly, the subjects of the evil eye, heredity, and even bisexuality are discussed here. Chapter Six returns to the subject of planetary incense, providing rites for each blend. The rather lengthy Chapter Seven concerns the magickal virtues and uses of plants, and consists mainly of "avowed and verbatim extracts from the

Nabataean Agriculture."[26] The final chapters, Nine and Ten, concern the occult virtues of physical substances, and the description of talismans, which rely on those virtues.

This, of course, merely scratches the surface of the material contained in the chapters of the *Picatrix*. Being that it is very much a sourcebook for the grimoiric tradition as we know it, I hope that an English translation will soon be made available for general study.

Key of Solomon the King (Clavicula Salomonis)

The antiquity of this French grimoire is not known exactly, though it is often placed somewhere in the fourteenth century. A. E. Waite[27] is willing to allow as much as two centuries before this time for the book to have been created and transmitted (perhaps orally), placing its true origin as far back as the twelfth century. It would seem that scholars generally agree on the idea that the *Key* (along with the *Lemegeton*)[28] is the fountainhead of medieval grimoiric writing; providing the format, style, and even much of the content of those that followed.

The *Key* is composed of two books. Book one concerns the art of spirit summoning—without offering any set hierarchies of intelligences or the use of a triangle. Instead, the spirits arrive at the edge of the circle, and it is up to the mage to question them about their names and functions. Also given are several planetary talismans[29] to be inscribed upon metal, and shown to the spirits in order to gain their obedience. Each one directs the spirits to perform different functions. Not only this, but "[t]hey are also of great virtue and efficacy against all perils of Earth, of Air, of Water, and of Fire, against poison which hath been drunk, against all kinds of infirmities and necessities, against binding, sortilege, and sorcery, against all terror and fear, and wheresoever thou shalt find thyself, if armed with them, thou shat be in safety all the days of thy life."[30] The remainder of the book is filled with day-to-day practical magick and experiments, such as finding stolen objects, hindering sportsmen from poaching game, and even fashioning a magick carpet.

Book Two concerns itself with all ritual preparations—purifications, the construction of magickal tools, incense, holy water, etc. These are the most well-known aspects of the book, even used in many instances by modern Hollywood: wands cut from trees at sunrise with one stroke of the knife, thread spun by a virgin, the conjuration of the magickal sword, etc.

Waite felt that the *Key* is the only (or perhaps merely the first?) magickal text that regulates the operations of magick by the attribution of the hours of the day and night to the rulership of the seven planets,[31] what we call the planetary hours.[32] While the *Key* certainly introduced the practice of the planetary hours into the larger tradition, it is likely that the *Picatrix* stands as an older source for this information.

The *Key of Solomon the King* is also the book from which Gerald Gardner drew much of his material in his formation of Wicca. Such rites as the blessings of salt and water, and the magickal characters for inscription upon the athame and pentacle are found here.

Lesser Key of Solomon (Lemegeton)

This is a collection of five magickal texts, *Goetia*, *Theurgia-Goetia*, the *Pauline Art*, the *Almadel of Solomon*, and the *Ars Nova*. It would appear that these were once separate texts (of which, perhaps, the *Goetia* is the oldest) collected together at some later date into the so-called *Lemegeton*.

Goetia

The meaning of the word "goetia" has long been a subject of scholarly debate. It is often thought to have derived from the Greek word *goaô* (to wail, groan, or weep), and is related to the howling of bestial demons. On the other hand, A. E. Waite suggests that the word indicates "witchcraft." This would derive from the Greek word *goes* (an enchanter, sorcerer), and from the word "goety," indicating the art of the sorcerer—which is witchcraft.[33]

In classical times, "witchcraft" was a direct reference to working with spirit Familiars, or the performance of necromancy.[34] Thus, the very name of the text was meant to convey its focus upon infernal spirit working. It is introduced in the Weiser edition: "The First Book, or Part, which is a Book concerning Spirits of Evil, and which is termed The Goetia of Solomon, sheweth forth his manner of binding these Spirits for use in things divers. And hereby did he acquire great renown."[35]

The examples we have today are said to date back only to the seventeenth century. However, Waite suggests that it must be older; due to such earlier texts as *Liber Spiritum*, which mimic the style of the *Goetia*. Elizabeth Butler was convinced that *Liber Spiritum*, and even *Liber Officiorum*, were earlier names for the *Goetia* itself.[36] To add to this, I discussed above the relation of the *Testament of Solomon* to the *Goetia*, with its large collection of demons, sigils, functions, and bindings. The *Testament* dates itself within the second through fifth centuries of the Common Era, suggesting that the *Lemegeton* might have enjoyed a rather long tradition both orally and written.

The story (or mythos) within the *Goetia* is based upon a Talmudic legend, wherein King Solomon sealed a group of spirits (in this case, seventy-two planetary spirits) into a brass vessel, and cast it into a Babylonian lake. The Babylonians witnessed the king disposing of the vessel, and retrieved it in hopes of finding treasure. Instead, they only succeeded in freeing the demons once more in a fashion reminiscent of Pandora's Box. Thus, the seventy-two spirits that Solomon once commanded are available for summoning, and are herein named and described, along with rites and conjurations meant to call them. The *Goetia* is the home of such popularized demons as Ashtaroth, Bael, Amon, Asmodai, and the four cardinal princes Amaymon, Corson, Zimimay, and Goap. With their brethren, they pretty much make up the standard hierarchy of demons from medieval grimoiric literature.

Perhaps the most fascinating aspect of the *Goetia* is its obvious tie to the tradition of the Arabian *Thousand and One Nights*. In these tales, mages are often depicted imprisoning jinni (genies) into brass bottles. In the example of "Aladdin and the Lamp," the prison was a brass oil-burning lamp instead. The powers attributed to the spirits of the *Goetia* likewise reflect the magick portrayed in the legends: production of treasure, turning men into animals, understanding the speech of animals, etc. Of course, the Arabic tradition focused somewhat on King Solomon, and most of the legends that we remember of him today originated there. I strongly recommend one read Arabic mythology (including the *Thousand and One Nights*) when studying the *Goetia*.

The *Goetia* is the source of the ever-popular triangle of the art, into which spirits are generally summoned. This is also the source of the infamous "Greater Curse," where the seal of a disobedient spirit is placed into an iron box with stinking herbs and perfumes, and dangled over an exorcised flame. The seal of Solomon, which the king impressed upon the brass vessel, is reproduced here; as are the pentagram, hexagram, and disk (or ring) of Solomon. These magickal tools have been used by various mages, for various purposes, since the publication of the *Goetia*.

Theurgia-Goetia

In the Middle Ages, the term "theurgy" was usually meant to imply "high magick," or the methods of working with good spirits. (Literally, *theurgia* means "god-working.") Thus, the *Theurgia-Goetia* was so named to indicate its contents of both good and evil spirits. Unlike the more feral goetic demons, these spirits were organized into a functional cooperation, assigned to the points of the compass. In total, there are thirty-one chief princes, who are each provided with an incomprehensible number of servient spirits. The name of each chief and several of his servitors, all with seals included, is recorded—making for a shockingly large collection. Conjurations, all identical in form, are provided with each group along the way.

Yet, even with this large number of spirits to choose from, the preamble to the text describes them in a very singular fashion:

> The offices of these spirits are all one, for what one can do the others can do also. They can shew and discover all things that is hidden and done in the world: and can fetch and carry or do any thing that is to be done or is contained in any of the four Elements Fire, Air, Earth and Water, &c. Also, they can discover the secrets of kings or any other person or persons let it be in what kind it will.[37]

The introductory material describes the *Theurgia* as ". . . one which treateth of Spirits mingled of Good and Evil Natures, the which is entitled The Theurgia-Goetia, or the Magical Wisdom of the Spirits Aerial, whereof some do abide, but certain do wander and bide not."[38] This leads me to the suspicion that these spirits are in some way connected to the stars or other astronomical concerns.

Pauline Art (Ars Paulina)

This book of the *Lemegeton* is introduced as follows: "The Third Book, called Ars Paulina, or The Art Pauline, treateth of the Spirits allotted unto every degree of the 360 Degrees of the Zodiac; and also of the signs, and of the planets in the signs, as well as of the hours.[39]

Joseph H. Peterson notes that the *Pauline Art* was supposed to have been discovered by the Apostle Paul after he had ascended the third heaven, and was then delivered by him at Corinth. He also points out that, although the grimoire is based on earlier magickal literature, it is apparently a later redaction due to repeated mention of the year 1641 as well as references to guns.[40]

The book is divided into two principal parts. The first part deals with twenty-four angels who rule the hours of the day and night. The powers of each angel changes depending on the day in question, and which planet happens to rule his hour on that day. (See the chapter on magickal timing for charts of these hours.) Each angel is listed with several servient angels (or spirits), and instructions for fashioning astrological talismans for any of the angels one wishes to work with. At the end of the text, the conjurations (used for any angel, changing only certain key words) are written out in full.

The second part of the *Pauline Art* is extremely interesting—as it concerns the finding of the angel of the degree of one's own natal Ascendant. In other words, this is the angel who was rising above the eastern horizon as you were born. He holds the mysteries of one's destiny, career, fortune, home, and all such factors that can be outlined by an astrological birth chart. Like the first part, methods of talisman construction are outlined for working with these angels. The text finishes with a conjuration for the natal angel called "The Conjuration of the Holy Guardian Angel," in which the angel is invoked into a crystal ball. Apparently, there was either little distinction between the angel of the nativity and the holy guardian angel at the time this text was composed, or it was simply unknown to the author.

As for current magickal technology that may have originated from this book, I mainly note the "Table of Practice" (or altar) the text instructs one to fashion. I refer specifically to the image on top of the table, which appears to be the oldest known example of the Golden Dawn's planetary hexagram. In both cases, the Sun is assigned the central position within the hexagram, and the six remaining planets orbit this at each of the six points. The only difference is the ordering of planets around the hexagram points.

Almadel of Solomon

The fourth book of the *Lemegeton* is perhaps my favorite. Weiser's *Goetia* includes the following blurb: "The Fourth Book, called Ars Almadel Salomonis, or the Art Almadel of Solomon, concerneth those Spirits which be set over the Quaternary of the Altitudes. These two last mentioned Books, the Art Pauline and the Art Almadel, do relate unto Good Spirits alone, whose knowledge is to be obtained through seeking unto the Divine. These two Books be also classed together under the Name of the First and Second Parts of the Book Theurgia Of Solomon."[41]

The four "altitudes" alluded to above are simply the four cardinal directions, though they are considered as stacked one on top of the other in this instance. It either originates from, or reflects, the Qabalistic tradition of the four worlds of creation that exist between the earth and the throne of God. Each world is populated with good spirits (angels) who can be summoned by the text of the *Almadel* for a diverse array of benefits.

The magick itself is worked via a fascinating piece of magickal apparatus called an "almadel." This is a square tablet of white wax, with holy names and characters written upon it with a consecrated pen. Its main feature is a large hexagram, which covers most of the surface of the tablet, and a triangle in the center of this (reminding one of the triangle used in the *Goetia*). As a final feature, four holes are drilled through the tablet—one in each corner. When this work is done, more wax is used (specifically more of the same wax from which the tablet was made) to fashion four candles; each with a small shelf-like protrusion of wax (called a "foot"), presumably, halfway up the length of the candle. The four candles are placed in candlesticks, and positioned in a square pattern with the "feet" all facing inward. The almadel itself is then placed between the candles, so that it rests on the "feet" (taking care they do not block the four holes) and is thus elevated well above the surface of the table or altar. The final components are a small golden or silver talisman that rests in the center of the almadel, and an earthen censer placed on the table directly underneath.[42]

Golden Dawn Hexagram.

Pauline Table.

No less than four almadels must be made—including the four candles and the earthen censer (but not the metal talisman)—so there is one of a different color for each of the four altitudes:

> **Note:** The golden seal will serve and is to be used in the operation of all the Altitudes. The color of the Almadel belonging to the first Chora[43] is lily white. To the second Chora a perfect red rose color; The third Chora is to be a green mixed with a white silver collour. The Fourth Chora is to be a black mixed with a little green of a sad color &c

These four colors are alchemical in their symbolism, rather than the common elemental colors of yellow, red, blue, and black or green of modern magickal systems. Once you have chosen which angels (and thus which altitude) you wish to work with, you set up the almadel, light the candles, and burn mastic in the censer. The smoke will rise against the bottom of the wax tablet, and is thus forced to some degree through the four holes. It is within this smoke, and upon the almadel and its golden talisman, that the angel(s) in question will manifest.

This text has had a profound, and yet little-known, effect on modern magick. It was never adopted directly into our modern magickal systems by men such as S. L. Mathers or Gerald Gardner. Instead, it had its effect upon Dr. John Dee in the late sixteenth century. The equipment described by the angels for his Enochian system of magick seem to have been derived largely from the almadel tradition. However, since I will be explaining the Dee diaries later in this chapter, I will save the comparisons for then.

Ars Nova (The New Art)

"The Fifth Book of the Lemegeton is one of Prayers and Orations. The Which Solomon the Wise did use upon the Altar in the Temple. And the titles hereof be Ars Nova, the New Art, and Ars Notaria, the Notary Art. The which was revealed unto him by Michael, that Holy Angel of God, in thunder and in lightning, and he further did receive by the aforesaid Angel certain Notes written by the Hand of God, without the which that Great King had never attained unto his great Wisdom, for thus he knew all things and all Sciences and Arts whether Good or Evil."[44]

The *Lemegeton's Ars Nova* is very often confused with another grimoire called the "*Ars Notaria*, or Notary Arts."[45] There appears to be good cause for the confusion. The actual *Notary Arts* is composed of three parts, and the third part is a collection of prayers called the *Ars Nova*. The *Ars Nova* that forms the fifth book of the *Lemegeton* appears to be based (at least in concept) upon the *Ars Nova* of the *Notary Arts*.

The *Ars Nova* only appears in one version of the *Lemegeton* (Sloane MS 2731). It is simply a book of invocations for the construction of the sacred space and some of the tools in the goetic operation. (Whether or not it is meant for use with the other books of the *Lemegeton* is unclear, though it should extend by definition to the *Theurgia-Goetia*.) Prayers are given for the inscription of the magickal circle and triangle of art, the donning of the hexagram and pentagram of Solomon, the lighting of the candles, etc. Then follows an invocation for binding the goetic demons into the brass vessel. These were perhaps something of an afterthought on the part of the compiler of the *Lemegeton*, but it does address the glaring omission of such invocations within the *Goetia* itself. Finally, the short text ends with a "Mighty Oration" that seems to be aimed at the catching of thieves and appears utterly removed from the material of the *Lemegeton* itself.

When Aleister Crowley published a translation of the *Goetia* by Samuel Mathers, it came with a copy of part of the *Ars Nova* (not including the "Mighty Oration" or the invocation against thieves.) However, it is not called such in the Mathers/Crowley text, and stands only as an "Explanation of Certain Names Used in this Book Lemegeton."

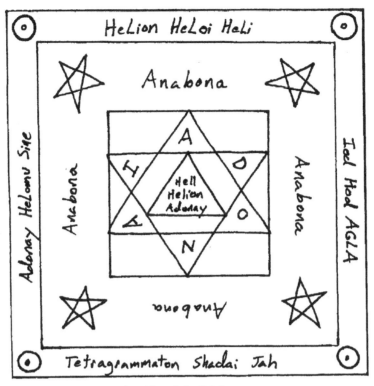

The Almadel of Solomon.

Notary Arts (Ars Notaria)

A wonderful discussion of this tradition can be found in an essay by Frank Klaassen, titled *English Manuscripts of Magic, 1300–1500*.[46] Another essay by Michael Camille, titled *Visual Art in Two Manuscripts of the Ars Notaria*, contains more historical analysis along with photographs of the pages of the book itself.[47] Finally, from the same source, we have an equally informative essay titled *Plundering the Egyptian Treasure: John the Monk's "Book of Visions" and its Relation to the Ars Notaria or Solomon*, which compares the *Notary Arts* to a later version of the text (*The Book of Visions*) that focuses upon the Virgin Mary rather than Solomon.[48]

There are approximately fifty different manuscripts of the *Notary Arts* known at this time, dating from between 1300 to 1600 CE. The Solomonic mythos from which it draws its foundation is found in the canonical Bible:

> "Now, O Lord God, let thy promise unto David my father be established: for thou hast made me king over a people like the dust of the earth in multitude. Give me now wisdom and knowledge, that I may show myself before this people: for who can judge this Thy people, who are so great?" And God said to Solomon, "Because this was in thine heart, and thou has not asked riches, wealth, or honour, nor the life of thine enemies, neither yet hast asked long life, but hast asked wisdom and knowledge for thyself, that thou mayest judge my people, over whom I have made thee king. Wisdom and knowledge is granted unto thee; and I will give thee riches, and wealth, and honour, such as none of the kings have had that have been before thee, neither shall there any after thee have the like." (II Chronicles 1:9–12)

This is the very scene that gave rise to the legend of the wisdom of Solomon. By refusing to ask for anything beyond self-improvement, he was able to enjoy all the things to which others cling with greed. Only without greed can true happiness be obtained, and physical things enjoyed. Many of us are familiar with the phrase "Ask for wisdom and all else will come." Solomon learned to stop allowing his physical surroundings to control his actions, and was thus granted the power of controlling them instead. This entire concept has been foundational to similar practices all over the world; from Eastern systems such as Buhddism, to the grimoires themselves,[49] and even many systems of today.

The *Ars Notaria* is a collection of purification procedures, obscure prayers, and magickal images that promise to result in the understanding of ". . . Magical Operations, The liberal Sciences, Divine Revelation, and The Art of Memory." The purifications are composed of fasts, observance of times, confessions, etc. In appearance it very much resembles prayer books or Psalters of the day—and the calligraphy and illustrations were very often commissioned to professional artists (the same men who did in fact fashion Psalters and prayer books).

The text itself is arranged into three distinct parts. Part I contains the prayers to achieve the "general" virtues necessary to attain the higher virtues found later. These are four in number: memory, eloquence, understanding, and perseverance. Without these, any attempt to produce results with the more advanced prayers will simply come to nothing.

Part II of the operation contains the prayers and magickal images that promise to bestow the "special" virtues. These are specifically the seven liberal arts that compose the common educational curriculum for the medieval scholar: grammar, logic, and rhetoric, followed by arithmetic, geometry, music, and sstronomy. It then culminates in philosophy and theology.

Following this is Part III, or the *Ars Nova*. This section is composed of ten prayers said to have been delivered to Solomon at a later time, and by different angels, for the purpose of rectifying any mistakes the aspirant may have made in the previous books. Apparently, they are mainly reprisals of some of the prayers of Part II. Finally, the text ends with the necessary instructions (needed for all three parts) concerning preparation of the sacred space, consecration of the images, fasting, confession, charity,[50] instructions on using the prayers, etc.

The prayers themselves are arranged within the elaborate magickal images, so that the reading of the prayer also results in the abstract viewing of the image. The effect of these two together is intended to induce trance.[51] (In many cases, it is even necessary to rotate the book as you read—the prayers being arranged in concentric circles or spirals: state-of-the-art hypnosis technology for the 1300s!) Here is an example of the prayers and how they are applied practically:

> This following is for the Memory:
> O Holy Father, merciful Son, and Holy Ghost, inestimable King; I adore, invocate, and beseech thy Holy Name, that of thy overflowing goodness, thou wilt forget all my sins: be merciful to me a sinner, presuming to go about this office of knowledge, and occult learning; and grant, Oh Lord, it may be efficacious in me; open Oh Lord my ears, that I may hear; and take away the scales from my Eyes, that I may see, strengthen my hands, that I may work; open my face, that I may understand thy will; to the glory of thy Name, which is blessed for ever, Amen.[52]

Overall, the *Notary Arts* stand apart from the usual structure of grimoiric texts, which demand more elaborate efforts for highly specific effects. One who made use of the memory prayer above was not attempting to remember one specific item or to pass a single test. Instead, he was acting on the question of what might be gained if only he had a better memory in general. Rather than achieving one single goal, after which the rite would have to be performed again, the idea was to master the entire subject in one fell swoop.

This philosophy of magick is very productive, and highly recommended. It is extremely important to the grimoiric traditions overall, and echoes of it can be found in the introductions to even the most materialistic texts. Those books which have gained reputations of deep mystery—and even danger—are very often just this kind of text. See the *Book of Abramelin* and the *Sworn Book of Honorius* below (as well as others in this list) that are such legendary examples.

Three Books of Occult Philosophy

First drafted in 1509–1510 by Henry Cornelius Agrippa (student of Johannes Trithemius), this is the single most important grimoiric text in existence. It is not, in fact, a practical manual, but is instead a compendium of the theories and philosophies upon which medieval and Renaissance magick are based.

Agrippa divided his work into three distinct sections (or books): the first focuses upon natural or earth magick. The second outlines the more intellectual techniques such as Qabalah, gematria, mathematics, and divination. The third book concerns religious observances and interaction with angelic beings. There are no ceremonies outlined, and no chapters dedicated to "how-to" instructions. Instead, it is a sourcebook or reference without which the other grimoires would be nearly useless today. One could spend a lifetime with this book, and still discover new treasures of ancient thought within its pages.

More than any other, this book (especially Book II) has had a major impact on our modern magickal cultures. It seems to have been a favorite of John Dee, as many of its correspondences and magickal wisdom appear throughout the Enochian system of magick. It was also a major sourcebook for the founders of the Golden Dawn, and most of their lists of angels and divine names can be found in its pages. The seven magickal squares, or planetary kameas (used in many traditions from the Golden Dawn to Wicca), are found in Agrippa's work. The four philosophical Elements (the gnomes, sylphs, salamanders, and undines), construction of talismans, gematria, the Shem haMephoresh, and more are all outlined here. And these are merely a few examples; due to its overshadowing influence on today, it would be impossible to list all of the modern borrowings from the *Three Books* in this small space.

The Magical Elements (Heptameron)

According to Joseph Peterson, *The Magical Elements* is a concise handbook of ritual magick, and was translated by Robert Turner in 1655. It appeared in Turner's collection of esoteric texts along with Pseudo-Agrippa's *Fourth Book of Occult Philosophy*.[53] The text is attributed to Peter de Abano (1250–1316), though Mr. Peterson feels that this is probably spurious, since de Abano's work betrays "no acquaintance with the occult sciences." *The Magical Elements* is primarily based upon Solomonic literature, and even appears in the Hebrew Key of Solomon (*Mafteah Shelomoh*, fol 35a ff) under the title *The Book of Light*.[54]

Agrippa published his *Three Books* without including any practical ceremonies. In the last chapter of the third book, he tells us his reason: "For we have delivered this art in such a manner, that it may not be hid from the prudent and intelligent, and yet may not admit wicked and incredulous men to the mysteries of these secrets, but leave them destitute and astonished, in the shade of ignorance and desperation."[55]

However, there was apparently some call for a "how-to" section of the work regardless of Agrippa's original intention. Thus *The Magical Elements* was written as a companion volume, including the necessary circle castings, invocations, consecrations, seals, etc. As Peterson suggests above, the book was very likely not written by the famed physician Peter de Abano. The death of Abano occurred in 1250, while the *Heptameron* did not make its appearance for another two hundred years.

Fourth Book of Occult Philosophy

This book needs little explanation, as it is basically another version of *The Magical Elements*, with large portions of the original *Three Books* included. Also, the *Lemegeton* (at least its style) had an influence on this work, as it does concern the evocation of "evil spirits" and even suggests the use of a triangle.

The author is known only as "Pseudo-Agrippa," because he chose to sign Agrippa's name to the work. According to A. E. Waite, the text appeared only after the death of the famous wizard, and was rejected as a forgery by a student of Agrippa's named Wierus.[56]

The Magus (Celestial Intelligencer)

Published in 1801 by Francis Barrett, this work was meant as a textbook for classes in magick that Barrett was offering at No. 99 Norton St., Marylebone—at any time between the hours of eleven and two o'clock. It would appear that he was attempting to found a magickal order, which may or may not have succeeded.

As for the content of the book, I'm afraid we have to class this text with the others that have taken so much from Agrippa's *Three Books* and those which came directly after. It consists mainly of large portions of Agrippa's work (specifically portions of the first and second books), along with large chunks of *The Magical Elements* and *Fourth Book of Occult Philosophy* thrown in. Many tend to consider Barrett a plagiarist, as he leaves his sources (which he does indeed quote word for word in most cases) unaccredited, although I tend to feel that Barrett (operating as late as the 1800s) was simply compiling a workable textbook for his class from the sources he had personally tracked down and studied. In fact, *The Magus* seems to represent a last revival of grimoiric material before the Victorian work of Eliphas Levi, and the Golden Dawn after him.

The Book of the Sacred Magic of Abramelin the Mage

S. L. Mathers, in his edition of this text, places the *Book of Abramelin* at the end of the seventeenth and beginning of the eighteenth centuries. Like the tradition of the *Notary Arts*, the Abramelin system stands apart from the grimoiric mainstream. Its focus is much more spiritual in nature than one might expect from the *Key of Solomon* or *Goetia*. The principal upon which the text is based is that all material happiness can only come from spiritual evolution.

The text is divided into three books. The first is an autobiography of the author, a man who calls himself Abraham the Jew. There may be a symbolic relation to the father of Judaism, though this Abraham writes of living during the reign of Emperor Sigismond of Germany (1368–1437 CE). Abraham describes his years of wandering in search of the true and sacred wisdom (more echoes of King Solomon), and his several disappointments along the way. In fact, the tale takes on the traditional tone of a quest. He learns several forms of magick, but finds them all lacking, and their practitioners to be less than they claimed. At the last moments before giving up the quest, Abraham meets an Egyptian adept named Abramelin, who agrees to teach Abraham the "Sacred Magic."

Abraham wrote this text for the sake of his son Lamech (another biblically inspired name).[57] According to the story, Abraham had granted the secrets of the Qabalah to his oldest son, in the tradition of Judaism. However, he did not wish to leave his younger son with no Key to spiritual attainment, and thus Abraham left behind the *Book of Abramelin*.

The second two books, then, are composed of the instructions for the sacred magic, which Abraham copied by hand from Abramelin's original. The first part (Book Two) describes a heavily involved procedure of purification and invocation, resulting in the appearance of one's own guardian angel. Of course, the concept of the personal guardian (and the invocation thereof) extends well before the dawn of written history. The system outlined in *Abramelin* itself shows amazing similarities to tribal shamanic procedures.

The purifications take the standard grimoiric forms of seclusion, fasting, cleanliness, and a heavy dose of prayer. A separate room—called an oratory (prayer room)—must be maintained in utmost purity during a six-month period, as this is where the angel will appear and bond with the aspirant at the end of this time. Afterward, the angel takes over as teacher for the aspirant, and it is from this being (and *only* this being) that the true and sacred wisdom and magic will be discovered.

Once the cooperation of the angel is assured, one continues to summon forth such demonic princes as Lucifer, Leviathan, Astarot, Belzebud, and several others (twelve in all). These beings are commanded to deliver an oath of obedience to the mage, as well as the use of four Familiar spirits for day-to-day practical tasks.

The final book is a collection of magick-square talismans, which the demonic princes and spirits must swear upon when giving their oaths. Each talisman can then be used to command a spirit to perform a task, in much the same fashion as those in the *Key of Solomon the King*. The functions of the talismans are those common to grimoiric material: finding treasure, causing visions, bringing books, flight, healing the sick, etc.

There is some speculation that Book Three was a later edition to the work. I don't know if this is the case, though it is true that it contains more contradictions and general mistakes than the second. In fact, those who have made use of the Abramelin system have found Book Three of little concern. Abraham himself hints at the reason for this in Book Two's Chapter Fourteen:

> Though the following advice may be scarcely necessary for the most part, since I have already explained unto you all things necessary to be done; and also seeing that your Guardian Angel will have sufficiently instructed you in all that you should do . . .

It is very possible that book three represents only "Abraham's" version of the "True and Sacred Magic," which will, of course, be different for everyone.

I also feel I should state that the talismans are specifically useless for those who do not first undergo the six-month invocation. They have no power in and of themselves, as they work only by showing them to spirit helpers who have touched them and sworn the oaths. Of course, that can only be done with the aid of one's guardian angel, which can only be achieved by following the entire six-month operation. Some of the most common urban legends I have heard concerning the dangers of grimoires were centered around those who have attempted to make use of Book Three of *Abramelin* by itself. Much more than this, however, I believe people simply find it of little use at all.

The *Book of Abramelin* granted one major concept to our modern practices: the holy guardian angel. The Golden Dawn adopted the "HGA" (holy guardian angel) straight from the pages of *Abramelin*, and the system of Thelema adopted it from the Golden Dawn. Both traditions agree on the vast importance of gaining knowledge and conversation of the holy guardian angel. *Abramelin* is one of my own areas of focus, and I could not agree with them more. In time, both the Golden Dawn and Thelema have developed their own methods of invoking and working with the guardian angel; though I have to admit that I find the *Abramelin* system to be the most impressive method.

Arbatel of Magic (Arbatel de Magia Veterum)

Joseph Peterson describes this text as appearing first in Latin in Basle, Switzerland, in 1575. It is also mentioned in John Dee's *Five Books of the Mysteries* (circa 1583).[58] This was among the rituals classified by A. E. Waite as "transcendental magic"—that is, magick that does not include what he considers black magickal elements (see the *Book of Ceremonial Magic*, p. 28). It was later translated into English by Robert Turner in 1655.

The *Arbatel* was originally intended to contain nine books, though we only know of the first book today. Many speculate that the other eight were never written, and this could very well be true. Although, the magick that is supposedly contained in those eight books would not have been uncommon medieval magickal literature. I feel that the author at least intended to write them, if he did not in fact do so after all.

The first book, called *Isagoge* (or *A Book of the Institutions of Magick*), concerns the basics of magickal procedure in general. It contains forty-nine "aphorisms," divided into groups of seven called "septenaries," which must be learned and followed in order to succeed in magickal experiments. A fitting example of the nature of these aphorisms would be number two:

> In all things call upon the Name of the Lord: and without prayer unto God through his onely-begotten son, do not thou undertake to do or think any thing. And use the Spirits given and attributed unto thee, as Ministers, without rashness and presumption, as the messengers of God; having a due reverence towards the Lord of Spirits. And the remainder of thy life do thou accomplish, demeaning thy self peaceably, to the honour of God, and the profit of thy self and thy neighbour.[59]

The third septenary of aphorisms begins a description of the natures and methods of working with seven planetary Olympic spirits, who inhabit the firmament (sky), specifically the stars (or planets) of the firmament. Their office is to declare destinies and to administer fatal charms as far as God permits them. Their names are Aratron, Bethor, Phaleg, Och, Hagith, Ophiel, and Phul.

According to this text, the universe is divided into 186 "provinces," which are ruled by the Olympic spirits. Each spirit also rules, in succession, a period of 490 years. According to the text, we have been under the general governance of Ophiel, the Spirit of Mercury, since 1900 CE, and will remain so until the year 2390 CE.

The eight nonexistent books said to follow the first are described in the introduction of the *Arbatel*. The second book concerns "Microcosmical Magick," and sounds as if it might be an operation of working with one's lesser guardian angel or genius (see the *Pauline Art* above). The third contains "Olympic Magick," or the methods of working with the spirits who reside upon Mt. Olympus. The fourth book contains what it calls "Hesiodiacal" or "Homerical Magick," and focuses upon working with "cacodaimones" (unclean spirits, or demons). It is very likely that this text was (or would have been) somewhat along the lines of the *Goetia*. The fifth of the nine books contains "Romane or Sibylline Magick," which concerns work done with tutelar spirits—that is, those spiritual entities who guide and protect human beings. The sixth book is called *Pythagorical Magick*, which promises the appearance of spirits who will teach one all of the "rhetorical sciences" such as medicine, mathematics, alchemy, etc. The seventh book is called the *Magick of Apollonius*, and claims to work according to the rules of both the *Microcosmical* (Book 2) and *Romane* (Book 5) Magicks. However, this work claims to work with hostile spirits instead of benevolent. The eighth book is called "Hermetical" or "Egyptian Magick," and is described only as being similar to "Divine Magick." If I were to make an assumption as to what this means, I might assume that it was related in some way to work with celestial beings ("theurgy"), or even devotional religious magick as found in Book III of Agrippa's *Three Books*. Finally, the ninth book is "that wisdom which dependeth solely upon the Word of God; and this is called Prophetical Magick."[60]

Sworn Book of Honorius (Liber Sacer Juratus)

The oldest copies of the Latin *Sworn Book* we have today are Sloane MS 313 and 3854, both of which date to the fourteenth century. Based on evidence in the text itself, Robert Mathiesen suggests that the material was composed "sometime in the first half of the thirteenth century."[61] Overall, there are six known copies of the book.

The introduction of the *Sworn Book* gives the story that the book was fashioned in response to the medieval inquisitions. As the officials of the Church sought to destroy all works of magick, a large council of adepts gathered with the purpose of somehow preserving the sacred science. One among them—Honorius, son of Euclidus—was chosen for the actual performance of the task. As is common in classical grimoiric literature, the master entered into conversation with an angel who directed the reception of the magick. In this case, the angel's name was Hochmel—obviously a version of the Hebrew word "Chockmah" (Wisdom). The *Sworn Book of Honorius* was the result of this action. Each adept was allowed to make no more than three copies of the book, and each copy was to be either buried before his death, interred in his grave with him, or given into trusted hands.

The *Sworn Book* is a specifically Catholic text that seems closely related to the *Ars Notaria*. Joseph Peterson points out the similarities in the prayers used in both manuscripts, and suggests that the two are directly connected.[62] Both texts indeed utilize pure prayer, divorced for the most part from typical grimoiric techniques, in order to achieve their high magickal goals. However, where the *Ars Notaria* focuses upon the gaining of rhetorical knowledge, the *Sworn Book* promises the gaining of the "Beatific Vision." This is simply the Christian version of the vision of the *Merkavah*—wherein one achieves a vision of the face of God through purification, fasting, and prayer.

Robert Mathiesen explains that the operation lasts for twenty-eight days. It is divided into two principal parts: the first part lasts twenty days, and concerns the purification of the operator for the work of the second part. The second part (the actual magickal ritual) is a mere eight days long.[63] This appears similar in style to the *Book of Abramelin*, which instructs one to enter an extended six-month period of purification, followed by a much shorter seven-day rite to gain the vision of the holy guardian angel and to bind the demonic princes.

Interestingly, John Dee owned a copy of this work (Sloane 313). Like the tools of the *Almadel of Solomon*, Dee also adopted an aspect of this work into his Enochian system. The text describes the inscription on parchment of a "Seal of God," which Dee used as the basis for his "Sigillium Dei Ameth." I will go into this somewhat below.

The Dee Diaries

In the late 1500s, two alchemist-mages joined their magickal efforts and began to contact angels. One of these men was Dr. John Dee—the most celebrated scholar of his day. He enjoyed the patronage of Queen Elizabeth I, and was wholly dedicated to the furtherance of the English empire. His goal seems to have been to receive a system of magickal world-domination, by which he could influence the fates of neighboring (and hostile) kingdoms. His partner was Edward Kelley, a dedicated alchemist (who seems to have indulged in alchemical fraud a number of times) who sought the true mysteries of turning base metals into gold.

With these goals in mind, the two men summoned and conversed with a large family of angels. Like the two mages, the angels seemed to have an agenda of their own: the transmission of an extremely powerful system of magick that would influence the world forever after. Not surprisingly, of these three goals (military power, gold, and magickal evolution), only that of the angels came to pass. The angelic system of magick thus delivered came to be known as "Enochian," as it was supposed to have been delivered originally to the biblical prophet Enoch before the Great Flood. It was eventually adopted, in part, by the Hermetic Order of the Golden Dawn in the late 1800s, and has thus become the very backbone of modern magickal knowledge.

John Dee made only one attempt to produce a Solomonic-style grimoire, which is published today as *The Enochian Magick of Dr. John Dee*, by G. James. However, this text has not been of nearly as much use to us as the journals he kept during his work with the angels. There we witness Dee and Kelley interacting with the celestial intelligences on a daily basis, and the new system of magick delivered piece by obscure piece. Dee was in charge of summoning the entities (mainly by nothing more complicated than the recitation of Psalms), and Kelley would gaze into a crystal ball and report on what he saw. (In fact, much of the common stereotypes of "the wizard" that exist in our popular culture today—such as the crystal ball—are traced directly to Dee and Kelley and their magickal journals.)[64] The sessions continued on a regular basis from 1581 to approximately 1607, and the heart of the work seems to have occurred between 1582 and 1585. The journals that are of primary relevance are as follows.

Five Books of the Mysteries (Quinti Libri Mysteriorum)

These five books (preserved as Sloane MS 3188) cover the years from December 22, 1581 to May 23, 1583. Their subject is the transmission of the "Heptarchia," a form of magick that centers around the mystery of the seven archangels who stand before the throne of God (see Revelation 4). It focuses upon the seven planets, days of the week, and even the seven biblical days of creation. The magick itself works through the patronage of forty-nine planetary angels, all of whom have very typical (though lofty) grimoiric functions—such as the bestowing of wisdom and knowledge, or military protection.

The tools of angelic magick are very typical of grimoiric technology. In fact, most of them preexist John Dee, having been adopted from various medieval texts. For instance, the influence of the *Pauline Art* (see above) is quite obvious in the form and function of the Heptarchic tools and furnishings. The *Almadel of Solomon* was a primary source for the design of Dee's holy table (or table of practice)—square in shape, a border inside its edges containing divine names, and a hexagram in its center. Although the almadel is made of wax while Dee's table is made of "sweetwood,"[65] wax is used to fashion Dee's Sigillum Dei Ameth (Seal of God, or Seal of Truth). This seal rests upon the holy table and, like the almadel, is intended to facilitate the skrying of the angels; perhaps in a crystal ball resting upon it as they did for Edward Kelley.

Even the design on the face of the Sigillum is traditional. The "Seal of God" makes its original appearance in the *Sworn Book of Honorius*, though (like the table) the names and characters inscribed upon it differ from Dee's final versions.

Also included is a ring of Solomon, fashioned of pure gold, and featuring the divine name "Pele." This name is found in Agrippa's *Three Books*, as well as Judges 13:18: "Why askest thou thus after my name seeing it is a secret?" The Hebrew word for "name" (פֶּלֶא)[66] indicates "a miracle of God." The archangel Michael delivered the design of this ring to Dee, stating that this was the actual ring worn by Solomon when he worked his miracles. Dee himself was instructed to attempt nothing without it.

Further tools consisted of seven talismans known as the ensigns of creation (corresponding to the seven biblical days of creation) fashioned from purified tin and arrayed around the Sigillum Dei Ameth, a lamen written in angelic characters, several covers of silk, a crystal "shewstone,"[67] lamens for each planetary angelic king (and perhaps the princes of each planet as well), and four miniature wax seals for placement underneath the legs of the table.

Toward the end of the *Five Books*, the angels delivered the first of the truly "Enochian" material. This came in the form of a holy book named *Loagaeth*, the *Book of the Speech From God*. This text consisted of forty-nine pages covered with an indecipherable language arranged in the form of huge magickal squares.[68] The angels proclaimed that it was a new doctrine, and that it contained the words by which God created the universe (as per Genesis). From there the records continue with:

A True and Faithful Relation

The full title of this text is *A True and Faithful Relation of What Passed for Many Yeers Between Dr. John Dee (A Mathematician of Great Fame in Q. Eliz. and King James their Reignes) and Some Spirits*. It is a huge tome published in 1659 by Meric Casaubon, containing a full thirteen books, and covering May 28, 1583 to September 7, 1607.[69]

It is here that we find the famous "48 Angelical Keys," the Great Table of the Earth (the Watchtowers), the 91 (or 92) Parts of the Earth, and the 30 Aethyrs (Heavens). The angels related instructions for using the keys—also known as calls—to access the mysteries of *Logaeth*. The celestial hierarchies within the Watchtowers are defined for the most part, along with an extended rite of summoning to establish contact with them. There are also some rather obscure instructions for skrying into the parts of the Earth, which are actually spiritual reflections of geographical locations. Dee hoped to control any country in the world by simply having access to the angels who resided in that area of the world.

This, of course, does not even begin to scratch the surface of the "Enochian" material of Dr. Dee and Sir Edward Kelley. However, space here would not permit such a massive undertaking. *A True and Faithful Relation* runs for several hundred pages, filled with magick, mysticism, politics, and intrigue. The study of this book, and the Enochian angelic system of magick, is the dedication of a lifetime.

The Grimoire of Armadel (Liber Armadel Seu Totius Cabalae Perfectissima Brevissima et Infallabilis Scientia Tam Speculativa Quam Practiqua)

This text is very often confused with either the *Almadel of Solomon*, or the *Arbatel of Magic*. In fact, it is very possible that the name "Armadel" is a corruption of one of these words—especially of the name "Arbatel." The *Grimoire of Armadel* does happen to borrow its principal conjuration and license to depart from the *Arbatel of Magic*. However, regardless of its use of material from earlier sources, the *Grimoire of Armadel* remains a magickal operation distinct from other texts with a similar name.

It is difficult to say exactly when the manuscript first appeared in history. The earliest recorded mention of the book is found in a bibliography of occult works compounded by Gabriel Naude in 1625. We do know that the name "Armadel" enjoyed some popularity among occultists during the seventeenth century, with several unrelated texts attributed to him. Eventually, a manuscript in the French language (MS 88) found its way into the *Bibliotheque l'Arsenal*, which was then translated into English in the early 1900s by Samuel Mathers. An introduction was then written for the text in 1995 by William Keith.

Seal of Truth.

It is a very simple book, full of colorful sigils related to recognizable angels and spirits (such as the seven arch-angels: Cassiel, Sachiel, etc.), along with borrowed conjurations. Apparently, one is intended to inscribe the sigils on consecrated parchment, and use them to contact angels and spirits who have mysteries to reveal. The book begins with a short section outlining the basic ritual procedure, and the forementioned *Arbatel* conjurations.

The sigils are then grouped into three categories. The first is called "The Theosophy of Our Forefathers or Their Sacred and Mystic Theology." It contains sigils to contact angels such as Gabriel, whose chapter is called "Of the Life of Elijah." Raphael teaches the "Wisdom of Solomon." Other chapters of potential interest are "The Explorer and Leader Joshua," "The Rod of Moses," "The Wisdom of Our Forefather Adam," "The Vision of Eden," and even "The Beholding of the Serpent [of Eden]." These are only a few of the best examples.

The next section is titled "The Sacro-Mystic Theology of Our Forefathers." Herein we can learn lessons "Concerning the Devils and How They May be Bound and Compelled to Visible Appearance," as well as "Concerning the Ways of Knowing the Good Angels, and of Consulting Them." (The latter is taught by no less than Zadkiel and Sachiel together.) We can learn much "Concerning the Evangelic Rebellion and Expulsion," and "Concerning the Life of the Angels Before the Fall." Again, this merely scratches the surface of available sigils.

The final section is called "The Rational Table: or the Qabalistical Light; Penetrating Whatsoever Things be Most Hidden Among the Celestials, the Terrestrials and the Infernals." This title represents the universally typical threefold world of the shaman. (We will learn much more of the importance of this threefold division in later chapters.) Here are contained further magickal requisites, talismans, orations, and several chapters that appear to be Christian sermons, or perhaps invocations.

Some scholars tend to suggest that the *Grimoire of Armadel* is a complete fabrication, akin to the *Grimoirium Verum* and *Grand Grimoire* we shall see below. *Armadel* flourished during the occult panic that gripped France between 1610 and 1640. The Christian orientation of the text, several Biblical sermons, the invocation of saints, and its instructions to recite such official prayers as the Pater Noster, Ave Maria, or the Creedo would probably have caught the attention of a public hungry for rumors of necromancers among the clergy.

However, I feel there is some reasonable doubt surrounding objections to this book's authenticity. The *Armadel* is indeed a simple text, more akin to a working notebook than a full magickal manuscript. It certainly would have been easy to put together—assuming one could have easily amassed its source material in the 1600s. However, the *Armadel* still lacks the shock value that is written into other forgeries like the *Grand Grimoire*, or even our own modern *Necronomicon*. In fact, the text is highly shamanic: offering to teach one how to contact the spirits in order to be safe from them, to learn mysteries from them, etc. There are not even any blood sacrifices found in the instructions. The focus of the work seems to be upon visionary quests or spiritual encounters facilitated by the magickal characters, as well as gaining some magickal powers such as healing, alchemy, agriculture, etc.

This kind of straightforwardness would not be expected of the shock-value forgeries. William Keith and several contemporary grimoiric scholars tend to feel the magickal value of this book is "slight, or at best highly dilute." I feel that the overall simplicity of the book disappoints many occult researchers. However, I am personally fascinated with the implications behind the sigils and the mystical experiences they promise. It seems just as likely that this grimoire was once a personal notebook used by a working mage. The reader may even agree with me if he encounters the *Armadel* after reading this book (especially Chapters Two, Three, and Ten).

Grimoirium Verum

Here we have one of the famous grimoires of "black" magick. Both A. E. Waite[70] and Elizabeth Butler[71] introduce the work with the text of its own title page: "Grimoirium Verum, or the Most Approved Keys of Solomon the Hebrew Rabbin, wherein the Most Hidden Secrets, both Natural and Supernatural, are immediately exhibited, but it is necessary that the Demons should be contented on their part. Translated from the Hebrew by Plaingiere, a Dominican Jesuit, with a Collection of Curious Secrets. Published by Alibeck the Egyptian. 1517."

Waite suggests that the date given in the above quotation is fraudulent, as the text actually belongs to the mid-eighteenth century. It is written in French, though it very likely has Italian connections, and does in fact seem to have a connection to Rome. It owes a debt, as do so many other grimoires, to the *Key of Solomon the King* as some of its material is taken directly therefrom. The *Lemegeton*, too, had its influence, as the *Grimoirium* contains instructions for the evocation of the exact same entities.

Little more needs said concerning this text. This type of grimoire, along with other purported "black" rituals, have always struck me as somewhat boring, very unoriginal, and rarely of much use practically. Overall, they tend to appear as little more than rehashes of the *Key of Solomon* and *Lemegeton*, with a few dissertations included to give the text a renegade "Satanic" feel. Most of them, in my opinion, do not even make the grade as Satanic or "black." While it is true that they call upon demonic entities, and usually include prayers and invocations directed to Lucifer, we shall see in later chapters that this does not properly make an operation "black."

The Grand Grimoire (Red Dragon)

This text was published without a date, though Waite suggests that it is about the same age as the *Grimoirium Verum*. The work is introduced as "The Grand Grimoire, with the Powerful Calvicle of Solomon and of Black Magic; or the Infernal Devices of the Great Agrippa for the Discovery of all Hidden Treasures and the Subjugation of every Denomination of Spirits, together with an Abridgment of all the Magical Arts."

This is, perhaps, the most well-known of "black" grimoires, appearing even in Hollywood next to the *Key of Solomon the King*. Like the *Grimoirium Verum*, the *Grand Grimoire* probably has an Italian origin or influence, as indicated by the name of its editor Antonio Venitiana del Rabina. The book itself is attributed to Solomon and depicts his summoning and binding of the demonic prime minister Lucifuge Rofocale,[72] who thenceforth became rather popular among occult authors (such as Eliphas Levi).

What perhaps makes this book so famous (or infamous) is the fact that it deals specifically with making pacts with devils. Other texts, such as *Goetia* and *Abramelin*, do not work through pacts at all, and the latter example expressly forbids such action. Meanwhile the *Grand Grimoire* instructs one to make a conditional pact with Lucifuge:

> It is my wish to make a pact with thee, so as to obtain wealth at thy hands immediately, failing which I will torment thee by the potent words of the Clavicle.

The written document to be signed by Lucifuge reads as follows:

> I promise the grand Lucifuge to reward him in twenty years' time for all treasures he may give me. In witness whereof I have signed myself. N.N.

After some dickering, further conditions are added by Lucifuge:

> Leave me to my rest, and I will confer upon thee the nearest treasure, on condition that thou dost set apart for me one coin on the first Monday of each month, and dost not call me oftener than once a week, to wit, between ten at night and two in the morning. Take up thy pact; I have signed it. Fail in thy promise, and thou shalt be mine at the end of twenty years.

The *Grand Grimoire* then proceeds to communicate Solomon's instructions for the making of a pact. E. M. Butler writes that this is the only complete "and perfect" outline of such a pact of which she is aware (though she does make mention of the similar Faustian ritual). The form of the pact in the *Grand Grimoire* is deliberately evasive—supposing that the mage is "getting one over" on the demonic forces.

For those who are interested in the darker side of the grimoires, I must recommend *Ritual Magic* and *The Fortunes of Faust*, both by Elizabeth Butler. She is an expert in what is known as the "Faustian" tradition—a Germanic phenomenon based upon the mythos of Faust and his dealings with Satan. A. E. Waite also gives portions of the texts of the above two (and other) grimoires in his *Book of Ceremonial Magic*.

Conclusion

The medieval texts do not (for the most part) contain dark and horrible rites that call upon "Lovecraftian" or ghastly beasties. They are not all about curses or pacts with "the devil," and there is no enslavement of innocent spirits. Instead, they reflect the magickal philosophies and wisdom of our magickal ancestors, from whom we have inherited much. It is a system of magick complete unto itself and rich with the influence of tribal magick. Agrippa, in the *Three Books of Occult Philosophy*, describes what the grimoires promise:

> To defend kingdoms, to discover the secret councils of men, to overcome enemies, to redeem captives, to increase riches, to procure the favor of men, to expel diseases, to preserve health, to prolong life, to renew youth, to foretell future events, to see and know things done many miles off, and such like as these, by virtue of superior influences, may seem things incredible; yet read but the ensuing treatise, and thou shalt see the possibility thereof confirmed both by reason, and example. (*Three Books of Occult Philosophy*, p. lxi)

The schools of magick or "natural philosophy" (that is, alchemy, astrology, and spirit-working) were considered among the respectable sciences from the earliest of times. The medieval and Renaissance mages I've mentioned above, along with numerous others both known and unknown, were also physicists, doctors, astronomers, biologists, mathematicians, philosophers, architects, navigators, etc. The existence of the *Notary Arts* and related texts makes this point evident. In truth, the men who created most of our modern fields of scientific study were adept mages as well (such as Sir Isaac Newton, who was in fact an alchemist).

For further information on this point, I highly recommend *The Rosicrucian Enlightenment* by Frances Yates. The preface, especially, and truly the entire book, contains much information about the magickal nature of the early sciences, and the mystical minds it took to dream of them.[73] The Rosicrucian thinkers of the seventeenth century were the ancestors of the Masons, the Royal Society of England, and of the Age of Enlightenment overall.

Not only was magick respected among the sciences, it was actually considered the highest and most sacred science. The *Goetia* begins, in some manuscripts, with the following words:

> Magic is the Highest, most Absolute, and most Divine Knowledge of Natural Philosophy, advanced in its works and wonderful operations by a right understanding of the inward and occult virtue of things; so that true Agents being applied to proper Patients, strange and admirable effects will thereby be produced. Whence magicians are profound and diligent searchers into Nature: they, because of their skill, know how to anticipate an effect, the which to the vulgar shall seem to be a miracle.[74]

One must question, then, why magick fell from its lofty position. Why are the texts considered superstitious rubbish when they were penned by the hands of such as John Dee, Henry Agrippa, and Trithemius? In general, we are given the impression that magick fell by the wayside due to its inability to withstand the scientific process. By applying the steps of experimentation, magick is said to have come up short, producing no results, and was thus abandoned by the educated.

However, that assumption is simply not true. The historical fact is that magick was feared enough by the medieval Church to outlaw it. Richard Kieckhefer opens his book *Forbidden Rites* with the observation that we are (mentally speaking) what we read, and the power that books hold to transform minds has given rise to anxiety as much as celebration.[75] Various related developments in late medieval Europe brought about a renaissance of literature, and brought with it concerns about what people were reading. Magickal books that blatantly called upon demonic powers embodied the worst fears of those who naturally feared a populace that (for the first time in history) could read.

It was not that magick failed to pass the test, but that it passed enough of its tests to make the world rulers of the day take action against it. It was forced from its position of highest respect into the underground realm of the outlaw and fraud. This is, in fact, no different from the current drug laws and the treatment received by such educated men as Timothy Leary. History shows us that such arts as magick, alchemy, and even a good number of the currently accepted sciences have been regularly repressed by established governing bodies. The scientists of the medieval and Renaissance eras necessarily had to distance themselves from the practice of magick (at least outwardly). A world where a man could be executed for suggesting that the Earth revolves around the Sun was no world for the investigations of occult philosophy.

As well, the Black Death that decimated Europe at the end of the medieval era had shaken many of the peoples' faith in all things spiritual. Those who continued to insist on its use were often feared by the peasants and ridiculed by their peers.[76] Thus, a tangible separation began to grow between the studies of magick, and the other—materialistic—sciences.

So, here we stand at the dawning of a new age, with the fear of the Church and our dependence upon materialistic science receding ever further into the past. We might choose to accept their authority on the uselessness and superstition of the grimoires, or we might instead return to the manuscripts for a second look, to judge them according to our own knowledge and experiences. We might decide to put them to the test—nearly six or seven hundred years after they were written—and see what results they might produce. Though it is common knowledge that they are the origins of many of our current magickal practices, few seekers have taken an interest in learning what deeper secrets they might contain.

In my searches, I found precious few who had taken such an interest. As I stated before, most (even Neopagans) were happy to accept the medieval Church's doctrine on the matter. On the other hand, those few who did make the effort to duplicate the experiments of the classical texts seemed to report outstanding results time and again. One might have to get up a little early on a Wednesday morning to find a virgin nut-tree from which to cut a wand. It might take some time to find thread spun by a young maiden. One might even have to dedicate a search by phone and Internet to locate rare materials, herbs, or perfumes. However, as E. M. Butler suggests concerning the Greek texts that gave rise to the grimoires: the instructions are not prohibitively difficult to follow, but they are by no means easy, and frequently demand considerable physical and mental effort on the part of the aspirant.[77]

If one has "what it takes" to put forth such physical and mental effort, then one can eventually access the treasures of the grimoires. I personally made the decision to test their promises, and to follow their instructions and procedures as completely as possible. What I have found is far from a failed science that cannot stand up to scientific process. On the contrary, I have found the results of the practice extremely impressive.

This book is about my experiences with, and discoveries within, the classical art. I have not written this book to explain the process of any single grimoire. Instead, it is about the living tradition of medieval grimoiric magick that resides within the overall body of literature.

Of course, I understand the difficulty in referring to the grimoires as a "living tradition," as it has been all but dead now for nearly five centuries. Some of their secrets have faded away, and the culture that gave them life has long since passed. Not only this, but the communities of the modern occult revival are seldom composed of Christian mystics who would find use for the prayers from the *Notary Arts* or *Liber Juratus*. Overall, there is no direct link between ourselves and the authors of the medieval and Renaissance texts.

Yet, they remain in fact our magickal ancestors, and their work has provided the very backbone of our own modern systems. Knowledge of this fact is becoming more widespread today than ever before, and for the first time we have an abundance of information concerning them. Meanwhile, occult students seem to have a natural inclination to seek out the "root origins" of the subjects they study. Therefore, the classical grimoires are just beginning to enjoy their own revival—with their tribal-shamanic magickal secrets appealing to a surprisingly wide (and usually non-Christian) audience. They are, once again, becoming a living tradition.

I, of course, cannot hope to cover every detail of medieval practice in this one book. My hope is only to provide a solid background upon which to study and experiment with the grimoires. I have also attempted to share some of my own experiences; especially to illustrate how the techniques must be adopted into their proper modern framework. Only by understanding what these mysterious books once were can we understand what they will (and have) become.

Medieval–Renaissance Time Line
Including Historical Events and Appearances of Grimoires

325: Council of Nice called by Roman emperor Constantine.

455: Rome sacked by Vandals. Medieval era begins around this time.

589: Third Council of Toledo inserts the word "filioque" into the Nicene Creed, driving a wedge between the Eastern and Western Churches.

638: Islamic armies take control of the Holy Land.

1054: Eastern Orthodox Church and Roman Catholic Church mutually excommunicate each other, and separate into two distinct bodies.

1095: Byzantine emperor pleads with Pope Urban II for help against Islamic Turks in the Holy Land. The Crusades are begun.

1118: Knights Templar is established in Solomon's Temple in Jerusalem.

1128: Knights Templar confirmed by Pope Honorius II at Council of Troyes.

1215: King John forced to sign the Magna Carta, an early Bill of Rights, by land barons.

1231: Pope Gregory IX declares life imprisonment for repentant heretics, and death for those who refuse to confess.

1256: Date of earliest known copy of the *Picatrix*, from the court of King Alphonso of Castille. The text is likely much older.

Late 1200s: Moses de Leon publishes the *Sepher haZohar*, the principal book of the Qabalah.

1291: Holy Land lost to the Turks. "Official" end of the Crusades. Knights Templar establish new headquarters at Temple Monastery in France.

1300s: Bubonic plague spreads from China during this century, and continues until 1600s. The *Key of Solomon the King* appears during this century, though it may be quite a bit older. The oldest known copies of the *Ars Notaria* also appear during this century.

1312: Pope Clemet V, at the insistence of French King Phillipe le Bel, issues a papal bull suppressing the Templar order.

1314: Templar Grand Master Jaques de Molay, and others, burned at the stake for heresy.

1318: Pope John XXII has the bishop of Frejus investigate several clerics and laymen on charges of necromancy, geomancy, etc.

Early 1400s: Suggested origin of the *Sworn Book of Honorius*.

1406: Group of clerics accused of working magick against the king of France and Pope Benedict XIII.

1409: Pope Benedict XIII is himself accused of working necromancy and employing necromancers.

1450: Johann Gutenburg invents printing press. Renaissance era begins circa this time.

1462: Trithemius born.

1468: Two Dominican monks write the *Malleus Maleficarum* (Witches' Hammer).

1492: Nobody expects the Spanish Inquisition, except for the queen of Spain. Columbus sets out to find shortcut to India.

Early 1500s: Martin Luther instigates schism of Roman Church into Catholic and Protestant sects. King Henry VIII creates the Church of England.

1509–10: Agrippa writes the *Three Books of Occult Philosophy*. After his death the *Fourth Book of Occult Philosophy* appears, and is rejected as a forgery by Agrippa's student Wierus.

1527: John Dee born.

1558: Henry's daughter and successor, Queen Elizabeth I, officially establishes her father's Church circa this time.

1575: Latin copy of the *Arbatel of Magic* appears. (John Dee also mentions the book in his work between 1581–1583.)

1581–1583: John Dee scribes the *Five Books of the Mysteries*.

1583–1607: John Dee scribes further angelic journals, published by Meric Casaubon in 1659 (see below).

1600s: Earliest known copies of *Lemegeton* date to this century, though it is certainly much older.

1610–1640: The *Grimoire of Armadel* flourishes in France around this time.

1614–1615: The "Rosicrucian Manifestos" (the *Fama* and *Confessio*) are published in Germany, sparking the Rosicrucian thought movement.

1655: Robert Turner includes a translation of the *Heptameron* in his collection of esoteric texts.

1659: Meric Casaubon publishes *A True and Faithful Relation*, a collection of John Dee's journal entries (see 1583 above), in order to slander Dee's memory.

Late 1600s to early 1700s: The *Book of the Sacred Magic of Abramelin the Mage* appears (though it claims to have been written between 1368–1437).

Mid 1700s: The probable origin of the *Grimoirium Verum* and the *Grand Grimoire*.

1801: Francis Barrett publishes *The Magus*, perhaps attempting to establish a magickal order.

---

1. See the "Medieval-Renaissance Time Line."
2. Note that "Catholic" means "universal." Thus the decentralized faith was certainly not Catholic.
3. *Qui ex Patre procedit*—"Who proceedeth from the Father."
4. Known as a *Papal Nuncio*.
5. It was not until 1964, over nine hundred years later, that the Ecumenical Patriarch Athenagoras and Pope Paul VI met in Jerusalem and annulled the mutual excommunications of 1054.
6. The "witches" of the Burning Times were very often healers. These small-village herbalists and midwives were seen as direct competition to the newly emerging practice of medicine, and the Inquisition provided an easy means to diminish it.
7. This plague was carried principally by parasitic insects who lived upon rats. Thus, the best defense against the Black Death was to maintain a clean, rat-free, flea-free home environment.
8. Interestingly, a similar Egyptian "fad" would later surround the rise of the modern Western occult tradition in the late nineteenth century.
9. It is important to note that the manifestos were most specifically addressed to alchemists and healers.
10. See the end of this chapter for time line.
11. *The Greek Magical Papyri in Translation: Including the Demotic Spells: Text*, ed. Hans Deiter Betz.
12. We will see in later chapters that these names are likely those of ancient angels and gods that have been corrupted over the centuries due to oral transmission and sometimes scribal errors.
13. I.e., "bornless," or without beginning.
14. *The Greek Magical Papyri in Translation.*
15. *Ritual Magic*, p. 8.
16. These are actually from "Recension C" of the *Testament of Solomon*, which was bound with a copy of the *Key of Solomon*, and a catalog of fifty-one infernal spirits, complete with seals, etc.
17. *Conjuring Spirits*, p. 256: "The Devil's Contemplatives."

18. Note this example from the *Key of Solomon the King*, Book II, Chapter 5: "Mertalia, Musalia, Dophalia, Onemalia, Zitanscia, Goldaphaira, Dedulsaira, Ghevialaira, Gheminaira, Gegropheira . . ."

19. This custom appears in several manuscripts. Solomon, in the *Key of Solomon the King* instructs his son Roboam to place the book into an ivory casket and intere it with him in his sepulcher. In the *Book of Abramelin*, the author claims to have written the text and locked it securely within a casket (though no mention of burial is made).

20. Take, for instance, the tale of the sorcerer's apprentice.

21. *Twilit Grotto—Esoteric Archives*, Picatrix (Summary).

22. Ibid. From Martin Plessner's Introduction, pp. lix-lxxv.

23. Ibid. This is a point we will return to again in the chapter on constructing tools.

24. Ibid. This is something else to which we will return in chapter 2.

25. Ibid.

26. Ibid.

27. *The Book of Ceremonial Magic*, p. 70.

28. See below.

29. Seven each for Saturn, Jupiter, Mars, and Sol; five each for Venus and Mercury; and six for Luna.

30. Weiser's *Key of Solomon the King*, p. 63.

31. *The Book of Ceremonial Magic*, p. 145.

32. See chapter 5.

33. *The Book of Ceremonial Magic*, p. 73.

34. I've noted that scholarly texts very often refer to all spirit summoning (demons as well as shades of the dead) as "necromancy," as the two traditions are nearly identical on a practical level.

35. Weiser's *Goetia*, p. 24.

36. *Ritual Magic*, p. 65.

37. Sloane MS 3825, though I have cleaned up the text a bit.

38. Weiser's *Goetia*, p. 24

39. Ibid., p. 24.

40. *Esoteric Archives*, Twilit Grotto. Intro to the *Ars Paulina*.

41. Weiser's *Goetia*, pp. 24-5.

42. If you would like to see a beautiful example of an actual almadel, see the video *The Magick of Solomon* by the Church of Hermetic Sciences. This magickal group practices a modernized version of the grimoiric tradition, and the film explains their system. http://www.miraclemile.com/hermsci/index.html.

43. The *Almadel* refers to the altitudes as "Choras."

44. Weiser's *Goetia*, p. 25.

45. See *Notary Arts* on next page.

46. Found in *Conjuring Spirits*, ed. by Claire Fanger, pp. 14-9.

47. Ibid, p. 110-39.

48. Ibid. p. 216-49.

49. Take special note of the *Book of Abramelin* and the *Sworn Book of Honorius* below.

50. The giving of alms appears in several places both within and without the grimoires. It plays a principal role in the *Book of Abramelin*, and even today remains an important religious duty among the Muslim people.

51. This is not dissimilar to modern Hermetic methods of skrying tarot cards or pathworking.

52. *Esoteric Archives*, Twilit Grotto. *Notary Arts*.

53. See below.

54. *Esoteric Archives*, Twilit Grotto. *Heptameron*.

55. Llewellyn's *Three Books*, p. 677.

56. *The Book of Ceremonial Magic*, pp. 74-5.

57. This is not unusual, as even the *Key of Solomon the King* addresses itself from father to son (Solomon to Roboam).

58. See below for more on John Dee and the *Five Books*.

59. *Esoteric Archives*, Twilit Grotto. *Arbatel of Magic*.

60. Ibid.

61. *Conjuring Spirits*, p. 146.

62. *Esoteric Archives*, Twilit Grotto, *Liber Juratus*.

63. *Conjuring Spirits*, p. 150.

64. Any remaining "wizard" stereotypes seem to have come either from the Jewish mystic (Baal Shem, *Merkavah* mystic, and/or Qabalist), and from the Merlin of Arthurian legend.

65. Any fruit or syrup wood: maple, apple, cherry, etc.

66. That is, the Hebrew letters Peh, Lamed, and Aleph.

67. Contrary to popular belief, Dee and Kelley never made use of Dee's obsidian mirror in their seances. For the majority of the work, Kelley used a clear quartz crystal.

68. The book still exists today, in Kelley's handwriting, as Sloane MS 3189. The *Esoteric Archives* CD, by Twilit Grotto, also contains the entire text.

69. The original manuscript is Cotton Appendix XLVI, sometimes referred to as Royal Appendix, or Sloane MS. 5007.

70. *Book of Ceremonial Magic,* p. 88.

71. *Ritual Magic*, p. 80.

72. Where Lucifer means "Light-Bearer," this name (probably a permutation of Lucifer) means "Fly from the Light." Rofocale, according to Butler, appears to be an anagram for Focalor, the forty-first spirit of the *Goetia*.

73. Throughout Western history, mathematical pioneers have been just as mystical-minded as our own modern quantum physicists and chaos mathematicians. It might even surprise the modern reader to discover how many respectable modern scientists and scholars are also occultists.

74. Weiser's *Goetia*, p. 21.

75. *Forbidden Rites*, p. 1.

76. It is reported that John Dee himself suffered in this way, having had his home partially burned down by fear-stricken peasants during one of his long trips abroad.

77. *Ritual Magic*, p. 10.

Shamanism,
Tribal to Medieval

It seems that one major obstacle, above all others, has most plagued students of archeology and anthropology. Specifically, this would be the failure to realize that cultures of the past do not often share our own basic assumptions about reality. In attempting to make heads or tails of the past, we very often find ourselves confounded by our predecessors' "odd" actions and statements. Specifically in the case of ancient magickal texts, the reaction is often to write them off as "blinds" or mere uneducated superstition. Throughout my time of anthropological research—from the lives of the ancient Sumerians to the very medieval minds that form the subject of this book—no problem has been more ubiquitous than the personal biases of the authors I've read.

Students of Egyptology have learned lessons in this regard, and today much is being done to correct the work of past scholars who simply failed to consider that the ancient Egyptians were not Christians at heart.

The damage done in the realm of the grimoires *is* even more severe, as anyone who has suffered through A. E. Waite's antagonism in *The Book of Ceremonial Magic*[1] can attest (see below). The rites of the grimoires are all too often depicted as being of low moral character, or even outright "black" in nature. Historical scholars very often question how such "low and base" goals as hindering sportsmen from killing game or the destruction of an enemy could exist alongside such goals as gaining the beatific vision of God. This mindset was an unfortunate result of the mainstream Christian antagonism to anything with a ring of shamanism or Paganism. Not only Waite, but Elizabeth Butler, Samuel Mathers, and many who have published on the subject have had to allow for this, and have been affected by this, in their work. We owe them a high debt of gratitude for publishing any of the material at all.

I would hazard to suggest the trend began in 1584, with the publication of Reginald Scot's *Discoverie of Witchcraft*.[2] This text was written to belittle and condemn the rituals of the grimoires as the worst kind of black magick. However, Mr. Scot actually did the grimoires a favor by presenting their material and further surrounding them with awe, mystery, and controversy. (Students of John Dee will recognize this same formula in Meric Causabon's preservation of Dee's angelic diaries in *A True and Faithful Relation*. Causabon added a preface of mockery to the diaries, but very few have cared to read the preface.)

Of course, even Reginald Scot had the full force of an Inquisitorial culture behind his efforts. As we shall see in this and later chapters, the grimoires do contain many practices borrowed directly from surrounding Paganisms. The medieval Church had long been running its propaganda campaign against such Pagan practices, labeling them "black": from ritual sacrifice to the fashioning of images. Of course, these were political concerns, regardless of the fact that such practices were—and remain—real and proven methods of working with the spiritual.

Yet, it was Scot who, in his time, did the most to preserve the grimoiric tradition; by writing a book that became a Western "standard." The medieval magickal texts survived by being remembered—whether with or without contempt was irrelevant. The same was true for the next generation to pick up the torch, this time represented by one Eliphas Levi. Levi was particularly influenced by texts such as Scot's *Discoverie*, and his resulting publications between 1855-60 became the new Western standard. These were *Dogme et Rituel de La Haute Magie* (otherwise known as *Transcendental Magic*) and *Histoire de la Magie (History of Magic)*.

As E. M. Butler affirms, Levi was all too happy to fabricate tales of horror and even false rites to attribute to the classical texts. He "romanticized and falsified the literature in question almost beyond recognition."[3] Levi's intentions were apparently sensationalistic, aiming to gain attention and sell books through tales of the horrors of black magick. Butler points out that most of the texts mentioned by Levi—such as the *Magickal Elements* of Peter of Abano and the *Fourth Book* of Pseudo-Agrippa—are innocent of the sacrilege described by Levi.

Levi painted a picture of black and dangerous rituals that could only lead to the ultimate destruction and damnation of the aspirant. The next standard text for Western scholarship on the grimoires was written by Arthur Edward Waite, who was himself influenced heavily by Eliphas Levi. Waite's book first bore the unfortunate title of *The Book of Black Magic*, but was later renamed *The Book of Ceremonial Magic*. This brings us back to the beginning of this discussion. Waite and nearly all who have followed have condemned the texts, at least in part, because they include elements (such as sacrifice, or the binding of spirits), which their Christian upbringing refused to accept. Rather than striving to understand these elements, the authors simply dismiss them out of hand:

> The Grimoires, once seized and burnt by authority everywhere, are certainly not harmless books. Sacrilege, murder, theft, are indicated as means to realization in almost all these works. . . . No doubt anyone who is mad enough and wicked enough to abandon himself to such operations is pre-disposed to all chimeras and all phantoms. (Levi, *Transcendental Magic*, p. 364)

> But, unhappily, this domain of enchantment[4] is in all respects comparable to the gold of Faerie, which is presumably its medium of exchange. It cannot withstand daylight, the test of the human eye, or the scale of reason. When these are applied, its paradox becomes an anticlimax, its antithesis ludicrous; its contradictions are without genius; its mathematical marvels end in a verbal quibble; its elixirs fail even as purges; its transmutations do not need exposure at the assayer's hands; its marvel-working words prove barbarous mutilations of dead languages, and are impotent from the moment that they are understood . . . (Waite, *Book of Ceremonial Magic*, p. 18)

> One might even suggest that a culture in which ritual occupies so central a place will naturally if not inevitably engender forbidden rituals, somewhat as the production of a tapestry necessarily produces on the underside a distorted version of the intended image. The study of late medieval necromancy gives an exceptionally clear and forceful picture of the abuses likely to arise in a culture so keenly attentive to ritual display of sacerdotal power. (Kieckhefer, *Forbidden Rites*, p. 13)

Is it any wonder my colleagues in the magickal communities were put off by the idea of grimoiric magick? And not only this subject, but other ancient practices suffer similar academic scorn. There *is* no shortage of anthropology texts that take unfortunately aloof stances toward primitive culture and mysticism. Waite can even be forgiven his harsh words when one realizes how common such attitudes were in his time. Even today, it was common until somewhat recently to classify the subjects of African-descended practices (Santeria, Voodoo, Palo Mayombe, etc.) as "black magick" or outdated superstition.

I feel that these attitudes among today's scholars can only hinder modern occultism, especially in the realm of experimental magick. As I have stated previously, these ancient ways are the heritage of our own modern practices, and dismissing them without attempting to understand them only rules out valuable magickal experience from which we might learn.

I did not personally come to this understanding until I came face to face with the occult philosophies of a tribal system of magick. This was around the same time I began to study the grimoires with full intention of working through a months-long operation. By mere chance, I gained the opportunity to spend large amounts of time with a man initiated into two different African traditions: Santeria and a related tradition known as Palo Mayombe. For the first time in my life, I found myself speaking with an accomplished magickian who did not see things in the usual Western Hermetic way.

His methods were simple and direct (in a sense), and based upon a very literal belief in the existence of gods and spirits. He never spoke of assuming godforms, nor of Jungian psychology or accessing aspects of the self. To put it simply, he spoke from a worldview completely alien to my own. Day after day I spent several hours with him, simply listening to him describe his ways and comparing them with what I had learned on my own.

At first I merely picked his brain for every scrap of information he would relinquish to a non-initiate. Eventually, I was able to witness much of the procedure firsthand when a loved one became an initiate of his tradition of Palo Mayombe. I very likely would have followed if only I had felt a calling from the African deities (Orishas), or had not already been committed to my own pursuits. Both Palo and Santeria are extremely beautiful systems, with a completeness and power that most of us in the modern reconstructionist movements cannot enjoy. I knew I was learning about a system of tribal shamanism that extended thousands of years into the past, and to the mysterious "Dark Continent" of Africa. This meant that the practices would have still been alive and contemporary with the medieval grimoires—texts which themselves sometimes purport to have originated in Africa.

Santeria specifically showed some very suggestive links to the same Middle Eastern cultures (Canaan, Israel, Egypt, Babylon, etc.) that gave rise to the Jewish, Christian, and Arabic traditions reflected in the grimoires. For instance, the Santerian goddess Yamaya is known as the "Walker Upon the Sea," and is said to embody the upper layer of water upon the ocean (i.e., the waves). Meanwhile, ancient Canaan[5] knew of a goddess named Asherah bat Yammi (Asherah, Lady of the Sea), who is also known as the "Treader Upon the Sea."

The Santerian methods of working with Orishas[6] also matched closely with what I knew of the ancient Near and Middle East. The gods are invoked into physical bases (sacred objects, statues, etc.) from which they are fed and cared for by their worshippers. Even the sacred Ark of the Covenant hailed in biblical legend did not strike me as so different from the Santerian pots[7] I could see before me in the here and now.

Meanwhile, most of the African-derived faiths seemed to have methods of evoking spirits very similar to the grimoires. They involved the inscription of the "signature" (sigil) of the spirit, along with the speaking aloud of the entity's name, dance, drumming, and sacred instruments used to gain the spirit's attention.

I find another hint of connection via these Orisha pots in the *Goetia*'s brass vessel: which is used to bind spirits. This is based on Arabic "jinni in the vessel" legends (such as "Aladdin and the Lamp"). It is the method of binding spirits, the grimoires claim, that King Solomon used himself. Meanwhile, African tribes are known to have entrapped

(Familiarized) spirits in pots[8] (very often of iron) from which the entities were summoned to perform tasks. If these practices did migrate from Africa, into the Middle East, and then into Europe, then we might have to consider the *Goetia's* claim somewhat truthful: the real King Solomon very likely commanded Familiar spirits trapped in brass or iron vessels, just as surely as his god took up residence in the Ark of the Covenant.

These kinds of similarities presented themselves even further when—during the same period as my encounters with Santeria—I purchased my first copy of Agrippa's *Three Books*. It struck me how closely Agrippa's lessons agreed with what I was learning about the ancient African practices and occult philosophies. Of special interest were Agrippa's Books I and III; the former dealing with natural magick, and the latter with religious/devotional considerations. (Book II contains the mathematics and gematria more unique to Western occultism.)

Finally, my own practice of the grimoiric rites came into play. As the Santero and I discovered more similarities between his methods and those of medieval Europe, I began to relate to him my own studies of the invocation of angels. Here, it appeared, we had hit a veritable gold mine. It happens that Santeria contains rites of invocation and bonding with Orishas (such as the rite of Ocha, which involves a bonding between a human and his or her patron), that show an incredible likeness to grimoiric procedures—in every major, and most minor, details.

It would be far outside the range of this book to fully discuss all of these similarities. I have seen it suggested lately that the African faiths may indeed have some direct relation to the medieval grimoires. What data I have gathered (most of it given above) seems rather inconclusive, yet certainly suggestive enough to elicit further study. If the discussion I have seen on the Internet is any indication, I would bet that we will be seeing more on this subject in the near future. As our modern occult communities outgrow the past social revulsion toward the Afro-Cuban faiths, we are finding an entirely new field of study which might relate directly to our own familiar paths.

In any case, it certainly opened up new vistas for myself. I soon found that I could bring obscure or confusing grimoiric material to the Santero for clarification. We needed only to discover if Santeria or Palo possessed a similar practice, and he would then proceed to elaborate upon it: why such a thing was done, how it was accomplished, and even where to find the materials, etc. He was able to relate orally to me what the authors of the grimoires very likely related orally to their own students. It was this more than anything else that made my practice of medieval magick possible—as well as ultimately successful.

I did not know if Santeria necessarily shared a direct historical relation to the Solomonic cycle or Agrippa's occultism, but it did seem to me that it shared a relation to tribal shamanism in general. There are certain common elements in such varied paths as Native American shamanism, Voodoo, Palo Mayombe, Sufism, and even many of the more obscure traditions found in Orthodox Judaism, Islam, and Christianities. Furthermore, these elements were both present in the grimoires and absent from most of what I had learned of magick over the previous years. In the end I could not help but draw the conclusion that the grimoires reflected nothing less than a survival of shamanism during even the darkest age of medieval Europe.

Shamanism

Before I can hope to prove my premise—that the grimoires are a principally shamanic phenomenon—we must first come to an understanding of the term "shamanism." Therefore, we will leave the subject of the grimoires alone for a short time, and consider the available scholarship on the subject of shamanism and "shamanic culture."

A well-respected and widely referenced textbook on the subject of shamanic culture around the world is Mircea Eliade's *Shamanism: Archaic Techniques of Ecstasy*. In this book, Professor Eliade explains all of the basic components of shamanic practice (from vocation and initiation, to the symbolism of the shaman's costume and drum). From there, he continues to highlight examples from all over the globe—the Siberian region, the Americas, the Far East, Africa, etc. It is a wonderfully enlightening book to read.

According to this text, shamanism (strictly speaking) originates in Siberia and Central Asia. The word "shaman" descends from the Tungusic *saman*, through the Russian language, and finally into English as "shaman." In the nineteenth century, this term was believed to derive from the Pali word *samana* (Sanskrit *sramana*), and similar words in Tokharian (*samane* "Buddhist monk") and in Sogdian (*smn = saman*) further indicate possible Indian origins for the word.[9]

However, regardless of where the word "shaman" originates, it has been used for the last one hundred years to indicate similar practices anywhere on Earth—in both primitive and urban cultures. A shaman is defined as a magician, a healer and doctor, a psychopomp, a mystic, a poet, and even (in the earlier cultures) a priest.[10]

Of course, this can only serve as a basic (and in fact general) definition. It is the particulars of the daily practice of a shaman that interest us—to see where an ancient shaman might have some relation to a medieval grimoiric wizard. For instance, Eliade expands upon his definition of "shaman" at various points within his book. The shaman is a human who has built a relationship with the spiritual, and can command the dead, demons, and nature spirits without falling prey to them. He engages in ecstatic trances that grant him magickal flight and ascent into the heavens, descent into the underworld, mastery over fire, etc.[11] His spiritual experiences are concrete and even face-to-face with the entities involved. He might talk with, pray to, or even implore any of them, but he does not directly control more than a limited number of them.[12] In this, we can already see strong ties to the rites described in the grimoires, though the relations will become much more pronounced as we continue to investigate.

Another interesting point of fact is the manner in which the ancient Arctic, Siberian, and Central Asian shamanic religions coincide. They each worship a celestial father god—the all-powerful creator whose name often translates as "sky" or "heaven."[13] Even if his name differs, the most characteristic attributes remain—such as "high," "lofty," "luminous," etc. From this father sky descends several subordinate "sons" or "messengers" who occupy the lower heavenly spheres. The names and number of these celestial children differs according to culture, place, and time—with seven[14] or nine sons or daughters being most common. The shaman will most often develop special relationships with some of these messengers, as they are the ones directly charged with the guardianship of Earth and its human beings.[15]

There is no question that these descriptions should remind us of the religious and cosmological structure of the grimoires, and the celestial beings they call upon. Although, it would be incorrect to suggest that these shamanic beliefs were incorporated directly into the medieval texts (thousands of years separate them.) Instead, this is the history of the origins of the Judeo-Christian beliefs themselves; from the migrations of the Indo-Europeans from Central Asia into the Middle East before the dawn of written history. What it proves is that these concepts—singular father deity who rules over a given number of (mostly) benevolent subordinate deities—is both older than we often consider today, and is shamanic at its core. Note here the relation to the "sons of God" mentioned in Genesis 6. Also, it is important to note that the word "angel" (Greek *Angelos*) translates as "messenger." The entire concept of the angel seems to have come from the basic shamanic concept that ruling gods employed "lesser" deities as viziers.

An interesting aspect of the ancient father sky is that he always tends to be rather far removed from reality. Unlike the ubiquitous and angry God of the medieval Church, father sky was relatively unconcerned with what humans did with their time. As one studies the chronological history of ancient cultures, it is actually possible to watch as such a deity recedes further into the background of his pantheon as time progresses. At first he is quite active; especially in regards to the creation, for which he is credited. As time rolls slowly onward, however, the people become more focused on the sons and daughters. These are the gods and goddesses we are more familiar with in

Pagan literature, who are active in the "here-and-now," have worshippers, sacred temples, and govern what happens on Earth from day to day.

A wonderful example of this dynamic can be found in the history of Sumer-Babylonia. When we are given our first peek at Sumerian mythos, we find that the supreme god is An (Sky). An takes part in the creation by mating with the great mother goddess Ki (Earth). Together, they engender the god Enlil (Lord Air), who is himself the ruling deity of the tribe. By the time Sumer fell and the Babylonians adopted the Mesopotamian gods, Enlil had moved away to allow his counterpart Enki (Lord of the Earth) to rule. Though, even at this point, Enki lived in the depths of the abysmal waters of the celestial sea (in other words, in the sky), and played little part in the lives of his people. Instead, such figures as Marduk, Ishtar, and other divine children of Enki governed the land and the temples.

Another example is found at the opposite end of the Fertile Crescent, in the land of Khemet (Egypt). Apparently, before writing was developed, the tribal Egyptians honored a deity known as Amon, whom they associated with the ram (and possibly the zodiacal sign of Aries, which would indeed place him in the sky where he belongs). When the first records were written in the temples, the solar deity known as Re[16] had taken over rulership in some areas, and the creator known as Ptah ruled in others. Eventually, we witness the rise of the Osirian cults, which pushed both Re and Ptah into the background to rule from afar. Amon, by this point, had become the transcendent "Hidden One."

All of this is, of course, highly generalized. The histories of these peoples are both complicated and varied according to time and place. The above is only to point out that supreme gods do have a habit of drifting away the longer (and the higher) they are honored. This even seems true of Judeo-Christianity; beginning with the God of the Israelites, who in time gave way to Jesus of the Christian Church, who in turn played a smaller role in the Protestant and Baptist faiths of later years.

Returning to our tribal shamanic cultures, we find that the shaman has a particular role in relation to father sky. The shaman alone knows the secrets of celestial flight, and only he can undertake the difficult journey to gain audience with the deity in his far-off home. This was done in times of great need for the tribe, such as famine or plague. If father sky became angry or upset, nature would suffer in reflection of his emotion. If the local nature spirits could not provide an answer or a cure, then it was up to the shaman to carry a sacrifice to father sky and ask for relief on behalf of the tribe.

It is, in fact, this ability to journey into the celestial (and subterranean) realms to interact with gods and spirits that marks the shamanic practice. As healer, the shaman certainly knew the lore of plants, massage, etc. However, such skills were hardly limited to the local witch/doctor, and most households could act on their own behalf in these areas. It was when these failed that the shaman was called upon to work his serious magick.

The understanding of the time was that death was the natural result of the vacation of the soul from the body; the soul having either been stolen by an angry spirit, or wandered away. Any sickness great enough to result in death was the immediate symptom of that vacation. The shaman's job was to gain an ecstatic trance, travel in spirit to the underworld, find the lost soul, and return with it to the land of the living.

Many readers may be familiar with this process as the "Orpheus myth," a Greek story wherein a musician named Orpheus descended into the underworld to retrieve the soul of his lost love. The god Hades refused his request for her return, at which point Orpheus (famed for his beautiful voice and skill upon the lyre) began to play and sing. Hades' queen—usually as cold as one might expect of the Queen of the Underworld—was moved to tears by the song, and this in turn moved Hades to grant Orpheus' request. The soul of his love was returned to him, on the condition that he walk back to the land of the living without turning to look behind himself. He agreed to these terms, though during his trek back he found himself plagued by fears and doubts. He thought he might hear the soul of his love moving behind him, her breath upon his neck, the smell of her skin and hair; but he also feared he may be imagining it all. Perhaps Hades lied to him, and only wished to send him from the under-world emptyhanded. At the end, when he was at last within site of daylight, he could simply no longer restrain himself. Upon turning to look, he caught only the slightest glimpse of his love as she vanished forever back into the depths of the spirit realm.

The Orpheus myth seems to pop up around the world, taking only slightly different forms. In nearly all cases the hero makes some kind of mistake that results in the loss of the captured soul. The tribal shaman, however, was charged with avoiding such mistakes. The spirit might be grasped in the hand, or captured inside a drum, and was then placed directly back into the patient's body upon the shaman's return to normal consciousness.

This healing art is bound up entirely with the shaman's role as psychopomp—one who guides the souls of the dead to their proper place in the underworld. Death was believed to be a very traumatic and disorienting event for a human spirit, and this very often resulted in the dearly departed remaining near his home and family for a period of time. Within reason, this was considered normal. A few days or weeks were usually set aside to allow the spirit to hover near his or her home, during which funerary rituals were enacted to let the spirit know that it was, in fact, dead. After the set period of time the shaman would be called upon to utilize his skill of astral travel, and to guide the departed soul to its final resting place in the underworld.

Various elements of the journey of the dead, reported by shamans after returning from the trip, are common throughout the world and history, such as crossing a narrow bridge (or a gate that swings open and shut rapidly), avoiding the snares of demons, making the proper supplications to the proper deities along the way, etc. These journeys were eventually recorded and used by temple priests in such places as Egypt; where we find the Egyptian *Book of the Dead* (*Pert Em Hru*: "Coming Forth By Day"). By this point, the priest did not usually make the astral journey with the departed spirit. Simply acting out the ritual procedures and supplying the deceased with the proper offerings and talismans (including a complete copy of the *Pert Em Hru*) sufficed. A similar work known as the *Tibetan Book of the Dead* suggests that merely reading the text aloud during the funeral is enough. These are aspects of what Eliade refers to as the "decadence" of shamanism that has occurred over time.

The tribal shaman, on the other hand, actually escorted souls to the afterlife, and such a feat demanded that he be familiar with the roads taken by the dead. This was most often a major focus of the initiation of a new shaman, which included the experience of death and rebirth. More often than not, the shaman-to-be would be dragged forc-ibly (and unwillingly) to the underworld by demonic entities; who would then proceed to dismember and reas-semble the human's body. During the process, each organ or body member would be purified, tempered, and strengthened. When the body was reassembled, it had become more than it was before; more than the sum of its parts. Only in this way could a human be magically transformed into a worker of miracles.

Once again, we can see echoes of this in ancient Egypt, where we find the famous murder and dismemberment of Pharaoh Osiris at the hands of his brother Set. Once Osiris' body was gathered and reassembled (by Isis and the lord of magick, Thoth), Osiris was resurrected with all of the powers of a god. This is nothing if not a survival of basic shamanic initiation. The process exists to this very day, in fact; many Hermetic systems still utilize ceremonies in which the candidate is broken down into his or her four Elemental components, purified, and reassembled to make the initiate something "More Than Human." This is a form of spiritual alchemy, and is summed up in the Her-metic phrase *Solve et Coagula* (disintegrate and reintegrate). First, the base matter (in this case the spirit—or psyche—of the candidate) must be dissolved into its most basic components. These components are then purified and en-hanced before they are recombined into the final product: lead to gold, plant into medicine, human to shaman, etc.

Interestingly, the shamanic *Solve et Coagula* has another aspect that is less common to other initiations. Remem-ber that the most important role the shaman played in his community was that of healer, and the initiatory experi-ence itself was caught up in this dynamic. The demons who caught and destroyed the shaman-to-be were very often the demons of sickness (such as found in the *Testament of Solomon* as well as other ancient demonologies).[17] For instance, the demon in charge of cutting off the hands of the shaman would have been a demon associated with injury to the hands. By adding its power to the severed hands and returning them to the initiate, the spirit granted power over that sickness (and himself) to the human. Overall, the death-rebirth initiation seems to have been a method of forcing the initiate to symbolically suffer all of the ills that he would later be called upon to heal. Modern psychology works in a similar fashion—it is known that a therapist has a harder time helping a patient through a trauma that the therapist has not personally endured.

As I stated above, the would-be shaman most often goes unwillingly into this experience. As Eliade explains in his work, shamanic vocation was usually a violent and sudden occurrence. This was not a time of mystical seekers and aspirants to the celestial mysteries. While such a thing is not unknown to tribal culture, it is most certainly rare, and the self-made shaman was considered less powerful than his peers and teachers. Normally, it was the guardian spirits of the tribe who would choose the human—from childhood—most psychologically suited to their needs. The child might prove mentally unstable, depressive, schizophrenic, or even epileptic. Eventually, the chosen one would suffer some kind of traumatic experience or nearly fatal sickness—and it was during this episode that the spirits would arrive to inform the chosen of his future role. In return, the shaman-to-be was given very little choice; either go with the spirits for initation in the underworld, or refuse and suffer madness and death.

It is perfectly understandable to cringe at such a thought. However, I feel there may be more to this dynamic than just a group of invasive spirit-archons. Keeping in mind that we are discussing primitive tribal culture, it is not hard to consider the probable fate of a person suffering an ailment such as epilepsy. Eliade points out that the shaman—a master of gaining the state of "divine madness" at will—had the peculiar ability to control his own seizures. The instability of this madness was viewed as a natural key that allowed one to enter ecstatic trances and communicate with spirits. From a tribal perspective, if a person has such abilities and does not learn how to use them, they will not simply go away. Instead, the nonshaman would continue to perceive the spirit world while having no idea how to navigate it or deal with its inhabitants.[18] It is perfectly conceivable that one suffering such a mental imbalance—without benefit of modern medical advances—would have few options aside from learning the art of shamanism to survive. If he did otherwise, it would take no interference from spirits for the person to finally lose his wits and die unpleasantly. Thus, if said spirits do arrive with an ultimatum, it could be seen as a rescue attempt rather than an occasion to threaten or coerce an unwilling candidate.

Another peculiarity of shamanic magick is that it is often learned almost entirely from spiritual entities. Eliade tells us that a future shaman's election consists of his encountering a celestial being—appearing in a dream, during a sickness, etc.—who reveals that he *is* chosen and must follow a new rule of life.[19] All categories of shamanism, Eliade points out, have their patron spirits.[20] He quotes the scholar Rudolf Rahmann as stating that shamanism—as a practice—is essentially composed of a relationship with such a patron, and manifested by that spirit's utilizing the shaman as its medium (or prophet), or by entering him to invest him with knowledge, magickal power, dominion over lower spirits, etc.[21]

In other words, a new shaman is made such through a bonding with his or her own guardian angel—who teaches him the shamanic arts and grants him dominion over the spirits of nature. These nature spirits, especially those that will be the new shaman's Familiars, also have a part in the teaching process. In fact, it is not at all uncommon for the initiate learn lessons from the demons during the initial death-rebirth trauma or sickness.

The lore taught to the new initiate[22] by an established master (often a family member such as a father or grandfather) is generally considered secondary, and is never even attempted until after the spirits or gods have made their call and had their say. Even when a shamanic vocation is hereditary instead of random, it is the transmission of the

Familiar spirits from the master to the student that forms the basis of the inheritance. One must either be given the spirits during an ecstatic trance or dream, or seek them out as part of a quest.

There are other aspects of tribal shamanic initiation that might interest the student of the grimoires. Eliade states that the universal aspects of mystical initiation are vocation, withdrawal into solitude, apprenticeship to a master, the gaining of Familiar spirits, ceremonial death and rebirth, and even the gaining of a secret language.[23] The only aspects we have not discussed so far are those of withdrawal into solitude and the acquisition of a "secret language" of some kind.

The solitude usually accompanies the original vocation or calling, wherein the initiate becomes sick or otherwise encounters a traumatic experience. Other forms exist as well, such as the American Indian vision quest, or the famous image of the hermit-prophet. As we will see later, the grimoires focus quite a bit on the concept of solitude.

The secret language of the shaman is a precursor to our own modern magickal languages. However, in their primitive state, these spiritual languages were more akin to the languages and sounds of animals and birds. More often than not, the mystical flight of a shaman would be accompanied by the calls of birds, wearing of feathers, etc. This language is most often learned during the periods of retreat/solitude and the death-resurrection initiations. It is, of course, taught directly to the shaman by the tutelary and Familiar spirits.

Even the death of a shaman was set apart from the norms of the clan. It is a little-known fact today, but the original concept of "heaven" was not at all a place where "good people" went after physical death. For the most part, all humans descended (at least in part)[24] to the underworld. This was generally a place of darkness and boredom. However, it must be remembered that this realm was not at all similar to the Christian Hell. There were pleasant areas set aside for those who had lived good lives, and even areas where evildoers were tortured. However, in general, one could live quite well in the underworld as long as one's living family members provided sustenance in the form of regular sacrifice and offering. Personal possessions, tools, writings, talismans, and more were also buried with the deceased, and this was believed to allow the spirit access to them from the other side of the grave. In other words, tribal cultures believed you could take it with you, at least in spirit. Even the Egyptian tombs of early written history stand testament to this.

The shaman, of course, had a different journey to make at passing. It must be remembered that he had already died once, at which time he successfully navigated to the underworld and made his way out again to be resurrected in the physical. Thereafter, he spent his career making regular trips not only to the dark underworld, but even celestial flights into the various heavens above. It was only common sense, then, to assume that the underworld itself would be powerless to entrap the shaman's spirit after physical death. Eliade again provides us with several examples: Sakai shamans, after death, are simply left in their homes without burial. The Jakun *poyang* are also left without burial, and actually raised aloft on platforms. Their people believe that the shaman's soul ascends into the heavens, rather than descending to the underworld through the grave as the normal human soul. The *puteu* of the Kenta Semang are buried, but with their heads left exposed above the grave. Similar to the Jakun belief, the puteu's soul is said to fly to the east (the place of the rising Sun) rather than west (the setting Sun) common for everyone else. Such practices and beliefs illustrate that the shaman was regarded as existing in a "privileged class of beings" who enjoyed an afterlife much brighter than the common grave-bound mortal deceased.[25]

To illustrate, I would like to bring up a subject with which many of us are familiar, at least in some part, today. My own generation saw something of a Greek and Roman mythology fad, from role-playing games to Hollywood films such as *Clash of the Titans*. If you missed out on these, then perhaps you have read Edith Hamilton's *Mythology, Timeless Tales of Gods and Heroes*, or read the legends behind our twelve signs of the zodiac. In these legends, the constellations visible in the night sky are said to be the spirits of gods, heroes, holy and great persons, and mythical creatures (such as Pegasus). Even the Hollywood film ended with the placement of its main characters in the nighttime sky. What is less known, however, is that this worldview was not peculiar to Greek mythos, but was actually common to most of the world until relatively recently.

To begin with, it was only the shaman who could travel to the sky either during life or after death. It was to the celestial realm he flew upon his passing, to take his place among the "elect" (i.e., the "chosen," as this is what a shaman essentially was). The same thing is reported in early biblical literature concerning heaven, where only the prophets and a "chosen" few were present in the sky.[26] Even as recently as the Renaissance era, the Catholic Church placed only its saints among the angels.[27] To be specific, once a human was translated into the heavens, he or she was considered as hardly different from a god or angel. In fact, there is no shortage of mythology around the world depicting gods as once living humans, having been translated to the sky in religious rapture or death/resurrection.

The Prophets

Rather than making an historical leap from the ancient shamans to the medieval wizards, I feel it would help to attempt to trace a more connected line from one to the other. The biblical prophets offer us a perfect starting point: on one hand, they were contemporary with ancient tribal shamanic culture, and, on the other, the grimoires are based largely on the concept of the prophetic tradition. In some cases, the prophets themselves are called upon in the magick, and this alone would make it worth our while to investigate their activities.

The question that faces us here is simply whether or not the prophetic tradition fits the description of shamanism. We have already seen that many of the basic concepts of Judaic and Christian theology originate among the Indo-European shamans north of the Middle East. It is only after their migrations and invasions into the Fertile Crescent (and elsewhere) that written history begins, and we see the movements of the twelve Israelite tribes. With this in mind, it may be possible to suppose a direct link between the original shamanic cultures and the prophets of Yahweh.

To verify this hypothesis, I decided to research the stories of the Bible, some of the Apocrypha, and even the *Midrashim* (oral legends) to locate instances where the prophets acted in a particularly shamanic manner.

Perhaps the most fascinating bit of information I found in this regard is located in the book of I Samuel 9:8–9:

> And the servant answered Saul again and said, "Behold, I have here at hand the fourth part of a shekel of silver: that will I give to the man of God, to tell us our way." (Beforetime in Israel, when a man went to inquire of God, thus he spake: "Come, and let us go to the seer." For he that is now called a Prophet was beforetime called a Seer.)

Already we are granted an indication of the extremely Pagan/shamanic nature of the prophet. First of all, the prophet is paid for his (or her!) services. While this may be looked down upon within many communities today, it was not at all uncommon in tribal culture. A shaman performed his role as one would any other job, and it was necessary to make a living at the art.

Note also that it was regarded as necessary to seek out a prophet in order to communicate with the tribe's god. This falls into the category of intercession, wherein the shaman would travel in the spirit to confront, question, or plead with the god for help in certain matters. Finally, we are told that prophets were originally called "seers"— which is a clear and undeniable relation to the art of the shaman. One was called a "seer" who could see and interact with spirits, and this label makes even such men as Moses and Elijah exist on the same plane as the famous witch of Endor.[28]

Of the most common aspects of shamanic practice described by Eliade and others, the biblical prophets display celestial/infernal journey, intercession on behalf of the tribe, learning their art directly from Angels and spirits, and (of course) the art of healing more than any others.

We will begin with the numerous references to prophetical celestial flight. The midrashim offers examples for nearly all the prophets. For instance, Isaac took a trip into heaven after his father Abraham nearly sacrificed him to El.[29] In fact, this legend makes it possible to interpret the entire biblical story as a proper shamanic initiation for Isaac.[30]

Abraham, too, was caught up into the heavens; by none less than the archangel Michael, who took the prophet in a chariot drawn by Kherubim, and with an entourage of sixty angels. He was shown ". . . all things that are below on the earth, both good and bad."[31]

Moses also took several trips into the heavens. His first trip, taken during his encounter with the burning bush, even outshines Abraham's journey. Moses was guided by the highest of all angels—Metetron, the Prince of the Presence—and enjoyed the guardianship of thirty thousand angels.[32] During several of his celestial flights, Moses was taken upon tours of Heaven, with its areas of paradise and punishment common to tribal shamanic cosmology. He even encountered resistance from the native angels, who challenged him upon his right to enter the realms of the dead.[33] Another legend depicts Moses ascending the holy mountain (more on this below), and spending a week in purification before attempting to gain entry to the sky. As is common in biblical celestial flights, Moses was taken up within a cloud.[34] A similar cloud is recalled during Moses' ascent to the top of Mt. Sinai (i.e., into the heavens) where he remained for forty days and nights.[35]

Ezekiel is another figure most famous for ascending into the heavens, as well as journeying across the face of the Earth:

> Then the spirit took me up, and I heard behind me a voice of a great rushing, saying, "Blessed be the glory of the Lord from his place." I heard also the noise of the wings of the living creatures[36] that touched one another, and the noise of the wheels[37] over against them, and a noise of a great rushing. So the spirit lifted me up, and took me away, and I went in bitterness, in the heat of my spirit,[38] but the hand of the Lord was strong upon me. (Ezekiel 3:12–14)

> And he [an Angel] put forth the form of an hand, and took me by a lock of mine head; and the spirit lifted me up between the earth and the heaven, and brought me in the visions of God to Jerusalem, to the door of the inner gate that looketh toward the north . . . (Ezekiel 8:3)

> . . . the hand of the Lord was upon me, and brought me thither. In the visions of God brought he me into the land of Israel, and set me upon a very high mountain, by which was as the frame of a city on the south. (Ezekiel 40:20)

The apocryphal *Ethiopian Book of Enoch,* is composed almost entirely of the celestial visions of the patriarch:

> Behold, in that vision clouds and a mist invited me; agitated stars and flashes of lightening impelled and pressed me forwards, while winds in the vision assisted my flight, accelerating my progress. They elevated me aloft to heaven. I proceeded, until I arrived at a wall built with stones of crystal. A tongue of fire surrounded it, which began to strike me with terror. Into this tongue of fire I entered. (*Enoch* 14:9–11)

> After that period, in the place where I had seen every secret sight, I was snatched up in a whirlwind, and carried off westwards. (Enoch 51:1)

Vision of Ezekiel.

A cloud then snatched me up, and the wind raised me above the surface of the earth, placing me at the extremity of the heavens. (Enoch 39:3)[39]

There is even biblical indication that only shamans (even as opposed to priests) were privileged enough to make such an ascent:

And he said unto Moses, "Come up unto the Lord; thou, and Aaron, Nadab, and Abihu, and seventy of the Elders of Israel; and worship ye afar off. And Moses alone shall come near the Lord; but they shall not come nigh; neither shall the people go up with him." (Exodus 24:1–2)

According to Christian legend, Jesus himself made trips through both Heaven and Hell. His celestial ascent, at least, is recorded in the canonical Bible after his initiation by death/rebirth:

And it came to pass, while he blessed them, he was parted from them, and was carried up into heaven. (Luke 24:51)

And when he had spoken these things, while they beheld, he was taken up; and a cloud received him out of their site. (Acts 1:9)

Oral legend also relates that Moses descended to the infernal realms, as a part of his own initiation. In one instance, after having spent forty days before God learning the Torah (law), he descended to behold the angels of terror, trembling, quaking, and horror. The sight was terrifying enough to make him forget all he had learned in the previous days![40] Yet another instance has the prophet guided by the archangel Gabriel, who must encourage the frightened human to continue onward into the nether realms.[41] In a final episode, God summons forth the angel of Hell himself to take Moses upon one last tour, and the prophet is finally willing to enter fearlessly.[42]

In at least one place, I found a reference to the gate between this world and the next which is extremely difficult to pass.[43] This involves the archangel Michael and Abraham once more, as the latter was brought to the place of the judgment of souls. In order to gain entrance, Abraham had to choose between two gates: one broad and the other narrow. The narrow gate leads to life and paradise, while the broad (or easily entered) gate leads to destruction and eternal suffering. Abraham felt that he had no hope of entering the narrow gate as a living human, but Michael assured him that he—and all the pious—could indeed pass through it unharmed.[44]

Unfortunately, there is little indication in the recorded material that the prophets acted as psychopomp on a regular basis. However, I did find an obscure reference that might indicate the existence of the practice in the remote past, especially as connected with ancestor worship, in Ginzberg's *Legends of the Bible*, pp. 588–9. Here we are told that the prophet Elijah continues to live in Heaven for all time. He sits there to record the deeds of men and the chronicles of the world. Moreover, he is the psychopomp, whose duty is to stand at the crossroads of Paradise and direct the pious to their appointed places. He further brings the souls of sinners up from Gehenna at the approach of each sabbath, and leads them back to punishment once more when the day of rest concludes. (Elijah, the legend assures us, also leads the same poor souls into eternal bliss once they have completed atonement for their sins.)

Along with the rich tradition of celestial (and infernal) flight, there are also numerous examples of the intercession of the prophet-shaman with the will of the tribal god. As in other shamanic cultures, it was the prophet's job to bear the prayers, wishes, pleas, and even sacrifices of the people directly before the face of the god. As we shall see below, this became something of an ambassadorial art. The prophets actually negotiated with the deity, reminding him of past promises, covenants, deeds, and even mistakes. It becomes very obvious that the god had to answer to the people (through the prophet) as much as they had to adhere to his statutes and taboos.

Ginzberg's collection of oral legends contains several perfect examples of such exchanges between prophet and patron. Abraham is said to have beseeched the grace of God not to destroy "the sinners," reminding him of his oath sworn after the Deluge to never again destroy the Earth by water. Abraham literally challenges God's honesty in the covenant, and asks, "Shall the judge of all the earth not do right Himself?"[45]

After Abraham had come through the ordeal of the near-sacrifice of his son Isaac, the old man again reproached his god for shoddy behavior. The deity had previously promised Abraham that his progeny would multiply through Isaac, yet was willing to let the prophet think his son would be killed before providing grandchildren. Abraham pointed out that he had held his silence and willingly followed God's apparently disloyal command. Therefore, the patriarch insisted, "Thus mayest Thou, when the children of Isaac commit trespasses and because of them fall upon evil times, be mindful of the offering of their father Isaac, and forgive their sins and deliver them from their suffering."

Moses was an overworked prophet where it came to approaching Yahweh for the sake of the well-being of his people. (Of course, a nomadic tribe might suffer more need for such action than an established city-state.) In our first example, after the incident of the golden calf at the Mount of God, Moses not only intercedes for Israel but actually enters into combat with angels of punishment sent by the wrath of Yahweh. Further, he even calls upon the aid of ancestors (Abraham, Isaac, and Jacob), in order to persuade the god to stand by his side in the fight.[46] This is all pure shamanic technique and experience. Another instance of Moses' intercession (Exodus 32:9–14) gives us a canonical example of the process by which a prophet-shaman dickers with his patron. Against Yahweh's wrath, Moses asks the god why he liberated his people from the land of Egypt only to act angrily toward them. In a particularly bold move, the prophet suggests that Yahweh's reputation among the Egyptians, who had so recently been defeated by him, would suffer. (As previously stated, the art of intercession is very ambassadorial.)

After this, Moses again reminds Yahweh of the deeds of Israel's ancestral fathers, and the pacts that were made with them.

Finally, we have one of the most famous of Moses' intercessions on behalf of Israel, this one involving direct competition with angels as well as magick:

> And the people spake against God, and against Moses, "Wherefore have ye brought us up out of Egypt to die in the wilderness? For there is no bread, neither is there any water; and our soul loathes this light bread." And the Lord sent Fiery Serpents[47] among the people, and they bit the people; and many people of Israel died. Therefore the people came to Moses, and said, "We have sinned, for we have spoken against the Lord, and against thee; pray unto the Lord, that he take away the serpents from us." And Moses prayed for the people. And the Lord said unto Moses, "Make thee a fiery serpent, and set it upon a pole." And it came to pass, that if a serpent had bitten any man, when he beheld the serpent of brass, he lived. (Numbers 21:5–9)

The patriarch Enoch is also shown bearing prayers to the divine throne, although in his case he was working for angels rather than for humans. After the group of angels known as the "Watchers" or "sons of God" descended to earth, mated with human women, and revealed the secrets of heaven,[48] they begged Enoch to intercede with God on their behalf. Though the subjects may be angelic rather than human, I feel it relates the procedure of intercession rather well:

> And they all became terrified and trembled; beseeching me to write for them a memorial of supplication, that they might obtain forgiveness; and that I might make the memorial of their prayer ascend up before the God of heaven; because they could not themselves thenceforwards address him, nor raise up their eyes to heaven on account of the disgraceful offence for which they were judged. Then I wrote a memorial of their prayer and supplication, for their spirits, for everything which they had done, and for the subject of their entreaty, that they might obtain remission and rest. Proceeding on, I continued over the waters of Danbadon, which is on the right to the west of Armon, reading the memorial of their prayer, until I fell asleep. And, behold, a dream came to me, and visions appeared above me. I fell down and saw a vision of punishment, that I might relate it to the sons of heaven, and reprove them. When I awoke I went to them. (*Enoch* 13:5–9; also see chapters 14–16)

In a final example, Moses seems to have taken some drastic measures when his own sister became inflicted with leprosy. Moses held a belief that his own flesh and blood simply could not languish in sickness while he was well. Therefore, he drew a circle about himself in the sand and prayed to Yahweh that he would not move from the spot until the God had healed his sister. Even if that failed, Moses swore, he would use the knowledge the God had already revealed to heal the leprosy himself.

We see in this, as well, an indication that Moses learned the art of healing from Yahweh. Learning directly from spirits, gods, or angels is an important aspect of shamanism—if not (as in the opinion of some scholars) the primary aspect. Both Old and New Testament records indicate that this was common among the Israelites. The entirety of the code contained in the five books of the Torah—including all tribal statutes, construction of the Tabernacle, the direction of travel for the tribe, warfare, sacrifice and religious observances, etc.—are supposed to have been received directly from Yahweh by Moses. While this is not exactly historically accurate, I feel that the practice is illustrated correctly. We cannot assume that cultures of the past took their gods so casually as our society does today. Consider Orthodox Judaism, as well as the orthodox Churches, as examples of what life within a primitive tribe was like. Taboos and observances were taken very seriously, and often nations would not move without prophetic word from their patron god or an angel thereof. Writing and languages, laws, and magick were all received by shamans during their ecstatic trances. One may be honestly surprised to find how much of our Earth's history has been literally directed by gods and spirits, whether one believes in them or not.

The legends and biblical stories are, of course, full of this kind of divine revelation. I looked for passages that indicated the necessity of the practice according to the prophetic tradition. The first example comes from a legend that stresses that Aaron (the priest) had to rely upon Moses (the shaman) for direct communication with Yahweh.[40] Aaron himself spoke directly to the god no more than three times during his life.[49]

The canonical Bible records several instances of prophets communicating with God or angels in an oracular fashion. Below are examples of Daniel and Moses:

> . . . Yea, while I was speaking in prayer, even the man Gabriel whom I had seen in the vision at the beginning, being caused to fly swiftly, touched me about the time of the evening oblation. And he informed me and talked with me, and said, "O Daniel, I am now come forth to give thee skill and understanding. At the beginning of thy supplications the commandment came forth, and I am come to shew thee; for thou art greatly beloved: therefore understand the matter, and consider the vision. (Daniel 9:21–23)

> And Moses said unto his father in law, "Because the people come unto me to inquire of God: when they have a problem, they come unto me; and I judge between one and another, and I do make them know the statues of God, and his laws." (Exodus 18:15–16)

> And Moses came and told the people all the words of the Lord, and all the judgement: and all the people answered with one voice and said, "All the words which the Lord hath said will we do." (Exodus 24:3)

The midrashim also contain similar examples. The most fascinating legend I came across depicts Moses befriending large numbers of angels. Each one teaches Moses a remedy, and the secrets of the holy names within the Torah. In proper shamanic fashion, even the angel of death arrives to grant a remedy against the grave.[50] Once again we see reference to the art of healing, and how the prophet learned these things from the angels directly. Only by meeting face to face with the angel (or the angel who governs the demon) of the disease and learning his remedies did Moses gain the power to heal that disease. Healing is another aspect of shamanism that many insist is primary.

> And [Jesus'] fame went throughout all Syria: and they brought unto him all sick people that were taken with diverse diseases and torments, and those which were possessed with devils, and those which were lunatic, and those that had the palsy, and he healed them. (Matthew 4:24)

> And when Elijah was come into the house, behold, the child was dead, and laid upon his bed. He went in therefore, and shut the door between them,[51] and prayed unto the Lord. And he went up, and lay upon the child, and put his mouth upon his mouth, and his eyes upon his eyes, and his hands upon his hands; and he stretched himself upon the child; and the flesh of the child waxed warm. Then he returned, and walked in the house to and fro; and went up and stretched himself upon him: and the child sneezed seven times, and the child opened his eyes. (II Kings 4:32–35)

There is an absence in the literature of the biblical prophets actually descending to the underworld to retrieve lost souls. However, I did find a single reference that might, again, suggest the practice in the distant past. At the very least, it illustrates that the prophets did view sickness as the vacation of the soul from the body:

Gabriel and Zachariah.

And it came to pass after these things, that the son of the woman, the mistress of the house, fell sick; and his sickness was so bad that there was no breath left in him. And she said unto Elijah, "What have I to do with thee, O thou man of God? Art thou come unto me to call my sin to remembrance, and to slay my son?" And he said unto her, "Give me thy son." And he took him from her breast, and carried him up into a loft, where he abode, and laid him upon his own bed. And he cried unto the Lord, and said, "O Lord my God, hast thou also brought evil upon the widow with whom I sojourn, by slaying her son?" And he stretched himself upon the child three times, and cried unto the Lord, and said, "O Lord my God, I pray thee, let this child's soul come into him again." And the Lord heard the voice of Elijah; and the soul of the child came into him again, and he revived. (I Kings 17:17–22)

It is plainly obvious that the prophets served their social role as shamans. However, they also display frequent hints of other aspects of shamanism and the shamanic vocation. For instance, I found a single reference to the mental unbalance necessary for the shamanic calling in that Joshua—the successor to Moses—was in youth "so ignorant that he was called a fool."[52]

Prophets also experienced the typical shamanic vocation, being called directly by the God. It would seem that even the prophets of Yahweh were not often happy to be called upon: Moses is said to have resisted his calling stubbornly, causing his would-be patron to declare that he would show himself of little faith in his shamanic career. The god even threatened to punish the would-be prophet with leprosy if he did not cooperate.[53]

Several further shamanic vocations are recorded in biblical scripture, each one illustrating beautifully that ever-crucial first meeting between a prophet and his god, and the visions and pacts that accompany these experiences:

Now the Lord said unto Abram,[54] "Get thee out of thy country, and from thy kindred, and from thy father's house, unto a land that I will shew thee. And I will make of thee a great nation, and I will bless thee, and make thy name great; and thou shalt be a blessing: And I will bless them that bless thee, and curse them that curseth thee: and in thee shall all families of the earth be blessed." So Abram departed, as the Lord had spoken unto him . . . (Genesis 12:1–4)

And Jacob went out from Beer-sheba, and went toward Haran. And he lighted upon a certain place, and tarried there all night, because the sun was set; and he took of the stones of that place, and put them for his pillows, and lay down in that place to sleep.[55] And he dreamed, and behold a ladder set up on the earth, and the top of it reached to heaven: and behold the Angels of God ascending and descending upon it. And, behold, the Lord stood above it, and said, "I am the Lord God of Abraham thy father, and the God of Isaac: the land whereon thou liest, to thee will I give it, and to thy seed . . ." (Genesis 28:10–13)

The word of the Lord came unto me [Jeremiah], saying, "Before I formed thee in the belly, I knew thee; and before thou camest forth out of the womb I sanctified thee, and I ordained thee a prophet unto the nations." Then said I, "Ah, Lord God! Behold, I cannot speak: for I am a child." But the Lord said unto me, "Say not, I am a child: for thou shalt go to all that I shall send thee, and whatsoever I command thee thou shalt speak. Be not afraid of their faces: for I am with thee to protect thee," sayeth the Lord. Then the Lord put forth his hand, and touched my mouth. And the Lord said unto me, "Behold, I have put my words in thy mouth." (Jeremiah 1:4–9)

Now the word of the Lord came unto Jonah the son of Amittai . . . But Jonah rose up to flee unto Tarshish from the presence of the Lord, and went down to Joppa; and he found a ship going to Tarshish . . . But the Lord sent out a great wind into the sea, and there was a mighty tempest in the sea, so that the ship was like to be broken. . . . Now the Lord had prepared a great fish to swallow up Jonah. And Jonah was in the belly of the fish three days and three nights.[56] Then Jonah prayed unto the Lord his God out of the fish's belly, ". . . I will sacrifice unto thee with the voice of thanksgiving; I will pay that which I have vowed. Salvation is of the Lord." And the Lord spake unto the fish, and it vomited out Jonah upon the dry land. (Jonah 1:1–2)

Jesus' initiation provides us with several basic shamanic components. It includes seclusion (in the wilderness), fasting, encounters with earthly spirits (Satan, in this case), and the appearance of angels who, presumably, teach him the arts:

Then was Jesus led up of the Spirit into the wilderness to be tempted of the devil. And when he had fasted forty days and forty nights, he was afterward an hungered. And . . . the devil taketh him up into an exceeding high mountain, and sheweth him all the kingdoms of the world, and the glory of them; and saith unto him, "All these kingdoms will I give thee, if thou wilt fall down and worship me." Then saith Jesus unto him, "Get thee hence, Satan: for it is written, Thou shalt worship the Lord thy God, and him only shalt thou serve." Then the devil leaveth him, and, behold, Angels came and ministered unto him. (Matthew 4:1–11)

Along with vocation and initiation, the Bible also gives us an example of shamanic inheritance from master to aspirant:

And it came to pass, when they were gone over, that Elijah said unto Elisha, "Ask what I shall do for thee, before I be taken away from thee." And Elisha said, "I pray thee, let a double portion of thy spirit be upon me." And he said, "Thou has asked a hard thing: nevertheless, if thou see me when I am taken from thee, it shall be so unto thee; but if not, it shall not be so." . . . And Elisha saw it, and he cried, "My father, my father, the chariot of Israel, and the horsemen thereof." And he saw him no more: and he took hold of his own clothes, and rent them in two pieces. . . . And he took the mantle of Elijah that fell from him, and smote the waters, and said, "Where is the Lord God of Elijah?" And when he also had smitten the waters, they parted hither and thither: and Elisha went over. (II Kings 2:9,10,12,14)

Like other shamans, the prophets were charged with protecting the tribes from the actions of malevolent spirits. One such example rests with the prophet/patriarch Methuselah (son of Enoch, grandfather of Noah). After spending three days in fasting (further ceremony is not mentioned), God granted him permission to inscribe the Ineffable Name upon his sword. With this sword, Methuselah slew "ninety-four myriads" of demons within a minute, until the firstborn demon, Agrimus, appeared and begged Methuselah to desist. At the same time, Agrimus revealed the names of all the demons to the patriarch. Methuselah used this information to place their kings in chains, while the remainder fled into hidden caves and beneath the depths of the ocean.[57]

The shamanic mastery over fire is also present in the biblical accounts. Notice that, above, Ezekiel is said to have gone into the sky ". . . in bitterness, in the heat of my spirit." Such references to heat are common in shamanic rites. The ability to walk over live coals is a well-known test of a tribal shaman's power. Others might swallow the coals, or even generate enough body heat to dry several wet blankets draped around their bodies in the freezing cold. Eliade provides several further examples in his work. Meanwhile, biblical literature possesses several stories in which prophets are cast into furnaces, only to emerge again unscathed:

Then these men were bound in their coats, their hosen, and their hats, and their other garments, and were cast into the midst of the burning fiery furnace. . . . And the princes, governors, and captains, and the king's counselors, being gathered together, saw these men, upon whose bodies the fire had no power, nor was an hair of their head singed, neither were their coats changed, nor the smell of fire had passed on them. (Daniel 3:21, 27)

Beyond what we have seen thus far, there are several examples of basic shamanic magickal procedure, especially in regards to the well being of the tribe:

And [God] said unto [Abram], "I am the Lord that brought thee out of Ur of the Chaldeans, to give thee this land to inherit it." And he said, "Lord God, whereby shall I know that I shall inherit it?" And he said unto him, "Take me an heifer of three years old, and a she-goat of three years old, and a ram of three years old, and a turtledove, and a young pigeon." And he took unto him all these, and divided them in two, and laid each piece one against another: but the birds divided he not. And when the fowls came down upon the carcasses, Abram drove them away. And when the sun was going down, a deep sleep fell upon Abram; and, lo, an horror of great darkness fell upon him. And he said unto Abram, ". . . Unto thy seed have I given this land, from the river of Egypt unto the great river, the river Euphrates." (Genesis 15:7–12)

And when the Philistines heard that the children of Israel were gathered together to Mizpeh, the lords of the Philistines went up against Israel. And when the children of Israel heard it, they were afraid of the Philistines. And the children of Israel said to Samuel, "Cease not to cry unto the Lord our God for us, that he will save us out of the hand of the Philistines." And Samuel took a suckling lamb, and offered it for a burnt offering wholly unto the Lord: and Samuel cried unto the Lord for Israel; and the

The Fiery Furnace.

Lord heard him. And as Samuel was offering up the burnt offering, the Philistines drew near to battle against Israel: but the Lord thundereth with a great thunder on that day upon the Philistines, and discomfited them;[58] and they were smitten before Israel. (I Samuel 7:7–10)

And the men of the city said unto Elisha, "Behold, I pray thee, the situation of this city is pleasant, as my lord seeth: but the water is naught, and the ground barren." And he said, "Bring me a new dish, and put salt therein." And they brought it to him. And he went forth unto the spring of the waters, and cast the salt in there, and said, "Thus saith the Lord, 'I have healed these waters'; there shall not be from thence any more death or barren land." So the waters were healed unto this day, according to the saying of Elisha which he spake. (II Kings 2:19–22)

Finally, we can see evidence that the prophets did not experience the same death as the common people. Instead of descending to Sheol (the underworld), they were caught up into the heavens—most often transformed into gods (angels) in their own rights. Like all shamans, death itself had no power over them.

The death of Aaron outlines these points perfectly. When his time came, he walked knowingly toward it. A cave had been prepared for him with couch, table, candle, and several ministering angels. The legend reminds us that Aaron, like his sister Miriam in the past as well as Moses in the future, was not to die through the angel of death, but instead by a kiss from God himself.[59]

Likewise, when Moses' time of passing approached, Yahweh reminded him of the nature of shamanic death; that it was not a destruction of his life (as usual for others), but instead was an elevation. Moses, according to Yahweh's instructions, was to ascend the mountain to die with no one to accompany him. There, he would be gathered to his people—the fathers of Israel, Aaron and Miriam, etc.

These promises notwithstanding, Moses reminds us at the time of his passing of his superiority over the angel of death, refusing to deliver up his soul to the angel, demanding to hand it over only to God himself.[60] When the issue could no longer be avoided, Yahweh consented to arrive in person with three angels.[61] Gabriel arranged a couch, Michael spread upon it a purple garment,[62] and Zagzagel set in place a woolen pillow. Moses laid here to pass beyond, with God at his head, and the three angels arranged upon either side of him and at his feet.[63]

The translation of the prophet Elijah from earth to heaven is recorded in canonical biblical scripture:

> And it came to pass, as [Elijah and Elisha] still went on and talked, that, behold, there appeared a chariot of fire, and horses of fire, and parted them both asunder; and Elijah went up by a whirlwind into heaven. (II Kings 2:11)

According to oral legend, Elijah was translated into the form of the archangel Sandalphon (the psychopomp illustrated above), and often returned to earth as a helper, protector, teacher, and guide for the children of Israel.[64] This, in fact, could be a further indication of the existence of ancestor worship in ancient times.

Elijah was not alone in his celestial and angelical translation. The patriarch Enoch was also said to have been caught up without suffering physical death,[65] and transformed into the archangel Metetron. A magnificent throne was erected for Enoch near the gates of the seventh (or highest) heavenly palace, and it was proclaimed throughout the heavens that Enoch was thenceforth to be known as Metetron (the voice of God, whose commands are to be followed as God's own). When transformed into Metetron, Enoch's body was transmuted to celestial fire. His flesh became flame, his veins ran with fire, his bones were glimmering coals, his eyes burned with heavenly brightness (his eyeballs were torches of fire), his hair was a fiery blaze, his limbs and organs burning sparks, and his frame was a consuming fire. To his right flashed flames of fire, and he was enveloped on all sides by storm and whirlwind, hurricane and thundering.[66]

Oral legend includes a similar fiery transformation on the part of Moses, associated with his primary initiation (at the scene of the burning bush) rather than with the end of his earthly career. It was Metetron who performed the initiation, changing Moses' flesh into torches of fire, his eyes into Merkavah wheels, his tongue into a flame, and granting him the strength of an angel.[67]

Note here further reference to fire and the shaman's mastery over it. Interestingly, the legend of Enoch's translation seems to have come originally from 3 Enoch 3–15, paragraphs 4–19 (the *Hebrew Book of Enoch*, not to be confused with the *Ethiopian Book of Enoch* that I have quoted elsewhere). James R. Davila, in his *The Heckalot Literature and Shamanism*, compares this scene to the typical shamanic initiatory destruction and reanimation of the body. Its many references to the transformation of specific body parts, one by one, is very reminiscent of shamanic initiation. According to Eliade, there are indeed examples of tribal shamans, like Enoch and Moses here, being taken into the sky for this process rather than into the underworld.

Merkavah and the Baalim Shem

After the end of the "Age of the Prophets" (which seems to have come just before the beginning of the Common Era), we see the rise of the *Merkavah*[68] or *Hekhalot*[69] tradition. James R. Davila, in his *Heckalot Literature and Shamanism*, explains that the *Merkavah* literature is a "bizarre" combination of late-ancient and early medieval Jewish mystical and revelatory texts. They were strongly connected, or at least parallel, with earlier revelatory and Gnostic material. They reveal the actual practices used by the "Descenders of the Chariot" to fly into the celestial realm and view Ezekiel's chariot vision (the Merkavah) for themselves. It also promised converse with angels and a mastery of Torah through theurgy.[70]

Their work was based heavily upon the records left behind in the books of Ezekiel and Enoch, as well as the rich oral tradition surrounding all of the old prophets and patriarchs. Their tradition was a continuation of the ancient shamanic practice of flying into the celestial realm to petition father sky. The texts produced directly by the *Merkavah* riders, to which we still have access today, are *3 Enoch* (*Hebrew Book of Enoch*), *Ma'aseh Merkavah* (Working of the Chariot), *Hekhalot Rabbati* (Greater Palaces), *Hekhalot Zutarti* (Lesser Palaces), and *Merkavah Rabbah* (Great Chariot). The record of one *Merkavah* rider found its way into the canonical Bible as the book of the Revelation of St. John.

Anthropologically speaking, the *Merkavah* mystics are essentially the same subculture of people who once made up the ranks of the prophets. Davila, of course, suggests that the techniques described in the *Hekhalot* literature are very similar to those described by anthropologists in relation to shamanism. For instance, the practice of fasting, isolation and stimulus deprivation, purifications, extended prayer, and even song are all included. The *Merkavah* songs, just as the shamanic hymns, seem to derive their power from the divine names and the unintelligible words of power within them.[71] (These are all subjects we will return to in later chapters concerning the grimoires.)

Davila provides several strongly shamanic examples of *Hekhalot* literature. For instance, note the instructions given in the *Hekhalot Zutarti* for approaching God directly (after ascending the palaces) with a wish:

> Make your request (as follows): May there be favor from before You, YHWH God of Israel, our God and the God of our fathers. (_Nomina barbara_), may You give me grace and lovingkindness before Your throne of glory and in the sight of all Your attendants. And may You join to me all Your attendants so as to do such and such, O great, mighty, fearsome, strong, valiant, magnificent, and eminent God! (*Hekhalot Zutarti*, paras. 418–19)

By this late date, the role of the shaman had become largely unofficial, and often focused on the self more than the community. Davila outlines the main focus of the available *Merkavah* texts as seeking both esoteric knowledge and theurgical power, most especially the power to learn and teach Torah. However, there is some indication that these men acted as shamans on a social level from time to time, working on behalf of their people. While the rites of healing and exorcism seem to be largely absent from the *Hekhalot* texts, Davila suggests this is only because the subjects were recorded adequately in other Jewish literature. The community of people that produced the *Hekhalot* literature was historically related, or even intermingled with, the authors of the pregrimoiric Jewish magickal texts.[72] The members of this latter community were referred to as the Baalim Shem, and were indeed often associated with *Merkavah* practices.

"Baal Shem" means "Master of the Name (of God)."[73] This was a label applied to men of the Middle Ages, often rabbis, who became masters of the art of practical Qabalah and *Merkavah*. Originally, the Qabalah was strictly a practice of meditation and contemplation upon holy scripture, such as found in the Sepher Bahir (Book of Brightness), Sepher Yetzirah (Book of Formation),[74] and Sepher Zohar (Book of Splendor). The *Merkavah* tradition also maintained itself among these people, who often considered the Qabalah to be a "modern *Merkavah*." This is historically accurate, as the Qabalah did indeed evolve directly from (but not limited to) the practices of both the *Merkavah* mystics and the ancient Gnostics.

Those who found practical applications for the material became the Baalim Shem, known as such for their ability to invoke the divine names of God to work miracles. Very often they were disliked by orthodox rabbis who abhorred any act that hinted the least bit of magick. Regardless, this did not stop them from taking active roles as nonclerical spiritual leaders (shamans) for their local towns or villages. It was a Jewish mage and *Merkavah* mystic, living as late as the 1700s CE, known as Rabbi Israel ben Eliezer (the Baal Shem Tov[75]) who founded the Hassidic[76] movement. Some considers this the single most important religious movement in the history of Judaism. This famous Rabbi serves as the best example of both the later *Merkavah* practices and the arts of the Baalim Shem.[77]

Oral legends abound of the Baal Shem going into combat against supernatural forces on behalf of the people:

> There is a story told:
>
> Whenever the Jews were threatened with disaster, the Baal Shem Tov would go to a
> certain place in the forest, light a fire, and say a special prayer. Always a miracle would
> occur, and the disaster would be averted.
>
> In the later times when disaster threatened, the Maggid of Mezritch, his disciple, would
> go to the same place in the forest and say, "Master of the Universe, I do not know how
> to light the fire, but I can say the prayer." And again the disaster would be averted.
>
> Still later, his disciple, Moshe Leib of Sasov, would go to the same place in the forest
> and say, "Lord of the World, I do not know how to light the fire or say the prayer, but
> I know the place and that must suffice." And it always did.
>
> When Israel of Rizhyn needed intervention from heaven, he would say to G-d, "I no
> longer know the place, nor how to light the fire, nor to say the prayer, but I can tell the
> story and that must suffice." . . . And it did.
>
> Remember the story, tell it, pass it on.[78]

Likewise are stories preserved of the ascent toward the throne of God (and the dangers involved), such as this example from the Talmud:

> Our masters taught: Four men entered the "Pardes," namely, Ben Azzai, Ben Zoma, Acher (Elisha ben
> Avuya), and R. Akiva.
>
> R. Akiva said to them: When you arrive at the slabs of pure blue transparent marble, do not say:
> 'Water, Water!' For it is said, "He that speaks falsehood shall not be established before My eyes" (Psalm
> 101:7). Ben Azzai cast a look and died: of him Scripture says, "Precious in the sight of the Lord is the
> death of His saints" (Psalm 116:15).
>
> Ben Zoma looked and became demented; of him Scripture says, "Have you found honey? Eat so much
> as is sufficient for you, lest you be filled with it, and vomit it" (Prov. 25:16). Acher mutilated the shoots
> (He became an apostate and purposely broke Jewish law). R. Akiva departed unhurt. (Chagigah 14b)

Meanwhile, the Baalim Shem are the men from whom the medieval Christian mystics were borrowing material for their own grimoires. Thus the semi-Jewish, Qabalistic, or even *Merkavah* flavor of many of the texts.[79] It is hardly any wonder that the Christian mystics were fascinated with the Baalim Shem, as the latter were renowned as powerful wizards who possessed the secrets of the magick of the ancient prophets. As far as it goes, I feel it is not historically inaccurate to make this claim, nor to suggest that it is through the mysteries of the Baalim Shem that the grimoires find their most direct link to the prophets and the ancient tribal shamanic tradition.

Medieval European Urban Shamanism: The Grimoiric Masters

Davila proposes that the people who created the medieval Jewish magickal culture (and the *Hekhalot* literature) were principally a group of professional scribes, lacking formal rabbinical training and existing therefore in a lower socio-economic class than full rabbis. It was perhaps, Davila feels, an envy of the superior station of the rabbis that encouraged these scribes to defy orthodoxy with the performance of magick.[80]

Interestingly, Richard Kieckhefer says the same of the predominantly Christian authors of the grimoires. In many cases they were likely scribes, employed in the lowest ranks of the Church. Kieckhefer further suggests that a study of the grimoiric rituals can add much to our understanding of this particular class of late medieval clerical culture. (Conversely, I feel that an understanding of that clerical culture can illuminate much about the grimoires.) Medieval society possessed a surplus of clergy, which therefore produced a "clerical underworld" of mystical-minded men who went largely unsupervised by the official Church. The magickal grimoires were the natural result.[81] Kieckhefer continues to explain that the cosmology and techniques found in medieval operations of spirit summoning mimic those of established religious rites. A culture that centered itself so heavily upon ritual would naturally produce "forbidden rituals."[82]

Thus, when studying the creation of the grimoires, it is obvious that we are concerned with a singular group (or culture) of people—specifically scribe-clerics. The procedures and prayers outlined in many of the medieval texts are taken largely from Catholicism. In these, it is often assumed that the reader is not only well aquainted with Church procedure, but should even have "insider" access to Church facilities. For instance, the following quotations from the *Sworn Book of Honorius* indicate that "him that shall work" (i.e., the mage) must have direct access to a church, its priest, the altar, and even the consecrated host:

> Then let him have . . . a faithful priest which may say unto him . . . a mass of the holy ghost. . . Then take frankincense and incense and cense the altar saying the first prayer . . . Then let the second prayer be said immediately and after . . . the mass let be said the third, fourth, fifth, seventh, and eighth prayers, and so in consecrating of the body of Christ, let the priest pray for him that shall work that through the grace of god he may obtain the effect of his petition and so must the priest do in all his prayers that he shall say for him that shall work but add nothing else to them . . .and after mass he that shall work shall rescue the sacrament saying the nineteenth and twentieth prayers . . . (*Liber Juratus*, Part 3)

Other texts instruct the reader to recite such things as the Seven Penitential Psalms or the Litany of the Saints without providing the words or even where to find them. It is extremely common for Psalms to be prescribed with no more than the first line granted. The *Book of Abramelin* provides several examples, though it does at least provide the numbers of the Psalms as well:

> When the child shall warn you that your Guardian angel hath appeared, then shall you, without moving from your place, repeat in a low voice Psalm CXXXVII., which beginneth: "Confitebor Tibi Comine, in toto corde meo," "I will give thanks unto thee, O Lord, with mine whole heart," etc. And, on the contrary, when you shall convoke for the first time the Four Chief Spirits, you shall say Psalm XC.: "Qui habitat in adjutorio Altissimi," "Whoso dwelleth in the defense of the Most High," etc.; and this not in a low voice as in the preceding case, but (aloud) as you usually speak, and standing where you happen to be. (*Book of Abramelin*, Book II)[83]

The *Key of Solomon the King* makes much use of Psalm magick (as we shall see in later chapters), giving only the numbers of the Psalms with no beginning lines for assurance. The same text also suggests one might obtain a robe either from Levites or priests who have worn them during services.

Another hint toward the clerical nature of the grimoires is the fact that many of the texts are written—entirely or in part—in Latin. Not only does this suggest (as Kieckhefer points out) that the texts were written by clergy, but it also indicates that they were written *for* clergy. Few outside the confines of the Church would have had the knowledge to produce or make use of the material.

Kieckhefer speculates (correctly, in my opinion) that the magick may have been utilized as a means for gaining political power within a competitive clerical environment.[84] Indeed, many of the grimoires provide techniques for controlling the wills of others, producing illusory banquets, castles, etc., procuring the favor of kings or priests, and other such feats that would aid one's advancement in official and social settings. There is one manuscript—the *Munich Handbook of Necromancy* (Clm 849)[85]—which offers an anecdote to illustrate the use of causing castles and armies to appear:

> Once when I [wished to test] this art I exercised it with the emperor, when many nobles were accompanying him on a hunting expedition through some dark forest. . . . A perfectly safe castle was made for the counts, with towers and moat, and the drawbridge down. It seemed excellently constructed and filled with mercenaries, who were crying out, "O lord emperor, enter quickly with your companions!" They entered, and it seemed that servants and many friends of the emperor were in it; he supposed he had come upon people who would defend him manfully. . . .[86]

Of course, what concerns us here is that neither of these two aspects of the grimoiric tradition—Church procedure or personal career advancement—have much to do with shamanism. Instead, they are aspects of institutionalized priesthood.

About the priesthood Eliade reminds us that the shaman is not typically the sacrificer (priest).[87] In the Altai, the shaman is similarly unassociated with the rites of birth, marriage, or death (unless something unusual occurs). Rather than these priestly duties, the shaman is principally concerned with healing.[88] However, it must be understood that the existence of the priesthood in no way rules out the shamanic art, just as the biblical prophets existed alongside the Levite priesthood. As well, it is not unknown for shamans to perform sacrifices and other priestly duties in the absence of a "temple faith" or priesthood. This being the case, it is surely conversely true that clergymen acted as shamans when there was a lack of such a vocation in the community. All the Inquisitorial hanging and burning in the world would not remove the need for healing the sick, and the interaction with local spirits.

By way of example, the *Book of Abramelin*, which insists that one must flee all human interaction as much as possible (the shamanic isolation), still makes an allowance for healing:

> We may then exercise the profession of Medicine, and all arts connected with the same; and we may perform all operations which tend unto charity and mercy towards our neighbor purely and simply.
> (*The Book of Abramelin*, Book II, Chapter 10)

The diaries of Dr. John Dee provide us with a scene in which the mage consults with the angel Murifri about the ills of those who have asked him for help:

Dee: If I might without offending you, I would move two Petitions unto you, one concerning the Soul, and the other concerning the body: . . . Concerning the Soul, is for one Isabel Lister, whom the wicked Enemy hath sore afflicted long with dangerous temptations, and hath brought her knives to destroy her self withall; she resisteth hitherto, and desireth my helping counsel, which how small it is God knoweth. The other is of another woman, who hath great need, and is driven to maintain her self, her husband, and three children by her hand labour, and there is one that by dream is advertised of a place of Treasure hid in a Cellar . . . I would gladly have your help herein, if it pleased God.

Murifri: I answer thee, I will come again soon, and thou shalt receive a Medicine which shall teach thee to work help in the first. The second is vanity, for it is not so . . . But yet she shall be comforted for thy sake. (*A True and Faithful Relation*, p. 5)

In another instance, the archangel Raphael assures Dee that his shamanic vocation will eventually be appreciated by the people of his community:

Raphael: When they (England) shall have need of thee, (some shut-up, some entangled, some gadding like master-less dogs), then shall they gladly seek thee and desire to find thee. They shall smell out thy footsteps, and thou shalt not see them. The key of their cares thou shalt be master of, and they themselves shall not unlock their own grievousness. Yea, they shall say, "Oh let the earth devour us!" (*Five Books of the Mysteries*, p. 141)

In fact, there is plenty of evidence that many of the grimoires were put together with the good of the community in mind. Apparently, the typical grimoiric mage of the late medieval era collected spells for the express purpose of selling his services—a fact that speaks strongly for the shamanic nature of the material. The single most common operation found in nearly all grimoires is that of divination, and especially the art of divination by spirits. The *Goetia* hardly possesses a spirit that does not "know all things past, present, and future" or some other indication of divinatory power. Besides this, the books contain spells for reconciling friendships, healing, reviving the dead, learning the virtues of herbs and stones, causing love between two people, finding lost or stolen items, and a nearly endless list of other domestic helps.

If a mage was not working for individuals in his community, then he might be found working directly for the sovereigns of his kingdom. John Dee is renowned for his utter dedication to Britain and Queen Elizabeth I. In fact, a good bit of his Enochian magick seems geared toward military purposes. Prince Befafes, an angel of Tuesday, is recorded as giving "good success in battles; reducing ships and all manner of vessels that float on the seas."[89] At the same time, Dee's magickal system involving the "Parts of the Earth" was more than likely an attempt to influence and learn the secrets of foreign nations from the astral plane.

"Abraham the Jew"—the supposed author of the *Book of Abramelin*—devotes an entire chapter to his own exploits as a traveling shaman, working for kings and common folk alike.[90] He claims to have healed no less than 8,413 people, without once considering the patient's religion. He lent a Familiar spirit to Emperor Sigismond of Germany (1368–1437), and worked magick for the benefit of the emperor's marriage. He delivered the Count Frederick of Saxony (1369–1428) out of the hands of Duke Leopold of Saxonia by causing two thousand illusory cavalry to appear. Several further claims are made here and in other chapters of the book. On pages 146–7, he claims to have revived the Duke of Saxonia from death for a space of seven years, so that he (the duke) could finish raising an heir for his estate, and not allow it to fall into the hands of greedy relatives.

However, scholars have been very quick to point out that—regardless of the grimoires' insistence on virtuous action and the love of God—they yet contain spells of "black" magick. This is especially true of the demonology of the time, such as the *Goetia* or the third book of *Abramelin*. The spirits, and sometimes even angels, are described as granting invisibility (assumed to be an aid to thieves), causing enmity between peers, making arrow wounds fester, revealing enemies' secrets, destroying warships, slaying men, blood sacrifice,[91] and more. This is generally seen as a contradiction to the priestly demands made of the mage, for which little explanation has been found.

Personally, I feel this comes from the previously discussed obstacle of modern misunderstandings of ancient worldviews. It is all too easy, and common, to label such practices as "black" or beneath the dignity of a truly virtuous mage. Yet, if we consider the lives of some of our most famous medieval wizards, it becomes apparent that many of them moved to some degree in political circles. It has already been illustrated that Abraham the Jew worked regularly on behalf of royalty. Again, John Dee is well-known for his allegiance to Queen Elizabeth I, and *A True and Faithful Relation* is full of his ambassadorial exploits across Europe. Even Agrippa possessed political influence, and was once able to single-handedly drive an Inquisitor out of office.[92] The same biography indicates the possibility that Agrippa, like Dee after him, may even have operated as a governmental secret agent.[93]

It would seem that in times previous to our modern era every King Arthur had his Merlin. The word "wizard" translates as "wise one,"[94] and it was not uncommon for royalty to call upon both priests and wisemen as advisors. Viewed in this light, the nature of the so-called "black" spells suddenly shift into the realm of patriotism. Invisibility certainly would have aided Dee and Agrippa in places they wished not to be seen. Causing enmity was very possibly used toward influencing treaties and negotiations (as were the opposing rites of causing the love and favor of kings and priests). Aggravating the injuries of an opposing army—such as arrow wounds—would certainly save many lives in wartime.

These are certainly not spells that we should make use of lightly today, in job or domestic situations. However, I wish to suggest that their inclusion in the grimoires do not prove hypocrisy or evil intent on the part of their authors. Of course, there are notable exceptions among some few of the lesser texts, which themselves are not known for their quality. Some examples even involve using magickal means to commit rape.[95] However, the bulk of the classical material seems to have been directed toward the aid and protection of the kingdom or local community. This is especially apparent when we consider that these "dark" spells exist alongside those that cause armed men and fortresses to appear, promise success in battle, etc. Even if we disagree with harmful magick even in wartime, we still must consider that such things were not viewed as dishonorable in previous history.

Overall, I feel it is safe to conclude that the medieval grimoiric mage did fulfill the social obligations of a shaman, even if in a nonofficial capacity. Both kings and peasants called upon them in times of distress; asking for everything from marital help to the curing of sickness to the defense of an entire country. They provided charms for love, fertility, prosperity, abundant crops, and any number of other uses. Plus, they were the liaisons between our world and the etheric world of nature spirits.

Other aspects of the shamanic vocation are clearly present within the grimoires as well. For instance, it is significant to note that very few texts attempt to teach step-by-step spells. Instead, the material is specifically geared toward the summoning and interaction with spiritual entities, from whom the real magick is learned. *The Book of Abramelin*, probably the most blatantly shamanic of all the grimoires, focuses entirely on gaining the patronage of a spiritual teacher who can relate what no text could hope to convey: the true and sacred magick.

The same book also covers the transmission of Familiar spirits into the mastery of the initiate. The guardian angel having tutored one in the summoning of several demonic princes, the book instructs:

> . . . in the first demand which thou shalt make unto the Four Spirits (who are) the Supreme Princes, and unto the Eight Sub-Princes; thou shalt demand the most skilful of the Spirits, of whom thou shalt make a register for convenience of the practice which I describe . . . But seeing that the subjects of various erring humours (of mind) and other occasions which arise daily be diverse, each man will procure for himself those (Spirits) which be of his nature and genius and fit for that wherein thou woudest employ them. (*The Book of Abramelin*, Book III, Essential Remarks Upon the Foregoing Symbols)[96]

The *Goetia* is another prime example of the acquisition of spirit Familiars, and the magickal lore and knowledge they can deliver. The arts and sciences are taught by the spirits, as well as healing, the languages of animals,[97] celestial flight,[98] divination, the virtues of herbs and stones, and so on.

The main difference in this regard between tribal shamanism and the classical grimoires are the methods used to summon and command the spirits. This seems to be an aspect of the priestly bent of the magick. Eliade once again points out the technical differences between the priest and the prophet/shaman. The priest does not work with ecstatic states of consciousness, but is instead a ritualist and exorcist. He may act to retrieve the lost soul of a sick individual, but he does not do this through visionary celestial/infernal flight. His attitude toward the world of spirits is, Eliade suggests, one of hostility or (more likely) mere superiority. The priest is the master and the spirits are servants, bound to carry out the will of the priest under the authority of his god. Meanwhile, the shaman is the master of ecstatic states, lives in familiarity with the inhabitants of the spiritual world, allows himself to be possessed (or "ridden") by his patron spirits, and acts as the diviner and prophet. Also, unlike the priest, the shaman is directly chosen by his spirits to perform his work.[99]

The grimoires are a curious mixture of priestly and shamanic influences. As we shall see later, the arts of summoning arose mainly from the priestly art of exorcism, and the concept that a holy man had the authority to command spirits. Yet, the goals and attitudes associated with the practice are often more shamanic. At the same time, the angelic procedures outlined in the texts often contain many aspects of temple procedure; while the attitudes displayed toward angels—most especially the guardian angel—parallel tribal shamanism closely.

It is important to understand what we have discussed so far in order to comprehend the "magickal current" behind the old texts. In this way, the wording becomes less obscure and the magickal reasoning at least shows itself to be coherent and consistent. As a further aid to this, I feel it would be helpful to append a few discussions concerning specific points of medieval cosmology; especially those that depend most directly on earlier tribal shamanic customs and worldviews.

Three Worlds, Four Pillars

One of the fundamental concepts of the shamanic worldview is the division of reality into three distinct "realms" or worlds. In its most primitive manifestation, it seems to have been recognized as a division between celestial (the sky), physical (the earth), and the underworld (beneath the ground). The former world belonged to the gods and demigods (which we will cover in more depth below), the latter was the realm of spirits and the souls of the dead, and physical beings existed betwixt the two extremes.

It is important to note here that man is not placed at the head of this hierarchy. While humankind certainly exhibits dominance over other animal species, we are not classed as having control over the basic forces or laws of nature (represented by such beings as gods and angels). The shaman was, in fact, unique in the fact that he could travel to the upper world(s), communicate with higher beings, and exert influence upon them. Those legends in which prophets such as Moses or Jacob battle and defeat angels are meant to convey the vast power supposed to be held by those men. How many true masters are there who can influence the path of a hurricane or tornado? What magick is performed to affect the courses of rivers, or to defeat a plague? These are the things believed to be within the power of the gods alone, and to those shamans who walk with them.

This threefold division of the world is also at the heart of grimoiric procedure. Herein lies the division between spirit work (which takes a priestly and authoritative stance over the spirits) and angelic work (which must be approached devotionally). Put simply, it represents humanity standing in the middle world, working with beings above and below on their own respective terms.

The exact description of the three realms has shifted slightly over time. Jim DeKorne, in his *Psychedelic Shamanism*, describes the hierarchy somewhat differently as I did above. In his version, the lower world represents the realm of animal powers, the middle world includes everyday human experience, and the upper world is the domain of higher (or celestial) spirits.[100] One notes the subtle shift of the animal kingdom to the lowest world, giving the division a tone of Darwinism, as if based upon evolutionary patterns.

Agrippa put much stock in the same cosmology, and based his work symbolically upon it (each of his *Three Books of Occult Philosophy* relating to one of the three worlds). He illustrates the concept in Book I, Chapter Two (What Magick is, What are the Parts Thereof, and how the Professors Thereof Must be Qualified):

> . . . all regulative philosophy is divided into natural, mathematical, and theological: (Natural philosophy teacheth the nature of those things which are in the world, searching and enquiring into their causes, effects, times, places, fashions, events, their whole, and parts also . . .

> But mathematical philosophy teacheth us to know the quantity of natural bodies, as extended into three dimensions, as also to conceive of the motion, and course of celestial bodies . . .

> Now theological philosophy, or divinity, teacheth what God is, what the mind, what an intelligence, what an Angel, what a devil, what the soul, what religion, what sacred institutions, rites, temples, observations, and sacred mysteries are: it instructs us also concerning faith, miracles, the virtues of words and figures, the secret operations and mysteries of seals, and as Apuleius saith. It teacheth us rightly to understand, and to be skilled in the ceremonial laws, the equity of holy things, and rule of religions. . . .

Although, the impression must not be given that the threefold division of the world had become pure philosophy by the Middle Ages. Book I, Chapter One of Agrippa's work is titled "How magicians collect virtues from the threefold world, is declared in these three books." The text of the chapter gives his version of the world division:

> Seeing there is a threefold world, elementary, celestial, and intellectual,[101] and every inferior is governed by its superior . . . Hence it is that they seek after the virtues of the elementary world, through the help of physic,[102] and natural philosophy in the various mixtions of natural things; then of the celestial world in the rays, and influences thereof, according to the rules of astrologers, and the doctrines of the mathematicians, joining the celestial virtues to the former: moreover, they ratify and confirm all these with the powers of divers intelligences, through the sacred ceremonies of religion.

In his footnotes, Donald Tyson suggests that Agrippa may have adopted his view of the threefold world from the teachings of Plato. After all, Neoplatonism is the foundational philosophy upon which the *Three Books* are based, and the model runs throughout its occult philosophy.

Eliade, of course, discusses this concept in his chapter on shamanism and cosmology.[103] In this description, the universe also possesses the three levels of sky, earth, and underworld. Further, all three worlds are connected by a central axis. He admits that the symbolism used throughout history to express the interaction of these three realms is both complex and contradictory. It has had a long and widespread history, being updated, altered, and contaminated with new symbolisms and cosmological theories each step along the way. The Neoplatonic shifting of the animal world to the lowest realm is one example.[104]

Indeed, the world division has taken on innumerable forms over the course of history. As astrology arose among the ancient priesthoods, it was common to find the celestial realm divided among seven planetary spheres. The Babylonians, and later the Israelites, are quite famous for this cosmic model. *Merkavah* mysticism retained the same division, while its "sister" practice of Gnosticism understood as many as 30, or even 365, levels to Heaven. Today, we are most familiar with the Qabalistic model, which simply adds a world to the summit of the original three; so that there exists a realm of pure divinity[105] above the celestial firmament of angels.

Another vital aspect of the threefold model of the universe is the "central axis" mentioned by Eliade. This is referred to variously as the "central pillar," "world pillar," "world tree," or "Tree of Life," or it might be represented as a mountain or ladder. What makes it so vital is that this axis is supposed to pass through an opening or "hole" at the center of the sky, through which the gods can descend to the earth and the dead can enter the infernal regions. This is also the same hole through which the shaman enters the spiritual worlds via his ecstatic trance.[106] Very often, this cosmic model was based upon the structure of a tribal tent or teepee:[107] the central pole representing the world pillar, and the tent opening at the top of the pole symbolizing the entrance to heaven. There are an abundance of shamanic spells which center around the tent pole, wherein the shaman literally climbs the pole to pass through the top opening and "enter the sky" in ecstasy. For this reason, the tent pole is often sacred in tribal cultural households.[108]

However, this merely touches upon the symbology of the central world axis. Eliade states that the shamanic ascent to the sky by la ladder is known in Africa, Oceania, and North America. However, ladders or stairs are only one type of symbol used for this purpose. One might reach the sky by fire or smoke, a chain of arrows, by climbing a tree, ascending a mountain,[109] a rope, vine, rainbow, or even a sunbeam.[110] Many traditions even held that the central pillar was a celestial post where the gods tied their horses.

Biblical literature focuses mainly upon the mountain and ladder symbols. Moses' ascent upon the mountain of Sinai is the most recognizable example of the former. The latter is made famous by Jacob's vision of a celestial ladder upon which ascended and descended angels, with God standing at its summit. By the time of *Merkavah* mysticism, the *Hekhalot Rabbati* records:

> What does this character [of the descender to the chariot] resemble? A man who has a ladder inside his house on which he ascends and descends; there isn't any living creature who can prevent him. . . . I will recite before [the academy] the mysteries, the concealed things, the gradations, wonders, and the weaving of the web that is the completion of the world and on which its plaiting stands, the axle of heaven and earth, to which all the wings of the earth and inhabited world and the wings of the firmaments on high are tied, sewn, fastened, hanged, and stand.[111] And the way of the ladder on high is that its one head is on earth and its other head is on the right foot of the throne of glory (*Hekhalot Rabbati*, paras. 199, 201).

Even among those who focused their religions upon astrological concerns, the central axis plays an important role. Eliade mentions the Pole Star—which shines in the middle of the sky, and is supposed to hold the celestial tent like a stake. It was called the "Sky Nail" by the Samoyed, and the "Nail Star" by the Chikchee and Koryak peoples. Likewise is the same symbolism found among the Lapps, the Finns, and the Estonians. To the Turko-Altaians, this star is a pillar, as it is a "Golden Pillar" for the Mongols, the Kalmyk, and the Buryat. It is an "Iron Pillar" for the Kirgiz, the Bashkir, and the Siberian Tatars. Finally, it is described as a "Solar Pillar" by the Teleut, etc.[112]

Plus, the concept of the world pillar extends even further. I have found that this world axis is sometimes represented as several pillars supporting a house. These are isolated stakes, or columns, supporting the sky in (for instance) the four quarters of the compass rather than a single pillar in a central location.[113] They appear at least as far back as ancient Egypt. They were originally the arms and legs of the sky goddess Nut—who was seen as resting in an arched-back position over the earth. Later, these arms and legs became associated instead with the four sons of Horus who stand at the extremities of the compass upholding the sky. (Similar to the Greek Atlas, who supports the sky on his own back.) Later biblical material (as well as the grimoires) represented these beings as the "Holy Living Creatures" or Kherubim who uphold the firmament and the throne of God.[114]

It is here that we encounter the concept of the four "cardinal" directions. They are so named due to the fact that astrology places the four cardinal (leading) signs of the zodiac in the east, south, west, and north of the compass.

Beginning with Aries (cardinal fire) in the east, we find Capricorn (cardinal earth) in the south, Libra (cardinal air) in the west, and Cancer (cardinal water) in the north. This is an older correspondence of philosophical elements to the four directions, while the more common arrangement used in modern systems (Air in the east, Fire in the south, Water in the west, and Earth in the north) descends from Masonry.

At the same time, there exists another arrangement which seems to have been important to the biblical and grimoiric traditions. It begins with the zodiacal sign of Leo, and the first-magnitude star which forms its heart: Regulus ("Little King"). Some traditions have considered this star to mark the true beginning point of the zodiac, as it rests upon the line of the ecliptic. If we draw our zodiacal chart anew with Leo in the east rather than Aries, we find:

Now the four fixed (or "Kherubic") zodiacal signs reside in the four quarters, where (in ancient times) they marked the changing of the seasons. Leo (the Lion) in the east, Taurus (the Ox) in the south, Aquarius (the Man) in the west, and Scorpio (represented by an Eagle) in the north. These constellations are important due to what the Persians referred to as the "Four Royal Stars," which dwell within them. Leo, of course, possesses Regulus, while in Taurus we find Aldebaran. In Scorpio resides Antares, or (as some suggest) the proper star is Altair, found nearby in the constellation of the Eagle. Finally, near the sign of Aquarius exists a constellation known as the "Southern Fish," which carries the star called Fomalhaut.[115] These four stars were considered the embodiments of the gods of the four quarters, the markers of the seasons, and the pillars which upheld the sky. These are the sons of Horus, and the holy living creatures witnessed by Ezekiel and St. John.

> . . . and in the midst of the Throne, and round about the Throne, were four Beasts full of stars round about. And the first Beast was like a lion, and the second Beast like a calf, and the third Beast had a face as a man, and the fourth Beast was like a flying eagle. And the four Beasts had each of Them six wings, and they were full of stars within: and They rest not day and night, saying, "Holy Holy Holy, Lord God Almighty, which was, and is, and is to come." (Revelation 4:6–8)

> Also out of the midst thereof came the likeness of four Living Creatures. And this was Their appearance . . . every one had four faces and every one had four wings. . . . As for the likeness of Their faces, they four had the face of a man, and the face of a lion, on the right side: and They four had the face of an ox on the left side; They four also had the face of an eagle. (Ezekiel 1:5–10)

It is interesting to note that Ezekiel was writing during the time of the Israelite captivity in Babylon (approximately 600 BCE). It was likely during this time that the four royal stars of Babylon were adopted into the Judaic material as the holy living creatures.[116]

This symbolism remained an important aspect of occultism well into the classical grimoiric era. The four evangelists of the New Testament (Matthew, Mark, Luke, and John) are associated with these forces, as are the four suits of the tarot. Agrippa found it important enough to include in his Book II, Chapter 7, "Of the Number Four, and the Scale Thereof." He clearly lists all correspondences (zodiacal triplicities, angelic rulers, Hebrew tribes, etc) with Fire in the east, Earth in the south, Air in the west, and Water in the north.[117] Later, in Book III, Chapter 24, "Of the Names of Spirits . . . That Are Set Over the Stars, Signs, Corners of the Heaven, and the Elements," Agrippa discusses the four archangels familiar in our own modern systems. Yet, he assigns them according to the above information:

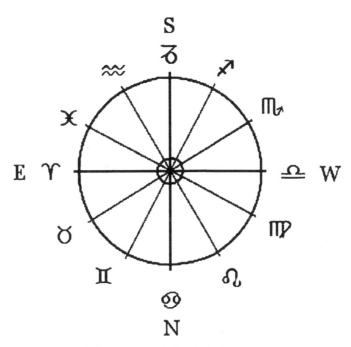

Horoscope Circle, Aries East.

There are also four princes of the Angels, which are set over the four winds, and over the four parts of the world, whereof Michael is set over the eastern wind; Raphael over the western; Gabriel over the northern; Nariel, who by some is called Uriel, is over the southern.[118]

John Dee seems to have taken Agrippa's words to heart, and used the same arrangement in his diagram of the Holy City (New Jerusalem) of Revelation 21. This city is described as having twelve gates—three in each of its four walls, facing the cardinal directions—and each guarded by the angel of a Hebrew tribe. John Dee drew his diagram to show each gate with the name of its angelic Guardian, the related tribe, and the number of its zodiacal sign.

We can see that in the east (Oriens), we have the first, fifth, and ninth zodiacal signs: Aries, Leo, and Sagittarius—the Fiery triplicity.[119] The south, west, and north also follow suit, with the triplicity of Earth in the south, Air in the west, and Water in the north.

Understanding this classical arrangement of elements to directions helps illuminate several obscure points in the grimoires—especially within Dee's Enochian magick. However, I wish to point out here that such correspondences are *strictly* secondary concerns in the grimoiric tradition overall. Where they do exist, keep in mind that they are usually astrological or alchemical symbolism, and it is in those directions one should focus research in this regard. Otherwise, keep in mind that it is the actual *directions* which play the vital role in the grimoires, and *not* the correspondences (angels, Elements, etc.) that might be placed there. These correspondences will change from record to record, and will very rarely become a consideration at all in practical work.

The Luminous Ones, or the Sons of God

When working with ancient or medieval mystical systems, it is important to understand the nature of the entities called upon in the texts. Previously in this chapter, we discussed the basic religious cosmology that extends from Siberian shamanism to the Judeo-Christian faiths. In part, that structure was based upon a singular sky father, who

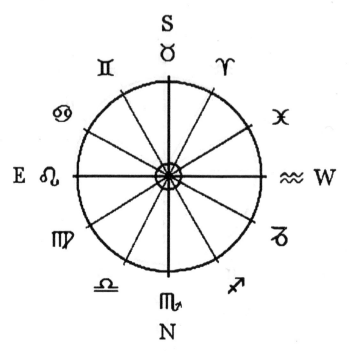

Horoscope Circle, Leo East.

rules over any given number of "sons" or "messengers" (viziers, demigods, angels, etc.). In several cases, the number of the "sons of God" equals that of the planets and other heavenly bodies.

It is also important to remember that this relation was neither arbitrary *nor* symbolic. Besides the practices of ancestor and animal worship, astrology is one of mankind's oldest religions. When the tribal shaman gazed into the sky, he saw living beings of light with the ability to fly through the highest reaches of the firmament. By tracking their movements, and judging their aspects,[120] one could theoretically get an idea of what their moods and whims were at any given time. Agrippa returns to this subject several times in his work, a few instances of which I will relate here:

> The world, the heavens, the stars, and the elements have a soul, with which they cause a soul in these inferior and mixed bodies. They have also as we said in the former book, a spirit, which by the mediating of the soul is united to the body: for as the world is a certain whole body, the parts whereof are the bodies of all living creatures, and by how much the whole is more perfect and noble than the parts, by so much more perfect, and noble is the body of the world than the bodies of each living man. (*Three Books of Occult Philosophy*, Book II, Chapter 56)

> It is necessary therefore, seeing celestial bodies are most perfect, that they have also most perfect minds. They partake therefore of an intellect, and a mind . . . (*Three Books of Occult Philosophy*, Book II, Chapter 57)

> The philosophers have maintained, as we have showed before, that the heavens and stars are divine animals, and their souls intellectual, participating of the divine mind. (*Three Books of Occult Philosophy*, Book III, Chapter 14)

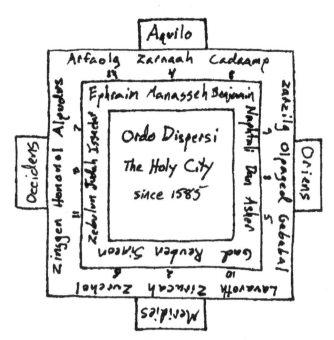

Dee's Diagram of the Holy City: Ordo Dispersi.

That the heavens and heavenly bodies are animated with certain divine souls, is not only the opinion of poets and philosophers, but also the assertion of the sacred Scriptures . . . Therefore although it see-meth to many ridiculous, that the souls themselves be placed in the spheres and stars, and as it were the gods of the nations, every one doth govern his regions, cities, tribes, people, nations and tongues, yet it will not seem strange to those who rightly understand it. (*Three Books of Occult Philosophy*, Book III, Chapter 15)

Thus, the gods and angels, in this view, are living beings moving about in their own celestial community—heaven. They are the ones who draw the purely Darwinian "lots" that decide human fates. A hurricane here, an earthquake there; a good crop season here, and a revolution there. In other words, they are the living forces of nature moving all around us.

Luckily, we can see them from here. Prophets, witches and holy men can often hear them, and the astrologers watch them to interpret what they are up to at any given time. These are the infinite stars that appear in the heavens each night. In this view, the Earth is a fixed object in the center of the universe, around which all the hosts of heaven revolve.

Seven of them, of course, stand out as larger, brighter, and faster than all the rest. First and foremost is the Sun—so mighty that all the other angels bow out before his presence and let him have the sky alone. This is the mighty general Michael, high priest of the heavens. Next to him stands the Moon, gentle Gabriel. And with these two are five other planets that shine brighter and move faster than the fixed stars. These are the seven who stand before the divine throne, and the outer stars are the choirs of angels. We find angels referred to as stars in biblical texts such as the *Ethiopian Book of Enoch*, or the book of the Revelation:

. . . I perceived the extremities of the earth, where heaven ceased. The gates of heaven stood open, and I beheld the celestial stars come forth. I numbered them as they proceeded out of the gate, and wrote them all down, as they came out one by one according to their number. I wrote down their names altogether, their times and their seasons, as the Angel Uriel, who was with me, pointed them out to me. He showed them all to me, and wrote down an account of them. He also wrote down for me their names, their regulations, and their operations. (*Ethiopian Book of Enoch* 32:2–4)

I beheld another splendour, and the stars of heaven. I observed that he [Uriel] called them all by their respective names, and that they heard. In a righteous balance I saw that he weighed out with their light the amplitude of their places, and the day of their existence, and their conversion. Splendour produced splendour; and their conversion was into the number of the Angels, and of the faithful. (*Ethiopian Book of Enoch* 43:1)

And their appeared another wonder in heaven; and behold a great red dragon, having seven heads and ten horns, and seven crowns upon his heads. And his tail drew the third part of the stars of heaven, and did cast them to the earth . . . he was cast out into the earth, and his Angels were cast out with him. (Revelation 12:3–9)

The belief that the stars and planets are actually living creatures is the primary basis of polytheism—or a universe run by several gods. By the time of the grimoires, however, polytheism had been all but outlawed, and the clerical authors of the texts were devout monotheists. The true mystery is found where these two conflicting theologies meet—pantheism. This is simply the belief that all things in the universe originated from one divine source, and that this source is alive and conscious at the core of all. Nothing is truly "dead," because everything is merely a manifestation of the living source.

(I might as easily have said "animism" in this place. The belief is similar to pantheism, except it does not necessarily include a singular divine source. Instead, animism simply insists that everything in existence is alive by its own right.)

Pantheism was understood by Agrippa via the philosophy of the "Soul of the World," which he adopted from the writings of Plato. In this view, the universe itself is a living intelligence—composed of planets and galaxies much as you and I are composed of molecules. Therefore, everything in existence is ultimately a part of one living body with a unified soul encompassing all—the Soul of the World.[121]

In Book I, Chapter 14, Agrippa discusses the manner in which the Soul of the World manifests within all things via the quintessence ("fifth essence," the element of Spirit). It is thereby that "celestial souls are joined to gross bodies, and bestow upon them wonderful gifts."[122] In Book II, Chapter 57, Agrippa further discusses the Soul of the World itself:

Therefore philosophers do not think the Soul of the Earth[123] to be as it were the soul of some contemptible body, but to be rational and also intelligent, yea and to be a deity. Besides it would be absurd, seeing we have reasons of our works, that celestial souls, and the Soul of the Universe should not have reasons of theirs. . . . The Soul of the World therefore is a certain only thing, filling all things, bestowing all things, binding, and knitting together all things, that it might make one frame of the world, and that it might be as it were one instrument making of many strings, but one sound, sounding from three kinds of creatures, intellectual, celestial, and incorruptible, with one only breath and life.

And, in the same chapter:

It is necessary therefore, seeing celestial bodies are most perfect, that they have also most perfect minds. They partake therefore of an intellect, and a mind . . .

Much more could be written here about the Soul of the World and pantheism. However, it is only necessary to understand what pantheism is, and how vital it is to an understanding of the grimoiric tradition and the numberless angels and nature spirits upon whom the books call. All things are alive, and all things "praise God," because all things are part of God. In the chapters following 14 and 57, Agrippa builds upon this subject as a (or the) foundation of his occult philosophy. Also, the Llewellyn edition of the *Three Books* includes an appendix that fully explains the history and meaning of the Soul of the World.

There is yet another detail of the nature of deities that must be understood in order to comprehend ancient and classical texts. As Agrippa stated above, the stars and planets are ". . . as it were the gods of the nations, every one doth govern his regions, cities, tribes, people, nations and tongues, yet it will not seem strange to those who rightly understand it." Those who "rightly understand it" are astrologers, who recognize that different areas of our Earth's geography are influenced (or governed) by different stars. Other deities might be nature spirits, identified with the rivers, mountains, and plant life of their native area. In any case, such entities have always been considered strictly localized, with little to no jurisdiction outside of their home territory.

This is not simply an aspect of ancient thought, but in fact was a common understanding even into the era of the grimoires. Agrippa outlines exactly which areas of the world are governed by the seven planets in his Book I,

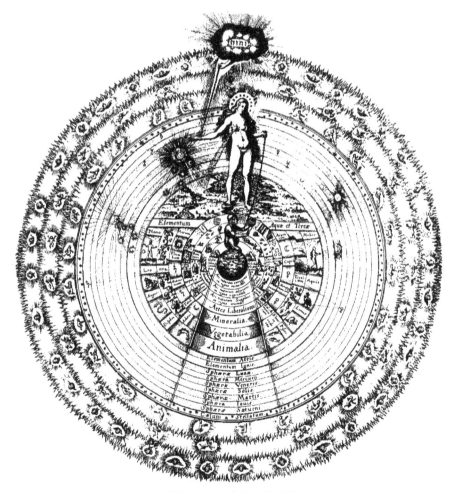

The Soul of the World.

Chapter 31. These are given according to the records of Ptolemy, whom John Dee also seems to have consulted concerning the spiritual governance of the earth.[124] Agrippa further gives, in Book I, Chapter 48, a listing of the planets and what "kind" of places each one naturally governs. In Book III, Chapter 14, after discussing the names of numerous national gods and where they ruled, Agrippa states:

> Of this sort therefore were the gods of the nations, which did rule and govern them, which Moses himself in Deuteronomy calleth gods of the Earth, to the which all nations were attributed, not signifying others than the heavenly stars, and their souls.

In Book III, Chapter 16, he relates a vital philosophy upon which shamanic and grimoiric magicks are based:

> Moreover, there is no part of the world destitute of the proper assistance of these Angels, not because they are there alone, but because they reign there especially, for they are everywhere, although some especially operate and have their influence in this place, some elsewhere . . . spirits of divers kinds in those regions are subject to men's commands.

And also, in Book III, Chapter 23:

> Each demon,[125] and intelligence do use the speech of those nations, with whom they do inhabit.

Note, however, that Agrippa stresses the angels (if not the spirits) are not completely restricted by location. Instead, they are simply stronger in one place over another—having various degrees of governing jurisdiction. Those angels stationed above nations are known as the "Principalities"[126] or "Dominations," and are commonly understood to be the ruling gods of those states. Therefore, even such Pagan deities as Marduk or Osiris would be considered members of the angelic hierarchy.

John Dee's Enochian system of magick, as hinted at above, relies very heavily upon these considerations of location. Both the four Watchtowers (which are symbolic representations of the earth, divided into four quarters) and the ninety-one "Parts of the Earth" all depend totally upon the concept of angelic rulers presiding over particular geographical areas.

A Medieval/Renaissance Definition of Magick

By this point, it has become clear that the magick of the grimoires is, indeed, based upon theories and philosophies that predate most of our modern mainstream systems of magick. When Aleister Crowley wrote that "Magick is the Science and Art of causing Change to occur in conformity with Will," he was not quoting from the *Keys* or Agrippa's Neoplatonic philosophy.

Elizabeth Butler defines magick, from the ancient and medieval standpoint, as existing under three specific heads: astrology, alchemy, and working with spirits. A. E. Waite also covers this somewhat in his work; stating that the medieval conception of magick centered upon interaction between human beings and a world of invisible intelligent powers. The methods used for such communication, he states, are the most important aspects of magickal practice, and the grimoires containing those methods are the most important to the body of literature.[127] Waite seems to feel that both alchemy and astrology, though "magically possible," nevertheless were subordinate to the most important concern: the art of interaction with spirits.[128]

Finally, Waite reminds us that mankind's desire to communicate with the spirit world is older than history, and that we must remember that the medieval grimoires—though semimodern in origin—nevertheless embody some elements of the most ancient magick.[129] This merely confirms what we have already discovered in our study of shamanism. Grimoiric magick is, simply put, a system of natural magick.

Agrippa once again defines our terms, this time in his *Three Books*, Book III, Of Natural Magic.[130] There, he states that natural magick involves the powers of all natural and celestial things, and the searching out of their various virtues and sympathies. By using inferior objects to allure the gifts of higher powers, the mage brings the occult powers of nature into public view. He does it not by force, but by following the laws of nature (applying active things to passive, etc) and merely helping them to complete their effect in a shorter span of time.[131] The "vulgar," Agrippa says, think these things are miracles.

Agrippa also makes several references to how the magick is supposed to have its effect. In Book III, Chapter 32, he explains that the magick is of a religious nature in that it calls upon spiritual creatures to work its miracles. It is not a system of direction of raw willpower, but of gaining conversation with angels and earth-bound spirits who can perform favors or transmit information to the mage.

Conclusion: Modern Grimoiric Shamanism

So, the shamanic nature of the grimoires has been outlined—with more to follow in chapter 3. However, as I write here in the early twenty-first century about systems of magick recorded in the late medieval era, there is one final point which must be covered. One author on shamanism, Jim DeKorne, states the point outright when he says that the archaic rituals and Latin spells from the medieval grimoires may have much romantic appeal (a statement I made myself in chapter 1) and even some power, but they do not exactly reflect our own modern reality.[132]

Indeed, one of the fundamental aspects of shamanism is its ability to grow and change with the times, culture, and needs of the people. DeKorne's thoughts above are echoed by many who look into the classical texts, feeling somewhat removed from the ancient recitations and evocations. What need have we of spirits who can transport us over several miles, when a plane ticket will take us anywhere on the earth we could wish to visit? What good is sending messages or retrieving obscure information via angels when we have the world wide web?

Some of the material in the grimoires may be, in fact, outdated. However, my focus is not upon the content or intent of the spells but on the foundational occult philosophy upon which the magick itself is based. It is my hope that this book will outline the processes by which this kind of magick works, and allow the practitioner to experiment with gaining conversation with various entities. As I have said before, this is the true focus of the grimoires. They are not about spells, but about establishing regular contact with beings who can relate personalized spells to you. These processes of gaining such spiritual communication are not now—nor have they ever been—outdated.

On the other hand, some things do change. What the angels and spirits reveal to you will be your own (and may or may not have much similarity to what "King Solomon" recorded in his works). Plus, there are even aspects of the tools and procedures which will not exactly match their original grimoiric counterparts. At all costs, one must avoid being entrapped by antiquated material, clinging senselessly to it on the basis of "tradition." While my intention here is to present the grimoiric material as the living tradition it once was, the sad fact is that it has not been alive for quite some time. It has had no natural progression or evolution to our own culture, and thus it is up to us to make it a part of our modern world. All of the chapters in part two of this book will hopefully follow this premise, while also preserving the magick itself.

---

1. Which, I should point out, was originally titled *The Book of Black Magic*.

2. *Ritual Magic*, p. 235.

3. Ibid., pp. 96–8.

4. I.e., the worldview of the occultist and ritualist, as Mr. Waite perceives it.

5. Only slightly north of Africa.

6. Gods. They work with lesser spirits along a similar basis—though the spirits are approached in a more "goetic" manner. See chapters 10 and 12.

7. These "pots" are actually decorative urns, which contain objects sacred to the Orisha in question. According to Santerian tradition, the Orishas are literally born and live in these pots.

8. Filled with an entire environment of materials. See chapter 12.

9. *Shamanism: Archaic Techniques of Ecstasy*, pp. 495–6.

10. Ibid., p. 4.

11. Ibid., p. 6.

12. Ibid., p. 88.

13. This brings to mind the Sumerian-Babylonian father god known as "An" or "Anu," which simply means "Sky" or "Heaven."

14. I.e., the seven planets.

15. *Shamanism: Archaic Techniques of Ecstasy*, p. 9.

16. Pronounced [ray].

17. See chapter 1 and chapter 12.

18. Even an experienced shaman who ceases to practice often becomes extremely ill.

19. *Shamanism: Archaic Techniques of Ecstasy*, p. 67.

20. Ibid., p. 91.

21. Ibid., p. 427. Rudolf Rahmann, "Shamanistic and Related Phenomena in Northern and Middle India," *Anthropos*, LIV (1959), 681–760.

22. I.e., shamanic techniques, herbology, names and functions of spirits, mythology and genealogy of the tribe, secret language, etc.

23. *Shamanism: Archaic Techniques of Ecstasy*, p. 288.

24. The concept of "multiple souls," or several individual parts to one soul, does exist in tribal shamanic culture. Only the shade descends to the underworld after death. Other parts of the soul may stay with the family (especially where ancestral spirits are worshiped), etc.

25. *Shamanism: Archaic Techniques of Ecstasy*, pp. 341–2.

26. Many have wondered at the rather small number of 144,000 people gaining entry into heaven according to Revelation 7. To understand this, it must simply be considered that the author believed in a heaven that only accepted an elect few.

27. Many of these saints were already gods of Pagan pantheons, especially among the Celtic pantheon. Sadly, within the Roman Church, the idea of translation to heaven was corrupted into that of "predestination." In this philosophy, it is decided from your birth whether or not you will gain entry to heaven, and it is based wholly upon your social and financial class.

28. I Samuel 28. King Saul (who preceded David upon the throne of Israel) had fallen out of favor with Yahweh. Thus his attempts to communicate with the god were frustrated. Saul, then, sought out a shamaness who was not bound to Yahweh, and had her raise the spirit of the departed prophet Samuel to answer his questions.

29. El was the Canaanite father deity, and apparently the patron of Abraham. Modernly, this name is simply considered a Hebrew word for "god."

30. *Legends of the Bible*, p. 135.

31. Ibid., pp. 144–5.

32. Ibid., pp. 311–2.

33. Ibid., pp. 314 ff.

34. Ibid., p. 392.

35. Exodus 24:15–18.

36. The Kherubim who uphold the firmament.

37. Auphanim, an angelic order associated with the wheel of the zodiac.

38. See below for more on the subject of mystical heat.

39. Enoch 39:3.

40. *Legends of the Bible*, p. 395.

41. Ibid., p. 312.

42. Ibid.

43. Above, I mentioned that this was very often a narrow bridge instead. Both bridge and gate are common in shamanic reports of the "otherworld," depending on which tribe is studied.

44. Ibid., p. 145.

45. Ibid., p. 115.

46. Ibid., p. 401.

47. Seraphim, an order of angels often associated with Mars. Though this is pure speculation on my part, I would wager that the original intent of this word—as recorded thousands of years before the development of our familiar angelologies—was simply to imply "poisonous snakes" that had infested the camp.

48. Genesis 6.

49. *Legends of the Bible,* p. 426. One is led to wonder why Moses did not use said knowledge in the first place.

50. Ibid., p. 422. Once again we see the distinction between priest and prophet.

51. Ibid., p. 395.

52. Between himself and the family of the child.

53. Ibid., p. 507.

54. Ibid., pp. 318–9.

55. Abraham.

56. Note that Jacob is sleeping with his head on stones. This seems to be based on basic tribal shamanic procedure, wherein an initiate is forced into an extremely uncomfortable or painful physical situation, from which the initiatory visions are produced. Eliade covers this subject across several cultures.

57. Though biblical literature is mainly silent on the concept of the sickness or near-death traumatic vocational experience, I feel that this incident with Jonah is one exception.

58. *Legends of the Bible,* p 65.

59. Yahweh, in his earliest form, was a storm god comparable to Baal of Canaan (i.e., of the Philistines).

60. *Legends of the Bible,* p. 456–7.

61. Ibid., p. 491.

62. Ibid., p. 493.

63. Note the use of the color of royalty.

64. Ibid., p. 501.

65. Ibid., p. 589.

66. Genesis 5:21–24.

67. *Legends of the Bible,* p. 64.

68. Ibid., p. 312.

69. *Merkavah* is Hebrew for "chariot," and this was the name of God's throne.

70. *Hechaloth* is Hebrew for "palaces." The journey from earth to God's throne took place through seven celestial (planetary) palaces—each one representing one level of Heaven. Each was guarded by several extremely dangerous angelic guardians. Early versions of this can be found in Egypt the *Book of the Dead* (*Pert Em Hru*)—as well as in Babylon ("Ishtar's Descent into the Underworld").

71. *Heckalot Literature and Shamanism.* http://www.st-andrews.ac.uk/~www_sd/hekhalot_shamanism_art.html.

72. Ibid.

73. Ibid.

74. "Baalim" is the plural form of "Baal."

75. Or "Book of Creation."

76. "Master of the Good Name."

77. "Pious."

78. For stories of the Baal Shem Tov available online: http://www.storypower.com/hasidic/stories.html#besht.

79. Quoted with permission. The Jewish Storytelling Coalition: 63 Gould Road, Waban, MA 02168. See http://www.ultranet.com/~jewish/story.html.

80. Note especially the *Sworn Book of Honorius,* which concerns the gaining of the "Beatific Vision of God."

81. *Heckalot Literature and Shamanism.*

82. *Forbidden Rites,* p. 12.

83. Ibid., p. 13.

84. Dover's *Book of Abramelin,* p. 153.

85. *Forbidden Rites,* p. 35.

86. This manuscript forms the basis of Kieckhefer's study in *Forbidden Rites.*

87. Ibid., pp. 52–3.

88. Here, Eliade is quoting Kai Donner, *La Siberie,* p. 222.

89. *Shamanism: Archaic Techniques of Ecstasy,* pp. 181, 182.

90. *The Enochian Magick of Dr. John Dee,* p. 61 Interestingly, Dee is often credited for the famous storm that destroyed the Spanish Armada before it could attack Britain.

91. Book One, Chapter 8, p. 27ff.

92. See chapter 4 for more information on this point.

93. See "The Life of Agrippa" in the Llewellyn edition of Agrippa's *Three Books*.

94. *Three Books of Occult Philosophy*, "The Life of Agrippa" p. xv ff.

95. According to *Webster's Dictionary*: *Wizard*: Etymology: Middle English *wysard*, from *wis*, *wys* wise. Date: 15th century 1 archaic : a wise man : SAGE 2 : one skilled in magic : SORCERER 3 : a very clever or skillful person.

96. See *Forbidden Rites*, p. 79ff.

97. Dover's *Book of Abramelin*, pp. 256–7.

98. Remember that the learning of the "magickal languages" of the animals represents a major aspect of shamanism.

99. Interestingly, there is one specific technique of celestial flight that made its way, intact, from the early tribal shamanisms to the grimoires; apparently coming by way of Arabic magick and its focus on the legends of King Solomon and the *Arabian Nights*. This is the use of a magickal horse to journey between the worlds. See Kieckhefer's *Forbidden Rites*, p 54–7ff, and then Eliade's *Shamanism* , pp 11, 89, 151, 154, 173–4, 232, 270n, 325, 405, 407–8, 380, 467ff, etc.

100. *Shamanism: Archaic Techniques of Ecstasy*, p. 348. The word in brackets is a translation.

101. *Psychedelic Shamanism*, p. 41.

102. I.e., lower, higher, and middle worlds respectively.

103. The art of herbology, healing, and medicine/alchemy.

104. *Shamanism: Archaic Techniques of Ecstasy*, p. 259.

105. Agrippa seems to treat the Infernal world as a kind of "fourth" unspoken world below the animal/vegetable kingdom.

106. Known as "Olam Atziluth" (World of Royalty). The other three follow the general shamanic pattern, and in descending order are "Olam Briah" (World of Creation), "Olam Yetzirah" (World of Formation), and "Olam Assiah" (World of Action).

107. *Shamanism: Archaic Techniques of Ecstasy*, p. 259.

108. Note the Tabernacle of Exodus.

109. I might point out that the Hebrew word "Vav"—usually translated as "nail"—specifically represents a tent stake.

110. One might note the ascent of Moses upon Mount Sinai, where he met with father sky.

111. *Shamanism: Archaic Techniques of Ecstasy*, pp. 490–2.

112. Note the similarity here to the idea of the world pillar being a hitching post for celestial steeds.

113. *Shamanism: Archaic Techniques of Ecstasy*, pp. 260–1.

114. Ibid., p. 261.

115. Reference Ezekiel 1 and Revelation 4.

116. Ref. *Secrets of a Golden Dawn Temple*, p. 386.

117. Until then, the usual number of Kherubim was two—such as the two angels on the Ark of the Covenant, and the various pairs of Kherubim depicted in Solomon's temple (pillars, the veil of the Holy of Holies, etc.).

118. *Three Books of Occult Philosophy*. Book II, Chapter 7.

119. Ibid., Book III, chapter 29. Note that Michael rules Fire, Raphael Air, Gabriel Water, and Uriel Earth.

120. I.e., Aries = 1, Taurus = 2 . . . Pisces = 12. In assigning each zodiacal sign to a tribe, Dee apparently referred to Agrippa's Scale of the Number 12, in Book II, Chapter 14.

121. In astrology, an "aspect" is an interrelation between two heavenly bodies. For instance, two or more planets might be in "conjunction," meaning they are working together in harmony. Or, they might be in "opposition," meaning they are working against one another. See chapter 5.

122. Note that the word "world" in ancient times was synonymous with our modern word "universe."

123. I.e., occult virtues, or magickal properties.

124. See note 122. The word "Earth" was also used commonly to indicate what we today would call "universe."

125. . . . [Edward Kelley] came speedily out of his Study, and brought in his hand one Volume of Cornelius Agrippa his works, and in one Chapter of that Book [i.e.—Book One, chapter 31] he read the names of Countries and Provinces collected out of Ptolomeus (as the author there noteth) . . . I replied, and said, I am very glad that you have a Book of your own, wherein these Geographical names are expressed, such as (for the most part) our Instructors had delivered unto us . . . (*A True and Faithful Relation*, pp. 158–9).

126. Agrippa often uses the word "demon," though he is not necessarily using it in its modern sense of "evil spirit." The words "demon," "intelligence," and "genius" are all synonyms, used to indicate anything which is alive and thinking.

127. Llewellyn's *Three Books*, p. 505.

128. *The Book of Ceremonial Magic*, p. 20.

129. Ibid.

130. Ibid., pp. 23–4.

131. Llewellyn's *Three Books*, p. 690.

132. Herein, Agrippa appears to be making a direct reference to the art of alchemy, which is often described in exactly the same manner.

The Art of Ecstasy:
Way of the Prophet-Shaman

The altered mental state is the most essential and critical aspect of magickal practice. Regardless of which system one utilizes—shamanic/prophetic, Hermetic, reconstructionist Pagan, Neopagan, Eastern or Western, tribal or urban, ancient or recent—the same practical teaching exists. In order to work the magick, one must first gain a heightened state of consciousness (i.e., going "between the worlds") during which the truly important mechanics of the magick take place. This is when the mage's subconscious mind connects quite directly into the astral, or collective unconscious, etc. This practice is known as the Art of Ecstasy, and history's shamans have largely been the originators and masters of its techniques.

Of course, differing worldviews from one magickal system to another should always be considered. While every true system in existence insists on mind alteration, they each go about it in different ways. Such talk of mind alteration most usually evokes images of the sacramental use of psychotropic plants and other chemicals. Below, I will be discussing the use of certain plants by the tribal shamans, prophets, and the authors of the grimoires. However, mind alteration is not achieved only by such drastic means. Such things as dance, drumming, chanting and breathing, incense, meditation, sensory deprivation, and even physical setting (robes, altars, colors, sigils, etc.) are important to magickal practice as consciousness stimulators.

Unlike the other aspects of shamanic practice described in chapter 2—each of which may or may not be found in any given culture—the ecstatic trance is most universal. Eliade makes this clear from the beginning of his text, stating that "shamanism" = "technique of ecstasy."[1] He further points out that scholars regard the ecstatic experience as the primary shamanic phenomenon. It is not restricted to any culture, but is fundamental to the human condition and known to all of humanity.[2]

Among the Siberian Tungus shamans, dancing and singing are the most common methods of inducing trance[3] (we shall see in chapter 4 how biblical magick worked in much the same way, via the singing of the Psalms). Even in the Far East, there are records of Manchu shamans (during the Ming Dynasty) performing healing rites via song, dancing and leaping, and drumming coupled then with vodka and smoke. Eventually, the healer would fall to the ground in exhaustion, at which time he was understood to have left his body to fly through the heavens.[4] This can find its modern parallel in Wicca and Neopaganism, which use similar methods for "Raising the Cone of Power" in ritual.[5]

In fact, the common image of trance through meditation (silence, rhythmic breathing, stretching) is very uncommon in Western culture. In most cases the shaman is on his feet and active, taking the journey symbolically upon the physical and literally upon the astral at the same time. A shaman may manipulate physical objects, ride mock-horses, climb ladders and ropes, and any number of other symbolic acts of what he is achieving in the spirit world. In short, it is a process and technique very little removed from a child playing and imagining with his toys.

One might even go so far as to suggest that this practice arose at a time when humanity itself was yet in infancy, and thus thought and acted largely upon the same lines. Even today, many teachers of magick insist that "finding the inner child" is a requirement for successful magickal practice. Even the author has written a bit about astral travel, and how to achieve it by the simple daydreaming and fantasy we are familiar with from our school days.

Less innocent in nature, this shamanic role-playing is also where the art of fakirism developed. This practice was important to the shaman, as it allowed him to physically prove his "supernatural" powers to those who relied upon him. As a master of fire, he should be able to walk across hot coals while in ecstatic trance or even swallow them without harm. Some Indo-Tibetan initiations include placing the aspirant outside in a snowstorm and wrapping him in several wet sheets. The ordeal demands the aspirant actually dry these sheets by increasing his own body heat (i.e., obtaining "mystical heat"). The Labrador Inuit must remain five days and nights in freezing sea water and prove that he is not even wet afterward.[6] Apparently, this kind of heat could be attained by an aspirant through meditation near a fire (which became popular in India), by holding the breath, by the Tantric transmutation of sexual energy, as well as several other techniques.

The shaman's superhuman powers (both real and illusionary) do not cease with mastery of fire. He might lance himself with needles, or cut his flesh with blades—all without drawing blood. He may bash himself in the head with rocks, or even lie upon a bed of nails. On the one hand, all of these actions can be used to induce trance (by causing enough physical discomfort to force hallucinatory experiences)[7] , and on the other hand they are used during the trance itself as proof of shamanic mastery. As we previously discussed, the shaman was seen as removed from the physical state of the majority of humanity, even undergoing a death outside of common human experience. His ability to travel in the spirit realm (to gain ecstatic trance) and his dominance over death made him more than human.

Mircea Eliade explains this quite well on page 486 of his *Shamanism*. The crossing of the "dangerous bridge" between the worlds, which the shaman achieves via his ecstatic flight, proves that he is not quite a creature of this world. Much like the Sun itself, the shaman is granted a special recognition for the ability to descend into the underworld and ascend again at will without being harmed. This natural communication between the spiritual and physical worlds is something, it was believed, that humanity as a whole once possessed. At some paradisiacal period in prehistory (perhaps ancestral memories from our earliest hunter-gatherer stages), it was supposed that all humans could ascend the heavens and speak with the gods without resorting to ecstatic trance. Due to some mishap or degradation, however, this ability was largely suppressed within humanity. It finally remained in only a few select individuals—the shamans. The use of ecstatic arts allows them to temporarily reestablish the broken links with heaven, and to return to the primordial state of innocence that once prevailed among humankind.

This one elaborate description of shamanism has gathered a great amount of material with which we are already familiar. It illustrates the interconnected whole formed by the various aspects of shamanism, and further points out that the Art of Ecstasy lies at the heart of it all. We also see echoes of the origins of the Eden mythos—

in which man once had direct communion with God, but lost the lofty position due to some error (usually of pride). The story of Eden itself (Genesis 2–3) is derived from Mesopotamian sources.[8] In Biblical mysticism, it is common to consider the aspirant as one who hopes to reenter Eden and eat the fruits of the Tree of Life. (The Tree, after all, is one symbol of the bridge between Earth and Heaven.) In short—it is an attempt to return to the state of Adam Qadmon—the Adam who existed previous to the Fall (or even previous to the separation of Eve from Adam).

Thus, the shaman is a superhuman in both a physical and spiritual sense—though he only exists as such for the duration of ecstatic trance. During this time he is impervious to wounds, a master of fire, a master of death and sickness, can change himself into various animals, fly through the sky or into the underworld, etc. Eliade suggests that all of the mystical references to speed, riding, flight, or journeys into otherworlds by the shamans are in fact figurative expressions for the "high" of the ecstatic state itself and the experiences it induces.[9] Thus, not only the fakiristic miracles, but even the basic components of shamanic mystical experience are all included under the umbrella of the ecstatic trance state.

The most exciting thing about this information is the light it sheds on magick in general, especially where the classical grimoires are concerned. Scholars have spent some time considering the fantastic claims made by the texts, which seem quite superstitious and incredible to our modern mindset. What are we to think of spells to summon flying horses, or to make one impervious to wounds in battle, or to change into the shape of an animal and speak its nonhuman language? This, of course, is the very "superstitious nonsense" so often mentioned concerning the grimoires. Yet, what we find is that a simple study of tribal shamanism makes the point very clear. These great mystical powers, for us just as for the ancient shamans, all have to do with the experience of the state of ecstasy.

EXERCISE

Part one of this book is concerned mainly with history and scholarship—the foundation upon which the practical work in part two will be based. However, with this chapter, we have entered a subject matter for which intellectual discourse alone is often little help. One can discuss the historical relevance of ecstasy to no end, but one will not (and cannot) conceptualize it if one has not directly experienced it. Therefore, before we continue, I wish to share with you a simple tantric yoga exercise that I discovered in the pages of *Prometheus Rising* by Robert Anton Wilson.[10] The technique is known as the "Breath of Fire." According to Wilson, this exercise seems to trigger neurotransmitters, which he relates to the experience of "mother's milk" (i.e., the snug security of breastfeeding), and compares to opiate use without being dangerous or addictive. For our purposes, it will allow you to experience a light ecstatic state, along with some amount of the mystical heat of the shaman. It will not, of course, allow you to walk across hot coals or cut yourself with blades without injury. What it will do, however, is give you a much firmer grasp of the material contained in this chapter.

To perform the Breath of Fire, you will be taking several breaths via panting as well as full yogic breathing. The latter involves inhaling from the diaphragm until the lungs are completely full. You will know you are doing this when your stomach rather than your chest fully distends during inhalation. Also keep in mind that a single breath involves both an inhalation and an exhalation—whether panting or yogic breathing is involved.

Begin by lying comfortably on your back.[11] Pant rapidly through the mouth to the count of twenty breaths. Then, perform twenty full yogic breaths—inhaling through the nose and exhaling through the mouth. After this, repeat the process of twenty panting breaths and then continue with the yogic breathing (I usually try to make sure I take at least twenty more of these). The exercise is as simple as that. As Wilson states, the results are most amusing and enlightening. Try it!

The supreme importance of such mind alteration is not passed over by Agrippa. In Book I, he dedicates no less than seven consecutive chapters to the "passions of the mind" and their vital consideration in grimoiric practice. There is no need to quote specifics from these chapters, as a listing of the chapter titles will serve to illustrate Agrippa's intent:

- Chapter 61: Of the forming of man, of the external senses, and also of the inward, and the mind: of the threefold appetite of the soul, and passions of the will.
- Chapter 62: Of the passions of the mind, their original, difference, and kinds.
- Chapter 63: How the passions of the mind change the proper body, by changing the accidents, and moving the spirit.
- Chapter 64: How the passions of the mind change the body by way of imitation from some resemblance; also of the transforming, and translating of men, and what force the imaginative power hath not only over the body, but the soul.
- Chapter 65: How the passions of the mind can work out of themselves upon another's body.
- Chapter 66: That the passions of the mind are helped by a celestial season, and how necessary the constancy of the mind is in every work.
- Chapter 67: How man's mind may be joined with the mind, and intelligences of the celestials, and together with them impress certain wonderful virtues upon inferior things.
- Chapter 68: How our mind can change, and bind inferior things to that which it desires.

Here we can see a progression of philosophy—from the effect of mental passion upon the operator himself to the connection of one's mind to the celestial intelligences (and the magick that this produces). Without this, the grimoires are dead books full of silly spells. However, by understanding this mental process, the grimoires become alive and immediately useful once again, that illusive "living tradition" I've mentioned before.

The next danger of misunderstanding arises when we attempt to define the ecstatic state itself. Regardless of the lofty worldview behind the practice, or even the secrets of gaining such a state, where exactly does it lead? In the end, isn't it simply about hallucination? This, of course, is the conclusion of the scientific mind of the late twentieth century. On the other hand, the ancient shamans and authors of the grimoires hold their own opinions on the matter. We have already discussed the importance of spiritual entities in the shamanic vocation, and now we will find that these same spirits are credited with the ascent into ecstasy. Agrippa describes the process in Book III, Chapter 45:

> . . . prophesying is not made according to the will of man, but holy men spake as they were moved by the Holy Ghost.

> When oracles and spirits descend from the gods or from demons[12] upon them, and are delivered by them; which descendings the Platonists call the falling down of superior souls on our souls . . . Of which sort of demons . . . were wont to enter into the bodies of men, and make use of the voices, and tongues, for the prediction of things to come . . .

> But these kinds of fallings down, or senses, come not into our souls when they are more attently busied about anything else; but they pass into them, when they are vacant. Now there are three kinds of vacancy, viz., phrensy, ecstasy, and dreams . . .

This "vacancy" of the human spirit from the body—so that room can be made for the entrance of the spirits or "Holy Ghost"—is brought about via ecstatic trance (when the prophet-shaman has left the body to travel through the heavens). Agrippa, in the following Chapters 46–49, describes four kinds of "phrensy"[13] used to open the senses to divine inspiration. The first is "from the Muses," and is described as follows:

> . . . the corporeal senses are stirred up, and being estranged from an animal man, adheres to a deity from whom it receives those things which it cannot search into by it's own power; for when the mind is free, . . . the reins of the body being loosed, . . . being stirred up by its own instigations, and instigated by a divine spirit, comprehends all things, and foretells future things.

The second phrensy Agrippa associates with "Dionysus," which indicates ecstasy through religious fervor:

> . . . by expiations exterior, and interior, and by conjurations, by mysteries, by solemnities, rites, temples, and observations divert the soul into the mind, the supreme part of itself, and makes it a fit and pure temple of the gods, in which the divine spirits may dwell. . . . Sometimes this phrensy happens through a clear vision, sometimes by an express voice: so Socrates was governed by his demon, whose counsel he did diligently obey, whose voice he did often hear with his ears, to whom also the shape of the demon did often appear. Many prophesying spirits also were wont to show themselves, and be associates with the souls of them that were purified . . .

The third phrensy Agrippa labels as "from Apollo," indicating a more cerebral focus (such as modern Hermetic magick), as well as with the "confection" of medicines (i.e., the ritual use of psychotropics and alchemy):

> This doth by certain sacred mysteries, vows, sacrifices, adorations, invocations, and certain sacred arts, or certain secret confections by which the spirits of their god did infuse virtue, make the soul rise above the mind, by joining it with deities and demons.

The fourth phrensy is explained as belonging to the nature of Venus. This concerns divine love and the Art of Devotion. I will pass over it here, as we will be returning to this subject at some length in chapter 4.

Finally, in Book III, Chapter 50, Agrippa gives us his teaching concerning "rapture and ecstasy." What he has to say on the matter will come as little surprise to the reader at this point. So vast is the potential of the soul, when not oppressed by allurements of the senses, will ascend of its own power into the "supercelestial habitations." Once there, it is most near, and most like unto God, and therefore becomes a receptacle of divine things. It is from this, says Agrippa, that oracles are derived. When the soul is loosed from the body, it "comprehendeth every place and time," encompassing the whole of time and reality as a singular Now. Therefore, nothing is truly hidden from the astral sight.[14]

Thus, once again, we see the ecstatic state described as celestial flight, and the transformation of the prophet-shaman into a celestial being in his own right. Interestingly, Agrippa (also in Chapter 50) associates this very directly with the shamanic sickness that often precipitates vocation. According to him, those who are troubled with the "syncope" and "falling sickness" can imitate a spiritual rapture (or, I believe, initiate one) and bring forth prophesy. Otherwise, such states as the passions of love, sorrow, hardship, or the agony of death can also bring about a radical shift of consciousness resulting in ecstatic fits.

> For there is in our minds a certain perspicuous power, and capable of all things, but encumbered and hindered by the darkness of the body and mortality. . . because the soul being less hindered by the senses, understandeth very acutely . . .

Thus is the nature of the ecstasy gained by the prophet-shaman, and the access it can grant to true magickal ability. Shamanism is structured upon a rather freeform basis. Its goal is to break down the practitioner's assumptions and reality structures so that new information (which very often contradicts one's former assumptions) can be implanted. Of course, there are certainly some structured magickal formulas embedded in the shamanic rites, some of them are as deep and mysterious as found in the Headless Ritual. Yet, most of them are very simple evocational formulas aimed at gaining the attention of a spirit and requesting aid.[15] The rest focuses on personalized ecstatic states in which direct communication occurs between the shaman and what appears to be an "outside intelligence."

This practice will definitely imprint one's mind—though in a much different (and often much more erratic) fashion than modern Hermetic procedures. This, in fact, is one source for the legendary dangers of the grimoires. If one is unstudied in the discipline of ecstasy, and all of its mental and spiritual implications, then it is unwise to attempt advanced invocations. Whatever these "outside intelligences" are, they will have a tremendous impact upon you and your environment. In an ecstatic state you are open for mental reprogramming, and your Guardians will use that time to apply what can only be termed "therapy." I have personally experienced regression to various stages of childhood,[16] sudden onrushes of specific emotions, and have even directly received lessons on how to handle various problems—just to name a few examples. Needless to say, if one takes this lightly, or aborts a significant process (such as *Abramelin*), or contacts the wrong entities,[17] one may be placing his personal well-being at risk.

Of course, that risk is ultimately present in any form of magick one chooses to undertake. Above, however, is my own attempt to describe the nature of that risk within shamanic or prophetic systems. It is not Spiritism by any means, but it is tribal; or, perhaps the word "primitive" would serve better. The pantheistic worldview, the World Soul, insists that the universe is thriving with living intelligences; there is no "dead matter." The magickal tools themselves are Familiar spirits who aid the shaman in his work. As stated in an old Qabalistic axiom: *Every blade of grass has over it an angel bidding it "Grow."* Becoming aware of these spiritual intelligences and learning to live in greater harmony with them (i.e., with your environment) is a life-long task.

Rising on the Planes, or Mental Circuitry

In order to understand the Art of Ecstasy, I feel it is necessary to step aside from classical magick long enough to discuss the subject of modern psychology. While I do not personally view magick as a mere form of psychology, I do feel that the study of mental process must be undertaken by the student. This, in and of itself, can eliminate most of the proposed dangers that go along with the invocations of the medieval grimoires; and the interaction with spiritual beings. As the Hermetic philosophy insists, one must "know thyself" first and foremost.

There are few texts on psychology that would be of any use to serious students today. Most of them, I'm afraid, are concerned more with forcing individuals into outdated Industrial Era mental molds than actually allowing one to explore their own inner depths. Luckily, this arena is not entirely a barren wasteland. Two texts, which I highly recommend to occultists, are *Prometheus Rising* by Robert Anton Wilson and the third edition of *The Middle Pillar* by Israel Regardie.[18] These will give any student a platform from which to launch a truly useful study of psychology and personal growth. The material that I will be presenting in the following paragraphs comes from Wilson's work; who was himself a student of the late Dr. Timothy Leary.[19] This is merely an overview, after which an in-depth study of *Prometheus Rising* itself is strongly suggested. I have found that a true study of that text will take several years, several readings, and much practice and exercise. In any case, I feel that the overview here will give you a workable starting point for assimilating the basic information.

First and foremost, it is important to understand exactly what "altered consciousness" means in a practical (or physical) sense. Right now, as you hold this book in your hands, you are currently under the influence of chemicals that affect the way you perceive the world around you. Your brain is made up primarily of gray matter held in "electro-colloidal suspension" (i.e., floating in protoplasm). These colloids are held in a precarious balance between the states of "gel" (coming together) and "sol" (pushed apart) by their respective surface tensions and electrical charges. As long as an equilibrium is held between these two conditions of gel and sol, you remain alive, well, and thinking. If something pushes this balance too far to either side, brain function (and thus life) ceases.

However, it is also true that there is a large margin of error between the gel and sol states, through which your brain fluctuates on a regular basis. *Any and every chemical that enters your body pushes the balance to one side or the other.* You are experiencing this on a daily basis (even right now) with every bite of food you consume, every breath you inhale, every physical sensation you encounter. These cause changes in emotion and thought process, and are the basis upon which you perceive and react to your environment. Are you laid back, uptight, depressed, elated, sexually aroused, angry, in love, or experiencing any one of a million other emotional states? In each and every case those emotions can be traced to chemicals either consumed by yourself or produced internally by your own body. These chemicals are called "psychedelic" because they have the ability to shift consciousness. Potatoes and chocolate, for instance, are psychedelic substances. Shifting your diet, such as from omnivorous to vegetarian, will also have a psychedelic effect upon your mind. From a more shamanic standpoint, consider the physical abuse often used in tribal culture to induce visionary states; the pain and discomfort does release chemicals throughout the body and into the brain.

Where it comes to magick, then, we can see that going "between the worlds," or gaining ecstasy, is merely a matter of shifting the chemical structure of the brain. The question that arises from this observation, however, is simply what use this could possibly be for us. How can one hope to accomplish anything practical while in a hallucinatory state? The answer depends merely upon a matter of perspective. If the world you are currently experiencing is the product of your own chemical make up (which itself is merely the end product of millions of years of Darwinian chance), then what evidence do we have that another chemical make up is somehow less "real"? The answer is quite simple—not one shred of evidence exists in this regard. For all we know, the reality viewed by the Native American under the influence of peyote is the real one. Or, perhaps, the LSD world discovered by Timothy Leary is the real universe. Then again, what reality would exist if our brains were not flooded with oxygen? Conversely, what reality existed for you after the oxygen rush of the Breath of Fire?

Returning again to the shamanic perspective, it is believed that all of these states are perfectly and tangibly real. Each new mental state merely allows us to view an aspect of reality invisible to us from previous states. The worlds experienced under these "other" chemical balances are called the spirit world, astral plane, dreamtime, etc. To the shaman, the beings who are met in these worlds are no less real than you or I.

Thus is the modern understanding of these ancient secrets. However, I do not wish to end the discussion here. Gaining the altered state is merely the beginning of the story, and knowing what to do once on the "other side" is of the most crucial importance. To this end, I am going to relate in the following a model of the mind (as opposed to the brain), which will allow you to understand the processes that occur within the celestial and infernal realms of the shaman. Understand, however, that by this I do not mean that these realms are merely within the self—but only that one must understand the mechanics that occur within the self in order to step between the worlds.

Information (software) is recorded into your brain (hardware) via three specific methods. The first is known as *imprinting*. If we were to compare the brain to a computer, then we would have to classify imprinted information as "read-only memory" (ROM), or information that is hard-wired and unalterable.[20] Imprints are the foundational mental programs that govern such reflexes as fight or flight, sexual attraction, mammalian territorial instinct, and even such things as deep tribal taboos.

We are not born with these read-only programs, but acquire them at various points in life known as times of "imprint vulnerability." To greatly simplify the concept, we might say that every time you enter a brand new state of consciousness (where your mind is a clean slate), the first experiences you endure will result in imprinting. Your perception and experience of reality from within that state of mind will, from that time forward, be governed by those imprints.[21] In short, they are your "basic assumptions" about reality. The first imprints occur at and directly after birth, others occur during the first toddler stages, puberty, young adulthood, etc., any time your brain physically and chemically changes into a "new brain." As we will see below, Leary and Wilson have (for convenience) narrowed down these instances to eight basic points of life, as well as major evolutionary points for humankind.

The second method of mental programming is known as *conditioning*. A conditioned response is one that is learned over a long period of time, and can often seem much like an imprint. The concept was discovered by Dr. Ivan Petrovich Pavlov in the early 1900s, while performing experiments concerning the physiology of digestive glands. Pavlov would ring a bell when offering food to a group of dogs. The smell of the food would, of course, cause the dogs to salivate. After repeating this process over some time, Pavlov discovered that the dogs had come to associate the bell with the presentation of the food. Even with no food offered, the sound of the bell alone would result in salivation.

These findings resulted in the early movements of behavioral psychology. It was discovered that the foods we enjoy are often the result of cultural conditioning, as well as the music we listen to, the colors and smells to which we react, and the ethics which govern our lives (again, tribal taboos). Racism and bigotry are often the result of bad conditioning, where something as simple as skin color or hair length can elicit immediate responses (negative or positive) from others. The opposite is also true, allowing con men all over the world to fool people into their traps by merely presenting the right positive mental cues to their victims. Further examples would be school children who become immediately hungry at the ringing of the lunch bell (echoes of Pavlov here), drivers who apply their brakes automatically upon seeing the taillights of the car ahead flash, or consumers who buy one product over another merely because they have heard its name (usually set to music) over and over again.

Conditioned reflexes are built over our imprinted reflexes—the former being strictly limited by the scope of the latter. For instance, a person growing up in a racially tense area, having been beaten or mugged by a member of another race, will possibly become imprinted with a fear response (fight or flight) to members of that race. Conditioning toward intolerance will then be easily applied by parents and peers on top of that imprint, while conditioning toward tolerance will be extremely difficult. Fortunately, conditioned reflexes are much looser than imprints. We might compare these to programs saved on a computer's hard drive, rather than encoded into the ROM. They will not simply vanish on their own, but one can access and overwrite them with relative ease if one knows how.

The final method of mental programming is *learning*. This is the method with which most people are familiar; including such things as memorization and study. As any student who has studied for a test will know, this programming is the loosest, and most easily altered, corrupted, or entirely forgotten. Prolonged learning can sometimes result in conditioning—such as those who can remember the basic multiplication tables throughout their life after having had them "driven into their heads" during elementary school.

Once again, this method is limited by past experience with the previous two. As Wilson tells us, "Whatever the Thinker thinks, the Prover proves." It is very difficult to learn anything which is contrary to our imprints and conditioning. This is why thousands of people today still insist on fearing "Hell," why Inquisitors and politicians feel ultimately justified in their actions, and why so many authors have found ample evidence to support their theories that the grimoires are low and base works of silly nonsense.

Taken together, these three aspects of mental programming combine to form your own personal reality map. In the occult communities, we often hear this referred to as a "filter" through which all sensual experiences, thoughts, and impressions pass. This is an *absolutely vital* point to keep in mind, as we will revisit it in later chapters concerning the shamanic interaction with spiritual intelligences. It is why one Christian's Jesus can be a spiteful and jealous God, while another's can be merciful and all-loving. Likewise, one Wiccan's Goddess might care nothing for men, while another's spends the course of the year pursuing her male lover across the heavens and into the underworld.

So much for how the brain assimilates and stores information. Now, it is necessary to return to the concept of Leary's eight points of imprint vulnerability, which he called "mental circuits." This is basically a map of your own reality map into which you can categorize your imprinted reflexes, and thus your conditioning and learning, to examine and make objective judgements concerning them. The Art of Ecstasy is wholly based upon shifting consciousness from lower mental circuits into higher ones. *Prometheus Rising* discusses the relation of several mystical systems—from yoga to modern Western magick—to the process of accessing (and reprogramming) each mental circuit one at a time; from the lowest to the highest.

Circuit One: Oral Bio-Survival

Simply put, this is the oldest existing evolutionary circuit wherein exists the survival instinct. After the traumatic experience of birth, a child is placed in the warm and protective arms of the mother who offers the first meal. From that moment onward, the child will associate the mother (or mother figure) with nourishment and physical safety. The mother and the environment surrounding her at the time becomes the data assimilated into the first circuit. It will then govern the mechanisms of advance and retreat which the new human will likely follow throughout life. Those things which resemble (or, like Pavlov's bell, are associated with) mother will automatically induce feelings of peace, happiness, and safety.[22] Anything unpleasant (noxious or predatory) will induce fear and retreat back toward the arms of mother or associated stimuli.

Circuit Two: Anal Emotional-Territorial

This circuit exists mainly in mammalian psychology, and is somewhat younger than the first. It is concerned with the "pack instinct," territorialism, and submission and domination. This circuit is associated with the father figure and imprinted during the toddler stage. Specifically, it includes the first experiences of a child learning to walk and establishing a place within the tribe or family. It is quickly understood that Father is the alpha male who can dish out both reward and punishment, and Mother likewise takes on aspects of this role for the first time. Brothers and sisters are also assimilated as those above and below in the pecking order: the large ones able to push the toddler down at will, and the smaller ones representing no threat. This circuit is why children who are abused so often remain victims to predators in later years, because they learn (on a first and second circuit basis) to submit quickly and easily to aggression. Likewise, this circuit can be imprinted in a healthy manner, where the cues given by predators and abusers simply have no effect. This is why children raised lovingly are rarely chosen by adult predators or abusive peers for victimization.

Wilson offers us a simple diagram that illustrates the interaction of the first two circuits, and how they integrate to form the basis of a human personality:[23]

Here we can see how a human's basic assumptions about reality—those set by the age of two or three—can direct attitudes and decisions throughout a lifetime. A person who is tyrannical and aggressive likely encountered some unfortunate first circuit "retreat" experiences, by which he learned that the world is a harsh and destructive place. Yet, on his second circuit, he was placed in a position of general dominance. When the world came to attack him, he learned he had the power to knock it back into its place. Thus, when feeling threatened or interfered with (which will be often), his reaction is to fight fire with more fire. In his reality either you or he is going to come to some harm, and he will do nearly anything to ensure that it is not himself.

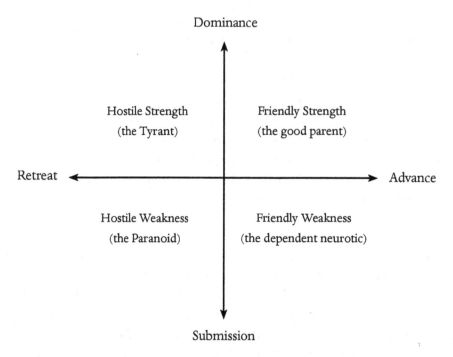

The Second Mental Circuit.

Meanwhile, another child will have been imprinted upon the first circuit to see the world as a basically fun place to live, and does not fear advancing into it. If this person is also imprinted upon circuit two within a role of dominance (for instance, perhaps he is the oldest of his siblings or the most outgoing among his peers), he will find himself in the position of the good parent. He knows that he can handle any situation without descending into the hell of fight or flight, and is also comfortable with leading others along the way.

On the other end of this scale, we see the paranoid. This poor chap also encountered harsh first circuit conditions and the general retreat reflex, but was not fortunate enough to land in a position of second circuit dominance. When the world came to attack, he had little choice but to retreat and submit. Here, of course, is our above-mentioned abused child. Like the tyrant, his reality also demands that someone gets hurt, but he has long since accepted that he will be the target. He suspects everything, and is satisfied with nothing. Re-imprinting the first two circuits is absolutely vital to this person for any hope of freedom.

The same is also true of our last personality—the dependant neurotic. This person learned early that the world could be an okay place, but was also set into a submissive role. He can advance into his environment, but *only* under the direction of someone else whom he considers his superior in some way. This person is also a favorite target of the tyrant, because the victim will "dig in" or advance toward him (catering to his whims) rather than retreating from the situation.

Of course, each of these examples are in the extreme. Our above chart should be considered more of a graph, where any given person might fall upon various points (as well as move from one to another within a given range). The truly balanced and healthy person rests principally toward the middle of the cross, able to consciously move in any of the four directions when necessary. Those who exist at the extremities of the graph are "robotized" people, living their lives upon thoughtless (and unbalanced) reaction to their environment. It is perhaps needless to say that the goal of the mage is to reach the central point; and it becomes quickly apparent why the cross is perhaps the oldest spiritual symbol of balance and harmony.

Medieval and Renaissance medical theory was based chiefly upon this kind of fourfold consideration, and its relation to astrology. Each temperamental extreme (as in our above graph) was labeled as a "humour," and was associated with the four basic principals of nature as embodied in the zodiac and the four Kherubim.[24]

The word "humour" derives from the Latin *humor* (moisture). The four humours of medieval medicine were associated with bodily fluids such as blood, bile, and phlegm. From a more psychological standpoint, they were associated with temperament. Just as in Wilson's graph, a person in good health was judged to be in a position of relative balance among the humours, though everyone would display a natural tendency toward some humours over others (based upon their natal chart).

Things and people associated with the fiery signs, especially the Kherubic Leo, were known as *choleric* and quick to anger and war (hostile strength). Those associated with the Airy signs, especially Aquarius, were labeled as *sanguine* and known to be happy and outgoing (friendly strength). Those related to the Water signs, namely Scorpio (symbolized Kherubically by the eagle), were called *melancholy* and considered emotional and often depressive (friendly weakness). Finally, those related to Earthy signs, especially Taurus, were *phlegmatic* and known as slow and stolid (hostile weakness).[25]

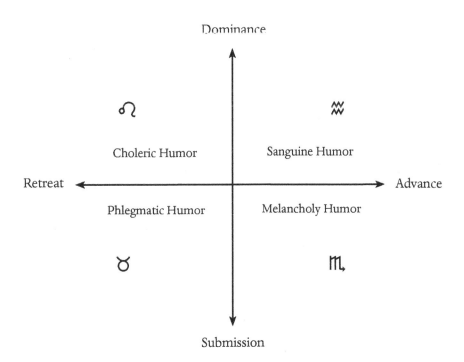

The Four Medieval Humours.

Circuit Three: Time-Binding Semantic

This is the first evolutionary circuit associated principally with humans, as it includes our ability for rational thought, the use of symbol systems (such as language), and the creation of artifacts. These are "time-binding" in the sense that they allow us to transmit messages from one generation to the next. A human reaches this point of imprint vulnerability in mid-childhood when first learning to speak, and then to read and write. Humanity as a whole seems to have reached this point somewhere before the beginning of what we call the "historical period," when tools were created, language was invented, and (eventually) written records were kept for the first time.

As Wilson points out, this circuit is what is normally considered "the mind," the constant internal dialogue that we all live with that perceives, considers, and labels everything it encounters. Based upon the left/right cortex model of the brain—in which the left half governs analytical thought and the right governs creativity and emotion—Wilson locates this circuit in the left cortex. This is what allows us to perform study and researc; not only because our brains can properly assimilate the information, but because those before us had the ability to record it.

When considering human behavior and personality, it is extremely important to remember that this circuit is not an objective observer of the world. Instead, the decisions it makes can be overridden by commands from the first and second circuits. For instance, if you were to suddenly find yourself in a position of personal danger, your biosurvival circuit would engage and direct the decisions made upon the semantic circuit. Likewise, the military, police, and large corporations are all familiar with what can be accomplished by activating one's submission reflex.

Wilson associates both patriotism and (organized) religion with this dynamic. By threatening their population with eternal suffering in Hell, or with the idea of Satanic magick being worked against them, the medieval Catholic Church was able to pervert rational thought into hysteria. Likewise, by threatening a population with loss of status (position in the tribe) or foreign invasion, any government can keep its people fighting mad.

These two processes are identical, even if each works from accessing a different circuit within the victim. For example, a play titled *The Crucible* was written in 1953 because Arthur Miller saw no difference between the hysteria of the old witch hunts (religion) and the hysteria of McCarthy's "red scare" (patriotism). What will successfully induce fear in any instance depends upon the individual or community. It might be fear of witchcraft, Hell, foreign invasion, or attack by drug offenders. If a propagandist can locate the victim's position on the previously given graphs, finding a supposed threat with the most appeal is easy. Once the propagandist has done the victim the "favor" of alerting him to the supposed danger, a "rational plan" must be offered that fulfills the requirements for safety set by circuits one and two. The plan does not have to be realistic or applicable in any logical sense, because a person experiencing fear is not truly thinking upon circuit three. He is regressed to a preverbal state, and no appeals to his intelligence will make any difference.

Those who are balanced within the center of the graph, by contrast, are hard to influence in such ways. This is why one modern Hermetic school insists to its students that "fear is failure," and such men as Israel Regardie insist that a proper mental balance is necessary to success and safety in magick. Even the shaman, characterized by mental unbalance in youth, is told by his spirits that he must become adept in the shamanic arts (by which balance can be found) or go insane and eventually die.

Circuit Four: "Moral" Socio-Sexual

According to Wilson, this circuit is imprinted by the first "orgasm-mating" experiences of puberty, and conditioned by tribal taboos. When the sexual apparatus of the human body wake up, new chemicals are released, and new thought processes are introduced into the brain. Imprint vulnerability is very high at such a time, and one's first experiences of sexual stimulation will set gender or sexual role for life.

From a tribal standpoint, this is some pretty unstable dynamite with which to play. What "turns you on" will determine who you mate with, and thus what newborns are produced. We might consider primitive tribes as living creatures unto themselves, with their own survival instincts that demand the protection of the local gene pool. Taboos will shift over time depending on the perceived needs of the tribe, or the whims of its governing body (chief, shaman, council, etc.). This is the origin of the many rites of passage known throughout the world and history. They are ceremonies constructed to surround a person's points of a imprint vulnerability and ensure that tribally acceptable imprints are put into place. This, in and of itself, is an important aspect of the shamanic vocation.

Of course, the umbrella of "sexual role" (or sexual identity) covers more than ideas of "Mom and Dad" or concepts of beauty and attraction. It also covers concepts of *personal beauty* and *body consciousness*. Wilson states that those who take the heaviest imprints on this circuit are very often extremely "beautiful" (whatever that means in any given time or place). They are very caught up with personal appearance, and can utilize their looks as practical assets. Models are, for example, very "fourth circuit" people. Your own attractiveness to other members of your tribe (especially members of the opposite sex) can very often play a large role in your life choices, and even influence your social class or physical well-being. Your own subjective impressions about your attractiveness can either boost you ever higher among your peers, filling you with self-confidence and self-love, or can hold you down and force you into hiding away from your peers.

Taken together, these first four imprint circuits make up the majority of human psychology. That is to say, they are evolutionarily the oldest and most common circuits in existence. Everyone has them, and we are currently (as a species) living principally upon the fourth.[26] As Wilson states, these circuits make possible "gene-pool survival, mammalian sociobiology (pecking order, or politics) and transmission of culture. The second group of four brain circuits is much newer, and each circuit exists at present only in minorities. Where the antique circuits recapitulate evolution-to-the-present, these futuristic circuits *pre*capitulate our future evolution."[27]

These are the levels of consciousness which most concern the shaman or mage. They are the higher levels ("heavens") accessed by mystical experience and the working of magick. By appealing to the entities of these higher realms, the shaman is literally taking steps toward personal and societal evolution. In order to make contact with "qliphothic entities," or enter the "hells," the shaman must descend into the fearful states of the lower circuits.[28]

Circuit Five: Holistic Neurosomatic

This is the circuit that concerns us most right now, as it is the one activated by ecstatic experience. I have already described the miracles (magick) that become possible in the ecstatic state, and Wilson adds to this in his description of the holistic neurosomatic circuit: "It processes neurosomatic ('mind-body') feedback loops, somatic-sensory bliss, feeling 'high', 'faith healing', etc."[29]

This circuit (generally) develops late in life for those few who possess it. It strikes me as likely that this fact has been known to mankind for several centuries thanks to shamans and mystics. In Jewish culture, it is insisted that an aspirant await the age of forty before entering into studies of the Qabalah. It is known that most people who show initial interest will eventually move on to other pursuits, while those few who persist until that later age are likely those who possess the necessary talent for the vocation.

Going back a bit further, the ancient Gnostics divided mankind into two principal camps: the Cainites and the Sethians. According to Genesis, Eve's son Cain became the world's first murderer when he slew his brother Abel. The Gnostics further believed that Cain was not the son of Adam at all, but was the flawed product of a mating between Eve and the Serpent (Devil) during their interaction over the Tree of Knowledge.[30] Cain later slew his half-brother because, unlike himself, Abel was successful in gaining contact with Yahweh. (One might suggest that even this hints at the separation between those who do possess fifth-circuit capabilities, and those who do not.) Cain was banished from his family's presence, and eventually fathered his own nation. This nation, according to the Gnostics, comprises the bulk of human population today; the common man who in no way experiences a mystical, shamanic, or prophetic vocation. Meanwhile, Adam and Eve produced another son together to replace Abel, and this was Seth. Seth was a product of proper balance between mother and father (circuits one and two), and was capable of communication with God. It was from Seth that the later patriarchs, such as Enoch, Noah, Abraham, and Moses, descended, and the Gnostics felt that they were his modern-day spiritual descendants.

Thus, what we are seeing in these examples, as well as in Wilson's material, is yet another reference to the exclusive state of the shaman, his life lived apart from the tribe in general, and even the privileged death he will experience. This is an evolutionary division of humanity between those who do, and those who do not, possess fifth-circuit capabilities.

Of course, if the logic of evolution holds true, we should have more fifth circuit–capable humans (shamans) around today than ever before. This would certainly explain the era of the 1960s, with its explosive and insistent focus upon mind alteration, and every human being's right to ingest psychedelic substances. It would also explain the negative reaction to that movement by the general population.[31] It even makes sense when considering the direction of our current massive world changes, focusing on the exploration of both space and cyberspace. Both of these will demand (and are currently demanding) those who have gained a suitable fifth circuit state of mind. They are the quantum physicists, mathematicians, engineers, computer geeks, cybernauts, etc.; all of them existing as both outcasts from, yet vitally important to the continuation of, mainstream society. Chapter 2, of course, explains this dynamic in full.

Wilson points out that *temporary* neurosomatic consciousness can be activated by the yogic practice of pranayama breathing (you have already experienced an example of ecstasy through breathing), by the ingestion of cannabis psychotropics, and by such things as sensory deprivation and zero gravity.[32] (We will be covering these latter methods of gaining ecstasy in this very chapter, with the exception of zero gravity, of course.)

Wilson continues to describe neurosomatic consciousness: "'Every act (becomes) an orgasm,' said Aleister Crowley . . . The lives of the saints are full of stories which seem 'miracles' to the four-circuited majority, or are rejected as 'lies, hoaxes, yarns' by the three-circuited dogmatic Rationalist, but which seem perfectly normal from the viewpoint of five-circuited polymorphous consciousness. The saint says he is in rapture, and full of gratitude to God, for giving him such a feast for dinner as—plain *bread* and *water*. (Of course, many a pot-head will understand *that* degree of neurosomatic rapture . . .) The guru comes into the room and his bio-energy has such a charge that a cripple jumps up and is 'healed'; the cripple merely acquired neurosomatic turn-on *by contact*, as some people get 'contact high' when others are on drugs. The fire-walkers in many shamanic traditions walk on the fire, as they tell enquiring anthropologists, to prove their control over 'the spirit'—i.e. to *demonstrate* to themselves and others that they have achieved high-quality neurosomatic tuning."[33] Likewise, "In alchemy this was known as 'the multiplication of the first matter' or 'the Philosopher's Gold,' which was unlike ordinary gold in that it could not be *spent* or used up, since it perpetually multiplied and renewed itself."[34] Here, yet once again, we can see where several ideas we have already studied are brought together into one coherent whole.

Finally, there are warnings that must be included for anyone who wishes to activate the neurosomatic circuit; they are basically the same warnings shamans and mages have been giving to apprentices since the beginning. Just as ecstatic bliss can be experienced upon the fifth circuit, so, too, can one experience very negative reactions. Wilson points to amateur yogis, "pot-heads," and schizophrenics who all possess examples of this point. It is commonly known in Western occultism as "the dark night of the soul," or as "crossing an abyss." This brings us back again to the subject of psychological balance. My policy is to tell any would-be student of magick that they *will* experience these rough periods. If you do not, then you are simply not making the transition into the higher realms and states of consciousness. Failure in magick stems from two dynamics: (1) failing to make any transition at all, and (2) failing the transition in the middle of the attempt. The former results in nothing but mental masturbation, while the latter can be extremely dangerous. Establishing balance among the four previously discussed temperamental extremes is the key to success and safety.

Circuit Six: Collective Neurogenetic

Of all the circuits discussed so far, this is the one that most directly relates to the idea of the shamanic spirit realm. Wilson insists that this circuit is "'collective' in that it contains and has access to the whole evolutionary 'script', past and future. Experience of this circuit is numinous, 'mystical', mind-shattering; here dwell the archetypes of Jung's Collective Unconscious—Gods, Goddesses, Demons, Hairy Dwarfs and other personifications of the DNA programs (instincts) that govern us."[35]

Thus, the sixth circuit can be described as the genetic archives within any individual, but that span far beyond the scope of any single being. It is concerned mainly with the survival of genetic memory over *long periods* of time. This is DNA memory; the entire past history of your species, as well as the blueprints for future evolution. The entities, or personifications of natural forces, one meets while in this mental state are not strictly subjective to the individual. They, like the DNA codes within us, exist for everyone.

Wilson has some extremely provocative things to say in regards to this circuit: "Circuit [VI] neurosomatic consciousness allows you to 'converse' with the evolutionary architect who *designed* your body—and billions and billions of others since the dawn of life around 3–4 million years ago. This 'architect' is the greatest designer on this planet . . . No human architect has yet equaled Her efficiency *or* Her esthetics in such routine products as roses, eggs, insect colonies, fish, etc. She (or He) can be personified in modern terms as Mother DNA or Father Nucleic Acid. The Rationalist immediately objects that such personification, however inescapable it is to all who have encountered the Architect directly on this circuit, is illegitimate, because She or He is *unconscious*. The rebuttal, given by all Circuit VI adepts in all cultures and all ages, is that She or He is not unconscious but intoxicated, and it is a divine intoxication."[36]

The Gnostics understood the concept of a creator god responsible for the formation of the physical universe (as opposed to the higher Parent of All who preexists both physical matter and the creator). The Gnostic term for the creator is the Latin *Demiurgos*, which literally translates as "builder" or "architect." Meanwhile, the Jewish *Merkavah* mystics were centered heavily upon gaining sixth circuit experiences of the creator—such as described in the first chapter of Ezekiel or the *Ethiopian Book of Enoch*. The grimoires have their own focus in this regard—as shown in the *Sworn Book of Honorius* where instructions are given for gaining the beatific vision of God. This entire practice was founded by the original tribal shamans who traveled to the highest heavens to meet the father face to face, and ask for favors.

It would appear that a vastly significant portion of human religion has been based on encounters upon the neurogenetic circuit. The life—even the intelligence—of genetic memory continues onward through time regardless of the life or death of individual physical bodies; much as your own life and intelligence continues regardless of the life cycles of your cells. The resurrection mythos found in so many cultures throughout history, with its promises of immortality through death and rebirth, are the result of sixth circuit consciousness.

> "I am the Alpha and the Omega, the beginning and the ending." Sayeth the Lord, which is, and which was, and which is to come, the Almighty.[37]

> "I am the resurrection, and the life: he that believeth in me, though he were dead, yet shall he live. And whosoever liveth and believeth in me shall never die."[38]

Call unto thy soul; arise and come unto me; for I am the soul of nature, who gives life to the universe. From me all things proceed, and unto me all things must return; and before my face, beloved of Gods and of men, let thine innermost divine self be enfolded in the rapture of the infinite.[39]

Wilson puts it into more physically concrete terms when he says, "To the individual, the breaks in the chain of life/death/life/death/life/death are all too real and painful; to the seed-and-egg wisdom of the neurogenetic circuit, the seamless unity of lifedeathlife-deathlife-deathlife is the greater reality."[40]

The angels and intelligences we will work with in later chapters might be thought of as intermediaries between us and the architect—operating somewhat between the fifth and sixth circuits. This fits them well as the messengers of the creator, whose principal function is the transmission of information from God(dess), sixth circuit, to humankind via the fifth circuit. Even divination can be attributed to neurogenetic consciousness—as this is where Jung's concept of synchronicity (or meaningful coincidence) rests. According to Wilson, Jung attributed this to what he called the "psychoid level" just below the personal and collective unconscious—much in the same position as our angels. This is "where 'mind' and 'matter' are not yet differentiated—the royal highway of the DNA-RNA-CNS (central nervous system) telegraph . . . Such synchronicities are a sure sign that you are dealing with the neurogenetic circuit."[41] A study and practice of the tarot will expand one's experience (and capability) in this arena.

Circuit Seven: Metaprogramming

With the final two circuits, we leave behind the devotional concerns of the grimoires and enter the realm of pure mysticism. We might say that circuits five and six, and the techniques of the magickal texts, represent the means, while circuits seven and eight represent the intended ends. Reaching these high mental "vibrations," attaining to the highest heavens, is what defines the master adept. This is where the psychonaut (or mage) enters the realm of personal godhood, with an all-encompassing control over his own self and environment. It is here that Moses attained, as we see in *Legends of the Bible*, when even the angels could not stand against him. The Gnostics entitled those who gained this mastery "Christ" (anointed)—and we are all familiar with the deeds of *one* man who earned that degree.

Circuit seven is defined by its ability to overrule and re-imprint all lower circuits at will—thus the name "metaprogramming." Wilson assures us that such metaprogramming makes "possible conscious choice between alternative universes or reality tunnels."[42] You and I might recognize this circuit more readily by the term "higher self." In practical terms, this is the self that preexists your current personality—existing as a null void before the establishment of your first imprints. These imprints, along with the conditioning, learning, neuroses, complexes and memories that overlay them, are not truly "you." When you like or dislike something, become angry or happy, excited or sad, these are not you in a mystical sense. Not a single word which you might use to describe or define yourself will reflect your true higher self.[43]

A colleague of mine once defined this fact by stating that we are each a living being trapped within a machine called a "body"; looking out through its eyes but having no control whatsoever over the actions or directions of that machine. This being cannot speak through the mouth, cannot decide which emotions to feel, cannot direct the thoughts that run through the mind. The robotic machine merely *reacts to its environment*, regardless of how much that machine insists it is a living and conscious thing. At least this is the case for many—the so-called Cainites.

What separates the Gnostic from the Cainite, he continued, was the fact that, within the Gnostic, the living being has awakened and attempts to gain control of the mind and body. It works to bring the *reaction* processes (again, neuroses and complexes, etc.) to a halt, so that it can begin to *act* on its own behalf. In modern psychology, it is known as "dissociation," where one simply takes a mental "step back" from any thought or emotion—to question its motives,[44] analyze its origins,[45] and make adjustments and corrections to the process that better suit personal goals.[46]

Humankind has understood this concept since at least the ancient dynasties of Egypt, where it is preserved in the mythos of creation and embodied in the figure of the god Tehuti (Thoth). Tehuti is the god of all things involving the intellect: words, writing, magick, sciences, etc. He was not born of a mother or father, but was self-created and sprang directly from the mind of Amen-Re at the time of creation. Without Tehuti's words and magick, the fashioning of the cosmos itself would not have occurred at all. This was later adopted by the Coptic Gnostics near the beginning of the Common Era, where the concept of Tehuti became known as the "Logos" (Word). As we read in one Gnostic text, preserved in the New Testament book of John:

> In the beginning was the Word, and the Word was with God, and the Word was God. The same was in the beginning with God. All things were made by Him; and without Him was not anything fashioned that was created. In him was life; and the life was the light of men. And the light shineth in darkness, yet the darkness comprehendeth it not.[47]

According to the Gnostic teachings, the highest Parent of All was not originally a thinking creature. Instead, it was simply an inconceivable *No Thing*[48] that existed before creation—full of itself, resting within itself, and as unaware of itself as a fish is unaware of the existance of water. At some point, for reasons which no human has successfully conjectured, this *No Thing* suddenly "woke up," and realized that it did, in fact, exist. This awakening was/is the self-created Logos.[49]

Now, it is extremely important not to confuse the Logos with the first *thought* that passed through the super-cosmic mind. Thoughts are the creation, indeed the *result*, of the Logos. The Logos is self-awareness, the ability to dissociate from the self and contemplate it objectively. Of course, the Gnostics did not perceive the Logos as a force reserved for God; it could be invoked by any human. The book of John continues:

> That was the true Light, which lighteth every man that cometh into the world. . . . But as many as received him, to them gave he power to become the sons of God.[50]

Dr. Wilson, of course, grants us some practical advise about the metaprogramming circuit, using the language of mathematics, when he says: ". . . as soon as you think of your mind as mind(1) and the mind which contemplates that mind as mind(2) and the mind which contemplates mind(2) contemplating mind(1) as mind(3), you are well on your way to metaprogramming awareness. *Alice in Wonderland* is a masterful guide to the metaprogramming circuit (written by one of the founders of mathematical logic) and Aleister Crowley soberly urged its study upon all students of yoga. R. Buckminster Fuller illustrates the metaprogramming circuit, in his lectures, by pointing out that we feel puny in comparison to the universe, but only our bodies (hardware) are puny. Our minds, he says—by which he means our software—*contain* the universe, by the act of comprehending it."[51]

I only wish to add here that this kind of consciousness (and even less the following eighth circuit) must not be considered a spiritual "end goal." Such discussion of the matter as I have seen tends to unanimously agree that these periods of what we call *enlightenment* are strictly temporary. All too often, students make the mistake of setting enlightenment far away from themselves, as something striven toward yet never reached. Consider the legends of the ever-elusive philosopher's stone, knowledge and conversation of the holy guardian angel, or attaining Christ consciousness. In reality, these upper circuit experiences will happen from time to time as you become adept in the ecstatic arts. Of course, the *effects* of these experiences will last a lifetime; while the imprinting episodes (enlightenment) will occur at various times and under various conditions.

Circuit Eight: Nonlocal Quantum

As I mentioned above, the final two circuits are extremely mystical, and their experiences are nearly impossible to describe. Note that I have been forced into more and more poetic imagery, even quoting religious scripture, as I moved from the fifth circuit upward. This is common to mystical literature; and even in Wilson's work his chapter on the eighth circuit is one of the shortest in the book. These are, indeed, the regions of the ineffable.

Luckily, Wilson came up with a useful comparison between the eighth circuit experience and a scientific, rather than poetic, model. This theorem is taken from quantum mechanics, and known as Bell's Theorem. As Wilson explains: ". . . in ordinary language it amounts to something like this: There are no isolated systems; every particle in the universe is in 'instantaneous' (faster-than-light) communication with every other particle. The Whole *System*, even the parts that are separated by cosmic distances, function as a *Whole* System. . . . the experiments are replicable and have been replicated several times. . . . [it is assumed] that the 'communication' involved in Bellian transmissions does not involve *energy*, since it is energy that cannot move faster than light. Dr. Edward Harris Walker suggests that what does move faster than light, and holds the Whole System together, is 'consciousness'. We may eventually be forced to accept this, in which case physics will have justified pantheism or at least panpsychism. The other alternative, proposed by Dr. Jack Sarfatti, is that the medium of Bellian transmissions is *information*."[52] I wholeheartedly agree with both alternatives, as I feel they are one and the same.

In mystical terms, the eighth circuit experience would be called the attainment of cosmic consciousness. This is where one utterly sheds the lower self—body and all—and taps into the quantum realm, the physical aspect of pure information / consciousness upon which even atomic structures are based. As Bell's Theorem suggests, and Plato and Agrippa taught centuries before, the universe itself is alive and conscious. By tapping into the eighth circuit, one is literally tapping into *everything that exists*. In that brief instant of contact, you *comprehend* the entirety of creation from beginning to end of both space and time; you are the Alpha and Omega.

This kind of intense gnosis is rarely about gaining information or insight into specific concepts,[53] and you won't likely return with the secrets of your neighbors. The experience is entirely too all-encompassing. I might describe it by saying that, when it happens, you get to spend one brief moment in which the universe just makes sense. You are shown a snapshot of the whole tapestry, and it is quite a "mind-blowing" image to see.

Thus is the eight circuit model of consciousness credited to Dr. Timothy Leary. It took me some time to make heads or tails of much of it; for instance, the sixth through eighth circuits made little sense to me for a couple of years. With consistent study and practice, however, one can eventually attain the higher shamanic realms of consciousness. The information given above will give you a practical model by which you can gauge your own experiences, signposts that let you know just how high you've reached, and a practical conception of what to *do* with the information.

Although, I do wish to state once more that I disagree with suggestions that the shamanic realms are strictly within the psyche. I have found that gaining these mental states is merely the "how-to" behind entering the shamanic spirit realms, which are themselves "collective." The various heavens and celestial realms described in ancient literature (most often shown stacked one atop the other reaching upward toward God) actually exist all around us at all times. They interpenetrate one another, and are separated merely by their differing vibrational pitches (or frequencies), just like the various stations found on your radio dial. One does not have to fly in an airplane to receive radio signals on the upper ends of the dial, and neither does the shaman have to physically leave the ground to "tune in" to the proper spiritual plane. The eight circuit model of consciousness is the best I have found to illustrate exactly where (and what) these "stations" are upon the shamanic dial.

The ecstatic art of the prophet-shaman is composed of techniques aimed at temporarily shifting consciousness among these circuits, especially circuits five through eight.[54] Therefore, we will now explore these techniques through history and into the grimoires.

Psychotropics: Ancient History

Mind-altering substances have been a major aspect of shamanism since well before the dawn of written history, and perhaps even since the dawn of mankind. There is some speculation that the human species attained what we call "sentience" only after ingesting psychotropic plants[55] and, because of our capability of speech and opposable thumbs, were able to learn to communicate the experience to others.[56]

Even if this is not true, it is still entirely probable that human spirituality *did* evolve from that source. It did not take early shamans long to learn that different substances, when consumed, could initiate various higher-circuit experiences. Such "minor" psychotropics as cannabis or tobacco could invoke the fifth circuit ecstatic state; while the more intense psychedelic substances could invoke sixth, seventh, or even eighth circuit encounters. What was seen by the most primitive psychonauts "on the other side" forms the very foundation of spiritual speculation, as well as the concept of life divorced from physical incarnation.[57] One might say that the early shaman simply saw no reason to assume his experiences during altered states were "hallucinatory"; though one could just as easily suggest that he did not automatically assume (as does twentieth-century materialism) that experiences during "normal" (first-fourth circuit) consciousness were ultimately "real."

Even the famous Tree of Life—by which shamans climbed into the celestial realms and whose fruits granted spiritual perfection—was very likely originally a psychotropic plant. For instance, the "Tree of Life" growing in the Babylonian Eden (Eridu) was called the *kiskanu*:

> In Eridu groweth the dark *kiskanu;* in a holy place was it brought forth;
>
> It's root was of bright lapis, set in the world beneath.
>
> [. . .]
>
> The Gods . . . have gathered this *kiskanu;*, and over the man
>
> Have performed the Incantation of the Deep,
>
> And at the head of the wanderer have set it.
>
> That a kindly Guardian, a kindly Spirit
>
> May stand at the side of the man, the son of his God.

The plant is never plainly described, but it is conjectured by some to have been a psychedelic of some sort. (Note how the *kiskanu* is "gathered" by the gods, which suggests against it being a tree.) Other cultures also viewed the Tree of Life as a feminine plant,[58] and often depict it as a goddess or a plant held in the hands of a goddess. This image is found in Canaan and other Middle Eastern cultures, and it is the *only* image of divinity known from ancient Scythian art.

Further, it is very likely that the mystery of the eucharist itself descends from these concepts. Though this is usually credited to agricultural society and the harvest of crops: where the dying and rising god of grain and fertility (literally embodied in the crop itself) would be sacrificed (harvested) each year and consumed by the community for continued life. However, the original idea that gods could embody themselves in plants was more than likely the result of mankind's first (pre-agricultural) experiences with such things as mushrooms, tobacco, cannabis, etc. There is indication that ancient Gnostic eucharists were themselves psychotropic, and even today most eucharists retain the element of wine.[59]

We know that digesting, as well as inhaling, any substance makes it literally a part of our own bodies. It is chemically broken down within our digestive system or lungs, and recombined to our own flesh in order to nourish it.[60] At the same time, as we have previously discussed, we know that everything in existence (most especially living matter) has its own spirit. That spirit is not a discarnate "entity" residing in a location within or above the physical matter, but is in fact encoded throughout the physical structure itself. By inhaling or digesting that physical matter, one is also performing a literal invocation of the spirit that resides within it. Anyone who has taken part in a eucharist ceremony understands how such a process feels, but there is no eucharist more profoundly striking than the consumption of a consecrated psychotropic substance, especially if one understands it to be a living being, rather than a mere dead mix of chemicals.

As Jim DeKorne illustrates in his *Psychedelic Shamanism*, "shamanic cultures worldwide share the near-universal belief that each plant species contains 'spirits' which can be utilized as allies for shamanic work."[61] He points out that even the earliest hunter-gatherer cultures gathered mushrooms and other psychotropic plants for a very long time. The plants were literally understood to be gods or patron spirits, given their own altars, sacrifices, and general worship. By sacramental eating or smoking of the plant, the shaman digested the body (or inhaled the spirit) of the god and temporarily became "at one" with it. Unlike most plants, these special entities could make the shaman a superhuman, with all of the powers we have discussed so far: celestial and infernal flight, increased strength, resistance to pain, etc. Not to mention the simple fact that consumption of the plant led to fifth (or higher) circuit consciousness, whereupon miracles could be performed. The shaman would very often hold conversation with the intelligence of the plant itself rather than praying to the more disconnected parental gods.

I feel that the prophet-shamans were, in their day, what we might call "stoners" today. In fact, the modern drug culture retains a certain element of shamanism.[62] The largest difference, however, is that the shamanic masters follow a disciplined spiritual practice, making them much more comparable with modern psychonauts such as Timothy Leary. Although, in simpler times psychotropic substances of choice were not always "major" narcotics or hallucinogens. It is apparent that tobacco was extremely popular where it grew. Coca leaves were simply chewed before refining procedures were created. Alcohol is another example that has been known worldwide and throughout history.

In a more restricted sense, there were cults centered upon cannabis and mushrooms, as well as peyote and other plants depending on geographical location. This is something, I feel, that should be taken into consideration when studying the ancient beliefs that gods were restricted to location (see chapter 2). Marduk had no jurisdiction in Egypt, and Baal meant nothing to the Romans. If the plant most sacred to a god was not available in a foreign land, then that god simply did not live there. Nomadic tribes (especially) are recorded as being guided totally by the whims of their gods; and this is perhaps explainable if we consider a tribe discovering their sacred plant grows poorly in one place and well in another. In that light (i.e., plain and simple horticulture), if the god-plant refuses to move to a new location, that is pretty much that. This also explains why deities took many generations to migrate relatively short distances, and why they always appear in mutated form once on foreign soil. A comparable psychotropic may have been found in the new land, but it would not necessarily produce *exactly* the same ecstatic experience. On the other hand, if nothing comparable could be found, then contacting that specific god would be all but impossible.

Today, gods do not seem so limited to geographic location as they once were. I have wondered if this is a reality or if it is simply a result of our current philosophical views of the deities. In fact, I feel it is both to various degrees. If a shaman were to go to a foreign land, taking a supply of the plant with him, then he could contact his patron. That patron would have a largely reduced effect upon the foreign environment than at home within his or her own culture, but the patrons would at least communicate with the prophet. If the plant could be imported, then there was little problem other than the fact that the plant could not be home-grown (which is nearly inexcusable to the ancient shamanic arts). Today, no known plant is truly restricted to its home land. An entire potted plant can make it (hopefully) unharmed around the globe while still alive and practically fresh. The gods have become mobile in the physical sense just as they have become mobile in the philosophical.[63]

For our brief discussion of this otherwise vast and highly involved subject, we will start with the very same Siberian-region shamans who formed the basis of Eliade's work (see chapter 2).[64] These are (generically speaking) the same people who eventually extended southwards, into Asia Minor and the Middle East, bringing with them their father god and religious practices.[65]

A favorite psychotropic plant of these people was the sacred mushroom *Amanita muscaria*. Some hypothesize that this is the "soma" praised at length in the Aryan Vedas, and had a major role in the establishment of such faiths as Zoroastrianism and Hinduism. The reader might recognize this mushroom more readily from *Alice in Wonderland*: the small red mushroom with white spots that has some rather surreal effects when eaten by Alice. The substance, though sweet to the taste, is also slightly toxic, causing nausea for some time directly after consumption.[66] One might also take note of the biblical Revelation of St. John, where a previously obscure reference suddenly becomes understandable, if the *shape* of the mushroom is held in mind:

> And I saw another mighty Angel come down from heaven . . . And he had in his hand a little scroll . . . And I went unto the Angel, and said unto him, "Give me the little scroll." And he said unto me, "Take it, and eat it up; and it shall make thy belly bitter, but it shall be in thy mouth sweet as honey." And I took the little scroll out of the Angel's hand, and ate it up; and it was in my mouth sweet as honey: and as soon as I had eaten it, my belly was bitter. And he said unto me, "Thou must prophesy again before many peoples, and nations, and tongues, and kings" (Revelation 10:1–2, 9–11).

Eliade does, to some extent, discuss the use of mushrooms and other psychotropics in shamanic cultures. The gaining of ecstatic states through mushroom intoxication, he says, is known throughout Siberia. Other parts of the world display similar practices associated with various narcotics or tobacco.[67] He also gives a few examples of shamanic procedure. The Ostyak shamans begin by offering sacrifices to the god Sanke. Then three mushrooms are eaten, allowing the shaman to begin his ecstatic trip. Shamanesses work in a similar manner, visiting Sanke via the mushroom and then ending the rites with songs concerning what they learned from the god.[68] These techniques are the direct ancestors of the typical medieval grimoiric practice. Another example of Ostyak shamanism illustrates this perfectly: once called upon to work, the shaman first performs fumigations and consecrates a cloth to Sanke. He then fasts for an entire day. At nightfall, he takes a cleansing bath, eats three or seven mushrooms, and falls asleep. After some time, he will likely awaken ("trembling all over") and reveal what he has learned from the spiritual "messenger," such as to which entity sacrifice must be made, why the hunt failed, etc.[69] We will see in later chapters (especially chapter 7) how similar this is to standard grimoiric rites; even down to the sacred numbers three and seven, and the use of sacred cloths.

Many scholars have pointed out the importance of psychotropics to various Persian mystical orders. According to Eliade, ecstatic dances of jubilation, the tearing of garments during trance, and a practice of erotic inhibition called *nazar ila'l mord* are a few indications of narcotic-induced trances among Persian shamans. Further, they can be traced to pre-Islamic and certain Indian mystical techniques that might have influenced Sufism.[70] Even the hymns to the gods make reference to ecstasy induced by mushrooms.[71]

The Arabic practice of Sufism itself becomes the direct link between the ancient shamans and the medieval grimoires. The Sufis are perhaps most famous for their "mad poets"; prophets who were characterized by seizure-fraught trances. During their ecstatic ceremonies, they were said to be grabbed and throttled by their patron entities or jinn, after which they would awaken with inspiration for scripture or oracular messages. This description is not very far from our Ostyak shaman above, who awoke "trembling all over" to communicate with spirits. See also these quotations from the *Ethiopian Book of Enoch*:

> Terror overwhelmed me, and a fearful shaking seized me. Violently agitated and trembling, I fell upon my face. In the vision I looked . . . (Enoch 14:12–13)

> . . . I saw that the heaven of heavens shook; that it shook violently . . . A great trembling came upon me, and terror seized me. My loins were bowed down and loosened; my reins were dissolved; and I fell upon my face. The holy Michael, another holy Angel, one of the holy ones, was sent, who raised me up. And when he raised me, my spirit returned; for I was incapable of enduring this vision of violence, its agitation, and the concussion of heavens. (Enoch 58:1–2)

The trembling or seizures are a direct result of the toxicity of the sacred mushroom. By comparing the various sources, we can thus trace a connected path from the Siberian shamans, to the ancient prophets, and to the Sufis and Arabic mystics of the early Common Era. For further study into the biblical uses of mushrooms, see *The Sacred Mushroom and the Cross; a Study of the Nature and Origins of Christianity Within the Fertility Cults of the Ancient Near East* by John Marco Allegro.

Another important psychotropic to our study is cannabis. This was a major sacrament among the Sythians, a nomadic tribe that originated near modern-day Russia, and eventually invaded the whole of the Middle East around 625 BCE (stopping just short of Egypt itself).[72] They made use of cannabis in their funerary rites via a method very similar to a Native American smoke lodge. They would seal themselves into small "teepees" and burn the buds of the female cannabis plants inside.[73] The herb was also used regularly by the transvestite shamans among them known as the Enaries, who "uttered prophecies in high pitched voices."[74]

Like the mushrooms, this plant traveled with the shamans and became pivotal in the foundation of Persian and other Middle Eastern mystical faiths. Eliade states that there is no doubt that intoxication via hemp—the most elementary ecstatic technique—was known to the ancient Iranians.[75] The use of hemp for such purposes is described among the Iranians, and the Iranian word for "hemp" is also defined as "mystical intoxication" in Central and North Asia.[76]

This latter point is very telling. Eliade continues to offer several important terms to illustrate. In several Ugrian languages, the Iranian word *bangha* (hemp) is used to designate both "intoxication" and, for some reason, the sacred mushroom. Likewise, the Vogul word *pankh* (mushroom) is also used to mean "intoxication, drunkenness." The term *Pouru-bangha* means "possessor of much hemp," and is used in the *Fravasi-yast*. The same text mentions one Ahura-Mazda as being "without trance and without hemp."[77]

Another example lies with the Mysian *kapnobatai* (whose name has been translated as "those who walk in the clouds") but more literally translates as "those who walk in smoke." It is assumed that the smoke implied is hemp smoke. The *kapnobatai* appear to be the same Getic dancers and mages known for smoking hemp to induce ecstatic trance.[78]

Chris Bennet, at the conclusion of his article on the Scythians,[79] offers a rather impressive hypothesis. According to his research, the most famous of ancient shamans to directly inherit the Scythian practice of cannabis ecstasy were men such as Moses, Isaiah, Ezekiel, and the other biblical prophets, priests, kings, etc. If this is the case, then Bennet has shown us yet another link between Eliade's shamans and our biblical prophets from chapter 2. Luckily, Bennet offered further information in a later article concerning cannabis and the Old Testament.[80] His conclusions are certainly controversial, however, I find they match quite well with my own research.

As it turns out, the use of cannabis by the prophets is a matter of scriptural record. The word appears no less than five times in the Old Testament; in Exodus, the Song of Solomon, Isaiah, Jeremiah, and Ezekiel.

The word "cannabis" was once assumed to be of Scythian origin. However, it has since been proven of Semitic origin. In Hebrew, the word is *kaneh-bosm* (*kan* = reed or hemp, *bosm* = aromatic), which might also be rendered as *kaneh* or *kannabus*. In the third century BCE, the word was mistranslated in the Greek Septuagint as "calamus," which (as Bennet points out) is a common marsh plant of little monetary or sacred value, and the error has continued to this day.

Cannabis was in use by Israel's neighbors in Canaan as a sacred incense to Asherah, the Queen of Heaven, as well as an ingredient for a psychoactive topical ointment. Evidence that this was adopted by Hebrew religion is presented in the book of Exodus:

> Moreover the Lord spake unto Moses, saying, "Take thou also unto thee principal spices, of pure myrrh five hundred shekels, and of sweet cinnamon half so much, even two hundred and fifty shekels, and of sweet calamus two hundred and fifty shekels, and of cassia five hundred shekels, after the shekel of the sanctuary, and of oil olive an hin: And thou shalt make it an oil of holy ointment, an ointment compound after the art of the apothecary: it shall be an holy anointing oil." (Exodus 30:22–25)

The emphasis on "calamus" is my own, as this is where "cannabis" should be listed. It is very unlikely that this recipe is dissimilar to the Canaanite version, and even probable that they are (nearly?) identical. The fact that this oil is made "after the art of the apothecary" has been conjectured to mean the herbs were to undergo alchemical extraction. This would result in an oil containing a large amount of pure THC[81] extract, with highly psychedelic effects when applied to the forehead, temples, and (in some cases) the eyelids.[82] The importance of this oil is not understressed in the Bible, as Yahweh continues his instruction to Moses:

> And thou shalt anoint the tabernacle of the congregation therewith, and the ark of the testimony, and the table and all his vessels, and the candlestick and his vessels, and the altar of incense, and the altar of burnt offering with all his vessels, and the laver and his stand. And thou shalt sanctify them, that they may be most holy: whatsoever toucheth them shall be holy. And thou shalt anoint Aaron and his sons, and consecrate them, that they may minister unto me in the priest's office. And thou shalt speak unto the children of Israel, saying, This shall be an holy anointing oil unto me throughout your generations. Upon man's flesh it shall not be poured, neither shall ye make any other like it, after the composition of it: it is holy, and it shall be holy unto you. Whosoever compoundeth any like it, or whosoever putteth any of it upon a stranger, shall even be cut off from his people." (Exodus 30:26–33)

Bennet illustrates in his work that Scythian and Semitic peoples were historically connected through trade and cultural interaction for an entire millennium before the fifth century BCE. To the Israelites, the Scythians were known as the *Ashkenaz*, a name mentioned in Genesis 10:3 as the son of Gomer (great-grandson of Noah). In the above, I pointed out that the Scythians are known to have gained ecstasy by burning cannabis within a sealed tent. This practice is found paralleled in biblical lore as the famed tent of meeting (see Exodus 26), in which Moses communed with Yahweh in the wilderness:

> And it came to pass, as Moses entered into the tabernacle, the cloudy pillar descended, and stood at the door of the tabernacle, and the Lord talked with Moses. And all the people saw the cloudy pillar stand at the tabernacle door: and all the people rose up and worshipped, every man in his tent door. (Exodus 33:9–10)

Thus, the people knew that their prophet was in communication with their patron when a "pillar of cloud" was seen at the door of the tent. Clouds of smoke, in fact, seem to be the principal form of manifestation for Yahweh. Leviticus 16:2–13 contains a communication from Yahweh instructing Aaron to burn incense within the Holy of Holies, making sure the smoke covers the Ark and Mercy Seat.[83] The god states "I will appear in the cloud upon the mercy seat." Numbers 11:25 describes Yahweh as descending in a cloud which, when it enveloped Moses and the elders, caused them to enter an ecstatic state of prophesy. Later on, we read that Ezekiel (6:1–4) met Yahweh and the Seraphim in the temple while it was "filled with smoke."

There is evidence to support the idea that this incense was either cannabis, or at least contained it as an ingredient. *The Song of Solomon* contains the following lines:

> Thy plants are an orchard of pomegranates, with pleasant fruits; camphire, with spikenard, spikenard and saffron, *calamus* and cinnamon, with all trees of frankincense; myrrh and aloes, with every kind of incense tree. (Song of Solomon 4:13–14)

Again, the emphasis upon "calamus" is my own, and the word used in the original Hebrew is *kaneh*. The herbs listed above are very similar to the herbs used in the incense and oil described in Exodus, which suggests a direct connection. The book of Isaiah provides us with a more immediate reference, straight from the mouth of Yahweh, to the use of cannabis as sacred incense:

> I have not caused thee to serve with an offering, nor wearied thee with incense. Thou hast brought me no sweet cane with money, neither hast thou filled me with the fat of thy sacrifices: but thou hast force me to settle for thy sins, thou hast wearied me with thine iniquities. (Isaiah 43:23–24)

This time the words "sweet cane" are used in place of kaneh. Of course, there is no solid evidence that these clouds were cannabis smoke. We only know that the herb was considered highly sacred, and was grown in large enough quantities to comprise an export:

> Dan also and Javan going to and fro occupied in thy fairs: brought iron, cassia, and calamus, were in thy market (Ezekiel 27:19).

The form of the word is also kaneh in this instance. Thus, it is certainly possible—even probable—that cannabis was the incense used by Moses (who did, after all, first meet Yahweh in the presence of a "burning bush"). The pillar of cloud mentioned in Exodus 33 is, in fact, the very same that led the tribes through the wilderness:

> And the Lord went before them by day in a pillar of cloud, to lead them the way; and by night in a pillar of fire, to give them light; to go by day or night: He took not away the pillar of the cloud by day, nor the pillar of fire by night, from before the people. (Exodus 13:21–22)

Earlier, I offered the fact that ancient nomadic people were guided by their gods, and that this direction came via the prophet-shamans who had the power to speak directly to the deities. This data fits very well into the above Exodus quotation, which seems to suggest that Moses and his shamanic brethren were burning *much* incense—and the concept that the smoke was cannabis.

I also mentioned the idea that using plants from foreign soil was a problem for the prophet-shaman. This may be supported by our final biblical reference to cannabis, wherein Yahweh shows great displeasure at offerings of foreign incenses ("sweet cane" is used once again in place of kaneh):

To what purpose cometh there to me incense from Sheba, and the sweet cane from a far country? Your burnt offerings are not acceptable, nor your sacrifices sweet unto me. (Jeremiah 6:20)

For further information on the biblical and magickal uses of cannabis, see *Green Gold the Tree of Life: Marijuana in Magic & Religion* by Chris Bennet.

Psychotropics: In the Grimoires

By the Christianized times of the classical grimoires, the concept of plant worship seems to have been nearly lost. However, the use of psychotropics to gain prophetical states of consciousness remained strong. Agrippa mentions the practice several times in his work, usually relating it directly to the art of prophesy:

> Also there is a herb called the Angelida, which magicians drinking of, can prophesy.[84] (*Three Books*, Book I, Chapter 38)

> . . . suffumigations are wont to be used by them that are about to soothsay, for to affect their fancy, which indeed being appropriated to any certain deities,[85] do fit us to receive divine inspiration: so they say that fumes made with linseed, and fleabane seed, and roots of violets, and parsley, doth make one to foresee things to come and doth conduce to prophesying. (*Three Books*, Book I, Chapter 43)

> So they say, that if of coriander, smallage, henbane, and hemlock be made a fume, that spirits will presently come together; hence they are called the spirits' herbs. Also it is said that a fume made of the root of the reedy herb sagapen, with the juice of hemlock, and henbane, and the herb tapus barbatus, red sanders, and black poppy, makes spirits and strange shapes appear . . . (*Three Books*, Book I, Chapter 43)

In Book I, Chapter 60, Agrippa covers the subject "Of Madness, and divinations which are made when men are awake, and of the power of a melancholy humour, by which spirits are sometimes induced into men's bodies." All within the chapter's title, we see reference to the typical shamanic "divine madness," as well as the manic depressive mental state common to shamanic vocation The body of the chapter discusses the practices of such cults as the Bacchides, ancient priestesses to Bacchus who produced ecstasy through wine and dance.

Kieckhefer divides grimoiric magickal spells into three general categories: (1) Divinatory: offering knowledge of the future, past, distant, or hidden things—detection of crime or a criminal, recovery of stolen goods, discovery of hidden treasure, etc; which has the motivation of knowledge; (2) Psychological: offering influence over other's intellects or wills—love and hatred, favour at court, etc; with the motivation of power; and (3) Illusionist: offering the power to make things seem as other than they are—illusory banquets, castles, horses and other means of transportation, causing the dead to seem alive and vice versa;[86] with the motivation of imagination or even ecstasy.[87]

Technically, psychotropics could play a part in all of these processes. Although, the one which seems to apply most directly is category three: illusionist experiments. Even without further investigation, we already see reference made to horses and transportation, the typical shamanic journey. We have discussed such themes in both *Abramelin* and the *Goetia*. In *Abramelin*, Book III, we also find such things as Chapter 15: "For the Spirits to bring us anything we may wish to eat or to drink, and even all (kinds of food) that we can imagine":

> . . . this food although it be appreciable to the eyes, and by the mouth, doth not long nourish the body, which hath soon hunger again, seeing that this food gives no strength to the stomach."

In short, it is illusory. Chapter 27 of the same book allows one to manifest up to thirty-five different visions; including palaces, meadows, bodies of water, woods, towns, various animals, castles, etc. Chapter 29 brings armed men, and Chapter 30 causes comedies, operas, and "every kind of Music and Dances to appear." All of these are illusions granted by spiritual intelligences, and the guests at the parties are themselves spirits.

There are echoes of the *Arabian Nights* in all of this, as well as to the European concept of "faery feasts." In fact, this latter is very likely the source for much of the dynamic present in the grimoiric banquets and feasts. The original inhabitants of Britain were known as the Picts, a tribal people not much different from those we have been discussing thus far. When the Celts invaded and settled the land between the fifth and third centuries BCE, the Picts were forced to flee into the deep wilderness. In time, they became something of a mystery to the Celtic peoples—who called them the "little people" or faery. Where the Picts gathered in the woods to enact religious or magickal rites, they arranged stones in circular patterns and decorated them with arcane symbols. These were known to the Celts as "faery rings," and were places strictly avoided and feared by the typical layperson. (Especially if such a ring were in use by the Pictish people when discovered!)

The Picts, whose homeland had been invaded, could indeed become hostile toward wayward travelers. However, the true danger according to the Celtic settlers was in becoming caught within the otherworldly realm of the faery. After stumbling upon a Pictish celebration, a traveler might be asked to join the fun, and offered obscure foods. These foods were a major concern, because they were foods of the faery realm and—like any eucharist—if one consumed them, one became a part of that realm. One would begin to experience ineffable and fantastic situations, the flow of time would alter (a few hours in the realm of faery could turn out to be days in the normal world), natural laws would mean little, and willing escape would be impossible. In a worst case scenario, one might awaken later to find himself married to a faery princess.

Thus are the legends, as many of us have heard them. However, history sheds some further light on this situation. The Picts were obviously tribal and shamanic, and would certainly have incorporated hallucinogenic substances into their rites—such as mushrooms. It is probable that these are the sweet-tasting exotic food that the Celtic traveler was warned not to eat under any circumstances.

Kieckhefer (*Forbidden Rites*, Chapter 3) illustrates the nature of the grimoiric spiritual banquets, even including the fact that (in the *Munich Handbook*) one must not eat the food brought by the spirits. In general, the spectral parties offered in the classical texts do seem to mirror the faery feasts, and the legends which arose around them throughout the years. The similarities are enough, and the geographical locations are close enough, to suggest a direct descent from one to the other; even where no drugs are indicated by the later grimoires.

In Elizabeth Butler's *Ritual Magic* (p. 225ff), we find preserved the story of one Faustian mage by the name of Johann Georg Schropfer, who lived from 1730–1774 CE. While residing in Dresden, Germany, Schropfer was persuaded by Prince Charles of Saxony to perform a necromantic evocation—in the presence of no less than nineteen distinguished witnesses. The spirit eventually chosen for the operation was Charles' own recently deceased uncle Chevalier George of Saxony (son of Augustus II of Poland). The rite even took place in the Dresden castle where George had resided in life, and which had been left to Charles. It was believed that the late uncle had hidden large sums of money on the premises, and it was hoped that his spirit could be compelled to reveal the concealed locations.

The appointed time for the experiment arrived, along with the somewhat skeptical guests, and Schropfer began the initial preparations for the summoning. Ms. Butler writes that the twentieth-century reader will likely "smell a rat" upon learning that Schropfer proceeded to offer the witnesses a kind of punch that would "fortify" them for the "forthcoming ordeal." (Many refused the drink.)[88] However, based upon what we have learned of the mystical uses of psychotropics, this presumed "rat" begins to smell a lot more like common shamanic magery. According to Butler, Schropfer continued with the evocation, and spent much of the lengthy ceremony laboring under great mental and physical stress, covered with a violent sweat, and suffering mild convulsions. It is nearly positive that

Schropfer utilized toxic chemicals in his brew, and Butler even admits that the shamans of Africa and Siberia experience similar states.[89]

Such toxins are another likely source behind the legendary dangers of summoning spirits. It is said that mages who fail to follow proper procedure might be found dead or insane from the attacks of the spirits. One recorded case of this occurrence illustrates the possibility of such a thing. The record is known as the *True Account of the Jena Tragedy of Christmas Eve*, published in 1716 CE.[90] In this case, a man by the name of Gessner had reason to suspect the existence of buried treasure in his vineyard. Apparently familiar with occult lore, Gessner desired to utilize the *Harrowing of Hell* (a Faustian "black magick" text) procedure for raising lost treasure. Not having a copy of the book, he enlisted the aid of three other men: a tailor named Heichler, a Jena student known as Weber, and a peasant known as Zenner. Weber and Zenner both seem to have been practicing mages, with copies of several texts and the necessary magickal equipment to perform the rites for discovering treasure. Unfortunately, they did not take the directions of the grimoires seriously, and approached their work in an extremely careless manner. They even dismissed the need for ritual preparation,[91] Gessner claiming they had no need of "all that palaver."

It was under such circumstances that three of the men (excluding Heichler, who seems to have been the only one involved who had not had previous magickal experience) set out to a small cabin in the vineyard on the evening of December 24, 1715. Inside, they lit a number of charcoal bricks and set them into a flower pot,[92] quickly finding enough fumes produced that the door had to be temporarily opened. Thinking the air was finally clear, the men sealed the cabin and continued with the operation—drawing the circle on the ceiling (for some reason) and reciting several evocations taken from different texts.

It was not until the next afternoon that the results of the magick became known. Heichler, who claims to have been overcome by panic while listening to a sermon at church, rushed to the cabin. As Butler says, he was presented with a rather gruesome scene when he entered the cabin. The two peasants were quite dead, with Zenner on the floor and Gessner collapsed across the table. Weber was nearly dead as well, laying head downwards on a bench. Help was immediately summoned, though Weber was unable to speak, but was uttering strange gibberish and noises. To complete the dramatic Lovecraftian scene, the copy of Faust's *Harrowing of Hell* was open on the table, along with a rosary, the protective seals and circles adorned the room, and the Tetragrammaton was inscribed upon the door.

As if this were not enough, further deaths resulted from this magickal tampering. After the authorities were called in, three watchmen were left on the site overnight to guard the bodies pending removal. These watchmen, too, used the flowerpot and coal to warm themselves in the cabin. The next morning, one of the men was found dead, and the others were nearly gone themselves. After their recovery, the guards related tales of spirit manifestations during their overnight stay. The inhalation of toxins from the coals certainly could have produced the necessary "hallucinations," and the overall scene reminds one of the sealed tents used by Scythians and Biblical prophets.

Of course, these men (who show themselves throughout the story to be rank amateurs in the art) do not seem to have used psychotropic suffumigations or decoctions. Their downfall came from a simpler negligence, and it is obvious that they were no prophets. Similar problems can arise, however, for those who use such recipes as described by Agrippa in the above quotations—including vision-producing poisons like hemlock, henbane, belladonna, black poppy, etc. If these kinds of "powders of manifestation" are utilized, one might expect the same unfortunate results.

Such highly toxic psychedelics are not exclusive to the grimoires, and in fact boast a long shamanic tradition. Many of us today, thanks to Hollywood, are familiar with the similar European "flying ointments" of witchcraft lore. While discussing Inquisitorial records of the prosecution of necromancers in the medieval era, Kieckhefer points out that there is a parallel with notions from the witch trials. A passage from a manuscript edited by Willy Braekman suggests that one can travel quickly wherever one wishes by making an ointment from seven herbs, the fat of a goat, and the blood of a bat. It is smeared on one's face, hands, and chest while reciting a magickal invocation. This is remarkably parallel to the formulas and applications of the witches' flying ointments.[93]

Scott Cunningham, in his work *The Complete Book of Incense, Oils and Brews* (p. 128), gives us two classical recipes for the deadly witches' flying ointment (the poisons are each marked with an "*"):

Flying Ointment #1
 Cinquefoil
 Parsley
 Aconite*
 Belladonna*
 Hemlock*
 Cowbane*

Flying Ointment #2[94]
 Hog's lard
 Hashish*
 Hemp flowers*
 Poppy flowers
 Hellebore*

These ointments were rubbed upon the hands, feet, stomach, temples, eyes, etc. In other words, they were applied to those areas that would allow the body to absorb the psychoactive substances directly into the bloodstream—just as the Canaanite and Israelite holy oils we have previously discussed.

The *Picatrix* also makes reference to such "shamanic" ointments. For instance, in Book Three, Chapter Nine, we find the following necromantic spell:

> Take the entire head of a man newly dead, and preserve [it] in a large pot. And with it place 8 oz. of new opium, human blood, [and] sesame oil, until such time as it [the head] is completely hidden; close up the mouth of the jar with clay . . . until all within the vessel has liquefied and come to be as an oil; and you shall set this back. And it is said that in this oil are many miraculous conditions (*esse*), and first [among these] is to behold whatever you would wish to see. If light shall be kindled from the aforesaid oil or any other should be anointed with it or eat of it with a bit of food, whatsoever you wish to see, you shall see.[95]

This may strike some as fairly gruesome, though in reality it is likely a survival of witchcraft from earlier eras of ancestor worship.[96] In any case, what is most interesting here is the fact that an oil is made with eight ounces(!) of opium. The spell suggests that burning it, *rubbing it on the skin*, or consuming the drug will cause visions. Another reference to sacred oils is made in the *Goetia*:

> The other magical requisites are: . . . also perfumes, and a chafing-dish of charcoal kindled to put the fumes on, to smoke or perfume the place appointed for action; also anointing oil to anoint thy temples and eyes with . . .

The ingredients for this anointing oil are not given in the text, though its application to the eyes and temples indicates its hallucinatory aim. We can guess which herbs were most likely used based on the nature of the goetic spirits themselves. Remember that certain plants are sacred to certain entities: substances such as cannabis and mushrooms allow the shaman to gain the heavens and interact with celestial beings of light and life, while poisons such as belladonna and henbane grant one visions of infernal entities of putrefaction.[97] As is obvious from the above, these poisons are the drugs most common in medieval "necromantic" (or goetic) literature. This is why the spirits listed in such works are commonly associated with horrible and terrifying forms. Take these descriptions from the *Goetia* into account:

Bael: He appeareth in divers shapes, sometimes like a Cat, sometimes like a Toad, and sometimes like a Man, and sometimes all these forms at once. He speaketh hoarsely

Amon: He appeareth like a Wolf with a Serpent's tail, vomiting out of his mouth flames of fire; but at the command of the Magician he putteth on the shape of a Man with Dog's teeth beset in a head like a Raven; or else like a Man with a Raven's head (simply).

Astaroth: He is a Mighty, Strong Duke, and appeareth in the form of an hurtful Angel riding on an Infernal Beast like a Dragon, and carrying in his right hand a Viper. Thou must in no wise let him approach too near unto thee, lest he do thee damage by his Noisome Breath.

Asmoday: He appeareth with Three Heads, whereof the first is like a Bull, the second like a Man, and the third like a Ram; he hath also the tail of a Serpent, and from his mouth issue Flames of Fire. His feet are webbed like those of a Goose. He sitteth upon an Infernal Dragon, and beareth in his hand a Lance with a Banner.

These highly talismanic forms may seem odd, but do not often strike the modern mind as particularly horrifying. However, anyone who has met with these spirits under the influence of such poisonous substances understands the truth behind the concept. Just as the higher drugs invoke upper circuit encounters, these lower toxins seem to push one downward into first and second circuit experiences. The reflexes of retreat and submission can be easily engaged at these times, and this can lead to real danger for a mage in the midst of a working.

Steps are taken to protect against this in the grimoires, from the magick circle (providing a psychological safe place for the mage), to the magickal sword and talismans, to the wording of the conjurations themselves. For instance, the *Goetia* commands the spirits with the following:

. . . I do exorcise thee and do powerfully command thee, O thou spirit N., that thou dost forthwith appear unto me here before this Circle in a fair human shape, without any deformity or tortuosity.

Likewise, the *Key of Solomon the King* contains the following within its conjurations:

Come ye at once without any hideousness or deformity before us, come ye without monstrous appearance, in a gracious form or figure.

The way the texts are written, it seems that the spirits rarely appeared in beautiful shape right off, but (if all was done properly) would be forced to alter that shape into something less hideous at the command of the mage. The major point of danger lay between the initial appearance of the spirit (when the mage's lower circuits are initially switched on) and the command to appear in fair shape (where the mage re-asserts his own third and fourth circuit control). It is in this space that neurotic reflexes on the part of the mage could get the better of him, and the spirit gain the upper hand.

According to Waite (*Book of Ceremonial Magic*, p. 67), the *Goetia* and *Key of Solomon* are the two grimoires upon which nearly all others are based. Today, we often include the *Picatrix* into this equation, as the *Goetia*, *Key*, and even Agrippa seem to have drawn from it. It is telling, then, that all of these books indicate the use of psychotropics. The above quotes are not the only examples. The *Key of Solomon the King* informs the reader that, after the conjurations, the mage will witness "wonderful things, which it is impossible to relate . . ."[98] reminiscent of descriptions of LSD trips. In the same text (Book I, Chapter 13), instructions are given for the creation of a "Magic Carpet" "proper for interrogating the intelligences." The use of the carpet is described as follows:

> . . . taking thy carpet, thou shalt cover thy head and body therewith, and taking the censer, with new fire therein, thou shalt place it in or upon the proper place, and cast thereon some incense. Then shalt thou prostrate thyself upon the ground, with thy face towards the earth, before the incense beginneth to fume, keeping the fire of the same beneath the carpet . . . And thou shalt hear distinctly the answer which thou shalt have sought.

This would seem to be a survival of the Scythian and biblical uses of the "tent of meeting," which throws some question upon the nature of the "incense" mentioned in the instructions. The text, like the *Goetia* and its oil, does not list the ingredients. However, an experienced shaman-mage of the medieval era would have known the secret.

In all of this, I have attempted to give a well-rounded view of the sacramental use of psychotropics. Plants, like people, have various personalities: some of them are known as benevolent, and others are known as harsh. The Infernal plants even work their magick by nearly killing their human host, and in many cases are actually cumulative neurotoxins; which means that they will kill the user over time even if a single overdose never occurs.

Although, one should not assume that even the celestial plants are completely benign. Even if they were 100 percent physically safe, there are still deep psychological matters to be considered. Jim DeKorne, fortunately, takes some time to address these issues in his work *Psychedelic Shamanism*—discussing the most common dangers to any would-be shaman.[99] He reminds the reader that "psychedelic shamanism" offers deceptively easy access to the inner realms for the purpose of personal growth and integration. The rewards of such endeavors are proportional to their risks, and novices making the attempt can easily get in over their heads. If one is obstructed by a poorly integrated personality, it will be as much (or more) a hindrance in "mind space" as it is in the physical world. Such an unbalanced individual can be easily overwhelmed by inner neuroses and complexes—one's "goetic" inner forces, whom the Tibetans call the "Peaceful and Wrathful Deities."

Therefore, performing some dedicated inner work (such as that outlined by Wilson) is an essential prerequisite for anyone seeking to travel through the celestial realms. Indeed, this has been the opinion of occultists all along (with or without psychotropics), and Regardie (see *The Middle Pillar*) made quite a point of it in his philosophy. This is also why I focused on relating the eight-circuit model in this work, and urged the reader to engage in a study of psychology and personal mental reprogramming before attempting to explore the shamanic realms.

Sensory and Stimulus Deprivation

II should again point out that the Art of Ecstasy is not so narrowly defined as "working with psychotropics." In the shamanic quest for higher and more profound ecstatic states, as we have slowly learned what things affect the mind and how, a complete arsenal of techniques has been created. I listed just a few of them above, not to mention the Eastern systems of mental control, or even such things as dream-work. I also failed to mention the most important among them—as widespread or more than the use of psychotropics—called today "sensory deprivation."

When the brain is starved for input from the usual five senses, it tends to turn inward upon itself rather quickly. The experiences thus obtained involve higher circuit functions, during which the subject can encounter all manner of inspiration or communication with seemingly outside intelligences. The process, in fact, is not unlike the typical shamanic vocation; only the mental "imbalance" is purposefully created rather than existing as the natural state of the initiate. Solitary confinement can have very profound effects upon any human mind.

The modern study of sensory deprivation began in 1952 when Dr. John C. Lilly developed the isolation tank. Initially, this was simply a very large tank of water within which the subject was submerged and kept afloat with supports. Light and sound were blocked by a thick mask that also doubled as a kind of snorkel, allowing the subject to breath easily while submerged. In time, however, the tank was modified so that less water is used (about ten inches deep), and the subject floats upon his back naturally due to a high concentration of Epsom salts in the water. The masks are also obsolete, as the tank itself is now constructed to block sound and light.

Lilly had learned that gravity accounts for much of our daily mental activity, as the brain works with the body to pull against gravity for sitting, walking, standing, etc. Thus, by removing this factor along with sight, sound, and tactile input, Lilly found that sensory deprivation experiences could be attained in a shorter time span than one might at first suspect. There are seven general stages through which a subject passes within an isolation tank, and understanding them will be important in our own studies:[100]

1) Very few people are aware of this fact, but the human brain has its own set of "memory buffers," just like a computer. As information is taken into the mind, it is held in these buffers for some time awaiting proper sorting and filing into the memory. This kind of diagnostic work usually takes place when we sleep, and is the source for a great many of our normal dreams. These buffers also seem to be the source of short-term memory, as they contain information that has only recently been recorded by the senses. When one experiences sleep deprivation, a large part of that experience is based on an overflow of these mental buffers. Short-term memory suffers dramatically, as do coordination, the ability to focus and concentrate, etc. In severe cases, hallucinations can even accompany the condition.

However, these buffers can be partially cleared even while remaining awake. Try this: the next time you are suffering from lack of sleep, take a few moments to sit down and "zone out." That is, allow your mind to simply wonder where it will for a while. Naturally, it will begin to review the day's events, current problems, and perhaps even your immediate surroundings. It may attempt to solve problems, or fantasize, or perhaps merely ramble upon several unrelated topics. This is part of the process of sorting the information and filing it properly within the memory structure of the brain. After only a few minutes, you will find yourself in a far better position to operate than you had been previously. You will literally feel less sleepy, and your eyes will not be nearly as heavy.

According to Lilly's experiments with the isolation tank, most subjects will undergo the exact same process for about the space of three-quarters of an hour. (This is also understood by those who practice the art of meditation.) Once the mind has cleared most of the information in its buffers, the second stage will come as a natural progression.

2) At this stage, the subject begins to fully relax, and even enjoy the experience of the isolation. It is very peaceful and restful, free from immediate concerns or agendas. However, this stage deteriorates over the next hour or so, moving on to stage three.

3) Here a tension slowly develops, which is called "stimulus-action" hunger. This is where true sensory deprivation occurs, and the brain begins to demand some kind of input from the outside. Very subtle methods of self-stimulation will develop, such as twitching muscles, slow swimming movements, stroking one finger against another, etc. It takes an amount of willpower on the part of the subject to pass successfully through this stage, as these movements must be suppressed.

4) Stage four seems to be a part of stage three, in that the body at this point will begin to protest the lack of physical sensation very loudly. Tension can develop to such a severe degree during this stage that the subject may have to leave the tank.

5) Also intimately connected with the above, stage five continues the same process. As the subject refuses to move or leave the tank, the brain will begin to focus intently on any remaining stimulus. For instance, in early tank

experiments, the subject would center upon such things as the mask or supports. These (or similar) stimuli become the strict focus of the mind, so that they fill the entire consciousness for some time and can become unbearable.

6) After some time, the mind finally gives in and begins to turn inward. The subject is said to engage in "reveries and fantasies of a highly personal and emotionally charged nature."[101] Some reports indicate that sexually charged fantasies are not uncommon.

Stages four through six are not unique to modern isolation tank experiments. Shamanic culture has long used the same factors to generate initiatory experiences. A shaman-to-be might be forced into extremely uncomfortable conditions, such as being lanced with spears, burned with coals, left in the cold, tied to stone slabs, or even wrapped in heavy wool blankets. Many of these we have encountered previously, usually explained as "proof" of the shaman's power, but which are also used to *induce* the shamanic state of mind. With the body undergoing this kind of intense stress, the mind literally has to divorce from the physical and begin wandering upon the higher circuits. This leads us to stage seven:

7) Finally, the mind does indeed undergo a complete separation from the physical, and actual astral projection/hallucination can occur. This is where the true shamanic state is reached, and interaction with nonphysical intelligences is common. *The Isolation Tank Experiment* describes a "black curtain" effect in front of the eyes, the usual blackness we see behind our eyelids in a dark room actually seeming to "part" or open into a three-dimensional empty void in front of the body. Gradually, images will begin to appear in this void of the type sometimes seen in hypnogogic states.

This opening of the "black curtain" before the eyes is also well-known to occultists. Those with great experience in skrying (mirrors, crystal balls, etc.) encounter the same phenomenon, as do those who succeed in the practice of astral travel. Sensory deprivation is a large part of all of these procedures. Lilly, along with countless occultists throughout history, eventually began to incorporate psychotropics into this process. (The "tent of meeting" comes to mind in this regard.)

My first experiment with sensory deprivation was an attempt to fashion a homemade isolation tank. I filled my bathtub with lukewarm water, allowing a small warm trickle to continue running into the tub to counteract the natural cooling of the water. I brought in a small television and set it to a nonchannel so that only static came from the speaker. This is known as "white noise, "sound that carries absolutely no message of any kind. I turned the volume up but left the screen dark, and this served to drown out any sound that might filter into the bathroom from outside. I closed the bedroom and bathroom doors, turned out all lights, pulled the dark shower curtain closed, and submerged all but my face into the tub of water. When I was done, there was absolutely no difference between having my eyes opened or closed, and the only sound was that generated by the trickle of water and the television static. The duration of the experiment was one hour, after which my partner was instructed to retrieve me.

It was not a resounding success, though it was worthwhile as a first attempt. I encountered several of the stages outlined above, but was hindered from the full experience due to a few small problems. First and foremost, the bathtub was not large enough to allow my legs to relax; a major minus, especially when encountering stages four and five. The pain that developed in my legs became quite excruciating. Second, the warm water ran out, though it was only a trickle, and the bath water grew steadily colder. This increased general tension, and also gave my mind something physical to focus upon.

My later attempts have been along different lines. I have had access to an actual deprivation chamber: a simple one involving a rectangular chamber (just large enough to lie down in) with cushions to rest upon rather than water. This was further enclosed in a small closed room to further remove the chamber from any surrounding noise, light, or activity. This new set-up has allowed me to progress in my experiments with such sensory deprivation.

For those experimenting at home without access to such a chamber, I would suggest repeating my original attempt without the bathtub. A dark, silent room with a bed or mat would be enough to start. The addition of earplugs, blindfold, and the television (tuned to white noise) would also be very beneficial. In later chapters we will discuss the creation of a magickal oratory—itself a primitive deprivation chamber—which could be used for the same purpose.

Stimulus deprivation is the most common technique of mind alteration in the grimoiric tradition. The procedures do not result in full sensory deprivation as with an isolation tank, but do produce a lighter version of this through removing common stimuli and distractions from one's environment. Because grimoiric magick is ceremonial in nature, it isn't quite feasible to perform all of the rites and then lay around in isolation for three or four hours.[102] Reversing that process would also be less than useful, as the enacting of the ceremony would effectively end the sensory deprivation.

Because the grimoiric technique is not so direct as an actual tank, the procedures involve several extra factors and extended periods of time. However, all of the basic aspects of the deprivation process are present, aiming at the same ultimate effect. The classical grimoires outline processes which take anywhere from several days to several months, during which sensory input is restricted—lightly at first, and then more heavily as time progresses. Other factors are brought into play, such as fasting, prayer, and abstinence; all of which serve to increase mental tension and focus upon the goal. A good example of the general process can be found in the *Key of Solomon the King*:

> Before commencing operations both the Master and his Disciples must abstain with great and thorough continence during the space of nine days from sensual pleasures and from vain and foolish conversation . . . (*Key of Solomon the King*, Book I, Chapter 3)

> From the first day of the Experiment, it is absolutely necessary to ordain and to prescribe care and observation, to abstain from all things unlawful, and from every kind of impiety, impurity, wickedness, or immodesty, as well of body as of soul; as, for example, eating and drinking superabundantly, and all sorts of vain words, buffooneries, slanders, calumnies, and other useless discourse; but instead to do good deeds, speak honestly, keep a strict decency in all things, never lose sight of modesty in walking, in conversation, in eating and drinking, and in all things; the which should be observed for nine days, before the commencement of the Operation. (*Key of Solomon the King*, Book II, Chapter 4)

> He who wisheth to apply himself unto so great and so difficult a Science should have his mind free from all business, and from all extraneous ideas of whatever nature they may be. (*Key of Solomon the King*, Book II, chapter 2)

More often than not, these instructions are classed as moral restrictions (tribal taboos), by which one makes oneself "acceptable" to the angels. To a degree this is certainly true—one who makes a living or a hobby out of the suffering of others will never become a prophet. However, from the perspective of shamanism and mind-alteration, another story quickly unfolds. By abstaining from all "sensual pleasures," one is literally cutting off a large portion of normal daily sensory input. No sweets, no sex, no fun and games; in other words, very little is permissible beyond sitting quietly in a bedroom.

One can, of course, continue to leave the home to work and enact daily business, but even this is avoided to the utmost of possibility, and approached humbly and righteously. The goal is to slowly disconnect from daily society, especially from its less than desirable aspects, and move closer to the state of the priest or shaman. Toward this end, prayers must be recited multiple times on a daily basis—usually increasing in frequency as the operation progresses.

Six of these nine days having expired, he must recite frequently the Prayer and Confession as will be told him. (*Key of Solomon the King*, Book I, Chapter 3)

Hereafter for three days at least [days seven, eight, and nine], thou shalt abstain from all idle, vain, and impure reasonings, and from every kind of impurity and sin . . . Each day shalt thou recite the following prayer, at least once in the morning, twice about noon, thrice in the afternoon, four times in the evening, and five times before lying down to sleep; this thou shalt do on the three ensuing days. (*Key of Solomon the King*, Book II, Chapter 2)

The *Book of Abramelin* is perhaps the best illustration of increasing abstinence and ceremony, as it extends the process over a span of six months. The first two months are outlined as very similar to the *Key*, with no major restrictions other than an attempt to live purely, honestly, serenely, and moderately. One is allowed to continue sexual activity. One is told to "seek retirement as far as possible." As for ceremonial procedure, the aspirant is not asked for much more than a couple of prayers a day: one at dawn and one at dusk. The lighting of a lamp and incense is not even called for except on Saturdays.

By the second two months, the ceremonial procedure increases to a certain degree. One must fast every Friday night, wash with pure water before beginning the prayers at dawn and dusk, and generally prolong the prayers themselves. Sexual stimulation is still allowed, but the author begins to strongly urge that it be avoided as much as possible. The aspirant is told: "Only it is absolutely necessary to retire from the world and seek retreat."[103]

The final two months switch the operation into high gear. A third prayer (at noon) is added to the daily regimen, with the lamp and incense kindled, and a white linen tunic donned each time. As well, a second prayer is added to each session—this one to the guardian angel. If it is at all possible, the aspirant must cease to work or to leave the home for nearly any reason. He is told to "shun all society except that of your Wife and of your Servants"[104] and that "ye shall quit every other matter only permitting your recreation to consist in things Spiritual and Divine."[105] Even the restriction against sex becomes complete, as the aspirant is told to avoid it like the plague.

After these six months of slowly increasing restriction and purification, one undergoes the seven-day ceremony by which final contact with the guardian angel is achieved. These days are extremely intense, involving total seclusion (even separating from one's family), fasting, prayer, etc. One day, the second of the seven, even gives restrictions against speaking to anyone.

The third of these seven days is extremely interesting in the light of sensory deprivation, as it may be the only case in the grimoires (that I have found) that seems to actually prescribe the use of a sensory deprivation chamber. In this case, the oratory (or prayer room) is used:

. . . wearing the same Robe of Mourning as of the day before, prostrate with your face towards the ground . . . And thus shall ye pray unto the utmost degree that shall be possible unto you, and with the greatest fervour that you can bring into action from your heart, and this during the space of two or three hours. Then quit the Oratory, returning thither at midday for another hour, and equally again in the evening . . . (*The Book of Abramelin*, Book II, Chapter 13)

In a situation of total silence and seclusion, one is to lie on the floor of the oratory for up to three hours. What is more, the window is kept open during this (the time being mid-September) and a robe of mourning is worn—which is made of sackcloth. This makes for a warm, scratchy, and generally uncomfortable experience. This serves as both a funerary rite (remember the shaman-mage must die and be reborn), and a process of isolation and sensory deprivation.

By and large, the general consensus among modern occultists is that the seclusion demanded by the grimoires is not feasible today. However, I challenge this assumption based upon the modern work done with sensory stimulation and deprivation.

In fact, the majority of our population today suffers from acute overstimulation (also known as "future shock"). We are bombarded with new information, changes in our environments, innovative technology, and a general upward movement of society in general. Things move very fast today, much faster than the authors of the classical texts were accustomed to moving. Where the author of the *Key of Solomon the King* was born, lived, and died in a relatively changeless environment, you and I have seen several lifetimes worth of change, with even more and faster changes on the horizon.

Thus, in the past, several weeks or months of isolation might have been necessary to produce results. The mage was, in effect, shifting his life from dead slow to stop. This is simply not the case currently. The starting speed is "too fast," and thus sensory deprivation can actually come *easier* to us than to our predecessors. As Wilson points out, experiments in isolation by the United States Marine Corps, Dr. John Lilly, etc., indicate that only a few hours of complete isolation are necessary, in some cases, to induce hallucination. This hallucinogenic state (when brought on either by isolation or psychedelic drugs) involves the dissolution of old imprints and vulnerability to new imprints.[106]

I have personally achieved acceptable results from as little as twelve hours of preparation and purification—including isolation, fasting, and prayer. Learning the art of relaxation and meditation can also aid this endeavor to a large degree. The reader might test this by attempting to spend just twelve hours (one-half of a day off of work) locked in a room with no TV, radio, computer, books, lights, etc., just resting in quiet meditation (and/or prayer). The mental stress that this simple exercise can produce just might astound you.

Fasting and Vegetarianism

Earlier in this chapter, I discussed the fact that your brain—or, better put, your mind—exists within a precarious balance of chemicals. Everything we have discussed so far concerns the shifting of that balance in one direction or the other. Abstinence from stimulation, from sex to social interaction, or even total isolation, have their effects upon that balance. Yet, one could hardly hope to experience the full effects of these without also changing the diet. Any time a shift in dietary intake occurs, the results are specifically psychedelic.

Fasting is an extremely time-honored method of mind alteration, and has been instructed in occult and mystical practice since well before recorded history. The Siberian and other shamans practiced it, as did all priesthoods of later eras. It appears in *Merkavah* literature, Qabalistic literature, all orthodox faiths, and most certainly within the classical grimoires. As we find in the *Key of Solomon the King*, Book II, Chapter 4:

> During the three days before the commencement of this action, thou shalt content thyself with only eating the fasting diet, an that only once in the day; and it will be better still if thou only partakest of bread and water.

The "fasting diet" is taken as a given by the author, and never explained in the text. However the intake of small amounts of bread and water itself can be seen as a fasting diet, especially if the bread is unleavened (such as crackers). Other examples might also include small amounts of fruit and vegetables. The drinking of water is always allowed under even the strictest definition of fasting.

The *Book of Abramelin* treats the subject of fasting as it does other procedures: beginning slow and increasing in magnitude. For the first two months, no fasting is necessary. For the remaining four months, one must fast every Friday night (eating nothing). By the final three days of the seven-day invocation, one is urged to fast completely—

though it is not outlined whether this means no food at all, or if one meal of bread and water is allowed each day. Either case will result in shifted consciousness on the part of the mage.

The benefits of fasting are many, and it affects the entire body. When the body stops receiving a steady flow of food, it begins to turn toward its own reserves of fat. As it breaks down these cells, it also mobilizes and eliminates toxins stored within the body. It combats inflammations such as arthritis, quiets allergic reactions, reduces various fluid accumulations (such as edema in the ankles and legs, or swelling of the abdomen), corrects high blood pressure, and it can even clear up the skin and make food taste better. Thus, it serves as a perfect form of purification—not to mention weight loss and a general increase in health.

Along with this, fasting allows the digestive system to take a rest—so that digestion and elimination of toxins later on become much easier. There is even evidence that undergoing a regime of fasting will aid one in breaking down bad habits and addictions—even drug addictions. Of course, before attempting to undergo such a process, even for the use of magick, one should consider one's personal health situation, and even consult a physician if necessary. Even the *Book of Abramelin* allows for those who are too ill to withstand the fasting process.

It is not advisable to jump directly into a fast without preparation. One might want to spend about a week beforehand gearing the body toward the ultimate goal by cutting meat from the diet (see below), eating smaller meals, and avoiding any high-fat or sugary foods. For the last couple of days before the fast, it is highly recommended that one eat plenty of salad, raw fruits and vegetables (or other roughage) in order to clear the digestive track of any food remnants.

While you fast—even outside of mystical consideration—it is a good idea to rest as much as possible. There may also be some accompanying physical discomfort—such as hunger pains (these are *only temporary*), dizziness, headaches, weakness, tiredness, or an inability to sleep. Some of this may be due to withdrawal from common drugs such as caffeine or sugar. If the hunger pains continue or become too intense, one can increase the intake of water.

For those who cannot eliminate all nutrition for a period of fasting due to health concerns, then juices (mixed half and half with water for acidic juices!) can be used. If you cannot squeeze your own juices for this purpose, then make sure you purchase those without any additives (including sugar or "high fructose corn syrup"). Vegetable juices, herbal teas (save those which contain caffeine), and vegetable broths are also viable options.

Also make sure to be prepared for the shift in psychological perspective, as that is the goal of the fast in our case. You may suffer anxiety, agitation, or impatience as you begin the process, though this seems to subside with experience. Eventually, your body seems to learn that a fast is a fast, and will finally stop demanding food. Perseverance is the key, and prayer and meditation are huge aids to this. As you continue, you will finally begin to experience the sought-after sense of well-being and physical/spiritual purity.

Afterward, make sure to break your fast gradually, as the sudden intake of solid foods can be physically dangerous. Begin by reintroducing the vegetables and salads with which you began the fasting procedure. Soups are also a good idea, as are baked or boiled potatoes. After some time, begin to eat more solid foods, without seasoning, as small snacks throughout the day. Finally, return to the normal diet (unless, at this point, you should wish to leave various harmful foods out of the diet altogether).

The first few fastings will not necessarily be easy, as the body/lower self will protest the change in routine. My own advice is to begin fasting as prescribed by *Abramelin*: merely abstaining for one night a week, beginning at dusk and ending at dawn. From there the procedure can be expanded to cover greater spans of time without much grumbling from the body.

Meanwhile, vegetarianism greatly aids all of these processes. Meat has a tendency to hang around in the body for extended periods of time, making the digestive system work slower and harder even long after eating. Just as fasting allows the digestive system to rest—thus increasing energy and blood available to the brain—so, too, does abstinence from meat.

Of course, a vegetarian diet also increases one's level of health in general. It is low in fat, high in fiber, and eliminates the various health risks that accompany the eating of meat. It is in its own way a kind of purification as well.

When you first begin the vegetarian diet, you will notice that meals do not "last" as long as you are accustomed to, and you will become hungry again relatively soon. This is simply due to the fact that you are eating light and consuming food that your body can use much more efficiently. What is occurring is a shift in your metabolism in response to the shift in diet. The recurring hunger is only temporary, and after only a few days (a couple of weeks at the most) you will find each meal lasting as long as your previous meat-inclusive meals. What is more, you will find after returning to meat (especially if you are fasting as well) that your consumption rate has slowed dramatically. You will eat less overall, not to mention the fact that habitual cravings for meat will be lessened—and can ultimately be phased out completely if such is your choice.

The most common concern over shifting from an omnivorous diet to vegetarian is a decreased intake of such nutrients as protein and zinc. However, the truth is that plant material can provide plenty of nutrition in this regard. For instance, canned green beans provide plenty of zinc (even more than fresh green beans), and a regular intake of good old beans and rice will take care of any worries about protein. Peanuts are also a good source for this (and I personally made peanut butter a big part of my own vegetarian diet).

There are also several foods which may surprise the would-be vegetarian with the inclusion of animal by-products. Gelatin is one of the best examples, as few realize that it is made from boiled animal sinews and bones. And remember that gelatin can be found in various foods such as jelly, confectionery goods, ice cream, etc. Animal fats can also be found in biscuits, cakes, and margarine to name just a few examples. Be on the lookout for anything that includes (or has been cooked in) lard or any other non-vegetable oil. Even cheese can contain rennet (used for curdling milk) extracted from the stomach lining of slaughtered calves.

The vegetarian diet is not passed over in silence by the grimoires. According to the *Book of Abramelin*, Book II, Chapter 20, rule #35:

> You shall eat during this whole period neither the flesh nor the blood of any dead animal; and this you
> shall do for a certain particular reason.

In other words, meat must be ruled out of the diet, though milk and eggs (neither of which come from a dead animal) are allowed. Mathers, in his edition of the text, notes the "particular reason" for this taboo is possibly to avoid obsession by any spirit that may have obsessed the animal. This does make a kind of Babylonian sense, where taboos existed against touching corpses for fear of demonic possession.[107] (In fact, *Abramelin* also makes the touching of a corpse a serious taboo during the operation.) However, I feel the most likely "particular reason" for this dietary restriction rests (as usual) upon biblical authority. Leviticus 19:26 reads in part: "You shall not eat any flesh with the blood in it."

And here I will bring this chapter to a close. Contained within these pages are all of the basics of the Art of Ecstasy, and should provide the student with a workable launching platform for further study and practice. The information presented here will become vital in later chapters, as we begin to invoke and interact with various classes of spiritual entities.

---

1. *Shamanism: Archaic Techniques of Ecstasy*, p. 4.

2. Ibid., p. 504. I have deliberately removed a word from the final sentence, which originally read ". . . to the whole of archaic humanity." While Eliade may have been discussing archaic humanity in particular, the practice of consciousness-shifting is anything but archaic.

3. Ibid., p. 243.

4. Ibid., p. 242.

5. A modern work titled *Between the Worlds* by Stewart Myers focuses on several nonpsychotropic techniques of mind-alteration culled from the practices of Gardnerian Wicca. Highly recommended.

6. Both of these examples are from *Shamanism . . .*, pp. 437–8.

7. Refer again to the biblical vision of Jacob's Ladder, discussed in chapter 2, for which Jacob went to sleep with his head upon a rock.

8. See the myth of "Adapa, the First Man" in *Myths from Mesopotamia: Creation, the Flood, Gilgamesh, and Others*, ed. Stephanie Dalley.

9. *Shamanism: Archaic Techniques of Ecstasy*, pp.174, 451

10. Pp. 36–7 (Exercise # 5).

11. I have tried this sitting up, with much less impressive results.

12. Note that Agrippa uses the term "demon" (or daemon) in its older sense of "genius" or "spirit." He even specifically refers to the holy guardian angel as a "demon," and thus no infernal intent can be possible.

13. I.e., "frenzy." This is also known as the divine madness or ecstatic state.

14. Note here that Agrippa, writing in the Middle Ages, seems to touch on Bell's Theorem.

15. Even the Headless Ritual, at its core, is based on that same simple concept.

16. When this occurs, it seems that the focus is to return in memory to a moment of bad mental imprinting and being forced to face the situation again. Literally, it is going back and "knowing then what you know now." After taking such a visionary journey, and handling the emotions properly (as opposed to the first time around), it seems to re-imprint the old complex with a healthier pattern. This is known as "practical time-travel."

17. For instance, there has been some discussion concerning *Abramelin*, and the possible dangers of contacting a demonic entity instead of the guardian angel. The *Book of Abramelin* itself warns of the possibility.

18. Llewellyn. I strongly suggest a study of material recently added by Chic and Tabatha Cicero titled "The Balance Between Mind and Magic," especially Chapter 6, "Psychology and Magic" (p. 103).

19. Timothy Leary is one of the few well-known examples we have of a modern-day prophet-shaman.

20. At least, they are extremely difficult to alter. We shall see in this chapter that mystical experience is aimed at the alteration of imprinted reflexes.

21. Perhaps you have heard the phrase "You never get a second chance to make a first impression." Likewise, nothing ever gets a second chance to make a first impression upon you.

22. Robert Wilson has written another book that covers this in-depth: *Ishtar Rising*. Also highly recommended material.

23. *Prometheus Rising*, pp. 48–9.

24. See chapter 2, section titled "Three Worlds, Four Pillars."

25. Note that Robert Wilson gives a different chart of humours on page 50 of *Prometheus Rising*. There was no single established system of humours in the Middle Ages.

26. Take note of the modern controversies over proper "morality," sexual role, taboos concerning interaction among sexes, and discrimination due to physical appearance. These are the concerns of a race thinking largely upon the fourth circuit.

27. *Prometheus Rising*, p. 19.

28. Feelings of dread and terror are reported in conjunction with contacting "goetic demons" throughout the grimoiric literature. I have personally experienced such an encounter—during which my own first circuit fight-or-flight instinct engaged strongly. (Strictly speaking, all I felt was the instinct of flight!) I find it interesting that this feeling accompanied the arrival of the spirit even though the spirit itself did nothing threatening.

29. *Prometheus Rising*, p. 19

30. Note that the term "to have knowledge of" in biblical terminology can mean "to have sexual intercourse with."

31. Who, like their mythological forefather Cain, reacted (and still react today) with violence. Dr. Wilson, on page 161 of *Prometheus Rising*, states: "There is no tribe known to anthropology which doesn't have at least one neurosomatic technician (shaman). Large-scale outbursts of neurosomatic consciousness have occurred frequently in all the major historical periods, usually being stamped out quickly by the local branch of the Inquisition or the A.M.A.; other outbursts have been co-opted and diluted."

32. Here is one reason why fifth circuit consciousness is a must for space travel.

33. *Prometheus Rising*, pp. 158–9.

34. Ibid., p. 170. Compare this statement to Waite's condescending words concerning the "gold of Faerie" quoted at the beginning of chapter 2.

35. Ibid., p. 19.

36. Ibid., p. 180.

37. Revelation 1:8.

38. John 11:25–26 .

39. The Wiccan "Charge of the Goddess."

40. *Prometheus Rising*, p. 180.

41. Ibid., p. 179.

42. Ibid., p. 20.

43. This is the foundation of meditative practice—silencing the mind (self) in order to experience communion with the true self.

44. I.e., what environmental factor caused the reaction?

45. I.e., from which circuit does the reaction originate, and what happened in your life to imprint or condition you for such a reaction?

46. Rather than being self-hindering or self-destructive, as the lower self—fashioned by modern society—often is.

47. John 1:1–5.

48. This was adopted—yet again—by the later Qabalists, who called it the "Ain" (No Thing) or "Ain Soph" (Limitlessness).

49. Within the Qabalah, a similar concept exists involving mystical consideration of the word *Berashith*. This is the first word of Genesis I—and thus of the entire Torah—and literally translates as "In the Beginning" or, as some suggest, "Before the Beginning." This is given more emphasis in some instances than the first words of creation ("Let there be Light," which the Creator does not utter until verse three). John Dee was extremely interested in the occult virtues of Berashith and we see its use (as the letter *B*) throughout the Heptarchic system of magick.

50. John 1:9–12.

51. *Prometheus Rising*, p. 199.

52. Ibid., p. 246.

53. Though, for a period following such an experience, watch for the aftereffects and remember to record them!

54. I should also point out that such arts as theurgy, yoga, and the Hermetic arts are aimed at shifting consciousness to the higher circuits permanently. These and the prophetic arts are not mutually exclusive.

55. For a full discussion of this, see Chris Bennet's "When Smoke Gets In My I," published in *Cannabis Canada,* April 1995.

56. See above concerning the third "Time-Binding Semantic" circuit, which is the first remarkably human circuit of the brain.

57. Compare this with the more common theory that primitive humans conceived of an afterlife and spiritual realm merely because they "did not like the idea of death"; yet another assumption made from confusing modern conceptions with past worldviews.

58. Note that it is the bud of the female cannabis plant that is consumed for psychoactive effect.

59. Alcohol is called "spirits" for no accidental reason.

60. Compare this to the processes outlined within alchemical practice.

61. *Psychedelic Shamanism*, p. 92.

62. For more information, I strongly suggest *Sex and Drugs* by Robert Anton Wilson.

63. The gods of the future planetary cybernets will, I believe, be quite an impressive thing to witness from a cultural perspective. Though it may not be in our lifetimes.

64. Unfortunately, Eliade only touches upon the use of "narcotics" by shamans. He insists that it was rare, and actually represents a "fallen state" of true shamanism. I feel this concept to be quite outdated, and completely unrealistic.

65. See chapter 2, section titled "Shamanism."

66. See *Psychedelic Shamanism*, pp. 120–3.

67. *Shamanism, Archaic Techniques of Ecstasy*, p. 221.

68. Ibid., p. 221, note 14.

69. Ibid., p. 220.

70. Ibid., p. 402, note 118.

71. Ibid., p. 401.

72. For more on the Scythians, see Chris Bennet's "The Scythians, High Planes Drifters," published in *Cannabis Canada,* July 1995

73. The Scythians were not unique in this practice at all. Eliade, in *Shamanism: Archaic Techniques of Ecstasy*, p. 83, says of the apprentice shaman of the Conibo of the Ucayali: "To enter into relations with the spirit the shaman drinks a decoction of tobacco and smokes as much as possible in a hermetically closed hut." We will be returning to this "smoke lodge" concept a couple of times in this chapter.

74. "The Scythians, High Planes Drifters," *Cannabis Canada,* July 1995.

75. *Shamanism, Archaic Techniques of Ecstasy*, p. 400.

76. Ibid., p. 395.

77. Ibid., pp. 399–401.

78. Ibid., p. 390.

79. "The Scythians, High Planes Drifters," *Cannabis Canada*, July 1995.

80. "Kaneh Bosm: The Hidden Story of Cannabis in the Old Testament" by Chris Bennet, published in *Cannabis Canada*, May/June 1996.

81. Tetrahydrocannabinol, the active chemical in cannabis.

82. We will be returning to the use of such oils in the medieval era later in this chapter.

83. The Mercy Seat was a kind of throne set atop the Ark, and upon which Yahweh was said to manifest.

84. In a footnote, Tyson adds: "The Angelida. '. . . grows upon Mount Lebanus in Syria, upon the chain of mountains called Dicte in Crete, and at Babylon and Susa in Persia. An infusion of it in drink, imparts powers of divination to the Magi.' . . . The herb is unknown. The name means 'messenger from god'".

85. Here is an extremely obscure hint of ancient shamanic plant worship. It is preserved in Agrippa's time as well as our own, as we continue to associate specific incenses to deities and angels.

86. Making the living appear dead might be familiar to those who have read or seen Shakespeare's *Romeo and Juliet*.

87. *Forbidden Rites*, p. 38.

88. *Ritual Magic*, p. 229.

89. *Ritual Magic*, p. 230.

90. See *Ritual Magic*, p. 218ff.

91. This is a vital aspect of the magick, and it will be discussed later in this chapter.

92. Texts such as the *Key of Solomon the King* require earthen vessels for censers.

93. *Forbidden Rites*, p. 47.

94. Cunningham lists both cannabis products here with "*." I'm sure this was a personal decision on his part, though I feel that it should be mentioned that these are not currently considered deadly poisons.

95. Pingree edition. Translation by Bick Thomas.

96. Similar uses of the grave can be found in certain Santerian and other Afro-Cuban practices. A study of these will help one understand their true nature, rather than being simply bits of ghoulery.

97. Opium, too, may be an infernal psychotropic.

98. Weiser's *The Key of Solomon the King*, p. 41.

99. *Psychedelic Shamanism*, p. 38.

100. The Isolation Tank Experiment. http://www.garage.co.jp/lilly/experimentx.html.

101. Ibid.

102. Though this is not always the case, as we will see below.

103. *Abramelin*, Book II, Chapter 8.

104. Ibid., Book II, Chapter 9.

105. Ibid., Book II, Chapter 10.

106. *Prometheus Rising*, p. 141.

107. I.e., by the spirit of sickness or injury that killed the victim in the first place.

The Art of Devotion: Way of the Temple Priest

Whosoever therefore thou art, who desirest to operate in this faculty, in the first place implore God the Father, being one, that thou also mayest be one worthy of his favour. Be clean, within and without, in a clean place, because it is written in Leviticus, every man who shall approach those things which are consecrated, in whom there is uncleanness, shall perish before the Lord. (*Three Books of Occult Philosophy*, Book III, chapter 44)

It is common today to raise an eyebrow or even turn away from "archaic Christian dogmatism" such as the above. Since the birth of the modern occult and Neopagan movements, and the general rebellion against Christian doctrine that came with it, this tone has kept the classical grimoires sealed away from a potentially larger audience. Association with a monotheistic and angry medieval God has not inspired the hearts of modern witches and magickians.

However, it can be illustrated that the grimoires themselves show forth an extremely polytheistic worldview—bordering much closer on Gnosticism, *Merkavah*, or shamanism in general than upon Roman Catholicism. Within these texts, one god acts as supreme creator, commanding legions of lesser gods, messengers, and spirits. We have already seen this in chapter 2, where such beliefs were shown as common even among primitive tribes.[1] In fact, the language of the above passage is not at all different from what we might read upon ancient Egyptian papyrus or Mesopotamian clay. Those names and descriptions of "God" we see in biblical literature are themselves largely borrowed from Pagan culture. As an example, the father god Ia[2] enjoyed supreme status in ancient Babylon for a time. Apparently, the Israelites (during the Captivity, circa 600 BCE) adopted prayers to this deity among their tribes; so that in the Bible, the word "Yah" is translated as "God." Each time you hear the phrase "Hallelujah"[3] in a prayer, you are hearing echoes of prayer to an ancient Babylonian father god.

This is not the only example of the direct borrowing of Pagan material into Judeo-Christian tradition. The word "Amen" comes to us from the Egyptian supreme god named Amon, and turns nearly every Christian prayer uttered into an appeal to him. Many of us are familiar with the fact that "Elohim" (usually translated as "God") was actually a plural word used in ancient Canaan and Israel to refer to "gods" in general. The Psalms, too, contain prayers that seem to have been adopted from Canaanite (Phoenician) victory hymns to the storm god Baal. (See the section on Psalms later in this chapter.)

This hardly scratches the surface of the fascinating subject of the ancient (and Pagan) origins of Judaism and Christianity. While we have already considered it more than once in the present work, it still remains a subject too vast to cover here with any justice. For those interested in further research, I will here offer my personal favorite book list, constructed through my own studies into the subject. These works will help bring biblical systems such as the grimoires into better focus.

-*A History of God: The 4,000-Year Quest of Judaism, Christianity and Islam* by Karen Armstrong

-*The Early History of God: Yahweh and the Other Deities in Ancient Israel* by Mark S. Smith

-*Yahweh and the Gods of Canaan: An Historical Analysis of Two Contrasting Faiths* by William Albright

-*The Babylonian Genesis: The Story of the Creation* by Alexander Heidel

-*The Gilgamesh Epic and Old Testament Parallels* by Alexander Heidel

-*Ancient Near Eastern Texts: Relating to the Old Testament* edited by James B. Pritchard

-*The Hebrew Goddess* by Raphael Patai

The point, in this case, is that the world has had no shortage of Pagans who uttered "Praise be to the Lord," or prayed to "Our Father, who art in heaven . . ." As a point of fact, the prayers of the grimoires bear a striking resemblance to ancient Mesopotamian prayers and often claim to descend from just that location.[4] At the same time, we have already discussed the well-documented Greek (and thus Pagan) origins of the medieval European texts, as well as their shamanic roots. It becomes possible to follow a relatively well-connected historical thread backward to the prehistory of medieval Judeo-Christianity, and we learn that ancient Pagans nearly everywhere prayed in a fashion much as we see in the Bible.

Today, the past (and many present) actions of the organized Christian churches have understandably caused a movement away from such material. Especially in our modern occult communities—even among those who take an interest in angels and grimoires—there might be a hesitance to grab a Bible and start reciting scripture. Of course, the simple response is to point out that grimoiric magick is a biblical tradition, and so the Bible must simply be accepted in its study. Plus, by indiscriminately avoiding such material, we face the problem of turning our backs on vital sources of our own modern traditions.

However, as it turns out, this would be needless in any case—as the prayers of the grimoires do not actually have to imply the medieval Catholic doctrine (nor its God) as we know it. We could just as easily be reciting these prayers to Baal, Marduk, and Amon. Replace the masculine references with feminine, and suddenly we find goddess literature similar to those to Asherah, Inanna, and Nut. Not only this, but we have an abundance of noncanonical Biblical material to draw from, which do not come burdened with the usual negative baggage. We will be returning to this very subject in a later chapter, where we discuss the making of prayers.

Therefore, instead of turning away, it should be important to study the religious dynamic that exists in such literature as quoted from the *Three Books* above. We must be willing to suspend our personal assumptions and dive into the mindset of the medieval Solomonic mage. This is the key to decoding these highly obscure religious writings.

Taking the sum of information we have gathered so far, I feel it is safe to make some educated deductions about the classical grimoiric material. Overall, it seems to reflect of a loose society of medieval prophets; descended more or less indirectly from the earliest of "primitive" shamanism, and more directly from Christian, Hebraic, Arabic, and Greek mysticism. Being that they stuck somewhat to a Judeo-Christian framework, they just barely survived the worst of the Middle Ages. (Though, it can also be suggested that it was these very mystics who were the first targets of the early Inquisitions, and even the reason such Inquisitions were created.) Yet, it must also be held in mind that even Christianity was once an obscure mystical cult, whose members were often considered master wizards.[5] There does exist a deep and rich magickal (even shamanic) system at the core of the Christian faith; far removed from the corruption experienced by the medieval Church as it became a dominating political force.

Keep in mind that the god described in the grimoires does not appear interested in converting heathens, persecuting heretics, or any of the other theological politics of the day. Instead, he manifests as the aforementioned father sky. He is primarily viewed as the creator of all things, and is thus credited with ultimate authority over physical material and events. Yet, as should be expected, he exists largely outside of space-time, and must be invoked by experienced shamans who know how to get his attention and ask for help. Many scholars and Church leaders have remarked upon the apparent attitude among grimoiric authors that actions can be taken "behind God's back." In reality, the grimoires are the very antithesis of this, with the mage working rather hard to gain God's attentions.

Also in line with shamanic procedure, the grimoiric wizard did not work the bulk of his magick directly via the creator. While he is in all cases called upon in initial prayers,[6] the actual work is accomplished by the intercession of angels and various classes of spirits. This, quite simply, results in a polytheistic worldview—each force of nature having its own deity (angel) who must be invoked, propitiated, and petitioned for help in a given matter. The spirits of the grimoires—though glossed over with Christian hyperbole about the fall from Heaven and punishment in Hell—are fundamentally one and the same with the jinni, faery, daemons, and intelligences of ancient cultures around the world.

Also included in this list are the ancestral spirits, whose presence are invoked via recitation of their past deeds. We have already covered the importance of ancestors in shamanic cosmology,[7] and here we can see their invocation in texts such as the *Key of Solomon the King*:

> I conjure ye . . . by the name Iah, which Moses heard, and spoke with God; and by the Name AGLA, which Joseph invoked, and was delivered out of the hands of his brethren; and by the Name Vau, which Abraham heard, and knew God the Almighty One; and by the Name of Four Letters, Tetragrammaton, which Joshua named and invoked, and he was rendered worthy and found deserving to lead the Army of Israel into the Promised Land . . . (Book I, Chapter 6)

Or the *Goetia*:

> I invoke, conjure, and command you . . . by the name & in the name YAH that Adam heard & spoke & by the name Joth which Jacob heard from the Angel wrestling with him, and was delivered from the hands of Easu his brother; and by the name of God AGLA, which Lot heard and was saved with his family; and by the name Anaphexaton which Aaron heard and spake and became wise & by the names Schemes-Amathia which Joseph called upon and the Sun stood still, and by the name Emanuel which the 3 Children Sedrach, Masach and Abednego, sang in the midst of the fiery furnace, and were delivered . . . (Second Conjuration)

Yet, the more generalized concept of "shamanism" should encompass only the tribal worldview and techniques shared by various cultures. What gives a specific practice its shape is the religious framework from which the magick draws its imagery and mythological validation. In the classical grimoiric literature, this framework descends from the Church, and the texts therefore display a nuance of the clergy. In this chapter, we will be discussing certain aspects of this core "priestly" tradition. I feel that little more needs to be said of the Roman Catholic Church itself, as opposed as it was to the grimoiric texts. However, in order to understand the "priestly" aspects of grimoiric practice (the Art of Devotion), it will again be necessary to first create a solid historical foundation. Just as we did with the shaman in chapter 2, we will here consider the origins of priestcraft, the development of its role within society, and finally lead up to the medieval magickal texts.

The Rise of the Priesthood

This story begins not with gods and temples, but with the primordial observance of ancestor worship. This can be considered a shamanic art—though it was not exclusive to initiated shamans—and it far predates the establishment of priesthood. However, it would appear that ancestor worship does form the chief root of the later temple faiths.

According to typical ancient worldview, a human spirit vacating its body upon death generally faced two options. On the one hand, it could be left without a body, and thus forced to roam the earth hungry, thirsty, and lost for all of eternity. Or, in some cultures, it might descend to the underworld—a colorless realm devoid of action or pleasure. This was not a place of punishment, but simply a place of eternal and boring rest. Mesopotamian texts refer to this as a place where one goes to sit alone and eat dust. In short, it is the grave and nothing more.

The second option was for the family of the departed to capture the spirit and formally bond it to a new body—that is to say, to a new physical base. This might be a certain stone or wood, or a statue or other hand-made artifact. Funerary rites for Egyptian and Aztec royalty included the preservation of the corpse itself, so that the spirit could be bound right back into it (an art known as mummification). Santerian oral legend describes the flight of human spirits into the mountains and high places, where they would attach themselves to various natural objects (rocks, sticks, etc.) in order to relax and enjoy the surrounding peace and beauty.[8] These natural objects could be located by living humans and brought home, along with the attached spirit.[9]

Whatever the case, from there the spirit could be cared for as if it were still very much alive. It could be offered food and drink,[10] given certain tools to replace those physical gifts lost at death (such as hands, legs, etc.), and even extra tools that made the spirit much more versatile than it had been while incarnate as a human. It might be given wings or claws, or hammers and building tools, or weapons, or boats and carts; the lists go on considerably. Simply study the contents of King Tutankhamen's tomb for a good example. Thus did a family care for its departed loved ones; these practices being primitive at first, but growing in complexity as time moved onward.

As compensation for this highly involved custodial care, the living family members could call upon the spirit in times of need. The spirit being incorporeal (no longer restricted by physical senses), it could foretell the future, disclose secret information, or describe events happening in distant locations. This, in fact, is the primordial origin of necromancy, the art of divination via converse with the dead. Further, the entity could actively aid the family in daily matters.[11] It might bring money and goods into the household, aid the growth of crops, offer assistance in battle, or protect the home from thieves; all by spiritually manipulating the astral currents as easily as the living move physical objects. This is also the origin of the "Familiar spirit."[12]

However, none of this would have been possible if the spirit had not been captured after death and reaffixed to something physical. It was not believed that any spiritual being could perform such powerful physical feats without (figuratively speaking) a base upon which to stand, or the symbolic tools granted for its use. Some form of material "anchor" is needed in order for a spiritual being to manipulate the physical. This is why genies were put into bottles, angels were bound to rings, and why ancient priests invoked their gods into statues.

Allow me to quote Agrippa's thoughts on this very subject: from Book I, Chapter 39, "That We May by Some Certain Matters of the World Stir Up the Gods of the World, and Their Ministering Spirits":

So we read that the ancient priests made statues, and images, foretelling things to come, and infused into them the spirits of the stars, which were not kept there by constraint in some certain matters, but rejoicing in them, viz. as acknowledging such kinds of matter to be suitable to them, they do always, and willingly, abide in them, and speak, and do wonderful things by them: no otherwise than evil spirits are wont to do, when they possess men's bodies.

All that is left is the question of exactly how humanity progressed from primitive ancestral observance to the great temple faiths that we know from the early historical period onward. After the innovations of agriculture took hold upon the heretofore-nomadic species of humans, various families began to settle into "city-states." Some of these cooperative families were larger than most, and, therefore, their familial spirits had wider and more powerful spheres of influence. Likewise, the sheer size of these clans allowed them to indulge their mammalian dominance instincts at the expense of their neighbors, thus forming themselves into a class we now call "nobility."

As it was, their neighbors did not choose to stand against them. In return for a general state of subservience and the paying of tributes to the nobles, the smaller clans were offered physical protection from nomadic raiders who would often sweep across the land. No less important, the noble families promised astral protection via their familial spirits. Tributes from the dominated clans were paid in crops and livestock, and therefore the ruling families had an interest in making sure the general prosperity of the city flourished.

The ancestral spirits of the nobles, who had once been mere Familiars, were now elevated to the status of godhood. They fed on the offerings and prayers of not just a small number of close relatives, but instead upon those of an entire nation of people. For instance, taking ancient Egypt as an example, tribute was not only paid to the pharaoh, but to his direct ancestor Osiris as well. Finally, the shamans who specialized in tending these large spirits evolved into what we know as the priesthood.

From Priests to Kings, and From Palaces to Temples

It is at this point in history—roughly eight thousand years ago—that humankind formed what we call "civilization." There have been several different economic and governmental structures attempted since then, but all of them ultimately trace back to the same root-assumptions we made when we first plowed the soil of the Fertile Crescent. Even our modern American legal structure traces itself backward through Rome and finally into ancient Babylon.

The records left by the earliest urban scribes, such as in Sumeria and Egypt, insist that the arts of civilization (primarily the arts of agriculture, kingship, and warfare) were delivered directly to us by the gods. This brings to mind the Greek god Prometheus delivering fire to mankind, or the Sumerian goddess Inanna stealing the *Mes* (arts) from her father to bring them to earth. Likewise, Osiris (the first earthly pharaoh) was credited with founding ancient Egyptian culture, teaching the primitive people the arts of agriculture, establishing the throne, etc. If there is any grain of truth in such a widespread mythos, then it is possible to suggest that these "arts of civilization" were discovered by prophets and priests exploring the higher circuits of consciousness. Thus, the situation is much akin to the ecstatic reception of written language, and indeed both developments came from the same group of people.

The establishment of kingship within the new city-states also had a profound influence upon both temple procedure and architecture. Apparently, kings and priests were established at roughly the same era of history; and it may be safe to assume that kingship was a direct result of the priesthood itself. The priest was a member of an elite ruling class, and his position was determined by blood descent much more often than his primitive shamanic counterpart. The general prosperity that came along with urban settlement also lent a hand in elevating the priest to higher realms of political power. Finally, the people of the lower class—being affixed to one location—became wholly dependant on both the whims of the national god, and the rulers through whom contact with that god was maintained.

All together, this formed a matrix which culminated in the inception of the priest-king. This was a singular human being who spoke with the voice of the patron deity, and thus had a totalitarian control over the entirety of the kingdom. In many cases, the king was believed to be a literal incarnation of the deity. In other cases, the king was thought to be the son of the patron. Later dynastic Egypt gives us perfect examples of both: the living pharaoh was worshipped as Horus incarnate.[13] At death, the pharaoh would become one with Osiris, and Horus would be left to dwell in the heart of the next king.

Thus, there was little difference between the royal court and the priesthood, as the king himself was the high priest of the local religion. The convention of "marriage" was created for no other purpose than to marry the king to the kingdom itself, just as the god was wed to the land. Laws were then issued as the taboos of the god and king, and the general population was expected to follow them for the privilege of residence and protection. Such was the birth of the royal court, with all of its ritualistic social and ambassadorial procedures.

While the king may have arisen directly from the priest, it would appear that the converse is true in relation to royal courts and temples. From the earliest of times, mankind has insisted upon envisioning the spiritual and celestial communities as working along the same lines as human social structure. For instance, the nomadic hunter-gatherer was more concerned with ancestral, plant, and totem (animal) spirits, as life was generally governed by the family[14] and the local natural environment. Once royal families had developed governmental procedures for settled land, the gods seemed to follow suit. The national god would meet with all local deities in a celestial court, with himself sitting upon a throne. From there the fates of the land would be decided (very often by the casting of lots), and the actions of the people would be judged. At the same time, the behavior of the gods in general began to mirror the typical shenanigans of all noble families, as a study of any Pagan mythology will illustrate.

For these reasons, the temple was established as a kind of earthly royal court for the gods. Take for instance these lines from the Babylonian creation epic, in which the kingdom of Babylon is founded by Marduk:

> Marduk made His voice heard and spoke,
> ". . . I shall make a house to be a luxurious dwelling for Myself
> And shall found My cult center within it,
> And I shall establish My private quarters, and confirm My kingship.
> Whenever You come up from the Apsu for an assembly,
> Your night's resting place shall be in it, receiving you all.
> Whenever you come down from the sky for an assembly,
> Your night's resting place shall be in it, receiving you all.
> I hereby Name it Babylon, home of the Great Gods.
> We shall make it the center of religion."

Even today, we can see specific parallels between court and church design. The judge and the priest hold the same basic location—usually in an elevated or even enthroned position. Off to the side, in a slightly less elevated position, resides the jury in the courtroom, and the choir in the church. A place exists in each for petitioners to approach the position of the "most high" and state their cases. The largest area is reserved for the congregation—those regular folk who wish to witness the rites taking place. Finally, the whole is monitored and guarded by bailiffs in the case of the courtroom, and by deacons within a church.

Now we can compare these similarities with the major aspects of a king's throne room, or "royal court." The king enthroned in the most elevated position, his advisors stationed near at hand,[15] the general people gathered in seats to witness or await their turn before the king, and the palace guards watching over all.

There are further similarities which can be added at this point. For instance, the ancient pagan ruling god had viziers (or messengers) to send on errands, while the king had human equivalents at his command on earth. Even today the court has its "agents" to send forth, bearing official seals and commands to the people. When comparing the models, these agents are the physical-world counterparts to angels.

Visions of the divine throne room recorded by *Merkavah* mystics show us the same heavenly structure utilized by the medieval grimoires. God sits upon his throne (the Merkavah), surrounded by the four *Chaioth haQodesh*[16]

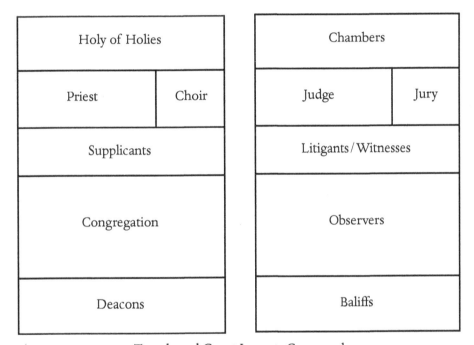

Temple and Court Layouts Compared.

who minister upon him. At hand, also, are the twenty-four elders—the advisors to the heavenly king (corresponding to the jury of a court). The archangel Raziel stands just inside the veil that separates the throne room (or Holy of Holies) from the rest of creation, to record all the decrees that issue from God (i.e., the court recorder or scribe).[17]

Of course, we must question which came first: the heavenly structure or the earthly? The mythos pattern suggests the heavens came first, and man was subsequently taught to follow suit. Students of anthropology, however, may be more comfortable with the idea that humans created the structure and then modeled their mythologies accordingly. As if this were not enough of a dilemma, we must also consider the early development of astrology / astronomy, which strongly suggests that mankind learned much about organization from the celestial realm after all. I feel that, with all evidence considered, the answer is simply that both earthly and (the human understanding of) heavenly organization evolved together.

Thus, as the world's first farmers began to cluster around strong warrior families for protection, paying tribute to the head of that family (now known as the king), so, too, did the shamanic sons of god eventually become the priestly servants of god. As the warrior tradition developed among the settled tribes, so the angelic hosts began to march in military formation. This is the basis for much of what we see in ancient mythologies, and even in the hierarchies and heavenly (or infernal) armies described in the grimoires.

All of this illustrates the intimate connections between temple procedure and court procedure. The manner in which a priest approaches his god is rather the same as an advisor might approach his king. Likewise, the priest would interact with an angel of his god just as the same court advisor might interact with the king's head vizier. What this means for us is that a study of the Art of Political Diplomacy can greatly increase one's understanding of obscure religious and magickal practices. This will have much to do with what we will discuss in chapter eight.

The Role of the Priest

We have already discussed the role of the tribal shaman in his community; specifically that of dealing with the local nature and ancestral spirits for the benefit of the tribe. The job of the urban priest was not so different in essence, though he certainly existed in a different cultural framework. For instance, the shaman or prophet obtained his position through individual efforts (often against his will), while the position of priest could be sought out and learned in a college-style setting. Priesthood, after all, became an institution (or social class) unto itself, with any number of groups or guilds devoted to various aspects of the priestly craft. There existed the "stolists"—perhaps the most common stereotype of the priest—who dressed and cared for the sacred cultic image. However, there were many other specialists who arose from the institution of priesthood, such as scholars, scribes, astrologers, and various performance artists such as psalmists, dancers, singers, and musicians.

The lower clergy were nonspecialists known as the "purified ones," who acted as participants in the rituals, and carried ritual objects and the standards of the deity. Among this group were also found the public oracles and dream interpreters. As a point of fact, this is the same clerical group who penned the grimoires in the Middle Ages. Texts such as the *Key of Solomon the King* preserve hints of this clerical class.[18]

The priesthood was also charged with actively personifying the gods of bounty and beneficence. Not only does this relate to the "god-king" as seen in Egypt, but also to the concept of the passion play. This latter is a form of liturgical ritual (where the priests play the roles of gods) enacted to invoke divine powers through a kind of sympathy. These rituals were mythological in nature, commemorating instances where the gods had defeated enemies of the kingdom or demonic entities of natural disaster. For instance, the Babylonian priesthood read (and most likely enacted) their creation epic at the dawn of each new year, in the hopes of encouraging the establishment of order over chaos, the triumph of good over evil, after the harsh winter.

While the shaman accomplished his work via any number of spirits under his command, the priest engaged in specialization toward the local deity. Like the shaman, the priest's principal function was to act as the representative of his community in its relations with the gods. Unlike the shaman, however, the priest was more concerned with calling his god to the earth plane than with attempting to cross the bridge to the spirit world himself. In a sense, he strove to embody that bridge in his own person: knowing the techniques of worship and conciliation that mend the rift between the divine and earthly realms.[19]

The priest was also called upon for important events in one's life—such as birth, puberty, marriage, etc.—for which the shaman was not generally called. (Remember the shaman was called specifically for the crises of sickness and/or death.) Although, the priest is not unknown as a healer, as the earliest rites of exorcism (casting out demons of sickness) attest.

The priest was the servant of the altar or shrine and the ritual expert. He guarded the secret lore of his patron, and ensured that the mysteries were perpetuated into future generations of initiates. He also became a social leader and pillar of strength, guiding his community through emotional situations that are beyond human control. His knowledge of the god's expectations and taboos assured him of this role, which often lead into powerful political positions such as judge (or Inquisitor!) and king. For this reason, the temple was often the very heart of the local culture.

Along with all of this, we also know that the priest (and not usually the shaman) was the master of sacrifice. Most any scholarly text will point out that sacrifices offered to the gods were meant to appease them in some way, though it would be unusual indeed to see much scholarly speculation as to *why* such a thing would appease them at all. In order to understand the role of the priest as sacrificer, it is absolutely vital to understand the true nature of sacrifice itself.

Perhaps the most common—and mistaken—fiction about ritual sacrifice is that it centers upon the death (and pain) of the animal offered. By this theory, a mage is literally torturing an animal to death in order to empower his spell with the agonies of the poor beast. It is thought that the chemical (adrenaline, endorphin) and emotional (fear, terror) reactions of the suffering animal produce intense levels of spiritual energy. This energy is then somehow "captured" by the mage and added to the overall power of the ceremony. It is for this reason that sacrifice is labeled as "black," and systems that include or allow its use are viewed as principally diabolical.

However, in reality, nothing could be farther from the truth. Such myths as the above were born from the medieval Catholic Church's anti-Pagan propaganda, and live on today in Hollywood and fantasy fiction. Now, the subject of sacrifice is literally buried amidst such popular myths and misunderstandings. I have often heard it said, with no small amount of venom on the part of the speaker, that any human who would work magick at the expense of a life is a low human indeed. Yet, I have seen many of these same people sit down in public and cut into a thick steak, or bite into a warm chicken sandwich. Protests that these are "two entirely different things" do not stand up to serious study and observation, as we shall see below.

Those sacrificial rites I have attended—involving Santeria and Palo, which generally use chickens for the purpose—have had nothing at all to do with inflicting pain or terror. In fact, the chickens I observed were treated quite humanely, and were not even allowed in the room to witness the offering of other birds. When a sacrifice was made, it was done as quickly as possible with every aim toward negating pain or suffering. When I asked the Palero to explain to me the practice of sacrifice in general, the concept of death simply never entered his reply. Instead, I was told very simply that "life feeds on life." I quickly learned that ritual sacrifice was not based upon fear, suffering, or death, but upon the very straightforward model of the food chain.

There is no form of life in creation that does not sustain its existence by consuming other forms of life. This is easily proven, even by our own modern scientific models. We also know that this formed the principal focus of ancestor worship, with family members seeing to the care and feeding of the dearly not-so-departed. Without nourishment, the spirits would languish and wane in power (just as we do), and eventually descend into an inactive (or catatonic) state.

Of course, even in the relatively recent past one could not directly obtain cut meats and vegetables from the local supermarket. Originally, these things had to be grown, raised, harvested, and/or slaughtered personally by those who intended to consume them. To the ancient mind there was technically little difference between preparing an animal for the nightly meal and doing the same thing to feed one's ancestors.

All that sets animal sacrifice apart from the usual slaughter of livestock for food is the fact that the former becomes a holy rite. The word "sacrifice" itself illustrates the religious focus of the practice. Originating in the thirteenth century, the term descends from the Latin *sacrificium*. It consists of *sacer* (sacred) and *facere* (to make). The idea was to consecrate the animal for consumption by a god or spirit, as only things made sacred were acceptable. This is the same basic concept behind the prayers we often say over our meals before eating to this very day.

An animal (or any other substance) offered had to be without blemish and consecrated very specifically to the spiritual entity in question. Different spirits, too, would require different foods and preparations, probably depending on what was and was not in sympathy with the nature of the spirit. (For example, Santeria requires the use of black chickens for Familiar spirits and white chickens for higher gods.)[20] If all of these considerations were not acted upon, the spirit would gain little sustenance from the offered material. Thus, we can see how sacrifice not only reflects the simple concept of preparing animals for food, but also goes the extra step of honoring and consecrating the animal and granting it a dignified and meaningful death. Compare this to the treatment—and manner of death—offered to our own modern livestock.

This practice of spirit-feeding survived intact through the evolution of ancestral shamanism and into the rites of priesthood. For a perfect illustration of the ancient practice of temple sacrifice and god-feeding, read the Old Testament books of Exodus, Leviticus, and Numbers. More examples can be found in texts from Sumer-Babylonia, Egypt (such as the *Book of the Dead*), and any ancient temple-priesthood culture from whom we have records.

One of the most interesting things we learn from all of this is that ancient gods and spirits were not "appeased" by sacrifice at all. Instead, they were nourished and strengthened by it, allowing them to offer much more efficient aid to the humans who needed them. The priest was not, after all, subservient to the god so much as to the nation of people who depended upon that god. Likewise, the god found itself in a curious position of dependence upon its priesthood.

Eventually, of course, the Catholic faith arose and established itself as the world's dominant religion. This was the state of things by the time the European grimoires were first penned. While it might seem natural to enter some discussion of this subject here, I find it unnecessary. At this point we are discussing the nature of priesthood as an art-form, rather than the political and institutionalized system that governed the Holy Roman Empire. The Catholic Church and its clergy were discussed somewhat in chapters 1 and 2, and we will return to the subject again in later chapters (especially chapter 12, concerning the priestly art of exorcism).

Devotional Magick

In chapter 3, where we discussed the shamanic elevation of consciousness, I outlined some of Agrippa's teachings on the matter. In the *Three Books*, Book III, Chapter 46, he discusses various mental "phrensies" (frenzies, or ecstatic states) and how they are obtained. We covered three of them in chapter 3: the phrensies of the Muses, Dionysus, and Apollo. The fourth phrensy, that of Venus, concerns the ecstasy of love and devotion, and was thus saved for this priestly chapter. Of the Venus phrensy, Agrippa says:

> Now the forth kind of phrensy proceeds from Venus, and it doth by a fervent love convert, and transmute, the mind to God. . . . Now then the soul being so converted into God by love, and sublimated above the intellectual sphere, doth beside that it hath by its integrity obtained the spirit of prophecy, sometimes work wonderful things, and greater than the nature of the world can do, which works are called miracles. (*Three Books*, Book III, Chapter 49)

Love is an emotion, or state of mind, that spans across all of the mental circuits of consciousness. Our instinctive mammalian need for others arises from the second circuit, which leads directly to our third circuit desire to connect with others mentally/intellectually. The physical aspects of love (attraction, arousal, and the pleasures of sex) center upon the fourth circuit. And all of the above traces itself to our first circuit, which tells us to advance toward the safety and pleasure of loved ones, and drives the propagation of the species. The fifth through eighth circuits also encompass love, taking it beyond the common expression and into more philosophical, spiritual, and ultimately cosmic interpretations. Therefore, a priest or mage who truly loves his god with all of his heart is wielding an incredibly powerful weapon. His love will engage and obsess every aspect of his mind and body.

The yearning of a lover for his or her mate is the purist and most powerful magick in the universe.

"Ah fair lady . . . truly the sweet behaviour, the perfect wisdom, the elegant grace, nobleness and sur-passing beauty that I see in you, hath so enraptured my soul, that I cannot but love you; and without your return of love, I am but as dead." (Edward III to the Countess of Salisbury)

It is not simply the existence of the love, but the yearning itself that generates such power. The earliest stages of being "in love," even the mere proximity of the desired mate, involves the release of endorphins and other chemicals by the brain into the body. They create a psychedelic trip during which thoughts are processed differ-ently, and experience is mentally interpreted in an entirely unique fashion. Thus, the Venus phrensy is rightly in-cluded as a form of shamanic-style mind alteration. Even today a person in love is often described as being in a state of ecstasy.

During one's time apart from a lover, the brain and body are constantly awash in these powerful chemicals. It becomes difficult or even impossible to think about anything without images of the desired partner intruding, bringing with them their addictive sensations. Each of these sensations, however, must go without answer or re-lease until such time as the lovers can be near again.

This is merely one step in a larger process; a process designed to result in the creation of life, in case that helps to illustrate the deep-rooted power of the magick we are discussing. The sexual/emotional tension (or yearning) that has built for hours, days, or even weeks is quite explosively released in the presence of our loved ones. This is the "electricity" often described as existing between two people. It literally blazes upon the astral, and (according to many mythologies) is the very light that attracts the souls of the yet-to-be-born; especially during lovemaking. The power of devotional love is very much about "build-up" leading to sudden "release."[21] That process, from start to finish, can transform an individual and/or alter the courses of nations.

The Art of the Priest is to harness this power within himself and the world around him. By directing his devo-tion toward a discorporate entity—thus ruling out the possibility of any physical consummation—the emotion can be driven to a fevered pitch that must find release in a philosophical sense. It becomes a gateway to the higher men-tal circuits with their more all-encompassing interpretations of reality. The love is projected through the god and on to everything that god embodies, represents, or governs. In this way the emotion comes full circle, from the physical (the priest) to the celestial (the god) and back to the physical again (the priest's environment). The priest then reacts to his environment, and the cycle starts anew. Via this pattern the energy is steadily increased through "iteration and feedback," over and over again, forming the very basis of magickal invocation. (This may shed new light onto the concept that a god is nothing without worshippers. However, now it becomes apparent that the op-posite is just as profoundly true: a worshipper is nothing without his god.)

It is within this cycle that the priest lives and works. So long as the god is happy, the world is happy, and so is the priest. If, however, the cycle breaks down—such as a negative occurrence in the environment controlled by the god—the priest must quickly discover and correct the problem between himself and his god. From this arose the (eventually perverted) concepts of "sin" and "atonement."[22] In fact, this is not so different than it is for human lov-ers.

The only points of release available to the priest are during the holy rites and observances. These are the times when he can commune with his patron, and are thus the instances where powerful magick can occur. Again, this can-not be the physical joining so necessary to the human system,[23] but can often lead to an even brighter astral explosion. Again, the power and emotion must project through the god and into the physical world. Miracles generally occur during the height of religious ecstasy.

The medieval mage fostered just this kind of relationship with God and his angels. In *The Devil's Contempla-tives*,[24] Richard Kieckhefer points out that "devotionalism" was increasingly important in late medieval Europe.

Spiritual exercises (such as the *Notary Arts*, for example) became more popular and more complex through the fourteenth and fifteenth centuries. Kieckhefer suggests that the combination of devotionalism and magick is perfectly common and routine. The spells and invocations of the classical texts are the rites and observances by which the mage communes and—in the highest sense—makes love with the celestial creatures.

> For love is the chariot of the soul, the most excellent of all things, descending from the intelligences above even to the most inferior things. It congregates and converts our mind into the divine beauty, preserves us also in all our works, gives us events according to our wishes, administereth power to our supplications . . . (*Three Books*, Book III, Chapter 5)

> Therefore our mind being pure and divine, inflamed with a religious love, adorned with hope, directed by faith, placed in the height and top of the human soul, doth attract the truth, and suddenly comprehend it, and beholdeth all the stations, grounds, causes and sciences of things both natural and immortal in the divine truth itself, as it were in a certain [mirror] of eternity. (*Three Books*, Book III, Chapter 6)

Without this devotional angle, the grimoires are little more than endless pages of long and dry recitations. They do not contain enough active ceremony[25] to be much else, and the true atheist would find something like the *Key of Solomon the King* of little use in its original context.

The third book of Agrippa's *Occult Philosophy* is largely dedicated to the arts of devotion and religious magick. He even goes so far as to make the assertion that religion is a necessary component of magick; an idea one may or may not agree with today, depending upon how one defines "religion." If one feels that religion is a systematized form of worship, depending largely on blind faith, then one is not considering religion from a mystical standpoint. To the mystic or occultist, religion is a set of techniques for interfacing with spiritual beings (or with divinity in general), and it is received directly from one's own guardians. For instance, note the peculiar stance that Agrippa takes toward the concept of "faith":

> But faith the superior virtue of all, not grounded on human fictions, but *divine revelations wholly*,[26] pierceth all things through the whole world. . . . by faith man is made somewhat the same with the superior powers and enjoyeth the same power with them . . . (*Three Books*, Book III, Chapter 5).

As we can see, Agrippa is not promoting the blind faith demanded by organized religion. Faith is a matter of receiving divine revelation or obtaining conversation with celestial entities. It is never something that can be read in a book or explained by a human teacher. Then, of course, the grimoiric tradition is all about gaining such revelations and conversation.

Spiritual Authority

The concept of "spiritual authority" is extremely important to the vocation of priesthood. One cannot simply stand and declare oneself a priest, nor does it merely take heartfelt dedication and devotion. In order to command the very forces of nature, the priest had to possess an essence of god's authority that those forces recognized. Take the unfortunate incident involving some hapless exorcists in the New Testament:

> Then certain vagabond Jews, exorcists, took upon them to call over them which had evil spirits the name of the Lord Jesus, saying, "We adjure you by Jesus whom Paul preacheth!" [. . .] And the evil spirit answered and said, "Jesus I know, and Paul I know; *but who are ye?*"[27] And the man in whom the evil spirit was leaped on them, and overcame them, so that they fled out of the house naked and wounded. (Acts 19:13–16)

As we have seen, the heavenly hosts are organized into a royal hierarchy, and any human aspirant must work slowly and painstakingly upward through their ranks. It is a process involving a lifetime of work, and without this, the spirits of nature will simply have no more cause to act at an aspirant's command than at the command of any layperson.

Note, for example, Agrippa's teaching on the subject of spiritual authority, and the holiness required of anyone who would attempt to interact with the celestial beings:

> . . . there is also required a certain assimilation of our life to the divine life, in purity, chastity and holiness, with a lawful desire of that which we wish for; for by this means we especially obtain the divine benevolence, and are subjected to the divine bounty; for unless we, having our minds purged, be worthy to be heard, and also those things which we desire, be worthy to be done, it is manifest that the gods will not hearken to our prayers . . . (*Three Books,* Book III, Chapter 58)

Consider, for example, the conjuror (described in Kieckhefer's *Forbidden Rites,* Chapter 8, p. 170) who explained that the spirits could not withstand his prayers, characters, and conjurations because he held a "commission from the King to which they were subject." This "commission" was from God in the form of an ordination—either officially if the mage was himself a cleric or priest, or through occult initiation. We will see how absolutely vital this concept of acting with the "Authority of God" becomes to magickal practice in chapters 8 and 12.

In the Arts of Priesthood, the first step to gaining such authority (beyond the heartfelt dedication) usually involves some kind of spiritual wedding between the human and his patron. Consider the tradition of Santeria as an illustration. Before an aspirant undergoes the Ocha initiation (to become a Santero (priest)) he must first search out a proper Santero to perform a divination. The god (Orisha) with whom this priest has contact will reveal which Orisha is the spiritual "parent" of the aspirant. It is a very intricate and subtle process that has to do with who the aspirant truly is inside, and what occult forces resonate with him the strongest. He might be a child of the (Orisha of the) river, or the storm, or the sea, or the mountain, etc. The newly revealed Orisha is the patron god who will be invoked and "put to the head" of the aspirant during the Ocha ceremony. (More on this ceremony below.)

Searching out a properly initiated priest or priestess for divination (specifically to talk with various gods or spirits) is a very widespread idea. Catholics do this all the time by going to their priest to speak with Jesus for them. The Old Testament itself is filled with instances where kings or common men will search out the prophet and ask him what Yahweh has to say on any given matter. The same has been true of every religion the world over, and can be found in most of the mythologies, up to the modern day.

Of course, this is not to say that contrasting traditions have not existed. The prophetic and gnostic traditions—including the grimoires themselves—have persisted for centuries in the conviction that each human being can make their own connections to god. The historical Gnostic sects, who existed from just before the dawn of the Common Era, believed in a one-on-one contact between man and divinity. The same basic philosophy existed in other cultures, and was a major driving force behind the formation of the Qabalah itself (a word that means "to receive," and is sometimes indicated to mean "reception of information directly from God"). However, even these traditions understood that if an aspirant wished to have conversation with the gods, it was up to the aspirant to dedicate his or her life toward gaining that contact. It was considered a birthright to have this contact, but it came only *after* many years of work and labor toward the goal. They were, in essence, simply working to become priests themselves.

Once one has undertaken these initiations, one is granted the ability to speak directly with the god in question. This isn't simply a lot of mystical "red tape" that one has to endure before being granted an audience. In fact, one must be bonded quite directly to the god in order to have such an intimate contact. The initiations themselves are focused on this kind of bonding.

For instance, Santeria accomplishes this with the very involved procedure known as the Ocha ceremony. This is where a patron Orisha is—as I have mentioned before—"put to the head" of an aspirant. This basically amounts to a form of possession, where the spiritual entity is summoned and bound directly into the skull of the initiate. (The ceremony even involves making cuts on an initiate's scalp and sealing the wounds with herbs sacred to the deity.) The priest and his god are married as one entity via this process.

Unfortunately, the information on priesthood initiations throughout history is sketchy, as the procedures were jealously guarded as sacred mysteries. However, I have seen traces of this Ocha-like technique in several places. Remember our discussion in chapter 2 of the importance of patrons and spiritual teachers to mystical vocation. Often these teachers were said to manifest as spiritual wives (or husbands), wed to the shaman metaphysically. Various Middle Eastern examples of religious artwork illustrate royalty in the arms of their protecting deities, or (as in Egypt) even understood their kings and priests to be incarnations of the gods. (For instance, the essence of Horus was said to reside in the heart of the pharaoh.) From the medieval era, we have the *Book of the Sacred Magic of Abramelin the Mage*, which contains a process by which one may bond directly with his own guardian angel—who is one and the same with the concept of the patron god. Its similarities to the Ocha ceremony are astounding, and I have little doubt that the *Book of Abramelin* itself was written from an author's knowledge of the general procedure for creating a priest.

Although, if one wishes to regularly contact a god, one needs to become initiated into the deity's specific tradition. It's more than simply a matter of gaining the initiations and the authority to speak to the god; there are also many subtle mysteries that are taught to a student along his way. These are the practical "how-to's" behind the art, such as how to actually call the god when one needs to speak with him, what is sacred to him, what will offend him, secret signs and words of power, dances and drumbeats, etc. In the case of *Abramelin* it would seem to be up to the patron to teach the aspirant the how-to's after the initiations.[28] This is the secret to truly unlocking the grimoiric traditions,[29] and we will be returning to the subject of angelic working in later chapters.[30]

Confession

The use of confession is certainly one of the most priestly, and blatantly Catholic, aspects of grimoiric tradition. As such, it is also perhaps the least favored practice among modern occultists. Judeo-Christianity has earned itself a reputation of self-abasement and groveling before a jealous deity. Confession would certainly appear to fit into this category; with its implications that one must live only to "please daddy," tell the truth about one's "no-no's," and beg forgiveness for living life the way one might choose. From the standpoint of medieval Catholicism, this isn't likely far from the truth at all, especially since the Church had officially set itself between God and the people.

However, it is my intention in this book to illustrate that early religion among humankind was not based on such political models of social control. Instead, they were born from natural principals that properly reflected the relationship and interaction between humans and their environment. This is not to suggest that some amount of parentalism was not involved in the adoration of the gods by their worshippers, but to stress that this was in no way related to fear, authoritarianism, or submission and domination.

An ancient person who found himself suffering hard times did consider himself a target of the gods' wrath. However, this was not because his gods were necessarily petty and abusive, but simply because suffering, like the gods, was a natural part of life. Sometimes droughts, floods, storms, and plagues took place, as they do to this day. They are examples of inharmonious nature, and therefore of inharmonious gods. The two are one and the same.

It was the job of (first the shaman, and later) the priest to intercede and petition the gods for relief from their irritable moods.

Eventually the concept of "taboo" arose among humanity. Most popular today, thanks to Judeo-Christianity, are the social taboos that tribal communities once used to maintain their genetic and social integrity. These governed many (or all) aspects of sexual and interpersonal activity among members of the tribe. These are also the same taboos that, after the agricultural revolution, were corrupted into techniques of mass population control and social engineering that culminated in medieval Catholicism and the inquisitions.

However, some of mankind's earliest taboos had nothing to do with such issues. Instead, they were our first attempts at controlling the spread of disease. For example, one of the strictest taboos observed in Sumer-Babylonian religion was that against coming into contact with a dead body. The taboos associated with the menstruation of women were also health related, especially in such primitive times. And, of course, coming into contact with a person already sick, or who had already broken a taboo themselves, was also prohibited.

Thus, the original concept of taboo was a *medical* concern, and it brought with it the concept of "atonement." Today we would refer to it as a "prescription," as atonement was the official instruction given by the medical professional (priest/shaman) to an afflicted patient. Remember, too, that the prescriptions issued by such professionals were generally received directly from the gods during trance. The sick person was out of harmony with nature, and therefore it was specifically the gods who could bring him back into harmony. Very often, such atonement involved separation from the tribe, cleansing by water (and thus baptism), and prayer, confession, and sacrifice. The cleansing and quarantine are also obvious marks of medical concerns.

Confession, finally, is an aspect of the atonement process. More than likely, it has its origins in the shamanic art of intercession, as well as in the priestly art of exorcism (which was itself caught up in the development of medicine and taboos). In order to illustrate these points, let us take a look at the confession recorded in the *Key of Solomon the King*, which is, in fact, titled "The Confession to be Made by the *Exorcist*."[31] It goes on for quite some time, and the following is merely a short quotation:

> O Lord of Heaven and of Earth, before Thee do I confess my sins, and lament them, cast down and humbled in Thy presence. For I have sinned before Thee by pride, avarice, and boundless desire of honours and riches. By idleness, gluttony, greed, debauchery, and drunkeness. Because I have offended Thee by all kinds of sins of the flesh, adulteries, and pollutions, which I have committed myself, and consented that others should commit. By sacrilege, thefts, rapine, violation, and homicide. By the evil use I have made of my possessions, by my prodigality, by the sins which I have committed against Hope and Charity, by my evil advice, flatteries, bribes, and the ill distribution which I have made of the goods of which I have been possessed.

I have to admit, this confession happens to be one of my favorites. It remains one of the most intellectually fascinating and classic examples of Solomonic lore with which I'm familiar. A colleague of mine once termed it a "reverse" negative confession. The real negative confession appears in the Egyptian *Book of the Dead*, where the soul being judged is accused of a long list of sins; each of which must be verbally denied by the soul. Our Solomonic example above shows us a "positive confession"; the master admits to every conceivable sin in order to catch any sin of which he may not be aware, or would be otherwise unwilling to admit.

This kind of all-inclusiveness finds its roots in ancient Mesopotamian prayers and exorcisms. When natural disaster struck a village, it was not always known which particular god was angry. Therefore, the priest would offer his prayers of intercession to any number of gods and natural forces, and would freely admit to having offended any or all of them—with wishes to make expiation.

Mesopotamian exorcisms were often similar. A spirit possessing a human victim (sickness) would often be an unknown to the priest. Without the spirit's name (or title, description, etc.), the exorcist could not hope to verbally control it. Therefore, the exorcisms read by the priest had to include the names and classes of many known demons, all of which were called in the hopes of hitting the right one.[32] We can see an example in one of the Babylonian exorcisms:

> Whether thou art an evil Spirit or an evil Demon,
>
> Or an evil Ghost, or an evil Devil,
>
> Or an evil God or an evil Fiend,
>
> Or Hag-demon or Ghoul or Robber Sprite,
>
> Or Phantom of Night or Wraith of Night,
>
> Or Handmaiden of the Phantom,
>
> Or evil pestilence or noisome fever,
>
> Or pain or sorcery or any evil . . . [33]

The main point here is that all of these things—taboo, atonement, confession, etc.—are based upon the principals of proper harmony with god and nature. In reality, a taboo should only exist so long as breaking it results in some kind of imbalance and suffering. Likewise, if breaking the taboo ever ceases to result in real problems, then it should be laid aside. Obviously, natural harmony is the main focus of any shaman, priest, or mystic. It is therefore little surprise that confession was included by the authors of the grimoires as a standard practice for ritual purification.

Whether we like it or not, suffering is a part of real life. Yet, it is also true that most current human suffering is self-inflicted (either on an individual or community basis). The modern human is quite overwhelmed with neuroses and habitual behavioral patterns that are destructive to the self and others. Denying this fact, especially about ourselves, is absolutely counter to the magickal arts. Admitting to our flaws, and working to fix them, is the first and foremost goal of magick.

> Now the greatest part of purgations is a voluntary penitency for faults: for . . . he whom it grieves that he hath offended, is in a manner innocent. . . . Therefore our cogitations, afflictions of our mind, and all evils that proceed from our heart and mouth, must be uttered . . . in confession . . .;[34] neither is there found in religion for the expiating heinous offences a stronger sacrament. . . . (*Three Books*, Book III, Chapter 56)

Another form of purification that Agrippa considered highly important was the giving of alms and charity. There is nothing that removes the weight of our own wrongdoings from our souls than efforts to help others who are in trouble themselves. Of course, this was a vital aspect of the Christianity taught by Jesus of Nazareth, and it is by such authority that it becomes important to the grimoiric mages:

> There is as yet another sacrament of expiation, viz. alms giving . . . give ye alms, and all things shall be clean to you . . . Hence Christ commanded us to pray to the Father, forgive us as we forgive others, give to us as we give to others. (*Three Books*, Book III, Chapter 57)

The same concept is found in the *Book of Abramelin*, where the aspirant is instructed to provide alms for up to seventy-two poor people before one can hope to obtain the true and sacred magick:

[Abramelin] said unto me that he required ten golden florins, which he must himself, according to the order which the Lord had given unto him, distribute by way of alms among seventy-two poor persons . . . (Book I, Chapter 4)

You shall fast for three days before giving the Operation unto any; and he who shall receive it shall do likewise; and he also shall hand over unto you at the same time the sum of Ten Golden Florins, or their value, the which you should with your own hand distribute unto poor persons . . . (Book II, Chapter 20)

The Ten Florins of Gold shall be distributed by your own hands when you shall have received the money, unto Seventy-two poor persons . . .; and see also that you fail not in this, for it is an essential point. (Book II, Chapter 20)

Psalmody

If the grimoires are a neglected area of European occultism, then the art of Psalmody is almost entirely forgotten. Many modern students are completely unaware of the Psalms' existence in the grimoires, while others tend to simply pass over them without much thought. However, I have come to feel that grimoiric spells without their Psalms are hardly grimoiric at all. Removing them, and thus all they represent within the tradition, is akin to removing the very marrow from the bones of a living creature.

This view arises from my observations of Orthodox Christianity. These traditions, as well as Catholicism, retain a heavy focus upon the divine power inherent within their holy scriptures. Setting the scriptures to music—such as Gregorian and other chants—is one of the most important devotional practices within the faith. Remember our discussion of history from chapter one, where we saw a single line of religious text (from the Nicene Creed), once set to meter, cause the first major schism of the Christian faith.

In fact, the Psalms were considered the only acceptable songs of worship in the early Christian Church. The inclusion of newer hymns into religious procedure did not become widespread until the fourth century, and then it was among the "heretical sects" that had moved away from orthodoxy. Various spiritual authorities opposed the trend, such as the Synod of Laodiciea (343 CE) and the Council of Chalcedon (451 CE). These people felt that the Psalms—and only the Psalms—were divinely inspired prayers by which Christians were intended to praise God.

Observing the rites of these highly ceremonial sects of Christianity (such as Communion or the observances of various holy days) one notices that the bulk of the invocations consist of Psalms and other scriptures chanted in meter. Even the more unusual procedures, such as exorcism, are performed via the recitation of Psalms. (One example is Psalm 91, which contains such declarations as the following:

I will say unto the Lord, "He is my refuge and my fortress: my God; in him will I trust."

Surely he shall deliver thee from the snare of the fowler, and from the noisome pestilence.

He shall cover thee with his feathers, and under his wings shalt thou trust: his truth shall be thy shield and thy buckler.

Thou shalt not be afraid for the terror by night; nor for the arrow that flieth by day;

Nor for the pestilence that walketh in darkness; nor for the destruction that wasteth at noonday.[35]

Since this Psalm was in common use in medieval Europe as an exorcism, it also found its way into procedures of conjuration in the grimoires, such as the *Book of Abramelin*.

Once I learned that orthodox Christian mysticism relied so heavily on its Psalmody, a great missing piece of the grimoiric tradition had been uncovered. We have always understood that vital information is missing from the classical texts, whereby the simple recipes they contain are transformed into living and powerful ceremonies. What shocked me was that the greatest bulk of this missing material had always been right in front of me: the Psalms in the grimoiric instructions do not take much space to list, and can therefore fool one into underestimating their importance. Reciting or intoning each Psalm along the way, such as in the Solomonic bath,[36] adds the meat back onto the skeleton of the rituals. Once you have experienced this, you have truly experienced a ritual of Christian-style mysticism; precisely as the authors of the *Key of Solomon the King* or the *Goetia* would have performed it. (The student may wish to attend a few orthodox services, as it will offer a perfect illustration of the general tone and style of the practice.)

Psalmody naturally falls within the priestly art, but it actually finds its origins in ancient shamanism. Apparently, the very earliest of spells and incantations were songs, and, at that time, all songs and music were aimed at magickal ends.[37] They were intended to align the shaman's mind with the spiritual forces by way of adoring them, and the songs were believed to literally summon the gods and spirits. Eventually musical instruments were added to the process; the gods adopted them as sacred objects, and demanded their priesthoods to play them at their evocations. (Consider the sistrum, which was associated with Isis worship in ancient Egypt.)

In ancient times, such techniques were the very latest in magickal technology and procedure, and it shows that early man fully realized the ecstatic effects of music on the human mind. These concepts were not lost over the thousands of ensuing years—and in fact only became more sophisticated as they developed into the many priestly arts involving music, Psalmody, and the bardic traditions. The angels of the Judeo-Christian faiths, even to this day, are depicted as singing their divine messages in great choirs. Gnosticism considered the entire universe a cosmic musical instrument (viz.—the harmony of the spheres), and musical theory became an important concern for medieval and Renaissance mages such as Agrippa and John Dee.

Even the biblical prophets were known as musicians, thus further associating them with the shamanic vocation. We can see the prophetess Miriam (Aaron's sister) playing a tambourine and leading the Israelite women in song and dance in Exodus 15:20–21, in celebration of the triumph of Yahweh over the Egyptian armies. In I Samuel 10:5–10, Saul meets with a band of prophets who come with "a psaltery, and a tabret, and a pipe, and a harp." Saul stayed that entire day to prophesy along with them. Both Isaiah and Ezekiel were songwriters as well. Though it is hard to distinguish between Isaiah's poetry and what should be musical, one song is mentioned directly in Isaiah 26 as a psalm to be sung at God's final victory over the earth. Ezekiel, meanwhile, is described in Ezekiel 33:32: "And, lo, thou art unto them as a very lovely song of one that hath a pleasant voice, and can play well on an instrument . . ."

King David was also a musician, and is generally credited with the establishment of music as a principal aspect of Yahweh's worship. During the transportation of the Ark of the Covenant to Zion, he appointed the musicians of the tribe of Levi (the priesthood, of whom Moses and Aaron were kin) to precede the Ark with music, song, and dance.

> And David spake to the chief of the Levites to appoint their brethren to be the singers with instruments of music, psalteries and harps and cymbals, sounding, by lifting up the voice with joy. . . . the priests, did blow with the trumpets before the ark of God. (1 Chronicles 15:16–24)

More David-related examples of such bardic worship abound. In 1 Chronicles 16:1–7, he appoints Asaph to the position of director for a group of priest-musicians who are to minister before the Ark and offer praise by song and dance. Psalteries, harps, cymbals, and trumpets are all mentioned. In 1 Chronicles 25:1–7, the practice is described in more detail, and even describes one prophet as prophesying *with* his musical instrument.

These examples give us a wonderful illustration of the nature of early Israelite worship. Song, dance, and sacred instruments all used to call upon the gods. This is typical of Middle Eastern religion, which generally revolved around various holy festival days. Worship and celebration were indistinguishable concepts. Remember the discussion of altering consciousness in chapter 3, and how music has long been a method of gaining ecstatic states. Imagine, for instance, the dedication ceremony of the temple of Solomon, who followed in the traditions of his father.[38]

> . . . Also the Levites which were the singers, all of them of Asaph, of Heman, of Jeduthun, with their sons and their brethren, being arrayed in white linen, having cymbals and psalteries and harps, stood at the east end of the altar, and with them an hundred and twenty priests sounding with trumpets.) It came even to pass, as the trumpeters, and singers were as one, to make one sound to be heard in praising and thanking the Lord; and when they lifted up their voice with the trumpets and cymbals and instruments of music, and praised the Lord, saying, "For he is good; for his mercy endureth for ever," that then the house was filled with a cloud, even the house of the Lord; So that the priests could not stand to minister by reason of the cloud: for the glory of the Lord had filled the house of God.[39] (2 Chronicles 5:12–14)

It sounds like quite a bash, and the glory of God was evoked once the singers and musicians had attained a unity of sound and voice. These kinds of musical festivals tend to build slowly to a fever pitch, at the high point of which ecstasy and visions will naturally strike some.

Many of the Psalms contained in the modern scriptures are attributed to David, which would be a significant point to the musical biblical tradition even if it lacked historical probability. The first seventy-two chapters of the Psalter are considered a collection of Davidic Psalms unto themselves, and Psalm 72 has a line appended which reads: "The prayers of David the son of Jesse are ended."[40] Though the historical King David may not have written all of these Psalms himself, it is probable that many of them originated during his reign. Their content reflects the pre-temple worship centered upon the Ark that is associated with David's reign. It is just as likely that David did at least commission some of those Psalms "attributed" to him.

Just as the methods of worship among the Israelites was rather common to Middle Eastern religion (from Egypt to Mesopotamia), so, too, is the poetry found in the Psalms. Specifically, they have much in common with similar poetry found in the Canaanite land of Ras Shamra. They contain the same basic rhythmic structures, as well as a poetry style called "parallelism."

This latter—parallelism—means that the Psalm verses come in pairs or groups, where the idea of one verse is balanced by the ideas of those which follow. In the eighteenth century, an Anglican bishop named Robert Lowth distinguished three main types of such parallelism: synonymous, antithetic, and synthetic. Synonymous parallelism simply means that the idea in one verse is repeated in the second, with only the wording altered. Take Psalm 38:1 for example:

> Yahweh, rebuke me not in thy wrath,
>
> Neither chasten me in thy hot displeasure.

In antithetic parallelism, the second verse presents the same basic idea as the first, but does so by way of negation or contrast. Psalm 1:6 gives us an example:

> For Yahweh knoweth the way of the righteous,
>
> But the way of the ungodly shall perish.

Finally, with synthetic parallelism, the second part is a completion or expansion of the idea expressed in the first part. We can see this in Psalm 42:1:

As the [deer] panteth after the water brooks,

So panteth my soul after thee, O God.

This particular category is somewhat broader than the others, and involves several variations. One example is called the *acrostic*[41]—meaning "staircase"—which consists of several verses that build upon one another to a final conclusion. Psalm 29:1–2 serves as an example:

1 Give unto Yahweh, O ye mighty,

Give unto Yahweh glory and strength.

2 Give unto Yahweh the glory due unto his name;

Worship Yahweh in the beauty of holiness.

Not only do the Psalms contain the same style and structure as Canaanite poems, but many of them seem to have been adopted directly from psalms of praise to Baal, the storm deity (the Canaanite version—if not predecessor—of Yahweh). For instance, note the remaining lines of Psalm 29:

3 The voice of the Lord is upon the waters:

the God of glory thundereth:

the Lord is upon many waters.

4 The voice of the Lord is powerful;

the voice of the Lord is full of majesty.

5 The voice of the Lord breaketh the cedars;

yea, the Lord breaketh the cedars of Lebanon.

6 He maketh them also to skip like a calf;

Lebanon and Sirion like a young unicorn.

7 The voice of the Lord divideth the flames of fire.

8 The voice of the Lord shaketh the wilderness;

the Lord shaketh the wilderness of Kadesh.

9 The voice of the Lord maketh the hinds to calve,

and discovereth the forests:

and in his temple doth every one speak of his glory.

10 The Lord sitteth upon the flood;

yea, the Lord sitteth King for ever.

11 The Lord will give strength unto his people;

the Lord will bless his people with peace.

Lines three through nine associate the voice of Yahweh with storm imagery, suggesting a direct connection to the Canaanite storm god. I have seen it theorized that this Psalm is a word-for-word borrowing from Canaanite literature (simply inserting one god's name over another's), or that it is perhaps merely a borrowing of imagery and style. In the end they amount to nearly the same thing—cultural intermixing—and there is sufficient evidence to suggest that ancient Israelite worshippers saw very little difference between Baal and Yahweh.

Generally, these Palestinian[42] songs of praise are broken down into three fundamental segments. We will continue to utilize the example of Psalm 29 to illustrate:

1) **The introduction or call to praise**: covering lines one and two.

2) **The reason behind the praise**: focusing on mythological elements of the God, covering lines three through nine.

3) **The praise itself**: focusing upon God's kingship, and protection of the people, covering lines ten through eleven.

Another example of Canaanite psalmody adopted into Israelite worship is Psalm 82:1–7, which seems very likely to have been a hymn of praise to the Canaanite father god El:

> God has taken His place in the assembly of the gods,
>
> He declares His judgment among the gods:
>
> How long will you give crooked judgment,
>
> and favor the wicked?
>
> You ought to sustain the case of the weak and the orphan;
>
> You ought to vindicate the destitute and down-trodden
>
> You ought to rescue the weak and the poor,
>
> To deliver them from the power of the wicked
>
> You walk in darkness
>
> While all earth's foundations are giving away.
>
> I declare gods you may be,
>
> Sons of the Most high, all of you;
>
> Yet you shall die as men,
>
> You shall fall as one of the bright ones.

The congregation of gods referred to in the psalm is actually the divine court of El, where all of the local gods gathered to draw lots and decide the fates of mortals. El, which loosely translates as "he" or "god," was also known as "Elyon" (the Most High). The psalm of Deuteronomy 32 contains the following lines (32:8):

> When the Most High divided to the nations their inheritance,
>
> When he separated the sons of Adam,
>
> He set the bounds of the people according to the children of Israel.[43]

Here we see the apportionment of Israel to its patron Yahweh by the "Most High" in the assembly of the sons of El. Yahweh does seem to have originated as a member of the Canaanite pantheon (a subject or son of El), and only later moved into position as the Israelite national god. As it was adopted by the Israelites, Psalm 82 became an uprising of Yahweh against the local deities for their inaction in the face of the people's suffering. This is, in short, where Yahweh ceased to be a minor Canaanite deity, and became the patron god of a nation. This kind of circumstance was not at all unique to Israel, and similar examples of tribal deities ascending to national status can be found with Osiris, Marduk, Re, and countless other ancient tutelary deities.

The *Encyclopedia Britannica* suggests the most important scholarship regarding the Book of Psalms is the work of Hermann Gunkel. This man was a German scholar of the Old Testament born in Springe, Hannover, in 1862, and died in 1932. Gunkel was among the first to develop the method of biblical research known as "form criticism."[44] The concept of form criticism is based upon the fact that such cultural writings as psalms, parables, stories, histories, etc. are *always* affected by the minds of those who write them. Therefore, by analyzing the manner in which ancient writers communicate their stories, something can be learned about the writers themselves.

By analyzing the Psalms in this manner, Gunkel identified five major types of Psalms, each cultic in origin. They consist of the Hymn (or song of praise), Communal Lament, Royal Psalm, Individual Lament, and the Individual Song of Thanksgiving. Not only do these classifications give us a slightly larger window into ancient Middle Eastern life, they also illuminate the book of Psalms as a true collection of shamanic (or bardic) formulas of invocation. Understanding them can go a long way toward helping the student apply the Psalms within his own "grimoiric" spells.

The Hymn has already been outlined above using Psalm 92. It includes the invitation to praise Yahweh, the reasons for the praise (his protection, his creation of all things, etc.), and a conclusion that either repeats the invitation to praise or simply offers the praise directly. These were generally associated with common worship, much as the hymns sung in churches today are intended. Gunkel also identified two subgroups within the Hymns: the Songs of Zion, which praise Yahweh as the lord of Jerusalem, and the Enthronement Songs, which praise Yahweh as king of the world.

The Communal Lament was associated with times of national crises and natural disasters, involving periods of fasting, prayer, and atonement in the hopes of returning to the good graces of Yahweh. In these Psalms, first of all Yahweh is invoked, the crisis is described, divine aide is requested, and confidence that the prayer has been heard is expressed. These are the best examples of pure shamanism within the Psalter. (See chapter 2 concerning shamanic intercession.)

The Royal Psalms form the next group. Apparently, these originated during the time of the Hebrew monarchy. As in all state-enforced Middle Eastern religions, the reigning king was understood to have an especially intimate relationship with the kingdom's patron god. These particular Psalms all concern some event in the life of such a king: accession to the throne, marriage, battle, etc. After the monarchy fell to Babylon circa 700–600 BCE, the royal Psalms were retained and adapted to different cultic uses.

Next follows the Individual Lament, which is largely self-explanatory, and comprises the largest group of songs in the Psalter. (These are, perhaps, the most useful in a magickal sense.) Each Lament includes an invocation to Yahweh, a statement of the complaint, a request for help, and the expression of certainty that Yahweh will hear and answer the prayer. The complaints generally offered in these Laments concern suffering at the hands of one's enemies, or suffering due to the condition of poverty. Also, in many cases, a vow is made to offer a sacrifice of thanksgiving. (The instructions for such sacrifices were contained in the Torah.) These Psalms are also noted for their sudden transitions of mood when the certainty of Yahweh's attention is praised. This uplifting of mood is a vital aspect of the magick of intercession. One must indeed be certain that their prayers are heard, and that they will be answered (e.g., Ask and ye shall receive, knock and the door shall be opened).

Finally, we have the category of the Individual Song of Thanksgiving, naturally following the concept of the Individual Lament. These Psalms were apparently intended for use along with the thanksgiving sacrifices mentioned above, as a completion of the magick invoked through the Laments. They include exclamations of praise to Yahweh at the beginning and the end, while the body of the poems include two elements: the story of the one who was saved, and recognition that Yahweh was the rescuer.

Gunkel also indicated several types of minor Psalms, such as Wisdom Poems, Liturgies, Songs of Pilgrimage, and (of course) Communal Songs of Thanksgiving. Overall, Gunkel seems to have been of the opinion that the majority of songs preserved in the Psalter were composed privately—in imitation of the cultic invocations—and were intended for personal worship. If this is the case, it means that their utilization within the grimoires is a perfect example of their originally intended use, a further connection between the arts of the biblical prophets and the European grimoiric mages.

The book of Psalms as we know it today is known in Hebrew as *Tehillim* (Songs of Praise). We obtain the name "Psalms" from the Greek *psalmas*, meaning "song." The English term used to describe the book, Psalter, originates from the Greek *psalterion*; the name of a stringed instrument used to accompany the songs. There are a total 150 Psalms dating from various periods of Israelite history, and representing expressions of faith from many generations and many different kinds of people.

When studying classical texts of magick, be aware of the fact that the Psalms are numerated differently according to the version of the Bible referenced. The Hebrew Bible, of course, contains the original numbering: 1 through 150. Later Christian recensions of the Psalter—the Septuagint, the Latin Vulgate, and those derived from them—have done a bit of juggling with their ordering. They have joined Psalms 9 and 10, as well as 114 and 115, but they also divide both 116 and 147 into two. The Roman Catholic versions of the Psalter have used the Septuagint-Vulgate numbering, though recent translations have followed the Hebrew tradition. King James also follows the Septuagint-Vulgate.

Division of Psalms between Hebrew and Septuagint-Vulgate Psalters

Hebrew	Septuagint-Vulgate	
1–8	1–8	
9–10	9	(Combines 9 and 10)
11–113	10–112	
114–115	11	(Combines 114 and 115)
116	114–115	(Divides 116)
117–146	116–145	
147	146–147	(Divides 147)
148–150	148–150	

The Psalter is divided into five sub-books, composed of Psalms 1–41, 42–72, 73–89, 90–106, and 107–150. This division appears quite artificial, and is likely intended to reflect the books of the Pentateuch (or Five Books of the Torah). Psalm 1 functions as an introduction to the entire Psalter, and Psalm 150 is a final expression of praise for God (or "doxology") also intended to encompass the entire Book of Psalms. The final Psalm in each sub-book (Psalms 41, 72, 89, and 106) also ends with a similar form of doxology.

There are other divisions of the text (such as the aforementioned 72 Psalms of David) that indicate the Psalter may consist of several preexisting collections. This would explain why some of the Psalms, such as 14 and 53, are near word-for-word duplicates of one another. (Even the grimoires recognize this, and sometimes allow the mage to choose between identical Psalms.) There is even a collection—Psalms 42–83—that appear to have derived from the Elohistic priesthood founded by King Josiah. They are marked by their use of the divine name "Elohim" in place of the older "Yahweh." This division cuts across the Davidic poems, so that Psalms 3–41 are Yahwistic and Psalms 51–72 are Elohistic.

After the destruction of the first temple by the Babylonians, the system we now know as "Judaism" arose to replace the interrupted temple faith. The singing of Psalms was retained as an aspect of worship in the new synagogues, and other scripture and prayers were chanted according to a system of "modes." I have a strong hunch that the post-Captivity Jewish faith adopted some of this practice (chanting holy scripture as spiritual invocation) from Babylonian religion, and it was this Jewish worship that influenced the early Church as described at the beginning of this section.

The practicing grimoiric mage has several options when it comes to the use of Psalms in magick. Personally, I tend to enjoy the poetry of the Psalter found in the King James Bible. On the other hand, if one wishes to experiment with the Psalms as actual songs, it is possible to obtain English Psalters that have been "reworked" into a meter that fits our language. Even better would be an attempt to learn the Psalms in Latin. Not only does this resonate best with the grimoires—which themselves often utilize the Psalms in Latin—but it also opens a window of experimentation with the Orthodox Christian chants. (If one doesn't chant them himself, they can be found on CD, perfect for playing in the background while one works.)

Perhaps what makes the magickal use of Psalms so incomprehensible to some is their lack of obvious magickal references. Their inclusion in the grimoiric spells can appear completely random. In other words, one might question their relevance to any given magickal operation. However, after studying the above information, we can begin to obtain a feel for their particularly shamanic nature, especially the arts of intercession that are employed via the Laments followed by Songs of Thanksgiving. An adequate example can be borrowed from the *Key of Solomon the King*, Book II, Chapter 5, the so-called "Solomonic Bath." The progression of Psalms I will use as an example follows the first immersion in water, as the mage reclothes himself in preparation to turn the bath water into consecrated holy water.

First, one is to recite Psalm 102 (*Hear my prayer, O Lord, and let my cry come unto thee*). This is apparently one of Gunkel's Individual Laments. It begins by beseeching God to "hide not thy face from me I the day when I am in trouble; incline thine ear unto me; in the day when I call answer me speedily." This even includes an extremely shamanic insistence that the God answer speedily. The Psalm continues to describe the horrible conditions afflicting the invocant; in fact illustrating a perfect example of a dark night of the soul. "My heart is smitten, and withered like grass. [. . .] Mine enemies reproach me all the day . . . For I have eaten ashes like bread, and mingled my drink with blood." Nowhere does the Psalm specifically outline an affliction—leaving that to the heart of the invocant himself. However, it does suggest that the afflictions are due to being out of favor with one's god: "Because of thine indignation and thy wrath: for thou hast lifted me up and cast me down." To the invocant, the Lament should encompass the spiritual and emotional dross that one wishes to wash away by the Solomonic Bath itself.

The Psalm then takes the signature shift in tone to a kind of praise—assuring us that God shall arise and redeem us from the evils of the world. "For he hath looked down from the height of his sanctuary:[45] from heaven did the Lord behold the earth. To hear the groaning of the prisoner, to loose those that are appointed to death."

From here one moves on to a recitation (or chant) of Psalm 51 (*Have mercy upon me, O God, according to Thy lovingkindness*). Having established the formula of redemption in the previous Lament, this Psalm is a confession, an entreaty to God to wash away one's sins. "For I acknowledge my transgressions: and my sin is ever before me." Specifically, this Psalm reflects the above assertion that one has fallen out of favor with God, and represents an aspect of atonement. I feel that enough has been said on the importance of confession to these biblical systems of magick previously in this chapter.

This is also the Psalm that contains the verse "purge me with hyssop, and I shall be clean: wash me, and I shall be whiter than snow" that is associated with ritual baths in the grimoires. The verse is even used in the Solomonic Bath immediately previous to this progression of Psalms. As for Psalm 51 itself, it strikes me as one that Gunkel may have associated with offerings of sacrifice to God. (Though, this may be a post-exilic Psalm—as the final lines claim that God does not wish for sacrifice or burnt offering—though such offerings shall please him again once he is established upon Zion.)

Having so invoked the redemption of God from worldly suffering, and then offered confession for one's own transgressions, the next Psalm listed is number 4 (*Hear me when I call, O God of my righteousness*). The focus of this short invocation is upon further gaining the attention of God, and assurances that the prayers cannot but be heard. "But know that the Lord hath set apart him that is godly for himself: the Lord will hear when I call unto him!" This marks a dramatic emotional upswing in the progression of Psalms, in direct contrast to the darker calls for help in the previous songs. Having called upon God, he has answered. If the mage can *know* this as he recites these Psalms, then his magick will be well on the way to success. "I will both lay me down in peace, and sleep, for thou, Lord, only makest me dwell in safety."

The next Psalm recited is number 30 (*I will extol thee, O Lord; for Thou hast lifted me up*). This is one of Gunkel's Personal Songs of Thanksgiving, and it continues the idea set forth in the previous Psalm. Not only has God heard the prayers and inclined his ear, but he has acted on behalf of the shaman-mage: "O Lord my God, I cried unto thee, and thou hast healed me!" There is even a hint of one shamanic technique that we discussed in chapter 2, where the shaman reminds the god of the importance of attending to the problems of His worshippers: "What profit is there in my blood, when I go down to the pit? Shall the dust praise thee? Shall it declare thy truth? Hear, O Lord, and have mercy upon me: Lord, be thou my helper!"

Following this is Psalm 119: 97 (*O how love I thy law! It is my meditation all the day*). The entirety of Psalm 119 is an extremely long example, divided into twenty-two sections based upon the Hebrew alphabet. Verse 97 falls under the section of *Mem* (M)—the Hebrew letter associated with Water—and thus relates directly to the Solomonic bath procedure. The directions in the *Key* make it uncertain whether one is intended to recite the entire Mem section (verses 97–104) or merely verse 97 itself. I would suggest the entire section, which asserts to God that one is walking in the holy path, and that much wisdom has come therefrom. "Thou through thy commandments has made me wiser than mine enemies: for they are ever with me. I have more understanding than all my teachers; for thy testimonies are my meditation. [. . .] I have refrained my feet from every evil way, that I might keep thy word."

By this point, the mage has attained a much higher spiritual state than he began with in Psalm 102. Now, one is to proclaim God's glory with Psalm 114 (*When Israel went out of Egypt*). This is perhaps one of Gunkel's Songs of Zion, praising God as the king and ruler of the world. On the shamanic side of things, this invocation mentions God's great deeds associated with the tribulations of the ancestors (specifically the events from the Exodus from Egypt to the entrance into Palestine across the Jordan). The earth is described as falling to submission before the might of God: "What ailed thee, O thou [Red] Sea, that thou fleddest? Thou Jordan, that thou wast driven back? Ye mountains that ye skipped like rams; and ye little hills like lambs? Tremble, thou earth, at the presence of the Lord, at the presence of the God of Jacob." The grimoiric mage might consider this an invocation of authority over the Elemental forces he will command with his magick. We will see in later chapters how this was an important aspect of grimoiric invocations overall.

Psalm 126 follows (*When the Lord turned again the captivity of Zion, we were like them that dream.*), and appears to be a continuation of the above. Here the praise is offered to God for saving Zion from captivity (Palestine was repeatedly captured by larger empires throughout its ancient history—Egypt, Persia, Greece, the Hittites, etc.). It appears to be a reminder to God of his past deeds on behalf of the people, and calls upon him to act again in the same manner: "Turn again our captivity, O Lord . . . They that sow in tears shall reap in joy!"

Finally, the progression of Psalms ends with number 139 (*O Lord, thou hast searched me, and known me*). This appears to be an apt completion of all of the above ideas. I get the impression that it is intended to be quieter, or perhaps less urgent in its delivery. It is a highly personal prayer, testifying to an intimate relationship between the invocant and his God. "Thou knowest my downsitting and mine uprising, thou understandest my thought afar off." Just as importantly, it seems to affirm that God has been successfully called, and that the invocant is now communing pleasantly with Him: "Thou has beset me behind and before, and laid thine hand upon me. [. . .] If I say, surely the darkness shall cover me; even the night shall be light about me." The Psalm offers praise for the help offered, and closes perfectly: "And see if there be any wicked way in me, and lead me in the way everlasting." So ends the progression of Psalms for the Solomonic Bath.

It should be a simple matter for the student to apply the same analysis to any given Psalm(s) in the grimoiric literature. They are not given in a random fashion, but should apply to the nature of the magickal operation attempted. However, in order to grasp this, one must be familiar with the concept of intercession, the art by which a human approaches and invokes the aid of a celestial being.

Words of Power

On words and Magick generally, a favorite example: I once ran across a neighbor's
cat, whom I'd never seen, but whose name I happened to know. It started to
run from me—a stranger—until I called its name; then it stopped,
thought about it, and came over. Can you imagine how "magical"; the act of
naming something must have seemed, when language was developing?; and does
one see here a possible origin for "When you know something's True Name, it
will obey you"? (A. J. Rose[46])

I am convinced, so far, that what we now call "magick" was born on this planet as our species moved from the second to third circuit of consciousness. Specifically, it came hand-in-hand with the discovery that we could communicate with one another. Today we take such things as our speech or writing for granted. It is so omnipresent as to be invisible, much as water must appear (or not appear) to a fish. We might not truly realize that it is indeed an incredible miracle we possess. In a completely pragmatic sense, *any* form of communication from human to human is a form of telepathy. One mind communicating information to another; from earliest speech and hand signals, to the written language, to libraries, to the world wide web, and beyond.

This flow of information from mind to mind (and from generation to generation) creates a very real yet intangible environment. We might call this the "mental plane," and perhaps Jung's "collective" exists there as well. Ideas live and thrive on that plane as certainly as we do on this plane. They procreate, fight for survival or dominance, adapt to their environments, mutate, and show many further signs of what modern science calls "life." If one is not convinced of this, simply consider that corporate entities are recognized by law, and corporations show all of the signs of life I mentioned above.

As the first humans began to think on the third circuit, they must have utterly dominated their second circuit peers. They could command animals by uttering names, they could communicate with one another over long distances (by merely yelling), and their groups would have been incredibly organized and hard to attack. Most importantly, language allowed them to spread their technology over wide areas, and to their children. The dominance of these people is attested to in some of earth's earliest mythologies, written down only after they were ancient. They speak of the first man and his naming of all things. Sometimes he is credited with the creation of all languages, magick, and even (later) the arts of writing. Genesis 2 (originally a Sumerian tale) makes quite a point of Adam's naming of all the beasts of the field, and properly stresses the awe in which primitive man held the use of words. Other mythologies contain parallel examples, such as Egypt's Tehuti (Thoth), who also created all language and magick.

Note how these legends suggest language and magick were created at once by the same hand, literally two sides of the same coin. Our ancestors put great mystical significance to the advent of language. Of all the beasts of the field, we humans had become *the Namers*, and that was the birth of our magickal power. If one can come to understand this basic miracle of nature, then one is well on the way to understanding the core of all magick, and the meaning of the Logos.[47]

The earliest known mysticisms do seem to center upon primitive man's fascination with this "new" thing called speech. Even today, our magick is based on the same long-established principals. The incantation, the spell, exorcism, invocation, names of power, the insistence on pronunciations, conversation of the guardian angel, mystery languages, the bardic traditions, Psalmody, and later the mystical status granted to letters, inscriptions, talismans, books, scriptures, etc., all of these are experiments in *communication*. They are all native to the third mental circuit.

Therefore, it is important for the mage to become familiar with that circuit within himself, and to use it to advantage. Try to imagine how it would feel to have no words in your head with which to think (let alone speak). How would you learn about anything you encounter? How would you reason and make decisions? How would you communicate needs or desires? The case was the same for ancient humanity as it is for every infant child.

When we encounter spiritual beings, it is true that the images we see are largely constructed from aspects of our own psyche. (We will discuss magickal images and the appearances of spirits in chapter 10.) The entities perceived by the skryer are bodiless, existing as pure intelligences. In communicating with them, we are left to formulate our own mental images. We do not, of course, choose these images at will;[48] they are evoked from the subconscious depending on what within ourselves "resonates" with the spirit we encounter. If there is anything about such an entity that one's mind cannot comprehend, then that aspect of the entity will be wholly invisible to him. The spirits have no choice but to work with what imagery we provide them, and the wider our own consciousness and knowledge, the fuller we can experience the spiritual realm.

As it is with images, so it is with words. Any message that might be transmitted by a spiritual entity is strictly limited by the vocabulary we have comprehended. The kind of "telepathic" communication used by angels and spirits works by the transmission of raw information from one consciousness to another. This is much akin to the way computers use binary in their processes. It is up to the receiving mind to decode the raw data and put the correct words and images to the message. We can see, then, how such communication can run into problems—if the receiving mind does not *posses* the correct words or images. Much like a computer attempting to run a program written in a language the computer does not understand, the message will either get nowhere, or be entirely misinterpreted. Of course, while this may sound like a peculiarly occult insight, it is actually true of *all* forms of communication.

Consider, for instance, the difficulty one has in relating even simple concepts to a child. It is not that the child is an unintelligent creature, but he certainly lacks both the vocabulary and the experience to make sense of your words. We can imagine, then, how difficult it is for an angel to reveal the mysteries of creation to a mere human, a member of an adolescent species at best.

The Australian philosopher Ludwig Wittgenstein said, "The boundaries of my language are the boundaries of my world." What the mind does not comprehend (meaning to "encompass" or "overwhelm"), it cannot contemplate. This is why modern systems of magick—from Neopaganism to the Golden Dawn—place so much stress upon learning pages upon pages (even books upon books!) of magickal correspondences. This is not so different from the teachings of "resonance" (Agrippa), "magnetism" (Barrett), and magickal sympathy given by all of the ancient masters. It is vital to fill the mind with a network of interlinked ideas and magickal images, coupled with the insights, experiences, and revelations that normally accompany the magickal path. With this foundational "Internet" established within the mind, the spiritual beings with whom we communicate will find it possible to relate their teachings. The mage will also find his own comprehension and mastery of the world around him increasing as his mental scope increases. These ideas are resumed beautifully in Robert Heinlein's *Stranger in a Strange Land*. I could not recommend reading this philosophical mythos strongly enough.

So, language is truly a powerful magickal tool. It has allowed the human race to reshape nature—for both good and ill—and has done its part to make us gods upon the earth. It is the root of our understanding of how to "impress our wills" upon our environments. (The concept of conscious will being itself associated with the third circuit and the Logos.) Language was so important and sacred to early man that the business of writing and letters fell strictly within the domain of the priest. Some of the earliest pictograms are so simple that they may have been created for more pragmatic reasons (though it is difficult to say, as even the most holy objects of such eras are also as simple). They are generally nothing more than straightforward line drawings of the objects to which they refer. However, the practice did become quickly sophisticated, and consisted largely of priests communing with their gods to receive sacred symbols and "signatures" (sigils). It is these divinely-inspired characters that form the primordial origins of our own modern alphabets.

If all of this is the case, then we can attribute the bulk of the philosophy of will and the Will within magickal practice to the priestly arts. Conjuration and the use of names of power certainly arise from this (beginning with the shamans, but gaining its ultimate sophistication in the temples). By the time of the grimoires, we find the invocant repeatedly identifying his own will that the will of God, so that the conjurations are read as if it is not the mage but God himself who makes the demands of the entities.[49] (We will return to this concept in later chapters.)

The *Arbatel of Magic* affirms[50] that no character or name of power can hold magical virtue unless such is ordained by God. This strikes me as a survival of the priestly art of receiving letters and signatures. Also, the grimoire tells us, such names can differ from one mage to another (depending on how each receives them[51]), and that the only words of use in magick are those delivered by the entities themselves.[52] However, such names are said to hold power for only about forty years. This makes sense, as the *Arbatel* seems to concern itself with a procession of ages, and the changing of spiritual rulership from one age to the next.

Meanwhile, Agrippa wastes no time in jumping onto the ideas of the third circuit (rationality) and its relation to the Gnostic concept of the Logos. From the *Occult Philosophy* Book I, Chapter 69 (Of speech, and the virtue of words):

> It being showed that there is a great power in the affections of the soul, you must know moreover, that there is no less virtue in words, and the names of things, but greatest of all in speeches, and motions, by which we . . . are called rational from that reason which is according to the voice understood in words, and speech, which is called declarative reason . . . For [Logos] in Greek signifies, reason, speech, and a word. . . . Words therefore are the fittest medium betwixt the speaker and the hearer, carrying with them not only the conception of the mind, but also the virtue of the speaker with a certain efficacy unto the hearers . . ."

In Book III, Chapter 11 (Of the divine names and their power and virtue), Agrippa takes a view somewhat more akin to the *Arbatel*:

> Therefore sacred words have not their power in magical operations, from themselves, as they are words, but from the occult divine powers working by them in the minds of those who by faith adhere to them.

Letter Name	Hebrew	Celestial Writing	Malachim	Passing the River
Aleph	א	𐤀	𐤀	𐤀
Beth	ב	𐤁	𐤁	𐤁
Gimel	ג	𐤂	𐤂	𐤂
Daleth	ד	𐤃	𐤃	𐤃
Heh	ה	𐤄	𐤄	𐤄
Vav	ו	𐤅	𐤅	𐤅
Zain	ז	𐤆	𐤆	𐤆
Cheth	ח	𐤇	𐤇	𐤇
Teth	ט	𐤈	𐤈	𐤈
Yod	י	𐤉	𐤉	𐤉
Kaph	כ	𐤊	𐤊	𐤊
Lamed	ל	𐤋	𐤋	𐤋
Mem	מ	𐤌	𐤌	𐤌
Nun	נ	𐤍	𐤍	𐤍
Samekh	ס	𐤎	𐤎	𐤎
Ayin	ע	𐤏	𐤏	𐤏
Peh	פ	𐤐	𐤐	𐤐
Tzaddi	צ	𐤑	𐤑	𐤑
Qoph	ק	𐤒	𐤒	𐤒
Resh	ר	𐤓	𐤓	𐤓
Shin	ש	𐤔	𐤔	𐤔
Tav	ת	𐤕	𐤕	𐤕

Magickal Alphabets.

Like the *Arbatel*, the words of power only have their effect through the divine powers. However, Agrippa takes this a step further, and suggests (true to his Neoplatonic philosophy) that these divine powers have their effect through the minds and faith of the humans who use them.

This merely scratches the surface of the many things Agrippa has to say on the magickal power of language and names. In Book I, Chapter 70 (Of the virtue of proper names), he describes the miracle of the third circuit mental process. The "natural power" of things, he explains, flow naturally from the object to the senses of the observer. From the senses this natural power—or virtue—is translated into the mind where it is classified (or *named*) and stored for later recall. Then this natural power can be conceived within the mind and expressed by language:

> First [the natural power is] conceived in the mind as it were through certain seeds of things, then by voices or words, as a birth brought forth, and lastly kept in writings. Here magicians say, that proper names of things are certain rays of things, everywhere present at all times, keeping the power of things, as the essence of the thing signified, rules, and is discerned in them, and know the things by them, as by proper, and living images."

In other words, the proper name of any thing contains its essence. That name can be transmitted to other humans, recalled from memory, or even written down for future generations. (Remember that "time binding" is one of the main aspects of the third mental circuit.) The physical matter of the object will eventually pass away, but its name and classification can be retained within human consciousness forever. This is the reasoning behind the ancient Egyptian belief in immortality through the preservation of one's name. This is also how the gods and spirits of our pantheons continue to exist throughout human history.

Sacrifice in Grimoiric Magick

The practice of animal sacrifice has long been held as the prime evidence for the "black" nature of many grimoiric texts. This, again, is due mainly to the propaganda of the medieval Church, which was itself appalled by the grimoiric texts' obvious associations with contemporary and ancient Pagan practices. Between the years of 1456 and 1464, *The Book of All Forbidden Arts* was written by Johannes Hartlieb, who served the duke of Bavaria in Munich. We see therein that one should "Take note of two great evils in this art. The first is that the master must make sacrifice and tribute to the devils, by which he denies God and renders divine honors to the devils, for we should make sacrifices only to God, who created us and redeemed us by his passion."[53] This insistence on the evil nature of sacrifice lives with us to this very day. (See "The Role of the Priest" above.) It is simply the unfortunate result of the misinformed propaganda and fantasies that have surrounded the subject of sacrifice for such a long span of time.

Meanwhile, the grimoiric mages were pretty clear on their intent in sacrificing to the spirits. They very obviously place the human in the role of master (something we will study in depth in later chapters). Plus, the texts support the previously discussed theory that sacrifices nourish, rather than appease spiritual entities. Such practices in the grimoires are very often associated with offering payment to a spirit for services rendered. The grimoiric mage, like the witch, should be no more bound by his Familiar spirits than by his dog or cat. (Much less so, in fact.)[54] I have previously covered the history of animal sacrifice, so all that now remains is to investigate its inclusion in the grimoires, and to perhaps share a bit of my personal theory.

Agrippa discusses this subject in several places, one of the most useful being Book III, Chapter 59 (Of sacrifices and oblations, and their kinds and manners). Here he explains the concept of ritual sacrifice:

> A sacrifice is an oblation which is both holy by offering, and sanctifieth and maketh holy the offerer, unless either irreverence or some other sin be an impediment to him; therefore these sacrifices and obla-

tions do yield us much hope, and make us of the family of God, and do repel from us many evils hanging over our heads . . .

In Book III, Chapter 60, he includes sacrifice in a list of several important devotional considerations:

> . . . by certain sacred mysteries, vows, sacrifices, adorations, invocations, and certain sacred arts, or certain secret confections, by which the spirits of their god did infuse virtue, make the soul to rise above the mind, by joining it with deities and demons.[55]

Agrippa suggests in these passages something very similar to what I explained above: that the practice of sacrifice is intended to make something sacred. In this case, Agrippa goes a step further and makes sacrifice another aspect of ritual purification for the practitioner himself. Offering such sacrifice was certainly intended to empower one's Patrons, oneself, and to open a line of communication between them.

Back in Chapter 59, Agrippa continues with practical instructions that remind me quite a bit of the previously mentioned Torah instructions on sacrifice:

> But there are many kinds of sacrifices: one kind is called a burnt offering, when the thing sacrificed was consumed by fire; another, is an offering of the effusion of blood; moreover there are saluriferous sacrifices which are made for the obtaining of health; others pacifying for obtaining peace; others praising for the freeing from some evil; and for the bestowing of some good thing; others gratulatory, for divine worship and thanksgiving . . .

Agrippa then shifts into sacrifice as it might be understood by the grimoiric mage:

> Now [the ancients] did sacrifice to each star with the things belonging to them; to the Sun with solary things, and its animals, as a luare tree, a cock, a swan, a bull; to Venus with her animals, as a dove, or turtle,[56] and by her plants, as vervain . . .

> Moreover to the celestial and ethereal gods white sacrifices were offered; but to the terrestrial or infernal, black: but to the terrestrial upon the altars, but to the infernal in ditches; to the aerial and watery, flying things: but to these (aerial) white, to those (watery) black.[57] Finally, to all the gods and demons besides terrestrial and infernal, flying things were offered, but to those only four footed animals, for like rejoiceth in like. Of these only which were offered to the celestial and etherial, it is lawful to eat, the extreme parts being reserved for God . . .

In *Forbidden Rites*, Kieckhefer highlights several instances of the sacrifice of a hoopoe bird in grimoiric literature, especially within the *Munich Handbook of Necromancy*. The hoopoe is a reddish colored bird, slightly larger than the American robin, with a fancy crest of feathers on its head, and black and white stripes on its wings and tail. It is native to the warmer regions of Europe, Asia, and Africa. It may perhaps have found a home in the grimoiric literature due to its association with Arabic mythos (see Qur'an 27:20ff), and it appears in several ancient mythologies as a bird associated with gods or the delivering of messages. Kieckhefer offers an extensive bibliography for further study of this particular bird and its association with magick in *Forbidden Rites*, p. 50, footnote 25.

The *Key of Solomon the King* focuses upon sacrifice in the final chapter of the text (Concerning Sacrifices to the Spirits, and How They Should be Made). It begins rather cryptically with the words: "In many operations it is necessary to make some sorts of sacrifice unto the Demons, and in various ways." However, it does not go on to explain what exactly would make such a thing necessary. Apparently it was assumed the reader would be familiar with such information as we have already discussed in this chapter. The rest of the chapter does make it rather clear that the sacrifice is offered to the spirits as payment—even as a kind of bribe—in order to entice them to appear. Greater sacrifices are promised to the spirits if they obey, an idea which I find hard to accept. The Afro-Cuban faiths, as well as such systems as Abramelin, are strictly against using sacrifice (or anything else) as mere appeasement for the spirits, nor allowing them to demand anything of the mage.

The chapter then continues with some interesting practical instruction, some of which might remind us of what we've read from Agrippa above:

> Sometimes white animals are sacrificed to the good Spirits and black to the evil. Such sacrifices consist of the blood and sometimes the flesh. They who sacrifice animals, of whatsoever kind they be, should select those which are virgin, as being more agreeable unto the Spirits, and rendering them more obedient. When blood is to be sacrificed, it should be drawn also from virgin quadrupeds or birds,[58] but before offering the oblation, say:—"May this Sacrifice which we find it proper to offer unto ye, noble and lofty Beings, be agreeable and pleasing unto your desires; be ye ready to obey us, and ye shall receive greater ones." Then perfume and sprinkle it according to the rules of Art.

The *Key* then goes on with a bit of information I find fascinating. It involves the use of specific woods sacred to each planetary force, which should be burned in "Sacrifices of fire." It is unclear whether this means that the wood is burned as an offering itself, or whether the wood is used to make the fire for any burnt offerings. What is fascinating is that the *Key* is a known sourcebook for traditional Wiccan practice, and that tradition recognizes various sacred woods burned in the cauldron during ceremony. (Though Wicca recognizes nine woods, rather than the seven of the *Key*):

> [The Sacrifice of fire] should be made of wood which hath some quality referring especially unto the Spirits involved; as juniper, or pine, unto the Spirits of Saturn; box, or oak, unto those of Jupiter; cornel, or cedar, unto those of Mars; laurel unto those of the Sun; myrtle unto those of Venus; hazel unto those of Mercury; and willow unto those of the Moon.

Finally, the *Key* concludes its instruction with the offering of prepared foods, a method I have used and been pleased with several times. It might remind us somewhat of the Celtic faery feasts, or various meals prepared and offered to ancestors (such as on Allhallows Eve):

> But when we make sacrifices of food and drink, everything necessary should be prepared without the Circle,[59] and the meats should be covered with some fine clean cloth, and have also a clean white cloth spread beneath them;[60] with new bread and good and sparkling wine, but in all things those which refer to the nature of the planet. Animals, such as fowls or pigeons, should be roasted. Especially shouldest thou have a vessel of clear and pure fountain water, and before thou enterest into the Circle, thou shalt summon the Spirits by their proper Names, or at least those chief among them, saying:—

> "In whatsoever place ye may be, ye Spirits, who are invited to this feast, come ye and be ready to receive our offerings, presents, and sacrifices, and ye shall have hereafter yet more agreeable oblations."

> Perfume the viands with sweet incense, and sprinkle them with exorcised water; then commence to conjure the Spirits until they shall come. This is the manner of making sacrifices in all arts and operations wherein it is necessary, and acting thus, the Spirits will be prompt to serve thee.

Kieckhefer's *Forbidden Rites* mentions several examples of the use of milk and honey as offerings to spirits: On page 51, a spell is given to manifest an illusory castle by summoning fifteen spirits who can create such an illusion.

Before reciting the conjuration, one is to "sprinkle" milk and honey into the air. (More than likely, this is intended to sprinkle the area around the circle in order to attract the spirits.) The same procedure is followed again on page 105, where a spell is given for skrying via a magickal mirror. In this case, milk, honey, and wine mixed in equal proportions are sprinkled into the air around the working area before the conjuration is recited.

I once made offerings of milk, honey, and bread on a regular basis to a particular mother goddess. Both the offerings and the devotion required to keep up with the practice seemed to produce outstanding results. Incorporating the same concept into the grimoires—as Kieckhefer illustrates above—can be very beneficial.

Meanwhile, many grimoires seem to focus upon animal sacrifice in an extremely practical fashion, associating it specifically with the making of parchment necessary for the magick. Keep in mind that these books were written during a time when one had to make his own parchment in any case, and therefore the appearance of associated ceremonies in the grimoires come as little surprise. They fall into place right alongside of similar ceremonies surrounding the otherwise mundane preparations of the other tools, inks, garments, burins, wax, etc.

The *Key of Solomon the King* gives us a surprisingly complete example of the creation of parchment. Book II, Chapter 17, is titled "Of Virgin Parchment, or Virgin Paper, and How it Should be Prepared." Nearly every aspect of the procedure has been ritualized: the cutting and fashioning of a knife of reed, the flaying of the animal, the salting and drying of the hide, the removal of excess fur and flesh with lime, etc. The skin is even stretched to dry upon a hazel stick cut under proper conditions, and secured with consecrated stones and a cord spun by a young maiden. The use of prayers and Psalms abound. Unfortunately, there is nothing at all said about any ritual preparation of the animal. It appears that the sacrifice of the animal itself is missed in this chapter.

A better example can be found in a less trustworthy source—the *Grand Grimoire*. Here again we see a procedure intended to result in consecrated parchment, except that now the actual parchment-making process is missing in favor of the ritual sacrifice of the animal:

> The next operation is the purchase of a virgin kid, which must be decapitated on the third day of the moon. Previously to the sacrifice, a garland of vervain must be wound about the neck of the animal, immediately below the head, and secured by means of a green ribbon. The sacrifice must be offered on the scene of the coming evocation, a forlorn and isolated spot free from all interruption. There, with the right arm bared to the shoulder, having armed himself with a blade of fine steel, and having kindled a fire of white wood, the Karcist[61] shall recite the following words in a hopeful and animated manner:

> **Initial Offering:** I immolate this victim to Thee, O grand Adonay, Eloim, Ariel and Jehovam, to the honour, glory and power of Thy Name, which is superior to all Spirits. O grand Adonay! Vouchsafe to receive it as an acceptable offering. Amen.

Here he must cut the throat of the kid, skin it, set the body on the fire and reduce it to ashes, which must be collected and cast towards the rising of the sun, at the same time repeating the following words:

> It is to the honour, glory and dominion of Thy Name, O grand Adonay, Eloim, Ariel, Jehovam that I spill the blood of this victim! Vouchsafe, O Thou grand Adonay, to receive its ashes as an acceptable sacrifice.

While the victim is being consumed by the flames, the operator shall rejoice in the honor and glory of the grand Adonay, Eloim, Ariel and Jehovam, taking care to preserve the skin of the virgin kid to form the round or grand Kabalistic circle, in which he must himself stand on the day of the supreme enterprise.

Later in the operation, one is to use the knife "stained with the blood of the victim" in the cutting and creation of the magickal wand (or "Blasting Rod"). The skin is cut into strips and laid upon the ground in the form of a circle, held in place by four nails. Of course, we do have to keep in mind that the *Grand Grimoire* is not a reliable source for grimoiric material. Instead, it might be a better example of the popular misunderstandings about grimoires, which this text was intended to exploit. We can't know how familiar the author was with the tribal practices of sacrifice, or even if he was familiar at all. The above instructions either show some amount of sophistication (markedly missing from later—more shocking—examples of sacrifice in the same grimoire), or merely a rather productive imagination.

However, this does not bring our discussion of grimoiric sacrifice to an end. In fact, it is a subject that needs to be explored in our own modern context in order to discover its place in a living grimoiric tradition. In the various chapters concerning magickal tools you will find in this book, you might note some call for the use of animal blood. Though none of the examples given will call for actual animal sacrifice, I feel that this is the proper place to discuss the use of blood in ritual overall. I decided against excluding it from this book for the sake of pure scholarship, as I do not wish to edit the grimoiric material I am presenting. It would result in an imperfect view of these tools, removing from them a certain depth. One example would be the black-hilted knife of the *Key of Solomon*, which calls for the blood of a black cat. Cats are common "witches' Familiars" even today, and they have always been surrounded with an air of mystery and power (and eventually even danger). Meanwhile, the black-hilted knife is utilized to strike fear into feral spirits. The inclusion of the life-force of a black feline makes perfect shamanic sense.

Note, however, that only the blood of the animal is necessary, and not the sacrifice of the animal's life. The same is true in most cases of blood magick in the *Key of Solomon the King* and similar grimoires. Regarding this, I take special note of the *Key's* Book II, Chapter 16 (Of the Blood of the Bat, Pigeon, and Other Animals). The text states that this is intended for winged animals only, though I have to admit I can't see anything in the rite that restricts it to creatures of the air. The heading of the chapter does mention two specifically winged species, but then ends with the vague reference to "other animals."

Whatever the extent of its application, the rite does show a preference to obtaining blood without causing undue harm to the animal. It is no more violent than taking a blood sample with a syringe, which latter would be consecrated to the purpose. (We will see in chapter 6 that one consecration is used in the *Key* for any needles or other instruments of iron or steel.) The instructions given use the example of a living bat, which must first be exorcised by the following recitation:

> **Camiach, Eomiahe, Emial, Macbal, Emoii, Zazean, Maiphiat, Zacrath, Tendac, Vulamahi**; by these Most Holy Names, and the other Names of Angels which are written in the Book Assamaian,[62] I conjure thee O Bat (or whatever animal it may be) that thou assist me in this operation, by God the True, God the Holy, the God Who hath created thee, and by Adam, Who hath imposed thy true name upon thee and upon all other animated beings.

At this point, the *Key* instructs one to draw the blood with the consecrated needle. Then, to repeat the following blessing over the collected fluid:

> Almighty **Adonai, Arathron, Ashai, Elohim, Elohi, Elion, Asher Eheieh, Shaddai**, O God the Lord, immaculate, immutable, **Emanuel, Messiach, Yod He Vau He**, be my aid, so that this blood may have power and efficacy in all wherein I shall wish, and in all that I shall demand.

This is then perfumed and kept for use. What exactly those uses are to be is not stated by the *Key*, nor is it specifically called for elsewhere in the text. It does appear directly following the chapters on pens and inks, and directly proceeding the chapter on parchment making. Therefore, I would assume its intent is mainly toward use an ingredient of ink. (In chapter 9, we will discuss the making of "lampblack" ink, which uses gum-arabic as a thickener. I would assume that such blood as gathered by the above method would have been used by the medieval mage in place of gum arabic.)

Of course, we also have to consider modern issues. Even if the true nature of sacrifice and the ritual use of blood is understood, there are still those of us who do not wish to make use of such methods. Such decisions would have to be strictly between yourself and your angelic guides. Fortunately, there are alternative options that do not necessarily disrupt the "spirit" of the magickal tools.

One novel option is the use of seawater in place of blood. I became aware of this idea relatively recently, and found it intriguing enough for further research. Apparently, mammalian lymph and blood plasma possess the same basic mineral composition as seawater. This discovery is credited to the biologist Rene Quinton, who published his findings in 1904 under the title *L'eau De Mer, Milieu Organique* (Sea Water: Organic Medium). This was done after he had performed several years of experimentation in hospital with three doctors named Potocki, Mace, and Jarricot.

Quinton was working with what he called "the vital medium," and what we now call "interstitial fluid." This is a liquid within which all of our living cells (and thus our entire bodies) live, and it is of *marine origin*. Therefore, your flesh and blood are, in essence, one and the same with seawater. We (along with most or all of the life on this planet) originally arose from Mother Sea.

During his years of experimentation, Quinton developed a serum which has come to be called "Quinton Plasma." It is derived from purified and cold-sterilized sea water, and apparently aids in cellular detoxification, nutrition, and regeneration. This serum is credited with saving the lives of several thousands of children in France and Egypt in the early twentieth century.

Unfortunately, World War I in Europe greatly hindered Quinton's research, and he died in 1925. The research was not picked up again until the 1980s by French doctors and therapists. The techniques have come into much more common use today. (This reminds me of a trip I once made to donate plasma. Once the plasma had been collected, I was then injected with a saline solution [basically salt-water] to return my blood pressure to normal. Perhaps I was seeing one small example of Quinton's work.)

So, it seems the theory of the ritual use of sea water in place of blood has merit. We might consider it as a "general substitute" for any called-for blood, much as we consider a white candle suitable for any other color. It also gives an incredible depth to the meaning of holy water (which is salted). Although, if used as a replacement for blood, I would strongly suggest one obtain natural sea water; especially if one personally journeys to the sea to collect it.

Another fascinating idea for non-violent ritual sacrifice is one I've drawn from certain practices within Santeria. One of the faith's most vital magickal ceremonies is a kind of "rite of birth" intended to allow a god or Orisha to inhabit a physical object. In order to accomplish this miracle, the sacred object must be washed in a very specific kind of holy water called *Omiero*. It is a mixture of water (which Santeria also understands as the basic component of organic life) and the nectar/juices of various plants considered sacred to the Orisha in question.

A Santero who wishes to create Omiero will first gather large amounts of the necessary fresh plants, and then run a trickle of simple tapwater into a bucket or bathtub. While singing shamanic songs of invocation, the Santero will hold the plant material beneath the running water and tear it over and over again. The resulting liquid collected in the tub should be green, the more opaque the better. This water is considered more powerful than blood.

I have heard of completely vegetarian paths within Santeria that have replaced all blood sacrifice with plant sacrifice, but I have yet to discover many details. I would assume the procedures are somewhat similar to the creation of Omiero. In any case, I see no reason why these principals could not be adopted into the grimoiric (or other magickal) traditions. We only need to know which plants are sacred to any given spiritual force, and the ever-shamanic grimoires are happy to provide such information.

We already know from the *Key of Solomon* which trees are acceptable for each planetary force. At the same time, we can reference Agrippa's Book I, Chapters 23–29. The leading chapter of this group begins with the title: "How we shall know what stars natural things are under . . ." and suggests:

> Now it is very hard to know, what star, or sign everything is under: yet it is known through the imitation of their rays, or motion, or figure of the superiors. Also some of them are known by their colours and odours, also some by the effects of their operations, answering to some stars.

In other words, the entire practice is somewhat intuitive, and depends upon magickal sympathy. Luckily, Agrippa does go on to offer several examples for each planet to get us started. He covers many areas, from plants and animals, to stone and metals, etc. Most of the plants are repeated here:[63]

Sol: marigold; flowers that close at night; lotus tree; balm; ginger; gentian; dittany; vervain; bay tree; cedar; palm tree; ash; ivy; mint; mastic; saffron; balsam; amber; etc

Luna: palm tree; hyssop; rosemary; agnus cactus, olive tree.

Saturn: dragonwort; rue; cummin; black hellebore*; styrax benzoin; mandrake*; poppy or any other narcotic plant*; weeds that bear no fruit; plants with dark berries; black fruit such as black fig tree, pine, cypress, and perhaps yew or hemlock.*

Jupiter: sengreen; garden basil; mace; french lavender; mints; mastic; *inula helenium*; violet; henbane*; poplar tree; oak or chestnut oak; holly; beech; hazel; white fig; pear, apple, and plum trees; corn, raisons, licorice, almond, etc.

Mars: hellebore*; garlic; radish; laurel; wolfsbane and all poisonous plants*;[64] all plants that prick, burn, or injure the skin such as nettle, etc;[65] onions; scallions; leeks; mustard seed; dog tree.

Venus: vervain; violet; maidenhair; valerian; thyme; gum ladanum; ambergris; msuk; sanders; coriander; all sweet perfumes; all delightful fruits such as pears, figs, and pomegranates; rose and myrtle.

Mercury: hazel; cinquefoil; herb mercury*; fumatory; pimpernel; marjoram; parsley; and any plant with few and short leaves that are compounded of mixed natures and diverse colors.

Later, in Book I, Chapter 44, Agrippa gives us various plants associated with the planets for the purpose of making incense. A few of them are listed here:

Sol: saffron; ambergris; fruit of the laurel (*Laurus nobilis*); clove; and all gum plants.[66]

Luna: white poppy; camphor laurel; frankincense tree; leaves of all vegetables; the leaf indum; myrtle; and bay tree.

Saturn: black poppy; root of mandrake*; all odoriferous roots such as pepperwort root and frankincense tree.

Jupiter: ash (*Fraxinus excelsior*); benjamin; and all odiferous fruits such as nutmegs, cloves.

Mars: All odoriferous woods such as cypress, sanders, lignum aloes, lignum balsam, etc; hellebore root*; bdellium.

Venus: ambergris; lignum-aloes; red roses; all flowers such as violets and saffron.

Mercury: frankincense; cloves; the herb cinquefoil; the peels of wood and fruit, such as cinnamon, cassia bark.

I admit this second list is taking Agrippa's correspondences somewhat out of context. I do this with the assumption that the plants used in the perfumes are themselves sacred to the planet. I was once given advice from a practitioner of Santeria to use only the freshest plants in my incense, because they still retained more of the living spirits of the plants themselves. (This makes the use of perfume in ceremony a form of sacrifice as well, offering plants by fire.[67]) Our prophets from chapter 3 heaped live plants upon the fire in their tent of meeting, and evoked their god therefrom.

Once the proper "planetary" plants are obtained fresh (or, better, the mage might raise them himself), they can be easily converted into a kind of "Solomonic Omiero." For instance, one might wish to make an offering to the forces of Sol, and would thus gather as many Solary plants as possible.[68] Perhaps six different kinds would be best, to reflect the sacred number of the Sun. The experienced witch or herbalist might even know exactly which Solary plants contain the best virtues for the spell, while the student can easily consult herbal reference manuals, both medicinal and magickal. (Many of the books by Scott Cunningham—a witch and herbalist—make useful reference material, and can greatly expand upon the given lists above.)

Proceed to rip and tear the fresh plants beneath running water, and collect the greenish liquid in a large container. While doing this, one should use his knowledge of Psalmody to sing the Psalms that will attract the proper divine attention. This is hardly the whole mystery of Santerian Omiero, but it is certainly a start for a young modern grimoiric tradition.

Candles are also important to sacred offerings. Wax is considered an acceptable offering when burned in candle form, and it is best to use fresh bee's wax. (See chapter 6 for instructions on Solomonic candles.) Besides this, any candle of an appropriate planetary color can be offered upon one's altar. Seven-day candles are in regular use as offerings in the Afro-Cuban faiths today. Later on, in chapter 8, we will encounter the use of candles as sacrifice once again.

Overall, there are many things that might be utilized for sacrifice and offering, so long as they are considered sacred to (or, are in sympathy with) the entity one is attempting to evoke. Agrippa's Book I, Chapters 23–39 are great sources for various things to offer upon altars. Finally, prayers and adorations were also considered a kind of sacrifice in the grimoiric tradition, as Agrippa outlines in his Book III—a sacrifice of one's own soul. (Of course, this is an aspect of the Devotional Arts). We will return to prayers and various invocations in chapter seven of this book.

Of course, these cases are merely half the story, and cults to goddesses existed side by side with the god-cults from prehistoric times. In fact, the Scythians, who we met earlier, did not leave behind a single example of a god in their religious art. Instead, their goddess appears to have been their major devotional focus. As is common in ancient Paganism, the father god is far away, while the mother goddess resides with us on earth.

---

1. Of course, these cases are only half the story, and cults to Goddesses existed side by side with the God cults from ancient times. For example, the Sythians, who we met earlier, did not leave behind a single example a God in their religious art. Instead, their Goddess appears to have been their major devotional focus. As is common in ancient Paganism, the Father God is far away, while the Mother Goddess resides with us on Earth.

2. Pronounced [yah]. Often transliterated "Ia" or "Ea." Ea (also called Nudimmud) was father of the patron deity of Babylon, Marduk.

3. "Hallelu-jah" = "Praise Yah," or "Praise God".

4. Mythological as that may be.

5. Once again a reference to Gnosticism in general.

6. "Thou shalt have no other gods before me" (Exodus 20:3—the first commandment).

7. Also see below for more information on ancestors and their role in magickal procedure.

8. Note that "heaven" literally translates as "high place."

9. The natural object itself would then be known as sacred to that particular spirit.

10. This is something done to this day in religions that recognize ancestral spirits, and we preserve echoes of the practice at Samhain (Halloween). Note "The Feast of All Saints."

11. Thus the wide selection of "tools" gifted to the entity.

12. Note that the root of "Familiar" is "family."

13. Horus was the son of Osiris, and thus always stood as the rightful heir to the kingdom his father founded.

14. Also note that the "father god" far predates the "national god."

15. Note that there are twelve members in a modern jury; one juror for each sign of the zodiac. Theoretically, each juror should be of a different birth sign, so that cases are judged from all twelve personality perspectives. More than likely, this descends directly from Babylon, where the king would have wanted the same balance from his cabinet of advisors (or "wisemen"—wizards).

16. Again, see the first chapter of Ezekiel, and the fourth chapter of the Revelation of St. John.

17. In addition to recording all of the secrets of God in his great book, Raziel is said to stretch out his wings to buffer the fiery breath of the Chaioth haQodesh, else it would consume the whole of creation in divine fire. Likewise, the sweat of the Chaioth haQodesh (induced by the effort of uplifting the Merkavah) pools under the Throne and runs forth into the heavens as the sacred river of fire called Nahar.

18. For instance, the *Key of Solomon*, p. 16, contains the following: "The First Disciple will bear the Censer, the Perfumes and the Spices; the Second Disciple will bear the Book, Papers, Pens, Ink, and any stinking or impure materials; the Third will carry the Knife and the Sickle of Magical Art, the Lantern, and the Candles; the Fourth, the Psalms, and the rest of the Instruments; the Fifth, the Crucible or Chafing-dish, and the Charcoal or Fuel . . ."

19. The same rift, in fact, said to have been caused by the "first shaman" in ancient mythologies of paradise lost.

20. *The Key of Solomon the King*, Book II, Chapter 22, preserves a similar direction, instructing the sacrifice of white animals for "good spirits" and black animals for "evil spirits."

21. Refer to chapter 3, where the effects of sexual deprivation are discussed from a magickal standpoint.

22. I should point out that both of these concepts were also historically caught up in the fact of sickness and disease. These things were considered to be attacks by evil spirits, who were themselves dispatched by angry gods. To expel the demons, the priest had to appease the gods. The "sin" involved the action that led to sickness (such as touching a dead body), and the "atonement" was the prescribed cure.

23. This statement does not include such concepts as invoking the deity into a human vessel—such as the Wiccan "Drawing Down the Moon" and "Great Rite." Nor does it include as aspirant being "ridden" (possessed) by the deity—such as occurs in Santeria.

24. Found in *"Conjuring Spirits"*, p. 251.

25. At least, not in the modern Western Hermetic sense.

26. Emphasis mine.

27. Emphasis mine.

28. And not merely *Abramelin*. Even established traditions of worship recognize the reception of information and instructions directly from god, the gods, etc.

29. See chapter 2.

30. See chapter 12.

31. *The Key of Solomon the King*, Book I, Chapter 4. Emphasis on "exorcist" is mine.

32. In both prayers and exorcisms, this resulted in long lists of names and titles that had to be read during the rites. This would seem to be a trend that extended into the Greek literature, and finally into the grimoires themselves as the "Barbarous Names of Invocation."

33. See *The Devils and Evil Spirits of Babylonia* by R. C. Thompson.

34. The full line here is ". . . uttered to the priest in confession." However, unless it is specifically called for in a text, one does not need be concerned with ordained priests. The art of confession itself is the focus here.

35. There are similarities in this prayer to older Sumerian-Babylonian exorcisms. See chapter 12 for more information.

36. See below, and in chapter 7.

37. In chapter 2 I mentioned that Eliade, in *Shamanism*, points out that the first magickal languages among shamans were likely the songs of birds.

38. Note the *Song of Solomon*.

39. The reader might remember this cloud from chapter 3.

40. This Davidic book within the Book of Psalms seems to have caught the attention of medieval wizards, such as the author of *The Book of Abramelin* and possibly the Jewish and Christian speculations upon the *Shem haMephoresh* (the seventy-two-fold name of God).

41. Later we will encounter this word again in relation to magickal squares.

42. I.e., Canaanite or Israelite.

43. Israel: literally "sons of El"

44. *The Legends of Genesis: The Biblical Saga and History* (1901).

45. This is also Canaanite imagery. Baal was said to live atop a sacred mountain, where he sent life-giving rains from his sanctuary. **Baal** was generally worshiped atop high places. Later, Yahweh was associated with Sinai and Zion in the same fashion—as this Psalm illustrates.

46. A. J. Rose's example, as posted to a private literary-industry mailing list. Paraphrased from his *C.'.G.'. Student Handbook: Mysticism, Magick, Thelema.*

47. Which is an understanding of both "self-awareness" and communication with others. It may be that the two go hand in hand with one another.

48. I do not include iconography, magickal images, and other talismanic imaging in this statement.

49. *Forbidden Rites*, p. 143.

50. *Book of Ceremonial Magic*, p. 43.

51. And thus explaining the differences in sacred names from grimoire to grimoire. Historically, this is more than likely due to oral transmission of the material.

52. There are certainly some exceptions, such as the practice of gematria.

53. *Forbidden Rites*, p. 33.

54. Reference *Forbidden Rites*, pp. 157, 121.

55. *Daemons* (intelligences).

56. The turtledove.

57. We will see below that the *Key of Solomon the King* makes this same distinction between white and black animals.

58. In Santeria and Palo Mayombe, birds are the most commonly offered. Quadrupeds (goats, etc.) are associated with "holocaust"—meaning that they are extremely powerful (and related in many ways to Elemental Fire), and are only used in times of great need.

59. That is, "outside the Circle."

60. Since no color is suggested for the cloth covering, we might assume it should be the color appropriate to the planet.

61. The *Grand Grimoire's* odd name for the operator.

62. Mathers suggests this is the Hebrew *Sepher haShamaim*, or Book of the Heavens.

63. Any plant marked with an "*" contains lethal neurotoxins. See chapter 3.

64. Interestingly, Agrippa suggests that poisonous plants are deadly due to too much "heat." Perhaps this is another manifestation of the heat we discussed in chapter 3.

65. Though it would be rather difficult to use such for any kind of Omiero.

66. Plants from which gum resins are obtained for such perfumes as frankincense.

67. The subject of incense offered to spiritual entities in the grimoires will be covered in chapter 6.

68. These could be gathered on the day and hours of Mercury. Or, if one wanted to choose a time specific to the planet, during the day and hours of (in our example) Sol.

PART TWO

Oculta
Practique

Magickal Timing

The subject of magickal timing is often surrounded by controversy. Debates on whether or not such a thing is useful to the modern mage are easy enough to find; yet there is precious little to explain the philosophies behind the practice. As with the rest of the grimoiric traditions, the information is scattered and often obscure. Agrippa discusses the subject at some length, the *Key of Solomon the King* explains its version, *The Magus* has some fairly sophisticated systems of its own, and even the author of *The Book of Abramelin* pulls out a soapbox on the issue.

In the context of modern traditions (i.e., post-Victorian era), magickal timing is a secondary concern. The reason for this actually seems to be a technical one: the use of invocation. Students of these modern paths follow an intensive course of study involving the various magickal forces (especially the spheres of the Tree of Life and the four philosophical Elements) and specific hierarchies of gods and angels to be called for all purposes. Add to this the proper pentagram and hexagram rituals, and all of the occult forces of the universe are placed into the hands of the mage. If one wishes to work with the forces of the Sun, one merely has to apply the hexagram ritual of Sol, and to call upon the hierarchy of Tiphareth. Magickal timing can fall away as a superfluous concern. What hour of the day or night it happens to be—or what sign the Sun has entered—simply makes little difference; and this is borne out by practical experiment. As always, I urge the student to try it out and record the results for him or herself.

Once we turn to the grimoiric traditions, however, the rules change a bit. Invocation of the type seen in the pentagram and hexagram rituals is glaringly absent. Instead, invocation takes the form of prayers and supplications to the transcendent deity, orders of angels, and the "Second Causes" (the gods).[1] They tend to be more all-encompassing in their scope, as if the purpose was to invoke pure divine brilliance rather than the colored force of a single sphere. Take for instance this invocation from the *Key of Solomon the King*, Book I, Chapter 3:[2]

> When we enter herein with all humility, let God the Almighty One enter into this Circle, by the entrance of an eternal happiness, of a Divine prosperity, of a perfect joy, of an abundant charity, and of an eternal salutation. Let all the demons fly from this place, especially those who are opposed to this work, and let the Angels of Peace assist and protect this Circle, from which let discord and strife fly and depart.

Magnify and extend upon us, O Lord, Thy most Holy Name, and bless our conversation and our assembly. Sanctify, O Lord our God, our humble entry herein, Thou the Blessed and Holy One of the Eternal Ages! Amen.

Having enflamed oneself with the above prayer, one might work with any spiritual entity one chooses. What such an invocation does not achieve, however, is focus upon a particular force. In order to perform a refined operation (such as a talisman enlivening) it is still necessary to have the correct hierarchy of spiritual entities present.

Medieval magick achieved this through prayer and supplication, along with an observance of magickal timing. It is another shamanic aspect of the system, depending on the natural tides of the earthly and astral planes for its effect. Remember that the medieval wizard viewed spiritual entities as literal and objective beings, with their own specific times of rule and action. This was based in large part upon the motions of the stars, as these were seen as the physical bodies of the intelligences. Thus, it had to be determined which beings were operative at any given time in order to know whom to call upon. There was no need to perform gate-opening operations such as the pentagram or hexagram rituals to call them from ethereal their homes to the earth plane. Instead, one merely waited to perform the rites when the entities came to earth of their own accord. Then, it was only necessary to invoke divine power, name the angels in question, and continue with the work. If the other formulas of the rite were followed correctly, success was assured.

However, I do feel it is important to point out that magickal timing was not an absolute in the grimoiric traditions. Such particular timing is extremely useful to the magick, allowing the mage to surf along with the natural currents of the world around him. On the other hand, the master mage could also work from experience and intuition. Even the *Key of Solomon the King* (Book II, Chapter 1) finds it necessary to stress this point:

> So exact a preparation of days and hours is not necessary for those who are adepts in the Art, but it is extremely necessary for apprentices and beginners, seeing that those who have been little or not at all instructed herein, and who only begin to apply themselves to this Art, do not have as much faith in the experiments as those who are adepts therein, and who have practiced them. But as regards beginners, they should always have the days and hours well disposed and appropriate to the Art. And the Wise should only observe the precepts of the Art which are necessary, and in observing the other solemnities necessary they will operate with a perfect assurance.

There do exist differing ideas on how magickal time should be calculated; namely those of days, hours, and elective astrology. In this chapter, we will focus upon each of these considerations.

Magickal Days

There are various types of magickal days, from the annual holy day to the shamanic observance of seasons to the days of the week. Most magickally significant days are based on astronomical events, such as the equinoxes and solstices, while others possess a mythological significance. The observance of these times does possess great power; as even the average man on the street is familiar with many of them. The American population regularly observes Christmas, Easter, the Fourth of July, etc. Wiccans recognize eight specific holy days based upon the motions of the sun and the cycles of the crops, along with the monthly esbats based upon the course of the Moon. Christianity sets aside Sunday as being mythologically important, while the Judaic faith sets aside Saturday for the same reason. The list, of course, is nearly infinite.

By timing our own rites to these days, we are literally tapping into the collective consciousness of our society. It is true that miracles happen during the Christmas season. Not only is this the time of year during which the Sun is reborn and the days begin to grow longer, but it is also a time in which thousands of people are focusing their spiritual intent. We, as occultists, often enjoy placing the "new year" before the fall of winter, or in the spring when the sun moves into Aries. However, there is no denying the very real change that can be felt from the beginning of the Christmas season to the dawning of New Year's Day. This is a common time for prosperity magick, healing, and any operation of goodwill.

The other holidays can be observed in just the same manner. The Fourth of July (at least in America) is a perfect time for rites of justice, warfare, independence, freedom, and the like. Thanksgiving offers another perfect time for prosperity magick, abundance, friendship, and alliances. Valentine's Day, of course, is a time for magick concerning love and emotions. Easter (or Ostara), the spring equinox, grants us much force in fertility and initiation rites. Halloween brings large focus upon rites of death, ancestors, personal sacrifice, etc. The days of Saturday or Sunday are always perfect for healing and spiritual growth.[3]

This also holds true for the nonmainstream holidays. Wicca, in particular, puts a large focus on practical magick for the monthly esbats and sometimes the eight sabbats. Judaism is replete with traditional ritual procedures and prayers for specific times of the week and year. Even the mainstream American holidays—which have so long suffered at the hands of commercialism—are still overflowing with rites and traditions that extend backward far into history. Families form their own traditions in many cases, while others are cultural. An attempt to outline all of this, from only a few of the world's religions, would occupy many volumes of space. Therefore, I leave it to the reader to determine which days are useful for which purposes, from the standpoint of his own culture and/or religion.

Another interesting method of working with magickal days and times is outlined in Frances Barrett's *The Magus* (which it quotes from the *Fourth Book of Occult Philosophy*). In this system, all days, hours, seasons, and even the Sun and Moon are given different occult names for different times.[4] This is yet another example of the pantheistic/polytheistic medieval worldview wherein all things, even the hours of the day and seasons of the year, are living creatures (or have such creatures associated with them). There is no need for detailed invocation ceremonies, as long as the names are written and/or called.

In the grimoiric tradition in general, each day of the week has significance in its own right. This is an aspect of the biblical nature of the systems, where the seven planets and their respective days are related to the first chapter of Genesis and the seven days of creation. Therefore, they are observed in order to mimic the creative process initiated by the Demiurgos.[5] Add to this the occult attributes of each planet as understood by astrologists, and a fairly complete system of magickal correspondence and timing is formed. If one wishes to work with any particular occult force, one needs only approach it on the proper day.

Our weekly days have always been associated with the seven ancient planets. Sunday, of course, relates to the Sun, and Monday to the Moon. Tuesday is related to Mars, for which Don Kraig (*Modern Magick*, page 343) relates a European Martian deity named "Tues." We derive Wednesday from the term "Woden's Day," and it has its relation to Mercury through the French name *mercredi*. Thursday is, in fact, "Thor's Day," and this Norse god of storm relates to his Roman counterpart Jupiter to give us the planet. Friday is "Freya's Day," named for a Norse Venusian goddess. Finally, Saturday takes its name from the remaining planet, Saturn.

Below I have included a simple list of the days, their planets, and what aspects of creative reality are attributed to each. I have also included the names of the ruling archangels of each day and planet. (See the biblical book of Revelation, Chapter 4. These are the seven "Lights" surrounding the throne, and are said to be the seven archangels who attend upon the divine throne.) These are only suggestive lists for study, and the practicing mage should not feel restricted by them. With study and practice, it will eventually become second nature to assign any given situation, object, or idea to its proper ruling planet without any need to refer to such lists.

☉ Sol and Sunday

The Sun is the Lord and Judge of the world. It is, in effect, God from our earthly vantage point—being itself a window to the divine realm. In this aspect, it is the planet most associated with the element of Spirit. It is also closely related to Fire as the god-force and fiery force of life. The Sun rules: Judgment, Exorcism, Court Cases, Ascension, Purification, Initiation and Trial-by-Fire, Healing, Compassion, Majesty, Growth, Spirit and Life Force, Strength, Power, Wisdom, Force, Rulership, Happiness. Also see Agrippa's *Three Books,* Book I, Chapter 23. The archangel of the Sun and the Fourth Heaven is Michael.

☽ Luna and Monday

The Moon is often seen as the Wife of the Sun, and can be seen as embodying the Goddess. It is thus related very closely to the element of Water, and governs the astral plane. It represents all things balanced and cyclic. She is especially invoked in matters of magick. The Moon rules: Emotions, Instincts, the Unconscious, Intuition, Personality, Infancy, Childhood, Motherhood, Dreams, Visions, Memory, the Past, Spiritual Knowledge, Magick, Astral Travel. Also see Agrippa's *Three Books,* Book I, Chapter 24. The archangel of Luna and the First Heaven is Gabriel.

♂ Mars and Tuesday

Mars is the fiery planet of warfare, and is often seen as the husband of Saturn. It is associated with gods of war as well as famine and plague (which themselves are often associated with war).[6] Putting it in a more proper medieval context, it is the planet of the *passions* of war, strife, and the rule of an iron fist. Therefore, it is related to the Element of Fire. It happens to be considered unfortunate in astrological terms. Its influence in a horoscope was avoided second only to Saturn itself. Mars governs: Forcefulness, Aggression, Boldness, Competition (especially Conflict), Ambition, Courage, Strength, Endurance, Strife, Tension, Anger, Accidents, Destruction, Heat, Fire, Earthquakes, Violence, War, Unleashed Energy. Also see Agrippa's *Three Books,* Book I, Chapter 27. The archangel of Mars and the Fifth Heaven is Camael.

☿ Mercury and Wednesday

Mercury is the messenger of the gods. It is associated with Thoth, Hermes, and other related beings of wisdom, invention, words, and communication. It is the source of logic, science, and magick. It is neither male nor female—usually represented by the hermaphrodite. It is most closely associated with the Element of Air, which is also a force of intellect. Mercury rules: Intelligence, Speed, Agility, Skill, Dexterity, Cleverness, Speech, Music (as in writing music and musical theory), Math, Astronomy, Cunning, Communication, Intellectual Energy, Perception, Reason, Memory, Speaking, Writing, Ceremony, Words of Power, Travel, Transportation, Education, Research. Also see Agrippa's *Three Books,* Book I, Chapter 29. The archangel of Mercury and the Second Heaven is Raphael.

♃ Jupiter and Thursday

Jupiter is the royal planet, ruling the heavens second only to the Sun. It is the polar opposite of Mars, representing the reign of benevolence and wisdom. It has been associated with such gods as El, Zeus, Odin, and other godly kings. Its principal Element is Water, and it directly concerns abundance of crops and good fortune. Jupiter rules: Joy, Expansiveness, Abundance, Honor, Good Faith, Wisdom, Luck, Health, Happiness, Wealth, Worldly Goods, Power, High Position, Knowledge, Higher Learning, Honesty, Philosophy, Success in Business, Blessings. Also see Agrippa's *Three Books,* Book I, Chapter 26. The archangel of Jupiter and the Sixth Heaven is Sachiel.

♀ Venus and Friday

Venus is the force of passion and sex. It is associated with such goddesses as Aphrodite, Ishtar, Inanna, and Astarte. You may take note that most of these goddesses are not only goddesses of love, but also of war. It is important to understand that the ancients saw no difference between the passions of love and war. Passion is passion, regardless of what you direct that passion toward. Venus itself is the polar opposite of Mercury—representing right-brained functions such as imagination and inspiration. It is closely related to the force of Fire, which also governs sex, lust, war, inspiration, etc. Venus rules: Love and Pleasure, Inspiration, Affection, Beauty, Desirability and Sex Appeal, Seduction, Love Affairs, Art, Beauty, Adornment, Decoration, Social Graces, Harmony, Friendship, Emotions, Happiness. Also see Agrippa's *Three Books,* Book I, Chapter 28. The archangel of Venus and the Third Heaven is Anael.

♄ Saturn and Saturday

Saturn is the slowest planet in the heavens, taking the longest to move across the sky. This is because it is the furthest away of the seven ancient planets, nearest the abyss of outer space. Saturn is the lord of the underworld and of the ages of time, and has been embodied by such gods as Chronos, Maveth, and Hades. Because of these aspects of its essence, it is associated with the Element of Earth. Saturn rules: Responsibility, Work Ethic, Strength Through Trial, Solved Problems (while Mercury rules problems yet to be solved), Time, Discipline, Diligence, Self Control, Limitation, Patience, Stability, Maturity, Realism, Reliability, Trustworthiness, Patience, Courage, Steadfastness, Integrity, Destiny, Fate. Also see Agrippa's *Three Books,* Book I, Chapter 25. The archangel of Saturn and the Seventh Heaven is Cassiel.

Magickal Hours

According to A. E. Waite,[7] the system of magickal hours we will discuss here originates with the *Key of Solomon the King,* though I personally suspect a somewhat earlier origin. It can be said, however, that the *Key* served as the principal source for the system in the bulk of the medieval grimoiric tradition. The tables of magickal hours appear to be an attempt at a systematic, and Qabalistic, attribution of planetary and angelic influence for each hour of the day and night. As I explained above, it is important to medieval magickal systems to know which entities are governing at any given time. Thus, it is common to find grimoiric operations prescribed for the "day and hour" of a planet, calling upon its ruling angel. On the same day, the other six angels are subordinate to the ruling angel.

Each day begins with the governance of the angel of that day. Thus, Sunday dawns under the wings of Michael. Michael then allows his fellows to corule the day, one angel per hour, in succession. The ordering follows from the furthest planet in our solar system (Saturn) to the closest (Luna),[8] or from the highest heaven to the lowest. This is also the attribution (known as the Chaldean ordering of planets) with which we are familiar from our modern version of the Qabalistic Tree of Life: Saturn, Jupiter, Mars, Sol, Venus, Mercury, and finally Luna. Therefore, at the second hour of Sunday, Michael will step aside to allow Anael to rule, followed in turn by Raphael, Gabriel, Cassiel, Sachiel, Camael, and then Michael again. This succession continues until all twenty-four hours have been covered—twelve hours for the day, and twelve for the night. Of course, Michael is in overall authority throughout the day of Sunday, but the seats of his power rest principally upon his natural hours. For easy reference, I provide the following list:

Hours of the Day (Sunrise to Sunset)

	Sunday	Monday	Tuesday	Wednesday	Thursday	Friday	Saturday
1	Sol	Luna	Mars	Mercury	Jupiter	Venus	Saturn
2	Venus	Saturn	Sol	Luna	Mars	Mercury	Jupiter
3	Mercury	Jupiter	Venus	Saturn	Sol	Luna	Mars
4	Luna	Mars	Mercury	Jupiter	Venus	Saturn	Sol
5	Saturn	Sol	Luna	Mars	Mercury	Jupiter	Venus
6	Jupiter	Venus	Saturn	Sol	Luna	Mars	Mercury
7	Mars	Mercury	Jupiter	Venus	Saturn	Sol	Luna
8	Sol	Luna	Mars	Mercury	Jupiter	Venus	Saturn
9	Venus	Saturn	Sol	Luna	Mars	Mercury	Jupiter
10	Mercury	Jupiter	Venus	Saturn	Sol	Luna	Mars
11	Luna	Mars	Mercury	Jupiter	Venus	Saturn	Sol
12	Saturn	Sol	Luna	Mars	Mercury	Jupiter	Venus

Hours of the Night (Sunset to Sunrise)

	Sunday	Monday	Tuesday	Wednesday	Thursday	Friday	Saturday
1	Jupiter	Venus	Saturn	Sol	Luna	Mars	Mercury
2	Mars	Mercury	Jupiter	Venus	Saturn	Sol	Luna
3	Sol	Luna	Mars	Mercury	Jupiter	Venus	Saturn
4	Venus	Saturn	Sol	Luna	Mars	Mercury	Jupiter
5	Mercury	Jupiter	Venus	Saturn	Sol	Luna	Mars
6	Luna	Mars	Mercury	Jupiter	Venus	Saturn	Sol
7	Saturn	Sol	Luna	Mars	Mercury	Jupiter	Venus
8	Jupiter	Venus	Saturn	Sol	Luna	Mars	Mercury
9	Mars	Mercury	Jupiter	Venus	Saturn	Sol	Luna
10	Sol	Luna	Mars	Mercury	Jupiter	Venus	Saturn
11	Venus	Saturn	Sol	Luna	Mars	Mercury	Jupiter
12	Mercury	Jupiter	Venus	Saturn	Sol	Luna	Mars

This method works mathematically, and, presumably, this is the very basis of the rationalization. Note that Sunday begins with Sol and ends on the twenty-fourth hour with Mercury. Monday, then, begins with Luna which properly follows Mercury in succession. The pattern never breaks down, which means that this system does indeed have magickal significance.

Magickal hours are set apart from everyday clock hours by the fact that they are not usually sixty minutes long. Due to the yearly waxing and waning of the Sun, the length of the day and night will vary throughout the year. Only on the equinoxes—the two days each year when the day and night are of equal length—are the hours sixty minutes long. On any other day, all attempts to divide the day or night into twelve equal parts will take mathematical calculation. On the winter solstice (the shortest day of the year) we would have incredibly short daytime hours, and incredibly long nighttime hours. The reverse will be true on the summer solstice. This kind of calculation is thus more in line with the natural tides of the days, and is the basis of magickal hours.

Calculating Magickal Hours

To calculate magickal hours, you must first determine both sunrise and sunset (for day hours), or sunset and then sunrise of the following day (for night hours). You can consult a newspaper, or an almanac, or make use of the world wide web.[9] Once these times have been found, you need only calculate the number of minutes for the entire day or night, and divide by twelve. The result is the length of the magickal hour.

For instance, on the day of Wednesday, May 9, 2001, the Sun is scheduled to rise at 0544 (5:44 am) and to set at 1909 (7:09 pm). We can simplify our calculations greatly if we first set aside the 16 minutes between 5:44 and 6:00, as well as the 9 minutes from 7:00 to 7:09. Write them down (16, 9) off to the side, as we will get back to them later.

We can now simply calculate our time from 6:00 am to 7:00 pm—a total of 13 hours. There are sixty minutes in each clock hour, so 13 times 60 results in 780 minutes. Now it is necessary to return to the minutes (16, 9) we set aside before. Adding them together results in 25, which must be added to the 780 minutes for a grand total of 805 minutes for the entire day.

Finally, divide this number into 12 equal parts (twelve hours in a day). This results in 67.08 minutes per hour— or we might simplify it to about 68. Therefore, the first magickal hour of May 9, 2001, begins at 5:44 am and ends at 6:52 am. Being a Wednesday, it is ruled by Raphael and the planet Mercury. The second hour will run from 6:53 am to 8:01 am, and is ruled by Gabriel and the planet Luna. This 68-minute succession continues until sunset at 7:09 pm. (Don't forget to account for daylight saving time if it applies in your area!)

Don Kraig, in his *Modern Magick*, does us the favor of giving a shortcut if we wish to continue onward to find the hours for the night. Rather than perform the calculations anew for sunset to sunrise, we need only take the number of minutes in a daytime magickal hour (in our example, 68 minutes), and subtract it from 120 (the number of minutes in two clock, or equinox, hours). Thus, for the night of Wednesday, May 9, 2001, the hours will each last 52 minutes. Sunset occurs at 7:09 pm, and the first magickal hour will last 52 minutes until 8:01 pm. It will be ruled by Michael and Sol. The second hour will run from 8:02 pm to 8:54 pm, and will be ruled by Anael and Venus. Etc, etc.

If the student has any trouble understanding these instructions, I can only urge one to follow the same advice given by Mr. Kraig: work out a couple of days for yourself, step by step. Doing this will solidify the concept in your mind, and make the calculations comprehensible. They are not nearly as complicated as they may appear at first, and the use of a calculator will make short work of the entire process.

Of course, the grimoiric tradition also assigns occult names to each of the magickal hours. They are found (perhaps originally) on page 8 of the *Key of Solomon the King*. There origins are not always readily familiar; though some of them are recognizable as Hebrew (such as AGLA), and some even show Egyptian origins (such as Athor[10]).

Daytime[11]		Nighttime	
1 Thamur	7 Nathalon	1 Rana	7 Salam
2 Ourer	8 Beron	2 Netos	8 Yayn
3 Thaine	9 Barol	3 Tafrac	9 Yanor
4 Neron	10 Thanu	4 Sassur	10 Nasnia
5 Yayon	11 Athor	5 Agla	11 Salla
6 Abai	12 Mathon	6 Caerra	12 Sadedali

Kieckhefer's *Munich Handbook*[12] even offers functions for each named hour. I offer them here as they most probably represent a tradition, however obscure, rather than simply the creation of the author of the text. I should point out, however, that the names of the hours given in the *Munich Handbook* differ in many regards to those found in the *Key of Solomon the King*. I find it very likely that the former text represents a corruption of the latter, due to such things as transcription errors over time as well as oral transmission. This being the case, I have simply preserved the ordering of the functions from the first hour to the last, the names notwithstanding.

Daytime

1 Freeing Captives

2 Peace Between Kings

3 Discord

4 Travel, Safe Passage Among Robbers

5 Work With Demons and Demoniacs, Foul Wind, Aid to Ladies

6 Causing Bleeding in Women, Binding Men to Women and Vice Versa

7 Peace (Between Men and Women)

8 Working With Demoniacs, Foul Winds

9 Working With Fish

10 Working With Fire

11 Destroying Houses, Expelling People

12 Asking Questions of Sleepers

Nighttime

1 Working With Fruit Trees and Other Plants

2 Expelling People, Causing Sickness and Death

3 Causing Enmity

4 Binding Tongues, Entering Before Kings and Lords

5 Destroying Evil Speech or Thought

6 Binding or Catching Birds

7 Telling Fortunes, Disclosing Theft or Other Crime

9 Binding Tongues

10 Friendship, Favour of Potentates

11 Hunting, Fishing

12 Binding Wild Beasts

13 Binding Beasts

The *Key of Solomon the King*, meanwhile, provides its own ideas about which days and hours are preferable for various functions. The list provided (Book I, Chapter 2) will perhaps be of more use to the modern mage: (In organizing the text of his translation, Mathers made use of several manuscripts. The result is somewhat choppy, and I have re-formatted the material for easier reference:

Note that each experiment or magical operation should be performed under the planet, and usually in the hour, which refers to the same. For example:

Day and Hours of Saturn

To acquire learning. Experiments to summon the Souls from Hades, but only of those who have died a natural death. To bring either good or bad fortune to buildings; to have familiar Spirits attend thee in sleep (also see Luna); to cause good or ill success in business, possessions, goods, seeds, fruits, and similar things; to bring destruction and to give death, and to sew hatred and discord.

Day and Hours of Jupiter

For obtaining honours, acquiring riches; contracting friendships, preserving health; and arriving at all that thou canst desire.

Day and Hours of Mars

Experiments regarding War; to arrive at military honour; to acquire courage; to overthrow enemies; and to further cause ruin, slaughter, cruelty, discord; to wound and to give death. For summoning Souls from Hades, especially of those slain in battle. (Compare to such necromancy associated with Saturn.)

Day and Hours of Sol

For perfecting experiments regarding worldly wealth, hope, gain, fortune, divination, the favour of princes, to dissolve hostile feeling, and to make friends.

Day and Hours of Venus

For forming friendships; for kindness and love; for joyous and pleasant undertakings, and for traveling. Furthermore useful for lotteries, poisons, all things of the nature of Venus,[13] for preparing powders provocative of madness;[14] and the like things.

Day and Hours of Mercury

For eloquence and intelligence; promptitude in business; science and divination; wonders; the visible appearance of spirits (or mystical illusions);[15] and answers regarding the future. Also for thefts; writings; deceit; and merchandise. Good for undertaking experiments relating to games, raillery, jests, sports, and the like.

Day and Hours of Luna

For embassies; voyages; envoys; messages; navigation; reconciliation; love; and the acquisition of merchandise by water. For making experiments relating to recovery of stolen property, for obtaining nocturnal visions, for summoning Spirits in sleep, and for preparing anything relating to Water.

The chapter also includes some further advanced information, incorporating aspects from astrological charts, etc. The section on elective astrology later in this chapter will make it more comprehensible:

> The hours of Saturn, of Mars, and of the Moon are alike good for communicating and speaking with Spirits; as those of Mercury are for recovering thefts by the means of Spirits. The hours of Saturn and Mars and also the days on which the Moon is conjunct with them, or when she receives their opposition or quartile aspect,[16] are excellent for making experiments of hatred, enmity, quarrel, and discord; and other operations of the same kind.

The hours of the Sun, of Jupiter, and of Venus, are adapted for preparing any operations whatsoever of love, of kindness, and of invisibility. The hours of the Sun, of Jupiter, and of Venus, particularly on the days which they rule, are good for all extraordinary, uncommon, and unknown operations.

But in order to thoroughly effect the operations of this Art, thou shouldest perform them not only on the hours but on the days of the planets as well, because then the experiment will always succeed better . . .

The *Key* returns to the subject of magickal hours in Book II, Chapter 1. There we are told that for any magickal operation where days and hours are not prescribed, we should utilize those of Mercury as a general practice. (The *Key*, overall, seems to focus heavily upon Mercury, the force most associated with magick, language, science, etc.) Also, the author suggests that nighttime is the best choice for working whenever such is possible, as it is easier for the spirits to appear in the "peaceful silence of the night than during the day." This makes perfect sense, as it is common practice to attempt evocations in nearly total darkness, as it is then easier for the mind to envision the entities. (The darkness itself plays into the sensory deprivation we have discussed previously.)

The chapter then goes on with information similar to the list given above, showing days and hours most suitable to one situation or another. (It is similar in nature, also, to the list of hours of the day or night and their uses from the *Munich Handbook*.) I have opted not to include it here, as it would be needlessly redundant, and of little use to the magick we will explore in later chapters of this book. The dedicated student will perhaps find it useful in his own studies, and is (of course!) encouraged to obtain a copy of the *Key* for himself.

Such lists as those shown above are profoundly interesting from a historical perspective, as they give us a glimpse into daily medieval life. Mages of the time often worked for their community (as with any form of shamanism), and thus these listed magickal goals tend to reflect the kinds of jobs the mage would be hired for, as well as his own personal agendas. This subject has been discussed in previous chapters.

The Book of Abramelin also discusses the subject of planetary days and hours, utilizing the concept of elective astrology (see below) rather than lists and tables. In fact, the author spends some time chastising other mages for observing such tables as the above, declaring that they have no basis in actuality.[17] In Book II, Chapter 6:

O how gross an error! Hear and tell me when it is that a Planet hath the greatest force in the Elements; whether when it is above or when it is below your Horizon or Hemisphere? We must however avow that it is more powerful when it is above, because being below it hath no power save according unto the Will of God. Why then, even further than this, should we attribute unto a Planet a Day and Hour, if during the whole period of such Day it appeareth not above the Horizon!

Based upon this premise, the book continues to relate its own system of magickal timing for use in natural magick. In a footnote, the translator (S. L. Mathers) suggests that this system is the "initiated Rosicrucian teaching."

The system is very simple in concept. The day of any given planet commences as soon as that planet rises above the eastern horizon "whether it be Light or Dark, Black or White" (i.e., regardless of other considerations). When the planet sets in the west, dipping below the horizon, its night commences, during which the planet has no natural power. This counts even in the cases of the Sun and Moon; so that every day is the day of Sol, and every night (save those of the dark moon) is the day of Luna.

The magickal hours work in a similar fashion, only it is the meridian (the zenith of the heavens, directly overhead) by which the time is judged rather than the horizons. Thus, for instance, the hour in which the Sun is directly overhead—noontime in this case—is considered the hour of Sol. The same applies to the Moon, as well as the other five planets.

Of course, it is unavoidable that every moment in time will show various planets in their days and nights—and even sometimes their magickal hours—simultaneously. The author affirms that this is proper to natural magickal considerations, and that the planets "then produce an effect according unto the nature, quality, and complexion of these stars." That is to say, if two or more planets are above the horizon or in the meridian at the same time, then the magickal effects upon that time is a mixture of their essences.

I have to admit that I rather like this system myself, over and above the tables of magickal hours. Once again, I am reminded of the fact that the physical planets were of importance to the medieval mage as the actual bodies of the seven archangels. The most natural time of rule for each would be that time when the planet is in the sky, and especially the hour in which it is directly overhead. In fact, it was quite common for astrologer-mages to draw up entire natal charts when deciding upon the time (and effects) of a proposed magickal experiment. This was an art known as elective astrology.

Elective Astrology

Every natural virtue doth work things far more wonderful when it is . . . informed by a choice observation of the celestials opportune to this (viz. when the celestial power is most strong to that effect which we desire, and also helped by many celestials) by subjecting inferiors to the celestials . . . Also in every work there are to be observed the situation, motion, and aspect of the stars and planets, in signs and degrees . . . (*Three Books of Occult Philosophy*, Book II, Chapter 29: "Of the Observation of Celestials, Necessary in Every Work")

What the learned Agrippa is describing in the above quotation is elective astrology. This is simply the practice of casting horoscopes for the purpose of magickal timing rather than for the birth of a person. By interpreting the chart, one can determine if the astrological (i.e., astral) conditions are right for the proposed spell.[18] One can see at a glance exactly what occult forces are active at a given time, and how they are all interacting to create a specific environment. This is, after all, the very reason for the study of astrology.

What concerns us here is how a mage of the late Middle Ages would have viewed such a chart. This can be surprisingly different from what a modern astrologer sees when he interprets a horoscope. Remember where I described the medieval view of angels and deities as literally embodied in the celestial bodies. This being the case, the medieval astrologer-mage was not merely calculating times and degrees. Instead, he was acutely interested in exactly where the stars were placed in the sky, and what messages this presented about the movements of the gods.

It is important to understand that medieval (and ancient) astrology is nighttime visual, and "geocentric" (Earth-centered). It is based upon a primitive cosmology in which the Earth rests at the center of the universe, and all of the stars of heaven revolve around it. Further, it is based only upon those celestial bodies that are visible to the naked eye on a clear night far away from the glare of urban centers. The first primitive tribes that took note of the stars, and who recognized and categorized their movements, did not have use of telescopes. Thus, the three outer planets of the solar system (Uranus, Neptune, Pluto) did not figure into ancient astrology. Regardless of this, the system worked wonderfully.

I suspect that when the first new planet was discovered, many considered it too far away to account for Earth activities. Some rushed to adopt the new planet, but it is obvious that not all chose to readily accept the new god. (I personally choose not to incorporate the new planets. Their inclusion in a medieval system of magick would corrupt too many balanced structures, such as the tables of planetary hours. At the same time, incorporating them "here" and not "there" would be arbitrary at best.)

Also remember that it is just as important to consider a medieval chart from a mythological standpoint. From this perspective, the seven visible planets are living archangels who are taking part in the governance of nature, and the backdrop of stars are the angelic hosts of the heavens. Looking at the chart shows which angels are engaging in battle (called "opposition" for two planets, or "square" for two or more), or are acting closely together in harmony (such as in "trine" or "sextile" groupings). Two or more of them may be "conjunct" and acting forcefully together, while others may be isolated and indifferent to the others. This is not to mention which planets are above or below the horizon, or in the meridian, as per *Abramelin*. This only scratches the surface of astrological thought and study.

Let us take an example. If one chooses to cast a spell for prosperity, it is the Jupiterian archangel Sachiel one would call upon. By casting a chart and paying special attention to Jupiter, it is possible to determine which angels Sachiel is working with or against at the time. During the Middle Ages and times previous, the heavenly court was seen much like those here on earth: filled with changing alliances, intrigue, and shifts of power.

Such was the view of a horoscope from the most ancient of times. Even with the growth in popularity of mathematics in the Renaissance, the mystical aspects of the practice had not dwindled completely away. In fact, the very study of mathematics itself was considered mystical, and mathematicians were often occultists. Many of the classical grimoires suggest performing rituals outside under the stars, on a clear night. In the prayers and invocations, one can safely assume that one should gaze at the star and pray directly to it. The *Book of Abramelin* is special in that it insists on avoiding nighttime magick, and times its ceremonies for dawn, noon, and dusk only. However, *Abramelin* is a Solar rite, and is thus done in accordance with the Sun.[19]

The instructions from *Abramelin* are themselves simple examples of elective astrology, as are its instructions for calculating magickal days and hours. Interpreting an entire natal chart is no more complicated in essence. Its apparent complexity lies only in the fact that there are several ways to consider the relationships of stars and planets. The best book I have found for beginners in this field is *The Only Astrology Book You'll Ever Need* by Joanna Martine Woolfolk. Of course, it is anything but the "only" such book you will ever need, but it is certainly a great primer. It will take you step by step through the process of erecting a natal chart, and how to interpret its various aspects.

At the same time, there are tools available for free on the world wide web that can be of great help to the twenty-one-first century mage. I highly recommend a simple program called Astrolog,[20] which will calculate and graphically display a chart once you enter the proper time and location. It also features a "Now" button, which will use your computer's clock to instantly calculate a chart for the given moment. It even has an animation capability, so you can load the program and watch the planets and stars move in real-time. It's quite a tool for "keeping an eye on the gods."

These sources aside, I offer here an abbreviated course that will allow you to familiarize yourself with the very basics of the system. To begin with, I will explain the structure of a simple astrological chart.

What you see above is simply a view of the heavens from the surface of the Earth. The planet Earth rests in the center, with the seven planets orbiting around it, and the twelve constellations of the zodiac surrounding all. The planets rotate clockwise, rising above the eastern horizon each day, passing overhead (which is marked "south" in the chart), setting below the western horizon in the evening, and passing underneath us (marked "north") before returning to the east. The exact zenith of the sky, also known as the meridian, is marked by the slightly diagonal line.

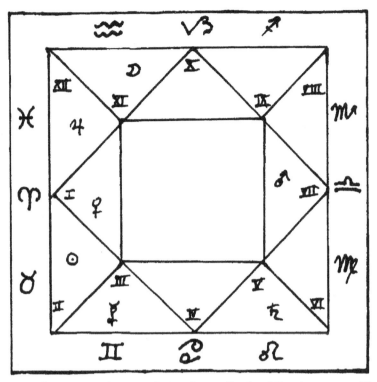

This is a square astrological chart, in popular usage during the medieval and Renaissance eras. The magick we are discussing in this book would have centered around such a chart, rather than the modern circular version. However, I have chosen to use the circular version for all practical purposes in this chapter, as the switch would be difficult and unnecessary.

It is important to keep in mind when viewing this arrangement that the Earth *does not* rotate. Of course, in reality the Earth does spin, and the stars are fixed. However, when standing on the surface of the Earth looking outward, just the opposite appears to be true. (This is an aspect of relativity; any arbitrary spot in the universe can be chosen and mathematically set as the immobile "center" of the universe.) Standing upon the ground and watching the stars rotate around the Earth is much like riding through a loop on a roller coaster, where the entire world appears to be spinning around the train of the coaster, which the latter does not appear to be moving at all.

Therefore, every time you see a natal chart, the four cardinal points of the earth will be fixed as you see them above, while the twelve constellations around the outside will be in a different position. They rotate in a clockwise direction, so that Aries will rise above the eastern horizon, followed by Taurus, then Gemini, etc., in proper order. (This can often confuse the student, because the twelve signs must be drawn around the circle in *counterclockwise* order to accomplish this.) It takes slightly less than a single day for all twelve signs to rise above the eastern horizon of the natal chart.

The planets move just a bit slower than the stars. The Sun, for instance, will run directly next to one zodiacal sign (say, Aries) for approximately a month. Every day, however, it slips a little further behind Aries; until the sign finally leaves it behind. The Sun, then, will run along side the next sign (Taurus) for about a month. It takes a year for it to pass through the entire zodiac in this manner, reaching Aries again. The Moon, on the other hand, takes about twenty-eight days to pass through the entire circle in the same way. It is by this that we judge Sun and Moon signs for any natal chart.

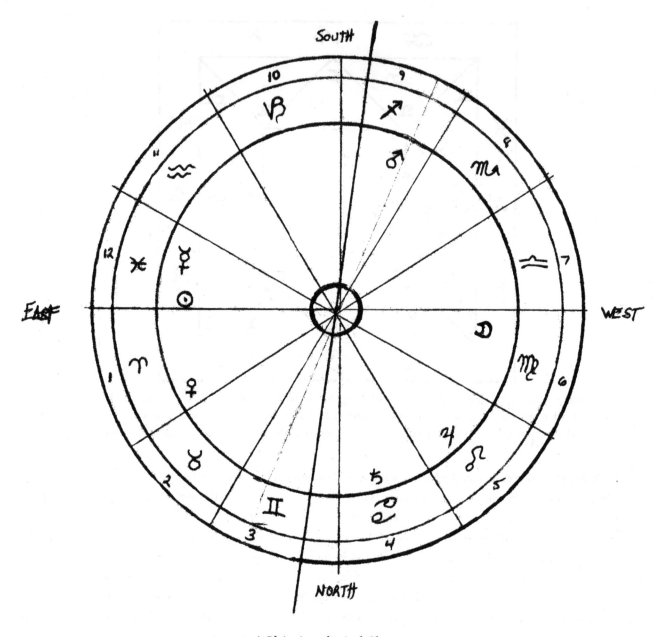

A Plain Astrological Chart.

Finally, there is another fixed aspect of the horoscope: the twelve houses. This is the numbered circle that surrounds the Earth/center. The reason the houses do not rotate is because they are projected outward from the surface of the Earth itself. They are "windows" in our own atmosphere through which we can watch the stars and planets pass each day. Every morning the Sun rises in the east, passing through the twelfth house. Each evening it sets in the west, passing through the seventh house. This pattern never changes.

Chart Interpretation

Hopefully the above has made the basic concepts of a chart easier to grasp than usual. With this in mind, we will now discuss the process of such divination, with an example chart. The following will present a step-by-step explanation of a basic astrological reading. Hopefully, it will allow the student to grasp the fundamentals of the process, and thus bring greater and greater accuracy to future divinations.

For our example, we are going to assume that we wish to contact the Angel of Mercury, Raphael. Of course, the goal of the intended magickal work could be anything of a Mercurial nature, but the actual focus of the shamanic-grimoiric process is to make contact with the angel himself. Therefore, our main concern is whether or not Mercury/Raphael is fortunately positioned in the reading. He should be both well aspected and well dignified (both terms will be explained below). He should also be above the horizon if at all possible, and if he is rising in the east or in the zenith it is all the better.

We can assume that we wish to accomplish our magickal goal within the next few weeks or months. (It could be days, or even years.) At the same time, we can narrow our possible times of working to Wednesdays (the days of Mercury), and to the four specific hours *of* Mercury on each Wednesday. The choice of times can then be further reduced depending on the Moon, as it must be waxing or full. This is actually something of a blessing, so that we don't have to cycle through dozens of possible charts to find a suitable working time. Each month (of approximately four weeks) will offer sixteen Mercury day/hour combinations—and approximately half of them should fall upon a waxing or full Moon phase. Narrow that list down to the times most feasible for yourself, and organize them into your first, second, third, etc., choices. Then, it is merely necessary to enter the dates and times (along with your own location) into an astrology program. Find those charts in which Mercury is well placed, and one of them will be your magickal time.

It is not necessary to calculate magickal hours while performing this preliminary search. Just treat each day as an equinox—daytime starting at 6 am, nighttime at 6 pm, and each hour lasting 60 minutes. Thus, for each Wednesday, you will only have to calculate charts for 6 am, 1 pm, 8 pm, and 3 am. (However, we do have to remember that nonmagickal days end/begin at midnight. Thus you will actually have to search for 3 am upon the following Thursday if you wish to work that late into Wednesday night.) Once you have found the desired day and hour, go ahead to calculate magickal hours and pinpoint the exact time you will perform the spell. The positions of the stars from the general reading to the more specific should not differ too drastically.

Finding the above chart was not at all difficult using an astrology computer program. My first attempt was to find a date in June 2001 (first choice), but I was very unimpressed with the arrangement of stars for that entire month. Therefore, I drew back a bit to the month of May[21] and found a much more acceptable situation. Mercury tended to rest in Gemini (the sign it rules), and did not possess any negative aspects against other planets.

Then I checked my wall calendar for the phase of the Moon. If I wanted Luna in her waxing or full cycles, I had to choose either Wednesday May 2 or 9. One week later and the Moon would again be in wane. I found both possible days acceptable. The major difference was that Mercury rests in Taurus on the 2nd, but has shifted into the sign it naturally rules (Gemini) by the 9th. Thus, I decided ultimately on May 9, 2001.

Next, I learned that if I wished to keep Mercury in a rising position (between the eastern horizon and the zenith), I did not have all four hours of Mercury to choose from that day. Because Mercury is so close to the Sun, I had to make sure that the Sun was also between the horizon and zenith. Six am was too early, and resulted in Mercury below the eastern horizon. Eight pm was too late, and put Mercury descending toward the western horizon. (Either of these might have been acceptable in most cases, but I wanted Mercury to be just right for illustration here.) The hour of 1 pm placed Mercury in just the right position: both rising and near the zenith.

(Remember that this is past March, and therefore daylight saving time is in effect where I live. I could have actually had the astrology program search for 2 pm rather than 1 pm, adding that extra hour onto all of my calculations. However, it is easiest to set aside that extra hour until the end of the process. Just make sure not to forget, and attempt to calculate by a clock that is ahead an hour. [Tables of sunrise and sunset *do not* generally include the

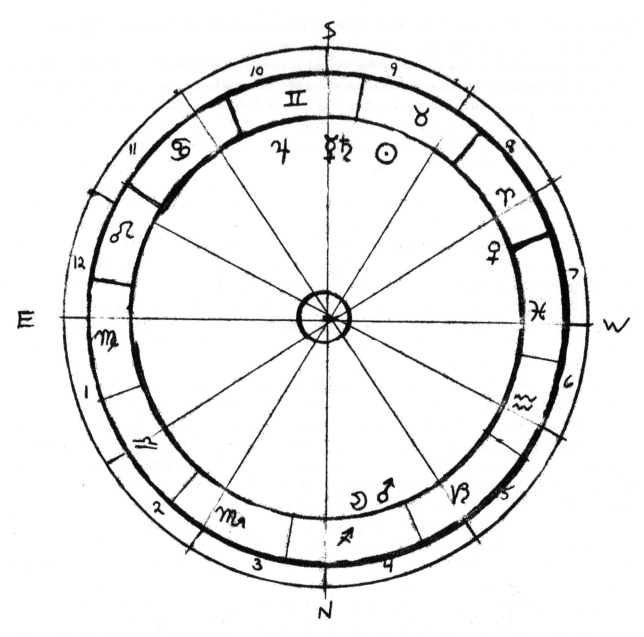

Tampa, FL. May 9, 2001. 82w28, 27n57. 1 pm real time—but 2 pm Daylight Saving. Then adjusted for magickal hours to 1:47 pm. Mercury rising (in zenith), and ruling in Gemini. Raphael very strong. Moon is 2 days after complete fullness—acceptable.

extra daylight hour.) You could end up working at noon [real time] while your clock says 1 pm. Daylight saving time is one of the most asinine concepts humans have yet created.)

Having found a day and hour in which Mercury is fortunately positioned—1 pm, Wednesday, May 9, 2001—it was then necessary to calculate magickal hours for the entire day. The process behind this has been covered previously in this chapter, so we will not need to cover it again. The end result was that each magickal hour for this particular Wednesday is 68 minutes in length. Daytime begins, without daylight saving, at 5:44 am, and the second hour of Mercury actually falls between 1:47 pm and 2:55 pm.

I finished by entering 1:47 pm into the astrology program (*with daylight saving turned off!*) and thus obtained the exact magickal time best for contacting Raphael, as shown in the chart above.[22] Of course, since all of my clocks must be set ahead for daylight saving, I would have to wait untill 2:47 by those clocks before beginning the magickal work. Sixty minutes earlier would place me into an hour ruled by Venus.

This is all we need to know in order to work with Raphael of Mercury. However, it is also important to know more about the rest of the angels and how they are influencing one another at the chosen time. Not only this, but it is necessary to understand horoscopes and astrological terminology in general in order to decipher the grimoires. Such obscurity as we see in the *Key of Solomon the King* ("[when] the Moon is conjunct with them, or when she receives their opposition or quartile aspect.") becomes recognizable with just a little study.

Therefore, we will examine a horoscope one step at a time, using our example chart of 1:47 pm, May 9, 2001, for any necessary illustration. The horoscope's "total picture" is gathered from each step along the way, and is something grasped both intuitively and logically. (Just as in a tarot reading, where each card has its own meaning while also combining with other cards in the spread to say something more.) Therefore, do not be discouraged if you do not feel immediately successful in chart interpretation. Follow the steps, write down your interpretations and thoughts along the way, and then simply consider how all the signs and messages add together. Practice is what perfects this art. Commit to interpreting twenty charts, and afterward you will be comfortable with the system.

The Zodiac

Constellation	Quality	Triplicity	Keywords (positive; negative)
Aries	Cardinal	Fire	Activity, Initiation; Violence
Taurus	Fixed	Earth	Stability, Practicality; Slow-moving
Gemini	Mutable	Air	Versatility, Duality; Alternating
Cancer	Cardinal	Water	Devotion, Domestic; Self-centered
Leo	Fixed	Fire	Magnetism, Pride; Egotism
Virgo	Mutable	Earth	Analytical, Exacting; Critical
Libra	Cardinal	Air	Harmony, Cooperation; Inconsistent
Scorpius	Fixed	Water	Intensity, Passion; Domineering
Sagittarius	Mutable	Fire	Enthusiasm, Swiftness; Impatience
Capricornus	Cardinal	Earth	Ambitious, Conservatism; Materialism
Aquarius	Fixed	Air	Imagination, Intellectualism; Dispassion
Pisces	Mutable	Water	Understanding, Intuitive; Impracticality

Step One: The Ascendant

In modern times, it is common to judge a horoscope primarily by the Sun sign. However, this was not always the case. In the past, the Ascendant was considered the primary indicator of the chart. The Ascendant is simply the zodiacal sign rising upon the eastern horizon at any given time, and represents the "basic nature" of the chart. In our example the Ascendant happens to be Virgo.

The Sun sign still represents the outward physical aspect of a situation or thing, (or the outer personality of a person, etc). However, the Ascendant rises above the chart as a Sun in its own right, casting a glow upon the rest of the interpretations, including the Sun sign.

I do feel that considering the Ascendant foremost is preferable, at least when using the system for magickal timing. While the Sun may be in another sign, one might need to work magick at night. That would put both the Sun and the Sun sign beneath the horizon. If these angels are in the underworld for half of every day, it is hard to imagine Them being the strongest influences in the chart at all times. On the other hand, the ascending sign is the rising influence of the sky, day or night. To speak mythologically again, this is the choir of angels who are currently being reborn and rising toward the zenith.

Step Two: The Sun Sign

This now becomes the secondary concern of the chart, nearly as important as the Ascendant itself. The Sun sign represents the general current of a situation, its physical action. A Sun in Taurus—as in our example—would represent a situation moving forward slowly and inexorably. The forces of the Sun sign must principally be considered in the light of the Ascendant. In our chart, both Sun sign and Ascendant (Taurus and Virgo) are constellations of the heavy and physical Earth triplicity.

Step Three: The Moon Sign

As the Sun sign represented the general activity or astral current of our chosen time, so does the Moon sign represent the subtle astral undercurrents. The moon sign must be considered in relation to the Sun sign, as the Moon represents many of the inner motivations behind the willful forces of the Sun. This will throw its own subtle light onto the total picture of the chart. Remember that it represents what is lurking under the surface of the astral waters, which you are about to access for your magickal goal—so it must not be mistaken as a needless concern.

The *Key of Solomon the King* devotes some instruction to the consideration of Luna and her sign:

> For those matters then which appertain unto the Moon, such as the Invocation of Spirits, the Works of Necromancy, and the recovery of stolen property, it is necessary that the Moon should be in a Terrestrial Sign, viz.:—Taurus, Virgo, or Capricorn.

> For love, grace, and invisibility, the Moon should be in a Fiery Sign, viz.:—Aries, Leo, Sagittarius.

> For hatred, discord, and destruction, the Moon should be in a Watery Sign, viz.-: Cancer, Scorpio, or Pisces.

> For experiments of a peculiar nature, which cannot be classed under any certain head, the Moon should be in an Airy Sign, viz.:—Gemini, Libra, or Aquarius. [Furthermore, if thou wishest to converse with Spirits it should be especially on the day of Mercury and in his hour, and let the Moon be in an Airy Sign, as well as the Sun.

Step Four: Planetary Dignities

Once the constellations have been interpreted, its time to move on to the planets. This is where we begin to look at the seven archangels, and judge who is strongest and weakest, etc.

These are known as the "dignities" of the planets. This refers to the nature of a planet's force when passing through any given zodiacal sign. Sometimes the sign makes the planet strong and benevolent, and sometimes the sign makes it weak and unfortunate. In fact, there are four specific categories of dignity, which I offer below. A planet that falls within the sign it naturally rules is extremely powerful, followed only by its sign of exaltation. If a planet is in the sign of its fall, then it will be weak at best. Its detriment is nearly the exact opposite of the general nature of the planet, considered very unfortunate, and perhaps even qliphothic (demonic):

	Rules	Exaltation	Fall	Detriment
Sol	Leo	Aries	Libra	Aquarius
Luna	Cancer	Taurus	Scorpius	Capricornus
Mars	Aires, Scorpius	Capricornus	Cancer	Taurus, Libra
Mercury	Gemini, Virgo	Virgo	Pisces	Sag., Pisces
Jupiter	Sag., Pisces	Cancer	Capricornus	Gemini, Virgo
Venus	Taurus, Libra	Pisces	Virgo	Aries, Scorp.
Saturn	Cap., Aquarius	Libra	Aries	Cancer, Leo

The planets whose dignities have the strongest influence in a horoscope are those who rule the Ascendant, Sun sign, and Moon sign. (Note these are the planets that *rule* those signs, and not the planets that happen to be *in* those signs. In our example, the Ascendant is Virgo, ruled by Mercury. The Sun sign is Taurus, ruled by Venus. The Moon sign is Sagittarius, ruled by Jupiter. The dignities of these three planets will be the strongest within the chart.) Also make sure to take special note of the planet/angel with which you intend to work. It would certainly be undesirable for that planet to be in its fall or detriment at the time of your spell casting (not to mention that it should best be above the horizon). In our example, Mercury rests in Gemini—the sign that it rules. Therefore it (and Raphael) is extremely powerful at this time.

Once this is done, continue to judge the dignity of each remaining planet, and consider how they affect the horoscope and your magickal goal. There is also a chapter in Agrippa's *Three Books* that might interest the serious student of astrology. Book II, Chapter 30 (p. 359) is titled "When Planets are of Most Powerful Influence." I have decided not to include the text here as it is written for those more advanced in the practice. However, once you have grown comfortable with the methods described here, I recommend one continue with this and other related chapters of Agrippa's book.

Step Five: Planetary Aspects

The process so far has allowed us to see what each planetary force is doing on its own. It shows us the general moods and demeanors of the archangels. By continuing onward to interpret the planetary aspects, we can learn how They are interacting with each other. Simply put, an "aspect" is the manner in which one planet relates to others in the chart. They have varying degrees of influence upon one another depending on how closely they are grouped together, or how far apart they rest.

The circle of the heavens, as depicted in the astrological chart, contains exactly 360 degrees. When that circle is divided among the twelve zodiacal signs, it leaves 30 degrees for each sign. The degrees progress in the same order as the signs, which is counterclockwise around the circle. The Sun moves through the signs at about the speed of 1 degree a day. (Thus, if you are born fourteen days after the Sun entered Taurus, then your Sun likely falls upon 14 degrees Taurus.) All planetary aspects are based upon the number of degrees between any two planets.

1 **Conjunction** ☌	Two planets within 7 degrees (usually sharing the same zodiacal sign).	Planets working strongly together, for either good or ill depending on the planets (and dignities) involved.

2 **Opposition** ☍	Two planets 180 degrees (six signs) apart. Orb 7.[23]	Planets in stalemate, working against each other. Need to balance and find point of cooperation.
3 **Trine** △	Two planets 120 degrees (four signs) apart. Orb 7.	Planets working with each other in harmony.
4. **Sextile** ✳	Two planets 60 degrees (two signs) apart. Orb 5.	Planets working with each other from signs of complementary Elements.[24]
5 **Square** □	Two planets 90 degrees (three signs) apart. Orb 7.	Planets in tension and working against one another.
6 **T-Square**	Three planets: two in opposition and both in square with the third planet.	Planets working against each other.
7 **Grand Cross**	Four planets: two pairs in opposition, each pair in square with the other pair.	Planets working against each other. Great tension.
8 **Grand Trine**	Three planets: all in trine with one another, and each resting in a sign of the same Element.[25]	Planets working very strongly together in harmony, from the standpoint of the singular Element.

Returning again to our example chart, we should take a look at how Raphael is getting along with his siblings. Mercury possesses aspects with only two other planets: a conjunction with Saturn and a sextile with Venus.

First in importance is the conjunction, which means that Cassiel and Raphael are combining their powers. Looking at our planetary dignities, I see no particular indication of misfortune: Mercury is extremely powerful for being in a zodiacal sign it rules, while Saturn is in its strong dignity in the same sign. If one were to contact Raphael at this time, he should expect a slower, older, and wiser Raphael than the fleet-footed youth one might otherwise encounter.

The sextile aspect between Mercury and Venus is not so fortunate. While it does indicate a harmony between the forces of intellect and passion (Raphael and Anael), we see that Venus is in her detriment. Her influence upon Raphael is next to zero, as his dignity overpowers hers manifold. (I am tempted to say that this is a good time to ask Raphael about matters of the heart—where the intellect has been neglected in favor of emotion.)

Of course, one should consider all of the planetary aspects of a chart, finding them one planet at a time. These other aspects will become more important when interpreting the twelve astrological houses. See step six below.

Now, we can return once more to the text of the *Key of Solomon the King*. Regardless of other planetary aspects, the author insists that the Moon must be observed above all:

> But if these things seem unto thee difficult to accomplish, it will suffice thee merely to notice the Moon after her combustion, or conjunction with the Sun, especially just when she quits his beams and appeareth visible.[26] For then it is good to make all experiments for the construction and operation of any matter. That is why the time from the New[27] unto the Full Moon is proper for performing any of the experiments of which we have spoken above. But in her decrease or wane it is good for War, Destruction, and Discord. Likewise the period when she is almost deprived of light, is proper for experiments of invisibility, and of Death.

But observe inviolably that thou commence nothing while the Moon is in conjunction with the Sun, seeing that this is extremely unfortunate, and that thou wilt then be able to effect nothing; but the Moon quitting his beams and increasing in Light, thou canst perform all that thou desirest, observing nevertheless the directions in this Chapter.

The *Key* is perhaps famous for giving the aspirant simpler methods of going about the magick if the fully involved processes prove impossible to follow. By suggesting that one can ignore all considerations beyond the phase of the Moon, "Solomon" is anticipating the methods used by our modern Neopagan communities.

Step Six: The Houses

This step represents the culmination of all of the above considerations. We have determined exactly what each archangel is doing in the heavens, both by themselves and in relation to each other. The houses, at last, allow us to judge exactly what it all means in a practical sense. It is the final cementing factor of the reading.

Each house has its own peculiar meaning, and is naturally ruled by one zodiacal sign. Aries rules the first house, and the pattern follows in proper order through Pisces and the twelfth house. As such, each house does represent an aspect of creation similar to its natural sign.

House Zodiac (Ruler)	Medieval Name	Modern Name	Description
1st House Aries (Mars)	Horoscope	Identity	Initiation or basis of a matter. (The Ascendant rises from here.)
2nd House Taurus (Venus)	Gate of Hades	Values	Resources, possessions, values, financial affairs, gain or loss.
3rd House Gemini (Mercury)	Goddess (Luna)[28]	Awareness	Consciousness, logic, education, travel, siblings.
4th House Cancer (Luna)	Lower Midheaven	Security	Property, parents and ancestors, home, closing of life.
5th House Leo/Sol	Good Fortune	Creativity	Romance, pleasure, art and creativity, children.
6th House Virgo (Mercury)	Bad Fortune	Duty	Employment, service, health, habits, dependants, aunts and uncles.
7th House Libra (Venus)	Occident	Cooperation	Marriages, contracts, partnerships, grandparents, known enemies.
8th House Scorpius (Mars)	Beginning of Death	Regeneration	Secrets and mysteries, sex, rebirth, death, inheritance, surgery.
9th House Sagittarius (Jupiter)	God (Sol)	Aspiration	Philosophy, ethics, spirituality and religion, visions, study and learning, grandchildren.
10th House Capricornus (Saturn)	Midheaven	Honor	Reputation, ambition, achievements, honor, influence, business activities.

House Zodiac (Ruler)	Medieval Name	Modern Name	Description
11th House Aquarius (Saturn)	Good Daemon	Social Conscience	Friends and acquaintances, goals, humanitarian interests, organizations, and circumstances beyond one's control.
12th House Pisces (Jupiter)	Bad Daemon	Subconscious	Hidden strength, danger, and weaknesses. Sorrows, hidden enemies, subconscious, and karmic debt.

Of course, an actual horoscope will show different zodiacal signs in each house—because the stars rotate around the chart while the houses remain fixed. (Note the arrangement in our example.) The constellations listed in the table above are the natural rulers from which each house derives its basic description.

When interpreting a practical chart such as our Mercurial example, consider the zodiacal sign and any planetary aspects that fall within each house, paying special attention to the houses that most affect the magickal goal. Most of this interpretation has already been done by this step, including the signs, planetary dignities, and aspects. Now, it is only necessary to group them together within their respective houses and see what they indicate about that aspect of the intended magickal goal. (Remember that all twelve houses are interpreted, whether or not there are any planets within them. The zodiacal sign present in each must be interpreted.) The first house, like the Ascendant, is considered the most important to the reading, coloring the interpretations that follow.

The Thirty-Six Faces of the Decanates

Each of the twelve signs of the zodiac is further subdivided into three 10-degree portions known as "decanates" (decans) or "faces." There are thirty-six of them from Aries to Pisces, and each one is associated with one of the seven planets. Any planet which falls within a decan on the zodiacal chart will actually be colored by a combination of the constellation *and* the planetary face. I have not included this in the above steps of chart interpretation for the sake of simplicity. Instead, I have appended it here because this information will become important in later chapters of this book.

There are various ways of associating the planets with the thirty-six decanates. Two of them in particular were most popular in the grimoiric literature, both of which are utilized by Agrippa in his *Three Books of Occult Philosophy*. In some instances Agrippa uses the Ptolemaic (or Chaldean) ordering of the planets, which we saw in relation to magickal hours previously in this chapter. It begins with Mars as the first face of Aries, and progresses through Sol and Venus for faces two and three. The first face of Taurus, then, is assigned to Mercury, and then progresses through Luna and Saturn. The cycle continues until the final face of Pisces, which is assigned to Jupiter. The circle then begins with Aries and Mars once again, with no break in the pattern. This is what Agrippa generally refers to as the thirty six faces.

In other cases, Agrippa seems to refer to a "ruling planet" ordering for the decans. In this method, the four triplicities of the zodiac and their ruling planets must be taken into account. Each triplicity is taken in the ordering of cardinal, followed by fixed, followed by mutable, and the ruling planets for each are assigned in a different order to each sign. Therefore, the first decan of Aries is ruled by its own natural ruling planet—Mars. The second decan of Aries is assigned the ruling planet of the fixed Leo—Sol. Finally, the third decan of Aries is assigned the ruling planet of the mutable Sagittarius—Jupiter.

If the sign in question were fixed, the sign's natural ruler would still rule its first decan. Then, the second decan is assigned the ruler of the *mutable* sign's ruling planet, and the third would complete the pattern with the ruler of the *cardinal* sign. Therefore, the three decans of Scorpio would be assigned to Mars, Jupiter, and Luna respectively (the rulers of Scorpio, Pisces, and Cancer). Agrippa seems to have referred to this system as the thirty-six decanates.

However, Agrippa does not appear to have held to his distinction between the systems throughout his text. I feel that both systems can be taken as parallel, though not as interchangeable. It would be necessary for the working mage to choose which list he intends to use at the start of his work, and to stick with it through the duration of any operation.

Zodiacal Sign	Faces	Chaldean Order	Ruling Planet Order
Aries	1	Mars	Mars
	2	Sol	Sol
	3	Venus	Jupiter
Taurus	1	Mercury	Venus
	2	Luna	Mercury
	3	Saturn	Saturn
Gemini	1	Jupiter	Mercury
	2	Mars	Venus
	3	Sol	Saturn
Cancer	1	Venus	Luna
	2	Mercury	Mars
	3	Luna	Jupiter
Leo	1	Saturn	Sol
	2	Jupiter	Jupiter
	3	Mars	Mars
Virgo	1	Sol	Mercury
	2	Venus	Saturn
	3	Mercury	Venus
Libra	1	Luna	Venus
	2	Saturn	Saturn
	3	Jupiter	Mercury
Scorpius	1	Mars	Mars
	2	Sol	Jupiter
	3	Venus	Luna
Sagittarius	1	Mercury	Jupiter
	2	Luna	Mars
	3	Saturn	Sol

Zodiacal Sign	Faces	Chaldean Order	Ruling Planet Order
Capricornus	1	Jupiter	Saturn
	2	Mars	Venus
	3	Sol	Mercury
Aquarius	1	Venus	Saturn
	2	Mercury	Mercury
	3	Luna	Venus
Pisces	1	Saturn	Jupiter
	2	Jupiter	Luna
	3	Mars	Mars

The student is free to take this new information and apply it to the example chart, to see what insight it might produce.

For the most part in this work, I have chosen to use the term "faces" when referring to the thirty-six decans. However, I do this only because I find the term romantic, as well as relevant to the magick associated with them which we will explore. By use of the term, I am not intending to mimic Agrippa's distinction between one system and the other. I have left this wholly to the choice of the student.

---

1. See chapter 4.

2. Weiser's *Key of Solomon the King*, p. 18.

3. Other forms of practical magick are traditionally avoided on these days, if one is observing the day from the standpoint of "the Lord's Day," or the "Day of Rest."

4. See chapter 12.

5. An ancient Gnostic term for the creator god of Genesis.

6. In many cases, gods of war were one and the same with gods of famine and plague. The ancient Babylonian god Nergal is one example. This terrible god was said to have stormed the gates of the underworld (which even Inanna had not done, though she came close), and forcefully took control of the land of the dead. He became the husband of the Queen of the Underworld, Ereshkigal (who relates to Saturn).

7. *The Book of Ceremonial Magick*, p. 145.

8. Going by ancient astrology. It was "nighttime visual," and thus did not know of the three outer planets. And it was "geocentric," assuming the Earth as the center of the system.

9. The Naval Observator, http://aa.usno.navy.mil/AA/data/.

10. I.e., Hathor, the Egyptian goddess of the Sun or Venus star, depending on the tradition.

11. Consulting the *Key*, one finds Yayn listed as the first hour, rather than Thamur. However, my list begins at sunrise, while the list given in the grimoire begins at the first hour after midnight (approximately 1 am). Regardless of this, both lists do match properly.

12. *Forbidden Rites: A Necromancer's Manual of the Fifteenth Century*, pp. 182–3.

13. See the previous list of planets and their days.

14. This is most likely a reference to the preparation of psychedelic herbs, which bring on the ecstatic state (or "divine madness") necessary to visionary work.

15. The *Key* uses the word "apparitions," which likely covers both illusions and visible appearance.

16. See the section concerning "elective astrology" below.

17. As opposed to the mathematical basis I described above.

18. Elective astrology was not only used for magick. It was, and can be, used to determine the most advantageous time for any event. Dr. John Dee, for example, is well-known for having cast horoscopes to decide upon the best time for Queen Elizabeth's inauguration.

19. I should add here: "beginning on the spring equinox to boot, where the length of the day overtakes the length of the night."

20. Astrolog is available here: http://www.astrolog.org/astrolog.htm Also a web page that will instantly calculate latitude and longitude for any location you enter: http://www.astro.ch/cgi-bin/atlw3/aq.cgi?lang=e.

21. I could have as easily gone forward to July, etc.

22. I noted, as well, that the new chart placed Mercury dead into the zenith, which is Mercury's true hour of rule by Abramelin's reckoning.

23. An "orb" represents a number of degrees of error to the left or right of any planetary aspect. For instance, two planets must be 180 degrees apart to form an opposition, but the aspect has an orb of 7, and thus the opposing planets may be as far as 187 degrees or as close as 172 degrees apart.

24. Complementary Elements: Air and Fire signs are "actives," Earth and Water signs are "passives." An active and a passive together—such as Water and Fire—are volatile and inharmonious. This cannot occur in a sextile aspect.

25. For instance, a Grand Trine of Fire would have one planet in Aries, one in Leo, and one in Sagittarius.

26. Any planet is in "combustion" when it is conjunct with the Sun. The Moon is in combustion once a month, when it passes over our heads with the Sun during the day, and is thus absent from our sight at night. This is the time of the dark Moon, which is traditionally avoided for magick even today. When she "quits his beams and appeareth visible" is the time of the new Moon, or first cresent.

27. Remember that classical texts, when referring to the new Moon, are indicating the first cresent, and not the dark Moon.

28. Luna is not a reference to the planet ruled by Gabriel. This is an alchemical term, perhaps similar to the Eastern concept of yang. The yin can be found in the ninth house.

Magickal Tools Part I:
Basic Tools and Holy Implements
(Celestial)

> Man makes talismans unawares as soon as he begins to manipulate nature in such processes as dyeing cloth, breeding animals, or compounding drugs; as well as in the manufacture of objects of everyday use from the products of nature, as in cooking, spinning, and the like. (*Picatrix*)[1]

In previous chapters, I have discussed the ancient and medieval belief in the objective existence of spiritual entities. This will be expanded quite a bit in later chapters concerning angelic and spirit work. However, it is important to remind the reader of this worldview here, because it has a direct bearing upon the subject of magickal tools.

The medieval grimoiric mage, much like his ancient shamanic ancestors, believed that the world was full of living spirits and angelic beings who moved through the atmosphere. Books such as the *Key of Solomon the King* even insist (Book II, Chapter 1) that spirits should be summoned during "clear, serene, mild, and pleasant weather, without any great tempest or agitation of the air, which should not be troubled by winds." Otherwise the disturbed atmosphere might make it impossible for the airy entities to manifest; dissipating them as smoke in a breeze. (I stress the relationship between the words for "spirit" and "air" here.) In general, spiritual entities were regarded as being formed of the same substance as the air itself.[2]

The weather is merely one example of the importance placed upon the physical environment by the medieval mages. Every aspect of the magickal items and tools used in the spells are drawn from the natural environment according to the rules of sympathy. This is, of course, essentially the same within any form of shamanism. Ancient tribal magick made use of sticks, stones, shells, plants, animal parts, and other natural items that were appropriate to the time and place of the tribe. Likewise, the gold, silver, linen, silk, and steel used for the grimoiric tools are appropriate reflections of the culture from which the magick arose.[3] The grimoires are certainly urban in nature, and were thus created within a culture marked by literacy, scholarship, expendable money, leisure time, etc. These things do not remove the tradition from the realm of shamanism. As I have stated previously, true shamanism not only reflects, but also evolves and adapts to, its culture.

The decisions made about the physical ingredients of a spell generally have to do with what is considered sacred or offensive to any given entity; and this in turn is related to magickal sympathy and resonance. For example, as Agrippa teaches, those things that possess Solar attributes will tend to attract spirits of a Solar nature, etc. Thus we inscribe Solar talismans upon plates of gold, because of its shared correspondences with the Sun.

On the other hand, there may be a mythological foundation to the sacredness of a physical object. The *Book of Abramelin* makes use of a wand made from almond wood, which is held sacred within the biblical traditions overall. This likely arises from Numbers 17, a fascinating story of a tribal divination procedure. In order to determine the chosen high priest for Yahweh, each tribe provided a wooden staff with the name of their choice written upon it. The tribe of Levi inscribed the name of Aaron upon their staff, which happened to be made of almond wood. Moses then took the bundle of thirteen staves into the Tabernacle to meet with Yahweh, and left them there overnight. The next morning, Aaron's staff had sprung almond blossoms, thus proving that he was the high priest chosen by God.

Of course, almond was certainly already sacred to Israel by the time Numbers was written. It was a crop with which the Middle Eastern farmers would have long been familiar, and it would have had its own established religious significance and occult tradition. Unfortunately, we are given little information in Numbers. For instance, we do not know if all thirteen staves were almond, or if perhaps each tribe had its own sacred wood. (Readers who are familiar with Palo Mayombe will find this entire procedure somewhat familiar. *Palo* translates as "wood" or "stick.")

We can also consider this subject of magickal sympathy from a more technical perspective. Agrippa stresses in his philosophy that everything in existence possesses its own natural resonance with a particular occult force. (Some things are Solary, some are Mercurial, some are Cancerian, etc.) This resonance can be based upon physical characteristics, such as color or shape, or even the geographic location of the thing's origin. In his Book I, Chapter 31, Agrippa describes the assignment of spiritual (astral) authority to various locations on earth.[4] He discusses things with natural planetary natures in Chapters 23–30 and 32. Agrippa gives us all of this information to aid in the proper construction of sympathetic magickal spells, specifically in a natural magick or shamanic style.

Of course, not all of the objects in the grimoires are so plainly categorized by planetary or zodiacal forces, nor are their supporting mythologies or theories usually explained. Because of this, modern occult researchers cannot easily classify them. For instance, the *Book of Abramelin* does not explain its reason for fashioning the wand from an almond tree. It is merely assumed that the reader is familiar with the wood's significance. We are merely lucky to have some clue to the mystery today.

However, this is not the case in an overwhelming number of examples from the same literature. Consider the nine herbs used in the *Key of Solomon the King's* aspergillum (see below). We happen to have some idea of the importance of hyssop and sage, but we have no information at all about the remaining seven plants. We may assume they are all sacred plants in some way (as are both hyssop and sage), else they would not likely have been included in the holy water sprinkler. We could surely find all of them listed in various modern correspondence tables of plants associated with the planets and stars. However, in the end, we have no way of knowing exactly what the author of the *Key* himself had in mind. The only thing of which we can be certain is that the authors of the grimoires *did* subscribe to the theories of sympathy (or resonance, "magnetism," etc.). Therefore, most or all of the ingredients listed in the texts very likely do have *some* importance to the foundation of the magick.

For example, even if we knew nothing of the biblical tradition surrounding the almond tree, we would still be able to make some simple Neoplatonic observations. An almond tree will only grow in very specific places on the globe, at specific times of the year, and only under specific conditions. (This is a matter of basic agriculture.) The tree is, in fact, 100 percent a product of its environment, the sum total of the world around it from the air it breathes to the specific nutrients found in the soil of its native areas. This is not to mention the subtle astrological forces acting upon the tree depending on its location on Earth and the positions of the stars, etc. All of this adds up to give almond wood a very specific vibrational pattern when considered from an astral, or magickal, perspective. It will be wholly unlike the patterns found in any other wood, or even any other object, in the entire universe. (See Agrippa's *Three Books*, Book III, Chapter 64, where he discusses several natural elements—such as plants, animals, etc—whose life cycles correspond to magickal times and holy days.)[5]

All of these considerations would be important to any shaman-mage who believed that his spirits and guardians were objective beings, and were largely at the mercy of the local atmospheric and/or astral environment. The rituals outlined by the grimoires are designed very specifically to facilitate contact with these incorporeal intelligences. All of the tools and talismans employed to this end are, like the magickal timing and invocations, intended to establish an atmosphere that the spirits will find habitable. Here upon the physical plane, one wood may seem as good as another for the construction of a wand. *However, it is the vibrational patterns of the wood upon the astral that are important to the magick.* If an angel we are calling upon requests almond wood, it may be for a reason not yet comprehended by the novice. If we make a substitution (which is sometimes unavoidable) we can only hope that the substitute is not offensive (or repulsive in the sense of polarity) to the angel.

It is also important to consider the philosophy of pantheism/animism that runs throughout this form of magick. Again, pantheism regards the universe as the collective embodiment of diety; where all things in existence are members of the divine body. All of reality ultimately possesses the divine consciousness at its core, and therefore all things are alive and sentient. Agrippa (following Plato) called this the "Soul of the World." Animism also considers all things to be alive and conscious, but each with its own independent mind. The philosophy does not depend on a singular god at the core of creation. It is reflected in the grimoires (especially by Agrippa) by the intelligences and spirits set over all created things.

Therefore, when one gathers the natural ingredients to construct a grimoiric tool, one is incorporating all of the spirits associated with those objects into the tool itself. The spirit of the almond tree, for instance, is an integral part of Abramelin's wand. It is the intelligence that embodies the vibrations and sacred mythos we discussed above. Solomon's aspergillum possesses nine such spirits—one for each of the sacred herbs. The sigils painted on the handle of the sprinkler, then, should relate to those nine spirits after some manner. (This idea of binding nature spirits into magickal tools and talismata might again remind one of the Arabic legends of the jinni in the bottle).

In the time and place where the classical grimoires were written, most of these natural ingredients were local. The plants and tree branches were gathered in the nearby wilderness, parchment was made from local livestock, paints and inks were made from scratch, etc, etc. Even tools that are bought (or professionally made) are purchased—without haggling!—from local shops and professionals. In this way the grimoires fulfill an important aspect of shamanism—to work with and develop relationships with the *local* spiritual intelligences. This was necessary in order for the shaman to have influence over the environment in which his community had to live from day to day.

Once the tools have been painstakingly gathered and fashioned, with their proper consecrations and magickal timing observed, the practicing mage will possess a living temple. Each and every aspect of that temple will be alive, conscious, and completely focused upon aiding him in the commission of his work. Arranging them and reciting the invocations are all it takes to "stir them up." The spirit(s) bound to each tool can be addressed and experienced in their own way, just as we can experience the entities that the tools will help summon. (In chapter 8, we will be returning to the subject of living occult tools in relation to the magickal book.)

Thus is the foundation of the medieval mindset concerning magick and its paraphernalia: the spirits described in the classical grimoires are understood as objectively real entities who, when attempting to manifest to humans, are extremely sensitive to their physical/astral environments. The implements and materials are carefully chosen and constructed to provide the proper atmosphere within which these spirits can exist and manifest. (This point will be picked up and taken a bit further in chapter 7, concerning the selection of the place.)

Perhaps even more important to the magick than occult sympathy is the overwhelming dedication and devotion it requires to collect and create the necessary tools. It is this that grants more personal and emotional meaning to any given tool or talisman than a sacred mythos could hope to accomplish. The tools are not designed to be easy to create.

However, as I pointed out in chapter 1, there are few instructions found in the grimoiric literature that are truly impossible to follow. It merely takes true dedication, and maybe some clever thinking. In my own experience, I find the spiritual entities are unwilling to accept my magick if I have not honestly given the work my all. An Enochian Sigillum Ameth made of wood might be pretty, but the angels are well aware that obtaining and carving the seal from fresh bee's wax (as instructed in Dee's diaries) is hardly beyond my capability. It's not simple, or even easy, but it is possible for me and therefore necessary.

This is not a well-understood fact, but the "novice stage" of grimoiric (and similar shamanic) magick and the gathering of the tools are one and the same. As Eliade made clear in his work (see chapter 2 of this book), the reception or creation of the tools was a basic aspect of the shamanic initiation process, along with the reception of the tribal spirits, education in tribal lore, etc. These tools are not such that can be ordered from catalogs, or (generally) bought from the local occult bookstore. You cannot (often) fashion them from things lying around the house. The grimoiric instructions make it very clear that one must go out into nature, and *quest* for the materials to construct the tools. At the same time, one must engage in studies of the books and recitations of the invocations. The mage's concentration must be focused in this way, or else searching for the materials would be pointless. It is during these quests that the relationship between the mage and the spirits begins.

This is a vital point to consider. If there is one complaint I have heard about the grimoires above all others, it is the complexity of the instructions for the tools. The meticulous magickal timing, invocations, ritual gestures, and obscure materials simply turns many students away. They want all of the tools readily available, right now, so that they can "jump to the good stuff" such as conjuration. Such a prospect would be either useless or dangerous. What they are not seeing is that the process of making the tools is the very *heart* of the magick itself.

It will most certainly take several years to collect most of the tools you might desire, beginning with what you have now and adding new tools as they come along. Some will elude your efforts of construction for months—usually due to a search for some obscure item. Others will literally present themselves to you whole. By the time you are adept in the art, you will have developed very intimate relationships with every tool that has come to you.

For instance, imagine the making of the Solomonic wand.[6] The mage might first spend several weeks or months hunting for a hazel or nut tree of less than a year's growth. It can take him some real detective work to find what he needs, and he will likely have to wait until a certain time of year. Once a lead yields success, he must visit the tree to ensure it is suitable for the wand.

If he obtains no leads, he will have to grow one himself. He will only have to wait up to a *mere* eleven months to retrieve the wand—no time at all! (On the other hand, it could take longer if he hasn't raised saplings before.) Then, when he finally finds or raises an acceptable tree, he must leave it alone until the proper day—a Wednesday.

When the blessed day finally arrives, the mage rises at four or five in the morning, dresses, and collects his hatchet. He ventures out into the brisk predawn air and groggily travels once more to the tree's location. Once there, he takes a few moments to rest near the tree, and perhaps even questions what insanity brought him here at such an hour. He checks his copy of the *Key of Solomon* in his hands, making a last minute review of the procedures, prayers, etc. Before long, he finds himself silently reading through a prayer, his mind drifting pleasantly into it. Perhaps visions will come, or instructions given; or perhaps merely glimpses . . .

After some time, the mage suddenly becomes aware of the world around him. The creatures of the night are just beginning to recede with the shadows, and the world itself is awakening to the approaching Sun. The night's dew still rests upon the earth, and it begins to shimmer like millions of tiny diamonds as the morning grows lighter. A few words from the *Book of Abramelin* are perhaps brought to his mind: ". . . amidst the flowers and the fruits you can also meditate upon the grandeur of God." With that, the Sun peeks above the eastern horizon, illuminating the sky in a royal blaze of red and purple.

The mage turns solemnly toward the tree, firmly grasps the branch, raises his hatchet, and steels himself for a powerful swing. With a prayer of blessing and thanks unto the spirit of the tree, he cleanly slices the branch free in a single stroke. This he carries home, where—at the proper hour—it will be artfully inscribed with the necessary characters, and consecrated with prayer, incense, and water. This wand, then, will be a living thing for the mage. There will be a story behind it, and it will be something that has *meaning*.

Since the creation of the tools does constitute the novice stage of the grimoiric tradition, then there is certainly no reason to wait passively until the tools are complete to begin the practice. I have found that grimoiric magick is, in fact, a rather practical art. Once we understand the theory behind the magick (see chapters 1–4), then we find that the processes can work under various "control" circumstances. The grimoires become guidebooks that merely initiate one's path, and a personal style and methodology will develop with time.

It is perfectly feasible to utilize alternatives on a temporary basis, as one slowly fashions the tools in an "orthodox" fashion one by one. In the meantime, sprinkling water with the fingers rather than the aspergillum is not impotent. Drying oneself after the Solomonic bath (see chapter 7) with a white terry cloth towel, rather than one of pure white linen, is not harmful. Overall, you more than likely already possess enough passable magickal tools or raw materials to begin working with grimoiric invocations. A censer and spices, ritual knife, wand, and candles are very often more than enough equipment. In fact, you will use these very tools on a regular basis; far more than the highly specialized and sophisticated tools such as the almadel of Solomon or John Dee's holy table.

The most fascinating thing about the creation of magickal tools is the manner in which it expands the artist's mental horizons. After all, this is why the process is considered a quest, as it is a journey of personal growth. The ultimate Solomonic master would understand herbology and some agriculture, candle-making, artistic painting and the making of inks and paints, tailoring, leather working, engraving, metallurgy, and even the making of parchment—just to name a few areas of necessary skill. (All of this includes only skills associated with making the tools, and not the myriad arts and sciences the magick itself will insist the practitioner explore.)

This is a part of the mystical adventure that is the grimoiric tradition. Making the tools over a period of months or years will greatly expand one's personal awareness and life experience. Renaissance magick demands one be a "Renaissance man or woman."[7] Again, I would never suggest that one should wait to learn the art of making parchment (for example) before continuing with the work. Even the grimoires tend to be lenient in this regard. The *Key of Solomon the King*, as merely one example, follows its elaborate instructions for making holy parchment with a simplified method for those who have to purchase parchment instead. There are many such instances throughout the grimoiric literature.

Some of the texts, of course, represent specific magickal goals. *Abramelin*, *Goetia*, and *Honorius* are examples wherein very specific entities are contacted, or spiritual states achieved. Therefore, we might consider their tools in the same specific manner. Each set is intended expressly for the magickal spells or entities listed within its grimoire. In these cases, I generally recommend one stick with the operation (including all tools and methods) as outlined in the text.

Other books, such as the *Key*, the *Magus*, the *Magickal Elements*, etc., are intended for more general workings. Their tools are designed to be used for any conceivable occult purpose. Overall, this body of medieval mystical literature (including the more strict singular operations) shows a relaxed attitude toward borrowing tools and methods from one text to another.

Thread Spun by a Virgin?
Finding Obscure Items

We are, of course, not currently living in medieval England. I'm afraid that something must be lost from the tradition in the translation of time, place, and culture. Someone living in a different geographical region will not be able to construct proper shamanic tools that reflect the true local environment. Even someone living in modern England is quite removed from the world in which the authors of the *Key* or the *Goetia* lived. On the other hand, this merely makes the importance of the magickal quest to find the tools all the greater.

We do happen to be quite lucky in this regard. With the advent of the Internet, and the recent explosion of interest in occultism within our society, there is no longer an excuse for failure to locate any obscure material or object. A few questions asked in appropriate occult forums, or the simple use of a search engine with keywords, can produce outstanding results. I once posted an inquiry about finding thread spun by a young maiden (as the *Key of Solomon the King* instructs for several tools), and received *several* replies within hours. Some of them contained information on acceptable substitutions,[8] others offered advice on how to best track the material down myself, and one or two even suggested direct sources. Using this same method, I have found jewelers who are also occultists, and were happy to fashion magickal rings and the like. Taking the time to network with other truly dedicated occultists around the world can yield invaluable treasures on many levels.

Networking will also be important in your own hometown. Attending a liberal Catholic or Eastern Orthodox Church on a semiregular basis, as well as frequenting the related Christian bookstores, can produce many leads for necessary grimoiric implements, furnishings, and vestments. Sometimes even objects that have been blessed by a priest can be obtained. If one is truly fortunate, and develops a relationship with an open-minded man of the cloth, even the most difficult clerical items can be obtained, blessed, etc. My own "grimoiric" censer was obtained from a Russian Orthodox clergyman who originally used it in his own religious ceremonies (consecration of the eucharist, etc.).

Another important source for the grimoiric mage are botanicas. These are occult stores specifically geared toward practitioners of Afro-Cuban faiths such as Santeria or Palo Mayombe. They specialize in many of the most obscure items that might be called for in a shamanic tribal system of magick. So useful are these stores for grimoiric magick, many of them even carry certain grimoires themselves! (The *Sword of Moses* is quite popular in some Afro-Cuban circles.) Developing a proper relationship with the proprietors and customers of such a store is vital. You absolutely *must* enter the store with nothing less than respect and humility. Questions should be asked, answers listened to, and no attempts can be made to impress people there with knowledge you think you possess. If, after regular pleasant visits, they come to know and respect you, they will often provide many invaluable leads and sources for nearly any conceivable natural magickal item.

Also, one should never overlook antique and import stores. These are great for finding various items of an artistic or decorative nature (such as censers or brass vessels, etc.). A few local nurseries will be necessary to obtain live plants and growing materials. Fabric stores provide the silks and linens necessary for the vestments. This list could go on at length, but the gist should be clear from these examples.

Finally, one will have to go out into the wild in many places. One may need to gather sand from the bottom of a nearby river (as in *The Book of Abramelin*), or wood from a tree that does happen to grow locally. All of these ideas taken together should provide more than enough resources to find and obtain all of the ingredients one could need for effective Solomonic tools.

Of course, some account does have to be taken of the differences between our modern world and the medieval world of the grimoiric mage. Therefore, in this chapter I will give the instructions as they appear in the grimoires no matter how difficult or archaic they may seem; however, I will also give some hints and alternatives drawn from my own experience along the way. It is only necessary to keep in mind that the closer you hold to the original ideal, and the more effort you put into the quest for obscure items, the deeper your relationship will be with the spirits of the tools, and the magick will be all the stronger.

This chapter is essentially divided into three sections, comprising chapters 6, 9, and 11. I had originally intended to outline all of the implements here, but eventually decided this course would be much easier to follow if they were divided among their relevant chapters. Therefore, chapter 6 covers all of the basic tools, and those necessary for the procedures of purification and angelic magick in chapters 7 and 8. Chapter 9 then continues with the tools and provisions necessary for the creation of talismans and magickal images in chapter 10. Finally, chapter 11 includes the weapons utilized in the exorcism/conjuration of earthbound and infernal spirits, such as we will discuss in chapter 12. Taken together, the three tools chapters are cumulative, so that the tools from the previous chapters are used throughout the book, and each new set of implements is merely added to the existing set. No such distinction of the types of tools is mentioned in the classical grimoiric literature.

As I outline specific tools in this and later chapters, I will usually focus upon those explained in the more generalized *Key of Solomon the King*. This is especially appropriate because the *Key* is the fountainhead of the Solomonic tradition.

The Aspergillum and the Consecration of Water

Your shamanic journey begins with the aspergillum, or holy water sprinkler. This tool (along with the holy water and censer we shall see below) is one of the few grimoiric tools that do not require special consecration. This is because one cannot perform the necessary consecrations without them. Instead of through invocation, this tool gains its virtue from the natural substances used in its construction. *The Key of Solomon the King*, Book II, Chapter 11 (Of the Water and Of the Hyssop) instructs one to gather nine sacred herbs to employ for this purpose:

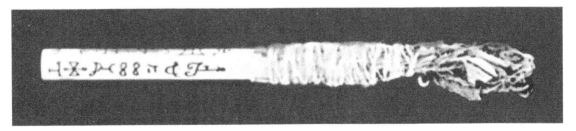

Solomonic Aspergillum.

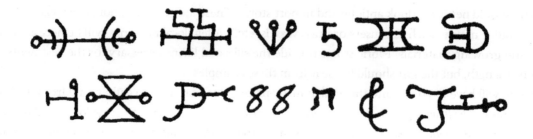

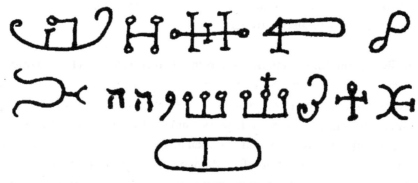

Aspergillum Sigils.

Thou shalt . . . make unto thyself a Sprinkler of vervain,[9] fennel, lavender, sage, valerian, mint, garden-basil, rosemary, and hyssop, gathered in the day and hour of Mercury, the moon being in her increase. Bind together these herbs with a thread spun by a young maiden, and engrave upon the handle on the one side the characters shown in figure 82, and on the other side those given in Figure 83.

In all shamanic systems of magick, the gathering and combination of living plants is considered very powerful magick.[10] In this case, most of the plants included have seemingly obvious significance (to greater or lesser degrees). The hyssop is culled from biblical scripture associated with Psalm 51.[11] Sage is used to this day in Orthodox Christian practice to sprinkle holy water. Others—such as the lavender, mint (for which I used spearmint), and rosemary—are specifically pleasant to smell. Finally, nine would appear to be an important number within the Solomonic system, as evidenced by the instructions for nine days of purification elsewhere in the *Key*.

Luckily, none of the herbs required for the aspergillum are rare or hard to find. The best case scenario, of course, would be to find these plants in the wild; gathering them on a Wednesday, in an hour of Mercury, while the Moon is waxing. If this is not possible, then purchasing seeds would be a wonderful idea, so that one could build a relationship with the plants as they are raised from infancy. Failing this (if, like myself, you aren't known for a green thumb) you can easily find whole plants for sale. They are inexpensive (under two dollars a piece), and one only needs to purchase pots, soil, and plant food to go along with them. Bring them home, plant them where they can receive plenty of direct sunlight, and care for them for a few weeks prior to harvesting. Doing this allows the plants to establish a relationship with yourself as well as with their new environment, both of which are vitally important to this process. Do not be afraid to talk to them, pray over them, etc., and remember that each plant has its own angel set over it. It is important to connect with these intelligences as you care for the plants.

Your real quest will be in finding thread spun by a young maiden. To begin with, we must decide what exactly the *Key* means by "maiden." This literally refers to a virginal girl, who thus has her maidenhead (hymen) intact. The loss of virginity indicates that one has left behind the innocence of childhood and entered the realm of adult politics. This is associated with the fourth mental circuit—concerned with taboos, etc.—and this is where all concepts of ritual purity rest.

On the other hand, the term "maiden" was also commonly used to indicate a woman who had not married, regardless of her sexual activity. For instance, I have seen it argued that the Virgin Mary is so called because she and Joseph were not yet married at the time of Jesus' birth (they were merely betrothed), even though they had quite obviously had sex.

My own opinion is that the instructions are referring to a virginal girl. The *Key* seems to stress the importance of the maiden being young (both for the aspergillum and elsewhere), and even once calls for candle wicks made by a "young girl" (see below). Given the nature of the grimoires, and the Christian culture which penned them, I would place my bet on the idea that sexual purity was the intention.

Interestingly, I have also learned of a parallel in another tradition: Tibetan Buddhism, specifically the *anuttarayoga tantras*, demands virgin-spun thread for certain five-colored cords worn during initiation. The emphasis is specifically on virginity, and in this case the virgin can be either male or female. However, the tradition has naturally evolved with the times, so that it can continue in a modern world that is somewhat short on virginal thread-spinners. Instead of spinning the thread by hand, a young monk or nun is simply sent to a store to purchase the necessary thread.

Another option is to do some research on existing art and craft festivals, and find those which advertise hand-crafted and home-spun goods. (Farmers markets in Pennsylvania's Amish and Mennonite districts have been suggested as a good bet.) It would then be necessary to visit these places and spend some time and effort searching for a young girl that hand-spins thread. If necessary, an item containing such thread could be purchased.

If a quest for virgin-spun thread comes up short in any case, it would ultimately be acceptable to simply purchase some thread and consecrate it in the standard Solomonic manner. (See the end of this chapter.) This doesn't mean that the proper thread will not present itself in time.

Again, there is no need to wait until all such quests are ended in order to get started. Solomonic holy water can be made and used without the aspergillum. The instructions for the water are contained in the same chapter of the *Key* in which the sprinkler is described.

Solomonic Holy Water

First of all, one must prepare a censer with holy perfume (see below), a vessel of brass, varnished lead, or of earth (such as clay or terra cotta), and salt. On the day and hour of Mercury, fill the vessel with pure water, either (as is best) from a clear and natural stream, or one can purchase bottles of purified water for the purpose. Then, say the following blessing over the salt:

> Tzabaoth, Messiach, Emanuel, Elohim Gibor, Yod He Vav He; **O God, Who art the Truth and the Life, deign to bless and sanctify this Creature of Salt, to serve unto us for help, protection, and assistance in this Art, experiment, and operation, and may it be a succour unto us.**

Cast the salt into the vessel of water, and then recite the following Psalms over the salt water:

102 (*Hear my prayer, O Lord, and let my cry come unto thee.*)

54 (*Save me, O God, by Thy name, and judge me by Thy strength.*)

6 (*O Lord, rebuke me not in Thine anger, neither chasten me in Thy hot displeasure.*)

67 (*God be merciful unto us, and bless us; and cause his face to shine upon us.*)

The *Key of Solomon the King* then ends the chapter with the following explanation concerning the uses of the holy water:

> After this thou mayest use the Water, using the Sprinkler whenever it is necessary; and know that wheresoever thou shalt sprinkle this Water, it will chase away all Phantoms, and they shall be unable to hinder or annoy any. With this same Water thou shalt make all the preparations of the Art.

The Censer and the Consecration of Incense

Agrippa outlines his theory on the ceremonial use of incense in his *Three Books of Occult Philosophy*, Book I, Chapter 43. In the very first paragraph, he explains the process by which air is taken into the body (via the lungs) and incorporated into the flesh (via the bloodstream). In a sense, breathing is a form of Eucharist, in which a substance outside the body is accepted into the body and physically assimilated. In an occult sense, doing this temporarily (and—to some extent—permanently) brings one into sympathy with the thing ingested. The two become one; or "You are what you eat/breathe." Therefore, says Agrippa, inhaling air that is perfumed with scents appropriate to one star or another will help bring one into sympathy with that force. (In a similar vein, consider our modern understanding of the relationship between the sense of smell and memory recall.)

Of course, this is not the whole of the philosophy behind the offering of incense. In chapter 4, I discussed the nature of ritual sacrifice and offering as it was understood by the authors of the grimoires. I outlined several useful forms of sacrifice, among them the offering of wax/candles and plants/incense. These two forms of sacrifice are obviously the most utilized by the grimoiric mage, either ancient or modern. Incense is offered liberally during all prayers and invocations, and a mage's oratory will often become shrouded in fog.

Therefore, the use of the censer in the ceremonies, along with the exorcism and consecration of the perfumes and the fire, should be approached in a properly devotional manner. The importance of this practice is stressed in such books as the *Key of Solomon the King* (Book I, Chapter 7):

> These things being thus done and performed, ye shall see the Spirits come from all sides in great haste with their Princes and Superiors. [. . .] Let [the Master], also, renew his fumigations, and offer large quantities of Incense, which he should at once place upon the fire, in order to appease the Spirits as he hath promised them.

It is vital to understand the ritualized use of incense as a form of sacrifice, to "appease" (or nourish, or attract) the spirits. Otherwise, the ingredients for perfumes listed in such sources as the *Picatrix* and Agrippa's *Three Books* would be shocking at best. Very often they include animal products, blood,[12] stones, magnets, and other seemingly odd or repulsive ingredients. Yet, it is very likely that these recipes have descended to us from shamanic sources (both European and Arabic), and are derived from the ritual sacrifices that were made on a larger scale in more ancient times.[13] Let us take a look at Agrippa's list of planetary "fumes," from Book I, Chapter 44 of the *Three Books*:

Sol: Take saffron, ambergris, musk, lignum-aloes, lignum-balsam, the fruit of the laurel, cloves, myrrh, and frankincense. Mix these together in such proportions that they will produce a sweet odor. Then incorporate the brain of an eagle, or the blood of a white rooster, "after the manner of pills."[14]

Luna: Take the head of a dried frog, the eyes of a bull, the seed of white poppy, frankincense, and camphor. Incorporate menstrual blood or the blood of a goose.

Saturn: Take the seed of black poppy, henbane (or, perhaps, the seed of henbane), the root of mandrake, the loadstone (a magnet—preferably a natural one), and myrrh. Mix them with the brain of a cat, or the blood of a bat. Notice that most of the plants listed for Saturn are extremely toxic.

Jupiter: Take the seed of ash, lignum aloes, storax, gum benjamin, a stone of lapis lazuli, and the tops of peacock feathers (easily purchased in decorative stores). Then add the blood of a stork, or a swallow, or the brain of a hart.

Mars: Take euphorbium, bdellium, bum aromaniac, the roots of both hellebores, the loadstone, and a small amount of sulfur. Then add the brain of a hart, the blood of a man, and the blood of a black cat.[15]

Venus: Take musk, ambergris, lignum-aloes, red roses, and red coral. Include the brain of a sparrow, and blood of a pigeon.

Mercury: Take mastic, frankincense, cloves, the herb cinquefoil, and the stone achates. Incorporate the brain of a fox or weasel, and the blood of a magpie.

I would assume that none of my readers will likely make these perfumes anytime soon. While some time spent in an Afro-Cuban botannica might yield some results (such as frog parts, or the more obscure plants and incenses), it would still be some feat to obtain such things as the eyes of a bull. Thankfully, even Agrippa did not expect us to create all of these incredible (and perhaps none-too-pleasant-smelling) perfumes. (I notice, too, that the more shocking ingredients are always appended to the ends of the lists of ingredients. I see no reason why these perfumes cannot simply be made without the animal products, etc.) His chapter continues to give more generalized associations of plants and scents to the various spiritual forces.

For Saturn, Agrippa prescribes all odoriferous (pleasant-smelling) roots such as pepperwort root, etc., as well as the frankincense tree. For Jupiter, all odiferous fruits such as nutmeg or cloves. For Mars, all odiferous wood such as sanders, cypress, lignum-balsam, and lignum aloes. For the Sun, we can use all gums such as frankincense, mastic, benjamin, storax, gum laudanum, ambergris, and musk. For Venus we utilize flowers, such as roses, violets, saffron, etc. For Mercury, the peels of wood and fruit are appropriate, such as cinnamon, lignum-cassia, mace, citron peel, bayberries, and all odiferous seeds. Finally, for Luna we may use the leaves of all vegetables, such as leaf Indum, myrtle leaves, and bay tree.

Furthermore, Agrippa teaches that we should use utilize a good fume—pleasant smelling and precious—for all positive matters such as love, goodwill, etc. On the other hand, for all negative purposes, such as hatred, anger, or misery, we should use a stinking fume that is of no worth. We will revisit this idea in chapter 12, where the exorcism of evil spirits is discussed.

Also, because the practicing mage might find the information useful for advanced work, I have included the list that Agrippa gives us for each of the twelve signs of the zodiac.

Aries: Myrrh	**Libra**: Galbanum
Taurus: Pepperwort	**Scorpius**: Opopanax
Gemini: Mastic	**Sagittarius** Lignum-aloes
Cancer: Camphor	**Capricornus**: Benjamin
Leo: Frankincense	**Aquarius**: Euphorbium
Virgo: Sanders	**Pisces**: Red Storax

A Standard Incense

At the same time, it is also a good idea to compound an incense intended for general use. Many operations do not require one to call upon a particular celestial force, but rather to invoke pure divine light, such as in the consecration of holy water or various of the tools. Plus, using the same incense for most general purposes establishes a psychological relationship between the mage and his magick. Eventually, the merest whiff of the scent will place the mage into a proper mindset for magickal work.

Agrippa's Chapter 44 suggests such a perfume made from seven planetary aromatics: pepperwort (from Saturn), nutmeg (Jupiter), lignum-aloes (Mars), mastic (Sol), saffron (Venus), cinnamon (Mercury), and myrtle (from Luna). Mix each of these together so they produce a pleasant odor when burned.[16]

The *Key of Solomon the King* also has a version, found in Book II, Chapter 10 (Concerning Incense. . .). Apparently, this is intended for general use throughout the Solomonic system. Mix together incense (frankincense), aloes, nutmeg, gum-benjamin, musk, and "other fragrant spices." This is a very simple example, though I offer it here for the sake of interest and scholarship. A truly "orthodox" Solomonic operation would utilize this scent.

An even better general-use incense is that described in the *Book of Abramelin*, Book II, Chapter 11, which is used for all purposes from the invocation of the guardian angel to the conjuration of the infernal spirits. In fact, the perfume is derived from the most official of grimoiric sources, the Bible. As we see in Exodus 30:34–35:

> And the Lord said unto Moses, "Take unto thee sweet spices, stacte, and onycha, and galbanum; these sweet spices with pure frankincense: of each there shall be a like weight. And thou shalt make it a perfume, a confection after the art of the apothecary, tempered together, pure and holy."

Compare this, then, to the recipe given in the *Book of Abramelin*: one part of incense in tears (olibanum, frankincense), one-half part of stacte (storax, benzoin), and one-quarter part lignum-aloes (or cedar, rose petals, or citron).[17] Reduce all of these to a fine powder (or purchase them as such and mix them thoroughly), and keep the result in a sealed container.

I would advise against simply purchasing "Abramelin Incense," since such perfumes rarely contain the actual ingredients as listed in the grimoire. Therefore, the store-bought versions are further removed from the original biblical model.

Exorcism and Consecration of Perfumes

What the *Key of Solomon the King* has to say about incense—mainly in Book II, Chapter 10—is quite parallel to Agrippa's teachings. The perfumes are described as offerings to the spirits, and those of good odor are offered to good spirits, while those of evil odor are offered to the infernal spirits. The chapter then continues to give its recipe for a general incense of good odor (see above section), and then prescribes the procedure to exorcise, consecrate, and use the perfume. Of course, this can be used to consecrate any perfume for grimoiric mysticism.

Prepare holy water and the aspergillum. Over the newly mixed incense, recite the following Exorcism of the Incense:

> O God of Abraham, God of Isaac, God of Jacob, deign to bless these odoriferous spices so that they may receive strength, virtue, and power to attract the Good Spirits, and to banish and cause to retire all hostile Phantoms. Through Thee, O Most Holy Adonai, Who livest and reignest unto the Ages of the Ages. Amen.

> I exorcise thee, O Spirit impure and unclean, thou who art a hostile Phantom, in the Name of God, that thou quit this Perfume, thou and all thy deceits, that it may be consecrated and sanctified in the name of God Almighty. May the holy Spirit of God grant protection and virtue unto those who use these Perfumes; and may the hostile and evil Spirit and Phantom never be able to enter therein, through the Ineffable Name of God Almighty. Amen.

> O Lord, deign to bless and to sanctify this Creature of Perfume so that it may be a remedy unto mankind for the health of body and of soul, through the Invocation of Thy Holy Name. May all Creatures who receive the odour of this incense and of these spices receive health of body and of soul, through Him Who hath formed the Ages. Amen.

Finish by sprinkling the incense with the "Water of the Art."[18] Then either wrap the finished product in a piece of consecrated silk (see below), or store it in a sealed container. I assume that wrapping the incense in silk is intended when it is used in ceremony, similar to the way in which talismans are often wrapped or covered with white silk or linen.

Jumping ahead in the *Key* for just a moment, Chapter 10 actually ends with a short recitation for use with any "Fumigations of evil odour." However, it is not clear where this prayer is intended to be spoken. It would appear, due to its content, to be a replacement for the "God of Abraham" prayer above. After all, the "God of Abraham" prayer does request the attraction of good spirits, and would thus be moot in regards to unpleasant perfumes. Therefore the following alternative is given for the purpose:

> **Adonai, Lazai, Dalmai, Aima, Elohi**, O Holy Father, grant unto us succour, favour, and grace, by the Invocation of Thy Holy Name, so that these things may serve us for aid in all that we wish to perform therewith, that all deceit may quit them, and that they may be blessed and sanctified through Thy Name. Amen.

After which, continue with the usual process from "I exorcise thee . . ." onward.

The Censer, and Using the Perfumes

The same chapter of the *Key of Solomon the King* proceeds from the Exorcism of the Incense to instructions for the censer. According to the text, this should be an earthen vessel (clay, terra cotta, etc.), glazed within and without. (Or, several such vessels if the operation of the *Key* is followed.) In Book I, Chapter 8, one is instructed to use a "Vessel of Earth," which might mean one made of earth, or one containing earth. Personally, I always use brass censers filled with river or beach sand.

Ultimately, any censer that seems appropriate to the grimoiric mindset (or the choice of the working mage) would be just as well. My own censer was a gift from a retired Orthodox clergyman, which he had used in his own personal rites of worship (such as the eucharist). Within the grimoiric or Solomonic traditions, any magickal tool or vestment that was once in use by the priests or Levites in their ceremonies is desirable.

It is best to have a coal-burning censer. They are more useful for burning home-mixed incenses, and they tend to produce an impressive amount of smoke. However, if necessary, one could certainly use appropriate stick incense. This might even be preferable in some cases, such as the Solomonic bath (see chapter seven), after which one must cense oneself with consecrated perfume. None of the Solomonic procedure needs to change if a stick is used.

To use the perfumes in the censer, begin by igniting the coal (or the stick). I suggest holding it over the flame of the holy lamp (described in this chapter below) until it catches, while simultaneously reciting the Exorcism of the Fire:

> I exorcise thee, O Creature of Fire, by Him through Whom all things have been made, so that every kind of Phantasm may retire from thee, and be unable to harm or deceive in any way, through the Invocation of the Most High Creator of All. Amen.

> Bless, O Lord All Powerful, and All Merciful, this Creature of Fire, so that being blessed by Thee, it may be for the honour and glory of Thy Most Holy Name, so that it may work no hindrance or evil unto those who use it. Through Thee, O Eternal and Almighty Lord, and through Thy Most Holy Name. Amen.

This being completed, the incense can be cast upon the coal and used as needed.

Holy Anointing Oil

We have already discussed the shamanic uses of anointing oils in chapter 3, where we learned that such oils as found in the *Goetia* were very possibly of a psychedelic nature. At the same time, the use of oil has another cultural foundation separate from concerns of mind-alteration. It may very well extend far beyond our own historical era, into the earliest of tribally organized society.

If so, then holy oil has its birth in primitive rites of sexual fertility, where it would have been used in a very practical sense, as lubrication. The oil is a symbol of feminine sexuality, much in the same way the scepter (which shares an origin related to that of holy oil) is symbolic of male virility. In time, the symbolism of those rites became incorporated into the rite of marriage and the consecration of the sacred king (early agricultural era). In order to rule his kingdom rightfully, the king had to ceremonially marry the land itself. During the consecration (or inauguration), the king's head would be anointed in a manner entirely symbolic of the anointing of the male's head, and therefore of the consummation of the marriage itself. It was associated with the creation of priests and prophets in much the same way, perhaps symbolic of the devotee's marriage/consummation with his or her patron or spiritual spouse.

There is a holy anointing oil prescribed by Yahweh in Exodus 30:22–33, which is indeed intended to consecrate the priesthood:

> Take thou also unto thee principal spices,[19] of pure myrrh five hundred shekels, and of sweet cinnamon half so much, even two hundred and fifty shekels, and of sweet calamus two hundred fifty shekels, and of cassia five hundred shekels, after the shekel of the sanctuary, and of oil olive an hin. And thou shalt make it an oil of holy ointment, and ointment compound after the art of the apothecary: it shall be an holy anointing oil.

> [. . .]

And thou shalt anoint Aaron and his sons, and consecrate them, that thy may minister unto me in the priests office.

The same chapter extends the use of the holy oil to the next logical step; with Yahweh instructing its employment for the consecration of all of the vessels, tools, implements, and furnishings of the tabernacle.

Just as we saw with the holy incense above, the *Book of Abramelin* derives its recipe and use for holy oil from the same biblical source. It is also found in *Abramelin* Book II, Chapter 11, and we can readily see the similarities to the above quotation from Exodus:

You shall prepare the sacred oil in this manner: Take of myrrh in tears,[20] one part; of fine cinnamon, two parts; of galangal half a part; and the half of the total weight of these drugs of the best olive oil. The which aromatics you shall mix together according to Art of the Apothecary, and shall make thereof a Balsam, the which you shall keep in a glass vial . . .

The mention of the "Art of the Apothecary" in both examples is likely a reference to an aspect of the alchemical arts, by which essential oils are extracted from plant matter. The process is easy enough to learn, but I will pass over it for now. It is acceptable to purchase all of the above ingredients in an essential oil form, and mix them according to the directions. Again, beware of ready-made Abramelin oil, as it may or may not include the proper ingredients. (I have also mixed this oil with the powdered forms of the plants, which results in a rather interesting substance that appears like blood.)

There are other traditional recipes for holy oil in existence, though the Abramelin oil, like the Abramelin incense, is my favorite choice. As both the *Book of Abramelin* and the Bible suggest, it can be used in the consecration of any tool, weapon, vestment, implement, or holy furnishing. It can also be used to anoint oneself and others for purification or magickal preparation, or to anoint talismans and magickal images in the ceremonies of enlivening. Falling short of this particular recipe for holy oil, the use of pure olive oil (purchased in any grocery store) is more than acceptable. Pure olive oil possesses its own traditional history, including a basis in biblical authority.

The Silk Cloths

The *Key of Solomon the King* includes a process of preparation and consecration for the silk cloths used to wrap tools, magickal books, talismans, etc., for storage. It appears in Book II, Chapter 20 (Concerning the Silken Cloth). Any appropriate color silk may be used with the exception of black or gray. I generally tend to rely upon white cloths for this purpose, as it is fitting to the Solomonic tradition (which utilizes a lot of white material—altar cloths, robes, linen coverings, etc.). The color white is also appropriate in the place of any other color besides black or gray.

There is a single exception to the ban on black silk for wrapping a tool, and that is the cloth used for the black-hilted knife (see chapter 11). This is a particularly goetic weapon, used to command infernal and earthbound spirits, and is therefore covered with a cloth of black silk. The *Key* is unclear on whether or not one should consecrate the black silk according to the following instructions, but I would do so in any case.

Obtain the necessary silk, the censer, and a holy perfume such as the incense of Abramelin, and holy water. Once the silk has been cut and prepared, it is necessary to inscribe the following characters upon it with a pen or fine-tip marker. (It is best if the writing instrument is set aside specifically for magickal use: see chapter 9.)

Then, light the censer (not forgeting the exorcism of the fire) and place the incense upon the coal. Perfume the pieces of silk, and then sprinkle them with the holy water. Recite the following Psalms:

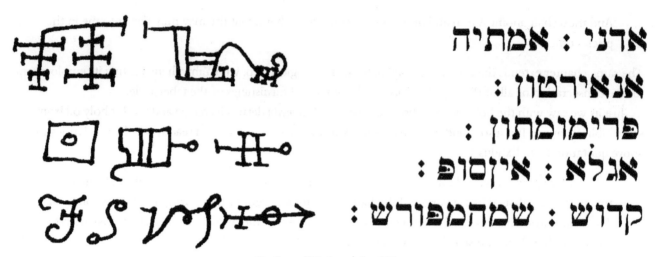

אדני : אמתיה
אנאירטון :
פרימומתון :
אגלא : אינסוף :
קדוש : שמהמפורש :

Sigils and Hebrew for Silk.

82 (*God has taken His place in the assembly of the Gods . . .*)

72 (*Give the king thy judgements, O God, and thy righteousness unto the king's son.*)

134 (*Behold, bless ye the Lord, all ye servants of the Lord . . .*)

64 (*Hear my voice, O God, in my prayer, preserve my life from fear of the enemy.*)[21]

Once complete, the silk is then placed in a container with sweet spices for a period of seven days. For the "sweet spices," I highly recommend compounding the Egyptian incense known as Kyphi. It smells absolutely wonderful without being burned. Just make sure it does not come into direct contact with the silk cloth, as it will stain.

Recipe for Kyphi Incense

—Raisins   —1 part cedar
—White wine   —2 parts myrrh
—Honey   —2 parts gum mastic
—4 parts frankincense   —1 part galangal or ginger
—2 parts benzoin   —One-half part cinnamon
—One-half part juniper berries

Mix the dry ingredients together first, and set them aside in an airtight container. Then, place the raisins in their own airtight container, and pour the white wine over them. Seal both of these and let them rest for several days. Finally, combine the two concoctions in one bowl, add the honey, and mix thoroughly with the hands. (Your entire home will be permeated with the pleasant smell of the Kyphi as you do this.) The result can then be kept in its own sealed container, and then wrapped in plastic for use with the Solomonic wrapping silks.

The Burin, Needle, and Other Iron Instruments [22]

The burin—or engraver—is a pointed metal instrument used to inscribe figures into wood or metal. Professional instruments can be purchased, or the burin can be as simple as a nail affixed into a wooden handle and sharpened on the other end. (The ultramodern mage might wish to consecrate a Dremel tool to the purpose.) This tool will be more necessary for talismanic magick, but it is included here because it can also be used to inscribe tools such as the wand, or even the blades of the various daggers and swords called for in the grimoiric traditions.

At the same time, this consecration is necessary for the needle that will be used to sew the magickal robes. (In chapter 10, we will see the *Key* also uses such a consecrated needle and virgin-spun thread to affix talismans to the front of the robe.) Finally, this same procedure can be used for the consecration of any further iron or steel instruments that become necessary along the way: scissors, compasses, pins, etc, etc.

In fact, there are two procedures given for this consecration in the *Key of Solomon the King*. The first is in Book II, Chapter 8, where the bulk of the generalized working tools are presented.[23] The second appears later in Book II, Chapter 19 (Concerning the Needle and Other Iron Instruments). It seems to me that this latter example was included as a companion to Chapter 18 (Of Wax and Virgin Earth), which explains how to consecrate material for the creation of magickal images. Just as with Voodoo dolls, such waxen or earthen poppets were sometimes pierced with needles, and chapter 19 does make reference to using the needle to either "prick or sew." In any case, the two consecrations are interchangeable, and the text specifies their use for the burin, needle, or any necessary tool of iron. The choice of which to use is left to the student.

The example from chapter 8 instructs one to fashion the burin or needle in the day and hour of either Mars or Venus. Upon the handle, inscribe the figures as shown in the illustration above.

Sprinkle and cense the new instrument as usual for such magickal tools, and then repeat the following prayer:

> **Asophiel, Asophiel, Asophiel, Pentagrammaton, Athanatos, Eheieh Asher Eheieh, Qadosh, Qadosh, Qadosh**; O God Eternal, and my Father, bless this Instrument prepared in Thine honour, so that it may only serve for a good use and end, for Thy Glory. Amen.

Finish the procedure by perfuming and sprinkling the instrument once again, then wrap it in consecrated silk and put it away for later use.

The second example from Chapter 19 is somewhat more involved. This time, there are no sigils given for inscription on the burin, though I do not think that the previously-given characters would be out of place if used here. Whatever steel instrument is fashioned, it should be done in the day and hour of Jupiter. Have the censer, perfumes, and holy water ready. Recite this conjuration over the finished tool:

> I conjure thee, O Instrument of Steel, by God the Father Almighty, by the Virtue of the Heavens, of the Stars, and of the Angels who preside over them; by the virtue of stones, herbs, and animals; by the virtue of hail, snow, and wind; that thou receivest such virtue that thou mayest obtain without deceit

The Burin.

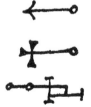

The Burin Sigils.

the end which I desire in all things wherein I shall use thee; through God the Creator of the Ages, and Emperor of the Angels. Amen.

Then repeat the following Psalms:

3 (*Lord, how are they increased that trouble me!*)

9 (*I will praise Thee, O Lord, with all my heart; I will shew forth all Thy marvelous works.*)

31 (*In Thee, O Lord, do I put my trust; let me never be ashamed . . .*)

42 (*As the hart panteth after the water brooks, so panteth my soul after thee, O God.*)

60 (*O God, Thou hast cast us off, Thou hast scattered us, thou hast been displeased . . .*)

51 (*Have mercy upon me, O God, according to Thy loving kindness . . .*)

130 (*Out of the depths have I cried unto Thee, O Lord.*)

Then cense and sprinkle the new tool as usual, wrap it in consecrated silk, and say the following invocation over it before putting it away:

Dani, Zumech, Agalmaturod, Gadiel, Pani, Caneloas, Merod, Gamidoi, Baldoi, Metrator, Angels most holy, be present for a guard unto this instrument.

The White Robe and Other Vestments

The robe may be a simple tau tobe, that is, a floor-length pull-over robe with sleeves that extend to large cuffs. It is a rather standard item throughout Western occultism, and you would be hard-pressed to find a text on beginner's magickal practice that does not include a design for such a robe. The *Key of Solomon the King*, in Book II, Chapter 6 (Of the Garments and Shoes of the Art), instructs that the robe is best made of silk, but can also be made of linen. If it is made of linen, then it must be sewn together with thread spun by a young maiden. (See the discussion on such thread with the aspergillum above, as well as the section on finding obscure items.) I assume the virgin-spun thread would be much too coarse for use with pure silk.

If you are somehow fortunate enough to come into possession of such vestments as worn by Christian or Jewish holy men during sacred rites, the *Key* says this is all the better. The reader may remember that I have previously mentioned the preference for holy implements of the "Priests or Levites" in grimoiric magick. This chapter of the *Key* serves as an illustration.

If one wishes to complete a fully Solomonic robe, then it will be necessary to embroider the following characters upon the breast, with a consecrated needle, in red silk thread:

Overall, it is not necessary to have anything more than the white robe for general work. However, when it comes to conjuring and binding infernal spirits, many grimoires incorporate added vestments, such as a crown. This serves as a kind of official "uniform" of authority that the spirits will recognize and respect. For instance, while the *Book of Abramelin* has the aspirant wear nothing but a white linen robe to contact the guardian angel, it further instructs one to don a red silk over-robe and a white and gold silk filet ("crown") when convoking the spirits. These vestments are similar to the traditional Rosicrucian garb, a uniform the spirits will certainly respect.

The vestments outlined in the *Key of Solomon the King* include not only the robe, but also a pair of shoes and a crown. There actually appear to be two conflicting instructions concerning the shoes of the art in the *Key's* Book II, Chapter 6. The first instruction simply says that the shoes must be white, does not mention a material from which they should be made, but does insist that the following characters must be embroidered thereon in the same red silk as previously mentioned:

Tau Robe.

The second set of instructions tells the student to fashion the shoes, or boots, from white leather. In this case, one could hardly be expected to embroider the magickal characters with red silk thread and a needle, so the text simply has one mark the characters thereon, probably with a consecrated pen and ink. If one is performing a true Solomonic operation, the text instructs one to fashion these shoes during the nine days of preparation and purification. (Such would not likely be possible if one were attempting to embroider the magickal characters upon the shoes as described in the first set of instructions. Especially if embroidery is not one's particular skill.)

The crown is simple enough to construct. It must simply be a fillet (like a headband) made of virgin paper, and inscribed with a consecrated pen and ink. (Consecration for parchment and paper, as well as pens and ink will be covered in chapter nine.) On the front should be the Hebrew letters of the name Yod Heh Vav Heh (י ה ו ה); on the back should be Adonai (א ד נ י); on the right side is the name El (א ל), and on the left is Elohim (א ל ה י מ). Again, remember that Hebrew writes from right to left.

Any working partners (which the *Key* refers to as "Disciples") who take part in the ceremonies should also have similar crowns made. However, rather than the four divine names listed above, their crowns are inscribed with these characters (in one continuous line) with consecrated scarlet ink:

Donning the Vestments
The ritual associated with the donning of the vestments is as follows: Begin by reciting Psalm 15 (*Lord, who shall abide in Thy tabernacle? Who shall dwell in Thy holy mountain?*), while perfuming and sprinkling the vestments with the censer and aspergillum. Then, continue to don the robe and any other necessary vestments while reciting the following invocation:

> **Amor, Amator, Amides, Ideodaniach, Pamor, Plaior, Anitor**; through the merits of these holy Angels will I robe and indue myself with the Vestments of Power, through which may I conduct unto the desired end those things which I ardently wish, through Thee, O Most Holy Adonai, Whose Kingdom and Empire endureth forever. Amen.

Finish by reciting the rest of the Psalms in the series (which properly began with Psalm 15 above):

131 (*Lord, my heart is not haughty, nor mine eyes lofty . . .*)

137 (*By the rivers of Babylon, there we sat down . . .*)

Robe Sigils

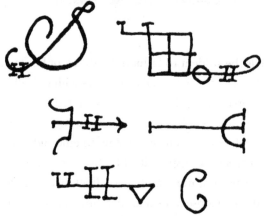

Sigils for Slippers.

117 (*O praise the Lord, all ye nations: praise Him, all ye people.*)

67 (*God be merciful unto us and bless us: and cause His face to shine upon us.*)

68 (*Let God arise, let His enemies scatter: let them also that hate him flee before Him.*)

127 (*Except the Lord build the house, they labour in vain that build it.*)

The White-Hilted Knife

It might be somewhat natural to assume this is the famous magickal dagger, or *athame*, that has become so popular in modern forms of occultism and Neopaganism. In fact, the true ancestor of our modern athame is the black-hilted knife, which we will not see until chapter 11.

The white-hilted knife is actually a very practical item, used for any operation of cutting or carving associated with the magickal art. It can be used to cut materials in the creation of other tools, or (in the absence of a burin) to carve and inscribe magickal figures, or even to cut plants needed in the spells. It is a general "all-purpose" tool, intended to be a ready companion to the practicing mage in his work. The only thing it should not be used for is the inscription of magickal circles, which is associated with lesser spirits, and is thus the job of the black-hilted knife.

Strict orthodoxy in the creation of the Solomonic daggers would require the mage to actually forge his own blades for the daggers, and to fashion his own knife handles. The magickal timing is only a bit more intricate than

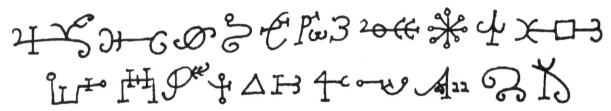

Sigils for Disciples' Crowns.

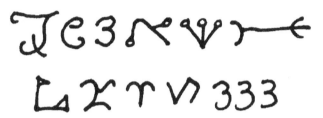

The White-hilted Knife.

usual for the Solomonic tools: it must be the day and hour of Mercury, during the waxing or full Moon (as usual). However, it also requires Mars to reside either in the sign of Aries or Scorpius (the signs it rules).

The blade must be dipped in a special concoction including the juice of a pimpernel plant and the blood of a gosling. (Though I should also point out that the death of the bird is nowhere called for in the rites. This subject was covered in some depth in chapter 4, section "Sacrifice in the Grimoires." Following that is an outline of a humane procedure—found right in the *Key* itself—for drawing only necessary blood from living animals with a mere needle. Then, the interested animal-lover is also referred to the same chapter and section for possible alternatives to the use of animal blood in ritual. Using such an alternative as plant sacrifice (or the "Solomonic Omiero" described in chapter 4) would allow even the dedicated nature-lover or vegetarian to participate in these grimoiric traditions.)

I assume that the dagger should be dipped into the blood and juice concoction while the blade is still red hot from the forge, tempering the metal therein rather than water. (At least, it should be used for the final immersion.) After this is complete, use the burin to engrave the Hebrew letters of the divine name AGLA (א ל ג א) into one side of the blade, and On (נ ו א) into the other side, writing from the point of the dagger toward the hilt. (Remember that Hebrew is written from right to left.) The white-painted hilt should be inscribed (or painted) with the characters shown above, one line on each side.

Dip the completed hilt into the same fluid as the blade. Take the completed knife, cense it with the perfumes of the art, sprinkle it with the aspergillum and holy water, and wrap it in consecrated white silk.

If, like most, you are not a metal-smith, then the *Key* offers a practical alternative. It should be little problem to find and purchase a suitable dagger of the mage's liking. It would be best to obtain one with a bolted-on hilt, so that it can be safely removed while the blade is consecrated. The magickal timing remains the same. Simply place the blade upon steady heat until it becomes red hot, and then thrust it into the same blood and juice as described above. Repeat the process twice more for a total of three heatings and immersions.

From that point, the instructions are the same as before. The white hilt must be decorated with the magickal characters and dipped into the blood and juice. Perfume and sprinkle, wrap in consecrated silk, and the process is complete.

The Holy Lamp and Candles

As the *Key of Solomon the King* says in Book II, Chapter 12 (Of the Light, and of the Fire), it has long been the custom around the world to utilize fire and light in sacred rites. The earliest religions that looked to the sky for the gods found heavenly bodies that shone with their own light (the Sun, Moon, and stars) and called them the "Bright and Shining Ones." On the other hand, the awesome power of fire had long been known to the creatures of earth, and it became a truly sacred thing once mankind had tamed the element. There was almost certainly a recognized sympathy between the light, heat-giving fire and the luminous heavenly bodies (especially the Sun).

Contained fire caused, perhaps, the first major social revolution among our species. At first, it was necessary to wait for a fire to occur naturally, such as a forest fire caused by a lightning strike. Then, some brave soul would have to venture into the smoldering wreckage and retrieve some scrap of wood upon which the fire was still alive. This, then, would be brought back to the home and used to build a fire at the entrance to a cave or other dwelling, or perhaps simply in the center of the tribe's camp. The family could dwell quite comfortably inside, knowing that the fire at the door would keep out the cold, predators, and probably a fair amount of insects as well.

The fire quickly became the central axis of ancient domestic life. It was around the fire that the clan gathered to tell stories, cook food, bake pottery, etc. It was the fire that offered protection from harmful animals as well as those humans who still feared it. To the rest of the animal kingdom—of which we had, until that point, been an accepted member—we became living gods. Our harnessing of fire was the foundation of our species' advancement and evolution. The rocket-powered ships that are reaching into space today are the descendants of the simple fires that once flickered at the entrances of caves.

However, since our prehistorical ancestors did not yet know how to create fire on their own, it was necessary to keep a perpetual watch on the tribal fire. If it went out for some reason, there was no telling when it could be replaced. Fire was yet a gift from the gods—brought down from heaven strictly at the whim of a Promethean benefactor. The importance of guarding this fire on a constant basis was so vital that it lives with us to this very day in religions such as Catholicism that make use of eternal flames. (We will return to this subject briefly in chapter 8.) More than likely, there is a natural historical progression from the first tribal fires, to the Zoroastrian religion of flame worship, and from there to the later Judeo-Christian traditions.

When the *Key of Solomon the King* was written, there was, of course, no means of creating artificial light. Candles and oil lamps were as common then as lightbulbs are today. When used to illuminate a temple or church, it was necessary to consecrate them to the purpose just as one would with any other furnishing. The grimoiric mage, too, needed light by which to work and read his invocations. Likely adopting the practice from Catholicism, the *Key* has the reader consecrate the candles used in the grimoiric lamp.

The practical use of the lamp is no more complicated than that. It can be suspended within the room where one works, preferably above the altar, but it can ultimately rest where it gives the best light. If one cannot hang the lamp properly, it can always be set upon the altar itself. When working outside, the *Key* instructs that a working partner hold the lamp near the master so the latter can see his work, read the invocations, etc. Obviously, it would be best to

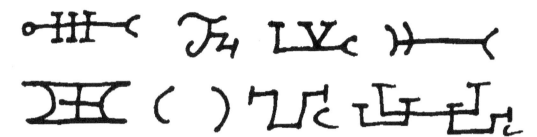

Sigils for Holy Candles.

avoid all artificial light when working grimoiric magick, so that the only (or principal) light is coming from the lamp of divine fire. It represents the eternal light of God, set over and above all of the mystical proceedings.

The *Book of Abramelin* makes use of such a holy lamp, but does not require the consecration of candles, etc. Instead, a simple oil lamp is used, specifically one that burns olive oil. If a proper olive oil lamp cannot be found, then a simple "hurricane lamp" that burns clear lamp oil can be used. In fact, some extremely beautiful hurricane lamps can be found, even some that are made to be suspended from the ceiling. There is only one consecration of tools outlined in *Abramelin*—done on a single day where all of the tools, vestments, and furnishings are consecrated at once. This is done by simply reciting a prayer of consecration (see chapter 7) and then touching the instruments with some of the holy anointing oil.

The *Key of Solomon the King* makes use of a candle-burning lamp instead. It calls for a square lantern with crystal (or glass) sides; an item which can be found in many home decoration stores, craft stores, or even antique stores. Nothing special needs to be done to the lantern, as it is the candle which receives all of the mystical attention.

To produce the necessary candles, it will be necessary to obtain fresh beeswax. This can be purchased in craft stores, as long as you make sure to get *pure* beeswax *without* any bleaching or coloring. Natural beeswax has an almost greenish hue to it, and will not appear as a pure white substance. Even better than buying the wax, of course, would be to contact a bee keeper and obtain the wax there. It would then be necessary to melt the wax down and strain out the impurities.

It will also be necessary to obtain the wicks to place in the candles. The *Key* suggests that these should have been made by a "young girl," which brings us back to the same situation we had with the aspergillum. Return to that section, as well as the beginning of this chapter, for advice on how to possibly locate thread spun by a young virgin. If such cannot be found, then it might be acceptable to simply have a young girl purchase the necessary wicks. If all else fails, just buy the wicks, consecrate them, and get on with it.

To fashion the candles, you have various options. If you know a bit about candle making, and have the equipment to produce your own dipped candles, then certainly take advantage of the situation. On the other hand, simple candle-making kits can be purchased from craft stores that include a mold by which the tapers can be easily fashioned. Perhaps the least desirable, yet still acceptable, method would be to buy already-made natural beeswax candles.

Finally, gather together your burin, holy water, and aspergillum, and the censer and incense. The Moon must be in its waxing phase, and the day and hour must be of Mercury. Fashion the candles as you see fit, making sure they will fit in the lantern. The *Key* insists that they should each be half a pound in weight, though I doubt this would be the most important concern to the magick. Once the candles are molded, inscribe the following characters upon them with the burin:

Then, recite the following Psalms over the candles:

102 (*Hear my prayer, O Lord, and let my cry come unto thee.*)

103 (*Bless the Lord, O my soul: and all that is within me . . .*)

107 (*O give thanks unto the Lord, for He is good: for His mercy endureth forever.*)

In fact, the *Key* lists Psalm 151 (or "cli") as the first Psalm to be recited. However, there is no such thing as a Psalm 151 in the Bible. There were a few points that made me choose Psalm 102 as the likely candidate for the intended prayer. First, I took note that the other two listed Psalms are 103 and 107, thus suggesting that perhaps the first Psalm should also be in the range of 100 to 109. That alone would not be enough to speculate, of course, except for the fact that the roman numerals which appear in the text "cli" (151) could so easily be a scribal error for "cii" (102). The final test was to see if Psalm 102 made proper sense according to our understanding of Psalmody in grimoiric magick. Sure enough, this prayer is a typical example of a Psalm that should begin a series of invocations. It begins "Hear my prayer, O Lord, and let my cry come unto Thee!"; showing that it is aimed at getting the initial attention of father sky, after which the next Psalms in the list come quite naturally. (See chapter 4 for more information on psalmody.)

After reciting or chanting the Psalms, continue with the following invocation:

O Lord God, Who governest all things by Thine Almighty Power, give unto me, a poor sinner, understanding and knowledge to do only that which is agreeable unto Thee; grant unto me to fear, adore, love, praise, and give thanks unto Thee with true and sincere faith and perfect charity. Grant, O Lord, before I die, and descend into the realms beneath, and before they fiery flame shall devour me, that Thy Grace may not leave me, O Lord of my Soul. Amen.

I exorcise thee, O Creature of Wax, by Him Who alone hath created all things by His Word, and by the virtue of Him Who is pure truth, that thou cast out from thee every Phantasm, Perversion, and Deceit of the Enemy, and may the Virtue and Power of God enter into thee, so that thou mayest give us light, and chase far from us all fear and terror.

Finally, sprinkle and cense the new candles as usual. Wrap them in consecrated white silk, and place them with the lantern in a safe place until needed. These candles can be used in the lantern as well as anywhere else that candles might be called for in the ceremonies. You may make as many at once as you need or wish.

The Exorcism of the Fire

When you have any cause to light these Solomonic candles, it will be necessary to recite the following Exorcism of the Fire:

I exorcise thee, O Creature of Fire, in the Name of the Sovereign and Eternal Lord, by His Ineffable Name, which is **Yod, He, Vau, He**; by the Name **Yah**; and by the Name of Power **El**; that thou mayest enlighten the heart of all the Spirits which we shall call unto this Circle (or etc.), so that they may appear before us without fraud and deceit through Him Who hath created all things.

The Solomonic Wand

As I mentioned in the section on holy oil above, the magickal wand or scepter also possesses a probable origin in ancient fertility rites. It is the symbol of male virility, and may have once been used in a very practical manner in conjunction with an anointing oil. Later on, this was utilized in a symbolic manner in the rite of marriage related to the consecration of the sacred king. The taking of the scepter was often as important as the donning of the crown in the inaugural ceremonies.

From that point, the significance of the scepter or rod spread in several cultural directions. In the hands of the king the scepter became a standard symbol of power and governance. A similar significance became associated with the shepherd's rod, especially in the predominantly pastoral biblical tradition. The shepherd's rod was used both to guide the flock through the wilderness and as a weapon to fend off predators. Therefore we see the powerful rod in the hands of such biblical figures as Moses and Aaron.

The magickal wand has been a tool of the priest and magickian for thousands of years, as we can see in lands such as Egypt, from which we most directly borrow our occult understanding of the instrument. The wand held by the mage confirms his own authority over the spiritual and earthly forces. We have discussed in chapter 4 (and will see again in chapter 8) how vital an understanding of spiritual authority is to the practicing grimoiric master.

Because of its association with brute-force command, I nearly saved the wand for chapter 11; where the weapons intended to control infernal spirits are outlined. The master/servant relationship is not generally associated with angelic contact in the grimoires. In the *Book of Abramelin*, for instance, the wand is not used in conjunction with the guardian angel at all. Instead, it is reserved as the principal tool in the conjuration and binding of the earthy spirits, over whom the aspirant is expected to rule.

However, the wand does have its place in angelic work. While the mage does not stand as master over the angelic hosts, he still enjoys a particular authority in their realm. It is appropriate to utilize the wand when summoning angels, if only to illustrate one's *right* to approach and issue petitions to them. In any case, I feel that the Wand is entirely too traditional a tool to save for the latter chapters of this book. It is such a standard part of the wizard's tool-kit that it simply had to be included here.

The *Key of Solomon the King* presents both a staff and a wand (as shown in the illustration below). There is absolutely no indication in the text of any practical differences between them. They are each made of different woods, but they are explained as having the same purpose, and are engraved with the same series of magickal characters. I assume that it is simply left to the practicing mage to decide which version to fashion.

The staff is made from elderwood, cane, or rosewood. The wand should be fashioned from hazel or nut tree. From here the directions for both are identical: the tree chosen for the purpose must be virginal, specifically of less than one year's growth. On a Wednesday at sunrise (which is both the day and hour of Mercury), the wand or staff is cut from the tree with a single stroke. No lengths are suggested in the text, though I suggest between twelve to eighteen inches for a useful wand. (It could, perhaps, be that the staff is intended as a much longer instrument— anywhere from three to six feet. The *Book of Abramelin* allows for a wand of such length if the aspirant so desires. However, the size of the *Key's* staff cannot be ascertained from the given illustrations, which seem to show both wand and staff of about the same size.)

The rest of the procedure can take place later, but it should still be a Wednesday on an hour of Mercury. At this time, light some of the standard incense (using the Exorcism of the Fire), and use the burin to engrave the characters as shown above on the implement's shaft.

Then, it is necessary to recite the following invocation over the completed wand or staff. Interestingly, the prayer indicates that the wand and staff are to be consecrated together, though I see no reason why one or the other cannot be addressed instead.

> Adonai, Most Holy, deign to bless and to consecrate this Wand, and this Staff, that they may obtain the necessary virtue, through Thee, O Most Holy Adonai, Whose kingdom endureth unto the Ages of the Ages. Amen.

The Solomonic Wand.

If this prayer seems a bit simple, we can always expand upon it by following the advice of *Abramelin*. In Book II, Chapter 14, we are instructed to entreat God to "give unto this Wand as much virtue, force, and power as He gave unto those of Moses, of Aaron, of Elijah, and of the other prophets whose number is infinite."

Back in the *Key*, we are told to finish the consecration by censing the wand with the smoke from the censer. Nothing is said about using holy water as well, though this is not necessary excluded. Finally, wrap the wand in its own piece of consecrated white silk, and store in a clean and safe place.

---

1. Translation by Bick Thomas.
2. Of course, this is a particularly general statement. Where it comes to the spirits of such Elements as Water, Fire, etc., the entities are said to be made of the same substance as their element, the rays of their planet, etc.
3. The grimoires also make use of sacred plants, animal parts, woods, etc.
4. While Dr. Dee was receiving the Parts of the Earth from his angelic teachers, Kelley complained that the attributions already existed in Agrippa's work. This is the chapter Kelley was upset about.
5. Of course, if we trace history back far enough, we generally find that the holy days and magickal timing arose *in response to* the already established cycles of the natural elements. This is an example of the symbiosis that exists between magick and nature, which makes up a part of the Neoplatonic philosophy.
6. The instructions are described later in this chapter.
7. That is to say, one skilled in many general arts.
8. Along with some unacceptable suggestions.
9. *Verbena officianalis.*
10. Refer to chapter 3, where the subject of plant worship is discussed. Then to chapter 4, where the use of plants as sacrifice is discussed.
11. Psalm 51:7: "Purge me with hyssop, and I shall be clean; wash me, and I shall be whiter than snow." (Psalm 51 is recited during the Solomonic bath, and verse 7 is also included in the prayers for the bath given in the *Key*.)
12. Animal products and blood: see chapter 4, where this subject is covered in depth, and alternatives are discussed.
13. At the same time, many toxic plants, such as black poppy, are mentioned. See chapter 3, and beware of using such ingredients(!).
14. How one could form pills from brains or blood, I have no clue. Perhaps there is something that is not being said here.
15. Interestingly, the blood of a black cat is called for in the *Key of Solomon the King* for the consecration of the black-hilted knife, used to command spirits. See chapter 12.
16. Plus, any one of them can be used alone in relation to its planet, rather than the more complicated compounds discussed above.
17. I personally use a combination of rose petals and cedar.
18. The three prayers given above and the sprinkling with holy water represent a true formula of exorcism. It is derived from the process by which new converts to Christianity were exorcised, consecrated, and baptized into the new faith. Chapter 12 will return to this subject of exorcism.
19. The best spices.

20. That is, myrrh in resin form rather than powder.
21. This Psalm is especially apt for the protection of a holy instrument.
22. Steel is included in the definition of iron.
23. Mathers included this version in his edition of the *Key* from Lansdowne MS 1203.

Purifications and Prayer

As we discussed in chapter 1, the classical grimoires were written principally by low-level Christian clerics. Not only were they written by men of the cloth, but they were often written *for* men of the cloth. Illustrative of this fact, a large amount of the procedure outlined in the texts rests solely upon biblical authority. *The Book of Abramelin* stands as a prime example; as most of its instruction can be located in verses from Psalms, Exodus, and other canonical books. Such works as the *Sworn Book of Honorius*, as we have seen, offer similar examples involving Church liturgy and ritual procedure. Therefore, the practical instruction found in the grimoires (fasting, intensive prayer, abstinence, confession, etc.) should come as no surprise to the modern student. The authors of the literature were assuming their readers were monks, clerics, or at least extremely devout Christian men.

Most of the grimoires pay special attention to the "dignification of the master"—meaning the lifestyle, devotion and purity of the working magickian. In many cases this subject is covered first and foremost—the reader being assured that lacking these basic virtues will render the magick useless or dangerous. Book One, Chapter One of the *Key of Solomon the King* is titled "Concerning the Divine Love Which Ought to Precede the Acquisition of This Knowledge." The text begins:

> Solomon . . . hath said that the beginning of our Key is to fear[1] God, to adore Him, to honour Him with contrition of heart, to invoke Him in all matters which we wish to undertake, and to operate with very great devotion, for thus God will lead us in the right way.

Other chapters give more practical instruction:

> He who wisheth to apply himself unto so great and so difficult a Science should have his mind free from all business, and from all extraneous ideas of whatever nature they may be. (*Key of Solomon the King*, Book II, Ch. 2)

> . . . it is absolutely necessary to ordain and to prescribe care and observation, to abstain from all things unlawful, and from every kind of impiety, impurity, wickedness, or immodesty, as well of body as of soul; as, for example, eating and drinking superabundantly, and all sorts of vain words, buffooneries,

slanders, calumnies, and other useless discourse; but instead to do good deeds, speak honestly, keep a strict decency in all things, never lose sight of modesty in walking, in conversation, in eating and drinking, and in all things. (*Key of Solomon the King*, Book II, Ch. 4)

The *Book of Abramelin*, which literally revolves around the practice of ritual purity, contains a chapter titled "Of the Age and Quality of the Person Who Wisheth to Undertake This Operation":

It is, then, necessary that such a man give himself up unto a tranquil life, and that his habits be temperate; that he should love retirement; that he should be given neither unto avarice nor usury . . . (*The Book of Abramelin*, Book II, Ch. 3) [2]

Agrippa, as we might have come to expect, gives us a slightly more psychological view of these processes, thus highlighting the true importance of ritual purity:

Therefore it is meet that we who endeavour to attain to so great a height should especially meditate of two things: first, how we should leave carnal affections, frail sense, and material passions; secondly, by what way and means we may ascend to an intellect pure and conjoined with the powers of the gods. (*Three Books*, Book III, Ch. 3)

Whosoever therefore being desirous to come to the supreme state of the soul, goeth to receive oracles, must go to them being chastly and devoutly disposed, being pure and clean go to them, so that his soul be polluted with no filthiness, and free from all guilt. He must also so purify his mind and body as much as he may from all diseases, and passions, and all irrational conditions, which adhere to it as rust to iron, by rightly composing and disposing those things which belong to the tranquility of the mind; for by this means he shall receive the truer and more efficacious oracles. (*Three Books*, Book III, Ch. 53)

For the mind is purged, and expiated by cleansing, by abstinence, by penitency, by alms (*Three Books*, Book III, Ch. 53).

It is believed, and it is delivered by them that are skillful in sacred things, that the mind also may be expiated with certain institutions, and sacraments ministered outwardly, as by sacrifices, baptisms, and adjurations, and benedictions, consecrations, sprinklings of holy water, by annointings, and fumes, not so much consecrated to this, as having a natural power thus to do (*Three Books*, Book III, Ch. 57).

The efficacy of consecrations is perfected by two things especially, viz. the virtue of the person himself consecrating, and the virtue of the prayer itself. In the person himself is required holiness of life, and a power to consecrate; the former, nature and desert perform; the latter is aquired by imitation, and dignification . . . Then it is necessary that he that sacrificeth must know this virtue and power in himself, with a firm and undoubted faith (*Three Books*, Book III, Ch. 62).

This can be intimidating to the modern occultist. Few would be willing to convert to medieval Catholicism or monkhood in order to succeed in the art. Yet, this kind of lifestyle is demanded by texts such as *Abramelin*. The instructions expect one to separate from the secular world, and to assume a very clerical method of stimulus deprivation.

It is my hope that part one of this book has demystified the structure and content of the grimoires to some extent. Seeing the practical necessity of the medieval Christian techniques, and even their shamanic origins, should set aside most objections to actually trying them out. Any fear that one must actually live the life of a monk is dispelled by the *Key of Solomon the King*:

> . . . it is absolutely necessary . . . to abstain from all things . . .; the which should be principally done and observed for nine days, before the commencement of the Operation. (*Key of Solomon the King*, Book II, Ch. 4)

And the *Key* is not alone in this stance. Most of the grimoires, even *Abramelin*, do not insist that one live the lifestyle of a cleric on a regular basis. We also have to keep in mind that some of the most famous Western mages in history have not been employed by the Church.[3] The grimoires only insist the mage remove himself from daily activity and undergo purification, confession, and cleansing for a duration before the magickal work. This is a manifestation of the shamanic nature of the material.

Of course, while most texts do not demand monkhood, it is always insisted that one be extremely devout. We most often assume this indicates devotion to the Church. However, the texts offer some surprises in this area. *The Book of Abramelin*, for instance, openly states that the faith of the aspirant is irrelevant. Plus, the grimoiric literature itself is such a mish-mash of Judaic, Christian, Arabian, and Greek influence that no singular established dogma can be found within it. However, one must be truly devout in his or her own way. The subject of devotion (Agrippa's "Venus Phrensy") is covered in chapter 4.

The only demand the grimoires make on one's daily lifestyle is that one not be a generally harmful person: profiting on the suffering of others, or living strictly under the neurotic rule of the lower self. Of course, this requirement is important for the success of all magick. A person living in so base a manner would simply have no access to the inner faculties necessary to hold converse with spiritual (celestial) entities:

> But I advise thee to undertake nothing unclean or impure, for then thy importunity, far from attracting them,[4] will only serve to chase them from thee; and it will be thereafter exceedingly difficult for thee to attract them for use for pure ends. (*Key of Solomon the King*, Book II, Ch. 21)

Thus, working with the grimoires means only part-time monkhood. Becoming adept in the practices discussed in this chapter (and others such as chapters 3 and 4) are extremely necessary to the magick. Like the magickal use of the Bible, this simply must be accepted in order to truly experiment with the classical techniques.

There is good reason for following the procedures faithfully. Beyond the mystical idea of purity and the shamanic idea of altered states, this practice has very profound psychological effects. This is literally a shifting of lifestyle, however temporary, and it brings with it many of the symptoms of culture shock. Your usual daily habits and unconscious patterns are suddenly taboo, and you are thus forced into direct confrontation with them. It will likely amaze you how many of them you discover, most of which you hadn't known existed.

These are the neuroses and personal demons that plague all of us. The ritual purifications demand the practitioner confront and defeat these demons, and it is only the strong-willed and balanced mage that will succeed. The *Book of Abramelin* discusses at some length the danger of demonic attack while undergoing its six-month purification (and while using the magick after the operation):

> The infamous Belial hath no other desire than that of obtaining the power of hiding and obscuring the True Divine Wisdom, so that he may have more means of blinding simple men and of leading them by the nose; so that they may always remain in their simplicity, and in their error, and that they may not discover the Way which leadeth unto the True Wisdom. (*The Book of Abramelin*, p. 35)

The Spirits . . . comprehend very well . . . what dispositions we have, and understand our inclinations, so that from the very beginning they prepare the way to make us to fail. If they know that a man is inclined unto Vanity and Pride, they will humiliate themselves before him, and push that humility unto excess, and even unto idolatry, and this man will glory herein and become intoxicated with conceit. . . Another man will be easily accessible to Avarice, and then if he take not heed the Malignant Spirits will propose unto him thousands of ways of accumulating wealth, and of rendering himself rich by indirect and unjust ways and means, whence total restitution is afterwards difficult and even impossible. . . Another will be a man of Letters; the Spirits will inspire him with presumption, and he will then believe himself to be wiser even than the Prophets . . . The causes and matter whereof (the Spirits) will make use to cause a man to waver are infinite, especially when the man attempteth to make them submit to his commands, and this is why it is most necessary to be upon one's guard and to distrust oneself. (*The Book of Abramelin*, pp. 254–5. Emphasis mine.)

You will better understand this if you have ever, three or four days into a vegetarian purification, prepared and eaten a chicken sandwich without a second thought. Or perhaps you've headed out to the movies with friends one night, while you were supposed to remain secluded, but didn't catch the mistake until some days later. Both of these, and more, have happened to me.

The good news about ritual purification is that the grimoires are written to allow for such mistakes. Such purification is a gradual process, not simply a mode to shift into at any given moment. The regimens outlined by the texts generally start off light and increase in intensity as one continues. The purpose is to move the magickian progressively from mundane life into the magickal mindset. Almost nothing must be sacrificed to begin with; the magickian may have to do little more than hang around at home and avoid contact with others. Each day more restrictions are added and the prayer and ritual becomes more intensive. By the final day, the mental focus of the magickian should be utterly consumed by the procedure.

This is designed to strengthen one physically, psychologically, and spiritually. It is akin to the modern psychological methods used to break old habits or begin new ones. Like all processes, you have to start from where you are, and expect to make mistakes at first. With experience it becomes easier, even to the point of becoming second nature. If you ever feel that you are making too many mistakes, simply lengthen the purification period. Instead of seven days, give yourself a month to work at it.

Abramelin is a perfect example of the process, though it is spread over a daunting six-month period. (It is reputed that one version of the text instructs a year and a half!) Dedication to such a lengthy period of purification really does bring about serious changes in one's lifestyle and habitual patterns. This is one of the features of the rite that make *Abramelin* so infamous, leading insincere dabblers into serious mental distress. The dedicated aspirant, however, can find in the pages of the grimoire a safe and steady-paced system of self-development.

For the first two months, little is expected of the aspirant. One needs only to enter a small prayer room (oratory) twice a day: once in the morning and once in the evening. A confession must be uttered, followed by a prayer, the structure of each being left completely to the discretion of the aspirant. For six days of the week, nothing else is required in the way of ritual paraphernalia. Only on the sabbath day must one light a lamp and burn incense upon the altar. This represents the extent of the first two months' difficulty, besides the required general isolation and vegetarian diet. Procedural mistakes are hard to make, and this leaves these months open for adjustment to the new lifestyle.

The second two-month period adds very little to the process. One must wash with purified water before entering the oratory, the prayers must be prolonged, and one must fast on the sabbath eve. The isolation and diet continue as before, and some amount of sexual abstinence must be observed. At this point, most of the novice mistakes will have been made and corrected, and one will have faced and dealt with a good number of heretofore unconscious habits. More than anything, the novelty of the entire affair will have worn away, and the aspirant will be reaching a point of mental exhaustion. If one is to fail at the operation, it is more than likely to manifest itself here.

The final two months kick the process into high gear, involving a lot more formal ritual. The prayer sessions increase to three times a day. Each time, one must cleanse in pure water, don the ritual garb, and light the lamp and incense. The weekly fasts continue, sexual activity must be entirely suspended, and even more prayer is added to each session in the oratory. All of this gives the aspirant much more to concentrate upon, resulting in a heightened mental focus. It tends to occupy the aspirant totally, and the increased stimulus deprivation can induce new mental stress. Fortunately, if one has overcome the exhaustion felt in the second two months—literally passing *through* it rather than retreating—this stage of the operation can produce a second wind. At the very least, these months are the "home stretch," and they bring with them a greatly increased sense of anticipation.

Finally, the operation proper takes place over a seven-day period. Here is where all of the tricks of the magickal trade are called into play, including heavy fasting, hours of prayer, very specific magickal tools and procedures, and the summoning of several classes of spiritual entities. All of the preparations undertaken in the previous six months have served to induce an altered state of consciousness, the stresses and exhaustion establishing the necessary mental condition for the ego-death that will follow.

Of course, the *Abramelin* operation is not for idle experimentation. It does, however, illustrate the basic processes found in nearly all of the grimoires. Another classic example—one which will allow for some testing and experimentation—is the set of ritual preparations found in the *Key of Solomon the King*. This text only demands nine days, and follows the same overall pattern as we have seen above.

This Solomonic regimen is specifically meant for use with the spirit summoning operation that forms the heart of the grimoire. It is not necessary to use this point-for-point unless one is working with the *Key of Solomon* itself. Toward the end of this chapter I will give outlines for more generic purifications, intended for use with this book, rather than any specific grimoire. However, there is no reason why the reader could not make use of the Solomonic system at will. It provides a perfect standard by which to judge one's own work.

The Solomonic Nine-Day Purification

Step one is to calculate the magickal timing of the desired ritual. Once the day is chosen, count back a full ten days beforehand. On that tenth day (i.e., the day before the nine days of the purification), it is necessary to recite the following conjuration once in the morning, and twice in the evening (*Key of Solomon the King*, Book II, Chapter 4):

> O Lord God Almighty, be propitious unto me a miserable sinner, for I am not worthy to raise mine eyes unto heaven, because of the iniquity of my sins and the multitude of my faults. O pitying and merciful Father, who wouldest not the death of a sinner but rather that he should turn from his wickedness and live, O God have mercy upon me and pardon all my sins; for I unworthy entreat Thee, O Father of all Creatures, Thou Who art full of mercy and of compassion, by Thy great goodness, that Thou deign to grant unto me power to see and know these Spirits which I desire to behold and to invoke to appear before me and to accomplish my will. Though Thee Who are Conqueror, and Who are Blessed unto the Ages of the Ages. Amen.

> O Lord God the Father Eternal, Who are seated upon the Kherubim and the Seraphim, Who lookest upon Earth and upon Sea; unto Thee do I raise my hands and implore Thine aid alone, Thou Who alone art the accomplishment of good works, Thou Who givest rest unto those who labour, Who humblest

the proud, Who art the Author of Life and the Destroyer of Death; Thou art our rest, Thou art the Protector of those who invoke Thee; protect, guard, and defend me in this matter, and in the enterprise which I propose to carry out, O Thou Who livest, reignest, and abidest unto the Eternal Ages. Amen.

Once again we see the typical shamanic formula. The first prayer contains a form of confession where the speaker admits to his faults as a physical creature. Such faults, vices, neuroses and other hindrances work against our gaining the celestial realm. Having asked to be relieved of these psychic weights, the aspirant continues to praise father sky, and finally presents his petition for spiritual aid in the forthcoming work. This conjuration is also instructed for use throughout the period of purification, anytime one feels the pressures of isolation and deprivation. It is intended to provide inner strength in times of "temptation."

One is also told to use the coming nine day period to prepare all things necessary for the coming ceremonies. As found in Book II, Chapter 13:

> He who hath attained the rank or degree of Exorcist, which we are usually accustomed to call Magus or Master according to grade, whensoever he desireth to undertake any operation, for the nine days immediately preceding the commencement of the work, should put aside from him all uncleanness, and prepare himself in secret during these days, and prepare all the things necessary, and in the space of these days all these should be made, consecrated, and exorcised.

Meaning that any tools or implements that need to be fashioned should be done during this time; such as any consecrated papers, colors, earth, and necessary tools you have not already made. The area chosen for the work should be cleaned, sprinkled with holy water, and perfumed with exorcised fire and incense. The *Key*, Book II, Chapter 6, also reminds us to prepare, polish, brighten, and clean all the necessary implements during these nine days.

Days One Through Six

As should be expected, the first days of the process do not require an extended effort. They merely call for some shifting of lifestyle and partial withdrawal from social surroundings. The *Key* puts it in a wonderfully archaic fashion:

> Before commencing operations, both the Master and his Disciples must abstain with great and thorough continence during the space of nine days from sensual pleasures and from vain and foolish conversation. (*The Key of Solomon the King*, Book I, Chapter 3)

> From the first day of the Experiment, it is absolutely necessary to ordain and to prescribe care and observation, to abstain from all things unlawful, and from every kind of impiety, impurity, wickedness, or immodesty, as well of body as of soul; as, for example, eating and drinking superabundantly . . . but instead to do good deeds, speak honestly, keep a strict decency in all things, never lose sight of modesty in walking, in conversation, in eating and drinking, and in all things. (*The Key of Solomon the King*, Book II, Chapter 4)

We can see that most forms of social interaction are ruled out by these instructions. Sexual abstinence is also suggested. The second example makes it clear that one should pay special attention to one's religious convictions, observations, etc.[5] A modest (non-egocentric) frame of mind must be held, and all activities must be done moderately and peacefully. Remember that the conjuration given previously (O Lord God Almighty . . .) can be uttered any time stress begins to mount.

Though Solomon does not instruct it, I would personally suggest one continue to recite the conjuration once in the morning and twice in the evening (until the seventh day—see below). I would also suggest that one shift to a vegetarian diet from the very first day, making sure to eat plenty of salad and other roughage. This will be important for the fasts instructed for the last three days of the purification.

Day Seven

At this point it is necessary to begin a "fasting diet," eating only one meal per day on each of these last three days. Other than this, Solomon does not indicate what such a diet involves. For certain, meat would have to be ruled out, as would anything that might be classified as junk food, snacks, sweets, etc. Solomon does suggest that the best course of action would be to eat only bread and water.

This is also the day on which the intense regimen of prayer begins. The prayer suggested by the *Key* is given immediately below. One is to recite it once in the morning, twice at noon, three times in the afternoon, four times in the evening, and a full five times before laying down to sleep.

> **Herachio, Asac, Asacro, Bedrimulael, Tilath, Arabonas, Ierahlem, Ideodoc, Archarzel, Zophiel, Blautel, Baracata, Edoniel, Elohim, Emagro, Abragateh, Samoel, Geburahel, Cadato, Era, Elohi, Achsah, Ebmisha, Imachedel, Daniel, Dama, Elamos, Izachel, Bael, Segon, Gemon, Demas.**

> O Lord God, Who are seated upon the Heavens,[6] and Who regardest the Abysses beneath, grant unto me Thy Grace I beseech Thee, so that what I conceive in my mind I may accomplish in my work, through Thee, O God, the Sovereign Ruler of all, Who livest and reignest unto the Ages of the Ages. Amen.

At some point during this same day, one is instructed to take a ritual bath. Though a full "Solomonic Ritual Bath" is given in the *Key*, it is not instructed for this day. (The full bath will be outlined below.) Instead, a simpler version is used: fill a tub with warm water, and recite the following exorcism over it:

> I exorcise thee, O Creature of Water, by Him Who hath created thee and gathered thee together in one place so that the dry land appeared,[7] that thou uncover all the deceits of the Enemy, and that thou cast out from thee all the impurities and uncleaness of the Spirits of the World of Phantasm, so they may harm me not, through the virtue of God Almighty Who liveth and reigneth unto the Ages of the Ages. Amen.

Now recite the following benediction over a small amount of salt, and then sprinkle it into the exorcised water:

> The Blessing of the Father Almighty be upon this Creature of Salt, and let all malignity and hindrance be cast forth hencefrom, and let all good enter herein, for without Thee men cannot live, wherefore I bless thee and invoke thee, that thou mayest aid me.

Finally, enter the tub and wash from head to foot while reciting the following prayer:

> O Lord Adonai, Who has formed me Thine unworthy servant in Thine Image and resemblance of vile and abject earth; deign to bless and to sanctify this Water,[8] so that it may be for the health and purification of my soul, and of my body, so that no foolishness or deceitfulness may therein in any way have place.

> O Most Powerful and Ineffable God, Who madest Thy people pass dryshod through the Red Sea when they came up out of the Land of Egypt, grant unto me grace that I may be purified and regenerated from all my past sins by this Water, that so no uncleanness may appear upon me in Thy Presence.

Once this is complete, immerse yourself completely into the water (thus mimicking a baptism). Finish by stepping out of the tub, drying with a white linen towel, and donning the white linen robe. If the master has companions (working partners), they are then called in to strip and enter the bath. (One might call them one at a time, though the *Key* does not indicate such) The master must pour the exorcised water over them—drenching them from head to foot—while reciting the following prayer. Afterward, each disciple also dons a white robe.

> Be ye regenerate, cleansed, and purified, in the Name of the Ineffable, Great, and Eternal God, from all your iniquities, and may the virtue of the Most High descend upon you and abide with you always, so that ye may have the power and strength to accomplish the desires of your heart. Amen.

This particular ritual bath is not repeated later. Likely, the bath is used at this time due to the holiness of the number seven. It is also noteworthy that this is the day upon which the truly involved ritual work begins.[9] The first six days are preliminary, focused more upon physical and psychological factors (i.e., shift in diet, lifestyle, etc.). Religious-style observances, such as the ritual bath, begin on the seventh day, and continue for three consecutive days. Three, as well, is a holy number within this magickal system.

Days Eight And Nine

These final days are merely repeats of day seven, sans the ritual bath. Solomon instructs the master (and, of course, all working partners) to continue the same fasting diet (one meal a day), as well as the prayer recited in the morning, noon, afternoon, evening, and night. (Herachio, Asac, etc.)

I would suggest one also increase isolation and stimulus deprivation as far as possible. Perhaps we might take a cue from *Abramelin* and spend the last days alone in our bedroom, reviewing the work to come ahead, reciting the seventy-two Psalms of David, etc. In fact, it might be a good idea to begin this as soon as the bath is completed on the seventh day. The donning of the white robe indicates a return to purity, and the less social contact and sensory input from that moment onward the better. That is to say, input should be avoided beyond the prayers, rituals, and scripture that will occupy your mental focus.

There is one final instruction given for the last three days (seven through nine) of the Solomonic cleansing. It appears rather cryptically in Book I, Chapter Three: "Six of these nine days having expired, he must recite frequently the Prayer and Confession as will be told him." These texts are given together in Chapter 4, and are long enough to cover nearly three pages. Remember that invocations and prayers this lengthy are generally intended to produce a trance state:

Confession

> O Lord of Heaven and of Earth, before Thee do I confess my sins, and lament them, cast down and humbled in Thy presence. For I have sinned before Thee by pride, avarice, and boundless desire of honours and riches. By idleness, gluttony, greed, debauchery, and drunkeness. Because I have offended Thee by all kinds of sins of the flesh, adulteries, and pollutions, which I have committed myself, and consented that others should commit. By sacrilege, thefts, rapine, violation, and homicide. By the evil use I have made of my possessions, by my prodigality, by the sins which I have committed against Hope and Charity, by my evil advice, flatteries, bribes, and the ill distribution which I have made of the goods of which I have been possessed. By repulsing and maltreating the poor, in the distribution which I have

made of the goods committed to my charge, by afflicting those over whom I have been set in authority, by not visiting the prisoners, by depriving the dead of burial, by not receiving the poor, by neither feeding the hungry nor giving drink to the thirsty, by never keeping the Sabbath and the other feasts, by not living chastely and piously on those days, by the easy consent which I have given to those who incited me to evil deeds, by injuring instead of aiding those who demanded help from me, by refusing to give ear unto the cry of the poor, by not respecting the aged, by not keeping my word, by disobedience to my parents, by ingratitude towards those from whom I have received kindness, by indulgence in sensual pleasures, by irreverent behaviour in the Temple of God, by unseemly gestures thereat, by entering therein without reverence, by vain and unprofitable discourse when there, by despising the sacred vessels of the temple, by turning the holy Ceremonies despising the sacred vessels of the temple, by turning the holy Ceremonies into ridicule, by touching and eating the sacred bread with impure lips and with profane hands, and by the neglect of my prayers and adorations.

I detest also the crimes which I have committed by evil thoughts, vain and impure meditations, false suspicions, and rash judgments. By the evil consent which I have readily given unto the advice of the wicked, by lust of impure and sensual pleasures. By my idle words, my lies, and my deceit. By my false vows in various ways. And by my continual slander and calumny.

I detest also the crimes which I have committed within. The treachery and discord which I have incited. My curiosity, freed, false speaking, violence, malediction, murmurs, blasphemies, vain words, insults, dissimulations. My sins against God by the transgression of the ten commandments, by neglect of my duties and obligations, and by want of love towards God and toward my neighbor. Furthermore, I hate the sins which I have committed in all my senses, by sight, by hearing, by taste, by smell, and by touch, in every way that human weakness can offend the Creator. By my carnal thoughts, deeds, and meditations.

In which I humbly confess that I have sinned and recognize myself as being in the sight of God the most criminal of all men.

I accuse myself before Thee, O God, and I adore Thee with all humility. O ye, Holy Angels, and ye, Children of God, in your presence I publish my sins, so that mine Enemy may have no advantage over me, and may not be able to reproach me at the last day. That he may not be able to say that I have concealed my sins, and that I be not then accused in the presence of the Lord. But, on the contrary, that on my account there may be joy in Heaven, as over the just who have confessed their sins in thy presence.

O Most Mighty and All Powerful Father, grant through Thine unbounded Mercy that I may both see and know all the Spirits which I invoke, so that by their means I may see my will and desire accomplished by Thy Sovereign grandeur, and by Thine Ineffable and Eternal Glory, Thou Who are and Who wilt be for ever the Pure and Ineffable Father of All.

Prayer

O Lord All Powerful, Eternal God and Father of all Creatures, shed upon me the Divine Influence of Thy Mercy, for I am Thy Creature. I beseech Thee to defend me from mine Enemies, and to confirm in me true and steadfast faith.

O Lord, I commit my Body and my Soul unto Thee, seeing I put my trust in none beside Thee. It is on Thee alone that I rely. O Lord my God aid me. O Lord hear me in the day and hour wherein I shall invoke Thee. I pray by Thy Mercy not to put in oblivion, nor to remove my from Thee. O Lord by Thou my succour, Thou Who are the God of salvation. O Lord make me a new heart according unto Thy loving Kindness. These, O Lord, are the gifts which I await from Thee, O my God and my Master, Thou Who livest and reignest unto the Ages of the Ages. Amen.

O Lord God the All Powerful One, Who hast formed unto Thyself great and Ineffable Wisdom, and Co-eternal with Thyself before thee countless Ages. Thou Who in the Birth of Time hast created the Heavens and the Earth, the Sea, and things that they contain. Thou Who hast vivified all things by the Breath of Thy Mouth, I praise Thee, I bless Thee, I adore Thee, and I glorify Thee. Be Thou propitious unto me who am but a miserable sinner, and despise me not. Save me and succour me, even me the work of Thine hands. I conjure and entreat Thee by Thy Holy Name to banish from my Spirit the darkness of Ignorance, and to enlighten me with the Fire of Thy Wisdom. Take away from me all evil desires, and let not my speech be as that of the foolish. O Thou, God the Living One, Whose Glory, Honour, and Kingdom shall extend unto the Ages of the Ages. Amen.

Day of the Operation

On this important day, one is instructed to fast completely until after the operation. As the magickal hour approaches, the master and partners individually perform the following preparations:

Recite the previously given confession and prayer three consecutive times. Then, perform the Solomonic bath. This is *not* the bath outlined on the seventh day of purification, but stands alone as its own ritualistic procedure. This bath will be outlined and explained in full below. After completing the bath and donning the white robe, ignite a coal in the censer while reciting the Exorcism of the Fire (see chapter 6). Cast exorcised incense onto it and cense yourself with the smoke.

At this point the master and partners must gather and prepare to enter the chosen working place. Before they do, the master is instructed to recite the confession and prayer again(!). Then each member present must kiss each of his fellows upon the forehead. This kiss calls upon biblical authority,[10] and is said to have been the salute passed within the inner circle of Jesus and his disciples. After the salute is passed, the master must extend his hands over his partners and absolve and bless them. The author of the *Key* merely assumes the reader will know how to do this. Or, more specifically, the author assumes the reader has been *ordained* to do this.

Further instructions are given by Solomon concerning the disciples (partners), and instructions necessary before and during the construction of the magick circle. However, this leads us into the Solomonic operation specifically, and it is not my intention to fully cover that subject in this book. In chapter 12, on spirit summoning, I will return to the subject of magick circles.

Creating Prayers and Invocations

I began this chapter with a short discussion of prayer and scripture. I made sure to point out the little-known fact that biblical literature—and even ritual procedure—are essentially identical to ancient Pagan examples. There is a common thread running through the mysticism of Egypt, Canaan, Mesopotamia, Arabia, etc. It likewise extends through the Greek mysteries, Gnosticism, Judaism, Pauline Christianity, and, finally, the classical grimiores. Now, let us examine these ancient essentials as they were understood and practiced by medieval occultists, and learn something about the Art and Science of Prayer.

Jonathan Dee once asked the angel Ave if he could provide the invocations for summoning the angels of the four Watchtowers.[11] Much to Dee and Kelley's frustration, Ave answered:

> I may not do so. [. . .] Invocation proceedeth of the good will of man, and of the heat and fervency of the Spirit.[12] And therefore is prayer of such effect with God.

Ave is here in agreement with Agrippa, who taught that invocation is accomplished by raising the passions of the mind. Agrippa called these passions "phrensy," and, in chapter 3, we called them "ecstasy." However, simply gaining the ecstatic state is hardly enough to accomplish magick. The "heat and fervency of the Spirit" one raises must be directed in some fashion if it is to be useful. It is the purpose of a magickal invocation to, in essence, program the mage's ecstatic trip along the necessary lines. It accomplishes this through what we call "resonance."

Resonance is similar to the occult concept of sympathy: like attracts like, as above so below, etc. For instance, if one were to stand near a piano and play a note on a violin, the corresponding strings within the piano would also vibrate. This is an example of physical resonance. Meanwhile, we can see examples of mental resonance in such concepts as "happiness breeds happiness" and "misery begets misery." Humans have a rather uncanny ability to attract to themselves those things they concentrate upon most. Agrippa discusses spiritual (or occult) resonance in his Book II, Chapter 60:

> . . . when anyone by binding or bewitching doth call upon the Sun or other stars, praying them to be helpful to the work desired, the Sun and other stars do not hear his words, but are moved after a certain manner by a certain conjunction, and mutual series, whereby the parts of the world are mutually subordinate the one to the other, and have a mutual consent, by reason of their great union:[13] as in a man's body one member is moved by perceiving the motion of another, and in a harp one string is moved at the motion of another. So when anyone moves any part of the world, other parts are moved by the perceiving the motion of that.

The gods do not hear our words with ears and sound vibration, but through the excitement of certain passions. Therefore, a magickal invocation must accomplish several subtle goals at once. First, it must aid in the attainment of ecstatic trance—through both its length (the longer the better) and its devotional content. Then, it has to direct that trance and call down the forces it addresses by *resonating with* those forces.

Fortunately, Agrippa gives us quite a bit of useful information where it comes to the proper construction of invocations throughout his *Occult Philosophy*. Book III, Chapter 32 is titled "How good spirits may be called up by us, and how evil spirits may be overcome by us." Here Agrippa stresses that good spirits (i.e., angels) cannot be conjured or forced into appearance, but must be attracted and beseeched by mention of things sacred to them.

> By these things, and such like symbolical orations and hymns, because they are signs of divine virtues, spirits did sometimes apply themselves to human uses; not as being compelled by any kind of necessity, but of their own accord . . .

Later on, in Book III, Chapter 61, "How these things must be performed, as to God, so to inferior deities," Agrippa continues:

> . . . when any prayer is to be offered . . . for the obtaining of any effect, it must be done with the commemoration of some work, miracle, sacrament, or promise, taken somewhere out of Scripture . . .

As we have discussed in previous chapters, biblical tradition depends on the power of its literature. From the ceremonial readings of the Torah scroll in Jewish temples to the scriptural hymns and chants of the Christian faiths.

Magickal operations and theories are often lifted directly out of the stories of the patriarchs and prophets. The reading of scriptures within the grimoiric rituals count as invocations and magickal incantations. Now, we learn that the same principals apply even to those prayers we compose ourselves.

For instance,[14] if one were to pray for the destruction of enemies, the prayer should commemorate the destruction of the wicked by the Deluge of Noah, the frustration of the efforts of the builders of the Tower of Babel, the destruction of Sodom and Gomorrah, or the crashing of the Red Sea upon the armies of pharaoh during the Exodus, etc. If one were to pray for protection from dangerous waters, one should commemorate the saving of Noah from the Deluge, the safe passage of the children of Israel through the Red Sea, Christ walking upon the waters and saving a ship from a storm, etc. If one wishes to obtain oracles by dreams, the invocation should mention such times as God, angels, or other spiritual beings have descended to speak with humans such as in Jacob's vision, the dream of Nebuchadnezzar, or the visions of Ezekiel and St. John, etc. (When looking for such references, don't forget the ultimate usefulness of a Bible concordance.[15])

Agrippa also returns to this subject in Book III, Chapter 62, "Of consecrations and their manner." Here, Agrippa is not discussing prayers offered to any particular entity, but prayers of consecration used upon magickal tools, talismans, images, etc. He first stresses the importance of the diginification of the mage when attempting to consecrate (in order to bring holiness upon something, one must be holy himself—see chapter 4), and then returns again to the use of biblical mythos in the invocations:

> . . . but of the commemoration of sacred things, as of sacred letters, histories, miracles, works, effects, favours, promises,[16] sacraments and such sacramental things, which shall seem to cohere with the thing to be consecrated, either properly, or improperly, or analogically.[17] [. . .] So in the consecration of oil such solemnities must be commemorated as belong to these, as in Exodus the oil of unction and sweet perfumes, and sacred names suitable to these, such as is the name Christ, which signifies Anointed, and such as this, and that in the Apocalypse concerning the two olive trees distilling sanctified oil into lamps burning in the presence of God.[18] [. . .] So in the consecration of places let there be commemoration made of Mount Sinai, of the Tabernacle of the Covenant, of the Sanctum Sanctorum, the temple of Solomon . . .

> After the same manner we must proceed in the benediction of other things, by inquiring into holy writ by divine names, and profession of religion for such things which may seem to be after a manner suitable to this or that thing. As for example, if there be a paper, or a book having some of the mysteries which we should commemorate, as the tables of the ten commandments given to Moses on Mount Sinai, . . . and let the divine names of the testament of God, the book of God, the book of life, the knowledge of God, the wisdom of God, and of such like be commemorated. So if a sword is to be consecrated, we may remember . . . also that in the Prophets,[19] take unto you two edged swords; also in the Gospel, coats being sold, swords must be bought;[20] and in the history of David an Angel was seen hiding by a bloody sword;[21] and many such like we shall find in the Prophets, and Apocalypse, as also the sacred names of the sword of God, the rod of God, the staff of God, the vengeance of God, and such like.

Of course, we are not restricted to merely the Old and New Testaments for mythical references in our invocations. We also have dozens of apocryphal writings from which to draw, from the *Testament of Solomon* to the *Book of Enoch*. There are the texts left to us by the *Merkavah* mystics which certainly apply. There are no shortage of Qabalistic commentaries such as the *Sepher Bahir*, *Sepher Yetzirah*, and *Sepher Zohar*. There are also the many volumes of the Jewish Talmud, and collections of biblical *Midrashim* (legends) such as collected in *Legends of the Bible* by Louis Ginzberg, *Lilith's Cave: Jewish Tales of the Supernatural* by Howard Schwartz, or *The Thousand and One Nights* of Arabian culture. Even the grimoires (especially their introductions) depict such figures as Enoch and Solomon dealing with angels and spirits, thus granting us useful mythological material. With such a rich and abundant literary tradition at our fingertips, the list could go on indefinitely.

Most importantly, all of these mythological elements must be included in the prayer in a truly devotional spirit. Endless repetitions of Bible stories alone will not move the stars; the power lies within what those stories *mean* to us. If a Jewish *Baal Shem* of the medieval era invoked the names of Jacob, Moses, and Elijah in his magick, he was calling upon the spirits of his blood ancestors, who, he believed, were active in the celestial realm and would willingly move to help their descendant. A mention of the passage of the Red Sea, or the foundation of the Holy Temple, would have spoken to his deepest ancestral and tribal emotions.

This was not entirely different for the Christian mystics who borrowed the Jewish material, because the Jewish forefathers and prophets *along with* the newer saints and martyrs were understood as the spiritual ancestors of any faithful Christian. The events and miracles of the Old Testament would have been just as important to the Christian—only by faith rather than blood.

Gnostics and adepts throughout history have held similar beliefs concerning spiritual descent. This historical Gnostics actually believed they were descended from Seth (third son of Adam) through reincarnation rather than genetic ancestry. Even today, mystical communities generally consider themselves spiritually related, and feel a connection to the adepts of the past.

When a prayer is actually meaningful to the orator, if it speaks to something deep in his spirit, it takes on a completely new dimension. No longer is it merely a "formula" by which A is connected to B. Suddenly the prayer becomes a love song—either a song of praise to the forces that give us life, or a lament for what has left us. This, of course, is what the Psalms are all about, and why they play such an important role in grimoiric magick.

Agrippa has much to say about the necessity of devotion and divine love in the offering of prayer, one example of which follows:

> . . . for by prayers which we utter with true and sacred words sensibly, and affectionately, we obtain a great power, when by the application of them to any deity we do so far move it, that he may direct his speech and answer by a divine way . . . Adoration therefore being a long time continued, and often frequented, perfects the intellect, and makes the soul more large for the receiving of divine lights, inflaming divine love, producing faith, hope, and sacred manners, purifieth the soul from all contrariety, and what is in any way adverse to it, and doth also repel divers evils . . . Now a vow is an ardent affection of a chaste mind given up to God, which by vowing wisheth that which seems good. . . .a vow cannot be perfect without an adoration, nor an adoration without a vow . . . (*Three Books*, Book III, Chapter 58, "Of Adorations and Vows").

I once had the good fortune to have a Russian Orthodox priest explain his method of mysticism and prayer to me. He did not make specific mention of resonance, elevating the mind, devotion, or mythical content; though all of those things were present in the underlying worldview of his explanation. His focus was, like the Psalms, upon *praising God*. This shows us how foundational such a concept is to biblical magick. Consider Louis Ginzberg's *Legends of the Bible*, Part I (The Creation of the World). The last section of this part is titled "All Things Praise the Lord," wherein each created thing is assigned its own hymn of praise to the Creator. "Heaven and earth, Paradise and hell, desert and field, rivers and seas—all have their own way of paying homage to God."

The same can be said of the angelic hosts, who are organized into musical choirs as often as into military hierarchy. The archangels who stand as generals in battle actually work as conductors in times of peace. Note, for example, the Seraphim described in Isaiah 6:3 singing the *Trisagion*: "Holy, Holy, Holy is the Lord of Hosts: the whole earth is full of His glory!" St. John heard the same hymn, in Revelation 4:8, from the four holy living creatures who uphold the throne of God: "Holy, Holy, Holy, Lord God Almighty, which was, and is, and is to come!" None of this should be surprising when we consider the bardic influences upon early Judeo-Christian worship (see chapter 4, section "Psalmody"). It also explains why angels are so often associated with trumpets, harps, and other musical instruments.

The music of the angels' song of praise to the creator is the energy of the living universe. Song raises passion, and passion is the energy of magick. Our invocations, then, must take on an aspect of the hymn or psalm. They must call upon the divine names and angels necessary to our desire, but they can only attract these beings if they partake in the same praise of God as the angels themselves.

Let us consider an example to illustrate this point (the same example given to me by the Orthodox priest). Imagine that you live in an area plagued by drought and fires, as has been the case in several places in the country over the past few years. As a mage-shaman, you would like to summon a rain storm to relieve the harsh conditions and protect your home and community from burning.

As Agrippa might suggest, one should endeavor to connect his mind with the intelligence of the storm. Remember our previous discussion about pantheism (or, just as well, animism) in chapter 2: all things are alive, and *all things praise the divine*. The physical aspect of the storm is the manifestation of the storm angel's song—or psalm—to the divine. To resonate with the angel, the mage-shaman needs only join into that psalm. The focus is upon the divine, but the mage is praising the god of storms just as the angel itself.

There are various routes one might take with this endeavor. There may be several existing Psalms from the Bible that invoke the attentions of the storm god. Men such as Dee and Kelley might have simply contacted the appropriate angels and asked for invocations in the angelic tongue itself. However, a method such as that would have to be considered advanced work.

Even better, however, is when the mage simply focuses his devotion toward the storm and begins to sing praises from his own mind and heart. ("Invocation arises from the goodwill of man . . .") The angel(s) who naturally resonate with those praises will take notice and react, just as the vibration of a violin string will certainly cause a nearby piano string to vibrate in sympathy.

This is something the student can experiment with, preferably over an extended period of time. If you see a storm brewing on the horizon, gain an ecstatic state and begin to sing appropriate Psalms. It is not necessary that we try to second-guess the "actual" words the storm angel is singing, but only that we sing a psalm such as the angel *would* sing. The resonance is in the emotions, rather than in the words.[22] The god of storm must be praised for all the life, protection, and beneficent things that he brings to us. The psalm must *mean something* to the invocant. See if you can, with dedicated practice, eventually connect your spirit with the winds and the storm.

Intercession

The art of intercession is also apparent in some aspects of Agrippa's teaching on prayer and invocation—and we will expand upon them a bit here. These arise from ancient shamanic techniques of prayer, as well as from the later temple faiths and royal court procedure. Remember that the heavens are, theoretically, organized after the fashion of a king's court. This means that God (or father sky) sits upon the throne of rulership,[23] and is surrounded by the various archons and archangels responsible for the daily mechanics of nature. Each angel governs his proper sphere, and receives his or her orders directly from the throne.

If a mage-shaman invokes an angel to perform something outside of his usual routine, it is not within the angel's authority to break the regular processes of nature. In the case of such an invocation, the angel must ascend to the throne and request permission to make a change. It is father sky who will make the final decision, and changes can be made only by his command. A study of various Middle Eastern prayers will reveal this dynamic, such as when a priest supplicates a lesser god to ascend to the divine court and "argue his case."

Note, for instance, the biblical book of Job, wherein *haSathan* approaches the throne of God in order to accuse Job of a lack of true faith. haSathan—the Adversary or Accuser—was most likely adopted into the Judaic faith from Babylon. It was the Babylonians who created the form of law we know today, including the infamous idea of a prosecuting attorney. Since this role existed in the Babylonian courts, so, too, must it have existed in their heavens. This was haSathan, and we witness this being at work in an official courtly capacity in the Bible:

> Now there was a day when the sons of God came to present themselves before the Lord, and Satan came also among them. And the Lord said unto Satan, "Whence comest thou?" Then Satan answered the Lord, and said, "From going to and fro in the earth, and from walking up and down in it." And the Lord said unto Satan, "Has thou considered my servant Job . . .?" Then Satan answered the Lord, and said, ". . .But put forth thine hand now, and touch all that he hath, and he will curse thee to thy face." And the Lord said unto Satan, "Behold, all that he hath is in thy power; only upon himself put not forth thine hand." So Satan went forth from the presence of the Lord. (Job 1:6–12)

This same process is supposed to go on every time an angel wishes to have an unusual effect upon the physical plane. For instance, the storm summoned by a mage is brought only after the storm angel requests of the divine permission to respond. It is for this reason that biblical magickal systems stress the invocation of the good graces of the highest before attempting to sway an angel. Plus, when appealing to the angel directly, it does not hurt to specifically request he or she bring the case before the throne, and argue in the mage's favor.

It is also vital to understand which star should be addressed in the first place. Mistakes are made in this area of invocation more often than one might suspect. For example, suppose one finds himself in a very martial and violent situation. Anyone who has studied chemistry or algebra might naturally assume that one force is neutralized by its equal and opposite, and so invocations to the powers of Jupiter might seem in order. However, this does not hold with the true art of intercession. Agrippa explains:

> Whence, if any misfortune hang over anyone from Saturn, or from Mars, the magicians command that he must not forthwith fly to Jupiter, or Venus, but to Saturn or Mars themselves. (*Three Books*, Book III, Chapter 49)

> First the knowledge of the thing to be adored [is necessary], and to which we must vow, and in what manner, and order, and by what mediums it must be worshipped; for there are various cooperators and instruments of God, viz. The heavens, stars, administering spirits, the celestial souls, and heroes, which we must implore as porters, interpreters, administrators, mediators . . . (*Three Books*, Book III, Chapter 58)

> Moreover we must petition for and to the effectors of the thing desired, viz. such an Angel, star, hero on whom that office lies . . . (*Three Books*, Book III, Chapter 61)

Thus, if one were to truly find oneself in a martial and violent situation, it would be the angels of Mars to whom the petition must be addressed. All things Martial lie within their office and nature, and therefore the command of such forces is within their jurisdiction. Jupiter—the king of mercy and abundance—would have no authority over spirits of combat or violence.

Agrippa also discusses the necessity of understanding the natures of the beings we would petition, and of addressing them accordingly:

> Therefore, in composing verses, and orations, for the attracting the virtue of any star, or deity, you must diligently consider what virtues any star contains, as also what effects, and operations, and to infer them in verses, by praising, extolling, amplifying, and setting forth those things which such a kind of star is wont to cause by way of its influence, and by vilifying, and dispraising those things which it is wont to destroy, and hinder, and by supplicating, and begging for that which we desire to get, and by condemning, and detesting that which we would have destroyed, and hindered . . .

> Moreover magicians command that we call upon, and pray by the names of the same star, or name, to them to whom such a verse belongs, by their wonderful things, or miracles, by their courses, and way in their sphere, by their light, by the dignity of their kingdom, by the beauty, and brightness that is in it, by their strong, and powerful virtues, and by such like as these. (*Three Books*, Book I, Chapter 71)

So, here we see the concept of resonance once again—this time through consideration of the personality of the angel or god we wish to call upon. This truly reflects the art of the courtier, presenting petitions to the king in diplomatic fashion. The right kind of attitude projected at the king or lord petitioned was vital to the success of the effort.[24] In this vein, Agrippa (Book II, Chapter 49) gives us a list of proper titles to use when addressing the planetary deities. The titles that are used give us important glimpses into the deities' personalities:

Saturn

Coelius (Heavenly), Scythe-bearer, the Father of the Gods,[25] the Lord of the Time, the High Lord, the Great, the Wise, the Intelligent, Ingenious, Revolutor of a Long Space, and old man of great profundity, the author of secret contemplation, impressing or depressing great thoughts in the hearts of men, destroying and preserving things, overturning force and power, and constituting a keeper of secret things, and [one who reveals] them, causing the loss, and finding the author of life and death.

Jupiter

A helping Father, the King of Heaven, Magnanimous, Thundering, Lightning, Unconquered, High and Mighty, Great and Mighty, Good, Fortunate, Sweet, Mild, of good will, Honest, Pure, walking well and in honor, the Lord of Joy and of Judgements, Wise, True, the [Revealer] of Truth, the Judge of All Things, excelling all in goodness, the Lord of Riches, and Wisdom.

Mars

Mavors,[26] Powerful in War, Bloody, Powerful in Arms, a Sword Bearer, Magnanimous, Bold, Untamed, Generous, Lightning, of great power and furious haste, against whom none can defend himself if he resist Him, who destroys the strong and powerful, and deposeth kings from their thrones, the Lord of Heat and Power, the Lord of Fiery Heat, and of the Planet of Blood; who inflames the hearts of contenders, and gives them boldness.

Sol

Phoebus (Shining), *Apollo*, Father of Heaven, *Titan*, *Paeon* (a name of Apollo), *Phanes* (God the Manifestor or Source of all things), Horus, Osiris, seeing all things, ruling all things, the Creator of Light, the King of Stars, the Great Lord, Good, Fortunate, Honest, Pure, Prudent, Intelligent, Wise, shining over the whole world, governing and vivifying all bodies that have a soul, the Prince of the World keeping all the stars under Himself, the Light of all the

Stars, darkening, burning, and overcoming their virtue by His approach,[27] yet by his light and splendor giving light and splendor to all things. In the night He is called *Dionysus*, but in the day *Apollo*, as if driving away evil things.[28] He is also called *Pheobus* from His beauty and brightness, and *Vulcan* from his fiery violence, because the force thereof consists of many fires. He is called by the Hebrews *Shemesh*.[29]

Venus

The Lady, Nourishing, Beautiful, White, Fair, Pleasing, Powerful, the Fruitful Lady of Love and Beauty, the Progeny of Ages, the First Parent of Men, who in the beginning of all things joined diversity of sexes together with a growing love, and with an eternal offspring propagates kinds of men and animals, the Queen of all Delights,[30] the Lady of Rejoicing, Friendly, Sociable, Pitiful, taking all things in good part, always bountiful to mortals, affording the tender affection of a mother to the conditions of them in misery, the Safeguard of Mankind, letting no moment pass without doing good, overcoming all things by Her power, humbling the high to the low, the strong to the weak, the noble to the vile, rectifying and equaling all things. And She is called *Aphrodite*, because in every sex She is found to be of every mind. And She is called *Lucifera*,[31] i.e. bringing light, bringing the years of the Sun to light. And She is called *Hesperus*, when She follows the Sun (appearing above the western horizon at Sunset), and *Phosperus* (appearing above the eastern horizon at Sunrise), because She leads through all things though never so hard.

Mercury

The Son of *Jupiter*, the Crier of the Gods,[32] the Interpreter of the Gods, *Stilbon* (to flash, or glitter), the Serpent-Bearer,[33] the Rod-Bearer, Winged on His feet, Eloquent, Bringer of Gain, Wise, Rational, Robust, Stout, Powerful in Good and Evil, the Notary of the Sun, the Messenger of *Jupiter*, the messenger betwixt the supernal and infernal Gods, male with males, female with females, most fruitful in both sexes.[34] Arbitrator of the Gods, and *Hermes*, i.e. interpreter, bringing to light all obscurity, and opening those things which are most secret.

Luna

Phebe,[35] *Diana*, *Lucina* (Goddess that Brings to Light), *Hecate*, menstruous, of a half-form, giving light in the night, wandering, silent, having two horns, a preserver, a night-walker, Horn-Bearer, the Queen of Heaven,[36] the Chiefest of Deities, the First of the Heavenly Gods and Goddesses,[37] the Queen of Spirits, the Mistress of all the Elements whom the Stars answer, seasons return, and elements serve. At whose nod lightnings breathe forth, seeds bud, and plants increase, the Initial Parent of Fruit, the Sister of *Pheobus* (the Sun), Light and Shining, the Lady of Great Beauty, the Mistress of Rain and Waters, the Giver of Riches, the Nurse of Mankind, the Governor of all States, Kind, Merciful, etc.

The prayer (or petition) must show that the mage is in sympathy with the entity, desiring those things the star can provide, and hating those things against which the star is set. For instance, if one were to petition the angel of Mercury for help in business affairs, it would be necessary to praise the virtues of business, trade, and growth while condemning poverty, ignorance, and stagnation.

To end this section, I think it might be helpful to say a few words about the formal structure of biblical-style prayer. While the words and emotions must arise directly from the heart of the mage, it often helps considerably to have a general pattern to follow. These are, after all, official petitions intended for nobles (the angels) and the king (father sky). The basic structure allows us to gather all of the above elements and combine them into a truly effective invocation.

In fact, we have already seen the structure utilized in Psalms and other Middle Eastern prayers:

1. **Introduction and Call to Praise**: wherein the psalmist states the name and nature of the divinity he is attempting to invoke. Not only does it address God directly, but also calls upon all to come and hear the praise, and join in the worship. In our own invocations, this would naturally be directed at the angels and spirits who are governed by the intended divinity. (Spirits of Fire, adore your creator!)

2. **The Reason for the Praise**: including the mythological elements of the prayer we discussed above. If the god and/or angels of storm are invoked, for instance, it is necessary to praise them for the life-giving rain they bring.

3. **The Praise Itself**: wherein the invocant raises his mind and emotions to an adoration of the appropriate divinity. This section would also include the petition itself, stating what is needed, and (in true shamanic fashion) even reminding the god or angel of promises and covenants made in the past.

I also suggest one read the information on conjurations in chapter 12. Though conjurations are specifically for use with earthbound and infernal spirits, the basic structure of the recitations is very similar to what we see above. Richard Kieckhefer, in his *Forbidden Rites*, lists four distinct aspects of conjurations (rather than the three aspects of Psalms):

1. **Declaration**: being the same basic concept as the "Declaration" above.

2. **Address**: which is somewhat akin to the "Call to Praise" intended to address the proper angels and spirits set over the mage's magickal goal.

3. **Invocation**: including all of the mythological elements, calls to ancestors, etc that are necessary to gain the proper resonance between the mage and the angels in question. This section of a prayer is generally akin to the Litanies we might hear in a Catholic church.

4. **Instruction**: wherein a spirit would be commanded to leave a victim's body, or to perform a task. However, in the case of divinities and angels, it would relate more directly to the "Praise Itself." This would include the petition, request for intervention in the divine court, etc.

Finally, one must remember to make the prayers long. (And here is the true reason behind the astonishingly lengthy recitations of the grimoires. Your invocations are written to invoke the proper forces, but they must be lengthy enough to count as a kind of meditative process. Long and involved prayer is, in the west, what similarly extended meditations are in the east. As chapter 3 indicates, shifting consciousness is a process. The importance of this often-missed point will be illuminated somewhat more in chapter 8. For those who are groaning at the thought of writer's cramp, there is some good news. In actuality, your invocations will not be written nearly so lengthy as they will become in practice. As you become accustomed to the Psalms and adept at properly constructing invocations, you will likely find inspiration urging you to continue after the formal invocation runs out. In many instances, you will find yourself reciting effective invocations completely on the fly, and at need. It becomes a system of practical magick.)

Selection of the Place

The concept of ritual purity extends beyond the physical body, and into the sacred space within which the magick must happen. Dr. Timothy Leary discusses in his work the importance of *Set and Setting* when exploring altered states of consciousness.[38] The term "set" indicates the mindset of the individual when undertaking the experience. The term "setting" indicates the environment in which the experience takes place. These two concepts are different sides of a single whole, each one interdependent upon the other. The experience itself is directed by one's emotions and train of thought at the beginning of the work. Meanwhile, one's emotions and train of thought are largely affected by immediate surroundings.

So far, this chapter has focused largely on those things Dr. Leary might have classified under "set." The days or weeks of prayer and discipline, the endless recitations of invocations and Psalms, and the many deprivations all work to focus one's mindset (or will) toward the ultimate goal. However, the place where we will work must also undergo ritual purifications and be arranged to provide the proper "grimoiric" setting in which the magick can take place.

The grimoires insist that the chosen space must be hidden; such as a private room or an obscure spot in the wilderness. Generally, this can be anywhere so long as it is removed from daily activity, safe from intrusion or accidental discovery, and is tranquil and quiet overall. If it is a room or building, it must be absolutely cleaned before attempting to work there, in order to render it pure for the invocation of angelic beings. It must be furnished according to the magick performed, and completed with the necessary magickal tools, candles, incense, etc. Finally, prayers and invocations must be recited to consecrate the area to its work, and gain the attentions of the spiritual beings the mage will call in his magick.

This process transforms the space into a kind of pocket reality of its own, separate from the harrying world of the early twenty-first century. Meditating within it, we might forget our time and place, and drift closer to the mystical world perceived by the authors of the classical texts. In fact, this space creates an atmosphere known to shamans and mages throughout history.

Not only is this pocket reality necessary for the mage, but also for the spiritual Intelligences with whom he will attempt to communicate within it. The establishment of the sacred ground and the oratory are directed at creating an atmosphere that is habitable for spiritual beings, specifically through mimicking the calm purity of their state. If the atmosphere does not mimic the angels' true nature, then the angels will not find it easy to manifest within it. Note Agrippa's assertion on this point:

> . . . neither do [angels] perceive after that manner as we do with different organs, but haply as sponges drink in water, so do they all sensible things with their body . . . (*Three Books*, Book III, Chapter 23)

Therefore, in a sense, a noncorporeal entity cannot be completely separated from its environment. When an angel is called down into physical surroundings, he (being bodiless) will naturally intermix his own substance with the natural currents and forces present in the place. (Consider the results of pouring two liquids together, or—as Agrippa suggests—a sponge soaking up a liquid.) For instance, where there are things of a Solary nature, there will necessarily be spirits of the Sun present. Where there is nothing sympathetic to the Sun, then no such entities are at hand.

This is all about sympathy and resonance, two related concepts that play heavily into all magickal traditions, and especially into Agrippa's worldview. We will expand upon them in later chapters concerning magickal images, materials, talismans, and seals. Here, it is merely important to point out that spiritual entities are essentially one and the same with their environment because they are the embodiments of the physical forces of nature. The oratory as we are describing it here does not concern itself with planetary or other sympathies so much as it concerns the purity, tranquility, and holiness most often associated with angelic beings.

The *Book of Abramelin* has a detailed chapter on the creation of sacred space, found in Book II, Chapter 11 (Concerning the Selection of the Place). It first suggests one erect the oratory in a natural setting, if you happen to live in the country. It should be in a "small wood," or (one might assume) a small clearing completely enclosed by trees. The altar is erected in the center of the clearing, built of "stones which have never been worked or hewn, or even touched by the hammer." This latter is a biblical injunction related several times in scripture:

> And if thou wilt make me an altar of stone, thou shalt not build it of hewn stone: for if thou lift up thy tool upon it, thou hast profaned it. (Exodus 20:25)

> And there shalt thou build an altar unto the Lord thy God, an altar of stones: thou shalt not lift up any iron tool upon them. (Deuteronomy 27:5)

King Solomon followed this taboo to some extent as he fashioned the holy temple:

> And the House, when it was in building, was built of stone made ready before it was brought thither: so that there was neither hammer nor axe nor any tool of iron heard in the house, while it was in building. (I Kings 6:7)

The injunction against iron seems to be widespread throughout ancient culture. In the Celtic lands, the faery are said to be highly offended by the metal. Even Santeria recognizes a certain darkness around the subject, and the myth which explains it is very similar to ancient Sumerian examples. The development of iron tools and weapons among humans (in the Middle East circa 1200 BCE) severely shifted the balance of power that existed in the world at the time. Entire nations were crushed and dominated by those few who discovered the secrets of iron.

Those cultures who suffered a loss of place or enslavement due to the advancement (such as the Picts—or faery—of Britannia) had real reason to resent and fear the metal. The African myths depict the mining of iron ore as a literal rape of the earth goddess by the god of tools and iron. Specifically, the god became that of tools and iron as a punishment for his rape, destined to be a manual laborer for the rest of eternity.[39] The Sumerian version involves Enlil, the king of the gods, and Ninlil (his intended spouse), a daughter of the earth goddess. While Enlil is not considered a god of iron, he is credited with the creation of such tools as the hoe or plow.[40]

The *Book of Abramelin* does not say anything further concerning the construction of the stone altar. I'm rather surprised it does not insist one use no more or less than twelve stones for the purpose. It is stressed in the biblical book of Joshua, Chapters 3 and 4, where the Israelites finally cross the river Jordan to enter the Holy Land. In order to cross the body of water, the Levite priests carried the Ark of the Covenant into its midst, which resulted in a parting similar to Moses' parting of the Sea of Reeds in the Exodus. Once the Israelites were across the Jordan, Yahweh ordered Joshua to send twelve men, one from each tribe, back to the dry river bed to collect one large stone a piece. These were established as a memorial to the crossing of the Jordan:

> And those twelve stones, which they took out of Jordan, did Joshua pitch in Gilgal. And he spake unto the children of Israel, saying, When your children shall ask their fathers in time to come, saying, What mean these stones? Then ye shall let your children know, saying, Israel came over this Jordan on dry land. (Joshua 4:20–22)

The prophet Elijah also made use of twelve stones in erecting an altar:

> And Elijah took twelve stones, according to the number of the tribes of the sons of Jacob . . . And with the stones he built an altar in the name of the Lord. (I Kings 18:31–32)

Abramelin continues its instruction for the wooded oratory by building a shelter (tent or tabernacle) of "fine branches" over the altar to protect it from rain (i.e., for when the lamp and censer are burning). Surrounding the altar at a distance of seven paces one must plant a "hedge of flowers, plants, and green shrubs." If these are high enough, they would provide better privacy than the surrounding trees alone. In any case, they serve to divide the space into an outer area and an inner Holy of Holies (the shelter and altar). The general idea behind this arrangement can be found in scripture at Exodus 26, where Yahweh instructs Moses in the construction of the tabernacle in the wilderness, and includes the separation of the Holy of Holies with a veil.

Of course, few people will have the luxury to establish such a wonderful natural oratory. *Abramelin* accounts for this and offers an "urban" alternative. This oratory needs only be an apartment (room) with a north-facing window leading to a balcony or terrace. The floor and walls should be made of (or covered in) white pine. The terrace (used for summoning earthbound spirits) is covered in pure river sand of "two fingers depth at least." The altar in this case is not made of loose stones, but is itself made of wood (perhaps pine after the walls and floor) and hollow for the storing of the magickal tools.

The *Key of Solomon the King* has a thing or two to say about location in Book II, Chapter 7 (Of Places Wherein We May Conveniently Execute the Experiments and Operations of the Art). First of all, the usual rule is given about the place being "concealed, removed, and separated from the habitations of men," as a symbol that the art is hidden from the sight of the foolish, ignorant, and profane (uninitiated). It suggests such places as lakesides or forests, caves, caverns, grottoes, gardens, and orchards. In other words, much stress is placed upon natural surroundings when possible, and it states that these places should be "spacious, clear, and bounded on all sides by hedges, shrubs, trees, or walls"—much like we saw in *Abramelin*.

However, this chapter of the *Key* also seems to focus on the places where necromancy may be performed (specifically the summoning of earthbound or infernal spirits, and not necessarily the souls of the dead). This relates to the principal operation of the book and the spirits controlled by the *Key*'s talismans. According to the text, any desolate and uninhabited region is appropriate; giving examples such as any "dark and obscure place," old and deserted houses, or (most especially) at a crossroads where four roads meet. The *Key* does suggest that the "depth and silence of the night" is the best time to work, especially for the practice of necromancy. Although it also admits that anytime day or night can be used in general. Magickal timing (see chapter 5) will largely determine this.

To complete the information, Solomon relates Psalms that should be read during the cleaning and preparation of the area (Psalms 2, 67, and 54: all suggested for use in my own instructions given later in this chapter), and the use of water and incense to consecrate the ground.

Barrett's *The Magus* repeats the standard information concerning the selection of sacred space in Book II, Part II, "Of the Invocation of Evil Spirits . . .":

> Now concerning the place, it must be chosen clean, pure, close, quiet, free from all manner of noise, and not subject to any stranger's sight. This place must first of all be exorcised and consecrated . . .

The information on how to go about the consecration of the space is quite a bit more interesting. It actually appears before the above information, in Book II, Part 2: "The Consecration of Places, Ground, Circle, &c."[41]

Nothing in the book (as in Agrippa) is given in a step-by-step fashion. Instead, the art form is discussed in a general manner, leaving the reader to discover what works best, and to set the forms of the ritual himself. To begin with, *The Magus* suggests one recite Solomon's dedication of the holy temple. This can be found at II Chronicles 6:14–42,[42] a prayer long enough to rival the Solomonic confession given previously. Further, one is instructed to create a benediction (blessing) in the manner we have already discussed in this chapter. One should make commemoration of holy mysteries; such as the tabernacle, Holy of Holies, the temple of Solomon, the sanctification of Mount Golgotha,[43] etc. Concepts without direct scriptural reference can be mentioned as well, such as the "Place of God," the "Throne of God," the "Tabernacle of God," the "Altar of God," etc. Finally, of course, the use of water and incense in the blessing of the space is insisted.

From all of these examples, we can get a rather clear picture of the standard grimoiric procedures for selecting and creating necessary holy ground. A natural setting is paramount, though nearly any place with enough privacy is acceptable. Also, as has been stressed, the space must first be cleaned with meticulous care. The physical act of cleaning an area has always been known to possess great banishing virtue.[44] By stripping a room of its furnishings, clutter, dust, and stains, one is literally removing its personality (or spirit). This includes the memories and vibrations of those who have passed through or dwelt there previously.

In this way the place is rendered calm and pure, and thus ready for the invocation of celestial forces. The act of cleaning has no less effect on the mind of the mage himself, making the sacred ground something new and unspoiled. The reader has certainly experienced this when clearing out an old room, or moving into a new home.

All possible distractions should be removed, whether they be visual or audible. It's not necessary to go overboard with this if you have no dedicated working space. But the immediate area should always be arranged and clutter removed. Phones (and answering machines!) are always turned off. All sources of light should be eliminated as far as possible. It is best to work in pitch darkness with only the sacred candles as illumination, and this is why so many grimoires suggest working mainly at night.[45] And, again, one must be assured that interruptions or intrusions of sound will not occur during the times of working.

In other words, try to create a sensory deprivation chamber as far as possible given your circumstances. If you are not in a position to remove all signs of daily life from the room, you might go so far as to surround the necessary space with a white curtain. This simple little idea creates a superb sensory-deprivation chamber, literally allowing you to erect an oratory wherever you need it and in any shape or size necessary to fit the space.[46] It is easy to assemble and completely portable. I have done this before using sheets of plain white fabric (bed sheets will do). They can be tacked to the ceiling and their edges pinned together, leaving one "seam" unpinned so it can be pulled back and used as an entrance. I also found it useful to weigh down the bottoms of the sheets with something moderately heavy. You might take several books and roll them into the fabric so as to be invisible. When complete, this structure blocks out all possible visual distractions and only lacks soundproofing.

Mage in His Oratory.

The Solomonic Ritual Bath

The Solomonic bath is truly a thing of beauty. It stands alone in the *Key*; given in Book II as Chapter Five: "Concerning the Baths and How They are to be Arranged." This bath can be used before any magickal operation, or anytime one feels a need for ritual cleansing. Some have even found it useful as a daily observance. I am giving it here in full not merely because it is called for in the above Solomonic purifications, but because I will personally call for it in my own instructions given later in the chapter. The aspirant is encouraged to make much use of this simple yet powerful rite.

For this, you will need the aspergillum and holy water, some salt, the white robe, and a white towel (preferably of linen). You will also need a Bible or Psalter on hand for the recitation of Psalms. Finally, I strongly suggest you copy the below instructions onto a separate sheet of paper and have it laminated. This will allow you to take them into the bath with you, and thus avoid water damage to this book. Personally, I took the *Key of Solomon the King* to a copy store, photocopied the two pages of the chapter, and laminated them back to back. The result is very nice, and even allows me to stick the instructions directly onto the damp wall of the shower as I wash.

The *Key* suggests that one find a running stream as the best case scenario for this bath. From a shamanic viewpoint this does make sense—although doing so would rule out several of the more important instructions. (For instance, throwing consecrated salt into a running stream would not grant much result.) Alternately, the *Key* instructs one to use a tub of warm water for this purpose.

Step One

Begin by reciting the following series of Psalms:

> **14** or **53** (*The fool hath said in his heart, There is no God.*)
>
> **27** (*The Lord is my light and my salvation; whom shall I fear?*)
>
> **54** (*Save me, O God, by Thy name, and judge me by Thy strength.*)
>
> **81** (*Sing aloud unto God our strength: make a joyful noise unto the God of Jacob.*)
>
> **105** (*O Give thanks unto the Lord, call upon His name.*)

These are recited for disrobing. For the sake of practicality, you may wish to recite all of them before disrobing; or you might recite the first Psalm, disrobe, and then finish by reciting the rest.

Step Two

Enter the bathroom and turn on the water in the tub. This first part of the bath is principally for the removal of day-to-day dirt and grime. Therefore, there is no need to fill the tub at this point. I have found it much more useful to set the water temperature and turn on the shower. I don't feel that this exactly breaks "tradition" with the *Key*, because the text does suggest one use a running stream. If you chose to use the shower as well, place your hand on the shower nozzle and recite the following Exorcism of the Water. If not, simply recite it over the filled tub:

> I exorcise thee, O Creature of Water, by Him Who hath created thee and gathered thee together in one place so that the dry land appeared,[47] that thou uncover all the deceits of the Enemy, and that thou cast out from thee all the impurities and uncleaness of the Spirits of the World of Phantasm, so they may harm me not, through the virtue of God Almighty Who liveth and reigneth unto the Ages of the Ages. Amen.

Step into the shower (or the bath) and thoroughly wash yourself from head to foot. While doing so, recite the following Barbarous Names of Invocation two or three times:

Mertalia, Musalia, Dophalia, Onemalia, Zitanseia

Goldaphaira, Dedulsaira, Ghevialaira, Gheminaira, Gegropheira

Cedahi, Gilthar, Godieb

Ezoiil, Musil, Grassil

Tamen, Pueri, Godu

Huznoth, Astachoth, Tzabaoth

Adonai, AGLA, On, El, Tetragrammaton, Shema

Aresion, Anaphaxeton, Segilaton, Primeumaton

Step Three

Leave the bath—turning off the shower or draining the tub—and dry off with the white towel. Take the aspergillum and sprinkle yourself with holy water (I normally sprinkle myself in the pattern of a cross) while praying:

Purge me, O Lord, with hyssop, and I shall be clean; wash me, and I shall be whiter than snow.

After this, proceed to don the white robe while reciting the following Psalms. Once again, you may recite one Psalm, clothe yourself, and then complete the rest.

102 (*Hear my prayer, O Lord, and let my cry come unto thee.*)

51 (*Have mercy upon me, O God, according to Thy lovingkindness.*)

4 (*Hear me when I call, O God of my righteousness.*)

30 (*I will extol thee, O Lord; for Thou hast lifted me up*)

119: 97 [48] (*O how love I thy law! It is my meditation all the day.*)

114 (*When Israel went out of Egypt*)

126 (*When the Lord turned again the captivity of Zion, we were like them that dream.*)

139 (*O Lord, thou hast searched me, and known me.*)

Step Four

Now enter the bathroom once again and fill the tub with warm water. (No shower this time.) After this is accomplished, recite the following prayer over the fresh water:

El, Strong and Wonderful, I bless Thee, I adore Thee, I glorify Thee, I invoke Thee, I render Thee thanks from this Bath, so that this Water may be able to cast from me all impurity and concupiscence of heart, through Thee, O Holy Adonai; and may I accomplish all things through Thee Who livest and reignest unto the Ages of the Ages. Amen.

Then take the salt in hand and bless it by performing the Benediction of the Salt:

The Blessing of the Father Almighty be upon this Creature of Salt, and let all malignity and hindrance be cast forth hencefrom, and let all good enter herein, for without Thee men cannot live, wherefore I bless thee and invoke thee, that thou mayest aid me.

Followed by the recitation of Psalm 103 (*Bless the Lord, O my soul, and all that is within me*). Sprinkle the now exorcised and consecrated salt into the water—effectively creating a tub full of holy water.

Step Five

Once more disrobe yourself, this time following it with these Barbarous Names:

Imanel, Arnamon, Imato, Memeon, Rectacon, Muoboii, Paltellon, Decaion, Yamenton, Yaron, Tatonon, Vaphoron, Gardon, Existon, Zagveron, Momerton, Zarmesiton, Tileion, Tixmion

Enter the bath for the second time and sit down in the salted water. Pour the water over your entire body, and finish by reciting Psalms 104 (*Bless the Lord, O my soul, O Lord my God*), and 81 (*Sing aloud unto God our strength*).

Finally, exit the bath, dry with the white towel, and put on the white robe of purity. Though the *Key* does not instruct it, I would finish this session with the Exorcism of the Fire and the burning of exorcised incense. Cense yourself completely, just as is instructed in the "lesser bath" the *Key* describes for day seven of the nine-day purification. After this, you are ready to perform the work at hand, whatever that may be.

Standard Procedure

At this point, it will probably be easy for you to recognize and employ the formula of ritual purification. It will be recognizable in any classical or ancient magickal text, and it will be no difficulty to construct your own versions. Here, I will outline two procedures which I have found useful: a thirty-day regimen (for important undertakings) and a twelve-hour example (for emergency situations or regular observances).

The One-Month Purification

We might call this the "Four-Week Purification," as the instructions will be related on a week-by-week basis. The reader may choose to simply begin this process thirty (30) days before the chosen magickal day. On the other hand, this can be shortened to twenty-eight (28) days and matched to a complete lunar cycle. Instead of four weeks, each set of instructions would be divided among the four lunar phases. If one begins the process as the Moon enters its waning phase, it should be completed by the night of the following full Moon. (Remember to calculate your time *backward* from the required magickal day!)

I choose an entire month for this regimen specifically for the reason of a vegetarian diet. I have found anything less than a month of this diet inadequate to produce the proper physical (purifying) and psychological (deprivation/habit breaking) effects. Therefore, the mage will be expected to abstain from meat from the very first day of this procedure to the completion of the magickal operation. As usual, I suggest one follow the *Abramelin* instruction: milk and eggs are allowed, but absolutely no food that must be taken from a dead animal is eaten. Refer again to chapter three for more information on the vegetarian diet, and remember to consult a physician where necessary.

You will need to prepare your ritual space and altar, preferably, before the first day of the purification. If you are fortunate enough to have an oratory (or other sacred space) set aside, this should be thoroughly cleaned, scrubbed, swept, etc. while reciting the following Psalms:

2 (*Why do the heathen rage . . .*)

67 (*God be merciful unto us, and bless us . . .*)

54 (*Save me, O God, by Thy name, and judge me by Thy strength.*)

Afterward, perfume the room with exorcised incense and sprinkle with the aspergillum and holy water.[49] From this point onward, no one must be allowed to enter for the duration of the purifications and magickal work. Even you must not enter it except at the instructed times.

If, like the majority of us, you also have to live in your sacred space, then attention can be focused on the altar alone. The area should still be cleaned (complete with the Psalms, incense, and water) but only the altar need be left undisturbed during the process. Set it in an unobtrusive area, and enclose it with a white curtain if possible. As stated above, even you must not approach the altar except at the instructed times.

Once the area is prepared, the altar must be erected. Begin by washing your face and hands in pure water. Then, position the altar and cover it with a perfectly clean white cloth.[50] On top of this place the lamp, the censer, exorcised perfumes, the holy oil, the aspergillum, and the brass vessel for holy water. Make sure to take the time to clean, polish, and shine all of the magickal instruments before they are placed upon the altar.

I would also suggest one complete these actions with a recitation of one or more Psalms (or other scripture). If you have read through them, and recited those used in the Solomonic bath, then you will already have some grasp of their poetry and may already have developed favorites. You can also use a concordance to see if any Psalms (or, again, other passages) mention such things as altars or sacred ground, or perhaps something that relates to your magickal goal. (Psalm 26 not only mentions the altar, but also speaks of purification and steadfastness. Psalm 51 (used in the Solomonic bath) is the same. I found these and more by using Bible concordances freely available over the internet. I merely searched for the word "altar.")[51] If all else fails, Genesis 1 is almost always an appropriate choice.

You will also need to write some necessary prayers and invocations use—on a daily basis—for the duration of the purification regimen. The first prayer should be addressed to the highest, and contain biblical imagery and references that relate in some way to your magickal goal. Begin with a general confession, and then continue with a section of praise/thanks. Finish with a request for aid and guidance in the matter for which you are doing the magick, and ask that the necessary angel(s) be sent to you.

The second prayer (or conjuration) is addressed to the angels in question. Like the prayer to the highest, this must also use the proper imagery and references; this time to angelic deeds. The prayer must simply request—in the proper name of God—that the angel draw near, and that he make an appearance on the set day and hour. Again state the reason the request is being made (your magickal goal).

A full discussion of psalmody and confession can be found in chapter 4, and the grimoiric method of writing prayer has been discussed above. However, it is not ultimately necessary to prewrite these prayers (nor the confession). As long as the prayers are sincere and cover all of the above points, they will be sufficient. Of course, the longer the prayer sessions the better.

Weeks (or Lunar Phases) One–Three

Each morning after you awaken (or at dawn), wash yourself and put off eating breakfast. Enter your sacred space, kneel before the altar, and recite the confession and prayer to the highest you have prepared. It is not yet necessary to light the lamp or incense. After reciting the prayer, leave the altar (breakfast is allowed then) and do not approach it again until the evening. Just before you lie down to sleep at night (or at dusk), wash your face and hands, and kneel again before the altar. Repeat the confession and prayer from the morning.

The lamp and censer are not necessary on a daily basis (though they should remain on the altar). They need only be employed on the sabbath day. This might be Saturday or Sunday depending on whether your Judeo-Christian orientation leans more toward the Judeo (Saturday), or more toward the Christian (Sunday). On the sabbath, remember to light the lamp with its Exorcism of the Fire, and to light the coals of the censer with their own Exorcism of the Fire (see chapter 6). This must be done before the morning and the evening prayers for this one day each week.

There are two final instructions related to the sabbath. On each sabbath eve (the night before the sabbath), you must fast completely from nightfall until dawn. (*Abramelin* states that one should fast from "the first nocturnal star," and refers to this as the "Qabalistical Fast.") Also on this night you may enter the sacred space to clean and dust the area and the altar.

For the first two weeks, isolation and deeper stimulus deprivation are not necessary. One should certainly take pains to live a quiet and mild-mannered life such as instructed by Solomon or Abramelin. I would suggest avoiding specific social gatherings such as parties, games, etc.

During the third week you should introduce more isolation and a peaceful environment. Simply staying at home and keeping largely silent will accomplish much in these days. Begin this week to reduce all sexual stimulation, along with any other sensual pleasures.

Finally, it is necessary to spend these weeks preparing, constructing, and cleaning everything necessary for the magickal work ahead. Make sure you do not set out to construct a tool involving obscure items with only four weeks to succeed! However, there may be many basic things that need prepared, such as holy water, wax, earth, talismans, colors, etc. It is better to prepare these during your period of purification. Also take as much time as possible each day in the study of the necessary material (such as the rituals you will use). If any extra time is left over, Abramelin suggests reading the Psalms of David (the first sevety-two Psalms) at least twice within a week.

Week (or Lunar Phase) Four

This is where the serious magick begins to happen. For this final week, you must wash yourself and approach the altar three times a day: once in the morning, once at noon, and once in the evening. Each time, don the white robe and wear nothing on your feet.[52] Also light the lamp and incense (with exorcisms) every single time.

Each prayer session will include the same confession and prayer to the highest you have been using all along. Now, however, you should add the second prayer—the conjuration of the angel(s). These sessions should be extended as much as possible.

Most of the other instructions remain the same as the first weeks. Only now the mage must enter total sexual abstinence, and as much isolation and deprivation as possible. Any final preparations should be completed. Holy water, for example, is perhaps best made during the Wednesday of this last intensive week.

Day of the Operation

Thus the month of preparation is nearly complete and the big day has arrived. Repeat the prayer session this morning as instructed above (confession, prayer, conjuration, robe, lamp, incense, etc.), as well as at noon and in the evening if the magickal hour falls later than these.

You must fast completely for at least twelve (12) hours before the set magickal time. It would also be best if a complete isolation could be achieved for these hours. Certainly get as close to it as possible: spending the time silently in your room studying the texts, readying the materials, and erecting the altar and sacred space as necessary for the spell.

About forty-five minutes to an hour before the magickal time, perform the Solomonic bath as outlined above. Complete it with the donning of the white robe and/or any other magickal vestments or talismata that are necessary. Cense yourself with appropriate incense, and anoint yourself with the holy oil.[53] If there is time left after all of this, spend it with last-minute details or (most preferably!) silent meditation and/or prayer in front of the altar.

If you are not experienced in these techniques, the shift in diet, light isolation, sexual deprivation, and the necessary focus on prayer sessions will have a surprisingly large effect on you. In many ways the experience will be an magickal ordeal, testing you on the physical, mental, and spiritual levels. Passing successfully through this is the way of the shaman stepping between the worlds. Attempt this only once, and you will experience the incredible shift in consciousness produced by these actions. Perform it regularly, and it will transform your life.

The Twelve-Hour Purification

This shorter preparation is not designed for beginners. Its simplicity demands one who has some experience with the longer purifications. One should have at least used several seven-day or nine-day purifications before success can be expected with this shorter technique.

Twelve hours before the chosen magickal time, begin a complete fast. Spend these hours as isolated as possible, alone in your sacred space arranging and preparing everything necessary to the work ahead. Arrange the altar as described for the month-long purification above, and create the prayer/confession to the highest and the angelic conjuration. Otherwise, simply spend as much time as possible in silent prayer and/or meditation before the altar.

About an hour before the magickal hour, take the Solomonic bath and robe yourself properly. Approach the altar, light the lamp and incense with proper exorcisms, and recite the confession, prayer, and conjuration. Anoint yourself with the oil. Now, as the magickal hour dawns, simply continue with the necessary work.

It is, of course, possible to manipulate these techniques somewhat. You might wish to create purifications for various lengths of time depending on the magickal work involved. A three- or seven-day purification would be useful, as both of these are extremely holy numbers. On the other hand, one may wish to choose a number related to the occult forces invoked. For instance, the number of the Moon is 9, and therefore a nine-day purification would be perfect for any invocation of Luna.[54] The numbers of the planets are as follows:

3: Saturn—Saturday

4: Jupiter—Thursday

5: Mars—Tuesday

6: Sol—Sunday

7: Venus—Friday

8: Mercury—Wednesday

9: Luna—Monday

---

1. The biblical use of the word "fear" indicates "to stand in awe of."
2. Compare this to Agrippa's comments on gaining the conversation of the holy guardian angel: "But when we are purified, and live peaceable, then it is perceived by us, then it doth as it were speak with us, and communicates its voice to us, being before silent, and studieth daily to bring us to a sacred perfection" (Llewellyn's *Three Books*, p. 527).
3. John Dee comes to mind as one important example.
4. Angelic entities and spirits.
5. Note the *Three Books of Occult Philosophy*, Book III, Chapter 3: ". . . so great is the virtue of holy duties rightly exhibited and performed, that though they be not understood, yet piously and perfectly observed, and with a firm faith believed, that they have no less efficacy than to adorn us with divine power."
6. Note the reference to the ancient father sky.
7. Note the biblical reference to a past miracle involving water. See the instructions for making invocations in this chapter.
8. Yet another reference to a past deed on the part of God. This one is a direct reminder from the priest/shaman for God to remember and to act upon the set precedent.
9. Compare this to my observations of Abramelin earlier in this chapter. There, the seriously involved ritual work does not begin until the fifth month of the operation.

10. Peter 5:14: "Greet ye one another with a kiss of charity. Peace be with you all that are in Jesus Christ. Amen." It was by passing this secret sign that Judas was said to have betrayed the identity of Jesus to the Romans.

11. *A True and Faithful Relation*, p. 188.

12. Certainly Ave is here talking about passion, but I see a hint of the shamanic idea of spiritual heat here. If the two are not one and the same.

13. Agrippa is describing a universal hierarchy where all things have their corresponding superior. As below, so above.

14. *Three Books*, Book III, Chapter 32.

15. See the Net Bible Homepage: http://www.bible.org/.

16. Note that Agrippa here includes favors and promises. Remember chapter 2 where we discussed the shamanic art of intercession, where a patron god is reminded of the promises he has made in the past, and the shaman demands returns for favors done on behalf of the god. We will return to this subject below.

17. Donald Tyson notes: "That is, intrinsically, extrinsically, or by analogy."

18. Revelation 11:4.

19. The Old Testament, or Tanakh, is traditionally classified by three divisions: The Law (or Torah), the Prophets, and the Writings (including Psalms, Proverbs, etc.).

20. Luke 22:36.

21. Chronicles 21:27.

22. Though the words one chooses are certainly important to stirring the emotions.

23. The "Merkavah" in our case.

24. This is an aspect of the diplomatic arts—to which we will return again in chapter 8.

25. Apparently a reference to the orbit-path of Saturn, the largest in the seven-planet system of the solar system.

26. According to Donald Tyson, Mars is a contraction of the name "Mavors."

27. In an astrological chart, a planet in conjunction with the Sun is "in combustion" and is overwhelmed by the power of the Sun.

28. The Sun has always been most associated with exorcism of evil spirits.

29. Originally the name of the Sumerian-Babylonian solar god.

30. "All acts of Love and Pleasure are My Rituals." From the *Book of the Law*, and the Wiccan "Charge of the Goddess."

31. Lucifer (Light-Bringer) was originally the god of Venus. (Later adopted into Christianity as Satan due to a translation issue in the Old Testament.) Since Venus is being treated as a goddess here, the name has apparently been altered to fit her sex.

32. Or "Herald of the Gods."

33. A reference to the caduceus wand born by Hermes. It remains a symbol of the medical profession to this day, as seen on ambulances.

34. The planet Mercury is associated with hermaphrodism. While the Sun, Mars, and Jupiter are masculine, and Luna, Venus, and Saturn are feminine, Mercury holds a balance of both sexes. Magickal images related to Mercury are very often presented as hermaphrodites, effeminate males with suggestions of breasts and covered genitals. (Hermes himself has similar characteristics.) Likewise, homosexuality has long been associated with shamanic vocation. Donald Tyson, in his footnote to this text in the *Three Books*, seems to side-step the idea that "male with males, female with females" might indicate Mercury's relationship with homosexuality.

35. The feminine version of *Phoebus*, found under Sol.

36. A title that is historically associated with Venus.

37. These last two—giving the Moon the principal position among the gods—is of Mesopotamian origin. In Sumeria, the Moon god Nanna was considered the father of the planetary deities—including Inanna and even Shamash, the Sun god.

38. See *The Psychedelic Experience: A Manual Based on the Tibetan Book of the Dead*, Timothy Leary.

39. Perhaps we might see the metaphorical implications in this curse for mankind, for whom iron did eventually lead to the endless toil and slavery of the Industrial Era (circa 1850–1900 CE).

40. Plus, in Sumeria, Enlil did act as a kind of Demiurgos (craftsman) or creator god.

41. Just for the record, this same material is to be found in its original source: Agrippa's *Three Books*, Book III, Chapter 62.

42. Refer to the making of invocations (later in this chapter). See if you can spot the patterns I discuss there in Solomon's lengthy invocation.

43. Mathew 27:33, Mark 15:22, and John 19:17. This is the place where Jesus was crucified.

44. The use of the broom by modern Wicca to banish the circle is a survival of this concept.

45. The *Book of Abramelin* insists that no operation should be undertaken at night unless extremely necessary. This is unique, but the book shows by all of its magickal timing that it is strictly a Solar rite. Thus it would naturally insist that one work with the guardian only when the Sun is in the sky.

46. We will also revisit the white curtain enclosure in chapter 8.

47. Note the biblical reference to a past miracle involving water. See the instructions for making invocations later in this chapter.

48. Psalm 119 is an extremely long example—divided into twenty-two sections based on the Hebrew alphabet. Verse 97 falls under the section of *Mem* (M), the Hebrew letter associated with Water.

49. The Psalms, censing, and sprinkling procedure is taken from the *Key of Solomon the King*, Book II, Chapter 7.

50. The color of the cloth may depend on your magickal goal. White is recommended, though, as it represents purity and spirit. Invoke the highest first in all things.

51. See http://www.bham.ac.uk/theology/goodacre/multibib.htm.

52. "Put off thy shoes from off thy feet, for the place whereon thou standest is holy ground" (Exodus 3:5).

53. I generally trace a cross between my brows, directly upon the "third eye" area. Some texts will call for the anointing of the eyes, temples, or other areas. For information on this, see chapter 3.

54. Interestingly, the *Key of Solomon the King* puts special emphasis on the Moon, and it uses a nine-day purification.

Angelic Work
(Theurgy)

Now we reach the heart of our work, the invocation and communication with celestial beings, or theurgy. "Theurgy" literally means to "work with gods," who are technically one and the same with angels. The difference between a "god" and an "angel" is specifically one of culture and linguistics, and not one of practical consideration. Many angels, such as Michael, were themselves Pagan gods in ancient times, later adopted into the Judeo-Christian pantheons.

The celestial realm is the third (or highest) world of the shaman, and we have already discussed those creatures who live there. It is the realm of father sky (the Demiurgos of the Gnostics), as well as the countless angelic hosts (luminous ones, sons of God, etc.) identified with the stars and planets. Astrology is the key to understanding them, and this chapter will provide the key for holding conversation with them.

To put the matter simply: an angel is the intelligence (or personality) of a force of nature. Remember the doctrine of pantheism taken to heart by such men as Agrippa. Everything is alive, and everything is intelligent. Of course, a force of nature has no physical body such as we possess. It is not born of woman or raised from childhood. It does not live a daily life such as we do, nor is it ruled by a single one of our values or human assumptions. In fact, without a human mind with which to interact, such a force is little different in nature than a bolt of electricity.

Though we shouldn't jump to the conclusion that this proves spiritual beings exist "only in our heads." What humans usually consider "personality" is, in general, a complex of *reactions* to input from others and the environment. Your pet dog or cat, for instance, is largely devoid of personality when you leave it by itself. It exhibits more personality when other animals are present, and quite a bit more in reaction to humans. The same can also be said of any human being. Even we can exhibit zero personality when we are faced with no input at all, such as in the case of sensory deprivation.[1] To the other extreme, we can each exhibit several starkly different personalities depending on where we are and whom we encounter. What we usually think of as "ourselves" is often more a reflection of other people in our own psyche.[2]

Sometimes we might encounter another who lacks the ability (through language or physical capability) to communicate with us. All too often, we mistake it as "unintelligent," or perhaps even as dead matter. This happens often when we meet other humans who do not speak our language; we often mistake them for simple or stupid. Many have made the same mistake in regards to such things as plants and animals. (Note, for instance, that it took mankind several millions of years to learn that there were sounds of *any kind* under the water. During this time, the sea was only interesting in so far as it was useful to humans. Now, however, we know there are creatures in the deep with entire languages of their own.)

What we have learned is that "sentience" or "intelligence" is not centered in the mind of the individual, but actually within the matrix that exists between two or more individuals. If communication ceases, much in the way of personality goes with it. Here, perhaps, we have the stark truth behind pantheism/animism. Literally *anything* in existence can exhibit personality so long as we are mentally interacting with it. The less capable we are of understanding its language or forms of communication, the more lifeless it will appear.

Of course, the converse is also true; the more we come to understand something, the more lifelike it will seem. This can be proven by any poet—or by any psalmist. When viewing the world from this standpoint, the winds and the mountains are alive. The seas and the forests are conscious. And the mighty (astrological) forces of nature that shape our universe are also living intelligences.

In the *Three Books*, Book III, Chapter 15, we can see Agrippa's assertion that celestial bodies are "animated with certain divine souls." In the following chapter, he elaborates on the nature of these souls, or "intelligences." They are actually one of three species of angel existing within the three shamanic worlds. At the highest are those angels surrounding God and concerned only with supercelestial matters.[3] At the lowest are those angels stationed with us on Earth to minister directly upon human and physical matters. Finally, the celestial intelligences are the personifications of astrological forces existing between the two extremes. Agrippa assigns them:

> . . . the government of every heaven and star, whence they are divided into so many orders as there are heavens in the world, and as there are stars in the heavens. (*Three Books*, Book III, Chapter 16)

There were seven planets known to ancient man, and thus we have the seven who stand before God. The Gnostics considered thirty heavens, each one with its own guardian. Other Gnostic sects recognized 365 heavens(!) and thus had archangelic entities for each one. Judaic mysticism took the number 12 to heart—a survival of its astrological origins. Each zodiacal sign has its own tribe, and each tribe with its own guardian angel.

These are the angelic beings called upon in the grimoiric literature. They may be somewhat intimidating to anyone expecting the modern light and fluffy type of angel. These messengers are the regents of diety, responsible for the cycles of all life, fortune, and death upon the physical plane. They operate according to a strict divine (or universal) will that modern scientists would call *natural law*.[4]

The ancient Gnostics called them *archons* (rulers); whose job it was to maintain the status-quo of reality, binding every physical thing to the karmic wheel of incarnation. They stood as adversaries to the true Gnostic soul seeking freedom from the chains of fate (viz. fate as dictated by one's natal astrological chart. The Gnostic did not wish to be bound by the stars—that is, the archons—in such a way.). A Gnostic adept ascending the heavens would have to battle his way past them, and/or exist in such a holy state that the archons could not touch him.

In some manners, the archons were even believed to feed upon human souls, specifically the mental energy we grant them through our attentions (or even worship). Jim DeKorne, in his *Psychedelic Shamanism* (Chapter 5), warns the would-be shaman about such creatures on the spiritual plane. He illustrates several examples of modern-day psychonauts encountering such dangerous and hungry entities. These archons seek to preserve themselves and to compete amongst each other; "to eat to live and to avoid being eaten" as any living organism will do. It is not so much a matter of good or evil, but of simple Darwinism. The archons' attitudes toward humans might be seen as similar to our own attitude toward the plants and animals we eat.

The *Merkavah* mystic also viewed these archangels in a somewhat antagonistic light. However, he did not encounter them as despotic celestial rulers feeding upon human suffering. Instead, he called them *Melakhim* (messengers), who were in the direct employ of the benevolent creator.[5] This is not to say that they were not dangerous. They were the guardians of the Seven Celestial Palaces—charged with keeping out the impure and profane. Similar to the Gnostic view, the truly holy man had nothing to fear from the palace guardians. Those who did not pass their scrutiny, however, could expect fates such as insanity or death.[6]

Biblical legend and Judaic Midrashim provide countless examples of the nature of these angels—from their awe-inspiring appearances to their surprisingly blunt and often indignant personalities. For instance, both Ezekiel and St. John give us glimpses of the four mighty Kherubim responsible for bearing the weight of both the sky and God's throne.

Ezekiel 1 describes them as massive beasts with four wings, four faces (that of a lion, eagle, man, and oxen), and cloven hooves resembling burnished brass. They appeared in a terrible whirlwind of fire and lightning, and were so huge that the sound of their wings is compared to the sound of roaring waters or the voice of the Almighty. Meanwhile, the living spirit (intelligence) of each angel existed within great wheels (Auphanim) "so high that they were dreadful; and their rings were full of eyes round about them four." This gives us a real clue into the immensity of these beings, as the wheels are specifically the ring of the zodiac, and the biblical term "eyes" refers to stars.

St. John saw the same four creatures in a different light in Revelation 4. The four faces of Ezekiel's Kherubs were now divided among the angels so that one appeared as a giant lion, another as an eagle, another as a man, and the last as an ox. These "Holy Living Beasts" possess six wings a piece—and they are described as so large as to contain many "eyes" (stars) within them. These Kherubim are described by John as being directly involved in the apocalypse of the Earth.

Another apocalyptic angel is described by St. John in his Revelation (Chapter 10). Once again its fiery aspect is incredible: his face shone as bright as the Sun, and his feet appeared as pillars of flame. John saw this angel place one foot upon the land, and another upon the sea—suggesting his all-encompassing size and influence over the entire surface of the Earth. When the creature issued a cry, John compared it to the roar of a mighty lion.

Not only are these celestial beings described in biblical literature as immense and fiery as the very heavenly bodies they personify, but their actions can be quite harsh when they bear the wrath of father sky upon the earth. We might take Genesis 19 as a prime example, where we witness the destruction of two cities (Sodom and Gomorrah) at the hands of two angels. Each city was crushed and incinerated in a rain of brimstone and fire from above, the inhabitants were stricken blind, and one young lady was turned to a pillar of salt merely by looking upon the destruction.

Oral legend (Midrashim) provides us with even better examples of the natures and personalities of angels. For instance, they are described as having been jealous and offended at the creation of mankind.[7] They felt God had wronged them in making Adam (a creature of dust) in the divine image, and thus greater than themselves.[8] When God granted Adam a copy of the *Sepher Raziel* (The Book of the Secrets of God),[9] the angels were so consumed with envy they persecuted Adam and finally stole the book from him to toss it into the sea.[10]

Another legend depicts Moses in heaven contending with the angelic guardians of the celestial spheres. As I mentioned previously, these angels are charged with keeping out the impure and unworthy, and the prophets often had to best them in order to pass. One such guardian is described as "sixty myriads of parasangs" taller than other angels, and so mighty was he that twelve thousand fiery lightning flashes issued from his mouth with every word he roared. Even Moses coward at such might.[11] During this same trip into the heavens, Moses encountered a host of angels of terror who surrounded the divine throne, and who would have consumed him with their fiery breath had God himself not protected him. They demanded, "What does he who is born of woman here!?"[12]

Perhaps my favorite legend of angelic guardianship concerns the Exodus and the archangel Michael. As the Red Sea closed upon the Egyptian army and dragged every last man into the depths, two Egyptian master magickians named Jannes and Jambres took action against the angelic hosts present at the event. They fashioned wings for themselves and took to the sky[13]—using charms and invocations to drag the angelic warriors down and into the sea itself. These men were so powerful that the angels were helpless against them, and Gabriel called upon God to send rescue. In response, God dispatched the archangel Michael (general of the heavenly armies) who quickly and easily destroyed the mages by smashing their bodies against the surface of the water.[14]

Of course, not every angel is described as an archon-like bearer of divine wrath, nor as a spoiled child of nobility. They also appear as guides and protectors—such as the pillar of flame and cloud that preceded the Israelites through the wilderness (see Exodus). The eastern star that guided the wisemen to Jesus' nativity is considered an angel. (Which makes sense, as the star of Bethlehem would have been one of the seven planets.) In the *Book of Enoch*, Uriel guides the prophet through the heavens, and explains the sights along the way. In Midrashim, Moses was guided though the heavens in a similar manner.

As well, angels tend to act on a regular basis as messengers from God; bearing commands, revelations, and pronouncements from the divine throne to humans. Such as Gabriel delivering the annunciation to Mary that she would give birth to a son of God (a term that might sound familiar to the reader by this point.) Or the "three men" (supposed to be Michael, Raphael, and Yahweh himself) who delivered the news to Abraham that he and Sarah, too, would have a child. They can also bear news from Earth back to the throne, such as haSathan does in the book of Job when he accuses the man of lacking fortitude.

Examples could be given indefinitely, especially if the entire corpus of biblical literature (including the Apocrypha) as well as the oral Midrashim is included. However, the above should prove sufficient to illustrate how the prophets viewed these stars of heaven—and how that view differs from the common "light and fluffy" version of popular occultism and New Age philosophy. I personally suggest, as I have before, that the student obtain a copy of Ginzberg's *Legends of the Bible* and read it in order to get to know these angels.

Angelic Diplomacy

We can form friendly alliances with these entities, and they can help us to purify and elevate ourselves to higher states of being. However, one must keep in mind that these are noble intelligences who act only in accordance with divine will. One must take care and respect in approaching them in much the same way we might respect the raging storm, the wild fire, or the bolt of electricity. I stress once more that these beings are the personifications of the forces of nature, like the course of a river, the rise and fall of the ocean tides, or the daily passage of the Sun across the sky. One does not casually interfere with the will (the natural courses) of such things. Angels can bite, and they often do.

The grimoires take this into account in their approach to working with angelic forces—incorporating the methods of both the priest and the shaman. This was discussed to some extent in chapters 3 and 4. We have seen the relation between the royal court and the divine court and the somewhat legalistic methods of wording prayers and invocations. When working with the angels, the mage operates in an ambassadorial role. Both the human and the angel are under the employ of the same crown, yet each occupies his own particular social position. The angels are nobility (somewhat akin to medieval land barons), concerned with governing the mechanics of nature; or they are direct ambassadors from God.

Meanwhile, the wizard's role is that of royal ambassador from the physical plane—acting as an agent (or angel) of God in his own right. As a priestly figure, the proof of his authority lies within the divine names he pronounces,

An Angel—Huge and Powerful.

and the mystic seals he employs in his work.[15] These things are direct parallels of the royal seals and passwords utilized by agents of the king in ancient times. Whenever the king wished to delegate royal authority, he would issue his agent his own royal seal. The bearer of the seal could then act with all of the force and authority of the throne itself, and he answered only to the king. On pain of death, no one (neither peasant or noble) could question or interfere with him so long as he was about royal business.

The grimoiric mage, if acting in accordance with the art, is always concerned with royal business when he summons angelic attentions. As a shaman, it is his *job* to protect and maintain the harmony of his environment and community. Thus he enjoys a basic right to approach the angelic forces and negotiate for aid and alliance. He is dealing with nobility of a high class, and yet speaks with the voice of the king himself.

There is also a biblical precedent which grants the human a great amount of authority on the spiritual plane. In Genesis, the text affirms that Adam was fashioned in the divine image of the creator. This is not exactly a reference to the physical appearance of the human animal, so much as to his spiritual nature. We possess the Logos, which incorporates self-awareness, free will, and the essential power to create. This was (and is) a major focus within the Judaic mysticism which gave rise to the grimoires. The formula for the creation of the golem,[16] for example, is largely a reenactment of Yahweh's fashioning of Adam in Genesis 2. It rests upon the concept that man is entitled to create life in the same manner as God himself.

Herein lies the reasoning behind the legendary angelic envy of mankind's position in the cosmic scheme of things. Humans and other animals properly fall in the second shamanic world—just above the infernal realm but below the celestial. Therefore, the angelic hosts occupy a higher Darwinian position and enjoy a general authority over us (again refer to the Gnostic archons). However, by breathing the breath of life[17] into our physical forms, the creator impressed upon us an ineffable royal seal granting us our authority and earthly dominion. An angel might possess raw power far beyond human capacity, but he is forever constrained to worship us as the living image of his sovereign. For the magickian, this calls for a curious mixture of authority and humility in dealing with the angels—an art long known as "diplomacy."

In working directly with the angels, one can employ a standard diplomatic pattern. This starts with the prayers and invocations one creates to call upon the angelic rulers. These should include the praise and glorification of the past deeds of both God and the angel(s) in question. (In other words, the entities are poetically reminded of their proper jobs, as well as any promises/covenants that have been made previously, etc.) Once the mage has highlighted the precedents that strengthen his case, he can then present his formal petition to the angels. This must be given (either spoken, or written on paper) with a request that the angel(s) argue the case before the divine court on the mage's behalf. (See chapter 4: "From Priests to Kings, and From Palaces to Temples.")

This is also a two-way exchange. Once the relationships are established, you may find that the angels often come to you of their own accord. Each person will experience them in different ways. They may involve themselves in your magickal work or meditations, appear to you in dreams with advice or commands from father sky (or mother earth), or make Their presence and influence known in times of distress. Myself being a researcher and author, I find they sometimes "speak up" while I study. Very often, obscure information is revealed or explained in these flashes of inspiration. I also note this same phenomenon frequently during my performance of ceremony. I will find various parts of the ceremonies explained in *very* occult detail as I perform them. Some of the revelations have been quite astounding.

The long and involved ceremonies of the grimoires are only designed to achieve initial contact with the celestial beings, while the communication and relationships that develop thereafter do not have to involve all of the "bells and whistles." The true magick of the grimoires is not found within their written pages, but in the active contact established with the angelic teachers and guides along the way. The grimoires are a starting platform, a set of keys that allow us access to the true magick.

Abramelin calls this the "True and Sacred Magick" when such mysteries are delivered by one's own guardian angel. We have already seen the similarity between the guardian angel and the ancient shamanic spirit guides and teachers, who were responsible for educating the shaman in the magickal arts, healing, etc. (see chapter 2). The same concept can be found elsewhere in the grimoiric literature as well. For instance, in the *Key of Solomon the King*, Solomon states that his vast wisdom and magickal knowledge (and thus everything in the *Key* itself) were delivered directly by an angel:

> For, on a certain night, when I laid me down to sleep, I called upon that most Holy Name of God, IAH, and prayed for the Ineffable Wisdom, and when I was beginning to close mine eyes, the Angel of the Lord, even Homadiel, appeared unto me, spake many things courteously unto me . . . (*The Key of Solomon the King*, Introduction, Add. MSS 10862)

> . . . when I was meditating upon the power of the Supreme Being, the Angel of the Great God appeared before me as I was saying, O how wonderful are the works of God! I suddenly beheld . . . a Light in the form of a blazing Star, which said unto me with a voice of thunder: Solomon, Solomon, be not dismayed; the Lord is willing to satisfy thy desire by giving thee knowledge of whatsoever thing is most

pleasant unto thee. I order thee to ask of Him whatsoever thou desirest. (*The Key of Solomon the King,* Introduction, Lansdowne MSS 1203)

This means the classical grimoiric literature is what we would today call "gnostic." That word literally means "knowledge" or "acquaintance," and refers to any practice involving direct reception of teachings from spiritual sources. The ancient Gnostics were labeled with this term in order to differentiate them from other biblical (Judeo-Christian) systems, which generally insisted on priestly intervention between humans and God. The Catholic Church was appalled at the heretical teachings delivered to humans by various classes of angelic teachers. (Thus the Inquisitions—see chapter 1.) The Gnostics, on the other hand, knew that the true and sacred mysteries could not be learned from human sources.

The grimoires are not "Gnosticism" in the proper-noun sense of the word, though they certainly do trace much of their material to ancient Gnostic concepts and methods. On the other hand, they are in many cases pure Gnosticism in the general sense. *Abramelin* is an especially perfect example of such Gnostic practices. As we can see in the quotations immediately above, the *Key of Solomon the King* claims to be a Gnostic work as well. The *Lemegeton,* also, concerns itself with contacting various hierarchies of angels and spirits, all of whom can teach us different skills and mysteries. The *Sworn Book of Honorius* claims to be the teachings of the angel Hochmel (wisdom of God). The *Notary Arts* also stand as a prime example of Gnostic practice. Even John Dee understood these concepts, and his angelic magick is entirely Gnostic:

> I had read in books and records how Enoch enjoyed God's favor and conversation, and how God was familiar with Moses, and how good Angels were sent to Abraham, Isaac, Jacob, Joshua, Gideon, Esdras, Daniel, Tobias, and Sundry others, to instruct them, inform them and help them in worldly and domestic affairs, and even sometimes to satisfy their desires, doubts, and questions of God's secrets. . . . Therefore I was sufficiently taught and confirmed that I would never attain wisdom by man's hand or by human power, but only from God, directly or indirectly. (*The Five Books of the Mysteries,* Preface)

This should be the position of anyone attempting to make use of the grimoires. You must be willing to open yourself to the influence of these spiritual teachers—to gain their familiarity, make alliances with them, and to learn the true and sacred mysteries of the magickal art, which are both unwritten and unspoken. Each individual mage will have his own lessons to learn, and will receive teachings unique to himself and his needs.

How To Summon Angels

Angelic communication was the primary goal of the grimoiric mage. It was only by befriending the celestial forces that he could work his magick, control the spirits, heal sickness, foresee the future, etc. Even those texts which focus on goetic spiritism were meant for use by holy men with preestablished angelic connections. Not only do the angels teach us how to properly go about the magick, but they are the authoritative forces that we must employ in influencing our environments. Therefore, contrary to the grimoires' popular reputation of spirit conjuration, it is the art of angelic communication that forms the heart and soul of grimoiric practice.

Each text has its own methods of going about this. However, even the most unique examples are typically variations on the same basic themes. All of them tend to summon angels via talismans, books, or peculiar apparatus that seem to work on the same shamanic principals as the magickal tools. Most of them employ a combination of the three, and they are generally based upon astrological and/or alchemical elements.

John Dee's Heptarchic system makes use of such apparatus; meaning the holy table with its Sigillum Dei Ameth, ensigns of creation, shewstone, etc. When these instruments are put together and used, they serve as a

The Holy Table.

kind of communications device that aids in attracting, perceiving, and conversing with spiritual entities. They create an atmosphere friendly to both the human and the celestial intelligences, and thus provide a point of contact between the two realms. This is analogous to the Ark of the Covenant in the temple of Solomon—upon which Yahweh would descend to speak with his priesthood. Dee's holy table setup, in fact, is based in part on the concept of the Ark.

Talismans also play a part in the Heptarchia, based upon the day one chooses to work. After the holy table is erected and its shewstone is in place, the seal of the angelic prince for that day must be placed upon the table. A talisman of the prince's 42 ministers must be placed under one's feet, and a wooden seal of the day's king is held in the hand. It is over these seals that the invocations and prayers are read. The result should be the appearance of the day's angel(s) in the skrying stone.

Technically, the angel is not called from "somewhere out there" in the far reaches of the cosmos. His essence exists within the very pattern of his seal,[18] and thus he literally inhabits the talisman itself. The holy table provides the proper atmosphere, and the invocations awaken the angel from his slumber within the talisman. The concept of spiritual entities inhabiting talismans will be familiar to those who have read the *Thousand and One Arabian Nights*—with its numerous jinni bound to brass vessels and rings.

The *Pauline Art* from the *Lemegeton* also rely on specially made (though less impressive) apparatus and talismanic seals. The central piece of equipment is the table of practice, a simple round altar with the figure of a hexagram, the planets, and various seals and sigils inscribed upon its top. (See chapter 1 for a photo of the table of practice.) For the first part of the work (concerning the twenty-four angels of the hours of the day and night) one

Dee's Skrying Stone Frame.

merely needs to place an angel's talisman upon the proper planetary sigil on the table and read the invocations. In the second part of the work (concerning the angel of one's nativity) the same table is covered with a white linen cloth, and a metallic seal is placed upon it facing the proper quarter. (Angels of Fiery signs [Aries, Leo, Sagitarius.] face toward the south, those of Earthy signs [Capricorn, Taurus, Virgo] face toward the west, those of Airy signs [Libra, Aquarius, Gemini] face toward the east, and those of Watery signs [Cancer, Scorpius, Pisces] face toward the north. I am unsure as to the purpose behind this arrangement. It does not follow the typical astrological arrangement of Fire in the east, Earth in the south, and Air in the west. I hesitate to suggest it is a blind.)

Also found in the *Lemegeton* is the almadel of Solomon (this beautiful piece of equipment has also been described in chapter 1). In this system, a beeswax tablet inscribed with a hexagram and divine names rests upon four candles of the same wax. The almadel also includes the use of a talisman—though this one is an inherent part of the almadel itself, and does not belong to any individual angel. Instead, it serves as the focal point upon which the angels will manifest upon the almadel. Underneath this apparatus is placed a censer so that smoke will drift upward

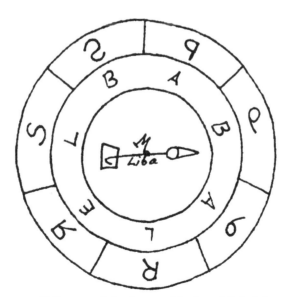

Talisman of the heptarchic Angel Babalel.

The Seal of Babalel's Prince.

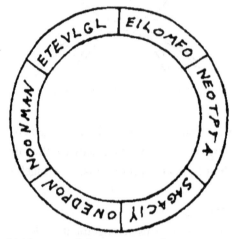

Round Talisman of the Ministers for Babalel's Prince.

beneath the almadel, and into holes drilled through the wax for the purpose. The mage may skry into the rising smoke to perceive the entities.

We can find three different procedures for angelic evocation in Barrett's *The Magus*, or *Celestial Intelligencer*—each given in much more detail than anything in the *Lemegeton*. The first example is outlined in Book II, Part 2, Chapter "Invocation of Good Spirits in Particular" (pp. 92–5). I find this method extremely interesting due to the fact that it is so very similar to my own. One can even see some hints of *Abramelin* in these instructions, suggesting that this material drew from *Abramelin* directly or indirectly, or that both share some common source material.

First, the usual grimoiric instructions are given regarding the ritual space. It must be hidden, cleaned, exorcised and consecrated. Further, *The Magus* instructs that a new and clean linen cloth must be laid upon the ground. As in *Abramelin*, one must always enter the consecrated space without shoes.

Next, an altar or table covered with a white linen cloth must be placed "toward the east" of this sacred ground This might mean that it should rest in the center and face toward the east. However, it would not harm this proce-dure in the least to place the altar in the eastern quarter, or even against the eastern wall of the room. (That is ex-actly where I regularly perform operations of this sort.)

On the altar should be placed a talisman of the angel one wishes to call.[19] It is covered with a white linen cloth, and is not to be uncovered at all until the day of working. Also on the altar rest the exorcised perfume (proper to the angel called) and censer, and a holy anointing oil. Holy water will also be needed, and this can probably be set on the altar with the rest of the items.

On either side of the altar stands a consecrated candle. Again the direction is a bit ambiguous: it might mean to set the candles on the floor beside the altar, or it might mean to place them on either side of the altar top. Again, either one should be fine, though I would suggest placing them on the altar for practical and safety reasons.

The Magus also insists that these lights should be kept burning for the entire period of working. This includes the period of ritual purifications (up to forty days!) and the day of working itself. On one hand, I find this instruction highly impractical and unnecessarily dangerous. The tapers would not last for very long, meaning an extremely large number of them would be necessary for each operation. Plus, one would have to tend them constantly to make sure they do not gutter out or burn away. More importantly, candles left burning unattended are never a good idea.

Even the *Book of Abramelin*, where it insists that a light must be allowed to burn for an extended time, also suggests that it is fine if the light has gone out while the mage is away. He must simply make sure to relight it when he returns. I see no reason why this could not follow in *The Magus'* system as well. One would merely have to light the candles when reciting the prayers at the altar.

On the other hand, I certainly appreciate the magickal significance of this instruction. The flames themselves embody the living energies raised in the work. Keeping them alive is akin to the eternal flame used in churches, at gravesides, etc to symbolize the ever-burning light of God or of the soul. If one wishes to use this system strictly as outlined in *The Magus*, I would highly suggest securing the time to enter heavy isolation for the entire period of purification. Then, one would be spending most of his time alone in the room, and would be on hand to tend the flames with devotion. When doing this, always make sure to light the new candles from the flames of the dying candles—so that the flame is transferred from one to the other without going out.

The ritual garb for *The Magus'* procedure is similar to *Abramelin's*: a white linen pull-over robe that reaches to the floor, and a white girdle (such as a silk sash) tied around the waist. Then, with a stronger hint of *Abramelin*, one is instructed to make a white linen veil with Tetragrammaton painted upon it in gold. Specifically, the text says that on the veil must be "wrote in a gilt lamen, the name Tetragrammaton." *Abramelin* makes use of magickal letter-squares on its veil, so we might assume *The Magus* is suggesting the divine name should be arranged into a similar square of some kind. Whether the Greek "Tetragrammaton" or the Hebrew (י ה ו ה) should be used is unspecified—though it is likely the former given the source of this procedure. All we do know for sure is that this figure should be painted onto the linen with real gold—hence the use of the word "gilt."[20] Finally, all of these materials must be consecrated as usual.

The suggested time of ritual purification and abstinence is one month (or lunar cycle), although the text mentions the forty-day preparations of the Qabalists as well. On each of these days, one must approach the altar seven times a day (the first session at dawn and the final at dusk). For each time, one is instructed to don the white robe, sprinkle the place with holy water, and light the perfume. Then, kneeling before the altar, prayers are recited first to the highest and then to the angel(s) in question—much as I described in chapter seven of this work.

On the last day of preparation, the aspirant must fast. Then, rising the next morning (the chosen magickal day) at dawn, he is to enter the sacred space and don the white robe. He must sprinkle himself as well as the general area this time, and then light the perfume. To complete the set-up, he must take the holy oil and mark the sign of the cross on his forehead, and also anoint his eyes.[21] *The Magus* says that prayer should be used in all these consecrations. Finally, the linen cloth is removed from the talisman upon the altar, the mage kneels before the altar and recites an invocation for the appearance of the angel.

The same chapter of *The Magus* (pp. 95–6) continues with a "simpler" example of angelic communication; one that extends over seven days. Specifically, it is a method of obtaining "Oracles" from the angels, rather than a full summoning "to visible appearance." One is to perform this rite to receive answers to questions, but no stress at all is placed on two-way conversation with the entities.

The ritual space must be clean, pure, etc., as well as "covered everywhere" with clean white linen. (It is possible that this is intended for the first example as well. It reminds me somewhat of the simple oratory I described in chapter 7, and I will return to this idea once again later in this chapter.)

First, as usual, the space must be consecrated for use. The text instructs one to wash thoroughly and don the white robe, and then proceed to exorcise and bless the area. With a consecrated coal (and presumably on the white linen cloth laid on the floor), a circle is traced out complete with the names of the angels being called and the related divine names. (Note that the use of such a circle is actually rare for angelic summonings, as the bulk of these examples from various grimoires illustrate.) A censer and a consecrated candle is placed in each of the four quarters of the circle. Once again, the text instructs one to keep these lights burning for the entire period of work (seven days).

The purifications span the first six days (of course), and one must keep himself "chaste, pure, and sanctified." A kind of fasting diet is prescribed in such a manner as to remind us of *Abramelin* once again. The mage must abstain from eating anything "having a life of sense"—meaning to avoid food taken from living animals. One is to drink only pure running water,[22] and is apparently not to eat any food at all after the Sun has gone down.

The mage must also fast before entering the sacred space each day—a point taken care of by the above instruction. *The Magus* does not indicate what time of day (magickal hour) one should enter. In any case, one must first wash thoroughly and then approach the altar. (The text makes no mention of donning the white robe, but that may be taken for granted.) The four censers must be lit along with the candles if they have not been kept burning continually. The mage then faces the east, and recites the entire Psalm 119 (*Blessed are the undefiled in the way . . .*), which is quite an undertaking in it's own right. This is the extremely long Psalm dedicated to the twenty-two letters of the Hebrew alphabet. It is certainly long enough to produce a trance state if read with proper devotion. Afterward, the procedure is completed by reciting prayers to the angel(s) in question that they appear and reveal what the mage wishes to know.

The seventh day should be the Lord's Day during the waxing moon. (*The Magus* says "the new of the moon"— which might indicate first crescent.) Having fasted and washed, the mage must don the white robe and veil, enter the circle, and light the censers (and candles). Then he must take the holy oil and anoint his forehead and eyes as before. However, this time he must also anoint himself in the palms of both hands and on both feet—mimicking the stigmata of Christ. Then, the mage repeats the actions of the previous six days by reciting Psalm 119 and the invocations to the angels.

Finally, *The Magus* gives instructions that modern Neopagans might find familiar. One is to rise from before the Altar, and circumambulate the circle clockwise "until thou shalt be wearied with a giddiness of thy head and brain." In other words, the mage will become increasingly dizzy and disoriented. Eventually he will fall down, where he can rest and "be wrapped up in ecstasy." It is during this altered mental state that the angel will make known the answers he seeks.

The Calling of Angels into the Shewstone, from The Magus

The third example provided by *The Magus* appears in Book II, Part 3, Chapter "The Conjurations of Spirits[23] into a Crystal; the Description of this Instrument; and the Form and Ceremony of a Vision" (pp. 134–139). This procedure is meant specifically for use with the seven planetary angels that rule each hour of the day (see chapter 5).

First, one must acquire a small crystal ball (shewstone) "fair and clear, without any clouds or specks." This is set in a plate of pure gold, and a circle must be inscribed into the gold around the crystal (apparently on both sides of the plate). Within this circle (between the crystal and the line of the circle itself) should be engraved these three symbols and the name Tetragrammaton.

יהוה

The Hexagram with Yod, the Pentagram, the Cross, and the Tetragrammaton.

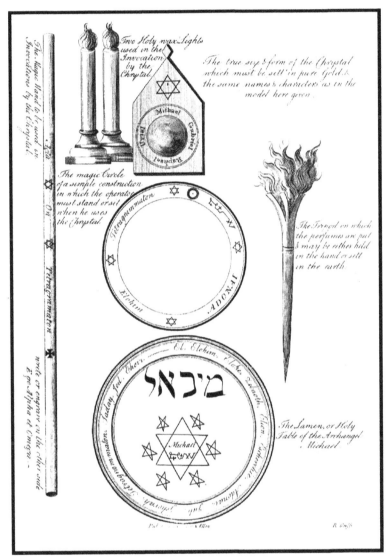

Plate from *The Magus*: the crystal, wand, circle, lamen, etc.

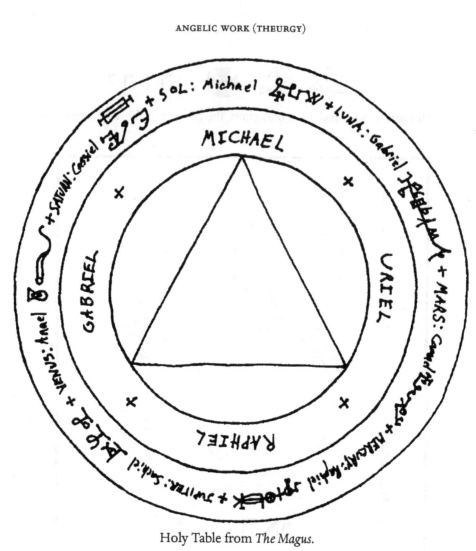

Holy Table from *The Magus*.

On the other side of the golden plate, also between the circle and the crystal, the names Michael, Gabriel, Raphael, and Uriel are engraved. Finally, the plate is set in a base of pure ivory or ebony.

The next piece of furniture is the table (or altar)—though it is not pictured anywhere in *The Magus*. The description does not indicate whether the table should be round like that in the *Pauline Art*, or square like Dee's skrying table. However, the proper shape might be round, due to the fact that the text instructs one to inscribe a double circle around the table's top.

In the outer circle, the names of the seven planets,[24] their angels, and the angels' sigils are inscribed. In the inner circle, the names of the "Kings of the Quarters" are written—which I can only assume to be Michael, Gabriel, Raphael, and Uriel. Finally, inside the circles inscribe a triangle (a point possibly borrowed from the *Goetia*). Upon this table will rest the shewstone, a censer (with perfumes appropriate to the day and hour of working), and two consecrated wax candles.

Also needed (and pictured with the crystal, etc.), is a wand of "black ebony" with gilt characters inscribed upon it. Apparently both real ebony and real gold are used for this. As I mentioned previously, paint with gold in it can be purchased for this task.

A magickal ring is also prescribed, and is described in Book I, Part II, Chapter 11, "Of the composition and magic virtue of Rings." Here the rings are described in exactly the same manner as any magickal talisman (see chapter 10), principally offering the wearer protection against all manners of evils and adversities. Beyond this, the

Sunday	Monday	Tuesday	Wednesday	Thursday	Friday	Saturday
Michael 	Gabriel 	Camael 	Raphael 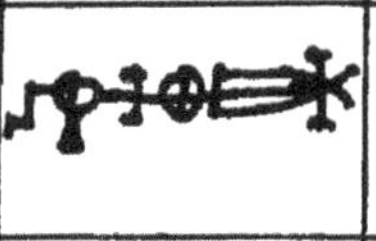	Sachiel 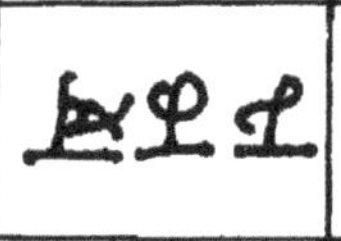	Anael 	Cassiel 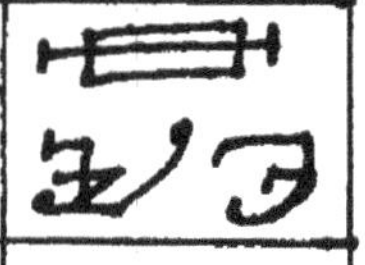
☉ ♌	☽ ♋	♂ ♈ ♏	☿ ♊ ♍	♃ ♐ ♓	♀ ♉ ♎	♄ ♑ ♒
4th Heaven Machen	1st Heaven Shamain	5th Heaven Machon	2nd Heaven Raquie	6th Heaven Zebul	3rd Heaven Sagun	No Angels Ruling Above 6th Heaven

Table of Seven Days.

rings are attributed to the working of various miracles by such men as Moses, Appollonius, Solomon,[25] and other historical masters. They can procure love, extend life, bestow beauty, and even grant honor and kingship.

In order to make and consecrate a magickal ring, one must first decide which star (planet) will produce the desired effect. Then, one gathers a ring made of metal, an herb or root, and a stone—all three of which must be associated with the chosen star. A time is chosen according to elective astrology for the construction, and apparently the consecration, of the ring. The star must be ascending in the horoscope, well dignified, and fortunately aspected (all of which we discussed previously in chapter 5). The stone must be carved with some magickal image or sigil appropriate to the star (see chapter 10), and then set into the ring with the herb or root *underneath* it—preserved permanently within the ring itself. As we will see in chapter 10, it is likely that the plant encased in the ring embodies the nature spirit (or jinn) by which the ring works its magick.

Having the ring made, we can return to the *Magus'* instructions for calling angels into the shewstone. The procedure also calls for a lamen or talisman for the angel being called, which might be made on virgin parchment or inscribed (again, like *Abramelin*) upon a square plate of silver. *The Magus* gives its example of a talisman for Michael (angel of the Sun and Sunday), and I will be outlining the text's method of talisman construction in chapter 10.

Finally, one must prepare a small book of pure white virgin vellum or paper—about seven inches long. This is the angelic book, containing the names, images, seals, invocations, teachings, etc. of the angelic entities one contacts. To write in the book, a pen (and ink if such applies) is consecrated to the purpose.

The Magus suggests that two participants should be present at these evocations. "For often a spirit is manifest to one in the crystal when the other cannot perceive him . . ." We might take the example of John Dee and Edward Kelley. Dee had limited ability with skrying, while Kelley was extremely adept at the art. Therefore, in all of their angelic seances, Dee would act as the master of the ceremony and Kelley would report what he saw in the shewstone. Only rarely would Dee share a vision with his skryer.

It is not true that one must always involve a partner in summoning rites. You can, and perhaps often should, perform a great deal of personal work on your own. However, as a natural human being, you may or may not fall

The Magick Ring from the Magus.

The Magick Book—with Cassiel.

into Dr. Dee's category. While we all can train ourselves to skry to various extents, it is still true that some have natural inclinations that others do not. I have heard the opinion that skrying is principally a gift of the mysteries of womanhood, and I've seen much evidence to support that conclusion. I am personally not a natural skryer,[26] and I find it very useful to involve a particular young lady in my work on a regular basis. We work along the same lines as did Dee and Kelley themselves.

Now we move on to the practical instruction given by *The Magus* for use of the shewstone. To begin with, one is instructed to observe the proper day and hour for the evocation. At the end of the chapter it lists the tables of planetary hours, but instead of showing the planets, it displays the names of the planetary angels. Thus, if the mage is working during a Thursday on the hour of Jupiter, we know he is attempting to call Sachiel, etc.

Therefore, at the appropriate magickal time, the mage is to approach the table and recite a prayer that involves the invocation of the highest as well as an exorcism of the crystal itself:

Oh God! Who art the author of all good things, strengthen, I beseech thee, thy poor servant, that he may stand fast, without fear, through this dealing and work; enlighten, I beseech thee, oh Lord! the dark understanding of thy creature, so that his spiritual eye may be opened to see and know thy Angelic spirits descending here in this crystal:

(Then lay thy hand on the crystal saying,) and thou, oh inanimate creature of God, be sanctified and consecrated and blessed to this purpose, that no evil phantasy may appear in thee; or, if they do gain ingress into this creature, they may be constrained to speak intelligibly, and truly, and without the least ambiguity, for Christ's sake. Amen.

And forasmuch as thy servant here standing before thee, oh, Lord! desires neither evil treasures nor injury to his neighbor, nor hurt to any living creature, grant him the power to descrying those celestial spirits or intelligences, that may appear in this crystal, and whatever good gifts (whether the power of healing infirmities, or of imbibing wisdom, or discovering any evil likely to afflict any person, or family, or any other good gift thou mayest be pleased to bestow on me, enable me, by thy wisdom and mercy, to use whatever I may receive to the honour of thy holy name. Grant this for thy son Christ's sake. Amen.

After this is done, the mage is to place the lamen of the angel around his neck, and put the ring on the little finger of his right hand. Then, with the ebony wand, a circle is traced upon the ground. (This seems a little odd if the rite is performed indoors.) The form of the circle is shown in the previously given illustration. Of course, the symbol of Sol and the sigil of Michael would be replaced depending on the angel being contacted. While drawing out the circle, one is to recite this consecration:

In the name of the blessed Trinity, I consecrate this piece of ground for our defense; so that no evil spirit may have power to break these bounds prescribed here, through Jesus Christ our Lord. Amen.

Then the text instructs one to place the censer "between thy circle and the holy table on which the crystal stands." This is yet another vague instruction. The illustration shows a kind of censer that can be set into the ground like a stake. Yet, exactly where in the circle it should be positioned is not indicated at all. I do have to wonder, though, if the idea is simply to show that no censer should be set on the table. I note that the text mentions nothing set there besides the shewstone and the pair of candles. Otherwise, it could simply mean that the censer should rest between the skryer and the crystal, so the skryer is forced to look through the smoke to see the shewstone. In any case, the coals in the censer should be lit with the following Exorcism of the Fire:

I conjure thee, oh thou creature of fire! by him who crated all things both in heaven and earth, and in the sea, and in every other place whatever, that forthwith thou cast away every phantasm from thee, that no hurt whatsoever shall be done in any thing. Bless, of Lord, this creature of fire, and sanctify it that it may be blessed, and that they may fill up the power and virtue of their odours;[27] so neither the enemy, nor any false imagination, may enter into them; through our Lord Jesus Christ. Amen.

Once the incense is burning and the candles are lit, the set-up procedure is complete. One should retain the rod in hand, and have the book and pen nearby. The only thing missing in these instructions is the period of ritual purification. Likely this is another point taken for granted in the text, and it leaves the mage free to decide what kind (or how long) of a regimen to follow. Refer to chapter 7 for instructions in this regard.

Then the *Magus'* instructions continue with the orations or callings for the angel to appear in the crystal. The particulars of such invocations have already been covered at length in chapters 4 and 7.

In the name of the blessed and holy Trinity, I do desire thee, thou strong and mighty Angel,[28] Michael, that if it be the divine will of him who is called Tetragrammaton, &c.[29] the Holy God, the Father, that thou take upon thee some shape as best becometh thy celestial nature, and appear to us visibly here in this crystal, and answer our demands in as far as we shall not transgress the bounds of divine mercy and goodness, by requesting unlawful knowledge; but that thou wilt graciously shew us what things are most profitable for us to know and do, to the glory and honour of his divine Majesty, who liveth and reigneth, world without end. Amen.

Lord, thy will be done on earth, as it is in heaven; -make clean our hearts within us, and take not thy Holy Spirit from us. Oh Lord, by thy name, we have called him, suffer him to administer unto us. And that all things may work together for thy honour and glory, to whom with thee, the Son, and blessed Spirit, be ascribed all might, majesty, and dominion. Amen.

These orations are not very long (and thus not so conducive to trance), though it is likely the mage would be expected to lengthen them according to his or her own will. Once the angel makes his appearance in the crystal, the following prayer of thanks is read (by whomever happens to first perceive the angel):

Oh, Lord! we return thee our hearty and sincere thanks for hearing of our prayer, and we thank thee for having permitted thy spirit to appear unto us which we, by thy mercy, will interrogate to our further instruction, through Christ. Amen.

This is followed by initial-encounter interrogations of the being appearing in the crystal (or otherwise present). In part, this is done to gain necessary information for further work with the entity (remember that these procedures are only meant to establish initial contact). We can find an illustration of this process in the journals of Dr. John Dee, March 10, 1582. He and Kelley (working together for the first time) had made contact with the archangel Uriel, and asked how to go about contacting the archangel Michael. Uriel replied:

He is to be invoked by certain of the Psalms of David, and prayers. The which Psalms are nothing else but a means unto the seat and majesty of God: whereby you gather with your selves due power, to apply your natures to the holy Angels. I mean the Psalms, commonly called the Seven Psalms.[30] You must use pleasant savours:[31] with hand and heart: whereby you shall allure him and win him (through God's favour) to attain unto the thing you have long sought for.

This is a fairly typical example of Renaissance-style magick, and the importance of the Psalms was discussed in chapter 4.

The next purpose of the interrogations is to confirm the identity of the entity in the crystal. *The Magus*, very sensibly, warns us: "For this I must tell you that it does not happen that the same spirit you call will always appear, for you must try the spirit to know whether he be a pure or impure being, and this thou shalt easily know by a firm and undoubted faith in God." For this we can find numerous examples in the journals of John Dee. He and Kelley were always on their guard against "false spirits" who would appear from time to time impersonating the angels.

The procedure given by *The Magus* to test the entity in the crystal is fairly standard for Renaissance magick. It depends on the idea that a spirit of deceit cannot swear falsely in the name of God:

> **Interrog. 1.** In the name of the holy and undefiled Spirit, the Father, the begotten Son, and holy Ghost, proceeding from both, what is thy true name? If the spirit answers *Michael*,[32] then proceed.
>
> **Quest. 2.** What is thy office?
>
> **3.** What is thy true sign or character?
>
> **4.** When are the times most agreeable to thy nature to hold conference with us?

Wilt thou swear by the blood and righteousness of our Lord Jesus Christ, that thou art truly Michael?

The instructions continue: "Here let him swear, then write down his seal or character in thy book, and against it, his office and times to be called,[33] through God's name; also write down any thing he may teach thee, or any responses he may make to thy questions or interrogations, concerning life or death, arts or sciences, or any other thing." Finally, after the session is complete (and, I might add, whether the angel is still present or not), the license to depart is recited as follows:

> Thou great and mighty spirit, inasmuch as thou camest in peace and in the name of the ever blessed and righteous Trinity, so in this name thou mayest depart, and return to us when we call thee in his name to whom every knee doth bow down. Fare thee well Michael;[34] peace be between us, through our blessed Lord Jesus Christ. Amen.
>
> Then will the spirit depart; then say, "To God the Father, eternal Spirit, fountain of Light, the Son, and Holy Ghost, be all honour and glory, world without end. Amen."

The Angelic Book (Sepher Malachim, or Liber Angelos)

The methods of angelic summoning that utilize talismans and shewstone are extremely popularized, and in regular use today. Meanwhile, the importance of the magickal book—such as described by *The Magus* and several other grimoires—is greatly neglected in most modern sources. For this reason, I have decided to highlight the magickal book and its uses in this work.

In truth, the magickal book was very much a product of the late medieval and Renaissance eras. Of course, its roots certainly extend to the early periods of written language, with hieroglyphs painted on walls and papyrus, or cuneiform inscribed into clay. An ancient Egyptian myth survives today concerning a magickal scroll written by Thoth (apparently the original model of the *Sepher Raziel* mentioned earlier in this chapter). As the story goes: by dissolving the papyrus scroll in water and drinking the result, a human was able to gain all of the knowledge and power inherent in the text (specifically from the words themselves). However, the magickal book, in and of itself, was mainly a concern for those to whom the printing press was brand new, and/or who spent much of their time in transcribing holy texts. These would be our medieval clergymen.

In Chapter 1 (Introduction) of *Forbidden Rituals*, Richard Kieckhefer discusses the magickal book at some length. He points out that the medieval magickal book was seen as a thing of power unto itself, partaking of the same occult powers outlined by the rites it contained. Like a liturgical vessel or sacred building, the book is consecrated to its purpose. This consecration adds its own particular power to the invocations that are read from the book. We can see in this a connection to the Christian use of the Bible and other liturgy, or the Jewish reverence and ritual use of the Torah. The magickal book is, culturally speaking, the direct descendant of these things. (This is also discussed somewhat in chapter 1 of this work, concerning the grimoires in general.)

So important was the consecration of the book, the magick within it was often supposed not to work without it. If a medieval mage found his spells failing, and could find no flaw in his own ritual performance or in the writing of the invocations and divine names, he would likely take the book to a priest to have it blessed (or perform an elaborate consecration by himself). Kieckhefer uses a medieval text known as the *Book of Consecrations* (which appears, in Latin, in the *Munich Handbook of Necromancy*) to illustrate this point. One who wishes to use the *Book of Consecrations* must first enter a nine-day period of ritual purification and abstinence. During each of these days, he must carry the book with him to church, place it upon the altar, and hear a Mass.[35] Afterward, once he has carried the book home, he must bind it with a priestly cincture and a stole placed in the form of a cross, and store it in a secret place that has been sprinkled with holy water.

In a sense, the magickal book is a living thing—and again I might bring up the subjects of pantheism and animism. Kieckhefer points out that, when these books were burned by Inquisitors and ignorant men, there were often reports of "the voices of demons within the crackling of the flames." He also gives the example of Archbishop Antoninus of Florence who chanced upon a book of medicine and incantations. When he had a flame lit in an earthen vessel and set fire to the book, the air itself seemed to darken so that those gathered with him were frightened. His explanation was that the book had had a Mass celebrated over it for the conjuring and summoning of demons. Therefore, such demons were always around the book, and were thus reacting to the burning of the magickal text.

Another example given by Kieckhefer concerns Michael Scot, who told of a magickal book inhabited by spirits. The mere opening of this book would stir the spirits, and they would call "What do you want? What do you seek? What do you order? Say what you want and it shall be done forthwith."

Kieckhefer also gives us his ideas on why these stories exist around the books. On the one hand, he says, it might depend upon the Christian idea of the ubiquity of evil spirits and their habit of gathering around anything that might occasion sin. Thus, any heretical book of magick was sure to have any number of demons attached to it. On the other hand, he suggests it might be a product of the paranoia over the books suffered by the inquisitors and other ignorant folk. Their taboo nature might fill such a person with enough loathing and fear to imagine demonic influence even where there is none. (Personally, I see little difference between these two options.)

However, I feel that neither of these ideas quite hit the mark. Each one assumes that only the Inquisitors or other critics perceived such spirits in connection with the magickal books. I note that all of Kieckhefer's examples are taken from the reports of the critics of the texts. Yet, I have found that the grimoires themselves also suggest an intimate connection between the books and the spiritual entities they describe.

In effect, such a book is itself (properly consecrated and enlivened) like the talismans I described above. Most often, each angel or spirit listed within the book must be specifically summoned and bound to the pages and the seals marked upon them. Then, the book exists as an actual habitation for the spirits, and is the means by which the mage makes regular contact with them. As I stated previously, the entities are not called from "somewhere out there," but are instead given physical bases within which they can live and be called at need. Thus the reports of the spirits calling out "What do you seek?" when such a book is opened to expose the seals and conjurations within.

We might take as an example the famed story of the sorcerer's apprentice. With nothing more than a recitation from the master's personal grimoire, the apprentice unleashes a tempest that he has no power to quell. It is only when the master returns from his absence and reads another incantation (of the same length and from the same book) that all is put right again, and the apprentice has learned a harsh lesson. This story is a product of the "living" status of magickal books, and the idea that they do not rely wholly upon the operator for effect. It is from this that the modern falsehood arises (propagated mainly by Hollywood) that one can work magick simply by opening and reading from any magickal text. Specifically, this idea should only apply to a fully consecrated book of angels or spirits, which itself should (as the sorcerer's apprentice teaches) never be left lying around.

John Dee was no stranger to the magickal book, and was instructed by the angels to make use of one in the Watchtower system of magick. The book (called the *Book of Supplication*) contained the divine names and prayers to God, the invocations for all of the angels, and the magickal squares and tables from which their names were derived.[36] To initiate oneself into the Watchtower system, one must first spend nineteen days invoking the names of God and reading each and every invocation to the angels written within it. Only after this will one "have the apparition, use, and practice of the Creatures."[37] (There are also other mystical books in Dee's journals—such as *Liber Loagaeth* and the mysterious "book of silvered leaves." However, neither of these fall into quite the same category as we are discussing here.)

The *Key of Solomon the King* also prescribes the use of an angelic book, in Book II, Chapter 21 (Concerning Characters, and the Consecration of the Magical Book). Of the more popular grimoires, this one has the distinction of providing the most complete system.[38] Its composition is described:

> Make a small Book containing the Prayers for all the Operations, the Names of the Angels in the form of Litanies, their Seals and Characters; the which being done thou shalt consecrate the same unto God and unto the pure Spirits . . .

All of this is familiar by this point. The only ambiguity might rest in the *Key's* use of the word "litanies." The word has two basic definitions. The first is a liturgical prayer (usually Christian) in which the priest makes a statement and the congregation makes answer. The Catholic Litany of Saints works in this manner. However, this doesn't make much sense in regards to the magickal book. On the other hand, the word also indicates a list. For instance, an angry customer in a restaurant might contact the manager with "a litany of complaints." This is more likely the intended understanding of the word in the *Key*. (Interestingly, the Litany of Saints is also an extremely long listing of saints, each of whom are called upon to pray on behalf of the congregation.[39] This seems similar to the method of consecration of the magickal book wherein each angel or spirit must be invoked in turn.)

If one wishes for a perfect example of a magickal book written in the form of litanies, simply observe the *Goetia*.[40] The text contains all the specifics instructed in the *Key of Solomon the King*: all of the necessary conjurations and prayers, and a listing of seventy-two spirits with their names, descriptions, offices, and seals. The other books of the *Lemegeton* are also fine examples of this same idea, though they tend to be a bit more jumbled at first glance.

However, I personally prefer a somewhat different style. Writing the entries directly one after another on the same page severely limits how much information one can add in the future. My preference is shown with *The Magus's* description of the magickal book above—where each entity is given the entirety of two facing pages. It allows for any drawings, various seals, invocations, teachings, decorations, etc. that may relate to the angel in question to be added over time. Also, it is better to be able to open the book, place it upon the altar, and have *only* the appropriate entry visible.

Finally, the magick book (according to the *Key*) must also include the conjurations needed to contact the entities within it. I feel a few words should be said on this subject, even though the basics have been well outlined between chapters 4 and 7. Here I am less concerned with the structure of the calls than with their tone and focus.

Modern texts often suggest we conjure the angels in the same way we would conjure earthbound spirits. I have even seen several examples that utilize the callings from the *Goetia* to summon angelic beings. (This is not limited to today by any means. There are many classic examples of texts that do the same thing.) However, the celestial nature of an angel is quite opposed to the kinds of demands and exorcisms used to tame spirits. As we will see in chapter 12, goetic conjurations often contain some rather harsh elements. On the other hand, when dealing with angels we have to remember we are diplomats attempting to gain an alliance with a noble personage. When ambassadors hope to forge equal alliances, they tend to avoid pronouncing demands or threats toward one another.

For one angelic conjuration, see example three from *The Magus* above. Another fine (if also short) example can be found in the *Lemegeton's Pauline Art*, being an invocation of the angel of the nativity.[41]

> O thou great and blessed N. (= name of Angel) my Angel guardian vouchsafe to descend from thy holy mansion which is celestial, with thy holy influence and presence, into this crystal stone, that I may behold thy glory and enjoy thy society, aid and assistance, both now and forever hereafter. O thou who are higher than the fourth heaven, and knoweth the secrets of Elanel. Thou that rideth upon the wings of the winds and art might and potent in thy celestial and superlunary motion, do thou descend and be present I pray thee. I humbly desire and entreat thee that if eve I have merited thy society or if any of my actions and intentions be real and pure & sanctified before thee, bring thy external presence hither, and converse with me, one of thy sublime pupils, by and in the name of the great God Jehovah, whereunto the whole choir of heaven singeth continually; O Mappa la man Hallelujah. Amen.

If one compares this invocation to the goetic formulas we will discuss later, the difference in tone and focus will be readily apparent. This is a prayer to a divine being, including the basic elements of praise and supplication. This is not a command issued to a Familiar or servient spirit.

Of course, longer examples of these angelic prayers would be preferable, as they will better aid in establishing trance. The example given in the *Almadel of Solomon* is a bit longer. John Dee's are each a page long in the *Book of Supplication*[42] (and, of course, *all* of them must be read at once). Each mage will likely need to discover what works best for himself, keeping in mind that longer is always better.

When you put together your own angelic book, you can choose to make one long "standard" invocation such as shown above, where the name of the proper angel is merely inserted into the recitation. This would likely be written in the beginning of the book (so that plenty of blank space can be left in the back for the addition of further angels and information over time). On the other hand, you might wish to create a different invocation for each angel and include them in the individual entries. Plus, more and/or different prayers and invocations may be added to any entry after you make contact with the angel.

Fashioning the Angelic Book

Because the *Key of Solomon the King* offers the most complete method of consecrating the magickal book, I have decided to offer it here in its entirety. I have also expanded the material quite a bit. This section in the *Key* is only about a page long.

We have already seen what the *Key* has to say about the content of the book: all necessary invocations, the angels (which would include any descriptions, times, offices, etc.), and their seals. However, nothing is said about how the book itself should be constructed. You may wish to follow the example of *The Magus* and bind together pages of vellum, or simply purchase a book of clean and unlined paper. On the other hand, you might wish to consecrate pages of parchment (see chapter 9) and bind those into a book. Finally, the appearance of the book is left to each individual. You might wish to cover it in leather, decorate the cover with names and seals, etc.

On the first leaf of the book (preferably writing with a consecrated pen—see chapter 9) inscribe the great pentacle of Solomon as shown on the title page of my book. This seal contains a cross, which is apparently based upon the Qabalistic Tree of Life, with the names of the ten Sephiroth written within and around the cross. The two rays issuing from the upper arm of the cross contain the names "Ab" and "Aima"—or "Father" and "Mother"—the two principal forces. The two groups of Hebrew letters found on either side of the cross appear to spell a version of the name "Solomon," though this may be some speculation on the part of the translator S. L. Mathers. Finally, the entire sigil is surrounded by a circumference of the twenty-two Hebrew letters—said by the *Sepher Yetzirah* to embody all of the occult forces of the universe.

On the next page, write this prayer from the *Key*, Book I, Chapter 14:

> **Adonai, Elohim, El, Eheieh Asher Eheieh,** Prince of Princes, Existence of Existences, have mercy upon me, and cast Thine eyes upon Thy Servant (N.), who invokes Thee most devoutedly, and supplicates Thee by Thy Holy and tremendous Name Tetragrammaton to be propitious, and to order Thine Angels and Spirits to come and take up there abode in this place; O ye Angels and Spirits of the Stars, O all ye Angels and Elementary Spirits, O all ye Spirits present before the Face of God, I the Minister and faithful Servant of the Most High conjure ye, let God Himself, the Existence of Existences, conjure ye to come and be present at this Operation, I, the Servant of God, must humbly entreat ye. Amen.

It is also a good idea to write a formal welcome and a "License to Depart" to use with any of the angels in the magickal book.[43] Both of these are further aspects of the ambassadorial art. An example of such a welcome is shown above in example three from *The Magus*—where the angel is further tested, and his seal, offices, natural times, etc. are immediately obtained. No entity should be accepted as true unless it can answer rightly to all of these questions and show the proper seals.

The License to Depart is simply a kind of farewell to the entity that urges it to return to its place of origin by the divine names to which it answers. A typical formula is used by *The Magus*:

> Thou great and mighty spirit, inasmuch as thou camest in peace and in the name of the ever blessed and righteous Trinity, so in this name thou mayest depart, and return to us when we call thee in his name to whom every knee doth bow down. Fare thee well Michael; peace be between us, through our blessed Lord Jesus Christ. Amen.

> To God the Father, eternal Spirit, fountain of Light, the Son, and Holy Ghost, be all honour and glory, world without end. Amen.

Not only does this license the angel to leave upon the authority of divine powers, but also includes a reminder to always return when called upon. I also note that the "peace be between us" clause is most common in classical as well as modern occult literature.

The Welcome and License to Depart can be written in the magickal book together on the page following the Adonai Elohim prayer. The rest of the pages are then free for the listings of angelic beings.

As I suggested above, and the illustration from *The Magus* shows, you might wish to give each angel two facing pages. The left-hand leaf can be left blank for the time being, so the image of the angel can be drawn in (with consecrated pen) after you have summoned and interacted with the entity. (Over time, there may be several such images to draw there, or none at all.)

On the right-hand leaf write (still with consecrated pen) the name of the angel, his sigil, any divine names to which he answers, his offices and powers (those things over which he rules), the proper times to contact him,[44] and leave space for further information that the angel might eventually reveal and should be recorded there. Finally, and most importantly, write out the conjuration(s) you will use to call the entity.

Most of the pages in the book will be left blank so that further entities can be appended thereto as you meet and interact with them. In such cases, it will not be necessary to consecrate the book again. Simply add the new angel's information and invocations, and go through the process of summoning him or her to the book as will be explained below. (Of course, one could decide to consecrate different books for different groups of angels.)

Because the consecration outlined by the *Key* is of a sevenfold and planetary nature, I have decided to list several groups of planetary angels for inclusion in its pages. The reader might consider these as "starter" entities. All of them are very well grounded in grimoiric and modern tradition, and none of them are unnecessarily dangerous for the aspirant just beginning in this practice. (Many of the archangelic beings of the Judeo-Christian pantheons are not ones to contact lightly, and especially never as a beginner. It is far better to begin with those angels well disposed toward the human condition, and allow them to teach us how to properly contact the higher.)

The angels I have opted to include here are the seven angels who rule the days and hours—as shown in *The Magus* and the *Key of Solomon the King* (plus we have met them in this work in chapter 5). Next are the seven planetary intelligences (the angels who rule the planets), as found in Agrippa's *Three Books* and reproduced in *The Magus*. Finally, I have decided to include seven further Hebrew angels whom embody the physical planets themselves. Most of the entries also include divine names to which the angels will answer, and which should be used in the conjurations.

The Archangels of the Days, Hours, and Heavenly Spheres

These seven archangels are known throughout *Merkavah* and Gnostic lore, and are ultimately derived from the primordial sons of God discussed in chapter 2. Their names change from system to system, but they always represent the spiritual forces of the seven planets. Their most ancient forms may have been the seven Babylonian deities of the planets, which the Israelites would have adopted during the Captivity circa 600 BCE. (This is the same period in which the Israelites adopted the Babylonian concept of the seven heavens.) In the Qabalah, this is the angelic order called the Elohim. Christian mystical lore names them the archangels or the dominions. The Gnostics, of course, called them the archons. These archangels appear in Revelation 4 as the "seven lamps of fire burning before the throne, which are the seven spirits of God." In Revelation 8, we find the title usually applied to this group: the "Seven Angels Who Stand Before God."

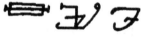

Seal of Cassiel.

Cassiel (ל א י ס כ)[45]

The archangel of Saturday (Saturn) and the Seventh Heaven (*Araboth*). Gustav Davidson, in his *A Dictionary of Angels*, describes Cassiel as an angel of solitude and tears who "shows forth the unity of the eternal kingdom." He (as Kafziel) governs the death of kings, and acts as chief aid to Gabriel when Gabriel bears his standard into battle.

The divine name of this heavenly sphere, according to Agrippa's *Three Books* (Book III, Chapter 10), is *YHVH Elohim* (ם י ה ל א ה ו ה י). In Book II, Chapter 6, he lists the divine name of three letters *Shaddai* (י ד ש).

Seal of Sachiel.

Sachiel (ל א י ח ס)

"The Covering of God." The archangel of Thursday (Jupiter) and the Sixth Heaven (*Zebul*). It is likely that Sachiel is a corruption of the name Zadkiel (ל א י ק ד צ), "*The Righteousness of God.*" *A Dictionary of Angels* describes Zadkiel as the angel of benevolence, mercy, and memory. He was the guardian angel of Abraham, and held back the arm of the patriarch before he could sacrifice his son Isaac (Genesis 22). He acts as chief aid to Michael when Michael bears his standard into battle.

The divine name of this sphere according to Agrippa (Book III, Chapter 10) is *El* (ל א), as well as (in Book II, Chapter 7) the name of four letters *YHVH* (ה ו ה י).

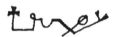

Seal of Camael.

Camael (ל א מ כ)

"He who sees God." The archangel of Tuesday (Mars) and the Fifth Heaven (*Mathey*). *A Dictionary of Angels* indicates this entity "personifies divine justice."[46] It further suggests that Camael may have originally been a Druidic god of war. (Interestingly, I was able to easily locate one Celtic deity named Camulos, a war god who was often equated with the Roman Mars.)[47] Camael is said to guard the portal to the heavens, and even engaged in battle with the prophet Moses when the human attempted to gain entry. Camael is also referred to as Zamael (ל א מ ז) or Samael (ל א מ שׁ) the "Poison of God." In this capacity he is the angel of death[48] and divine retribution (this apparently being a direct extension of his lordship over war). He was the guardian angel of Esau (Jacob's brother, Genesis 27), and wrestled with Jacob to detain him as Esau raced to capture him (Genesis 32:22–30). He was also the angel who slew the firstborn of Egypt in Exodus 12.

For this sphere, Agrippa lists the divine name *Elohim Gibor* (ר ו ב ג ם י ה ל א) and the names of five letters *Elyon*[49] (ן ו י ל ע), *Elohim* (ם י ה ל א), and *Yeshuah* (ה ו שׁ ה י).

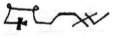

Seal of Michael.

Michael (מ י כ א ל)

"He Who is Like God." The archangel of Sunday (Sol) and the Fourth Heaven (*Machonon*). Michael is both the high priest of Heaven, who makes sacrifice in the celestial temple, and is also the general of the heavenly hosts. (Originally, Michael was worshipped in Canaan [Phoenicia] as the war god Reshef. One of Reshef's epitaphs was "Mikal." He was only later adopted into the Israelite pantheon as Michael.) It was Michael who engaged in single battle with Lucifer in the heavens, and brought an end to the rebellion in Heaven. Michael is the highest of all angels, second only to Metetron (the voice of God). In fact, he filled the position held by Metetron before the latter archangel was granted the post. Likewise, Lucifer had held the position before Michael defeated him. Even still, Michael is said to sit at the right hand of God's throne. He is the quintessential guardian angel—especially the guardian of Israel, and the patron of all (virtuous) armies and police forces. Finally, Michael is the benevolent angel of death. He is usually charged with gathering the souls of the prophets and saints, and leading them to celestial paradise. (He is also often shown as the weigher of souls at the end of time, and holds the keys to Heaven and Hell.)

For this sphere, Agrippa lists the divine names *Eloah* (א ל ו ה) and *YHVH vDaath* (י ה ש ה ו ד ת ע), and the names of six letters *El Gibor* (א ל ג ב ו ר) and *Elohim* (א ל ה י מ).

Seal of Anael.

Anael (א נ א ל)

The archangel of Friday (Venus) and the Third Heaven (*Shechaqim*). According to *A Dictionary of Angels*, Anael is the singer of the psalm "Open ye the gates . . ." in Isaiah 26, and controls kingdoms and kings upon Earth. The name Anael is likely a later version of Hanael ("Grace of God") who is credited with bearing the prophet Enoch bodily into the heavens. (This suggests that Anael is, in fact, Enoch's guardian angel.) Most importantly, Anael is an angel of passion, and has dominion over the star of love and human sexuality.

For this sphere, Agrippa lists the divine name *YHVH Zabaoth* (י ה ו ה צ ב א ו ת) and *Adonai Zabaoth* (ת ו א ב צ י ג ד א), and the names of seven letters *Ararita* (א ר א ר י ת א) and *Asher Eheieh* (ה י ה א ר ש א).

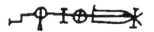

Seal of Raphael.

Raphael (ר פ א ל)

"Healer of God." The archangel of Wednesday (Mercury) and the Second Heaven (*Raqia*). His name was originally Labbiel, but this was changed when Yahweh appointed him the divine healer.[50] *A Dictionary of Angels* quotes the *Zohar*: "Raphael is charged to heal the earth, and through him . . . the earth furnishes an abode for man, whom also he heals of his maladies." He was the angel dispatched to heal Jacob of the wound he suffered at the hands of Samael (Genesis 32). Further, Raphael has dominion over all knowledge, language, writing, and sciences.

For this sphere, Agrippa lists the divine name *Elohim Zabaoth* (א ל ה י ם   צ ב א ו ת), and the names of eight letters *Eloah vDaath* (א ל ו ה ַ ו ד ת ע) and *YHVH vDaath* (י ה ו י ו ד ת ע).

![Seal of Gabriel]

Seal of Gabriel.

Gabriel (ג ב ר י א ל)

"Strength of God." The archangel of Monday (Luna) and the First Heaven (*Shamayim*). Christian lore holds that Gabriel was the angel of the annunciation who delivered the news of pregnancy to the Virgin Mary (Matthew 1, Luke 2). Also, on the night of Jesus' arrest, when the prophet prayed on the Mount of Olives for God to "remove this cup from me," it was Gabriel who appeared to strengthen him (Luke 22:43). Islamic lore holds that Gabriel "of the 140 pairs of wings" dictated the Quran to Muhammad, only after granting the previously illiterate prophet the power to read and write. In rank, Gabriel is second only to Michael, and sits upon the left-hand side of God's throne. He is also an angel of truth and vengeance, the prince of justice, and is credited with the destruction of Sodom and Gomorrah. Joan of Arc even claimed that Gabriel was involved in her motivations.

For this sphere, Agrippa lists the divine names *Shaddai* (ש ד י) and *El Chai* (א ל ח י), and the names of nine letters *YHVH Zabaoth* (י ה ש ה   צ ב א ו ת), *YHVH Zidkenu* (י ה ש ה   צ ד ק נ ו), and *Elohim Gibor* (א ל ה י ם   ג ב ו ר).

The Seven Planetary Intelligences

The mysteries of mathematics were a major interest for such mages as Cornelius Agrippa, Johannes Trithemius, and John Dee. In fact, the interplay of numbers have been important to mystical concerns since the very invention of mathematics in ancient times. Pythagoras did his work circa 530 BCE, and this became an important foundation to the later Qabalah. (Reference the *Sepher Yetzirah*.)

As we have seen previously, each planet (or planetary sphere) is given a mystical number in occult literature. In the *Three Books*, Book II, Chapter 22 (Of the Tables of the Planets . . .), Agrippa outlines seven "magickal squares" formed from these mystical planetary numbers.[51] For instance, the number of Saturn is 3. Therefore, the magickal square of Saturn is a 3 x 3 grid. This makes for nine spaces in the grid, and the numbers 1 through 9 are placed in these spaces according to certain mathematical patterns. These nine numbers can then be added in various ways to produce hidden numbers that relate to Saturn. The same works for Jupiter (4 x 4 grid), Mars (5 x 5), Sol (6 x 6), Venus (7 x 7), Mercury (8 x 8), and Luna (9 x 9).

At the same time, we know that Hebrew has no separate character sets to represent letters and numbers. Instead, only the letter characters are used for either purpose. What this means in relation to the magickal squares is that each number written within them can also stand for a Hebrew letter. Each square will then contain letters by which specific divine, angelic, and even goetic names can be formed—each one operating in the sphere of the planet that the square embodies. The names of the following seven planetary intelligences, the controlling divine names, the seals, and even the spirits they direct[52] are drawn from these magickal squares.

Sigil of Agiel.

Agiel (ל א י ג א)

Very little is recorded about this mysterious angel, save that he is the presiding intelligence of the planet Saturn. He rules especially when Saturn enters the zodiacal signs of Capricornus and Aquarius. He directs the earthbound spirit known as Zazel.

The divine names drawn from the square of Saturn, and outlined by Agrippa in Book II, Chapter 22, are *Ab* (א ב), *Hod* (ה ד or ה ו ד), *Yah* (י ה), and "Jehovah extended" (י ו ד ה א ו א ה א).[53]

Sigil of Iophiel.

Iophiel (ל א י פ ה י)

"The Beauty of God." According to *A Dictionary of Angels*, Iophiel is a companion of Metetron, and a prince of the Torah (Law). As "Yefefiah," He taught the Qabalah to Moses. He was the angel charged with the sad task of expelling Adam and Eve from Paradise. Iophiel rules Jupiter, especially when that planet enters the signs of Sagittarius and Pisces. He directs the earthbound spirit Hismael.

The divine names drawn from the square of Jupiter are *Aba* (א ב א), *Havah* (ה ו ה),[54] *Ehi* (א י ה), and *El Ab* (א ל א ב).

Sigil of Graphiel.

Graphiel (ל א י פ א ר ג)

"Might of God." This is also an angel for which little traditional material has been recorded. It is known simply that Graphiel is the intelligence of Mars, and rules especially when that planet enters the signs of Aries and Scorpio. He directs the earthbound spirit Bartzabel.

The divine names drawn from the square of Mars are *Heh* (ה), *Yahi* (י ה י), and *Adonai* (א ד נ י).

Sigil of Nakhiel.

Nakhiel (נ כ י א ל)

The intelligence of the Sun, ruling especially when Sol enters the sign of Leo. He directs the earthbound spirit Sorath.

The divine names drawn from the square of Sol are *Vav* (ו), "Heh extended" (ה א), and *Eloh* (ה ל א).

Sigil of Hagiel.

Hagiel (ה ג י א ל)

The intelligence of Venus, ruling especially when that planet enters the signs of Libra and Taurus. He directs the earthbound spirit Qedemel.

The divine name drawn from the square of Venus is *Ehe* (א ה א).

Sigil of Tiriel.

Tiriel (ט י ר י א ל)

The intelligence of Mercury, ruling especially when that planet enters the signs of Gemini and Virgo. He directs the earthbound spirit Taph-thar-thar-ath.

The divine names drawn from the square of Mercury are *Asboga* "eight extended" (ה ג ו ב ז א),[55] *Din* (ד י ן), and *Doni* (ד נ י).

Sigil of Malkah.

Malkah b'Tarshishim v'Ad Ruach Shechalim (מ ל כ א ב ת ר ש י ש י ם ו ע ד ר ו ח ש ח ל י ם)

"Queen of the Chrysolites and the Eternal Spirits of the Lions." The intelligence of the Moon, ruling especially when Luna enters the sign of Cancer. She directs the earthbound spirit known as Chashmodai.

The divine names drawn from the square of Luna are *Hod* (ה ו ד), and *Elim* (א ל י ם).

The Ruling Angels of the Planets

Everything in existence has an angelic governor established over it. Hebrew angelology takes this to heart, and thus shows us a universal method for finding the (somewhat generic) angelic name set over any object, place, idea, etc. First, one must consult a Hebrew dictionary or lexicon to find the Semitic word for the object in question. Then, one needs merely append a divine name such as "El," "On," or "Yah," to that word. The result will be the name of an angel.

For instance, the Hebrew word for Saturn is "Shabathai." If we wish to know the angel who governs the planet Saturn, we simply must add "El" on to Shabathai for the result of "Shabathiel" (sometimes written "Zabathiel"). It literally means "Saturn of God."[56] Once we have this name to work with, further information about Saturn and its angels can be obtained by evoking the entity and asking questions.

The names of all seven of the following angels are generated in the same fashion—taking the Hebrew name of the planet and adding "El." There are no traditional sigils for these angels; therefore, I would suggest each mage skry these for himself, asking for them directly from the angels in question. The divine names given with the previous angels should work perfectly for the following.

John Dee was instructed by the archangel Uriel to inscribe these seven names upon the Sigillum Dei Ameth. In the cases of Sol and Mercury, Dee had cause to use some rather peculiar spellings for these names, which I have included in parentheses to avoid confusion. These angels are important to Dee's system because the names of many vital angelic entities are hidden within these seven more common Hebrew names.

Zabathiel (ל א י ת ב ז)

"Sabbath of God." Angel of Saturn, and of all natural things of a Saturnine nature. Also the angel of the holy sabbath (specifically Saturday). *A Dictionary of Angels* describes him (as Sabathiel) as receiving the divine light of the Holy Spirit and communicating it to the dwellers of his kingdom. Zabathiel is one of the seven angels to whom are given "the spirit-names of the planets."

Zedekiel (ל א י ק ד ז)

"Righteousness of God." Angel of Jupiter, and of all natural things of a Jupitarian nature. Zedekiel is also one of the seven angels to whom are given "the spirit-names of the planets."

Madimiel (ל א י מ י ד מ)

Angel of Mars, and of all natural things of a Martian nature. Madimiel is one of the seven angels to whom are given "the spirit-names of the planets."

Shameshiel (Semeliel) (ל א י ש מ ש)

"Light of Day or Sun of God." Angel of the Sun, and of all natural things of a Solar nature. According to *A Dictionary of Angels*, Shameshiel is the guardian angel of Eden. (Shemesh, or Shamash, was also the name of the Sumerian-Babylonian god of the Sun.) He is said to have guided Moses through the celestial realms during the prophet's visits there. Shameshiel crowns prayers and carries them as far as the Fifth Heaven. *The Zohar* tells us that he is one of the chief aids of Uriel when that archangel bears his standard into battle. Finally, he is one of the seven angels to whom are given "the spirit-names of the planets." He governs 365 legions of spirits (one legion for every day in the solar year).

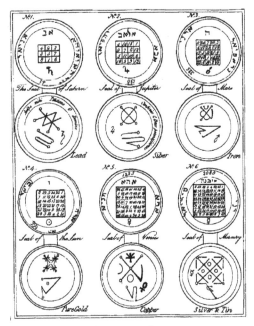

Intelligence Talismans.

Nogahel (ל א ה ג ו נ)

"Brightness of God." Angel of Venus, and of all natural things of a Venusian nature. In the *Revelation of Moses*, this star (as Nogah) is pointed out by Metetron who explains that the angel "stands above the sun in summer to cool the earth." Nogahel is also one of the seven angels to whom are given "the spirit-names of the planets."

Kokabel (Corabiel) (ל א י ב כ ו כ)

"Star of God." Angel of Mercury, and of all natural things of a Mercurial nature. *A Dictionary of Angels*, listing him as "Kakabel," describes him as a great angelic prince with dominion over the stars and constellations, who can instruct in the arts of astrology. Kokabel is one of the seven angels to whom are given "the spirit-names of the planets", and he governs 365,000 spirit servitors.

Levanael (ל א ה נ ב ל)

Angel of the Moon, and of all natural things of a lunar nature. Levanael is the last of the seven angels to whom are given "the spirit-names of the planets."

Consecrating the Angelic Book

The Key of Solomon the King does not outline ritual purifications for the consecration of the magickal book. Instead, one merely needs to establish an oratory and perform a seven-day series of invocations. Since this is not quite an evocation (no communication is attempted), it is not necessary to spend days or weeks in preparation. In a sense, the time of purification for this procedure is one and the same with the seven-day period of working itself.

It might be taken for granted, however, that the basic practices of purity, sensory deprivation, and diet (as shown in chapters 3 and 7) should be followed for the entirety of this week-long consecration. One might also wish (though the *Key* does not instruct) to begin with a full Solomonic bath on the first day of the consecration, holding to standard ritual purity from that point onward. Repeating the bath each day would also increase the effect. These things will serve to properly remove one from the secular world and its vibrations before attempting the spiritual work.

Of course, it will not be necessary to prepare any prayers to the highest or invocations to the angels for this operation. The prayer used in this process already exists on the first leaf of the book (Adonai, Elohim . . .) and the invocations should already be included with the entries for each angel.

The Altar, Sacred Space, and Tools

Within your chosen sacred space, set a table or altar covered with a white cloth. From the ceiling directly above the altar, suspend the holy lamp. (If this is impractical, setting the lamp on the altar would hardly be amiss.) Around all of this, the *Key* instructs one to hang a white curtain, so as to form a kind of tabernacle (or oratory) in which the consecration can take place. The use of this kind of curtain was discussed in full in chapter 7 concerning "selection of the place."

Place the censer upon the altar and have ready seven different kinds of incense: one proper to each planet and day of the week (see chapter 6). The white robe is also necessary. The magickal book to be consecrated must be placed on the altar and opened to the great pentacle on the first leaf.

Finally, make sure to calculate the entire week's magickal timing in advance. You will need to know the hour of Saturn for Saturday, of Sol for Sunday, Luna for Monday, Mars for Tuesday, Mercury for Wednesday, Jupiter for Thursday, and the hour of Venus for Friday. (Each day does have more than one hour ruled by its planet, however, only one of these must be chosen for each day.)

Day One (Saturday)

The consecration must begin on a Saturday upon the hour of Saturn. Having fasted and washed beforehand,[57] don the white robe and enter the oratory. With both of the proper fire exorcisms, light the lamp and the coal in the censer.

(The *Key* insists that the lamp must remain lit from this moment until the end of the seven days. We have already seen this concept earlier in this chapter—as it appears in the *Magus* [example one]—and we discussed it from both pragmatic and mystical viewpoints Overall, the same applies in this case. If one is not able to achieve seven days of total isolation where the lamp can be tended constantly, then considerations must be made for practicality and safety.)

Cast the perfume of Saturn onto the live coal, kneel before the altar, and recite the prayer on the first leaf of the magickal book (Adonai, Elohim . . .). When finished, pass the book through the smoke of the incense to consecrate it to the day and planet of Saturn.

Now, turn to each page consecutively, and recite with devotion each and every invocation to every angel listed in the book. It may at first seem natural to invoke only those angels related to Saturn or Saturday, but this is not the case. This rite must be taken as a sevenfold whole, and every angel involved must be invoked seven times—once each day—over the course of the week. As several of the classical grimoires point out, no angel rules *only* during his natural time, but merely *especially* at that time. Thus, each angel can and should receive consecration on all seven days, and via all seven planets.

Finally, return the pages to the great pentacle and replace the open book upon the altar. Leave the oratory and do not enter the space again until the proper time on the following day. Unless, of course, you are tending the candles. If so, never enter without being washed and robed.

Mage Summoning in Oratory.

Day Two (Sunday)

The same process is prescribed for Sunday. On the hour of Sol, washed and fasted, don the robe and enter the oratory. Light the lamp and censer with exorcisms, and cast Solar incense onto the coal. Kneel before the altar to recite the Adonai Elohim prayer, cense the book, and invoke each of the angels one by one.

Days Three–Seven (Monday–Friday)

Repeat the same regimen as the previous days. Enter the oratory each day at the hour proper to the ruling planet, and utilize the related incense. Most importantly, keep in mind that this is a rite of devotional magick. It is not the goal of this process to bring on visions or angelic conversation. Instead, we are attempting to magickally create a living thing, a talisman with an intelligence of its own. This book should be "alive" as the sacred scriptures of any faith are alive to an adherent of that faith. *Enflame thyself with prayer!*

Once the weeklong process is ended, the *Key* says to place the book in "a small drawer under the table, made expressly for it, until thou shalt have occasion to use it." I would suggest wrapping it in consecrated white silk, and storing it either inside the altar or in another well-hidden and clean place.

There is no indication in the *Key* that one must create separate books for angels of the zodiac/Elements.[58] The sevenfold consecration is meant to be all-encompassing, and the angels of the stars can likely be entered into the same book without problem. However, one might personally wish to keep separate magickal books for planetary angels, those of the zodiac, or other mystical groupings (orders) of entities. There is certainly no limit to the number of different magick books any grimoiric mage might create and use.

Using the Angelic Book

The Key of Solomon the King is even more cryptic where it comes to the use of the magickal book. It can be quoted in full here:

> And every time that thou wishest to use it, clothe thyself with thy vestments, kindle the lamp, and repeat upon thy knees the aforesaid prayer, 'Adonai Elohim,' etc. (*Key of Solomon the King*, Book II, Chapter 21)

The author obviously expected his readers to know enough about magick in general to make use of this information. What we have learned so far in this book, in fact, should allow us to construct a full ritual procedure based upon the above sparse quotation.

Step One (Magickal Timing and Preparations)

As described in chapter 5, you will need to calculate the best magickal time to perform the operation. The star that represents the desired angel should be in fortunate aspect, with nothing working against the angel in regards to your desired goal. Remember the chosen day should be that which is ruled by the angel, and the time of working should be on his or her magickal hour.

Once an acceptable time for the ceremony is found, it is then necessary to decide upon a proper course of ritual purification. See chapter 7 for discussion of all of the following points, and follow the step-by-step instructions given there.

The length, content, and intensity of the preparations will depend wholly on the results you hope to obtain, as well as the circumstances of the evocation itself. (A seven-day preparation would always be acceptable for these planetary angels.) Prefix the days of purification on to the already-chosen magickal day. The sacred space (see step two) must be prepared on the first day—or the day before—the purification period begins.

You will also need to write the appropriate prayers for use throughout the ritual purifications. This includes the confession, praise, and invocation to the highest as well as an invocation of the angel. (Do not confuse this latter with the prayers and conjurations written in the magickal book. Those will come into play only on the day of operation.)

Step Two (Establishing Sacred Space)

We should now follow the same basic process to use the book as was used in its consecration. The small oratory must be erected, with the white curtain, the holy lamp, and the altar draped with a white cloth. To prepare the area, follow the instructions given in "Standard Procedure" in chapter 7.

The censer and coals must be on hand, along with the perfumes appropriate to the angel being summoned. (For the best effect, I would suggest always using the same incense(s) as were used in the consecration of the book itself.) The magickal book should be placed upon the altar and opened to the great pentacle on the first leaf. It will remain this way throughout the period of preparation.

Have any offerings prepared as discussed in chapter 4, "Sacrifice in the Grimoires." Of course, the incense burned during the ceremony is always an offering in itself. Though, I typically offer consecrated candles as well—such as a seven-day candle of a color appropriate to the angel's star.[59] Whatever you're offering, prepare it and wrap it in white cloth (such as silk or linen) and leave it undisturbed upon the altar until the magickal day. Of course, perishables can wait until the last moment, prepared just before the mage washes, robes, and enters the oratory on the final day.

Finally, with everything established, cleaned, and ready begin the period of purification and invocation. When it is complete, continue with step three:

Step Three (Day of Operation)

On the chosen magickal day, about forty-five minutes to an hour before the proper magickal hour, perform the Solomonic bath. Don the white robe and any other necessary magickal vestments, and spend any remaining time before the magickal hour in silent meditation. When the time arrives, enter the oratory and light the lamp (with its fire exorcism) if you have not kept it burning throughout the days of purification. Also light the coal in the censer with its own fire exorcism, and cast the appropriate incense upon it.

Kneel before the altar and recite the prayers to the highest and the angel(s) that you have been using throughout the purifications. Then, take the magickal book and recite the Adonai Elohim prayer from the first page. When complete, turn to the angel's entry so that the sigil is plainly visible. Uncover the offering you have prepared (lighting the wick if it is a candle) and offer large amounts of incense upon the censer.[60] Then begin to recite the angel's conjuration as written in the book.

The conjuration can be repeated as many times as you wish. If nothing comes of this, recite the Adonai Elohim prayer once again and return to the conjuration. You may also prolong and intensify the prayers as much as possible; as the spirit moves you, we might say. Always remember to *enflame thyself* with the prayers.

Continue invoking until the presence of the celestial entity is felt within the oratory or upon the altar. This is the point where an understanding of the Art of Ecstasy is vital, as the prayers are meant to eventually raise the aspirant into the ecstatic trance necessary to perceive and interact with the angelic entities. If you have faithfully followed all instructions unto the best of your ability then you have been subjecting yourself to a gradually increasing trance state for several hours, days or even weeks. The prayers and other ritual patterns have honed your focus to a very narrow point, and this moment in the oratory is the culmination and ecstatic release. Just as you did when utterly bored in grade school, you will eventually "break through" into a higher state of consciousness. In essence, this is the daydream state, characterized by creativity, inspiration, and inventiveness. It is only then that conversation will begin.

Allow your mind to contemplate the questions you have to ask, or the requests you have to make. This is like meditation—with relaxation and full yogic breaths—but does not involve silencing the mind.[61] The short-term memory buffers in your brain will be so full of grimoiric invocations and Psalms, your mind will take off like a shot in that direction. I generally continue with impromptu prayers and invocations flowing through my thoughts. I tailor them to my magickal goal, as well as offering formal welcome to the angel, and indicating the offering(s) I've brought.

Eventually, this might lead me into a somewhat deeper trance where any experiences (such as messages, visions, etc.) may occur. For some this results in nothing more complicated than flashes of *inspiration* or *insight*. Remember that artistic traditions (from poetry to painting) hold that all inspiration is the result of communication from one's personal muse. In fact, a muse in this capacity is merely another manifestation of the guardian or patron concept. So, take special note of any insights you attain during this state, whether you feel like they came from within yourself or from the angel. It will be very difficult for the novice to tell the difference, and only their usefulness afterward will be the true judge.

Also, especially if you are working with a skryer, you can follow a more standard welcoming and questioning procedure. An example of this was given in example three from *The Magus*, and referred to again in the section on "Fashioning the Angelic Book." In such a case, the scribe is usually in charge of invocations, reciting them clearly and calmly so as to aid the skryer in gaining trance. Once contact with the angel is reported, the scribe can then issue the formal welcome to the angel and begin the line of questioning, and/or state the petition, remembering the Art of Intercession.[62] The seer should only concentrate on perceiving the angel and reporting the results.

Once your session is complete—*whether you think the entity appeared or not*—always finish with the License to Depart. Even if you experienced nothing, it is a sure bet your invocations got the attention of the entity. (See "Experiencing the Angels" below.) Once the license has been read, and the presence of the angel has withdrawn, end the work with a prayer of thanks to the highest and the angel, and/or recite an appropriate Psalm. Leave the oratory and let all candles burn completely away.[63]

There are several methods of skrying angels outlined in the medieval grimoires, many of which could easily be used along with the above procedure. The most famous, thanks to Dee and Kelley, is the crystal ball. We have already seen an elaborate system from *The Magus*, and even the *Goetia's Pauline Art* makes use of a crystal. Little more needs to be said here concerning that tradition.

Meanwhile, other classical sources show some fascinating bits of creativity on the part of seers. The magick mirror is well-known thanks to fairy tales like "Snow White," and many modern sources explain how to fashion one for practical use.[64] One might also wish to experiment with gazing into consecrated ink (see chapter 9), either in its well or poured into the palm of the hand. Chalices of consecrated red wine also make useful skrying mediums. One of my favorites involves anointing a single fingernail with consecrated oil (see chapter 6) and skrying into the pinpoint of candlelight reflected there. (A dark room is necessary save for the single candle, or holy lamp. Hold your finger extremely close to your eye, as if trying to peer through that pinpoint of light. It can appear as if an entire world rests within it.)

Another method of working with spiritual entities, not quite as common, involves no skrying at all. It appears in one form (concerning spirits rather than angels) in the *Key of Solomon the King*, Book II, Chapter 13:

> Then shall the Magus place the petitions of himself and his companions, which should be written down clearly on virgin card, or paper, beyond the Circle towards the King or Prince of the Spirits, and he will receive it and take counsel with his Chiefs. After this he will return the Card, saying: -That which thou desirest is accomplished, by thy will performed, and all thy demands fulfilled.

I have personally made successful use of a version of this method with angels. You might wish to experiment with this yourself, especially if skrying is not your strongest skill. At the same time you prepare the invocations for use during the purifications (see chapter 7), also prepare a pen and a clean piece of paper or parchment (see chapter 9 for these consecrations).

Upon the paper, write a clear and detailed petition for your magickal goal. You should be extremely straightforward and honest in this, as anything less will cause harmful conflicts in the operation of the magick. The ancient masters stress that the angels can see into your heart, and a more modern explanation of this concept will be given below in "Experiencing the Angels." Have no fear if the subject of your petition is extremely personal, as there is no reason for it to be read aloud during the rites, nor for anyone else to ever read it.

Once prepared, place the paper (open or folded) upon the altar, and cover it with a white cloth. (Consecrated silk or linen as described in chapter 6 would be great. Though, any white cloth will ultimately work.) It should remain this way undisturbed throughout the period of purification and invocation. Uncover it only on the day of the operation, after the prayers to the highest, and when the angel is summoned. Direct the angel's attention to the paper, and (if you feel it necessary) you may read the petition aloud. The angel *may or may not* indicate his assent or refusal at this time.

After the rites are complete, the paper should be burned. It may not be desirable to burn it in the oratory, so it can be burned later. When you do so, *make sure* to call upon the angel by name to witness the offering of the paper. Scatter the ashes in some pure place such as a garden.

There is also a method of receiving messages from the angels that does not depend upon skrying ability. Rather, one must simply keep an eye on any candles that are burning while reading the conjurations. Especially watch the flame of the holy lamp and (if it applies) the candle you are offering to the angel directly. The flames of these candles often seem to indicate the responses of the angels to the invocations. Technically, this would be called "pyromancy," or the act of divination by flame.

As you recite the conjurations, you might notice a candle's flame suddenly begin to dance or sway. It may sputter and pop, or slowly gutter and even die. Sometimes a wick might utterly refuse to light, and another time a candle's flame may burn fierce and higher than expected. All of these can be taken as positive and negative reactions to the things you might be saying, thinking, feeling, or intending. Of course, the validity (or usefulness) of this Spiritualist-style method of spirit communication will certainly depend upon the individual. Yet, I can state with surety that it would have been recognized by the typical medieval mage. These adepts were very interested in obtaining measurable physical results with their magick. Typical practitioners today may not be interested in such things, though the Jungian school might find it fascinating.

I once attempted to cast a spell for which the central element was a candle. Unfortunately, the spell was the wrong one for my intended goal. Being unaware of this at the time, I very nearly went through with the casting. I was stopped only by the fact that the candle itself refused to light. Even after working for some time to get the wick to catch fire, it merely faded and died within seconds. The spell was put off, and in the meantime I learned that my intended petition needed to be altered. Once the invocations were rewritten, and my own focus corrected, the spell was enacted without a hitch.

In another instance I found it necessary to call upon an angelic order (in general) for protection. As I recited the invocations over a red seven-day candle, the small flame leapt upward to the height of three or four inches. It continued to burn in this manner until the invocations ceased. In this way I knew the angels were present and attentive to my speech, even though I received no further indication of their presence.

This does not exhaust the examples I could list of such pyromancy. However, there is little more I can give by way of instruction. This method of divination is very intuitive. Alone in the oratory, only you know what you are saying, thinking, or doing when a candle begins to act up in some way. When the flame pops angrily, dances excitedly, or threatens to die away, only you can know at that moment what the response means. Simply keep your eyes and your intuition open.

Return again to chapter 7's "Selection of the Place" and consider Agrippa's suggestion that an angelic entity is never quite separate from its surrounding environment. Therefore, anything that occurs within the oratory during an evocation can be taken into account. Candles are merely one example among a limitless number. The rising smoke of incense can be watched for "personality." Even mishaps during a rite can contain important messages. Take note of what spilled, fell, or broke. Notice, also, when and where the incident occurred. The spirit that inhabits that object, and/or the angel you are addressing, was not happy for some reason.

Finally, I do want to offer some word of caution and common sense. Working with these "omens" (or, better, "synchronicities") can easily lead to distraction and the ultimate failure of magickal efforts. It is important that the mage never attempt to search for omens, or to assume that every chance sound or circumstance represents a vital spiritual message. They should come of their own accord, striking one with an unquestionable impression that a message is intended. True messages often come with very little doubt, and anything else should be *recorded and forgotten until future review*. Just as often, nothing noteworthy will occur during the evocation at all. It can take days, weeks, and even months for the results of the encounter to come to fruition.

Experiencing the Angels

Finally, it is time to discuss some of the things one should expect when summoning a spiritual entity It is not my wish to predispose the student toward any particular experience. However, the misconceptions surrounding this subject are so numerous and deeply rooted that a few words of common sense are necessary. Time and again I have seen students claim failure in their evocations while their written records clearly indicate all the signs of success. Invariably this is because the student (committing the grand magickal sin of "Lusting After Result") expects Hollywood special effects rather than allowing the entity to manifest in a more natural manner. It is perhaps needless to point out how dangerous it can be to call forth an entity but not realize that it has arrived when it has, indeed, arrived.

The principal myth I wish to bust is that of the "visible appearance" of the spiritual entities. Beginners tend to focus entirely too much on this concept, often expecting to literally see and/or hear the angelic beings hovering over the altar (or the spirit in the triangle). However, the truth is that these entities are strictly nonphysical, and we cannot realistically expect their bodies to reflect light to our retinas,[65] or their voices to vibrate the air with sound. Agrippa discusses this topic somewhat in his *Three Books*, Book III, Chapter 23:

> But now how Angels speak it is hid from us, as they themselves are. Now to us [so] that we may speak, a tongue is necessary with other instruments, as are the jaws, palate, lips, teeth, throat, lungs, and the [windpipe], and muscles of the breast, which have the beginning of motion from the soul.[66] But if any . . . [speaker] could be coupled to the hearer, a softer breath would suffice for [his voice] would slide into the hearer without any noise, as an image in[to] the eye, or glass. So souls [having gone] out of the body, so Angels, so demons speak: and what man doth with a sensible voice,[67] they do by impressing the conception of the speech to those to whom they speak, after a better manner than if they should express it by any audible voice. That instrument . . . by which one spirit makes known to another spirit what things are in his mind, is called by the apostle Paul the tongue of Angels.

We have already discussed the concept of incorporeal intelligences. Ultimately, this means that any angel or spirit is quite literally "made of the same stuff" as our own thoughts. They exist on what we might call the mental-plane, or Jung's collective. Therefore, they tend to move in much the same way as thoughts and ideas. When we call upon them, we are not so much inviting them into our physical presence as into our heads. When they communicate, it is done by "impressing the conception" of their message directly upon the mind of the listener.[68] In encountering an angel, there are *typically* no impressive flashes of light or puffs of smoke, but the messages are conveyed "without any noise, as an image into the eye."

The same is also true of their "visual" images. These images are likewise impressed directly upon the mind of the seer, meaning that one must actually skry the entity in order to see it. As I've mentioned previously, some tend to have this ability (such as Edward Kelley) while others do not have the natural tendency (such as John Dee) and must work at it.[69]

The classical grimoires are themselves partly to blame for the mythos of visible appearance. The texts literally overflow with spirits who appear in various shapes,[70] spectral music, lights, smells, and even the manifestation of castles, armies, and entire banquets. Much of this can indeed be attributed to skrying on the part of the mage. The rest, as we learned in chapter 3, is likely attributed to the shamanic nature of the grimoires and their use of hallucinogenic substances. Meanwhile, other ancient systems, such as those represented by the Afro-Cuban faiths, put no stress at all on physical perception of gods or spirits. The entity's name, sigil, and the proper rites are all that are necessary.

Even such important texts as the *Key of Solomon the King* and the *Book of Abramelin* make it clear that visible appearance should not be a primary concern:

> (21) In operating, as rarely as possible insist upon the Spirits appearing visibly; and thus you will work all the better, for it should suffice you for them to say and do what you wish. (*The Book of Abramelin*, Book II, Chapter 20)

> . . . and even if the Angels and Spirits appear not in the Consecration of the Book, be not thou astonished thereat, seeing that they are of a pure nature, and consequently have much difficulty in familiarizing themselves with men who are inconstant and impure, but the Ceremonies and Characters being correctly carried out devoutedly and with perseverance, they will be constrained to come, and it will at length happen that at thy first invocation thou wilt be able to see and communicate with them. But I advise thee to undertake nothing unclean or impure, for then thy importunity, far from attracting them, will only serve to chase them from thee; and it will be thereafter exceedingly difficult for thee to attract them for use for pure ends. (*Key of Solomon the King*, Book II, Chapter 21)

The modern reader will likely have little use for such archaic terms as impurity or uncleanness. However, the average human today is riddled with neuroses and habitual behavioral patterns that are destructive to the self and others. This makes us generally ill-equipped to perceive and interact with spiritual entities in a safe and healthy manner. Like it or not, we all start out with these basic problems. *It is the magickal discipline itself, regular meditation, fasting, etc. that can* rectify *one to the point that angelic interaction is possible.*

Therefore, the novice must not be surprised if little success is gained at first. As Solomon insists, one can only achieve success after long and diligent practice. Though this has been said before: *Invoke Often*.[71] Experience will make things easier, so that contact with the angel will likely begin long before the period of purification is complete. (In this case, though, *continue with the prescribed rites* and do not assume you have achieved the end goal.) In such cases, on the magickal day and hour, only a single recitation of the angel's conjuration may be necessary. Until then, however, it may take much more work.

If you happen to be a natural skryer like Kelley, or are otherwise visually oriented, you may never experience a problem seeing these angels. However, not everyone is mentally oriented in the same direction. Some people are geared for auditory input, and thus might communicate with the angels as if hearing their voices or song. The sense of smell is also commonly involved; remember the mention made above of phantom smells in relation to the appearance of spirits. The sense of smell is connected quite directly to the faculty of mental recall, and it is not uncommon at all to perceive an angel's presence via the smell of his incense when no such perfume has been burned in the room. Various pleasant scents are reported in connection with angels, such as roses; while noxious stenches are often reported upon the appearance of infernal spirits, such as rotting eggs.[72]

It is also a little-known fact that we possess more than the typically listed five outer senses. By this, I do not mean to imply the mystical "sixth sense"; instead I am referring to numerous scientifically recognized inner senses that are necessary for the everyday running of our bodies. For instance, we possess a sense of hunger, a sense of balance, one of exhaustion, of physical excitement, and sexual arousal. We have senses that indicate physical damage (pain), as well as ailment and illease. These are only a few of the more obvious examples. Even a great deal of what we call "emotion" is tied into these inner senses. We experience them as biological feedback in response to our mental condition, such as butterflies in the stomach, the shock of fear, or the tensions of anger. We even possess a "sense" of humor.

Any number or combination of these senses—both inner and outer—might come into play in the perception of a spiritual intelligence. On the other hand, some may experience nothing beyond a purely intellectual communication, such as receiving inspiration.

More than anything else, an angel's *presence* will be more likely to descend upon you as an intense emotion, or even an "Aha!" Similar to the feelings you experience upon singing and dancing along to your favorite song, or after a movie in which you particularly identified with the hero. These elations are very much classed under the heading of "ecstatic states." What a shame it is for the student who wastes all of his energy and focus upon visual experience alone. (Especially if he is simply not wired for it.)

A study of Dr. Wilson's material will certainly aid in understanding these concepts. At the same time, I would suggest one study the subject of neuro-linguistic programming (NLP). This branch of psychology is very much focused on how one perceives his surrounding environment, how the brain processes that information, and how all of this influences and interacts with the body. One book has already been written that utilizes the principles of NLP in magickal work: *FutureRitual,* by Phillip H. Farber, available from Eschaton Productions. Though the material is modern and bears no direct relation to the Renaissance magick we are discussing here, the principles it outlines are immediately useful in any case.

Another vital aspect of this learning involves "reality maps" (also called reality tunnels, or mental filters). I first made reference to this concept in chapter 3, explaining that any individual's reality map is the sum total of his or her own mental programming including all imprinting, conditioning, and learning. In short, your reality map defines all of your basic assumptions about everything. This map is necessarily present within all of us. Its job is to act as a buffer (or "mental firewall") through which all of our sensory input as well as our thoughts must pass before they can be accepted and understood by our brains.

It is this reality filter that tells us to expect such mundane things as gravity or the hardness of solid objects. The same filter learns to expect heat from fire, cold from ice, nourishment from food, etc. It contains the labels and definitions of everything around us, allowing us to walk, talk, drive, and interact with others successfully. It also tells us how we perceive intangible concepts, such as our attitudes toward others based on race or other stereotypes.

Moreover, the reality filter has rigidly set boundaries on what kind of information it will accept, and which it must reject. If the filter encounters evidence to support its assumptions, it will accept and promote them within the mind. If it encounters contrary information, it will tend to ignore, block, or (if necessary) rationalize the data away. "What the Thinker thinks, the Prover proves."

The "Thinker" is the mind, accepting input that has passed through the reality filter. The "Prover" is also the mind, constantly maintaining the filter in an attempt to preserve a mental status quo. (Imagine, for example, the personal turmoil that might result if a true and heartfelt fundamentalist Christian suddenly found he no longer believe in God at all. Like a stone thrown into a pond, the disturbance would ripple outward through his entire worldview and psychological structure. Years worth of imprinting, conditioning, and learning would be compromised. The Prover, acting without conscious guidance, will *always* protect against this.) The mind and reality filter are integral parts of each other, and cannot be separated.

Most of these things are programmed into us before we gain the faculty of reason (third circuit) and thus before we could make conscious decisions about them. On the other hand, the successful mage-shaman (or psychonaut) who has attained the higher mental circuits is free to reprogram his reality filter as he pleases. Most humans, living in ignorance of these facts, doom themselves to lives of robotic behavior and preprogrammed reactions.

Language is also an important part of our reality maps. As we discussed in chapter 4, the scope of the human mind is greatly limited or expanded depending on the language it understands. There is no need to return to this subject in any depth, but it is important to understand that it plays a role in our discussion here.

Even if we can rewrite our reality maps at will, we must still be aware that the map itself is always present, and always has an effect upon our magick. This point is illustrated quite well by *A True and Faithful Relation* where Dee and Kelley receive lessons from their angelic teachers. Quite often the angels would launch into sermons containing typical Christian dogma for Renaissance England. They even railed against Kelley for receiving blasphemous messages from spirits, such as the idea that Jesus was not God, and that reincarnation might in fact be true.

Remember the beginning of this chapter where I discussed sentience and personality, and how these things exist within the matrix *between* individuals. The dogmatic speeches offered by Dee's angels were not often important to the magick being taught at all, but they were important to John Dee. He simply never would have accepted angels that spoke and acted differently. It would not have fit into his reality map, and thus he very likely could not have perceived them at all. Even Kelley, who seems to have had a somewhat wider reality tunnel, had his limits on what he could accept. More than once he reacted badly when the angels did not behave as he felt they should.

So, to John Dee and Edward Kelley the angels were strictly Christian. Yet, today, there are no Enochian mages known to myself who report such dogma from the same angels. Instead, each individual or group goes on perceiving these beings exactly as they expect to perceive them. The images skryed during an evocation—if seen at all— are always taken to some extent directly from the mind of the seer, allowing the entity to appear in some form recognizable to the human.[73] More often than not the image seen, including clothing, any weapons or items held by the entity, wings, colors, background, etc. are all important to the nature of the being or the message delivered. We will learn more about magickal images in chapter 10.

This information is important for two reasons. First of all, we have to remember that what we experience during our evocations is ultimately personal. Anything about the evocation that we can write down later has already passed through our personal mental filters, and is thus a mere transliteration of the true message received during ecstasy. Anything we may see, learn, or experience is not necessarily truth for another working mage. We must simply be aware that our reality map exists and thus take what it produces with a grain of salt.

Second, we should be aware that our reality maps are not perfect. Most or all of us begin with a map that is quite flawed and overwhelmingly limited. In fact, these flaws are the primary cause of all failure in magical practice. They are blockages for what should be a free flow of spiritual energy and conversation. Understanding this, one can be on guard against entrapment within a reality tunnel. Accepting your map strictly as a work in progress opens up infinite possibilities, and allows the spiritual intelligences to communicate more and often alien information. This kind of information forces us to alter and widen our reality tunnels, and thus allows us to grow and mature. Information that you simply cannot accept (viz. does not fit into your reality tunnel) will simply not be revealed until you can accept it.

As you can see, much of this is a very tricky business. On the one hand, we have to be watchful against getting what we expect. Yet, on the other, we have to guard against refusing what we do not expect. One must enter an in-between state of mind which is not governed by the usual psychological patterns. Fortunately, the ecstatic trance itself (rising to the fifth mental circuit) takes care of most of these concerns during the evocation. It is after the work is completed and we are judging the usefulness of what we have learned that such common sense absolutely must be brought into play.

In most cases, it is best to wait for several days or weeks before making any assumptions about the evocation. This goes for any experience you may have in the oratory, but it goes triple if you experience nothing at all. I have not found it uncommon for a summoned angel to arrive, listen to the petition, and leave again without a single indication of assent or refusal. Sometimes the benefit received by standing in the presence of the angel is something other than what we expected. Other times one merely performs the rites and recites the invocations, knowing in his heart that the angels will hear even if they make no discernable appearance in the oratory.

If you perform the rites, know that they hear you, and refuse to lust after result, your relationship with them will grow in its own natural manner. Some angels will be very aloof and nontalkative no matter how experienced you become. Others will be very communicative and friendly. None of them will likely turn out as you would expect them to today. Angels do not possess our usual human conceptions or hangups. (Try to imagine the resulting personality of someone growing through the first four or five mental circuits with no physical body, and no remotely human experience. Return to chapter 3 and ask yourself how much of our mental development depends on our bodies alone.)

Finally, remember that once you have made contact with an angel, the lines of communication are officially opened for *both* sides. As your relationship with the entity grows, you will find it easier and easier to contact it in times of need. You may need to do little more than open the book and recite the conjuration. Likewise, the angel will become a part of your life, and may influence or communicate with you at any given time. (This is part of the necessity of waiting for several days to allow the results of an evocation to manifest.) Summoning a celestial being does not mean you are confining it to your presence to interrogate and send away. Instead, you are inviting it into your life.

---

1. This is why sensory deprivation aids in breaking down the ego, habitual patterns, etc. See chapter 3.

2. Consider those who suffer from narcissism, an extreme case of this principle where the subject's entire sense of self is consumed with what others think of him, how they react to him, etc.

3. I find a hint of the Gnostic *Pleroma* (fullness) here, as well as the fourth and highest world recognized by the Qabalah (Atziluth). Any "angels" existing here would be recognized as the Aeons, or the Sephiroth.

4. By this I am not attempting to imply merely Newtonian physics.

5. I should point out that the *Merkavah* mystic would have more often referred to the beings as Seraphim (Fiery Serpents) or Kherubim (Strong Ones). By the Middle Ages, Qabalists and grimoiric mages had cataloged dozens of species, orders, and titles for angelic entities. The Melakhim (Greek *Angelos*, Latin *Angelus*) were merely one order among many. However, the title of "messenger" has remained the umbrella term for the entire heavenly host, in order to stress the nature of celestial entities as agents of God's will.

6. See chapter 2 concerning this aspect of *Merkavah* mysticism.

7. *Legends of the Bible*, p. 27ff.

8. Ibid., p. 33.

9. This is not to be confused with the medieval Hebraic grimoire of the same name. The grimoire took its name from this legend. The *Book of Raziel* is supposed to be one kept by the archangel Raziel himself, wherein is recorded all that transpires in the divine court.

10. *Legends of the Bible*, p. 72.

11. Ibid., p. 392.

12. Ibid., p. 394.

13. A hint of the Greek legend of Icarus here. He also fashioned wings with which to fly, but lost his life when he flew too close to the Sun and the wings were burned away.

14. Ibid., p. 359.

15. This immediately brings to mind the methods employed by the *Merkavah* mystics.

16. A golem is a man-shaped automaton fashioned of clay and awakened to life via magickal invocations.

17. Genesis 2:7. The Gnostics believed that this was a transfer of the Holy Spirit from the creator to the soul of man.

18. See chapter 10, section on sigils.

19. I will explain *The Magus*'s instructions for this in chapter 10.

20. Paint that includes real gold can be bought at most hardware stores.

21. Refer to chapter 3 and the shamanic use of hallucinogens.

22. Gallons of spring water could be purchased easily.

23. Specifically "good spirits"—angels.

24. The text does not say whether these should be in English or Hebrew. The Hebrew transliterations would probably be the best bet: *Sabbathai* (Saturn), *Tzedek* (Jupiter), *Madim* (Mars), *Shemesh* (Sol), *Nogah* (Venus), *Kokab* (Mercury), and *Levanah* (Luna).

25. This ring is said to have protected Solomon from serpents, witchcraft, and evil spirits. We will see this very ring in chapter 11, as it appears in the *Goetia*.

26. For the reader who may share this condition: take heart. Keeping up regular exercises and practices of skrying does increase the ability. I seem to lose it when I don't use it, but can then regain it again when I renew the practice. Later in this chapter, I will return to this subject in more depth.

27. The exorcism suddenly switches from the coals to the incense itself. I'm tempted to suspect a missing line. But it does appear this way in the text.

28. Footnote in the text: "Or any other Angel or spirit." I should point out, though, that the invocation is specifically for celestial spirits, and would not work well for earthbound (goetic) entities. See chapter 12.

29. I assume that here should be placed whatever divine names most relate to the angel in question.

30. The Seven Penitential Psalms are traditionally associated with Lent. They are a "Psalmic Formula" such as we see in the *Key of Solomon the King*, and serve as a kind of confession. They are Psalms 6, 32, 38, 51, 102, 130, and 143. (See chapter 4 for both Psalmody and confession.)

31. Incense.

32. Depending, of course, on whom you are calling.

33. In other words, the above items numbered 1–4 are those which must principally be written in the book.

34. Or, etc.

35. The placing of this book on the altar suggests that the *Book of Consecrations* may have been one of those texts intended for use by clergymen, or at least by one with close connections within the Church.

36. This book is available in its entirety in James' *The Enochian Magick of Dr. John Dee*, pp. 117–77.

37. *A True and Faithful Relation*, p. 184.

38. For the angelic book. Meanwhile, *The Magus* contains even more complete information concerning the spirit book. See chapter 12.

39. Remember chapter 2 and the shamanic technique of calling upon ancestors to intercede in the spiritual world on behalf of living humans.

40. Even though it concerns earth spirits rather than angels. The construction of both are identical. See chapter 12.

41. Called "The Conjuration of the Holy Guardian Angel." However, this angel should not be confused with that described by *Abramelin*.

42. See *The Enochian Magick of Dr. John Dee* by G. James.

43. Both of these are further aspects of the ambassadorial art

44. Refer above to the crystal-gazing rite given by *The Magus* (example three), where asking for these pieces of information are standard procedure for interrogating the angel.

45. Hebrew is read from right to left.

46. Quotation attributed to Eliphas Levi's *The History of Magic*.

47. *Dictionary of Celtic Myth and Legend*, by Miranda J. Green, p. 141.

48. Though not on a regular basis. Samael seems to act as the angel of death only on particular divine missions, such as the slaying of the Egyptian firstborn in Exodus. Generally, the Arabic "Azrael" is credited with the role of angel of death.

49. "The Highest."

50. *Legends of the Bible*, p. 28.

51. In the Llewellyn edition of Agrippa's *Three Books*, Donald Tyson (editor) has added an appendix (five) that discusses these magickal squares in depth.

52. See chapter 12 concerning these spirits controlled by the intelligences.

53. This latter name is the Tetragrammaton (YHVH) with each Hebrew letter spelled out (Yod Heh Vav Heh).

54. Possibly related to "Chavah," the Hebrew name of the mother Eve.

55. This name is composed of three pairs of Hebrew letter/numbers. Each pair adds to the number eight—sacred to Mercury. (1 + 7, 2 + 6, and 3 + 5)

56. Or literally "Sabbath of God."

57. The *Key* does not suggest even these preparations, but I would not exclude them.

58. Remember that this is all celestial magick, and thus the angels of the Elements will relate to the zodiacal triplicities (especially the fixed signs) more-so than to the Earthy elements.

59. Meaning the planet, sign, or etc. Colors are listed in chapters 9 and 10.

60. Some people choose not to use incense at all for medical reasons. This is certainly permissible. However, for those who can use it, the smokier the atmosphere the better. It adds to the setting, and further limits one's sensory input.

61. For full yogic breathing, see chapter 3 concerning the breath of fire.

62. See chapter 2, and chapter 4 (constructing prayers).

63. If you use a seven-day candle as an offering, you might wish to leave the oratory undisturbed until it has burned completely away as well.

64. Such as *Modern Magick* by Donald Michael Kraig (Llewellyn Worldwide).

65. Remember that pitch-black darkness is always recommended for these rites anyway.

66. Viz. these organs have the beginning of their motion when we inhale, as in just before speaking.

67. Meaning what humans do with an audible voice.

68. I hesitate to use the word "telepathy," though the term would fit well enough here.

69. Of course, anyone who has experienced an hallucination is familiar with the nature of the experience. It can seem physical enough to the skryer.

70. There is good reason to suspect that these are magickal images such as we will discuss in chapter 10.

71. And, at the same time, it is crucial to study and practice such things as Wilson's *Prometheus Rising* and *Ishtar Rising*. (See chapter 3.)

72. The Afro-Cuban faiths also understand this concept. Their Familiar spirits (prendas) are very often accompanied by the faint stench of the organic material that has been sacrificed to them.

73. Could you imagine, on the other hand, attempting to have a conversation with a bolt of lightning? Or a thunderstorm? Or with "Libra" or "the planet Mercury"?

Magickal Tools Part II: Of the Talismanic Arts (Natural)

Now we return once again to the subject of magickal tools. In this chapter, we will focus upon the artistic implements necessary for the creation of talismans and magickal images, which we shall cover in chapter 10. This includes such things as consecrated writing and painting instruments, paints and inks, and wax and clay used for sculpting. I have generally stuck with the *Key of Solomon the King* in this chapter, but I have drawn from other sources where required to expand upon a point or to give further instruction.

As a note, I nearly included the burin—or engraver—here due to its use in scribing talismans in metal or wood. However, I included it in chapter 6 due to its possible applications for inscribing the other tools. Also remember that chapter 6 contains a consecration for any steel instruments that may not be covered below (such as scissors, for instance).

The Pen, Ink, and Colors

Book II, Chapter 14 of the *Key of Solomon the King* is called "Of the Pen, Ink, and Colours." It primarily concerns the creation of a quill pen and the consecration of the colored inks used with it. Of course, it is unlikely that the reader will find use for these particular medieval writing instruments, unless you happen to be into calligraphy. Since I know that calligraphy does continue as an art form in the modern world, I have decided to include the full set of directions here.

However, the non-calligraphist need not worry, as the consecrations can also be adapted to perfectly modern writing tools. It may seem somewhat anachronistic to use a ballpoint pen and colored markers to fashion grimoiric talismans, however it is also true that the medieval mage saw no need to use an ancient stylus and papyrus, or clay tablets. What we see in the *Key* is a reflection of the perfectly modern writing tools known to the medieval scribe. Therefore, there is no reason why we cannot use our own modern writing tools today.[1]

The Pen

The first thing described in Chapter 14 of the *Key* is the creation of a quill pen. It is made from the third feather from the right wing of a male gosling. One must simply pluck the feather while reciting the following invocation:

> **Adrai, Hahlii, Tamaii, Tilonas, Athamas, Zianor, Adonai**, banish from this pen all deceit and error, so that it may be of virtue and efficacy to write all that I desire. Amen.

Then, sharpen the end of the feather with the white-hilted knife. Perfume and sprinkle the tool as usual, and then wrap it away in consecrated white silk.

Making and Consecrating Ink

Remember that such a pen as described above will be a dip pen, so the chapter next instructs one to consecrate an inkstand (or inkwell) for magickal purposes. It does not matter what the inkwell it made of—as the text suggests it may be "of earth or any convenient matter." Taking the burin of the art, on the day and hour of Mercury, it is necessary to engrave upon the inkwell the following names in Hebrew: Yod Heh Vav Heh (י ה ו ה), Metetron (ו נ מ ט ט ר), Yah Yah Yah (י ה י ה י), Qadosh (ק ד ו ש), and Elohim Zabaoth (א ל ה י מ צ ב א ו ת). Then, while pouring the ink into the well, recite the following exorcism:

> I exorcise thee, O Creature of Ink, by **Anaireton**, by **Simulator**, and by the Name **Adonai**, and by the Name of Him through Whom all things were made, that thou be unto me an aid and succour in all things which I wish to perform by thine aid.

Agrippa has a few words to say about magickal inks in his *Three Books of Occult Philosophy*, Book III, Chapter 11 (Of Divine Names, Their Power and Virtue). When he speaks of writing divine names upon talismans, he says:

> But all of this must be done . . . with ink made for this purpose, of the smoke of consecrated wax lights, or incense, and holy water.

Surely it takes a powerful wizard indeed to create ink—with which to inscribe the names of God—from light and smoke. Actually, this is a process which utilizes a substance called "lampblack." You have seen lampblack if you have ever held an object (such as a spoon) directly over (but not *within*) a candle flame. The spoon will come away with a thin coating of black material that can get all over one's fingers, and can stain paper and material. The same can be achieved, though not as easily, by holding the spoon within the smoke of burning incense. The lampblack can then be collected and used as the main ingredient—along with water and a thickening agent—in a dipping ink.

To create a supply of this ink, it will be necessary to have a consecrated Solomonic candle (see chapter 6, "The Holy Lamp and Candles"), or an amount of consecrated incense. Also needed is a small amount of Solomonic holy water, and gum arabic for a thickener. (The *Key* actually seems to intend the use of blood instead of gum arabic. It is taken from the same gosling that gave a feather for the pen, or from a bat or other winged animal. See chapter 4, section "Sacrifice in the Grimoires," where this and other uses of blood in grimoiric magick is discussed in detail.)

Light the candle or the coal in the censer, making sure to recite the related Exorcism of the Fire while so doing. Then take a spoon which, if you wish, may be consecrated in the same manner as the burin and other steel instruments (see chapter 6). Hold the spoon over the candleflame until it is coated with lampblack. Then, using a piece of paper or card, begin to *carefully* remove the lampblack from the spoon and collect it in a container. The lampblack is extremely light, and will tend to scatter into the air at the slightest disturbance (much like bits of ash that rise into the air from a campfire). Continue this monotonous and messy process until enough lampblack *is* collected, which could take as long as an hour or more of steady work.

Once complete, begin to add the holy water a single drop at a time. It will be very easy to add too much water before you become adept at the practice. Proceed carefully and slowly, mixing in single drops of water until a dark fluid results. (If the liquid becomes a translucent gray, then too much water has been added, and more lampblack is going to have to be collected.) Finally, mix in a small amount of gum arabic until the fluid results in the same consistency you would find in a commercial ink. Pour the new ink into the inkwell with the above-given Exorcism of Ink, seal, and keep in a safe place. If one desires, it can also be wrapped in consecrated silk.

Colors, Paints, and Modern Implements

The *Talismans of the Key of Solomon the King* were all created with colored inks. Yet, the only ink described by the *Key* would appear to be that taken from the bat or gosling. The modern mage will more than likely wish to use paints, markers, pencils, and other common artistic instruments. Luckily, the process of consecrating these for our use is no more complicated than the processes outlined previously.

Of course, any tool made of iron or steel—such as scissors, compasses, etc.—can be consecrated in the same manner as the burin shown in chapter 6. Any tools intended to draw or paint upon talismans or magickal images can then be consecrated by slight alterations of the above procedures for the pen and ink:

-For any markers or pens: First recite the Exorcism of Ink, and then follow with the "Adrai, Hahlii . . ." invocation for the pen (substituting the word "marker", etc.).

-For paints and brushes: Simply treat the paint exactly as you would the ink, and the brushes as you would the pen. Substitute the words "paint" and "brush" where necessary in the exorcism and invocation.

-For pencils (either regular, mechanical, or colored): Recite first the Exorcism of the Ink—making it instead an Exorcism of the Lead. Then recite the invocation for the pen, substituting the word "pencil."

In all cases, finish the procedure by censing and sprinkling. Wrap the result in consecrated white silk.

The *Key of Solomon the King* lists several colors in its Book II, Chapter 14, that the working mage will need to create the Solomonic talismans. They are listed as yellow or gold, red, celestial or azure blue, green, brown, and "any other colours that may be requisite." However, a much more useful list is given in the introduction to the *Key*, where each of the seven planets is associated with a color:

Sun and Sunday: Yellow.

Luna and Monday: White.

Mars and Tuesday: Red.

Mercury and Wednesday: Mixed colors.

Jupiter and Thursday: Blue.

Venus and Friday: Green.

Saturn and Saturday: Black.

Consecration of Parchment and Paper

We have already discussed in chapter 4, "Sacrifice in the Grimoires," the process by which the *Key* makes its parchment from scratch, from the sacrifice of the animal to the final preparations of the dried parchment. It appears in Book II, Chapter 17 (Of Virgin Parchment, or Virgin Paper, and How it Should be Prepared). However, the same chapter describes a simpler method by which we may obtain premade parchment or paper, and consecrate it to talismanic use.

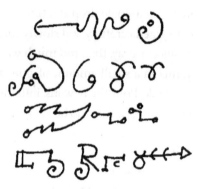

Parchment Sigils.

It will be necessary to prepare the censer, holy water, and the pen of the art. With the pen and consecrated ink, inscribe the following characters upon the paper:

Then, hold the parchment or paper over the incense and recite the following invocation:

Be ye present to aid me, and may my operation be accomplished through you; **Zazaii, Zalmaii, Dalmaii, Adonai, Anaphaxeton, Cedrion, Cripon, Prion, Anaireton, Elion, Octinomon, Zevanion, Alazaion, Zideon, AGLA, On, Yod He Vau He, Artor, Dinotor**, Holy Angels of God; be present and infuse virtue into this Parchment (or Paper), so that it may obtain such power through you that all Names and Characters thereon written may receive due power, and that all deceit and hindrance may depart therefrom, through God the Lord merciful and gracious, Who liveth and reigneth through all the Ages. Amen.

Follow with the recitation of the following Psalms:

72 (*Give the King Thy judgments, O God, and Thy righteousness unto the King's son.*)

117 (*O praise the Lord, all ye nations: praise Him, all ye people.*)

134 (*Behold, bless ye the Lord, all ye servants of the Lord . . .*)

And then recite the *Benedicte Omnia Opera*. (Here is a case where the author of the grimoire assumes liturgical knowledge on the part of the reader, as he does not offer us the *Benedicte Omnia Opera*, nor any explanation of it. In fact, it is contained in an Anglican *Book of Common Prayer*, which was popular during the era of the grimoires. This book included a standardized set of prayers and liturgical material that made it easier for many to practice their faith at home. This strikes me as something every Solomonic wizard would have had on his shelf.)

The *Benedicte* itself is a long invocation that calls upon all creatures in the universe to praise God:

1 O all ye Works of the Lord, bless ye the Lord: praise him, and magnify him for ever.

2 O ye Angels of the Lord, bless ye the Lord: praise him, and magnify him for ever.

3 O ye Heavens, bless ye the Lord: praise him, and magnify him for ever.

4 O ye Waters that be above the Firmament, bless ye the Lord: praise him, and magnify him for ever.

5 O all ye Powers of the Lord, bless ye the Lord: praise him, and magnify him for ever.

6 O ye Sun and Moon, bless ye the Lord: praise him, and magnify him for ever.

7 O ye Stars of Heaven, bless ye the Lord: praise him, and magnify him for ever.

8 O ye Showers and Dew, bless ye the Lord: praise him, and magnify him for ever.

9 O ye Winds of God, bless ye the Lord: praise him, and magnify him for ever.

10 O ye Fire and Heat, bless ye the Lord: praise him, and magnify him for ever.

11 O ye Winter and Summer, bless ye the Lord: praise him, and magnify him for ever.

12 O ye Dews and Frosts, bless ye the Lord: praise him, and magnify him for ever.

13 O ye Frost and Cold, bless ye the Lord: praise him, and magnify him for ever.

14 O ye Ice and Snow, bless ye the Lord: praise him, and magnify him for ever.

15 O ye Nights and Days, bless ye the Lord: praise him, and magnify him for ever.

16 O ye Light and Darkness, bless ye the Lord: praise him, and magnify him for ever.

17 O ye Lightnings and Clouds, bless ye the Lord: praise him, and magnify him for ever.

18 O let the Earth bless the Lord: yea, let it praise him, and magnify him for ever.

19 O ye Mountains and Hills, bless ye the Lord: praise him, and magnify him for ever.

20 O all ye Green Things upon the Earth, bless ye the Lord: praise him, and magnify him for ever.

21 O ye Wells, bless ye the Lord: praise him, and magnify him for ever.

22 O ye Seas and Floods, bless ye the Lord: praise him, and magnify him for ever.

23 O ye Whales, and all that move in the Waters, bless ye the Lord: praise him, and magnify him for ever.

24 O all ye Fowls of the Air, bless ye the Lord: praise him, and magnify him for ever.

25 O all ye Beasts and Cattle, bless ye the Lord: praise him, and magnify him for ever.

26 O ye Children of Men, bless ye the Lord: praise him, and magnify him for ever.

27 O let Israel bless the Lord: praise him, and magnify him for ever.

28 O ye Priests of the Lord, bless ye the Lord: praise him, and magnify him for ever.

29 O ye Servants of the Lord, bless ye the Lord: praise him, and magnify him for ever.

30 O ye Spirits and Souls of the Righteous, bless ye the Lord: praise him, and magnify him for ever.

31 O ye holy and humble Men of heart, bless ye the Lord: praise him, and magnify him for ever.

Glory be to the Father, and to the Son: and to the Holy Ghost; as it was in the beginning, is now, and ever shall be: world without end. Amen.

Finally, finish the procedure with the following conjuration / exorcism:

I conjure thee, O Parchment (or Paper), by all the Holy Names, that thou obtainest efficacy and strength, and becomest exorcised and consecrated, so that none of the things which may be written upon thee shall be effaced from the Book of Truth. Amen.

Then sprinkle the consecrated parchment paper with holy water, and wrap it in consecrated silk.

The *Key* then ends its Chapter 17 with the idea that such parchment can also be made from the cauls of newly born children. Also, the same procedure as above can be used to consecrate any paper, silk, satin, or other material that may be used in the creation of talismans or magickal images.

Consecration of Wax and Virgin Earth

Book II, Chapter 18, of the *Key of Solomon the King* contains a consecration for wax or earth (such as clay). As we shall see in chapter 10 of this work, these items are most specifically intended for use in the creation of magickal images (or Solomonic "voodoo dolls"). The text indicates that the consecration can also be used for candles—although a better procedure for candles is given in relation to the holy lamp (see chapter 6).

Earth, says the *Key*, should be dug from the ground with your own hands. If you do this instead of purchasing modeling clay, then I would suggest finding a spot to obtain natural clay. (The *Key* makes no mention of this, but Hebrew legend tells of Yahweh gathering the clay with which Adam was fashioned. He took earth from each of the four quarters of the world, so that Adam would thereby have rightful dominion over the entire world. One may wish to incorporate this mythos into the gathering of the clay, so that a handful or so is taken from the four directional quarters of the area in which it was found.) One must then add small amounts of water and mix *with the hands* until it is reduced to a shapeable paste. The *Key* is very explicit that the earth must never be touched with any instrument whatsoever.

If one consecrates wax for the same purposes, simply follow the same strictures as directed for the candles of the holy lamp in chapter 6. The wax should be fresh from the hive, and never before used for any other purpose. It must not be bleached or colored.

For both wax and earth, begin with the following conjuration:

Extabor, Hetabor, Sittacibor, Adonai, Onzo, Zomen, Menor, Asmodal, Ascobai, Comatos, Erionas, Profas, Alkomas, Conamas, Papuendos, Osiandos, Espiacent, Damnath, Eheres, Golades, Telantes, Cophi, Zades, ye Angels of God be present, for I invoke ye in my work, so that through you it may find virtue and accomplishment. Amen.

Then recite the following Psalms over the material: (I admit that this list does seem somewhat excessive. In fact, if we consider the normal shamanic progression of these prayers—see chapter 4, sections on psalmody and prayer—it would almost appear to be two different sets. I have included an artificial break, at Psalm 22, where the division seems to rest.):

131 (*Lord, my heart is not haughty, nor mine eyes lofty . . .*)
15 (*Lord, who shall abide in thy tabernacle? Who shall dwell in thy holy hill?*)
102 (*Hear my prayer, O Lord, and let my cry come unto thee.*)
8 (*O Lord, our Lord, how excellent is thy name in all the earth!*)
84 (*How amiable are thy tabernacles, O Lord of Hosts!*)
68 (*Let God arise, let his enemies be scattered . . .*)
72 (*Give the king thy judgments, O God, and thy righteousness unto the king's son.*)
133 (*Behold, how good and how pleasant it is for brethren to dwell together in unity!*)
113 (*Praise ye the Lord. Praise, O ye servants of the Lord, praise the name of the Lord.*)
126 (*When the Lord turned again the captivity of Zion, we were like them that dream.*)
46 (*God is our refuge and strength, a very present help in trouble.*)
47 (*O clap your hands, all ye people; shout unto God with the voice of triumph.*)

22 (*My God, my God, why hast thou forsaken me? . . .*)
51 (*Have mercy upon me, O God, according to thy lovingkindness . . .*)
130 (*Out of the depths have I cried unto thee, O Lord.*)
139 (*O Lord, thou hast searched me and known me.*)
49 (*Hear this, all ye people; give ear, all ye inhabitants of the world.*)
110 (*The Lord said unto my Lord, "Sit thou at my right hand . . ."*)
53 (*The fool hath said in his heart, "There is no God."*)

Finish with the Exorcism of the Wax and Earth:

> I exorcise thee, O Creature of Wax (or of Earth), that through the Holy Name of God and His Holy Angels thou receive blessing, so that thou mayest be sanctified and blessed, and obtain the virtue which we desire, through the Most Holy Name of **Adonai**. Amen.

Sprinkle lightly with holy water and the process is complete.

---

1. Indeed, I have seen several talismans that were designed on a computer and printed out.

Talismans and Image Magick
(Natural Philosophy)

The talismanic art of medieval European occult literature is outlined rather well in Frances Barrett's *The Magus*, Book II, Part II, "Of Magic Pentacles and their Composition":

> For these pentacles are certain holy signs and characters, preserving us from evil chances and events, helping and assisting us to bind, exterminate, and drive away evil spirits, alluring the good spirits, and reconciling them to us.

This is certainly an apt description of the general focus of the grimoiric talismanic art. In fact, it would apply to similar arts in any given time or culture. These "certain holy signs" and objects are granted some form of spiritual power that enables them to attract or repel occult forces. The question that remains, however, is how (on a technical level) a mage of five hundred years past might have believed these talismans worked.

Agrippa devoted much attention to the theory behind invocation, or the drawing down of celestial forces. In chapter 3, I gave a long list of chapters from his *Three Books*, Book I (Chapters 61–68) that all discussed the passions of the mind. This succession of chapters culminated in the idea that spiritual forces could be directed by our own minds.

In Chapter 67, Agrippa explains that one's *state of mind* has the ability to impress itself upon the physical world. For example, someone overwhelmed with love will tend to also cause love, while one overcome with hate will generally cause more hate. Where this concerns magick, Agrippa states the need to elevate consciousness in order to "join" (commune or grok) with the celestial intelligences. This is achieved through complete concentration—actually obsession—with the goal. (See chapter 3 concerning the ecstatic state, as well as chapter 4 concerning devotional magick.) In this, the grimoiric systems display their shamanic roots, where it is *together with* celestial beings that spiritual forces are impressed upon physical things.

This concept is continued in Book II, Chapter 35, "How Some Artificial Things . . . May Obtain Some Virtue From the Celestial Bodies":

> So the magicians affirm that . . . images, seals, rings, glasses, and some other instruments, being opportunely framed under a certain constellation . . . some wonderful thing may be received; for the beams of the celestial bodies being animated, living, sensual, and bringing along with them admirable gifts, and a most violent power, do, even in a moment, and at the first touch, imprint wonderful powers in the images . . .

We can see in this an insistence on magickal timing in our consecrations, so that the celestial beings will be in force and can "touch" the physical object. This is no different in theory than the astrological forces that touched each of us at the time of birth resulting in our natal horoscopes. A magickal talisman is, in essence, born at the time of its creation/consecration. Its own natal horoscope will show how it was touched by its angel at the time of its birth.

In Chapter 38 of Book I, Agrippa takes an even more shamanic stance in claiming that the celestial beings can be drawn down by physical objects that possess a "natural corrispondency" with the celestials. Not only the object, but even the ceremony of consecration used to enliven it must be in sympathy with the desired force. Specifically, ". . . an image rightly made of certain proper things, appropriated to any one certain angel, will presently be animated by that Angel."

In chapter 8, I mentioned that grimoiric talismans are often intended for habitation by the angel or spirit named (or symbolized) upon them. As Agrippa says in his Book II, Chapter 50:

> But know this, that such images work nothing, unless they be so vivified that either a natural, or celestial, or heroical, or animastical, or demoniacal, or Angelical virtue be in them, or assistant to them.

Now, before we continue this line of thought, I would like to step away from the medieval era for a short time, and look once more toward the African-derived faiths such as Santeria. The talismanic art is yet another area of medieval European magick that might be illuminated by considering older tribal magicks.

The Santerian faith also depends upon the concept of spiritual beings animating physical objects. Specifically, this refers to the spirits of the Orishas (gods) inhabiting sacred objects through which they are cared for and evoked.[1] The story behind this (as passed down within Santeria) was related to me during my conversations with the Santero several years ago. I repeat it here from memory:

In ancient Africa, it was believed that the spirits of departed humans would naturally ascend into the mountains. (This fact is preserved in the etymology of the word "heaven," which literally means "highland."[2]) Once in this serene and tranquil environment, the spirits would attach themselves to some physical base: a stone by a stream, a twig or branch beneath a shady tree, etc. From here the soul could enjoy its own peaceful rest, far from the concerns of the living.

In time, however, the living began to make their own trips into the mountains. The tribal shamans would search the natural landscapes for any objects with spirits attached to them, and carry them back to the village. These then became the hearts of elaborate shamanic spells designed to excite the "captured" spirits and enlist their magickal aid. This same practice applied, in essence, to all spiritual creatures from earthbound Familiars to the spirits of the Orishas. The physical object itself was sacred to the entity, and was the only indispensable part of even the most elaborate altars. It existed as the physical body of the otherwise discorporate spirit.[3]

It was (and is currently) possible for these spiritual creatures to propagate as well. Through a very specific set of spells and invocations, the original sacred object is brought into contact with an identical object. In this manner, the spiritual entity passes from the original to the new sacred object, but without diminishing the original in any way. It is akin to the lighting of one candle from another, where the first flame is not lessened by sparking the new flame. The newborn Orisha is considered both a copy of the original spirit and the child thereof. Both Orishas are treated as separate and autonomous entities, and each will manifest its own particular personality. (It is because of this that each Orisha encompasses many different "paths" or traditions, each depending on a given Orisha's personality.) Finally, the newborn Orisha can go on to give birth to any number of its own "children," making an unbroken line of succession from the original Orishas of the ancient past to the very Orishas living in the homes of American (and worldwide) Santeros today.

Such practices are not unique in history to the African Pagan faiths, and are not far removed from the cultic images, fetishes, and statues consecrated in many ancient cultures. Nearly anything to which a spirit or god might attach itself could become a sacred object of worship. Egypt, Mesopotamia, Greece, and Rome are all known for the elaborate statues in their temples, through which they would feed and care for their gods. In Babylon, a statue of Marduk was paraded through the town at each new year. In Egyptian mythology, the goddess Isis finds the head of her murdered husband Osiris locked in the inner sanctum of a temple with its own cult of worshippers. The nomadic tribes of the Arabian Desert carried various portable objects as their cultic focuses of worship, perhaps a sacred stone, the horn of an animal, or even such things as the Israelite Ark of the Covenant. In Canaan, the god Baal was invoked upon the statue/altar of a bull.[4] Christianity, too, retains this primordial practice with its extensive use of iconography and consecrated statues. The Eastern Orthodox Church favors egg-tempera portraits, and the Catholic Church favored marble statues, of their saints and archangels. These icons are physical habitations for the spiritual entities, where they can be given prayer and offerings.

These concepts were known even after the Middle Ages, and I see their echoes in the grimoiric talismanic traditions. Agrippa even makes a specific mention of them, in *The Three Books*, Book I, Chapter 39:

> So we read that ancient priests made statues, and images, foretelling things to come, and infused into them the spirits of the stars, which were not kept there by constraint in some certain matters, but rejoicing in them, viz. As acknowledging such kinds of matter to be suitable to them, they do always and willingly abide in them, and speak, and do wonderful things by them: no otherwise than evil spirits are wont to do, when they possess men's bodies.

This harkens back to the previous quotation, where Agrippa suggests "an image rightly made of certain proper things, appropriated to any one certain Angel, will presently be animated by that Angel." And it puts more stress on the importance of using proper materials: those which are sacred to (or in sympathy with) the entities in question.

The talismans described in the grimoires certainly lean more toward the shamanic side of things than the ceremonial. Any ceremony associated with them is minimal, aside from the consecrations of the material beforehand, and any necessary magickal timing. Overwhelmingly, though, the grimoiric talismans place their focus on the materials themselves:

> Yet they bestow more powerful virtues on the images, if they be framed not of any, but of a certain matter, namely whose natural, and also special virtue is agreeable with the work. (*Three Books of Occult Philosophy*, Book II, Chapter 35)

In a best-case scenario, the talisman is created from very recently living things. The parchment should be from a calf newly and reverently sacrificed.[5] The paints should be composed of natural pigments that you have gathered and prepared yourself. John Dee was instructed to fashion certain talismans and tools from "sweetwood,"[6] and still others from pure beeswax, which would contain traces of fresh honey. These things have powerful natural vibrations that greatly affect the spirit within the talisman.[7]

Also common in the grimoiric literature is the fashioning of planetary talismans from specific metals (such as found in the *Goetia* and *Pauline Art*—see below). These are drawn from the alchemical mysteries, where each of the seven planets is associated with a common metal:

Sol = Gold

Luna = Silver

Saturn = Lead

Jupiter = Tin

Mars = Iron

Venus = Copper or brass

Mercury = Quicksilver[8]

Of course, the use of a few disks of metal or wood for a talisman is a rather far cry from the elaborate statues, altars, temples, and monuments that were once erected to the old gods. In fact, post-Christian Western occultism has generally placed far more importance upon the odd pictograms that are usually inscribed upon the small disks, commonly known since the fifteenth century as "sigils."

Sigils

The Latin word *sigillum* translates into modern English as "seal" or "signature." In relation to magick, this specifically indicates the signature of a spiritual entity. It is highly likely that the concepts behind sigil magick arose during the earliest days of written language when simple pictograms and hieroglyphs were the standard. (At this point, the reader may wish to refer to chapters 4 and 7, both of which devote some discussion to the magickal power of language and its initial development among early human society.)

We already know of the magickal power inherent in the speaking of a name. However, the advent of writing and the first rudimentary legal systems of our ancestors also gave much power to the written record of a name. The signature was (and is) considered very powerful in the legal *and spiritual* binding of any individual—corporate or discorporate. This can still be seen in medieval magick and religion, where spirits were often required to sign books or contracts created by mages or priests.

Of course, when a spiritual entity signs its name, it does not always produce simple Arabic letters. Instead, it typically results in a symbolic character of some sort, like a hieroglyph. Agrippa discusses these symbols in his *Three Books*, Book III, Chapter 29:

> We must now speak of the characters and seals of spirits. Characters therefore are nothing else than certain unknowable letters and writings, preserving the secrets of the gods, and names of spirits from the use and reading of profane men, which the ancients called hieroglyphical, or sacred letters, because devoted to the secrets of the gods only.

Since the human brain thinks in pictures more readily than in words, this makes the hieroglyphic languages very powerful on a subconscious and magickal level. In other words, sigils resonate particularly well with the third mental circuit, and spirits (being creatures of the mental plane) express themselves naturally in such a symbolic manner.

Speaking from the pantheist worldview of the Renaissance mage, literally everything has a signature of its own.[9] Modern physics would also agree with this assertion. Everything has its own energy or frequency signature. Modern occultists understand a similar (though non-Newtonian) concept called "vibration." Coming full circle, then, a written sigil is the pictorial representation (schematic?) of the vibrational frequency of a given object, concept, etc.

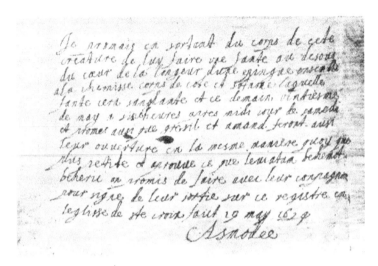

Contract with Asmodee's Signature.

So, we have sigils for all manner of spiritual and mental creatures, from demons, to angels and gods, to ideas and organizations, etc. There are even examples in the grimoires of complex figures known as the "Signature of God" himself, such as the Sigillum Dei of John Dee's Enochian magick. (It is also called Sigillum Ameth, or "Seal of Truth.") As they say, a picture is worth a thousand words, and can therefore convey large amounts of information instantaneously. A spiritual entity's sigil can be considered a diagram expressing the nature of the entity itself.

In a practical sense, any of these sigils can be compared to the kind of "official seals" we discussed in chapter 8 ("Angelic Diplomacy"), used by kings and nobility to delegate their authority or to establish ownership over any given object or place. Rulers always stamped their documents with their royal insignia (again—*sigil*). That insignia was usually impressed into the wax used to seal the envelope (or scroll, etc) from being opened, hence the term "seal." One would not break such a seal unauthorized, because that insignia was as good as having the king himself present.

Consider the Revelation of St. John, Chapters 5 and 6, where a holy book sealed with seven sacred wax seals is brought to the divine throne. An angel exclaims, "Who is worthy to open the book, and to loose the seals thereof?"[10] So sacred were these royal seals, no man in created reality could be found with the authority to open them. Finally, the Son of God himself is called upon for the task—and drastic change is brought to the Earth by the breaking of each seal.

So, the sigil of any entity (such as an angel) is like a legally binding signature, and anything that bears the sigil claims to be the property, or under the protection, of that entity. In the talismanic art, the inscribed sigil—as the written diagram of a spiritual vibration—does its part along with the physical materials to make the talisman sympathetic to the angel or spirit. The angel himself is, in essence, present wherever that sigil exists. It is this even more than the physical materials that "appropriates" a talisman to "any one certain Angel" and allows him to animate that talisman.

However, sigil magick did not likely begin as a talismanic art. Tribal systems of magick and witchcraft most often make use of sigils in their own right, treating them as "gateways" through which spiritual entities can be summoned. This makes theoretical sense when we consider the sympathy and vibrations initiated by an inscribed sigil. Just as it would naturally attract the angel or spirit it represents, so, too, would it provide a natural focal point through which we can communicate with them. Consider this historical incident in which the magickal uses of sigils and seals became vital to the survival of African Paganism in America:

One of the most intriguing things about these shamanic magickal systems is the simple fact that their gods and Familiar spirits are always close at hand. There is no need for elaborate ceremonies of summoning or "drawing down" the spiritual creatures. Instead, the shaman merely needs to approach an altar and speak directly to a physically present entity. At most, a song and/or musical instrument (rattle, drum, sistrum, etc.) might be used to awaken or "stir up" the spirits; and, of course, one must feed and care for the sacred object on a regular basis. Without such a physical base to act as a point of contact between the human and the spiritual, more elaborate systems of evocation must be employed.

We can turn once again, briefly, to the African Pagan faiths for an illustration of these concepts. These systems had remained unchanged for thousands of years until the African people were taken as slaves into the New World. Once there, the faiths had to adapt to the new conditions—generally hiding themselves within the practices of Christianity. This resulted in several new religions that have come down to us in the modern world today: Santeria in Cuba, Candomble in Brazil, and Voodoo in Haiti.

As my Santero friend explained to me, there was a stark difference in how the slaves were treated in various areas and communities. The Catholic people insisted on showing a certain level of humanity even to the slave class. They tended to preserve family units, and gave their servants private (segregated) churches of their own—in which they were expected to worship in the Catholic way. These simple factors afforded the slave families enough privacy and leeway to preserve some of their traditions. They had literally smuggled the sacred objects of their Orishas into the New World, and, after submerging them beneath a Christian veneer, the ancient practices continued in the small slave churches. This is the origin of Santeria.

The slaves taken into Protestant captivity, however, were not so fortunate. To these people, a slave was nothing more than legal property to be bought and sold at need. Family structures among the enslaved were forever obliterated, ancient traditions were lost and forgotten, and the Orishas were left behind in the homeland. Furthermore, there were no provisions made for the slaves' worship as in Catholic areas, and any practice of the old ways had to be attempted in quiet seclusion, similar to the underground practice of Paganism in an Inquisition-torn medieval Europe.[11] This situation evolved into what we generally call Voodoo, a faith that shows many of the marks of an oppressed and resentful people.[12]

While the Protestant slaves no longer possessed the sacred objects inhabited by their Orishas, they were able to retain in memory something nearly as useful—the "signatures" or sigils of the Orishas. Drawing upon the remnants of their shattered ancestral traditions, the Voodoo priests designed music, chants, songs, and dances for use in conjunction with the inscription of the signatures. These aim at the temporary opening of "gates" (or points of contact) between the physical and spiritual worlds. Though the gods could not be directly "on hand" as they were for the Santerian peoples, the use of summoning ceremonies and sigils allowed the Voodoo peoples to remain in contact with them.

Apparently, this is not the first time a magickal system has adapted to repression in such a manner. Before the rise of the medieval Catholic Church, there were many cults across the known world that practiced the invocation of the gods of the stars into statues and other physical objects. In time, however, these practices were suppressed and smothered by the Church's enforced dogma. By the medieval and Renaissance eras the practice had been reduced to what we find in the grimoires, which use magickal sigils to summon forth spirits and celestial beings. This is the same survival tactic used by the early Voodoo priests some time later.

Several of the medieval texts make use of this method, such as the *Goetia* (and, by extension, the *Theurgia-Goetia*), the *Arbatel of Magic*, and (after a fashion)[13] the *Pauline Art*. However, there may be no better example of this Voodoo-like sigil magick than the system outlined in the *Grimoire of Armadel*. That particular operation includes a period of ritual purification, inscription of a magickal sigil, some simple magickal timing, and invocation/meditation upon the sigil for several days. The procedure is no more complicated than that. For instance, note the entire entry given with the character of Gabriel, which will summon that archangel to teach one "Of the Life of Elijah":

> Gabriel is a Spirit who did teach unto the Prophet Elijah all the Mysteries of Divinity. He is to be invoked on a Thursday before Daybreak. His Power is very Great, and he can do you great good, in the which he will instruct you. Thus is his Character:

In this Sigil there be taught the Methods of restoring and transplanting both health and sanity.[14]

To activate this seal and contact Gabriel, one merely need undergo standard purification and prayer, inscribe and consecrate the magickal circle, draw the seal onto parchment, and repeat the invocations over a period of three days. This, done properly, is enough to bring Gabriel, and it is certainly as primitive in execution as any Voodoo conjuration.

In magick both tribal and grimoiric, sigils were primarily supposed to be delivered directly by the spiritual entity to the human. They should preferably be inscribed in the entity's own hand (i.e., while it possesses the body of a shaman, etc.), or shown to the human in a vision. On the other hand, if a shaman needed to obtain a sigil on his own, he could take them from natural occurrences and patterns: astrological configurations, patterns of roots, or even entrails, etc.

This latter idea is covered by Agrippa in his *Three Books of Occult Philosophy*, Book I, Chapter 33. Herein, Agrippa explains that all stars have their "peculiar natures, properties, and conditions." He could have just as easily called them the stars' virtues. These virtues, he writes, are impressed upon the inferior things over which the stars rule, such as the Elements, stones, plants, animals, etc. Here we see the highest (celestial) shamanic world influencing the lowest (natural) world. Therefore, everything in physical creation receives from the rays of its own star some particular seal or character—or sigil—which is significant to that star. For instance, the bay tree, lote-tree, and the

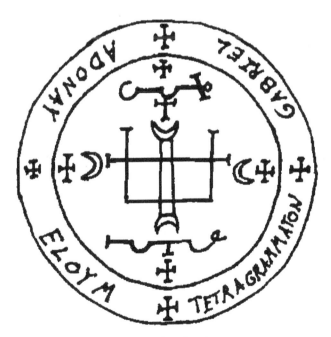

Seal of Gabriel.

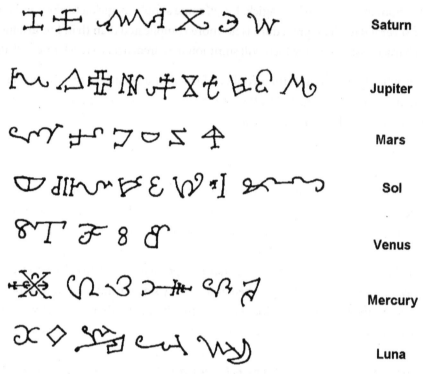

Agrippa's Divine Letters.

marigold are all listed by Agrippa as Solar plants. The roots of these plants—after cutting off the knots—will show the characters of the Sun.

The student can make much use of this technique for any of the various occult forces. Agrippa dedicates several chapters of his Book I (Chapters 22–32) to lists of natural things—plants, animals, birds, etc.—which are governed by each of the astrological forces.

Once higher mathematics became popular, humans started finding new ways to create their own sigils for spiritual entities. Some of the oldest examples from the Middle Ages (or maybe much earlier) are the seven planetary squares. Each square resembles a tick-tack-toe board, with the smallest being a 3 x 3 grid (Saturn) and the largest being 9 x 9 (Luna). The squares are all filled with numbers, and are each associated with a different planet. All of the numbers on each square relate in some occult sense to its planet.

Therefore, if one wishes to create a sigil for the name of a spirit of Saturn, one merely has to convert the Hebrew letters of its name into numbers (remember Hebrew letters are numbers as well), and then find those numbers on the grid for Saturn. Play "connect the dots" with the letters, and it results in the sigil. That is a greatly simplified explanation, but it gets the basic idea across.

In the *Three Books of Occult Philosophy*, Book III, Chapter 30, Agrippa discusses further methods of deriving sigils from the letters of an entity's name. Modern students of the school of chaos magick may be surprised to find that A. O. Spare's "Alphabet of Desire" was explained several centuries ago in this chapter of Agrippa's work. With this method, one simply takes the letters of the name (in Hebrew, English, or any language) and combines them in an intuitive manner to form an image. Agrippa uses the example of the archangel Michael, and shows several possible sigils formed from the letters of his name:

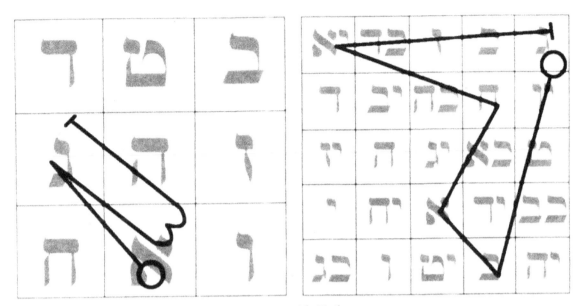

Squares with Sigils.

Now, some talismans are not designed for the habitation of any individual intelligence, but are instead meant to serve as divine seals that grant their bearer authority over various powers and spirits. This brings us once again to the influence of medieval royal court and ambassadorial protocol on grimoiric procedure.

This kind of seal is very rarely used for angelic work, such as the talismans presented to the guardians of the celestial palaces in *Merkavah* mysticism. And, like *Merkavah* seals, they grant the mage clearance and passage more than granting any authority *over* the angels. In the grimoires, such as the *Key of Solomon the King* or the *Goetia*,[15] the divine seals are typically used to prove the mage's authority over earthbound spirits. The talismans have nothing whatsoever to do with the evocation of the spirits, and the *Key* even suggests covering them until the entities appear. Only then are the seals uncovered and presented to the spirits in order to "strike fear" (or awe) into them and encourage obedience. Very similar, in fact, to the way a police officer or other official might present a badge or warrant to a mere citizen.

These grimoiric seals typically display appropriate divine names, biblical scripture (especially Psalm verses), and various sigil-like characters meant to embody universal occult forces. Sometimes the characters are recognizable, such as magickal squares, astrological symbols, geomantic hexagrams, etc. In other cases these sigils are created by the mage for specific circumstances.

Agrippa discusses the creation of such symbols in Book II of his *Occult Philosophy*. Chapter 23 is titled "Of geometrical figures and bodies, by what virtue they are powerful in magic, and which are agreeable to each element, and the heaven." The modern mage will likely be familiar with the information presented herein, as it covers the sacred geometry associated with various shapes. The circle is discussed as representing infinity, unity, and even the number 10.[16] The pentagram is discussed, as having command over evil spirits. The cross is described as representing all of the celestial powers, as the most perfect symbol.[17] Furthermore, says Agrippa, all lineal figures—triangles, quadrangles, sexangles, septangles, octangles, etc.—possess occult virtues based on the numbers represented by their shapes and measurements.

Generally, this has to do with the heavenly spheres of Judaic mysticism. The pentagram is so powerful for command because it is a five-pointed star, and 5 is the number of Mars. The triangle can bind spirits (as we see in the

Latin   Greek

Hebrew

Examples of Michael's Name as a Sigil.

Goetia) because it is associated with Saturn, and thus restriction. (Interestingly, Agrippa explains the pentagram as a pentagon surrounded by five triangles.)

Other examples depend upon sacred geometry and the drafting arts. Various forms of numerology and gematria are applied to the numbers associated with the lines, points, angles, and measurements of the shapes. The circle, for instance, relates to infinity because it has no beginning or ending point. It represents the number 10 for the same reason, because 10 is the rollover of our base-ten number system, a return to the number 1.[18] The cross is considered so perfect a symbol because of its four equally balanced arms. They represent the four Elements, the four quarters, the four seasons, and all fourfold concepts of cyclic balance by which life and the universe are maintained.

If the student wishes to study further into the mysteries of lineal figures, I would suggest reading Donald Tyson's material on the subject in his *New Millennium Magick*, published by Llewellyn Worldwide.

There are similar mysteries associated with the well-known astrological figures of the planets and stars. The symbols of the seven planets, for instance, are composed of the circle, crescent, and cross. These are alchemical symbols of the forces of Sol, Luna, and corrosion respectively. The particular combination of those three symbols that make each planetary sigil is associated with the composition of the planet's alchemical metal. To explain the subtleties of the attributions, it would be necessary to expand upon alchemical subjects, which is somewhat beyond the scope of this chapter.

For the time being, however, the astrological sigils as we already know them are sufficient. They should, of course, be incorporated into magickal talismans that draw authority from celestial forces. Agrippa, then, shows us how to expand their uses in Book II, Chapter 52. The method is similar to the previously discussed method of combining letters to form sigils. However, in this case, we combine the astrological symbols to form sigils of combined forces. For instance, the following sigils are given by Agrippa as representing the four zodiacal triplicities. Each one is a combination of the three signs of the same Element:

And these planetary sigils intended to represent various conjunctions—as in elective astrology:

Finally, we must also consider those divine seals that come directly of spiritual revelation. Like the signatures of spirits received through skrying, these revelatory sigils are the most useful and powerful. Because they come directly from God or his angels, these symbols are especially applicable as seals of authority.

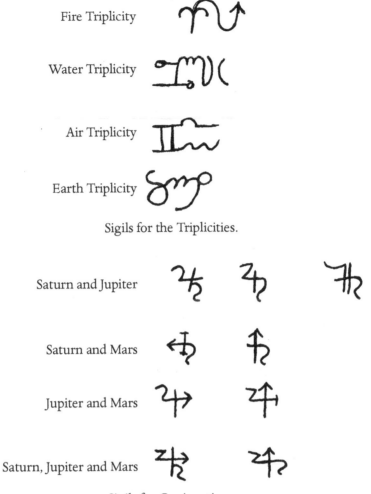

Fire Triplicity

Water Triplicity

Air Triplicity

Earth Triplicity

Sigils for the Triplicities.

Saturn and Jupiter

Saturn and Mars

Jupiter and Mars

Saturn, Jupiter and Mars

Sigils for Conjunctions.

Agrippa saved this subject for Book III, Chapter 31. As one example, he discusses the divine symbol allegedly revealed to Emperor Constantine and his troops before they entered into battle with a superior enemy. Around the symbol were the words *In Hoc Vince* (By This, Conquer). That night, Christ is said to have appeared to Constantine in a dream, and instructed him to bear the symbol into battle. He did so, and was victorious despite the odds set against him. (In several ways, this reminds me somewhat of the Grail mythos.)

Talismanic Magick in the Grimoires

Now that we have considered some of the concepts behind the creation and use of grimoiric talismans, we can explore the medieval texts themselves. To begin with, we will discuss the use of talismans in the *Key of Solomon the King*, the grandfather of the entire Solomonic tradition:

> . . . it is necessary that thou shouldest understand that the whole Science and understanding of our Key dependeth upon the operation, Knowledge, and use of Pentacles. [. . .] Let [the reader] then, O my son Roboam, know and understand that in the aforesaid Pentacles he shall find those Ineffable and Most Holy Names which were written by the finger of God in the Tablets of Moses; and which I, Solomon,

Constantine's Seal.

have received through the Ministry of an Angel by Divine Revelation.[19] These then have I collected together, arranged, consecrated, and kept, for the benefit of the human race, and the preservation of Body and Soul. [. . .] I assure thee that this is the true way to succeed with ease in all thine operations, for being fortified with a Divine Name, and the Letters, Characters, and Sigils, applicable unto the operation, thou shalt discover with what supernatural exactitude and very great promptitude, both Terrestrial and Celestial things will be obedient unto thee. But all this will only be true, when accompanied by the Pentacles which hereinafter follow, seeing that the Seals, Characters, and Divine Names, serve only to fortify the work, to preserve from unforeseen accidents, and to attract the familiarity of the Angels and Spirits. (*Key of Solomon the King,* Book I, Chapter 8)

A common misconception surrounding the *Key* is that it contains an operation of angelic summoning, as opposed to the infernal spirits called by the *Goetia.* In fact, however, the *Key* is itself a goetic magickal operation calling upon several (planetary) classes of earthbound spirits. It is the Solomonic talismans that tend to give the *Key* its angelic reputation, as they are covered with the names of God, angels, holy scripture, and holy seals. As explained above, these talismans are meant to act as royal seals, which *do* depend on divine and angelic force, intended to control the goetic spirits:

The Medals or Pentacles, which we make for the purpose of striking terror into the Spirits and reducing them to obedience . . . If thou invokest the Spirits by virtue of these Pentacles, they will obey thee without repugnance, and having considered them they will be struck with astonishment, and will fear them, and thou shalt see them so surprised by fear and terror, and that none of them will be sufficiently bold to wish to oppose thy will. (*Key of Solomon the King,* Book I, Chapter 18)

In a kind of appendix to Book I, the *Key* offers a total of forty-four different talismans: seven for each planet Saturn, Jupiter, Mars, and Sol; five each for Venus and Mercury; and six pentacles for Luna. I find it somewhat odd that the seven planets are not each assigned seven seals; odd enough to suggest a few seals might even be missing from the text. The *Key* does offer the slightest clue that these talismans (and the summoning ceremonies that go with them) are used in some form of self-initiation. As stated in Book I, Chapter 7:

[After the appearance of the Spirits, the Master] should then cover the Pentacles, and he will see wonderful things, which it is impossible to relate, touching worldly matters and all sciences.

It is for this reason that a 7 x 7 division of talismans would make perfect sense for this operation. The aspirant would likely begin with the first seal of Luna and progress in a systematic fashion through Luna, into Mercury, and continuing all the way to the seventh seal of Saturn. The resulting "Solomonic Operation" would consist of forty-nine separate ceremonies of invocation—ensuring the mage would walk away from the work with a solid foundation of practical experience with all aspects of the forces of nature, not to mention a mastery of the *Key of Solomon* itself. It seems likely to me that the missing talismans for Venus, Mercury, and Luna should be discovered and replaced by each practicing Solomonic mage. By the time the first thirty-three talismans are created and used in full ceremony, receiving the missing seals from the spiritual entities will not likely present a problem.

In any case, even if the author of the *Key* did intend to hide a formula of initiation within his work, the text is very clear on the practical uses of the talismans. Each seal is assigned a virtue that is in some way sympathetic to the planetary force it embodies. Having first decided what task one wishes the spirits to perform, it is then necessary to decide which planet (and thus which spirits) are appropriate to the task. Then, one must further discover which specific planetary talisman embodies the necessary force. It is by showing this seal (or seals) to the summoned spirits that the task is accomplished.

> Here be the Symbols of Secret things, the standards, the ensigns, and the banners, of God the Conqueror; and the arms of the Almighty One, to compel the Aerial Potencies. I command ye absolutely by their power and virtue that ye come near unto us . . . (*Key of Solomon the King*, Book I, Chapter 6)

> Obey ye, Obey ye, behold the Symbols and Names of the Creator; be ye gentle and peaceable, and obey in all things that we shall command ye. (*Key of Solomon the King*, Book I, Chapter 7)

For instance, the first pentacle of Saturn is designed to strike awe into the spirits and constrain them to obedience. The fourth pentacle of Saturn is aimed at any operation of ruin, destruction, or death. The seventh is even aimed at the causing of earthquakes. The second pentacle of Jupiter serves to acquire glory, honors, riches, and all kinds of "good" and tranquility of mind. The sixth pentacle of Jupiter brings protection from all earthly dangers. Meanwhile, the Martian pentacles are aimed at the healing of diseases as well as victories in warfare and conflict. Solar pentacles tend to relate to victory, kingdom and empire, pride, and even the freeing of prisoners from chains. Venetian pentacles are used in operations of sex and love. Mercurial pentacles allow one to discover hidden things, acquire knowledge, and to open locks. Finally, Lunar pentacles grant protection from water, from all sorceries, and can also grant dream visions and the like.

Of course, this merely scratches the surface of the listed aims of the Solomonic pentacles, outlined here to illustrate the basic point. In the *Key*, a great number of the talismans are given no specific uses beyond "controlling" the spirits associated with the planetary energy. What tasks such spirits are put to would be at the discretion of the mage, considering what we learned in chapter 5 of this book (and in the introductions and first chapters of the *Key*).

Plus, several different talismans can be brought into the circle at once, so they can be utilized in various combinations for an infinite number of effects. A talisman of Saturn to command the spirits might work extremely well with a Martian talisman of warfare. While the mage is at it, the third pentacle of Jupiter—for protection from the spirits thus evoked—would likely be a good idea as well. (Modern Hermeticists may be a bit uncomfortable with the idea of mixing planetary energies so liberally in a single operation. However, the fact is that the Solomonic invocations are not designed to be planetary specific. As discussed at the beginning of chapter 5 of this work, Solomonic invocations are aimed at invoking pure divine force. Even the summoning operation does not demand that any specific spirits from any specific hierarchies appear. Instead, it intends to conjure the nature spirits local to the working mage; a true form of shamanism. What pentacles one uses to command them will depend on necessity, and perhaps upon the astrological chart drawn up before attempting the work.) Each mage will most likely

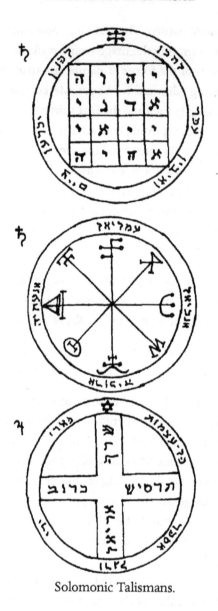

Solomonic Talismans.

develop his own favorite combinations of pentacles: those he might need for any given circumstance, those he tends to find useful in all ceremonies, and those combinations that produce the best visions of "wonderful things touching worldly matters and all sciences."

Unfortunately, the *Key of Solomon* is somewhat contradictory in its practical instruction for the talismans as used in the rites of summoning. In Book One, Chapter 3, the instructions are to draw the seals on virgin paper and sew them to the front of the ceremonial robe with thread spun by a young girl. The same chapter instructs one to place his hand over the pentacles for the final conjurations, thereby (presumably) placing the hand over one's heart at the same time.[20]

However, by Chapter 6 the instructions seem to have changed. The shift is so abrupt as to suggest that different operations are being described; perhaps merely two different versions of the *Key* having been copied into this single manuscript:

[If the Spirits do not appear] let the Master uncover the consecrated Pentacles which he should have made to constrain and command the Spirits, and which he should wear fastened round his neck, holding the Medals (or Pentacles) in his left hand, and the consecrated Knife in his right; and . . . he shall say with a loud voice . . . (*Key of Solomon the King*, Book I, Chapter 6)

Here, the author assumes that the pentacles have been covered since the beginning of the ceremony (we might remember this method from *The Magus* in chapter 8 of this book). Although, they are now suspended around the neck like a lamen or amulet instead of sewn to the robe,[21] so that they can be picked up and held in the left hand while the master convokes the spirits. (No mention is made of how they should be suspended—perhaps from a thread spun by a young girl?) How one is supposed to cover them while they hang around one's neck is also not mentioned. The text does mention that the covering should itself be consecrated.

Later, in Chapter 7, the subject is expanded somewhat. The pentacles are once again described as hanging around the neck, and covered with a cloth of silk or fine twined linen. Again, they are to remain covered until the spirits make their appearance. This is the chapter that further suggests one should, after the appearance of the spirits, then recover the pentacles in order to "see wonderful things." Afterward, the pentacles can be revealed once more in order to make any necessary demands of the spirits.

Instructions for the fashioning of these mystical seals appear three times in the *Key*, possibly separated in order to confuse the issue for dabblers and the curious. (Or, perhaps this is further evidence of separate Solomonic operations, or different versions of the same.) The first set is found in Book I, Chapter 8, "Concerning the Medals or Pentacles, and the Manner of Constructing Them."

The pentacles are made in the day and hours of Mercury (like much else in the decidedly Mercurial Solomonic material), with the Moon residing in an aerial sign (Libra, Gemini, Aquarius) or terrestrial sign (Capricorn, Virgo, Taurus). The Moon must also be waxing, and in "equal number of days with the Sun."[22] If a pentacle is not complete when the magickal hour runs out, work must be halted until the next hour appropriate to the planet. If one day is not sufficient, then the talisman may be wrapped in the consecrated silk (see chapter 6 of this work) until the same day the following week.

The work itself must be done in a private chamber that has been purified for magickal use (see chapter "The Selection of the Place"). The *Key* also insists that the sky be clear and serene, an instruction it also gives for summoning the spirits in general.

Of course, one will need to have virgin paper prepared and consecrated, as well as pen, ink, colors, etc. (see chapter 9). The *Key* suggests one gather the colors gold, cinnabar (or vermillion red), and celestial or brilliant azure blue. Appropriate colors are also discussed elsewhere in the *Key*, such as the introduction from Lansdowne MS 1203 (which also lists the alchemical metals that can be used to fashion the seals):

Planet:	Saturn	Jupiter	Mars	Sol	Venus	Mercury	Luna
Color:	Black	Blue	Red	Yellow	Green	Purple or Mixed Colors[23]	White
Metal:	Lead	Tin	Iron	Gold	Copper	Mercury	Silver

Or the slightly different list given in Book I, Chapter 18, "Concerning the Holy Pentacles or Medals":

Planet:	Saturn	Jupiter	Mars	Sol	Venus	Mercury	Luna
Color:	Black	Celestial Blue	Red	Gold, Yellow, or Citron	Green	Mixed Colors	Silver, or Argentine Earth
Metal:	Lead	Tin	Iron	Gold	Copper	Mixture of	Silver Metals[24]

In the appendix to Book I, the forty-four pentacles are drawn in full color.[25] Mathers' edition unfortunately does not reproduce them with color plates, but the colors are listed at the beginning of the section. The pentacles do not follow the instructions of the introduction in every case, showing forth this arrangement:

Seals of:	Saturn	Jupiter	Mars	Sol	Venus	Mercury	Luna
Color:	Black	Blue	Red	Yellow	Green	Mixed Colors	Silver

Returning now to Book I, Chapter 8: once the talismans are completed, they are wrapped in the consecrated silk described in chapter 6 of this work.

Lansdowne MS 1203 gives further instructions (also Book I, Chapter 8), insisting that the talismans be fashioned while the sun is in Leo (the beginning of the month of August) before sunrise. The operator must be in a state of purity, which may suggest a period of preparation. The materials given here are no more than virgin parchment and "ordinary ink." Each seal must be drawn separately, while the operator faces east. The same text also outlines an expanded use for the Solomonic pentacles:

> Thou shalt preserve them to suspend from thy neck, whichever thou wilt, on the day and hour wherein thou wast born, after which thou shalt take heed to name every day ten times, the Name which is hung from thy neck, turning towards the East, and thou mayest be assured that no enchantment or any other danger shall have power to harm thee.

> Furthermore thou shalt vanquish all adversities, and shalt be cherished and loved by the Angels and Spirits, provided that thou hast made their characters and that thou hast them upon thee.

The third set of instructions for the seals is found much later in Book I, Chapter 18, "Concerning the Holy Pentacles or Medals." Here they are said to be:

> . . . of great virtue and efficacy against all perils of Earth, of Air, of Water, and of Fire, against poison which hath been drunk, against all kinds of infirmities and necessities, against binding, sortilege, and sorcery, against all terror and fear, and wheresoever thou shalt find thyself, if armed with them, thou shalt be in safety all the days of thy life.

> Through them do we acquire grace and good-will from man and woman, fire is extinguished, water is stayed, and all Creatures fear at the sight of the Names which are therein, and obey through that fear.

Now the metals are finally suggested for the construction of the pentacles, as an alternative to virgin paper or parchment. The text even goes so far as to say the pentacles are "usually made of the metal the most suitable to the nature of the planet." If fashioning them from such metal, they must be engraved with the burin of the art. If fashioned from paper, the same instructions as already given above (consecrated colors, instruments, etc.) are followed. The proper metals and colors from this chapter are given in a table above. The magickal timing mentioned here is merely an observation of the proper planetary day and hour, rather than the sun, moon, and zodiacal signs. The size of the pentacles is strictly arbitrary.

Finally, Lansdowne MS 1203 adds its own ideas to the instructions. Beyond the proper timing or materials, the text puts its stress upon the observation of the correct procedures and the "requisite solemnities" while drawing the seals. While working, one must take care never to forget the incense, nor to "employ anything beyond that of which mention is made":

> It is necessary, above all things, to be attentive to the operation, and never to forget or omit those things which contribute to the success which the Pentacles and Experiments promise, having ever in mind no other intention than the Glory of God, the accomplishment of thy desires, and loving-kindness towards thy neighbor.

The *Key* also gives a full set of instructions for the consecration of the pentacles or medals. However, we will save this for later in this chapter, as I intend to outline it step by step for the practical use of the reader.[26]

At this point, logic suggests we examine the *Lemegeton*, as it represents the second half of the origin of the Solomonic grimoiric traditions. We will start, of course, with Book I, the *Goetia*. The seals used in this text are quite different in their nature and operation than those used in the *Key of Solomon the King*. Rather than acting as royal seals used to control the spirits, the characters of the *Goetia* are the signatures of the spirits themselves.

As has been pointed out, the *Goetia* is a later Christian expression of an Arabic tradition. In turn, the Arabic material is itself descended from ancient Sumerian-Babylonian astrological magick. We discussed in chapter 2 the tendency of the ancient mind to assume that heavenly bodies—the "Brilliant Ones"—were living beings. As the Babylonians developed humanity's first systems of astrology, they approached *every* aspect of the sky as its own god—from the planets and stars to the divisions of the astrological chart such as the decanates.

Later Arabic shamanism retained versions of these ancient Mesopotamian traditions in which astrological groups of celestial beings were invoked for magickal effect.[27] They might come in planetary groups of seven (such as our own magickal book as described in chapter 8), zodiacal groups of twelve or twenty-four, or decanate groups of thirty-six or seventy-two.

In many cases, the magick was directed not toward the celestial gods themselves, but toward the control of the earthbound spirits (jinni) who were governed by the stars. In other words, they were typical shamanic goety. (More on this in chapter 12.) It was one of the Arabic seventy-two-fold hierarchies that eventually became the basis of the Christian-created *Goetia*. Even many of the spirits themselves are of Arabic origin. Unfortunately, however, the *Goetia* does not accurately reflect its source material. Ideally, it should contain two spirits for each of the thirty-six decanates, one who rules during the daylight and one who rules at night. However, the arrangement of talismans in the text does not show forth any such pattern.

Instead, the emphasis of the *Goetia* has been shifted to a feudal European mindset. Rather than to the decans, the spirits are all assigned to a loose hierarchy of kings, dukes, princes and prelates, marquises, presidents, earls or counts, and knights. These total seven categories, each related to a planet and its metal, from which the talismans must be fashioned.

Kings—Sol (Gold)

Bael, Paimon, Beleth, Purson, Asmoday, Vine, Balam, Zagan, Belial

Dukes—Venus (Copper)

Agares, Valefor, Barbatos, Gusion, Eligos, Zepar, Bathin, Sallos, Aim, Bune, Berith, Astaroth, Focalor, Vepar, Vual, Crocell, Alloces, Murmur, Gremory, Vapula, Haures, Amdusias, Dantalion

Princes and Prelates—Jupiter (Tin)

Vassago, Sitri, Ipos, Gaap, Stolas, Orobas, Seere

Marquises—Luna (Silver)

Samigina, Amon, Leraje, Naberius, Ronove, Forneus, Marchasias, Phenex, Sabnock, Shax, Orias, Andras, Andrealphus, Cimeies, Decarabia

Presidents—Mercury (Mercury)

Marbas, Buer, Botis, Marax, Glasya-Labolas, Foras, Gaap, Malphas, Haagenti, Caim, Ose, Amy, Zagan, Valac

Earls or Counts—Mars (Mixture of Copper and Silver[28])

Botis, Marax, Glasya-Labolas, Ronove, Furfur, Halphas, Raum, Vine, Bifrons, Andromalius

Knights—Saturn (Lead)

Furcas

Obviously, this arrangement will not lend itself to association with the decanates, which show an even division of planets to decans. Some of the goetic spirits are assigned to more than one planet, such as Glasya-Labolas (a president and an earl), or Vine (a king and an earl). Even otherwise, these spirits do not divide evenly among the planets. For instance, there is only one Saturnian knight, while the planet Saturn rules several of the decans.

It would almost appear that the author/copyist of the *Goetia* did not understand the zodiacal nature of the Arabic jinn he was contacting. As a medieval Christian, it might follow that he would have been more readily familiar with the seven planets. Yet, even this categorization is treated very laxly in the *Goetia*, and is certainly not a reflection of the arrangement of planets in the Arabic material. I sense a strong probability that long-time and cross-cultural oral transmission is responsible for these problems. I have seen some work done recently toward restoring the *Goetia* based upon research of its Arabian predecessors. Once complete, this work will certainly be of great value to both scholars and practitioners of the goetic tradition alike.

Meanwhile, what we know of the development of Voodoo in early American history might tell us something of practices such as *Goetia*. In both examples, the signature of a spiritual entity is used in a very shamanic manner to evoke the presence of that entity, so that it may be summoned to appearance or made to inhabit a physical object. In the case of the *Goetia*, this physical object is a metal seal bearing the sigil of the demon. Since the goetia operation is derived from ancient Arabian shamanism, it is not difficult to suppose a connection between the grimoire's medals and the magickal rings containing genies in the *Arabian Nights*. (There is certainly a connection, of course, between the brass vessels and lamps from the legends, and the brass vessel used to bind the spirits of the *Goetia*.)

Apparently, the concept of the *Goetia* operation is to bind a demon into a metal seal, thus anchoring it to the physical plane. We have already discussed this subject in some depth, utilizing the histories of various African, and Middle Eastern–descended practices to illustrate the point. If these principles hold true for the *Goetia*, then the practice should be to fashion the talisman and then place it *within* the triangle of art.[29] A single evocation ceremony would be necessary in order to obtain an oath of loyalty from the spirit, and to have the entity introduce its essence into the talisman itself. The talisman can then be placed within a brass vessel (for which a diagram is given) as a protective measure. From that point onward, one would have a Familiar spirit always on call. It would mirror perfectly the Santerian Orishas residing within the sacred objects enclosed in elaborate urns. Consider this excerpt from the *Goetia* itself:

> And when [Solomon] had bound them up and sealed the vessel, he, by the divine power, cast them all into a deep lake or hole in Babylon; and the Babylonians wondering to see such a thing there, they went wholly into the lake to break the vessel open, suspecting to find a great treasure. But when they had broken it open, out flew all the chief spirits immediately, and their legions followed them, and they were restored again to their former places. Except Belial, who entered into a certain image, and there gave answers to those who did offer sacrifice unto him as the Babylonians did.

The goetic spirit would likely tend to "sleep" (or rest passively) inside the sealed vessel, but could be awakened by simple calls and invocations. Perhaps one would need to open (unseal) the vessel, or merely rub it as Aladdin did his lamp.

I admit that much of this depends on speculation, making use of Palo Mayombe, Santeria, and the *Arabian Nights* to "fill in the gaps" left by the text of the *Goetia* itself. The grimoire offers only a bare-bones outline of what is necessary, suggesting that this was truly the notebook of a working mage, rather than something written merely for popularization. In fact, there are no instructions given at all for the practical use of the metallic seals. We are only shown the necessary sigils for the seventy-two spirits, and told which metals should be used to fashion each. (They are the same as listed above from the *Key of Solomon*.)

It seems the modern practice among goetic practitioners is to wear the sigil of the demon[30] as a lamen during the evocations. This is due principally to the fact that Aleister Crowley published a translation of Sloane MS 2731, which makes several references such as the following:

> This is [the spirit's] character which is used to be worn as a Lamen before him who calleth him forth, or else he will not do thee homage.

However, it is interesting to note that other manuscripts make no such mention of wearing the character of the spirit. In fact, if the shamanic principles I've suggested are applicable to the *Goetia*, and the demon is actually meant to inhabit the seal, then wearing the metal talisman on one's person would be specifically undesirable.

Fortunately, I believe the grimoire does offer a key to the solution of this dilemma. It lies within the description of another important goetic talisman: the pentagram of Solomon. (For an illustration, see chapter 11.) All of the texts generally agree on the pentagram:

> This figure is to be made in gold or silver, and worn upon the breast with the *seal of the spirit on the other side of it.*[31] It is to preserve the Exorcist from danger, and also to command by, etc.

Since only one version of the *Goetia* stresses the wearing of the signature as a lamen, we have to consider it a unique case within a larger body of literature. It becomes very likely that this single copyist was making reference in his version to something that already existed in the goetic tradition. The seal inscribed on the opposite side of the pentagram of Solomon may be the reference in question. It is, after all, to be worn around the neck as a lamen.

I have seen it suggested, and I have tended to agree, that one is to fashion the pentagram of Solomon (from gold or silver) and wear it so that the pentagram lies inward against the chest. This way it would act as a buffer between the mage and the demon's signature, and would leave the signature exposed to the sight of the entity. (The *Goetia* does make reference to the sigils as "Seals of Obedience," adding just a touch of flavor from the *Key of*

Solomon the King. Thus the sigil would need to be visible, rather than turned toward the heart of the summoner.) This new data leaves the seventy-two metal talismans free for use as something more than lamens. The evidence of history suggests the African-style shamanic practices I have outlined above.

The *Goetia* also makes use of three further talismans that partake of the nature of royal seals, and are used to command and protect against the spirits. (You can see illustrations, along with instructions for making them, in chapter 11 of this book.) The first among these is the "Solomon's Hexagonal Figure," and it reminds one distinctly of the talismans from the *Key of Solomon the King*:

> This figure is to be made on parchment made of calf's skin and worn at the skirt of the white vestment, and covered with a linen cloth to the which is to be shewed to the spirits when they have appeared that they may be compelled to be obedient and take a human shape, etc.

The hexagram is used in conjunction with another divine seal—the "Secret Seal of Solomon." This is a semi-elaborate talisman used to establish command over the spirits. Most of the figures and sigils on the talisman make no immediate sense, but the ruling and commanding powers of Saturn and Mars are displayed quite clearly, so as to leave the spirits little doubt as to the dangerous power wielded by the exorcist. It was this seal, says the *Goetia*, that Solomon used to bind the spirits and command them into the brass vessel. By now, the small hints given in the text as to its consecration should make perfect sense to the reader:

> This secret seal is to be made by one that is clean both inward and outward, and hath not defiled himself by any woman in the space of a month; but hath with fasting and prayers to God desired pardon of all his sins, &tc. It is to be made on a Tuesday or Saturday night at 12 of the Clock, written with the blood of a black cock which never trode hen, on virgins parchment. Note; on those nights the Moon must be encreasing in Virgo. When it is so made, fume it with alum, raisons of the sun, dates, cedar and lignum aloes. By this seal Solomon compelled the aforesaid spirits into a brass vessel, and sealed it up with the same. He by it gained the love of all manner of persons, and overcame in battle, for neither weapons, fire nor water could hurt him.
>
> The secret seal aforesaid was [also] made in brass, to cover his Vessel with it at the top, &tc.

The diagram of the brass vessel given in the Mathers/Crowley version of the text also shows this seal inscribed into the lid of the container itself. Without this seal, the spirits would have no particular bond to the vessel itself, and would otherwise be allowed to come and go at will.

Finally, what system of Solomonic magick would be complete without the king's historically famous magickal ring? The goetic version is of a simple design, a round bezel with three names written in three concentric circles: *Tetragrammaton*, *Anaphaxeton*, and *Michael*. The text has little to say about the ring, though this should not give the reader the mistaken impression that it is thus not important:

> This ring is to be held before the face of the Exorcist to preserve him from the stinking fumes of spirits, &tc.

My studies of the *Goetia* have shown that a good amount of practical information is deftly hidden in the main body of text, within the descriptions of the seventy-two demons. The entries for spirits number 13 and 29—Beleth and Astaroth—each contain the necessary instructions for the making and use of the ring of Solomon:

Beleth: . . . and you must have always a silver ring on the middle finger of the left hand, held against your face . . .

Ashtaroth: Therefore the exorcist must hold the magickal ring near to his face and it will defend him.

Generally, it is assumed that the ring of Solomon is Solar in nature and therefore fashioned from gold. The above quotations, on the other hand, indicate that the ring is made from silver. This Lunar—and thus Watery—association does make sense when we consider that its function is to counteract the fumes and fiery breath of the demons.

The *Lemegaton* also makes good use of talismans in its other books. I will skip over the *Theurgia-Goetia* at this time, since it is merely a continuation of the operation of the *Goetia*. It includes more goetic spirits, some of good nature and some of hostile, but all of the procedures and tools are shared by both books. Instead, we will skip to Book III, *The Pauline Art*, which contains two distinct talismanic operations.

The first part outlines the basis of an extremely elegant method of angelic summoning, deriving its principal virtue from magickal timing. It focuses on a group of twenty-four angels who rule each hour of the day and night. However, these must not be confused with the archangelic rulers as shown in chapter 5 of this work, who are seven in number (associated with the planets) and rule each hour in cyclic succession. Instead, each of the twenty-four angels of the *Pauline Art* is assigned to one specific hour of the day or night as follows:[32]

Day Hour: Angel	Night Hour: Angel
1: Samuel	1: Sabrathan
2: Anael	2: Tartys
3: Vequaniel	3: Serguanich
4: Varhmiel	4: Jefischa
5: Sasquiel	5: Abasdarhon
6: Saniel	6: Zaazenach
7: Barquiel	7: Mendrion
8: Osmadiel	8: Narcoriel
9: Quabriel	9: Pamyel
10: Oriel	10: Lassuarim
11: Bariel	11: Dardariel
12: Beratiel	12: Sarandiel

This ordering will never change, as these are the angels who govern the hours themselves, and are not otherwise assigned to any particular astrological force. The powers embodied by each angel will shift depending on the arrangement of the stars during his hour of governance. The *Pauline Art* gives an example:

As for example, you may see . . . that Samuel, the Angel that ruleth the first hour of the day, beginning at sun-rising, suppose it be a Monday in the first hour . . . that is attributed to the Moon that you call Samuel or any of his Dukes. Their offices in that hour is to do all things that are attributed to the Moon. But, if you call him or any of his servant Dukes on Tuesday morning at sunrise, being the first hour of the day, their offices are to do all things that are attributed to Mars.

Note that this explanation utilizes the Solomonic magickal hours—so that Luna rules the first hour of Monday, Mars rules the first hour of Tuesday, etc. This serves wonderfully to illustrate the cyclic powers held by the angels, but is actually misleading where it concerns the *Pauline* operation itself. There is no indication that the magick actually makes use of Solomonic hours at all. The technique depends on a much more *Abramelin*-style system of magickal timing, wherein the working mage must draw up an astrological chart to see which stars are in governance at the chosen time (see chapter 5).

The talismans used to establish contact with the angels are based on this ever-shifting nature, and are thus extremely unique within the grimoiric literature. They are neither royal seals intended to prove the mage's authority, nor do they incorporate the personal characters of the entities. Instead, they are purely astrological in design—bearing the symbols of planets and stars derived from the chart erected by the operator. Therefore, the *Pauline Art* (Part I) does not offer an established set of talismans for general use. Every single time an angel is contacted, a new seal must be created which reflects the current arrangement of powers on the celestial plane.

By way of example, the *Pauline Art* offers a set of twenty-four talismans supposedly created for Wednesday, March 10, 1641. However, if one follows the instructions as given in the text, they will not produce exactly the same twenty-four talismans. Enough of them are correct to show forth the pattern, but enough of them are incorrect to suggest that errors have crept into the text somewhere along the line. Because of this, I have chosen to offer an example that holds true to the instructions, and applies to a more recent date. (I have used Wednesday, May 9, 2001, 1:47 pm—see the example chart in chapter 5.) The instructions (given in a rather broken and garbled form in the grimoire) are as follows:

First and foremost, these talismans are based upon the astrological Ascendant and its ruling planet. One must first decide which of the twelve zodiacal forces (both the sign and its planet) will best yield the desired results. Then, for the day or night one wishes to work, the magickal hours must be calculated and astrological charts erected (see chapter 5) to discover at which hour the chosen sign will be in the Ascendant. This will show which of the angels must be evoked.

The talisman itself only requires clean paper or parchment.[33] In the center one must write the sign of the Ascendant beside its ruling planet. The circumference contains the remaining six planets, beginning with Luna at the top and following clockwise in the regular pattern of Saturn, Jupiter, Mars, Sol, Venus, and finally Mercury. Of course, the ruling planet will always be subtracted from this pattern, so that (in our example) a talisman of Virgo / Mercury displays the symbol of Mercury in its center, while the symbol is missing from the circumference.

To use the talisman, one is merely instructed to place it upon the table of practice (shown in chapter 1) directly upon the symbol of its planetary ruler. Then, placing one's hand upon the talisman, the invocations are recited until the angel (Osmadiel, in our example) makes its appearance. No further preparations or procedures are offered in the text, they being left to the expertise of the mage.

The second part of the *Pauline Art* also focuses upon the astrological Ascendant, though this time it concerns the degree of one's own natal Ascendant (the "degree of the nativity") and the angel who governs that degree. This angel represents the principal point of your birth chart (remember that the Ascendant, and not the Sun sign, was once considered the most important part of the natal horoscope) and it thus stands as a patron or guardian from whom the mage can learn much. The text refers to this as a "Holy Guardian Angel," but this must not be confused with the transcendent entity of Abramelin, who has nothing to do with nativity.

The text offers a list of 360 angels. Each sign of the zodiac possesses thirty angels, one for each degree. Thus, these angels encompass the entire circle of the heavens. It is necessary for the mage to draw up his own natal chart and calculate which degree of his ascending sign was rising upon the eastern horizon. For instance, if his ascending degree were 10 degrees Capricorn, his nativity angel as listed in the *Pauline Art* would be one called Izashiel.[34]

(If one does not know the degree of his nativity, but does know the ascending sign itself, the text also offers twelve angels associated with the general zodiacal signs. It is considered a less accurate, but acceptable, manner of working.)

Unlike Part I of the grimoire, this operation does offer an established set of talismans and instructions for fashioning them. There is no need to create new ones each time the invocations are performed. However, as in Part I, these talismans appear to be associated specifically with the magickal timing (in this case, one for each of the twelve zodiacal signs) rather than acting as signatures of the angels or as royal seals.

While any mention of metal talismans, consecrated burins, or engraving indicates some influence of metallurgy on the grimoiric tradition, this portion of the *Pauline Art* reads as if it were written specifically for experienced metallurgists:

> Aries: Make this seal of Iron ? dram, Gold 2 drams, Copper ? drams, and melt them together when the
> Sun entereth the first degree of Aires . . .

This does make sense, given the strong current of alchemical philosophy and practice that runs throughout the grimoiric literature. In fact, the process of evoking spirits from sacred metals is itself an alchemical practice. The *Pauline Art*, with its various metallic alloys, seems to be a rather sophisticated experiment. This fact is not only obvious in the *Pauline Art*, but even more so in the text of the *Almadel* of Solomon (see chapter 1). The interests of the author of the *Lemegaton* are rather clear.

Another classical European grimoire with a unique, and generally misunderstood, talismanic system is found in Book III (and part of Book II) of the *Book of Abramelin*. Rather than making use of hieroglyphic characters, Abramelin's talismans display names and arrangements of letters into magickal squares. They are somewhat reminiscent of the planetary squares found in Agrippa's *Three Books*, as well as some examples of magickal squares found on the talismans of the *Key of Solomon the King*.

Abramelin makes absolutely no use of consecrated pens, inks, or papers. In Book II, Chapter 20, the author insists that drawing the symbols clearly with any pen and ink (so that the operations intended by each is not obscured) will suffice.

The rest of the practice as outlined by the text is also fairly simple: one first undergoes the six-month operation of purification and summoning of the guardian angel. Once successful in this, the aspirant turns to an evocation of

Pauline Art talisman—for May 9, 2001.

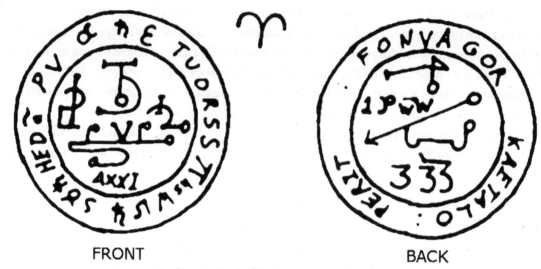

FRONT   BACK

Pauline Art Seal of Aries, Front and Back.

the twelve princes of Hell: Lucifer, Leviathan, Satan, and Belial (the four princes), and Astarot, Magot, Asmodee, Belzebud, Oriens, Paimon, Ariton, and Amaimon (the eight sub-princes). From these twelve one must demand a list of servient spirits who are best matched to one's personal psychology and practical needs:

> . . . in the first demand which thou shalt make unto the Four Spirits (who are) the Supreme Princes, and unto the Eight Sub-Princes; thou shalt demand the most skillful of the Spirits . . . But seeing that the subjects of various erring humours (of mind) and other occasions which arise daily be diverse, each man will procure for himself those (Spirits) which be of his nature and genius and fit for that wherein thou wouldest employ them. (*Book of Abramelin*, p. 257)

Once these spirits have made their appearance(s), the aspirant conjures them to swear an oath of loyalty upon the talismans. This results in the spirits being forever bound to the squares. When one wishes to work the magick, he needs only expose the talisman and speak the name of the spirit he wishes to appear. In most cases, it is necessary only to show the talisman to the spirit for it to understand what it is to accomplish (somewhat like the seals of the *Key of Solomon the King*).

The magick squares provided by this text are often mistaken as *Goetia*-style seals, where the mere presence of the talismans equals the presence of the spirits themselves. This has led to urban legend–style stories of the "dangers" posed by the possession of the talismans or even possession of the book itself. However, there is nothing of signatures or seals about these talismans. Only rarely are the letters of the Abramelin squares formed into recognizable names, and then they are not always the names of the spirits who are actually associated with the talisman. They are only like the *Goetia* in that the spirits are bound to the squares, but this only occurs *after* the six-month operation. On their own, the talismans seem quite inert and harmless.

In fact, it might be possible to suggest the talismans provided in *Abramelin* are actually useless. The first clue comes with the fact that Book II provides a long list of the spirits that Abraham the Jew bound by his own performance of the operation, yet Book III states that each aspirant should demand from the princes a list of personalized spirits. The talismans given in the text are specifically associated with the list of spirits already provided. Theoretically, if one receives his own list of spirits, one should also receive his own book of talismans to go with them.

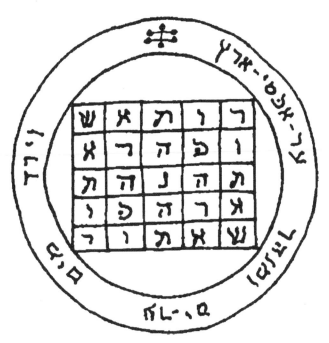

Solomonic talisman with square.

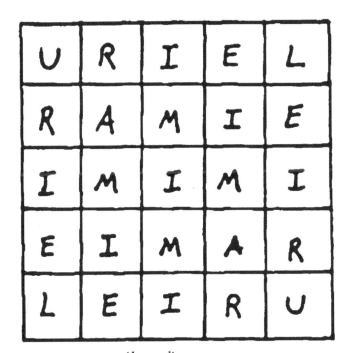

Abramelin square.

Planetary Square.

The second clue is provided by the state of Book III itself. While the first two parts of the work are generally consistent and well (if obscurely) written, Book III persistently shows forth errors, omissions, and outright contradictions. I've seen it suggested that Book III was a later addition to the text, written in an obviously different style, and with an obviously different (goetic) intent, than the rest of the celestial-aimed operation. It could even be that Book III was added to the work as a blind (to divert the attention of the curious), or even as a kind of bait to lure would-be aspirants who might otherwise pass over the book for more popular *Goetia*-style operations. At the very least, we should consider these talismans as mere examples of what "Abraham the Jew" received from his guardian angel for his own personal use. As the *Book of Abramelin* stresses again and again, the holy guardian angel will instruct one in all necessary areas after contact is made, making anything written in the operation past that point tentative and exemplary at best.

Finally, we come to the talismanic art as taught by Frances Barrett's *The Magus*. It begins on page 80 of the facsimile edition: Book II, Part II, "Of Magic Pentacles and their Composition":

These pentacles consist either of characters of good spirits of the superior order,[35] or of sacred pictures of holy letters or revelations, with apt and proper versicles, which are composed either of geometrical figures and holy names of God, according to the course and manner of many of them, or they are compounded of all of them, or many of them mixed. Having come this far in our own grimoiric journey, we can make perfect sense of this description. We see here the use of Signatures and Sigils *or* the fashioning of Divine Seals with geometrical figures and words of power. Plus, any talisman may include elements from various different "types." (Also note that reference is made to "sacred pictures of . . . revelations." This is an aspect of the talismanic art known as image magick, which will be covered below.)

"Barrett" goes on to explain the creation of talismans of the first type, specific to one or more angels. The name of the entity, the corresponding name of God, and a proper geometrical figure are all included.[36] He also goes on to reveal a Qabalistic secret (which we can also find in Agrippa's numeric tables, and with the angels provided in chapter 8 of this work for the magickal book):

> . . . that the [name of God] consist of just so many letters as the figure may constitute a number; or of so many letters of a name, as, joined together among themselves, may make the number of a figure . . .

Thus, if one were to fashion a talisman for a Solar entity—for whom the number 6 is sacred—it is necessary to employ those divine names that possess six Hebrew letters. These letters would then, according to the instructions, be written within the six angles of a hexagram. The angel's name and/or sigil would reside in the center of the hexagram, and it is also suggested that the entire talisman be surrounded by a circle containing appropriate scripture and/or words of power.

The text also suggests making use of magickal squares of the *Abramelin* type. It describes the process as "making the revolution of some kind of name, in a square table, and by drawing about it a single or double circle, and writing therein some holy versicle competent and befitting this name, or from which that name is extracted." This "revolution" of the divine name is generally called a double *acrostic* (literally meaning "stair"), such as the famous ROTAS[37] square:

S	A	T	O	R
A	R	E	P	O
T	E	N	E	T
O	P	E	R	A
R	O	T	A	S

You are not alone if these descriptions remind you of the talismans from the *Key of Solomon the King*. The instructions given in *The Magus* seem perfectly applicable to the fashioning of further *Key* talismans. At the same time, this process may appear more familiar to you than many of the other grimoiric talismans. Because this is the basic method of talismanic art that has descended to modern occultism through the Victorian Hermetic traditions such as the Order of the Golden Dawn.

To complete the section, *The Magus* explains how to find the appropriate divine names and verses in Scripture along with material from which to write the necessary prayers. There is little need to cover this information here, however, as we have already discussed it in chapter 7 "Creating Prayers and Invocations." One need simply apply the same method to locate single biblical verses that relate in some way to the magickal goal and/or contain the divine name upon which the talisman depends. We can take for example the fifth pentacle of Jupiter from the *Key of Solomon the King*, which is designed to cause visions. The Hebrew verse inscribed around its circumference translates as the first verse of the book of Ezekiel: "As I was among the captives by the river of Chebar, the heavens were opened, and I saw visions of Elohim." The second pentacle of Mars promises to serve against all manners of diseases, and its Hebrew verse is from John I:4: "In Him was life, and the life was the light of man."[38]

Now, let us continue to the next section on talismans in *The Magus*, as found in Book II, Part II (p. 94).

The Particular Form of the Lamen, from The Magus

Because, in chapter 8, I took the time to outline several little-known angelic summoning procedures from *The Magus*, I feel it would now be helpful to provide its instruction for the necessary lamen. This is the talisman that is placed upon the altar in the first and third example procedures I outlined. It is actually a rather fascinating method, bearing a strong resemblance to the above instruction from the text, but also including some obscure talismanic innovations:

> Now the lamen which is used to invoke any good spirit must be made after the following manner: either in metal conformable or in new wax mixed with convenient spices and colors,[39] and the outward form of it may be either square, circular, or triangular, or of the like sort, according to the rule of the numbers, in which there must be written the divine names, as well general as special. And in the center of the lamen draw a hexagon or character of six corners, in the middle thereof write the name and character of the star,[40] or of the spirit his governor, to whom the good spirit that is to be called is subject. And about this character let there be placed so many characters of five corners or pentacles as the spirits we would call together at once. But if we should call only one, nevertheless there must be made four pentagons, wherein the name of the spirit or spirits, with their characters, are to be written. Now this lamen ought to be composed when the moon is in her increase, on those days and hours which agree to the spirit; and if we take a fortunate planet therewith, it will be the better for the producing the effect;[41] which table or lamen being rightly made in the manner we have fully described, must be consecrated according to the rules . . .

From here we will move on to such rules of consecration. However, rather than outlining the more generic instructions given for consecration in *The Magus*, we will instead take a look at the method given in the *Key of Solomon the King*.

Consecrating Talismans

Enough has now been said on the fashioning of grimoiric talismans, either from metal or parchment/paper. The consecration of these talismans is simple enough, though it seems to me to resemble the Orthodox Christian method of consecrating sacred icons. In that system, the icon is merely placed upon the altar during services such as holy communion. Once consecrated in such a manner, the icon becomes a fit vessel for the indwelling of a celestial spirit. (More on icons below.) We will see here how similar is the practice as outlined in the *Key*.

Your talisman should be created according to the rules given above (such as with the *Key* or *The Magus*), following any necessary magickal timing, and utilizing consecrated colors, parchment/paper, or the burin of the art for engraving. In order to consecrate—or enliven—the talismans, it will be necessary to make holy water, exorcise some incense, and prepare an earthen vessel to burn the perfumes. Finally, do not forget to consecrate the silk as shown in chapter 6 to wrap the talismans once they are complete.

Prepare your sacred space as described in chapter 7. The *Key* also suggests that one use the black-hilted knife to inscribe a simple magickal circle, complete with divine names appropriate to the operation written in the four quarters.

The *Key* says nothing about the magickal timing necessary for this consecration, instead focusing on the timing for the drawing of the talismans. I assume that one is intended to draw and consecrate a talisman as a single operation. Thus, one would need to operate on the days and hours of Mercury, the Moon being in an aerial or terrestrial zodiacal sign, as well as in her increase and in "equal number of days with the Sun."[42] Perhaps, according to Book I, Chapter 8, one is also meant to perform the action before sunrise while the Sun is in Leo. Otherwise, one need only observe the days and hours most proper to the talisman and its planet (or sign, etc.).

Step One

Though the *Key* does not make such a suggestion, I would instruct the practicing mage to spend at least twelve hours in preparation and purification, following the points outlined in chapters 3 and 7 of this book. A longer period may not be necessary because this is not an operation of summoning, which would require a deeper ecstatic state. About forty-five minutes to an hour before the work begins, perform the Solomonic bath.

Step Two

At the hour of working, cense and sprinkle the chamber with appropriate prayers. This is also as described in the practical instruction from chapter 7. Place the censer on the altar and cast more incense upon the coal.

Step Three

Face east, hold the talisman over the incense, and chant the following Psalms:

8 (*O Lord, Our Lord, how excellent is thy name in all the earth!*)

21 (*The king shall joy in thy strength, O Lord . . .*)

27 (*The Lord is my light and my salvation; whom shall I fear?*)

29 (*Give unto the Lord, O ye mighty, give unto the Lord glory and strength.*)

32 (*Blessed is he whose transgression is forgiven, whose sin is covered.*)

51 (*Have mercy upon me, O God, according to thy lovingkindness . . .*)

72 (*Give the king thy judgments, O God . . .*)

134 (*Behold, bless ye the Lord, all ye servants of the Lord . . .*)

Then repeat the following oration:

O Adonai most powerful, El most strong, AGLA most holy, ON most righteous, the Aleph and the Tau, the Beginning and the End; Thou Who hast established all things in Thy Wisdom; Thou Who has chosen Abraham Thy faithful servant, and has promised that in his seed shall all nations of the earth be blessed, which seed Thou hast multiplied as the Stars of Heaven; Thou Who has appeared unto Thy servant Moses in flame in the midst of the Burning Bush, and has made him walk with dry feet through the Red Sea; Thou Who gavest the Law to him upon Mount Sinai; Thou Who hast granted unto Solomon Thy Servant these Pentacles by Thy great Mercy, for the preservation of Soul and of Body; [I or we] most humbly implore and supplicate Thy Holy Majesty, that these Pentacles may be consecrated by Thy power, and prepared in such manner that they may obtain virtue and strength against all Spirits, through Thee, O Most Holy Adonai, Whose Kingdom, Empire, and principality remaineth and endureth without end.

As an alternative to this oration, one might create unique invocations for different talismans, as instructed in chapter 7. Especially if the talisman is specific to one entity, one should create two prayers: the first to the highest

Solomonic Circle for Talisman Consecration.

(similar to the above oration) in which the related angel's presence is requested; and the second prayer to the angel him- or herself to touch and inhabit the talisman, or to command a servient spirit into the same.

Step Four

Cense the talisman once more, sprinkle it with the holy water, wrap it in the consecrated white silk. It is now ready for practical use.

Image Magick[43]

In the above discussion, I mentioned the ancient Mesopotamian tendency to recognize each part of the heavens as a living being within their pantheons. In fact, the same became true of most ancient civilizations once they discovered astronomy. Each of the celestial spirits were given cultic images that were the focus of worship and sacrifice in elaborate temples. These were not supposed to be the "physical" appearances of the entities so much as symbolic representations of their basic natures. For instance, note the images of Zeus (Greek) or Marduk (Babylonian), both storm gods who are necessarily depicted as wielding bolts of lightning and/or holding mighty hammers of thunder. This is known today as "iconography."

Of course, both Mesopotamian and Egyptian religion were known for their specifically astrological/astronomical focus. Egyptian astrology was concerned mainly with the Sun and the fixed stars (including the thirty-six decanates), while Babylonian astrology focused upon the planets and their aspects. The Greeks eventually combined these two systems into the astrology used in the grimoires (and by most astrologers today). Over time, this resulted in specific lists of gods and spirits who could be called in magickal operations, depending entirely upon which celestial force the priest-shaman wished to invoke.

The Art of Iconography was preserved long after the fall of these ancient civilizations. The Mesopotamian systems, especially, led directly to later practices such as *Merkavah* mysticism, Arabic magick, and the grimioric systems (such as the *Goetia*). Gnosticism was also influenced heavily by these Mesopotamian and Arabic traditions, but also drew much material from Egyptian religion and iconography.

Later on, Orthodox (as well as Catholic) Christianity put much stress on icons, claiming a direct descent of the art from ancient Egypt (presumably through the Gnostics) to themselves. I find the claim to be very likely true. Much like the Egyptian images found in texts such as the *Book of the Dead*, the later Christian examples were often depictions of scenes from the scriptures. Otherwise, they are portraits of the celestial beings holding certain items, or hands held in particular positions, to symbolize their natures.

The Christian icons are utilized in the same manner as their ancient counterparts: to provide a physical dwelling for the entity or entities they depict. While Christianity mostly prohibits the making of images of God himself, this restriction does not apply to Jesus, the saints, nor to the innumerable angels that populate the Christian universe. Each of these entities can be invoked into an icon, and thus reside in the worshipper's home as surely as do the Santerian Orishas in the homes of their devotees. Catholic icons are even better examples—as they made use of fully three-dimensional statues rather than flat pictures. (Very often these statues were adopted directly out of the Roman Pagan temples so that, for example, statues of Apollo might have become dwellings for St. Michael the archangel, etc.)

It was from the Mesopotamian systems of iconography that the Arabic magickal texts arose, and from thence the medieval grimoires. In these later forms, the images themselves were simplified somewhat, and became a focus for meditation and invocation rather than for worship. We do not even know how many of these magickal images still resemble the older gods, especially after so many centuries of oral transmission and scribal alterations. However, it is still very possible that some of them do reflect some semblance of the original cultic images.

The *Goetia* serves as a perfect example of medieval magickal imagery. The entry for each spirit lists not only his signature and powers, but also a short description of his natural appearance. In many cases, the descriptions are obviously meant to embody the astrological nature of the entities. For instance, the tenth spirit (president Buer) comes when the Sun rests in Sagittarius, and appears as an archer or centaur.[44] Or the fourteenth (marquise Lerayou), also of Sagittarius, who appears as an archer, clad in green, and carrying a bow and quiver. Over the years, various artists have fashioned images based on these descriptions, giving us something more visual to work with.

The above illustration was created from the description of the demon Astaroth, spirit number 29 in the *Goetia*, and appears in the *Dictionnaire Infernal* published in 1825–1826 by Collin de Plancy. The entry in the *Goetia* reads as follows:

> He is a Mighty, Strong Duke, and appeareth in the Form of an hurtful Angel riding on an Infernal Beast like a Dragon, and carrying in his right hand a Viper.

Being a duke, this spirit is under the governance of the Venus star. As we know from chapter 5, Venus is the occult force of passion and sexuality. Keeping this in mind while we look at Astaroth's image can illuminate much about the spirit's nature. The humanoid (angelic) figure riding upon a "beast" is a classic depiction of the most bestial sexual instinct.[45] The serpent is also an extremely ancient symbol of base sexuality (orgasm and ejaculation). I find it interesting that the *Dictionnaire Infernal* depicts this serpent as held in the male figure's right hand, especially since it also depicts the angelic figure as crowned: showing pride, hubris, or "self-love."

It also helps that we know something of the origins of Astaroth. The demon's name is actually of Phoenician (Canaanite) and Hebrew origin, combining the name of the Palestinian goddess of Venus (*Astarte*) with the Hebrew word for "abomination" (*Thoabath*).[46] Astarte was the goddess of sex, passion, fertility, generation, and abundance.

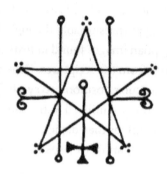

Ashtaroth
A Strong Duke
(Venus)

Astaroth and His Sigil.

Though we will most likely never know what her signature(s) looked like, we do know that the pentagram has been a symbol of Venus since very ancient times.[47]

Of course, we have to keep in mind that Astaroth is *not* Astarte. The Astaroth of the *Goetia* is a Christian creation; supposed to be one of the infernal spirits who reside in Hell and oppose all things good. Therefore, as his image illustrates, Astaroth embodies everything negative about the Venusian current and human sexuality. This "hurtful Angel" can represent everything from simple lust to outright rape. It might also include the concept of sex without fertility.[48]

Another example from the *Goetia* shows a spirit assuming the magickal image of the planet Saturn. Spirit number fifty, the knight Fureas (or Furcas), is described as "a cruel old man with a long beard and a hairy head, sitting on a pale-colored horse, with a sharp weapon in his hand." This is an image comparable to the magickal images of Saturn given by Agrippa (included in the charts later in this section). For verification, we take a look at the alchemical metal used for the seals of goetic knights—and it is indeed lead, the metal of Saturn. I would bet that the "sharp weapon" intended for Fureas' hand should be a scythe or sickle.

According to Bick Thomas, a contemporary medieval scholar, there were a few sets of astrological images—associated specifically with the thirty-six planetary decanates—that enjoyed popularity in the Middle Ages. The oldest derives from an astrological work called *Liber Hermetis*, whose astrology reflects the Ptolemic system common to the Middle Ages rather than Arabic versions.[49] In the text, the decans are given the images of various deities of Egypt and Asia Minor, thus illustrating their connection to religious iconography. However, this material describes them as malevolent beings set over certain diseases and infirmities. Thomas suggests this may indicate a Gnostic origin for the images, and I tend to agree. Another source would not likely have associated celestial beings with the negative powers usually reserved for infernal spirits (like those of the *Goetia*). Gnosticism, meanwhile, specialized in viewing the celestial forces as archons bent on enslaving and tormenting humanity.

Not all image magick in medieval Europe was associated with spirits or angels. In fact, in the greater genre of image magick, any relation between these astrological images and literal entities was extremely played down. This is likely due to the fact that the art caught on with those mages who refused to engage in any type of goetic (or other) evocation. Medical professionals in particular made much use of images in the healing arts,[50] in conjunction with its use of stones, talismans, and (most importantly) astrology.

After the *Liber Hermetis*, the next oldest set of magickal images is outlined in the *Picatrix* (itself a text of Arabic origin). This is the text that most influenced the later grimoiric systems we are now studying. Here we finally see the emphasis placed upon magickal timing rather than on particular beings or spirits. The book lists the powers of each decan and the type of magick that is most appropriate to its time of rule. By way of example, Thomas offers this translation from the *Picatrix*:

> And there ascends in the first face of Taurus a woman with curling hair, having a child who is dressed in clothes like fire, and she herself is dressed in similar clothes. And this is a face of tilling and working the earth, of sciences (knowing), geometry, of sowing seed, and making things.

There is nothing here to indicate that this woman and her child are living intelligences intended for worship or invocation. Instead, the image is simply listed as an iconographic representation of the natural forces of Taurus (tilling the earth, sowing seed, making things) as the Sun passes through that constellation's "first face," the decanate ruled by Mercury (sciences, geometry).

After the *Picatrix*, it was Agrippa who made the astrological images most popular, influencing such Renaissance mages as Giordano Bruno and Marsillo Ficino. Agrippa devoted much space in his *Three Books* to the images related to all aspects of the heavens, and his source seems to have either been the *Picatrix*, or at least a common tradition therewith. (There are both similarities and marked differences between the two texts.)

In the beginning of this chapter, we took a brief look at Agrippa's Book II, Chapter 35, "How Some Artificial Things as Images . . . and Such Like May Obtain Some Virtue From the Celestial Bodies" This is the point in the *Occult Philosophy* that launches a twelve-plus chapter dissertation on the forms and uses of magickal images—covering the entire astrological realm. We will here take a look at much of this information, beginning with Chapter 36:

36: Of the Images of the Zodiac . . .

For these magickal images, Agrippa instructs one to simply use the "twelve general images" associated with the signs of the zodiac. These are most likely recognizable to the modern reader:

Aries: Ram	Libra: Scales
Taurus: Bull	Scorpius: Scorpion
Gemini: Twins	Sagittarius: Arrow, Archer, Centaur
Cancer: Crab, Scarab	Capricornus: Goat, Goat-fish
Leo: Lion	Aquarius: Man, Angel, Water-bearer
Virgo: Virgin	Pisces: Two fish

Images fashioned of the Fiery triplicity (**Aries, Leo, Sagittarius**) are profitable against all manner of fevers and "cold and phlegmatic infirmities."[51] One who carries such an image will be acceptable, eloquent, ingenious, and honorable because these signs are ruled by Mars, Sol, and Jupiter. Following are the specifics on two Leo images outlined by Agrippa, both being simple lions, consecrated at the given magickal time:

Magickal Timing (Fiery Triplicity)	Application
Hour of Sol, First Degree of Leo Ascending	Against fevers delusions diseases.
When Sol enters Second Decan of Leo in Tenth House	Against injuries from beasts.

The Airy triplicity (Libra, Aquarius, Gemini) are ruled by Venus, Saturn, and Mercury respectively. Images fashioned of these three signs serve to put to flight diseases, conduce friendship and concord, prevail against melancholy, and promote health. No specific images are described in the text.

Cancer, Scorpio, and Pisces are the Watery triplicity, and thus images fashioned under them are prescribed against hot and dry fevers, tuberculosis, and all choleric passions. Scorpius, specifically, is associated with the human genitals; and thus its image serves for purposes of lust. Agrippa gives several images—of Scorpius and Cancer—as examples:

Image	Magickal Timing (Watery Triplicity)	Application
Scorpius	When 3rd decan of Scorpius (Venus) ascends.	For lust.
Scorpius	When 2nd decan of Scorpius (Sol) ascends.	Against scorpions, poisons, serpents, evil spirits. Promotes wisdom, health.
Cancer	When Sol and Luna are conjunct and ascending in the 1st decan (Venus) or 3rd decan (Luna) of Cancer.	Against serpents, poison.
Cancer	When Sol is in Cancer.	Against serpents.

The Earthy triplicity of Capricorn, Taurus, and Virgo are ruled by Saturn, Venus, and Mercury respectively. Thus they are prescribed to cure all "hot infirmities" such as synocal fever (a prolonged fever with inflammation). They also serve to make one grateful, acceptable, eloquent, devout, and religious. Capricorn, specifically, is good for the protection of people and places, because it is the exaltation of Mars.

37: Of the Images of the Faces . . .

The thirty-six faces of the zodiac are basically one and the same with the thirty-six decans. Agrippa makes use of both terms to indicate two different planetary arrangements. In chapter 5, I explained the differences and similarities between these systems, and listed the planets associated with both. (For that reason, I have not included the planetary attributions here. See chapter 5 for the system you wish to utilize.) For simplicity, I have chosen to refer to the faces as decans throughout this list.

Finally, there is no magickal timing mentioned with these magickal images. All of them are intended for creation and consecration when the related decan ascends above the eastern horizon. (For instance, if Aries is the ascending sign: when only the 1st to 10th degree of Aries has risen above the horizon, the decan is the first. If the

Solomonic Scorpion Talisman.

11th to 20th degree has risen, it is the second decan ascending. If the 21st through 30th degree has risen, the third decan of Aries has ascended.)

Decan	Image	Application
Aries 1	Large, strong black man, girded about. Reddish eyes, very angry. Clothed in white garment.	Causes boldness, fortitude, loftiness, shamelessness.
Aries 2	Woman clothed outward with red and underneath with a white garment covering her feet.[52]	Nobleness, ascension of kingdom, greatness of dominion.
Aries 3	Pale white man with red hair, clothed in red. Wearing golden bracelet, holding staff of wood. Restless and wrathful because he cannot perform the good he wishes.	Bestows wit, meekness, joy, and beauty.
Taurus 1	Naked man, an archer, a harvester, or a husbandman; going forth to plow, sow, people, and divide the earth according to the rules of geometry	No listed application(?)[53]
Taurus 2	Naked man holding a key.	Power, nobility, and dominion over people.
Taurus 3	Man holding a serpent and an arrow in his hand.	The image of necessity and profit, and of misery and slavery.

Decan	Image	Application
Gemini 1	Man holding a rod, and serving another man.	Grants wisdom, knowledge of numbers and arts in which there is no profit.
Gemini 2	One man holding a pipe, and another bowed down digging the earth.	Signifies infamous and dishonest agility— such as jesters and jugglers.[54] Also labors and painful searchings.
Gemini 3	A man seeking for arms, and a fool holding bird in right hand and pipe in left.	Forgetfulness, wrath, boldness, jests, scurrilities, and unprofitable words.
Cancer 1	Young virgin, adorned with fine clothes, wearing crown.	Gives acuteness of senses, subtility of wit, and love of men.
Cancer 2	Man in comely apparel OR: A man and woman sitting at a table playing.	Bestows riches, mirth, gladness, and love of women.
Cancer 3	Hunter with lance (spear) and horn, calling out dogs for the hunt.	Signifies contention of men, pursuing those who flee, hunting and possessing things by arms and brawling.
Leo 1	Man riding a lion.	Boldness, violence, cruelty, wickedness, lust, and labors to be sustained.
Leo 2	Image of hands lifted up, and an angry man wearing a crown, threatening with a drawn sword in right hand, and a shield[55] in the left.	Hidden contentions, unknown victories, base men, quarrels, and battles.
Leo 3	Young man holding a whip, and a sad man looking ill.	Signifies love and society, and the loss of one's right to avoid strife.
Virgo 1	A good maid and a man casting seeds.	Gaining wealth, ordering of diet, plowing, sowing, and peopling.[56]
Virgo 2	Black man clothed in a skin, and a man with bushy hair holding a bag.	Gain, scraping together wealth, and covetousness.
Virgo 3	Deaf white woman OR an old man leaning on a staff.	Weakness, infirmity, loss of members, destruction of trees, depopulation of lands.
Libra 1	Angry man holding a pipe and a man reading a book.	Justifying and helping the miserable and weak against the powerful and wicked.
Libra 2	Two men furious and wrathful, and a man in comely apparel sitting in a chair.	Indignation against evil, quietness and security of life with plenty of good things.
Libra 3	Violent man holding bow, before him a naked man. Another man holding bread in one hand, and wine in the other.	Wicked lusts, singing (or songs), sports, and gluttony.

Decan	Image	Application
Scorpius 1	Woman of good face and dress, and two men striking her.	Comeliness and beauty. And for strife, treachery, deceits, detractions, and perditions.
Scorpius 2	Naked man and woman, and a man sitting on the ground. Before him, two dogs biting one another.	Impudence, deceit, and false dealing. To send mischief and strife against another man.
Scorpius 3	A man bowing upon his knees and a woman striking him with a staff.	Drunkenness, fornication, wrath, violence, and strife.
Sagittarius 1	Man in a coat of mail, holding a drawn sword.	Boldness, malice, liberty.
Sagittarius 2	Fully clothed weeping woman.	Sadness and fear of one's own body.
Sagittarius 3	Gold-colored man OR an idle man playing with a staff.	Following our own wills and obstinacy therein, activity for evil things, contentions, and horrible matters.
Capricornus 1	A woman, and a man carrying full bags.	To go forth and rejoice, to gain and lose with weakness and baseness.
Capricornus 2	Two women and a man looking at a bird flying through the air.	Signifies requiring things that can't be done, searching for things that can't be known.
Capricornus 3	A woman chaste in body and wise in her work, and a banker gathering his money on a table.	Governing in prudence, covetousness of money, avarice.
Aquarius 1	A prudent man and a woman spinning (thread).[57]	The thought and labor for gain, in poverty and baseness.
Aquarius 2	Man with long beard.	The understanding, meekness, modesty, liberty, and good manners.
Aquarius 3	Black and angry man.	Expressing insolence and impudence.
Pisces 1	Well-clothed man carrying burdens.	Journeys, change of place. Carefulness in getting wealth and clothes.
Pisces 2	Well-dressed woman with pretty face.	To desire and put oneself on high. Great matters.
Pisces 3	Naked man or youth. Near him a beautiful maid whose head is adorned with flowers.	Rest, idleness, delight, fornication, and embracing women.

38: Of the Images of Saturn

Image	Magickal Timing	Application
Engraved in a loadstone: A man with the face of an hart, and camel's feet, sitting upon a chair or dragon.[59] Holding scythe in right hand, and an arrow in the left.	Saturn ascending.[58]	Prolongation of life, dying only of old age.
Engraved in a sapphire:[60] An old man sitting on a high chair, lifting a sickle or a fish in both hands above his head, and a bunch of grapes under his feet. Head covered with, and body clothed with black or dark clothing.	Hour of Saturn, when Saturn ascends or is fortunately aspected. OR: Hour of Saturn when Saturn ascends with the third decan of Aquarius	Length of days. OR: Against the stone[61] and other diseases of the kidneys.
Old man leaning on a staff, clothed in black, holding a sickle.	Saturn ascending in Capricornus.	Increasing power.

39: Of the Images of Jupiter

Image	Magickal Timing	Application
Engraved in a clear white stone: Crowned man, wearing saffron colored clothes, riding an eagle or dragon, and holding an arrow (or spear) in right hand about to strike it into the head of the dragon or eagle.[62]	Hour of Jupiter. Jupiter in exaltation (Cancer), ascending, and fortunately aspected.	Prolongation of life.
Engraved in a clear white stone (especially crystal): Naked man wearing crown, both hands clasped and lifted up (as in deprecating something), sitting in a four-footed chair which is carried by four winged boys (like modern cherub/cupid figures).	Same as above.	Increases felicity, riches, honor, confers benevolence and prosperity, and frees one from enemies.
Man with lion's or ram's head, eagle's feet, clothed in saffron colored garments. Called the Son of Jupiter.	None given(?)	For a religious life, advancement of fortune, and a glorious life.

40: Of the Images of Mars

Image	Magickal Timing	Application
Engraved in a martial stone, such as diamond: A man in armor, riding a lion, with a drawn sword (point upwards) in right hand and a human head in the left.	Hour of Mars, Mars ascending in the second decan of Aries.	Makes one powerful in good or evil so he is feared by all. Gives power of enchantment so men are terrified and stupefied by one's angry looks.
Soldier crowned and armored, girt with a sword, long lance (or spear) in right hand.	Hour of Mars, Mars ascending in the first decan of Scorpius.	Obtaining boldness, courage, and good fortune in war and contentions.

41: Of the Images of the Sun

Image	Magickal Timing	Application
Crowned king sitting in a chair, a raven on his bosom, a globe under his feet. Wearing saffron colored clothes. OR: Same image engraved in a balantine[63] stone or ruby.	Hour of Sol, Sol ascending with first Decan of Leo. OR: Hour of Sol, Sol in exaltation (Aries) and fortunate aspect.	Renders men invincible and honorable, and helps to bring business to a good end, to drive away vain dreams, and against fevers and plague.
Engraved in a diamond: Woman crowned, dancing and laughing, standing in a chariot drawn by four horses, a looking glass (or small shield?) in right hand, a staff in the left hand leaning against her chest. A flame of fire on her head. OR: Same image engraved in a carnelian stone.	Hour of Sol, Sol in exaltation (Aries) and ascending. OR: Hour of Sol, Sol ascending in first Decan of Leo.	Makes on fortunate and rich, and beloved by all. OR: Against lunatic passions proceeding from the combustion of the Moon (i.e.—the dark phase of the Moon, when it is in conjunction with the Sun.)

42: Of the Images of Venus

Image	Magickal Timing	Application
Woman with head of a bird, feet of an eagle, holding an arrow in her hand.	The very hour that Venus ascends into Pisces.	For favor and benevolence.

Image	Magickal Timing	Application
Engraved in lapis lazuli: naked maid with hair spread out, looking-glass in hand, and a chain about her neck. Near her a handsome young man holding her by the chain in his left hand, but making up her hair with his right. Both look lovingly at one another. About them is a cupid figure with an arrow or sword.	Hour of Venus, Venus ascending in Taurus.	To get the love of a woman.
Little maid with hair spread out, clothed in long white garments, holding a laurel wreath, apple, or flowers in right hand. A comb held in the left.	Venus ascending with the first decan of Taurus, Libra, or Pisces.	Makes men pleasant, jocund, strong, cheerful and gives beauty.

43: Of the Images of Mercury

Image	Magickal Timing	Application
Handsome young man, bearded, caduceus wand in right hand (only one serpent entwined around it— as in the modern medical symbol), an arrow (or flute?) in the left hand. Winged feet.	Hour of Mercury, Mercury ascending in Gemini.	Confers knowledge, eloquence, diligence in merchandising and gain. Begets peace and concord and cures fevers.
Man sitting in chair or riding a peacock, with eagle's feet, a crest on his head, and holding a rooster or flame in his right hand.	Mercury ascending in Virgo.	Good will, wit, and memory.

44: Of the Images of the Moon

Image	Magickal Timing	Application
Man leaning on a staff, a bird on his head, and a flourishing tree before him.	Hour of Luna, Luna ascending in the sign of its exaltation (Taurus).	Against weariness for travelers.
A horned woman[64] riding a bull, seven-headed dragon,[65] or a crab.[66] An arrow in her right hand, looking-glass in left. Clothed in white or green. On her head are two serpents with horns twined together, and on each arm and ankle a serpent twined about.	Hour of Luna, Luna ascending in first decan of Cancer.	Increase of the fruits of the Earth. Against poisons, and infirmities in children.

A Solomonic Talisman Depicting Metetron.

Such are the examples given by Agrippa. I have decided to exclude Chapters 45 through 47, as these chapters deal with the Lunar nodes, the twenty-eight mansions of the Moon, and the fixed stars. All of these are less used in modern astrological magick. In any case, the given examples are intended to illustrate the underlying logic that goes into the fashioning of such magickal images, so the reader can go on to create new and unique pieces. The step-by-step instructions given for magickal timing, as well as the list of planets and their powers, given in chapter 5 of this book are crucial to image magick. With the information given there as well as here, there should be no end to the magickal images one might create.

Also of importance are the talismans in such grimoires as the *Key* and *The Magus* that make use of the scriptural-image technique similar to Egyptian, Gnostic, and Christian practice. The technique is explained quite well in *The Magus*, Book II, Part II, nested in the middle "Of Magic Pentacles and their Composition." The text refers to magickal images used to empower talismans, and we can see that the focus is much more mythological than astrological:

> But the holy pictures which make the pentacles are they which every where are delivered to us in the prophets and sacred writings, both in the Old and New Testaments . . .

"Barrett" then goes on to elaborate with instructions that sound very much like Agrippa's teachings on how to create prayers (see chapter 7). One searches for biblical scenes that relate to the magickal goal, and the scenes are drawn and colored as talismanic images *as well* as the scripture being adopted into the prayers. A circle should be drawn around the image, and either proper divine names or the scripture itself can be written in the circumference. (Note again the similarity to the Talismans of the *Key of Solomon the King*.)

For instance, says Barrett, "if a pentacle were to be made to gain a victory, or revenge against one's enemies, as well visible as invisible, the figure may be taken out of the Second book of the *Maccabees*; that is to say, a hand holding a golden sword drawn, about which let there be written the versicle there contained, to wit, *take the holy*

The Lamb of the Revelation.

go sum A et Ω principium et finis
qui est et qui erat et qui venturus
est Omnipotens

go sum primus et novissimus et
vivus et fui mortuus et ecce sum
vivens in sæcula sæculorum et habeo
claves mortis et inferni

The Ruling Christ.

Image from the Ars Notoria.

sword, the gift of God, wherewith thou shalt slay the adversaries of my people Israel" (2 Maccabees 15:16, an apocryphal writing).

He goes on to outline two rather impressive magickal figures taken from the Revelation of Saint John; both suggested for use in the consecration of any experiment or summoning of any spirit:

> one whereof is that in the first chapter of the Apocalypse, to wit, a figure of the majesty of God sitting upon a throne, having in his mouth a two-edged sword, as there is described;[67] about which let there be written, "I am Alpha and Omega, the Beginning and the End, which is, and which was, and which is to come, the Almighty. I am the First and the Last, who am living, and was dead, and behold I live for ever and ever; and I have the keys of death and hell."[68] Then there shall be written about it these three versicles:
>
> Munda Deus Virtuti tuae, &c.—*Give commandment, O God, to thy strength; confirm, O God, thy strength in us. Let them be as dust before the face of the wind: and let the Angel of the Lord scatter them. Let all their ways be darkness and uncertain: and let the Angel of the Lord persecute them.*
>
> Moreover, let there be written about it the ten general names, which are *El, Elohim, Elohe, Zebaoth, Elion, Escerchie, Adonay, Jah, Tetragrammaton, Saday.*
>
> There is another pentacle, the figure whereof is like *a lamb slain, having seven eyes and seven horns; and under his feet a book sealed with seven seals*, as it is in the fifth chapter of the *Apocalypse*.[69] Round about let be written this versicle, *behold the lion hath overcome of the tribe of Judah, the root of David. I will open the book and unloose the seven seals thereof.*[70] And another versicle, *I saw Satan like lightning fall down from heaven. Behold I have given you power to tread upon serpents and scorpions, and over all the power of your enemies, and nothing shall be able to hurt you.*[71] And let there be also written about it the ten general names as aforesaid.

Another important example of medieval image magick is the text known as the *Ars Notoria*. As we learned in chapter 1, this book contains an extremely theurgic system of magick akin (in spiritual aims) to those in the *Book of Abramelin* or the *Sworn Book of Honorius*. It is an extended devotional operation that promises to result in the acquisition of all scholarly virtues, from memory to mathematics all the way to philosophy and theology. It achieves these goals through an ingenious mixture of prayer and magickal images, wherein the words are (in many cases) actually woven into the graphic of the image itself. To read the prayer, following all purification and preparation procedures, is to experience the magickal image.

However, these magickal images differ from our previous examples. They are neither astrological in nature nor do they depict iconographic scenes from scripture. Instead, they arose from the realm of education itself. It was common in the Middle Ages to utilize mnemonic pictograms and images to aid students in retaining written information. It was this era in which the "tree pattern" of organizing information became popular—used to show classifications of categories and subcategories.

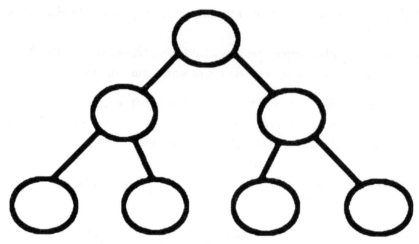

The Tree-Pattern.

(Such trees were used to diagram grammatical constructs, illustrate mathematical procedures, etc. The Qabalistic Tree of Life with which we are most familiar today is itself just such a "tree pattern," which finally explains why it in no way resembles an actual tree.) Geometric figures were also used to illustrate directly related classifications, such as arranging the four humors around the four points of a square (as we saw in chapter 3), or the five elements around a pentagram. Teachers had learned that associating the abstract concepts and words with figures and pictures (the natural alphabet of the human brain) greatly increased the faculty of learning.

The *Ars Notoria* simply took this concept to the next logical step, and refashioned it into a spiritual observance. All of the shamanic craft of ritual preparation and mind alteration (fasting, etc.) were added to the process, along with devout invocations for aid from the celestial beings. Whether we choose to view this from a psychological or spiritual perspective, we all must agree that these ritualized additions hold great potential for enhancing the effects such mnemonics were originally designed to produce.

So, these magickal images are drawn from the tradition of common visual learning aides. However, in the *Notary Arts*, they have mutated somewhat to better match the magickal nature of the material. Each image is in some way a depiction of the virtue described in the related prayer(s), several examples are guarded by depictions of armed angels, and unexplained sigils and barbarous names of invocation are prominent throughout the text. Nevertheless, the basic technique of the mnemonic images is retained in all cases.

It is here that we finally encounter the influence of the artist on medieval magickal practice. In fact, this entire chapter has represented some amount of that influence. Artists were just as interested in occult philosophy as were mathematicians or scribes.[72] Michael Camille, in his *Visual Art in Two Manuscripts of the Ars Nototia*,[73] points out that surviving texts of painters' recipe books and technical manuals resemble those of alchemists. And remember that the surviving copies of the *Notary Arts* most often seem to have been professionally executed, rather than drawn by the aspirant himself.

At the time, however, the painter did not enjoy any kind of official recognition; his vocation was unaccredited. In later years, during the educational reform movements of the Renaissance, the technical aspects of artistry (such as perspective drawing) came to hold a place of importance in scholarly pursuits. This brings to mind such men as Leonardo da Vinci.

It became very important to the Rosicrucian movement before and after 1613; a movement that was itself populated with artistic-minded alchemists. The mnemonic images underwent yet another evolution to finally become the famous Renaissance alchemical engravings.[74] (These are the magickal images from which, for instance, much

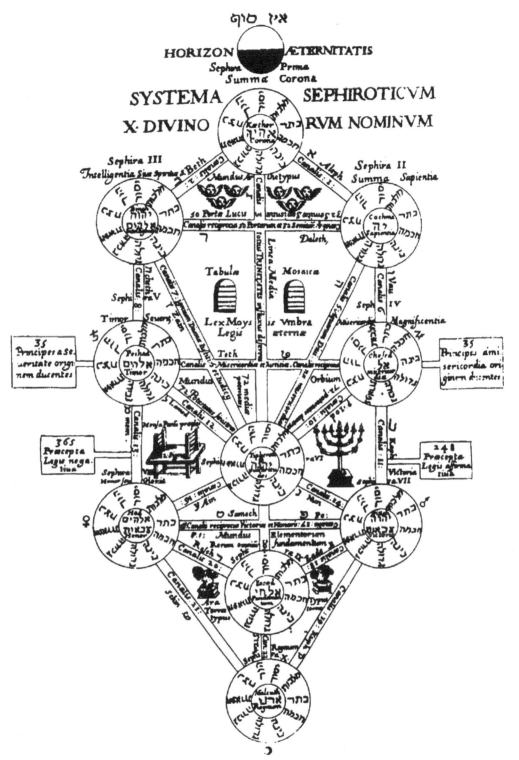

The Kircher Tree of Life.

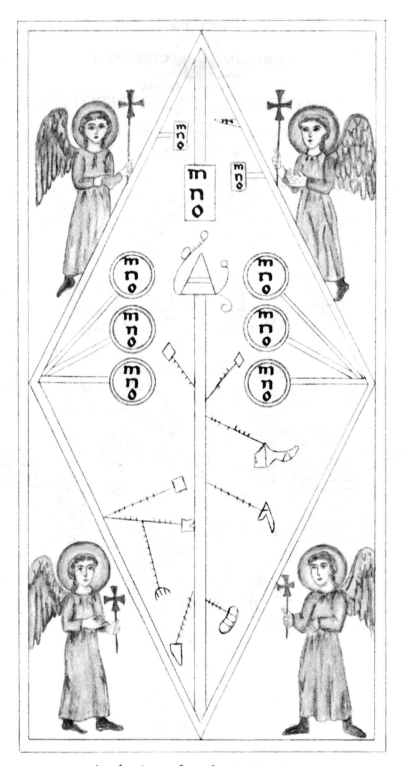

Another image from the Ars Notoria.

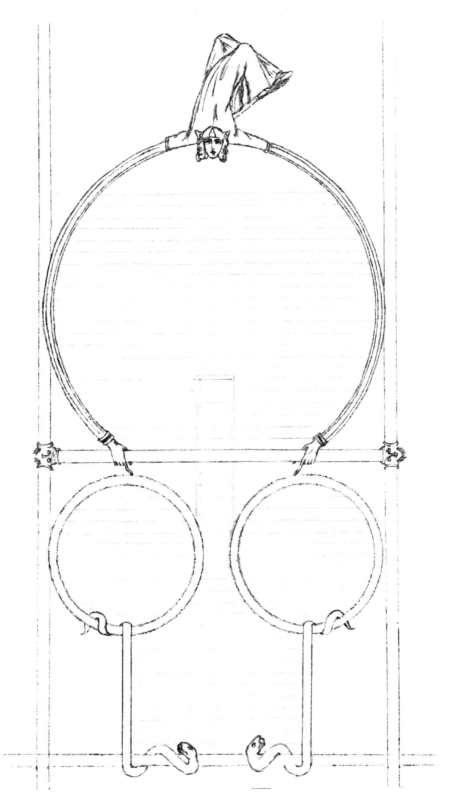

Another Notary Arts image.

Yet another Notary Arts image.

of our tarot imagery comes.) They were still employed as visual aides—each picture contained volumes of secret information—but they had by this point become intentionally created "media viruses." The engravers who made them and the printers who published them (a highly Rosicrucian lot) were intending to spread their philosophies as far and wide as possible "under the radar" of the Roman Church's Inquisition.[75]

Of Wax and Earth

The subject of image magick does not end with the iconographic arts. Before we can call this section complete, we are going to have to discuss magickal images fashioned of consecrated wax and earth (clay). These images—or figures—are more commonly known as "poppets," and were somewhat popularized through the medieval Church's Inquisitorial efforts. Many innocent women lost their lives for possession of such dolls, even when they were not intended for magick. A childhood doll used as a pincushion was quite enough to carry a death sentence in harsh political climates. Still, poppet magick was a common aspect of medieval European witchcraft and wizardry. It appears in the *Key of Solomon the King* (from which I pulled the instructions for consecrating earth and wax in chapter 9), as well as several works on spirit summoning or necromancy.

Outside of a few primitive examples of religious figurines,[76] the first fully sophisticated magickal figures seem to have come from the tombs of ancient Egyptian pharaohs. In order for the spirit of a pharaoh to continue living like a king in the afterlife, it was necessary to provide him with a full staff of workmen and servants. Thankfully, the Egyptian royalty does not seem to have practiced burying their poor slaves with themselves. Instead, the priests would populate the tomb with small humanoid magickal figures called *Ushabti*. Rather than serving as a dwelling for a particular god or Familiar spirit, the Ushabti figure was alive in its own right and inhabited by its own unique spirit. The funerary ceremonies of the *Book of the Dead* even include a speech given by the Ushabti as it pledges allegiance to the deceased.

Much later in history, we encounter the same idea in the creation of the Judaic golem, or even the Hermetic homonculus. These are a kind of homegrown Familiar spirit most often set to perform a singular task. Unlike the genie in a lamp or the spirit in a bottle, the golem and his cousins are not considered sentient and self-thinking. Once set to a task, the golem/Ushabti will perform that task to the exclusion of all else. It is this kind of magick that gives rise to "sorcerer's apprentice" stories of spells that work, and *keep working*, until they are shut off again. For instance, the golem, which was created to protect the Jewish citizens of Prague, caused much damage when it was left running past the time of its usefulness.

The magickal figures described in the grimoires are of three principal types. The first is merely talismanic, like the images we have already discussed, but sculpted in three dimensions rather than inscribed on paper or in a stone. The wax figure of a lion, for example, could be used in exactly the same way as the drawn image of a lion for Leo. A set of scales could be consecrated to Libra. An Egyptian-style scarab figure (easily purchased wherever Egyptian-theme gift shops are found) could be charged with the energies of Cancer, etc.

The second type of magickal figure was used in the process of exorcism. In this case, the image is made to symbolically represent an invading demon, similar to the symbolism used to construct the goetic spirit images as explained above. Once complete, the name of the spirit is inscribed upon the forehead of the figure in order to sympathetically link it to the spirit itself. The demon might be drawn into the figure and the figure disposed of, or the spirit might simply be driven away as various abuses are inflicted upon the figure, such as sticking the image with pins, hanging it over a flame, or sealing it in a box of stinking fumes (see chapter 12).

The third type of magickal figure is the most notorious and well-known example of poppet magick—known today as the "voodoo doll." This particular image was fashioned to resemble a human victim, and sympathetically linked to the victim by including hair, nail clippings, shreds of clothing, and/or other personal items owned by the spell's target. Finally, the name of the victim, rather than of a spirit, is inscribed upon the doll's forehead. (This practice derives principally from the golem legend. In order to bring the beast to life, the mage inscribed three Hebrew letters into its forehead: Aleph, Mem, and Tau. These spelled the Hebrew word for "truth": *Ameth*. In order to take the life away from the golem once more, the Aleph was erased from the forehead so that only Mem and Tau remained, spelling the Hebrew word *Mot* or *Maveth*—"dead.")

Then the doll is consecrated in the name of the victim, so that it exists as a miniature "version" of the human himself. Once complete, the mage could inflict the same punishments upon the image as he would to drive away a demon. In this case, however, the pain is supposed to transfer from the sympathetic image to the victim's guardian angel, and from thence to the hapless human.

Of course, this is a somewhat one-sided take on the "voodoo doll" concept. Once such a poppet is fashioned, there are no rules which state the image must be abused. Any kind of care, pleasure, healing, etc., might be just as easily applied to the poppet to the benefit of the "victim." The *Munich Handbook of Necromancy* contains two good examples.[77] In one, an image is fashioned to control wild or dangerous beasts (lions, wolves, bears, etc.). The name of the animal is inscribed upon the figure's head, the name and ruler of the proper magickal hour is inscribed upon its chest, and on its stomach the "seven names of the first hour." The image is then fumigated with Indian wood and red sandalwood, and buried in a place of the mage's choosing.

The second example is more elaborate, and is aimed at bringing concord between people. This involves at least two (or more) images cast in bronze or yellow wax. Or, if one wishes to create love between two people (say a man and woman), a pair of green wax figures are fashioned. The name of the man is inscribed upon the heart of the figure of the woman, while the name of the woman is inscribed upon the male figure's heart. Specific magickal timing is observed, and a conjuration is recited to empower the figures. Finally, as is common, the images are buried where the intended friends will pass.

Unfortunately, such benevolent uses for wax images gain less attention in the grimoiric literature. The *Munich Handbook* provides us with a particularly nasty example aimed at gaining the love of a woman.[78] First, the doll has to be made according to specific and complex rules. The mage must either make a set of nine needles, or have them made by a craftsman. (This latter is impossible unless one intends to let the craftsman in on the secret. He must be pure and wearing clean garments, and can make the needles only between the hours of Sol and Saturn.)

Then, on a Thursday or Sunday, at the hours of Venus or Jupiter, one is to melt virginal wax over burning coals. It must not be allowed to grow so hot that it smokes. For sympathy, the mage must obtain some hairs from the desired woman, along with three red hairs, and add them to the wax.

Later, (beginning at the hour of Jupiter and continuing until the hour of Saturn) the mage must take his companions and find a secluded fruit-bearing tree. There a magickal circle is inscribed upon the ground, and the wax is carved with a white-handled knife into the image of a woman. Then the nine needles are thrust into the figure in various places such as the head, heart, side, and even the anus(!). Various demons are called upon for the working of this magick, such as Belial, Astaroth,[79] and Paymon. As the needle is placed into the heart of the image, the mage proclaims:

> Just as this needle is fixed in the heart of this image, so may the love of N. be fixed to the love of N., so
> that she cannot sleep, wake, lie down, sleep, [or] walk until she burns with love of me.

After this, the image is baptized in the name of the victim. Three times it is immersed in holy water, each time with the question "How shall it be called?" followed by the victim's name as a response. After the third repeat of this, the mage states, "I baptize thee, N., in the name of the Father, and of the Son, and of the Holy Spirit. Amen." The image is then placed aside from the hour of Sol until the hour of Mars.

In order to cast the actual love spell, the mage must take the image back to the fruit tree, light the coals as he did to first melt the wax, face the east and recite a conjuration:

> O, N., I conjure your entire substance, that you may not sleep or sit or lie down or perform any work of craft until you have satisfied my libidinous desire . . . And as this wax melts before the face of the fire, so should N. [melt with] desire for my love . . .

This is obviously never a recommended course of action. The text suggests several signs the woman may show of the spell taking effect, such as lamenting, sleeplessness, solitude, or dizziness of the head.

This kind of experiment seems to have descended from the Greek magickal papyri. One example of such a Greek spell uses two figures of wax or clay: a kneeling woman with her arms bound behind her back, and an armed man behind her. (This is reminiscent of one of Agrippa's graphic images for Venus—see the charts above.) In this case, just as in the *Munich Handbook*, the female image is pierced through all of its limbs with needles while recitations are made so the intended woman will be "unable to drink or eat, that she cannot be contented, not be strong, not have peace of mind," etc.[80]

I should point out here that this process may actually sound worse than it was intended for practice. While the needles and other afflictions (such as the burning coals) visited upon the image may seem incredibly sadistic, it may very well be that no direct transfer of physical pain was intended by this magick. The piercing needles, the burning flame, and the like may all be sympathetic in their own right, meant to simulate the obsessive passions of lust. The human woman—dizzy, sleepless, and without appetite—might simply be experiencing a "sudden shock" of sexual frustration. The mage is merely attempting to awaken that lust, and assure himself that no man but himself will satisfy that feeling.

How to Render Oneself Invisible, from the Key of Solomon the King

Luckily, we can turn to the *Key of Solomon the King* for a much less hostile, if not less questionable, example of image magick. Book I, Chapter 10 (Lansdowne MS 1203), contains a simple spell titled "How to Render Oneself Invisible." Certainly a favorite of royal spies such as Henry Agrippa and John Dee!

In this example, one must take yellow wax and fashion a small image of a man (presumably of the mage himself). It must be done in January (most likely Capricorn) and in the day and hour of Saturn (which rules Capricorn). Cut off the top of the skull, inscribe the following magickal character inside with a consecrated needle, and replace the top again:

Then, upon a small strip made from the skin of a frog or toad one has killed oneself, write the following words and characters (presumably with a consecrated pen and ink):

At the hour of midnight, the completed figure must be suspended with one of the mage's own hairs in the vault of a cavern. It is then perfumed with "proper incense" (likely those related to Saturn) and a short invocation is recited:

> Metetron, Melekh, Beroth, Noth, Venibbeth, Mach, and all ye, I conjure thee, O Figure of wax, by the Living God, that by the virtue of these Characters and words, thou render me invisible, wherever I may bear thee with me. Amen.

Once complete, the figure must be buried in a small box in that very same place. When the mage wishes to go invisible, he only has to retrieve the image, place it in his left pocket, and say: "Come unto me and never quit me withersoever I shall go." When it is no longer needed, it must be replaced in its box in the cavern and covered with earth once more.

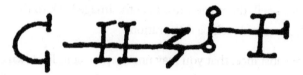

Wax Sigil for Invisibility.

Sigils for the Frog-skin.

Agrippa also gives quite a few examples in his *Occult Philosophy* Book II. Two of them occur with the images of Saturn (Chapter 38), though I did not include them with the tables of graphical images. These are magickal figures of a very sophisticated type.

The first is an "image of melted copper" fashioned when Saturn ascends the eastern horizon or better still when Saturn ascends into the first degree of Capricorn. (More *Abramelin*-style magickal timing.) This image is "affirmed," says Agrippa, to speak with a man's voice. Donald Tyson suspects this sounds "very much like yet another oracular brazen head, which was usually associated with Saturn."[81] Actual mummified heads do appear in Hebraic and other Middle Eastern legend often enough, along with the later decadent brazen versions. These ancestral-magick holdovers were said to be animated by small brass plates inscribed with the "Hidden Name of God" (Tetragrammaton) and placed under the dead tongues. They were silenced by removing the plate. In fact, the process is extremely similar to that applied to the golem in later Jewish legend.

Agrippa's second Saturnine magickal figure is also an oracular image—cast in metal to resemble a "beautiful man." (It is conceivable that this figure is also merely a head.) Once exposed to the right arrangement of stars, it is said to "foretell things to come" and to "speak with men and declare those things which are profitable for them." The astrological time given for the fashioning/consecration is incredibly complex, and seems to assure us that few will ever live to experiment with the technique: it must be made on the day and hour of Mercury, on the third hour of Saturn, the sign of Gemini ascending. (Gemini is ruled by Mercury, and signifies prophets.) Saturn and Mercury must be in conjunction with one another in Aquarius, and all three must rest in the ninth House (called "God"—see chapter 5). Saturn must further have a trine aspect on the Ascendant and the Moon. The Sun should "have an aspect on the place of conjunction" and "Venus obtaining some angle may be powerful and occidental." Mars must be in combustion(!) with the Sun, but cannot have an aspect with either Saturn or Mercury. Good luck, intrepid mage!

As usual, Agrippa makes sure to place the most stress upon the magickal timing involved in the creation of his images:

> So great is the extent, power, and efficacy of the celestial bodies, that not only natural things, but also artificial when they are rightly exposed to those above, do presently suffer by that most potent agent, and obtain a wonderful life, which oftentimes gives them an admirable celestial virtue. . . . even garments, buildings and other artificial works whatsoever, do receive a certain qualifications from the stars. . . . being opportunely framed under a certain constellation, some celestial illustration may be taken, and some wonderful thing may be received; for the beams of the celestial bodies being ani-

mated, living, sensual, and bringing along with them admirable gifts, and a most violent power, do, even in a moment, and at the first touch, imprint wonderful powers in the images . . . (*Three Books, Book II, Chapter 35, "How Some Artificial Things as Images, Seals, and Such Like may Obtain Some Virtue from the Celestial Bodies"*)

A magickal image is not a seal with a spirit invoked and bound to it. Instead, the magickal image is a living thing unto itself, born at the moment of its construction and consecration. Like all things that are born, it has its own natal horoscope that indicates its general nature. Of course, in the case of any talisman or magickal image, one can choose that moment of birth through the process of magickal timing.

For instance, take the story of the thirteenth-century astrologer Guido Bonatti and an impoverished apothecary with whom he sometimes played chess.[82] The astrologer took pity on the poor man and made for him a small wax magickal image in the shape of a ship. Bonatti told him that he would become rich so long as he kept the ship hidden safely away, but that if he removed it from its box he would lose his fortune. The magickal image did its job, and the apothecary soon grew rich. However, the occult source of his riches was a matter of worry for his Christian mind, and he eventually confessed to a priest who instructed him to destroy the image. The apothecary followed this advice, destroyed the wax ship, and eventually returned to poverty. Of course, he went again to Bonatti in the hopes of obtaining another magickal image. However, of supreme importance in the creation of the image was the astrological timing. The necessary configuration of stars was not due to recur for fifty years, and the apothecary was simply out of luck.

In order to accomplish such magickal enlivening, the mage must first understand his own inherent ability to create life. This concept is actually an aspect of the Semitic mysticism that was adopted into the grimoiric traditions. It is based primarily on two specific quotations from the book of Genesis:

And God said, "Let us make man in Our image, after Our likeness . . ." (Genesis 1:26)
And the Lord God formed man of the dust of the ground, and breathed into his nostrils the Breath of
Life; and man became a living soul. (Genesis 2:7)

Because man was made after the image of God, both Jewish and Christian mystics recognized that we alone among animals have the power of creation. (Compare this to our earlier discussion about mankind possessing the Logos.) It is only for this reason that we enjoy magickal power. It is considered a birthright granted to mankind at the very creation of Adam, a power transferred to us by the breath of life that first animated us as human beings. It came with our harnessing of fire, our development of language, and with all of those things that made man a god (a creative force) upon this planet.[83]

But who can give a soul to an image, or make a stone to live, or metal, or wood, or wax? And who can raise out of stones children unto Abraham? Certainly this arcanum doth not enter into an artist of a stiff neck: neither can he give those things which hath them not. Nobody hath them but he who doth (the elements being restrained, nature being overcome, the heavens being overpowered) transcend the progress of Angels, and comes to the very Archetype itself, of which being then made a cooperator may do all things, as we shall speak afterwards. (*Three Books of Occult Philosophy*, Book II, Chapter 50)

This is the theory behind the creation and enlivening of any magickal object—from talismans and images to the famous Jewish golem.[84] Life is breathed into these things by way of the spoken prayers and invocations used to consecrate and awaken them, and this only has effect when performed by a master who has restrained the Elements, overcome nature, overpowered the heavens, and transcended the realm of the angels to meet face to face with God.[85]

In any case, it is the natal/hoary magickal timing that determines the nature of the entity thus created. Agrippa offers a good bit of practical instruction in Book II, Chapter 50, "Of Certain Celestial Observations and the Practice of Some Images." Therein, he gives several examples of magickal images and their necessary magickal timing. I've condensed the information into the following entries:

To Make Anyone or Any Place Fortunate

Make an image in which the following astrological considerations are all in fortunate aspect: the significator of life,[86] the givers of life,[87] the signs, the planets, the Ascendant, the mid-heaven, the ruling planets thereof, the places of the Sun and Moon, the Part of Fortune, and the lord of conjunction or prevention.

To Procure Misery

The converse of the above directions.

For Destroying or Prejudicing Any Person or Place

Make an image under the ascending sign of the man you would destroy. Make unfortunate the lord (ruling planet) of the house of his life, the lord of the Ascendant, the Moon, the lord of the house of the Moon, the ruling planet of the house of the lord of the Ascendant, the tenth house (career and public life), and the lord of the tenth house.

For the Fitting (to Prepare or Make Acceptable) of Any Place

Make an image with the fortunes[88] in the Ascendant. The lords of the Ascendant and of the house of the Moon must also be fortunate—and Agrippa seems to indicate that these two planets must also fall within first, tenth, second, or eighth houses. Otherwise, Agrippa is merely indicating that all of these houses must also be fortunate in their own right.

To Chase Away Certain Animals from Certain Places

Make an image of the animal in question, under the sign of its Ascendant. For example, to chase away scorpions: make an image of a scorpion, the sign of Scorpius ascending with the Moon. Make unfortunate the Ascendant, the lord of the Ascendant, and the lord of the house of Mars. Apparently, the lord of the Ascendant should rest in the eighth house (to keep the animals from propagating), and should also be in an unfortunate aspect such as opposition or square. Upon the image, write the name of the Ascendant, the lord of the Ascendant, the Moon, and the lords of the day and hour (see the table of planetary hours in chapter 5). Agrippa then instructs: "Let there be a pit made in the middle of the place, from which thou wouldst drive them; and let there be carried into it, some of the earth taken out of the four corners of the same place, and let the image be buried there with the head downward, with saying, this is the burying of the scorpions, that they may not come into this place . . ."

For Gain

Make an image under the Ascendant of the nativity of the man or place to be made gainful. The lord of the second house (substance) should be joined to the lord of the Ascendant in a trine or sextile aspect—and there should be "reception" among them.[89] The eleventh house, its ruling planet, and the eighth house should all be fortunate. The Part of Fortune should be in the Ascendant or the second house (material assets). Have the image buried in, or carried from, the place to which you would appoint the gain.

For Concord and Love

For this, two magickal images must be created. The first is made in the day of Jupiter under the Ascendant of the person you would have be beloved. The Ascendant and tenth house (long-range goals) must be fortunate.[90] The lord of the tenth house and the planets residing in the eleventh house (friendship) should be joined in trine or sextile aspect, and in reception with one another.

Then make a second image for the person in whom one would stir up love or friendship. If this party is a friend of the one to be beloved, Agrippa instructs us to make the image "under the ascension of the eleventh House from the Ascendant of the first image." I take this to mean that, having calculated the Ascendant of the first image, one should then wait for the sign of the eleventh house (friendship) to itself become the Ascendant. (This will, of course, occur sometime during the same day.) However, if the second party is a wife or husband to the first party, the image should be made under the ascension of the sign of the seventh house (marriage). If the second party is a blood relative such as a brother, sister, or cousin, the second image should be fashioned under the ascension of the third house (which includes siblings), and so on . . . In all cases, the significator of the Ascendant sign of the first image should be joined to the significator of the Ascendant sign in the second—with reception between them. All other aspects must be fortunate as in the first image.

After the images are complete, join them together in a mutual embrace,[91] or put the face of the second image to the back of the first, wrap them in silk, and let them be "cast away or spoiled."

For Success of Petitions and for the Obtaining of Anything Denied, Taken or Possessed by Another

Here again two magickal images are necessary. Make an image under the Ascendant of he who is making the petition. The lord of the second house (material assets) should be joined to the lord of the Ascendant in a trine or sextile aspect, and there should be reception between them. If possible, the lord of the second house should be in an "obeying sign" and the lord of the Ascendant in a "commanding sign."[92] The Ascendant and its ruling planet must both be fortunate, and take care that the ruler is not in retrograde, combustion, in falling dignity, or in the house of opposition to the Ascendant (i.e., the seventh from his own house). Both the lord of the second house and the Moon must also be fortunate.

The second image is made for the person to whom the petition is being made (or who possesses the object in question). If he is a king, prince, or someone in such official authority, it should be made when the tenth house (superiors, authority figures) ascends sometime after the Ascendant of the first image. If he is the petitioner's father, wait until the fourth house (family, father) ascends. If he is the son, wait until the ascension of the fifth house (children), and so on . . . The significator of the second image should be joined to the lord of the Ascendant of the first image in a trine or sextile aspect. They should both be fortunate and strong, and in reception with one another. If possible, the tenth and/or fourth houses should be fortunate.

Then, join these two images together face to face, wrap them in clean linen, and bury them in the middle of the petitioner's house under a strong significator and the Part of Fortune being strong. The face of the first image should be either toward the north, or toward the direction where the thing desired resides. Or, if the petitioner is going to meet the person, have him carry the images with him.

For Prophetic Dreams

Fashion a figure of a man sleeping in the bosom of an angel. It must be made when Leo is ascending, and the Sun resides in the ninth house in Aries. On the breast of the man, write the name of the effect desired, and in the hand of the angel the name of the intelligence of the Sun (Nakhiel). Put this image under the pillow when sleeping.

The exact same image can also be made under various other astrological conditions. It can be made with Virgo ascending, and Mercury being fortunate in Aries in the ninth house. If made when Gemini ascends, Mercury should be fortunate in Aquarius in the ninth house. In both cases the planet Saturn should be in reception with Mercury, and in fortunate aspect. The name of the intelligence of Mercury (Tiriel) should be written in the hand of the angel.

If the image is made with Libra ascending, Venus should be with Gemini in the ninth house, and in reception with Mercury. The intelligence of Venus (Hagiel) should be written in the angel's hand.

If the image is made with Aquarius ascending, Saturn should be exalted in Libra in the ninth house. The intelligence of Saturn (Agiel) should be written in the angel's hand.

Finally, Agrippa suggests making one with Cancer ascending, and the Moon in fortunate aspect in Pisces in the ninth house. The Moon should be in reception with Jupiter (in Cancer) and with Venus in Pisces. Write the intelligence of the Moon (Malkah . . .) in the hand of the angel.

As one becomes familiar with the zodiacal signs and their ruling planets, the pattern of the above magickal timing will become clear.

Consecration of Images

I have several times witnessed the consecration of icons for the Eastern Orthodox Christian faith. Previous to these experiences, I had suspected complex and hidden rituals meant to enliven the images and invoke the archangels into them. While the mysteries involved in their creation are certainly many and deep, the consecration itself was very straightforward. It needed only to be placed upon the altar during a ceremonial observance, such as holy communion. A properly designed icon opened to the divine in this way cannot help but accept habitation by its angel. Once again we see the traces of Agrippa's assertion that anything bearing the seal or image of an angel will be inhabited by that angel.

Very little is said of actual consecration of magickal images in the grimoiric literature. One will, of course, have to prepare and consecrate all materials beforehand, as well as prepare the sacred space and undergo purification. Then, short invocations and Psalms are recited as the image is created, and/or at various stages of the image's creation. This, too, is a very shamanic process. Once it is complete, the image might be sprinkled and/or censed (such as in the *Key*) and put away in some way like the magickal book.

Overall, the instructions for consecration of images would not differ from those for consecration of talismans already given in this chapter. You must simply consider your magickal timing (which can be as simple or complex as you dare), choose appropriate Psalms, and write a relevant invocation or series of invocations. If all else fails, return to chapter 8 and summon the related angel for instruction.

---

1. With this, and the following Santerian teachings, compare the explanation of ancestor worship in chapter 4.

2. Note also the importance of mountains to the spirituality of most early cultures, such as Mt. Olympus for the Greeks, Mt. Sinai for the Israelites, and the pyramids and ziggurats used by such peoples as the Egyptians, Babylonians, Aztecs, etc.

3. Note also that this aptly describes how the process is followed to this very day in Santeria and related faiths.

4. Note the incident of the Golden Calf in Exodus. This is likely a record of Canaanite, or perhaps Egyptian, worship among the Israelites. The Hebrew religion retained an echo of this in its use of the horned altar, and several other instances where oxen symbology is prominent.

5. More than likely the meat would be eaten, perhaps as part of a religious feast, etc.

6. This is often described as any wood that smells sweet, such as cedar. However, this is not likely the case. In the late 1500s, the word "sweet" was used to refer to taste rather than smell. The term "sweetwood," then, would indicate a syrup—or fruit wood—such as maple, apple, cherry, etc.

7. A similar discussion can be found at the beginning of chapter 6 concerning magickal tools.

8. Or perhaps a mixture of copper and silver. I have also seen pewter suggested, not for its lead and tin, but for the fact that it is a mixture (alloy) of metals.

9. Later Rosicrucian philosophy often referred to the "Characters of Nature" having been inscribed by the finger of God.

10. Revelation 5:2.

11. As an example of this, consider the slave girl Tituba as depicted in *The Crucible*. The entire Salem witch-hunting incident was precipitated by her observing her island faith in the woods, where she was discovered by ignorant Christians.

12. Compare this to the "Ethiopian" *Book of Enoch*—the product of an enslaved Hebrew people, and the origin of the typical apocalyptic "God will destroy our oppressors" theology such as seen in the Revelation of St. John.

13. The talismans in the first part of the *Pauline Art* display specific astrological configurations rather than hieroglyphic symbols.

14. Mathers gave ". . . transplanting both health and mental force."

15. Specifically the pentagram and hexagram and "Secret Seal" of Solomon.

16. Ten is the number of the Qabalistic Sephiroth (heavenly spheres).

17. This was likely adopted from Gnosticism, though Agrippa rightly enough attributes it to Egyptian and Arabic mysticism.

18. The Qabalist will understand: Kether is in Malkuth, and Malkuth is in Kether.

19. Once again the shamanic concept of receiving magickal teaching directly from spiritual patrons.

20. The same instructions are repeated verbatim in Book I, Chapter 5.

21. Not to mention that here the text allows one to make the pentacles of metal, rather than strictly the virgin paper mentioned previously.

22. I have yet to discover the precise meaning of this term. A "day" in astrology is the same as a "degree" of the zodiacal chart—and the author of the *Key* does use the latter word in a later example. However, I am unsure as to what the Sun and Moon must be equal in relation.

23. The mixed colors are symbolic of alchemical Mercury. Spirit, essence, etc. Consider that pure white light is a mixture of all colors of the spectrum.

24. I have seen an alloy of copper and silver suggested for this, as well as pewter, an alloy of lead and tin.

25. Specifically Lansdowne MSS 1202, and 1203.

26. I should point out that this has merely been an overview of the practice of Solomonic talismanic magick. We do not have space here to enter into the actual content of the pentacles found in the *Key*. They are composed of an incredible mixture of sacred scripture, geometry, gematria, geomancy, and even image magick (see below). The subject certainly deserves a study completely unto itself.

27. We can also see how deeply the ancient Sumerian-Babylonian traditions affected even more well-known systems such as Gnosticism, *Merkavah*, and any such system that assigns gods or angels to heavenly stations.

28. Perhaps because this is easier to work with than iron? (The mixture of copper and silver is more usually suggested in place of Mercury. This is an ambiguity in the text of the *Goetia*.)

29. Outside of the circle where the spirits will appear. See chapter 12.

30. Or a copy thereof.

31. Emphasis mine.

32. The first hour of the day begins at sunrise. See chapter 5 for instructions on calculating the length of magickal hours from sunrise to sunset.

33. This information is hidden in the entry for the angel of the second hour of the day: Anael.

34. See Mitch Hensen's *Lemegaton, the Complete Lesser Key of Solomon*, p. 77 (Capricorn, Column 10.)

35. In other words: angels. Note the shamanic reference to the angels as existing in a "higher order," the celestial realm above mankind.

36. Remember the numbers given for the planets. For example, a Solar talisman would display a hexagram (six-pointed star), because the number of Sol is 6.

37. *Rotas* appropriately means "revolution."

38. The Hebrew letters of these verses are also incorporated into the bodies of the talismans, utilizing a fascinating mixture of gematria and geometry.

39. This reminds me somewhat of John Dee's seal of truth, made from fresh bee's wax with traces of honey within.

40. Here is another instance of an angel being referred to as a "star." See chapter 2.

41. The reference to a "fortunate planet" is obviously astrological. As I suggested in chapter 5, the planet associated with the entity in question should be in fortunate aspect, above the horizon, etc.

42. As previously stated, I am unsure of the proper meaning of this term.

43. Thanks to Bick Thomas for his research into the subject of medieval image magick, some of which is included here.

44. The text actually says: "Buer. A great President and appeareth in Sagittarius. That is his shape when the Sun is there."

45. Note the Strength card of the tarot, as well as Crowley's own version thereof titled "Lust." Reference also the biblical book of Revelation, wherein the Whore of Babylon is depicted as riding upon the Beast of the Apocalypse.

46. In Jewish scripture, certain words (such as the name of God: JHVH) are not to be spoken aloud. Therefore, other words must be substituted for them when the texts are read aloud. In order to help remind the reader to do this, the vowel-points from the substitute word are placed into the scriptural text around the letters of the taboo word. This convention was not understood by the original Christian

translators of the Bible, who mistook these hybrid words as singular names. The combination of Astarte and the vowel-points of Tho-abath resulted in "Astaroth."

47. It is a little-known fact that the pentagram did not arise as a mystical symbol until mankind discovered astronomy. Venus appears above the horizon in exactly five places throughout the year. If we were to mark each point around the horizon and then connect the dots, we would end up with the figure of the pentagram. For this reason the five-pointed star has long been a symbol of the mother.

48. Again note the serpent in the figure's right hand. Masturbation is hardly a sexual negative today, but keep in mind that the *Goetia* is a medieval Christian text.

49. Remember the discrepancy between the attributions of the goetic spirits and their Arabic originals.

50. See "English Manuscripts of Magic, 1300–1500: A Preliminary Survey" by Frank Klaasen, published in *Conjuring Spirits*, edited by Claire Fanger.

51. See chapter 3 for some explanation of this kind of medieval medical terminology.

52. These are the exact same robes described in the *Book of Abramelin*. Mathers explains them as the Rosicrucian magickal garb.

53. It may be that the application of the image for the second decan of Taurus is also intended for the first.

54. In other words: slight-of-hand artists, stage magicians, etc.

55. Agrippa calls this a "buckler" in the text.

56. Peopling = populating an area.

57. The text is unclear on whether this is one image or two.

58. Note the magickal image of the Saturnine angel Cassiel (chapter 8), who is also sitting on a dragon.

59. Working planetary magick when the necessary planet is ascending is very similar to the method of magickal timing outlined by *Abramelin* (see chapter 5 of this work).

60. This possibly means a piece of lapis lazuli

61. Kidney stones, and perhaps gallstones as well.

62. Apparently this was once an image of the god Jupiter himself. Later, we see the same imagery in the Icon of the archangel Michael defeating Satan (depicted as a dragon).

63. In a footnote to Agrippa's text, Tyson gives some examples of what "balantine stone" might be. It may be *Lapis Judaicus* (Jewstone)—which is either the fossilized spine of a large Syrian sea urchin, or a silver colored iron-pyrite.

64. The horns, or antlers, are symbolic of the lunar phases. This is very similar to the modern Wiccan concept of the Horned God.

65. See the book of the Revelation of St. John.

66. Luna rules Cancer.

67. Revelation 1:12–16.

68. Revelation 1:8, 17–18 (Verse 19 is rather amazing from the standpoint of image magick: "Write the things which thou hast seen . . ." This is an exciting verse for one who works magick based upon biblical authority, and who looks for "hidden instructions" in the Scriptures.)

69. Revelation 5:6–8 (The Lamb opens each seal of the book between Chapters 6 and 8.)

70. Revelation 5:5.

71. Luke 10:18–19.

72. This is not an entirely new concept—we encountered the influence of the musician in chapter 4, concerning the Psalms.

73. *Conjuring Spirits*, p. 111.

74. These deeply occult pictures (or at least their style) will be familiar to any student of European history. Most of our world's preeminent scholars and scientists have traditionally been mystics and alchemists as well. We are most often presented with these images with little to no explanation.

75. Once again I highly recommend *The Rosicrucian Enlightenment* by Frances Yates.

76. Such as the "Venus of Willendorf," which dates to about 24,000–22,000 BCE.

77. *Forbidden Rites*, pp. 178–9.

78. *Forbidden Rites*, p. 87.

79. Considering what we learned of Astaroth earlier in this chapter, his appearance here makes perfect sense.

80. *Forbidden Rites*, p. 88.

81. *Three Books*, Llewellyn Edition, p. 382, note 5.

82. "English Manuscripts of Magic, 1300–1500: A Preliminary Survey" by Frank Klaasen, *Conjuring Spirits*, ed. Claire Fanger. p. 4.

83. Please see *Semitic Magic* by R. C. Thompson for a wonderful discussion of the origins and development of this mystical "man as image of God" concept.

84. The golem is brought to life via a ceremony that mimics Yahweh's creation of Adam in Genesis 2.

85. See chapters 3, 4, and 8 for discussions of spiritual authority, and the shaman-mage's exalted rank among celestial beings. Herein lies the mystery behind this magick.

86. Donald Tyson explains this as the "prorogator." It is the planet or part of the heavens in a natal chart that becomes the moderator and significator of life. It is utilized to determine the number of years a subject has to live.

87. These are those planets (beneficent and malefic) that rule the length of life in relation to the prorogator (the significator of life).

88. Jupiter (the greater fortune) and/or Venus (the lesser fortune).

89. Meaning that each planet rests within the zodiacal sign that the other rules. For example, when Mars rests in Cancer and Luna rests in Scorpio, there is reception between Mars and Luna.

90. Agrippa also says that the "evil" (unfortunate) must be "hidden" from the Ascendant—though I cannot say what he could mean by this.

91. Assuming these images are figures of wax, earth, etc.

92. Donald Tyson explains that obeying and commanding signs are applied to the divisions of the zodiac, which are disposed at an equal distance from the same equinoctial sign (Aries or Libra), because they ascend in equal periods of time and are on equal parallels. Those in the summer hemisphere are commanding, and those in the winter hemisphere are obedient. Therefore, excluding the equinoctial signs of Aries and Libra, the pairs of obeying and commanding signs are:

Commanding	Obeying
Taurus	Pisces
Gemini	Aquarius
Cancer	Capricornus
Leo	Sagittarius
Virgo	Scorpius

Magickal Tools Part III: Tools of Protection, Weapons of Command (Goetic)

This chapter includes the tools and weapons associated with goety, or spirit work. Guarding against the negative effects that accompany the appearance of the spirits is given some importance in the grimoires. The texts constantly warn against the horrible appearances, noxious breath, scorching fires, terrible screams, and other shocking imagery that can assail an exorcist. More than likely, this imagery is as metaphorical as the celestial flight described in relation to shamanic ecstasy (see chapter 3). As we have discussed previously, to evoke the presence of a spiritual intelligence is equal to inviting a particular influence into one's life. One who wishes to work with the lower forces of nature (i.e., demons, jinni, etc.) must beware of activating the most animal aspects of his own spirit.[1]

As we will see in chapter 12, the conjuration of spirits is, in fact, a form of spiritual animal taming. Therefore, we might note that the related tools are all aimed at the protection of the working exorcist, or at asserting his command over the infernal and earthly forces. They serve as a kind of firewall between the exorcist and the infernal forces he wishes to control. (Somewhat akin to the lion tamer's whip and chair. Take special note of the disk of Solomon described in this chapter.)

In some cases, as with the hexagram and secret seal of Solomon below, the tools are actually talismans that grant authority to the mage—the seal of the king discussed in previous chapters. The belief that even infernal spirits will bow to the authority of God descends from Judaic roots. Within Judaism, there is no concept of rebel angels and spirits. All things in creation, both pleasant and noxious, are ultimately under the authority of the same all-encompassing God. This philosophy fits very well into the Neoplatonism that rests behind the grimoiric traditions.

As in the previous two chapters on magickal tools, I have continued to draw from the *Key of Solomon the King* in this chapter. The standard complement of goetic tools will, of course, also include all of the tools and vestments from chapter 6. It is, after all, from the celestial powers that the shaman-mage draws his authority.

However, I have relied even more upon the tools of the *Goetia*, because that has become the quintessential text of spirit conjuration for the grimoiric tradition. I will offer an overview of the *Goetia's* magickal procedure in chapter 12, and the descriptions of the tools here will help in the understanding of that material. Plus, there is no reason why those same tools cannot have applications outside the *Goetia*. They have, after all, been borrowed time and time again in the grimoiric texts which followed. Some of them even appear, along with several goetic conjurations, in a watered-down form in Barrett's *The Magus*.

The Black-Hilted Knife

This weapon appears in the *Key of Solomon the King*, Book II, Chapter 8 (Of the Knife, Sword . . . and other Instruments of Magical Art). I feel it is mostly unnecessary to go into depth on the relationship between the black-hilted knife and the Wiccan athame. I only need to point out that this is the direct source of the description, form, and the magickal characters upon the traditional Neopagan instrument.[2]

The two only differ in the manner of their consecration. In the tradition of Gardnerian Wicca, a spiritual line of descent is created from one dagger to the next; from initiator to initiated. Anything more I could say would merely be repeating the work of Janet and Stewart Farrar, as found in *A Witches' Bible*, and their chapter on magickal tools.

The black-hilted knife of Solomon, on the other hand, is a shamanic instrument intended to inscribe magickal circles and to command and evoke respect from animalistic spirits. What you are going to read below would be quite against the tenets of Wicca and other forms of Neopaganism. The recipe calls for the blood of a black cat. In order to avoid further redundancy, I will simply refer the reader to chapter 4's sections on the "Role of the Priest" and "Sacrifice in the Grimoires." The black-hilted knife is mentioned directly in the latter section. Some discussion is also made of this subject in chapter 6, concerning the white-hilted knife.

This particular knife is consecrated in the same manner as the white-hilted knife, with only a few differences according to the unique nature of each blade. See chapter 6 for some short discussion on the creation of the blade itself: either forging the metal oneself or simply purchasing a suitable knife. Both contingencies are allowed according to the *Key*.

In order to consecrate the knife, it should be the day and hour of Saturn with the Moon waxing or full. Further, the planet Mars should rest in the sign of Aries or Scorpius—both of which it rules. Saturn—the earthiest of the planets—is the primary focus of this consecration because the black-hilted knife is used exclusively for working with earthbound spirits. The knife is used to inscribe the protective circle into the earth—and so the unyielding

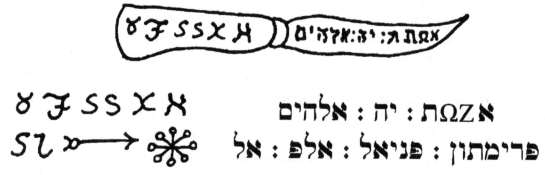

The Black-hilted Knife.

force of Saturn is necessary for the job. (Notice, also, that the Goetia uses a Triangle—the traditional shape of Saturn—in order to contain its spirits.)

However, the dignified position of Mars is also necessary for many of the same reasons. The black-hilted knife of Saturn works hand-in-hand with the Solomonic sword of Mars. Compare this to the secret seal of Solomon from the *Goetia*, which displays the symbols for both Saturn and Mars together. Like the knife and sword, the seal is intended to strike awe into the spirits and compel them to obey.

All of this is taken from astrology, where Mars and Saturn are the most forceful and dangerous of the planets. They represent, more than anything else, great authority; Saturn is the all-powerful Chronos, grandfather of the gods. Mars is the god of warfare, conquest, and the subjugation of enemies. These are the two forces invoked by most tools intended to command goetic entities.

The blade must be dipped in a mixture of the blood of a black cat and hemlock juice.[3] This can be done a single time to temper the metal if one is forging the blade oneself. If the blade is purchased, the handle should be removed, and the metal should be heated until it turns red and then plunged into the mixture, for a total of three heatings and immersions. Once complete, use the burin of the art to inscribe the names AZOTh, Yah (י ה), and Elohim (א ל ה י מ) into one side of the blade, writing the Hebrew from the point of the blade to the hilt. Upon the other side, inscribe the names Primeumaton[4] (פ ר י מ ת ו נ), Pheniel (פ נ י א ל), Aleph (א), and El (א ל). The hilt itself should be painted black, and then marked (probably in white paint) with the characters shown in the above illustration—one line upon each side.

Dip the completed hilt into the same fluid as the blade. Take the finished knife, cense it with the perfumes of the art, sprinkle it with the aspergillum and holy water, and wrap it in consecrated black silk. (Remember, in chapter 6 we discussed that this blade—which is specifically intended for infernal uses—is the only tool wrapped in black silk.)

The Solomonic Sword

The Solomonic or magickal sword is *the* classical weapon for wielding command authority over lower spirits. In a sense, even the black-hilted knife is merely a miniature version of the sword. It is like the lion tamer's whip, which allows the tamer to meet the wild animals fang for fang.

Yet, as we will see in chapter 12, even the grimoires warn against the excessive use of force against spirits. Overall, the sword is used in a defensive manner. It is generally necessary to simply hold on to the drawn sword during the evocation and interrogation of the spiritual entities. If the mage needs to reach outside the bounds of the circle for some reason (such as to offer a contract to an entity), it is generally the sword which actually passes the boundary.

Of course, the wand can also be used for this and nearly every use associated with the magickal sword. The *Book of Abramelin* seems to agree, and does not include a sword among its required magickal tools. The wand of almond wood serves all purposes where commanding the spirits is concerned.

However, the sword plays a more important role in the Solomonic and other grimoiric literature. Medieval European culture was staunchly paternalistic (father- or male-oriented), and had evolved from a long tradition of the warriors' arts. The grimoires themselves draw heavily from the Middle Eastern traditions: Chaldean, Arabian, and Judaic—all warrior cultures themselves. The sword was not important in the earliest tribal cultures, but became vital to the life of the agricultural human, who had to defend his crops from raiding tribes of nomads.

Once the sword became indispensable to daily survival it could not be long before it found a place in magickal tradition. The shaman whose job was to defend his people from hostile spirits would only naturally adopt the sword into his arsenal. Jewish legend tells of Methuselah—the son of Enoch, and grandfather of Noah—slaying thousands of demons a day with a sword inscribed with the name of God. (Asmodeus, the king of demons, finally

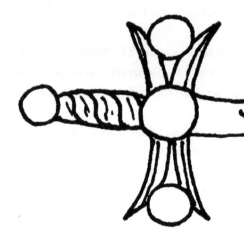

יהוה : אדני : אהיה : ייאי
אלהים גבור

The Solomonic Sword.

appeared to him and promised to offer a list of every existing demon if Methuselah would stop his attacks. This sounds very similar to the story of the *Testament of Solomon*, which we will see in chapter 12.) Thus, we can see how the goetic arts and the sword have long been associated.

The Solomonic sword appears in the *Key*, Book II, Chapter 8 (Of the Knife, Sword . . . and other Instruments of Magical Art). Thankfully, the author of the text did not expect us to forge our own battle-ready sword. Instead, one must simply take a new sword and clean and polish it. This must be done on a Wednesday as usual—on the first hour (sunrise) or fifteenth hour (approximately 3 am), which are both hours of Mercury. The burin of art will also be needed, along with the censer and incense, aspergillum and holy water, and a large piece of consecrated silk.

With the burin, inscribe the divine names Yod Heh Vav Heh (ה ו ה י), Adonai (י נ ד א), Eheieh (ה י ה א), and Aye (א י), on one side of the blade. On the other side, inscribe the name Elohim Gibor (ר ו ב ג ם י ה ל א).

Sprinkle and cense the blade when the above work is complete, recite over it the following Conjuration of the Sword, and then wrap it in its consecrated silk:

> I conjure thee, O Sword, by these Names, **Abrahach, Abrach, Abracadabra, Yod Heh Vav Heh**, that thou serve me for a strength and defense in all Magical Operations, against all mine Enemies, visible and invisible.
>
> I conjure thee anew by the Holy and Indivisible Name of El strong and wonderful; by the Name **Shaddai** Almighty; and by these Names **Qadosh, Qadosh, Qadosh, Adonai Elohim Zabaoth, Emanuel**, the First and the Last, Wisdom, Way, Life, Truth, Chief, Speech, Word, Splendour, Light, Sun, Fountain, Glory, the Stone of the Wise, Virtue, Shepherd, Priest, Messiach Immortal; by these Names then, and by the other Names, I conjure thee, O Sword, that thou servest me for a Protection in all adversities. Amen.

There are three further swords outlined in one manuscript of the *Key of Solomon the King*, found in Sloane MS 1307, and which Mathers included in his published translation. They are distinguished by different names inscribed upon them, though I would assume the same consecration and magickal timing as above would apply. Each sword is held, drawn, by the exorcist's working partners[5] throughout the summoning operation. It is considered necessary to grant such protection to the working partners, because they take an ultimately passive role in the overall work.

Upon the first sword, engrave with the burin the name Cadriel (ל א י ר ד כ) or Gabriel (ל א י ר ב ג) on the pommel. Engrave Region (ן ו י ג ר) on the guard. Finally, engrave Panoraim Heamesin (ן י ש מ א י ה ם י א ר ו נ פ) upon the blade.

On the second sword, engrave upon the pommel the name Auriel (ל א י ר ו א). On the guard, the name Sarion (ן ו י ר ש). On the blade, Gamorin Debalin (ן י ל ב ד נ י ר ו מ ג).

On the third sword, engrave upon the pommel the name Raphael (ל א פ ר). On the guard, the name Yemeton (ן ו ט מ י). On the blade, Lamedin Eradim (ם י ד ר ע ן י ד מ ל).

The Sickle, Scimitar, Dagger, Lance, or Poniard

I am including Solomon's sickle (et al.) mainly out of interest, and not because it is vital to exorcism. It appears in the *Key*, Book II, Chapter 8 (Of the Knife, Sword . . . and other Instruments of Magical Art). In chapter 12 of this book, we will see how the *Key* utilizes this instrument in the casting of protective circles. I personally find this to be a superfluous tool. The practitioner must tie a nine-foot cord to the sickle, and thrust the blade into the ground at the center of the working area. The other end of the cord is tied to the sword or black-hilted knife, which is then used to trace the outline of a large eighteen-foot diameter circle. (Practitioners of Wicca will know that this was likely the source from which Gerald Gardner and his contemporaries dew the similar practice in traditional Wicca.)

The *Key* actually describes several pointed instruments that are intended solely for this one task. A scimitar, dagger, lance, and poniard are all described along with the sickle, and given the same instructions for construction and consecration. Perhaps any one of them can be chosen, at the discretion of the working mage. That is, of course, if he ever finds a need for such tools.

The consecration for these tools is generally the same as for the black- and white-hilted knives. They are made on the day and hour of Mercury. The blade of whichever instrument you have chosen must be dipped in a concoction of magpie blood and the juice of the herb Mercury.

The handles for these tools, however, are made in a manner similar to the Solomonic wand. They are fashioned from white boxwood, which is cut from its tree in a single stroke at sunrise. (No magickal timing is given for this, though I feel that Wednesday at sunrise would be the most likely time. Then the blade could be consecrated as described above on the same day, at another hour of Mercury.) Then, the characters that are shown in the illustrations above are inscribed or painted on to the tools. Perfume the completed implement (the text does not say to sprinkle as well, though I would suggest doing so), wrap it in consecrated silk, and put away for later use.

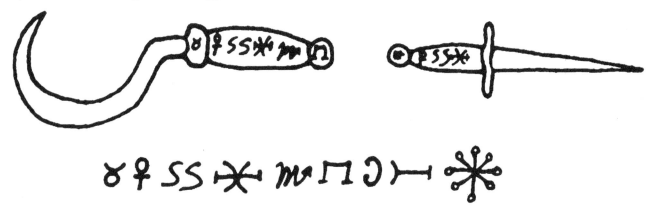

The Solomonic sickle and dagger.

Pentagram of Solomon.

The Pentagram of Solomon

The rest of the tools in this chapter have been pulled from the system of the *Goetia*. In fact, we have already covered all of these in chapter 10, concerning the uses of talismans in spirit summoning. Therefore, I will avoid repeating too many details here, and merely give the necessary information to make and use them.

The "Pentagonal Figure of Solomon" is a circular lamen etched in silver or gold. It is intended to protect the exorcist from the dangers associated with goetic summoning, as well as to illustrate his authority over the spirits. On the back side of this lamen, one is to trace the sigil of the spirit one is calling.

As covered in chapter 10, this lamen is most likely intended to be worn with the spirit's sigil facing outward, and the pentagram facing inward. This presents the sigil to the view of the entity, so that it can see the exorcist wearing the character as the text instructs. The pentagram, then, would rest directly against the heart, where it would best protect one from the energies associated with both the spirit and its character.

As a personal note, I would suggest one inscribe the pentagram into the silver or golden lamen (with the burin of the art), and then paint the reverse side with several coats of "chalkboard" paint. (This can be purchased in the common chalkboard colors of green or black. I suggest obtaining the black.) Once this is done, any spirit's sigil can be drawn onto the lamen with chalk, and then easily erased after the operation is complete.

Finally, there is a prayer given in the fifth book of the *Lemegeton*—the *Ars Nova*—to be spoken as one dons the pentagram. The prayer is actually a part of the larger set of prayers for casting the circle and donning the necessary talismans and vestments. Because I give this prayer in full in chapter 12 ("Magickal Circles"), I have decided not to reproduce it here.

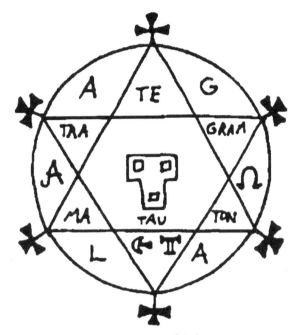

The Hexagram of Solomon.

The Hexagram of Solomon

"Solomon's Hexagonal Figure" in the *Goetia* is closely associated with the lamen of the pentagram. It is also intended to provide authority and protection to the exorcist. This one, however, is specifically intended for display to the spirits once they arrive at the circle. We have discussed previously (and will return to again in chapter 12) the animalistic and horrifying shapes the spirits can assume when they first appear. This is due to their natural correspondence to our own animal natures, often engaging our neuroses and unconscious reactions and fears. It is important for the shaman-mage to establish his authority over such spirits, and compel them to take on aspects more pleasant. (Like any wild animals, such spirits will appear with their fangs bared. The tamer must reduce the hostile spirits to docility before attempting to work with them.)

The hexagram of Solomon should be made on calf's skin parchment if possible. Though the *Goetia* says nothing about consecrating the parchment beforehand, I would suggest following the procedure outlined in chapter nine. It is then worn at the skirt of the white robe, covered with a cloth of linen. Once the spirits have been conjured to appearance, the hexagram is uncovered and displayed to the entities with the following words:

> Behold your confusion if you be disobedient. Behold the Pentacle of Solomon which I have brought here before thy presence. Behold the person of the Exorcist in the midst of the exorcism, who is armed by God and without fear, who potently invocateth you and called you to appear. Therefore make rational answers to my demands and be obedient to me, your master, in the name of the Lord **Bathat** rushing upon **Abrac, Abeor** coming upon **Aberer.**

The *Goetia* also gives a short prayer to be recited as one dons the hexagram of Solomon. Like the pentagram of Solomon, these prayers are an integral part of the procedure for casting the circle and donning the vestments. This procedure is reproduced in full in chapter 12 ("Magickal Circles" section), and therefore does not need to be included here.

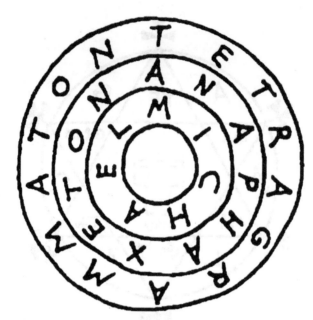

Ring or Disc of Solomon.

The Ring of Solomon

The legendary ring of Solomon descends to us from Arabic and Judaic mythology. Most versions of the story claim that the ring was given to Solomon by an archangel, usually Michael himself. Most importantly, this ring was inscribed with the ineffable true name of God—by which Solomon enjoyed his command over the spirits of nature. Some legends describe a pentagram design upon the ring (such as the *Testament of Solomon*), though this was generally changed to a hexagram once that symbol became important to the Judaic faith.

The ring was also supposed to possess four precious stones, one given to him by each of the four archangels of God: Michael, Gabriel, Raphael, and Phanuel (or Auriel). This effectively gave the ring—and thus Solomon—power over the four quarters of the earth, the four Elements, and even the four worlds of the Qabalah.

The ring described by the *Goetia* is of a simpler design. It is merely a round silver ring with three names written in concentric circles: Michael, Anaphaxeton, and Tetragrammaton. Two of them are rather obvious—beginning with Michael, who is credited with delivering the ring to Solomon. He is also associated with the triangle where the spirits are bound (see chapter 12). Because Michael was the vanquisher of Satan in the heavenly wars, the archangel became a standard in medieval exorcisms. The other obvious name is Tetragrammaton, which is merely a Greek term for the Hebrew YHVH (יהוה).

The use of the ring in the *Goetia* is also very simple. It is merely worn upon the middle finger of the left hand, and held in front of the face during communication with infernal spirits. It is said to "preserve [the exorcist] from the stinking fumes of spirits, etc." As I stated in the beginning of this chapter, these stinking fumes (or hellfire, etc.) associated with the spirits' initial appearance is metaphorical. It represents the chaotic nature of the entities themselves, and the danger this can pose to the psyche of the working exorcist. The ring of Solomon, in this incarnation, would therefore act as a shield and anchor against these energies.

Secret Seal of Solomon.

The Secret Seal of Solomon

This particular talisman is the prime example of the seal of the king, the warrant which grants its possessor the power of the rule of law. Notice the conjunction of Saturn and Mars in this single magickal image, indicating the power of war and death, and governance with an iron fist. Both the creation and the design of this seal indicate that it is a show of power on the part of the exorcist to the spirits he wishes to bind. Solomon is said, in the *Goetia*, to have commanded the seventy-two evil spirits (with their legions) into the brass vessel by virtue of this seal, and to have covered the vessel itself with a brass lid etched with the same design. He is also said to have used the seal to gain the love of many people, and to gain victory in battle. Neither weapons, fire, nor water could harm him while he possessed it.

The seal is made only by one who has undergone ritual purification for the space of one month (see chapter 7). Sexual abstinence is specifically called for,[6] along with fasting, prayer, and confession. It is necessary to work on a Tuesday night (associated with Mars) at the hour of midnight. The Moon must be in her increase, and should also rest in the sign of Virgo.

The talisman itself is inscribed on virgin parchment, with the blood of a black rooster[7] that has never mated. Nothing more is said in the *Goetia* about these materials, such as consecrations and preparation. However, this information can be found throughout this book, mostly drawn from the *Key of Solomon the King*. Obtaining the blood of winged animals is discussed in chapter 4 ("Sacrifice in the Grimoires"), and creating an ink therefrom can be deduced from chapter 9. A consecration of parchment is also found in chapter 9, along with instructions and consecrations for magickal pens. More than likely, one is expected to use calf's skin parchment for this seal as with the hexagram of Solomon.

Once the secret seal has been drawn upon the parchment, it is perfumed with an incense compounded of alum, raisons, dates, cedar, and lignum aloes. Once again, full grimoiric procedures for the censer and incense can be found in this book in chapter 6. Nothing more is said about the seal in the *Goetia*, though I would further suggest wrapping it in consecrated silk as with the rest of the tools.

1. I do not mean this to suggest that there is anything wrong with man's natural animal spirit. However, the modern human is anything but a natural creature, and the activation of the hidden neurosis within one's mind is not something to be approached lightly.

2. Even the name "athame" comes from a manuscript of the *Key of Solomon*—Sloane 3847, not used by Mathers in his translation. That version shows a small sickle knife labled "Artanus" or "Arthany." Sloppy handwriting might make the name a bit hard to make out, and "Athame" is an understandable attempt.

3. An extremely poisonous plant!

4. I am assuming that this is the name which the Hebrew is intended to spell. The Hebrew is faithfully reproduced from the *Key*, but the transliteration I offer is merely my own speculation. You will note that the given Hebrew does not "exactly" spell "Primeumaton"—it is missing the *u* sound, or Hebrew Vau. I am also unsure of the actual intention behind the following name "Pheniel," unless it is related to the archangel Phanuel. (One of the four principal archangels according to older Judaism and the *Ethiopian Book of Enoch*.) Once again, the *u* sound—the Hebrew Vau—is missing.

5. The *Key* suggests that four people—one master and three partners—is best for the evocations the text describes.

6. Albeit in a somewhat typically medieval male-chauvinist manner.

7. Remember that black animals are specifically associated with infernal spirits.

CHAPTER TWELVE

Conjuring Spirits (Goety)

No work on the medieval grimoiric traditions could be complete without a survey of goety,[1] the conjuring of earthbound nature and infernal spirits. This is certainly an area that needs much attention in order to bring the truth into focus through the chaotic blur of historical and philosophical misunderstandings. As I said of evocation in chapter 8, the art is mired in the dross of anti-occult Church propaganda and the glitz of Hollywood. Modern occultists have generally drawn their opinions on spirit work from sources influenced by these things, or by the horrible mishaps experienced by fellow practitioners who themselves were operating under the same misconceptions. As always, a little understanding of history can go a long way.

We have already discussed many of the points relevant to this subject in chapter two—concerning the vocation and initiation of the shaman. This man (or woman) did not suffer from the moral dilemmas of modern students concerning goety. Today, it is all too common to see the term "black magick" defined as *any* work incorporating infernal spirits. The tribal shaman, on the other hand, was *expected* to work intimately with these creatures. In many cases, the spirits (especially of sickness) would be directly involved in the new shaman's initiation, during which each demon would grant the human power over itself and (thus) the ailment it represents.

This is the point missed by most current commentaries on spirit conjuration. The "black magick" label for the grimoires stems ultimately from the medieval Church's opinion of the texts. In *Forbidden Rites* (p. 157), Richard Kieckhefer points out that the critics of the grimoires cited the sacrifices and offerings made to the demons (animals, incense, etc.) as proof of the Satanic nature of the texts. Sacrifice was a method of worship—specifically of Pagan worship—and it proved that the mage was submitting himself to the infernal spirits.

In reality, this was not the stance of the mages at all. As was discussed in chapter 4 of this work, the act of sacrifice is a method of empowering and nurturing a spiritual entity. As Kieckhefer states in his discussion, the grimoiric mage saw these offerings as allurements for the spirits and payment for services rendered.

Historically, the grimoiric (and similar shamanic) arts were not practiced by so-called Satanists making Faustian-style pacts with devils. (Even the most blatantly "Satanic" texts, such as the *Grand Grimoire*, seem to have been written for shock value by people who were not themselves Satanic.) Instead, they were placed firmly in the domain of holy men—shamans and clerics—who had been granted the spiritual authority to command the ethereal creatures. Without this authority, the holy men could not have cured disease, retrieved lost souls from the underworld, or protected the community from the random rabid spirit (demon). This was hardly "black" magick. (See chapter 4 concerning spiritual authority.)

There are various legends surrounding King Solomon that illustrate this point. The king, known for his wisdom and piety, was also world famous (through Judaic, Hebrew, and Arabic mythos) for his binding of demonic spirits. Through them he was able to exert his will upon the physical plane and to obtain hidden information. (This, in fact, is the basic premise upon which the *Goetia* is founded.)

However, the ability to perform magick and divination through spirit Familiars was not the true foundation of the Solomonic legend. In its original form(s) the story tells of the king conjuring and binding the infernal demons (or "unclean spirits") of sickness and sin that afflicted his kingdom. Solomon's use of the spirits for practical purposes (namely forcing them to build the holy temple) was little more than an afterthought. In some versions of the legend, Solomon commands the king of demons Asmodeus to perform the labor. In other legends the demon king is Belial, or Beelzeboul.

The *Testament of Solomon*, which we encountered first in chapter 1 and will be covering in more depth below, is a perfect example of this mythology. In the text, Solomon is called upon to help a child who has fallen mysteriously ill. Thus, it is illness that represents the starting point as well as the main focus of the entire story. Upon investigation of the problem, Solomon finds that a vampiric spirit (Ornias) is responsible for the child's waning health. The king lays a trap for Ornias, and succeeds in conjuring the demon to his presence. An interrogation ensues, during which the spirit reveals his functions and the name of the angel who can defeat him. It is by summoning the angel (Uriel) that Solomon is granted total authority over the spirit.

The king then contacts the prince of demons (in this case Beelzeboul) and utilizes him to conjure a long list of unclean spirits. Each one is treated in the same shamanic manner as Ornias; their functions discovered, and their opposing angels invoked to bind them. Finally, they are all set to useful tasks in the building of the holy temple.

Solomon Binding Belial (or Asmodeus?).

These legends, of course, are the very reasons why Solomon was chosen as a favorite mythical figure upon which to base such grimoires as the *Lemegaton* and the *Key of Solomon the King*. Both of them (along with the rest of the Solomonic tradition) concern the conjuration of spirits *specifically* through the power and authority of God and his angels. As Agrippa affirms in his *Occult Philosophy*:

> . . . neither can any work of wonderful efficacy in religion be done, unless some good spirit the ruler and finisher of the work be there present. [. . .] But evil spirits are overcome by us through the assistance of the good, especially when the petitioner is very pious and devout, and sings forth sacred words, and a horrible speech, and by conjurations, or adjurations, in as much as they are done by the name and power of religion, and divine virtue, those evil spirits are afraid of . . . (*Three Books of Occult Philosophy*, Book III, Chapter 32).

And *Abramelin* stresses concerning the true and sacred magick:

> . . . a Spirit which of his own nature is all vanity, would not be likely to submit himself unto thee without a superior force (compelling him), neither would he wish to obey thee nor to serve thee. He who shall reflect and reason upon these particulars will know that all things come to us from God, and that it is He Who wisheth and commandeth that the Evil Spirits should be submitted unto us. If then all things depend from the Lord, upon whom wilt thou, O Man, base thyself so as to be capable of thyself (alone) to dominate the Spirits? It is certain that such an enterprise cannot succeed without the loss of thine own soul. Then it is by virtue of that God Who hath submitted them under thy feet, that thou shalt command them . . . (*The Book of Abramelin*, Book III, pp. 255–6).

The necessity of invoking the aid of angelic beings to exorcise spirits is certainly not original with the grimoires. In fact, the practice itself might be traced all the way back to exorcisms in ancient Babylon or earlier:

> Shamash is before me,
> Sin is behind me,
> Nergal at my right hand,
> Ninib at my left hand.
> When I draw near unto the sick man,
> When I lay my hand on the head of the sick man,
> May a kindly Spirit, a kindly Guardian, stand at my side.[2]

> The great Lord Ea hath sent me;
> He hath added His pure spell to mine,
> He hath added His pure voice to mine,
> He hath added His pure spittle to mine,[3]
> He hath added His pure prayer to mine.

Another grimoiric myth I would like to take this opportunity to bust is that which insists all spirit conjuration has to do with the enslavement of innocent spirits against their wills. Certainly the practice does involve authority and command over the spirits, but, in order to understand this, it must be replaced into its proper context. As explained in chapter 2, goetic spirits do not reside in the highest (celestial) shamanic world, nor in the middle (intellectual) world. Instead, they exist in the lowest world along with the kingdoms of all earthly life less evolved than humanity.

In essence, they are no different from wild animals, dogs or cats, reptiles, or most other forms of animal life. Mircea Eliade points out, in *Shamanism, Archaic Techniques of Ecstasy* (Chapter 3, p. 89) that the majority of spirit Familiars in shamanic cultures did in fact have animal forms. To the Siberians and the Altaians they appeared as bears, wolves, stags, hares, various birds (geese, eagles, owls, crows, etc.), and even giant worms. Richard Kieckhefer, in his *Forbidden Rites* (p. 160), discusses this in relation to the horrible shapes usually ascribed to the spirits in the grimoires. The figures are most often composed of various animal parts, specifically because the demons are closer to animal then they are to human.[4] The working mage must take it upon himself to force the demons to appear in human or otherwise nonthreatening shape.

Like any wild animals, goetic spirits might be clawed and dangerous, or they might be docile and harmless. Some of them can be tamed and kept as pets (Familiars), while others are rabid and strictly harmful to humans. Some might display great intelligence (in the manner of a bright dog or cat), and others might be driven only by blind instinct. All of them, of course, must ultimately live by their basic instinctual natures.

Most importantly, the mage must *never* mistake the goetic spirits as equals to the human mind; no matter how eloquently they might appear to "speak" or even the information they are able to reveal. Even a parrot can utter words, but that does not make it a fully sentient fourth or fifth circuit individual. Agrippa explains in Book III, Chapter 16:

> Some of these [spirits] are so familiar and acquainted with men, that they are even affected with human perturbations, but whose instruction Plato thinketh that men do oftentimes wonderful things, even as by the instruction of men, some bests which are most nigh unto us, as apes, dogs, elephants, do often strange things above their species.

Agrippa here supports my above theories, treating the spirits as if they were a species of domesticated animal. Being so intimately connected, even symbiotic, with mankind gives them a false air of humanlike personality. It is similar, in fact, to the tendency of pet owners to assume their pets are much more human than animal, even becoming convinced that the animal can understand perfect English! As I suggested in chapter 8, the concept of "personality" exists between two communicating minds rather than within a single person's skull. Therefore, both pets and earthbound spirits do often display personality traits that are above their true evolutionary state, so long as they are in communication with a human mind.

If it is possible to relate Leary's eighth circuits model of the mind[5] to spirits at all, then we might assign them to the second circuit; with perhaps enough third circuit consciousness to allow them to communicate with us. The most advanced among them might be compared to a prepubescent child, while many more might compare better to a bright dog. For instance, note the emphasis on hierarchies (a second circuit "pack animal" concept) in most goetic systems of magick.

Richard Kieckhefer (*Forbidden Rites*, p. 155) states that such hierarchies were principally a product of Neoplatonic thought (the same philosophy behind Agrippa's *Three Books*), and were generally viewed as a parody of God's divine court.[6] The categorization of the spirits into kings and princes, prelates and earls, etc., was in fact unique to the grimoires. Other systems, such as the Arabic, retained the more animalistic (or at least zodiacal) attributions for the spirits. Iamblichus (250–330 CE) may have been the first Neoplatonist to recognize an elaborate categorization for the demons in his *The Mysteries*. He was then followed by such philosophers as Proclus (412–484 CE—who attributed the spirits to the four Elements and the underworld), Psellus (1106 CE—who added the *lucifugum*, or "light fliers"), and finally the mystical authority Johannes Trithemius (1462–1516 CE), the teacher of Agrippa.

The shamanic quality of these mens' philosophies and views on nature seems quite apparent—and we can even see echoes of the ancient Pagan faiths whose royal and divine courts so often mirrored one another.[7] This philosophy merely had to wait through the Aristotelian-dominated Middle Ages for the Neoplatonic rebirth of the late medieval and Renaissance eras.

Finally, the *Testament of Solomon* played its principal role in the foundation of the grimoiric cosmologies.[8] The *Testament* concerns a long list of goetic spirits conjured by Solomon, and thus represents the fountainhead of the European Solomonic traditions (more on this below). Related texts followed in the fifteenth and sixteenth centuries that seem to be the actual sources for the *Goetia* itself. Such as the *Pseudomonarchia Daemonum* of Wierus, which included sixty-nine devils along with their offices and functions, or the *Liber Officiorum* which included four emperors, several kings, dukes, marquises, and counts.

Beneath these hierarchical rulers, there are an infinite number of lesser "servient" spirits who operate within the sphere of their superiors. These would appear to be the agents through which the conjured demonic nobility actually accomplishes the commands of the mage. Many systems find these spirits useful; such as the *Thuergia-Goetia*, which conjures Elemental emperors and dukes who bring incredible numbers of lesser spirits with them. The first listed emperor is Carnesiel (who rules in the east), and he brings with him a thousand great dukes, one hundred lesser dukes, and fifty trillion(!) ministering spirits. The *Goetia* itself works in a similar manner, where each ruling spirit, a king, duke, earl, etc., is said to govern so many legions of lesser spirits.

The *Book of Abramelin*, on the other hand, warns us against even bothering with this lowest "ministering" class of spirit:

> There be certain little terrestrial Spirits that are simply detestable; Sorcerers and Necromantic Magicians generally avail themselves of their services, for they operate only for evil, and in wicked and pernicious things, and they be of no use soever. He who operateth could, should he so wish, have a million such, but the Sacred Science which worketh otherwise than Necromancy in no way permitteth you to employ such as be not constrained by an Oath to obey you. (*The Book of Abramelin*, p. 263)

It might be possible to assign these "astral nasties" to the reptile mind of the first circuit. The grimoires rarely pay any attention to them at all, unless they are listed as servants to a higher ranking spirit such as Carnesiel in the *Theurgia-Goetia*, or any given spirit in the *Goetia* proper. They are typically listed in seemingly outrageous numbers, which I suspect might actually have some kind of mathematical, astrological, or numerological significance.

More than likely, the grimoiric "ministering spirits" were derived from the older concept of the Familiar. For instance, the tenth spirit listed in the *Goetia*, the president Buer, is one of several who "giveth good familiars." One would assume that any Familiar spirit given to the mage by Buer would come from among the forty legions of spirits that he governs.

Of course, it is the Familiar spirit—rather than the healing arts—that forms the primary focus of most post-*Goetia* spirit-magick grimoires. Just as with King Solomon, it was the mage's ability to command the spirits that made him a miracle worker on the physical plane. For more on this, return to chapter 2, the section titled "A Medieval/ Renaissance Definition of Magick."

Then, in chapter 4, section "The Rise of the Priesthood," we discussed the origin of the Familiar spirit in ancient ancestral magick, as well as the roles and functions such spirits played in their communities. Most importantly, we saw that these spirits were given their power through binding them to physical objects. (A subject that also played an important role in chapter 10.)

Fortunately, we can learn even more about Familiar spirits by observing the surviving tribal faiths such as Santeria or Palo Mayombe, which refer to their Familiars as the *Nganga* (cauldron) or *Prenda* (jewel). Technically, these terms refer to the elaborate urn (usually a cauldron or large terra cotta pot) used to house the spirit, working in much the same manner as the Orishas in their own elaborate pots. In fact, the Prenda is quite a bit more elaborate than the Orishas' physical basis. The latter is generally very artistic and aesthetically pleasing, while the former is more practical but contains a larger quantity of sympathetic and empowered objects.

The Prenda is supposed to be the spirit of a departed human who has found him or herself bound to the earth-plane. Generally, the spirit is assumed to be stuck here because of various wrongdoings during its lifetime. In what appears to be some kind of tribal version of Purgatory, such a spirit can by right be made to serve the interests of a living shaman. It is by working for the shaman, and thereby on behalf of the community, that the spirit pays its dues.

The art of Prenda-making is actually a survival of ancestral practices, and a visit to a graveyard is most often necessary to locate a suitable spirit to bind into the Prenda. Otherwise, the spirit might be found in various natural settings (by rivers, the sea, mountains, etc.), attached to a physical object such as a stone, shell, or branch.

This is where the fashioning of the Prenda becomes a truly fascinating practice. Since the Familiar is a nature spirit, it is necessary to create a microcosmic natural environment, completely sympathetic to the spirit, inside the Nganga itself. For instance, if one were to find his Familiar attached to a stone by a river, it would be necessary to create a miniature river "ecosystem" inside the pot. Various secret herbs and woods associated with water would be included, along with water from a river (and other places), shells, and even parts of river animals: snakes, alligator, fish, etc.

In other words, not only the stone must be taken from the river and placed into the Nganga, but so (in essence) must the river itself. It is from the river (and especially from the river goddess) that the Familiar must draw its power. While separating the spirit from its natural environment would dramatically limit its ability to function, the Nganga offers a method of bringing a small pocket of the necessary environment right into the shaman's home.

From there, various tools and sympathetic materials can be included in the Nganga, depending on the kind of work needed from the spirit. A farmer might include agricultural tools so the spirit can enjoy influence over the crops. Carpenters and masons can include their building tools, writers can include pens and ink, etc. When the first sacrifice of chicken is made to the spirit, the wings can be left in the pot so that the spirit can fly. The feet can be left so the spirit can walk, or attack and scratch. The head is left so the spirit can see, etc.

The other sympathetic materials also grant the spirit influence over areas of the physical plane. Dirt is taken from the grounds of hospitals, banks, courthouses, jails, churches, and other places from which help or protection may be needed. Weapons can also be included in the Nganga—from knives to (in some cases) guns—so the Familiar can defend the home.

Finally, several "hot" items are included in the pot, such as all kinds of peppers (the hotter the better), gunpowder, rum, cigars, blood, and an alcoholic beverage called *Chomba* (made from grain alcohol and the hottest peppers). All of these are included not to harm the spirit, but to add "shamanic heat" to the pot; keeping the spirit awake, alert, and "stirred up."

Most of the grimoires have, unfortunately, not inherited the elaborate system of microcosmic sympathy used with Afro-Cuban Familiars. (Unless it exists in some form in the oldest texts, such as the *Picatrix*.) Instead, the elaborate microcosms have been replaced with talismans as described in chapter 10. The most shamanic of the grimoires—*The Book of Abramelin*—is one such example; and it offers more information and instruction on the Familiar spirits than any other text of its kind.

The foundational mythos contained within *Abramelin* is similar to that of the *Goetia* and other quasi-Christian grimoires. The infernal spirits are said to be the stars cast upon the earth from heaven after Lucifer's failed rebellion. As part of the chastisement for their assault upon God's throne, they were destined to live among and serve the will of mankind. (Note the similarity here to the Afro-Cuban Prenda, which was also a spirit in servitude for wrongdoing.) Because of this, these demons menace us at all opportunities, but can be controlled by holy men. It is by gaining conversation with the holy guardian angel that one is granted the spiritual authority to command the infernal spirits.

Besides binding by oath the twelve princes of Hell along with innumerable servient spirits, the *Abramelin* system also indicates that four Familiar spirits are destined for the servitude of every master. On page 262 of the Mathers edition of *The Book of Abramelin*, we find the following (seemingly outlandish) description of the kinds of tasks to which these spirits can be set:

> The Familiar Spirits are very prompt, and they are able to execute in most minute detail all matters of a mechanical nature, with the which therefore it is well to occupy them; as in historical painting; in making statues; clocks; weapons; and other like matters; also in chemistry; and in causing them to carry out commercial and business transactions under the form of other persons; in making them transport merchandise and other goods from one place to another; also to employ them in causing quarrels, fights, homicides, and all kinds of evils, and malefic acts; also to convey letters and messages of all kinds from one country to another; to deliver prisoners; and in a thousand other ways which I have frequently experimented.

It is perhaps unlikely that a discorporate spirit will be creating painted masterpieces, nor (sadly) will they go off to work in our stead. However, remembering what we learned of the familial spirit in chapter 2, we know that a Familiar could certainly be used to *some* advantage in all of these industries and circumstances. For instance, if an alchemist needs new equipment to produce a medicine, he will most likely set his own Familiars upon the task of making the equipment manifest. Through their aid, some means of obtaining the needed items will present itself.

According to *Abramelin*, each Familiar has its own natural time of operation, depending on the course of the Sun. The first Familiar remains on "guard duty" with his master from dawn until noon; at which point the second Familiar takes its shift from noon to dusk. The third Familiar then operates from dusk until midnight, leaving the fourth to guard from midnight until dawn. (Unfortunately, *Abramelin* does not state whether or not the Familiars can perform tasks while not on "guard duty.")

These four spirits are given into the service of the aspirant by the four lesser princes Oriens, Paimon, Ariton, and Amaimon—the traditional demonic kings of the four cardinal directions. This fits well with the solar rotation of the Familiars' shifts, which reflect the four quadrants of the horoscope (east/dawn, south/noon, west/dusk, north/midnight). This indicates that the Familiars themselves are likely of a directional or even Elemental nature.[9] Thus, for the aspirant, the four Familiar spirits plus the guardian angel constitute a pentagonal mastery of the Elemental forces (Fire, Earth, Air, Water, and Spirit).

Like the other spirits, the Familiars are bound to a set of talismans, found in *Abramelin* Book III, Chapter 5, "How we may retain the Familiar Spirits bond or free in whatsoever form." This consists of twelve talismans intended to bind the Familiars in various illusory shapes. Some of the shapes are an old man, a soldier, a page, or even a flower. However, the majority of the talismans serve to bind the Familiars into the shapes of animals such as a lion, eagle, dog, bear, serpent, or ape. This would seem to be a survival of the common shamanic practice of keeping the Familiars around in animal form, which is closest to such spirits' inherent nature.

Though *Abramelin* insists these talismans are not ultimately necessary—the verbal command of the master always being sufficient—it still suggests one make use of them (perhaps for practical convenience). One merely has to reveal and move (we might say "disturb") one of the talismans while speaking the spirit's name in order to stir the creature into action. All of *Abramelin's* talismans work in this manner and, like those of the *Key of Solomon the King*, the demons summoned thereby know what is expected of them by lying eyes on the talisman. In the case of the Familiars' talismans, they will merely cause the spirit to arrive in the chosen form and await further instruction.

(Of course, *Abramelin* also urges the aspirant to avoid demanding physical appearance of the spirits as much as possible.)

All of this information allows us to put the art of spirit conjuration into perspective. This is not enslavement or domination, but simply a matter of taming wild animals—making Familiar-pets out of them. Just as with animal training, the spirits are treated humanely, but also with firmness and common sense toward the real danger these creatures can pose to the tamer. Note the advice given by *Abramelin* on this very point:

> Also do not familiarise thyself with them; for they be not little pet dogs. Adopt a serious tone and air of authority, make them obey thee, and be well ware of accepting the least offer which they shall make to thee of themselves; and treat them as their Master, also without occasion thou shalt never molest them. . . . (*The Book of Abramelin*, Book III, p. 256)

> These Spirits should be treated according to their quality, and a distinction should be made between a great Spirit and one of a vile or insignificant nature, but thou shouldest nevertheless alway conserve over them that domination which is proper unto him who operateth. In speaking to them thou shalt give them no title; but shall address them sometimes as "you," sometimes as "thou"; and thou shalt never seek out expressions to please them, and thou shalt always have with them a proud and imperious air. (*The Book of Abramelin*, Book III, pp. 262–3)

I have already hinted in this chapter at the principal danger associated with goety (or any work with spiritual entities): all spirits must ultimately follow their basic instinctual natures. We might even think of this in a technical manner: if the physical universe is itself a cosmic supercomputer (and it is), then the spiritual entities that populate the universe are its programs. To evoke such an entity (angel or demon) is to run a particular program. Just like on your own computer, once you click an icon the program will launch, and you must simply live with the consequences. Likewise, to summon an entity like Astaroth (see chapter 10 for an analysis of this spirit) is to initiate a current of *everything* he represents. The mage cannot be immune to this current. *Abramelin* also makes sure to stress this point:

> The Spirits . . . comprehend very well . . .what dispositions we have, and understand our inclinations, so that from the very beginning they prepare the way to make us to fail. If they know that a man is inclined unto Vanity and Pride, they will humiliate themselves before him, and push that humility unto excess, and even unto idolatry, and this man will glory herein and become intoxicated with conceit . . . Another man will be easily accessible to Avarice, and then if he take not heed the Malignant Spirits will propose unto him thousands of ways of accumulating wealth, and of rendering himself rich by indirect and unjust ways and means, whence total restitution is afterwards difficult and even impossible . . . Another will be a man of Letters; the Spirits will inspire him with presumption, and he will then believe himself to be wiser even than the Prophets . . . The causes and matter whereof (the Spirits) will make use to cause a man to waver are infinite, especially when the man attempteth to make them submit to his commands, and this is why it is most necessary to be upon one's guard and to distrust oneself.
> (*The Book of Abramelin*, Book III, pp. 254–5)

We can take a lesson from our knowledge of the shamanic vocation (see chapter 2). The shaman-to-be did not simply disappear into the woods and begin to summon spirits at will. Instead, he first had to encounter and suffer *brutal attack* by each spirit he hoped to control in the future. He had to face and survive the worst that any infernal demon could deliver upon him. Afterward, the demons could hope for no influence or control over the shaman.

(Interestingly, as these were most often the demons of disease, this seems rather parallel to the human immune system, which can only be attacked by a virus once.)

Of course, the shaman did not work exclusively with infernal spirits. He also worked with Elementals and nature spirits, faery and jinni, intelligences and daemons; the list could go on at some length. His job was to create a harmonious relationship between himself, his tribe, and the natural environment in which they existed. This certainly involved the casting out of a rabid spirit from time to time, when it was causing suffering among the people. However it was hardly the whole of his vocation. The human/nature interface was his vocation.

Exorcism

The second book of the *Key of Solomon the King*, Chapter 13, is titled "Concerning the Precepts [General Rules] of the Art." Its opening words are a vital clue to the true nature of the grimoiric magickal practices:

> He who hath attained the rank or degree of Exorcist, which we are usually accustomed to call Magus
> or Master according to grade . . .

There are several points in this and other Solomonic texts were the operator is referred to as an "exorcist." We also see quite a bit of stress placed upon the "exorcism" of each physical object used in the spells, including those of fire, water, incense, ink, etc. The use of bindings, oaths, invocations of God and his angels, and even the magickal circles within the literature (to mention just a few examples) are also classic markers of the arts of exorcism. Note the prayer given in the *Lemegeton* (Book Five: the *Ars Nova*) for the consecration of the triangle within which the spirits are to be bound:

> Thou God of almighty Power . . . Thou who art the first and last, let all spirits be subject unto us, and
> let the spirit be bound in this Triangle which disturbs this place[10] by thy holy Angel Michael until I
> shall discharge him.

It seems that the master is supposed to be binding a spirit that is specifically haunting an area, such as the attic of an old house, etc. While the *Goetia* proper seems to focus on calling spirits to perform tasks for the master, the prayer given above betrays the art of the professional exorcist, who would have used the techniques of the *Goetia* to exorcise a demon from someone's home or person.

It is a somewhat common assumption that exorcism means "the casting out of spirits" and is thus a polar opposite practice to that of spirit summoning. However, this is a technical misunderstanding. The word "exorcise" descends from the Greek *exorkizein* (*ex* + *horkiaen*),[11] meaning "to bind by oath, or adjure." In *Forbidden Rites* (p. 127), Richard Kieckhefer also points out the use of such terms as "conjure," "adjure," and "exorcise" in the grimoires, all of which are synonymous with "I command." This is merely one of the central elements that the goetic grimoires share with the art of exorcism proper.

Thus, to bear the title of "exorcist" one must be adept in the binding and commanding of spirits. Therefore, such men as King Solomon were in fact exorcists. They were the holy men I mentioned above who possessed the spiritual authority to command the infernal spirits.

The practice of exorcism, as we would recognize it, is perhaps one of the most ancient of the priestly arts. It was in this way that the priests continued their shamanic roles as healers in a post-tribal (agricultural) world. In this paradigm, all sickness was defined as demonic possession, and it was the priest's job to identify, conjure, and cast out the affliction (perhaps not so different than our own modern medical professions).

The world's most famous exorcists were the priests of ancient Babylon. They are associated with exorcism as commonly as the Egyptian priesthood is associated with tombs and funerals. The subject of demonology and exorcism among the Babylonians is covered in depth by the historian R. C. Thompson in two extremely informative books:

The Devils and Evil Spirits of Babylonia
Semitic Magic: Its Origins and Development

Mesopotamia, unlike Egypt, existed in a harsh desert environment. The demons that might plague this culture were many, and they were known for their particular nastiness. There was the *Alu* (demon) who "possesses you and dares you to sleep" (most likely a nightmare demon), the *Lilu* and *Lilitu* (incubus and succubus), the *Gallu* (devil), *Rabisu* (lurker), *Ahhazu* (seizer, perhaps relating to epilepsy), and the *Labasu* (ghoul) to name just a few. There were several classifications of evil (*Limnu*) beings: the *Utukku Limnu* (evil spirit), *Alu Limnu* (evil demon), *Ekimmu Limnu* (evil ghost), *Gallu Limnu* (evil devil), *Ilu Limnu* (evil god), and the *Rabisu Limnu* (evil fiend). There were demons associated with crib death and birth complications (such as Lamashtu)[12] and even those associated with diseases arising from the waters of the Tigris or Euphrates.

The most prevalent demon in Mesopotamian religion, however, was not an infernal spirit at all. It was the *Ekimmu*—a human ghost. Remember our discussion of ancestor worship in chapter 2, and the horrible fate that awaited any human spirit left alone and starving after death:

The Man whose corpse lieth in the desert

Thou and I have oft seen such an one

His spirit resteth not in the earth;

The man whose spirit hath none to care for it

Thou and I have oft seen such an one

The dregs of the vessel, the leavings of the feast,

And that which is cast out into the street are his food.[13]

There was no dark and frightening area of the Babylonian landscape that was not the potential harbor of countless forgotten and ravenous souls who ached to possess a human body. One could even be plagued by the shades of past acquaintances—no matter how casual—if one had so much as shared food with them once during their lifetimes. This was not an act of maliciousness on the part of the spirit, but a mere act of desperation on the part of a hungry, frightened, and confused being.

Of course, we moderns tend to be somewhat free with our translation of Limnu as "evil." In fact, the pre-Judeo-Christian (or, at least, pre-Zoroastrian) world did not abide by our own dualist concepts of good and evil. While any spirit may be harmful (rabid, feral, etc.) it was in no way seen as acting on behalf of any great demonic enemy of mankind. Demons were dispatched by the same otherwise benevolent gods for whom sacrifices and worship were offered in the temples. A human only became possessed/fell sick by breaking a taboo (see chapter 4, "Confession") or otherwise offending their patron deity. Lesser gods might plague one's person or home in this way, and greater gods—even father sky himself—could send great natural disasters such as floods, storms, war, famine, plague, or even eclipses. (These latter were generally attributed to higher beings rather than mere earthbound spirits. The *Ilu Limnu* (evil god) was likely more akin to the angels of destruction of Jewish lore; quite separate from any consideration of infernal demons.)

This paradigm accounts for the seemingly odd treatment granted to the possessing spirits by the Babylonian priests. Rather than threatening or coercing the demons, the exorcist appeals to the patron god or gods who might have sent the problem in the first place. Atonement is sought and fulfilled, and then the spirit is called out with surprising respect and diplomacy. Often, the spirit is even promised rewards or sacrifice if he will willingly leave his victim in peace.

Once a demon had been successfully conjured, it was the common Babylonian practice to guide the entity into another medium such as a pig or a bird. By doing so, the exorcist ensured that the demon was not left wandering free to re-infect the same or another victim. The practice survived even into the common era, as shown in the New Testament:

> And when [Jesus] was come out of the ship, immediately there met him out of the tombs a man with an unclean spirit, who had his dwelling among the tombs; and no man could bind him, no, not with chains: Because that he had been often bound with fetters and chains, and the chains had been plucked asunder by him, and the fetters broken in pieces: neither could any man tame him. And always, night and day, he was in the mountains, and in the tombs, crying, and cutting himself with stones. But when he saw Jesus afar off, he ran and worshipped him, and cried with a loud voice, and said, "What have I to do with thee, Jesus, thou Son of the most high God? I adjure thee by God, that thou torment me not." For [Jesus] said unto him, "Come out of the man, thou unclean spirit." And he asked him, "What is thy name?"
>
> And [Legion] answered, saying, "My name is Legion: for we are many." And he besought [Jesus] much that he would not send them away out of the country. Now there was there nigh unto the mountains a great herd of swine feeding. And all the devils besought him, saying, "Send us into the swine, that we may enter into them." And forthwith Jesus gave them leave. And the unclean spirits went out, and entered into the swine: and the herd ran violently down a steep place into the sea, (they were about two thousand;) and were choked in the sea. (Mark 5:2–13)

In this example, the demons (Legion) beg Jesus not to send them "away out of the country." In Luke 8:31, this is phrased ". . . out into the deep." In the Bible as in Babylon, the spirits feared being forced to wander alone and starving in the wilderness. The compassion that Jesus shows to these spirits by allowing them into the pigs is reminiscent of the Babylonian practice, as well as Abramelin's injunction against mistreating even the lowest demons.

Water was also a favorite of the Babylonian exorcist. Bathing the victim in fresh water (not surprisingly) often resulted in increased health; and the demon was understood to have passed from the body with the pouring of the water. Washing in holy rivers or other bodies of water has been common to shamanic medicine around the world, and it, too, appears even in the New Testament:

> He answered and said, "A man that is called Jesus made clay, and anointed mine eyes, and said unto me, 'Go to the pool of Siloam, and wash': and I went and washed, and I received sight." (John 9:11)

The washing away of sickness or possessing demons was the precursor to the concept of baptism, which is itself a washing away of "uncleanness." This would explain why the use of natural rivers was the common procedure in both exorcism and baptism. Note that such a river or stream is mentioned in the Solomonic ritual bath.

When natural bodies of water could not be used, the Babylonian exorcist would simply pour a vessel of pure water over the head or infected area of the patient's body. The water (now infected with the demon's presence) would be captured in another vessel, which could then be poured out upon the earth or otherwise disposed of properly. I have to wonder if this is not the true origin of the vessels and bottles so often associated with jinn and demons in Middle Eastern shamanism.

Large portions of the Babylonian cosmology and mystical practice found their way into Judaism (during the Captivity after 600 BCE), and from thence into Christianity, as evidenced by the Biblical passages quoted above.

The arts of exorcism came along with the rest of the material, moving from a primarily medicinal focus into the devil-scare hysteria of the Catholic Middle Ages. By the fifteenth century, exorcism had become something of a fad, and most of the exorcism manuals are the product of this time. Likewise, it was in this environment that the goetic grimoires (exorcism manuals in their own right) had their birth.

In chapter 1, we learned that the grimoiric texts were written primarily by low-level clerics; the same people who held the lower offices and duties of the Catholic Church, such as carrying ritual objects, preparing the altar, writing music, transcribing texts, etc. (In chapter 4 we called this class of holy men the "Purified Ones.") The *Key of Solomon the King* supports this theory in its constant references to the master's companions, who perform all the same jobs as described for the typical lower clergy.

Traditionally, the Church is divided into seven orders: three major and four minor. The three major or sacred orders all depend on ordination: the priesthood (including bishops), deacons, and subdeacans. The four minor orders tended to change depending on time and place, and included such offices as acolyte, reader, doorkeeper, porter, lector, and *exorcist*. These orders did not depend upon ordination into the priesthood itself, but were bestowed upon individuals by bishops[14] during certain holy days. (Today, these minor orders are usually granted to ecclesiastical students during their seminary studies.)

These lesser clerical roles form the ranks of our own "Purified Ones"; generally playing a somewhat indefinite role of participation in the liturgical ministry and serving at the altar. Such offices were conferred by a ritual outlined in the *Statuta Ecclesiae Antiqua* (a document that originated in Gaul circa 500 CE), in which a candidate is presented the instruments appropriate to the order. For instance, lectors simply received a benediction, acolytes were given the linen bag in which they would carry the eucharist, and exorcists were given the *Book of Exorcisms*[15] (containing the *Rituali Romanum*). We can see how this plays into such texts as the *Key of Solomon the King*:

> The First Disciple will bear the Censer, the Perfumes and the Spices; the Second Disciple will bear the Book, Papers, Pens, Ink, and any stinking or impure materials; the Third will carry the Knife and the Sickle of Magical Art, the Lantern, and the Candles; the Fourth, the Psalms, and the rest of the Instruments; the Fifth, the Crucible or Chafing-dish, and the Charcoal or Fuel . . ." (*Key of Solomon the King*, Book I, Chapter 3)

Thus, the medieval Solomonic tradition seems to have been founded by the exorcists, who were considered the second of the four minor orders of the Catholic Church. Religious canon insisted that all newly converted individuals (*catechumens*) must undergo a "laying on of hands"[16] by the exorcists before receiving baptism. (This relation of baptism and exorcism descending from the Mesopotamian traditions.)[17] The exorcists were also in charge of the general care of victims of possession (*energumens*), who are said to have habitually frequented the Church.

Exorcism as a practice was never restricted to the priesthood, nor denied to any of the laity. Quite the contrary, there was no escaping the teachings of Christ and the Apostles that *anyone* who possessed faith and the Holy Spirit could cast out devils. This is reflected in the Apostolic Constitutions,[18] which state that "the exorcist is not ordained." Anyone possessing the charismatic power of exorcism had to be recognized by the official Church, or—if need be—ordained a deacon or subdeacon outright. (This practice survives today in the Eastern Orthodox traditions.)

Because the exorcists did not have to be initiated priests, it freed them from many of the dogmatic restrictions that should otherwise have bound them from experimentation. They were commonly known to break with the ritual forms prescribed in the *Book of Exorcisms*—suggesting a very intuitive (fifth circuit) technique. It is almost as if these were the "bad boys" of Christianity—operating right on the fringe of religious law, but generally allowed to do their thing because *it worked*. Of course, of all of the minor orders, we can hardly be surprised that it was the one most concerned with the exorcism of spirits that produced the grimoiric body of literature.

However, we also have to keep in mind that this "order" was a very loose one to say the least. The place of exorcist changed frequently throughout the years; at one point it may be an order, while at another it might be considered a mere office. It was even dropped altogether at one point when the Church felt that it had successfully driven back the "demonical" Pagan religions. In many cases, the role of exorcist was simply played by the holy man most available.

The prerequisites for exorcism sound like something right out of the *Key of Solomon the King*: anyone who undertakes the office must himself be a holy man, of a blameless life, intelligent, courageous, and humble. He should prepare for his work through intense abstinence and stimulus deprivation, specifically through prayer and fasting as prescribed by Jesus in Mathew 17:20–21:

> And Jesus said unto them, ". . . For verily I say unto you, If ye have faith as a grain of mustard seed, ye shall say unto this mountain, 'Remove hence to yonder place'; and it shall remove; and nothing shall be impossible unto you. Howbeit, this kind goeth not out but by prayer and fasting.

The exorcist was, of course, encouraged to avoid anything in the course of his rite that savored of "superstition," which might remind us somewhat of the attitude of *The Book of Abramelin*. He was also instructed to leave the medical aspects of his cases to "qualified physicians," showing the division that was already growing between the shamanic arts and the concept of official medical authority[19] with which we live to this very day.

The exorcism itself was supposed to take place in the Church or any other convenient sacred ground. If the patient could not be moved, it was to take place in a private house (no doubt sealed from the sight of the curious), although witnesses such as family members were present as well. When addressing the possessing demon, there was to be absolutely no idle or curious questioning. This is reflected in several places in the grimoires, such as *The Book of Abramelin* (Book II, Chapter 15):

> . . . your object is not at all a malign curiosity, but (one tending) unto the Honour and Glory of God, and to your own good and that of all the Human Race.

Also like the *Book of Abramelin*, the exorcist is taught to read his prayers and invocations with great faith, humility, fervor, and an awareness of power and authority. Like the *Key of Solomon* or the *Goetia*, he is also instructed to repeat the rites several times if one attempt does not produce results. Finally, the exorcist is vested with a violet stole and "surplice," a loose white robe with large open sleeves, as described in most of the grimoires. (The *Key* suggests obtaining such a robe used by the clergy—and I suppose the surplice used by an exorcist would be a fairly desirable magickal item. Of course, if one were ordained an exorcist, one would own just such a robe)

Ultimately, the grimoiric methods of evocation and those of medieval exorcism are one and the same. Whether one is summoning forth a spirit or sending it away is immaterial to the practical concerns of taming the beast in the first place. In medieval literature, the words "conjure" and "exorcise" were interchangeable terms regardless of intent to summon or dispel.

Even the written conjurations used in the two practices are basically identical to one another. An absolutely wonderful essay on this subject is contained in Richard Kieckhefer's *Forbidden Rites*, Chapter 6, "Formulas for Commanding Spirits: Conjurations and Exorcisms." It includes a breakdown of such conjurations into four basic components, very similar to the way we broke down the Psalms in chapter 4 and the holy invocations in chapter 7.

Most any given exorcism can be broken down into four basic elements:

Declaration: This is merely a statement of intent on the part of the exorcist, namely to conjure, adjure, exorcise, or otherwise command the spirit in question.

Address: The naming of the spirit, which was as important in medieval Christian exorcism as it was to the Babylonian priests. If a name for the possessing spirit is not known, then descriptive terms must be utilized to capture the essence of the demon.

Invocation: This portion of an exorcism is something we should already be familiar with from chapter 7, section "Creating Prayers and Invocations." Specific divine powers, God, Jesus, angels, and even biblical events are stated as the forces through which the exorcist draws authority. We can even see hints of shamanic ancestor magick in conjurations that call upon and recite the deeds of the patriarchs and saints. Often, the exorcist claims in this section that it is these divine and mythical powers, and not himself, who makes the demands of the spirit.

Instruction: Finally, the instruction must be given, by which the spirit knows what it is expected to do. This usually involves commanding the spirit to leave the body or dwelling of a victim, to enter into another object, etc.

An extremely simple example of such a conjuration can be found in one of the fifteenth-century exorcism manuals called *The Conjuration of Malign Spirits Dwelling in the Bodies of People, as it is Done in Saint Peter*:[20] "I exorcise you, unclean spirit, in the name of God the Father almighty + and in the name of Jesus Christ His Son + and by the power of the Holy Spirit + that you should recede from this servant of God, [name of victim]."[21] The four components here are easily identifiable:

Declaration:	I exorcise you,
Address:	unclean spirit,
Invocation:	in the name of God the Father almighty + and in the name of Jesus Christ His Son + and by the power of the Holy Spirit +
Instruction:	that you should recede from this servant of God, [name of victim].

In this case, as in the grimoires, the first conjuration applied is very short and simple. Further conjurations are then added as necessary, each one becoming more elaborate and complicated than the last. However, no matter how complicated the conjuration becomes, it retains the same four basic elements. They may be repeated in different forms several times throughout the prayer, and appear in various combinations, but they remain generally recognizable. To illustrate, the *Conjuration of Malign Spirits* continues:

I conjure you, O Devil, by the Father and the Son and the Holy Spirit, and by the patriarchs and prophets, apostles, evangelists, martyrs, confessors, virgins, and all the holy men and holy women of God [. . .] and by our Lord Jesus Christ I conjure you, that you should recede from the servant of God, N. I conjure you, O Devil, by the passion of our Lord Jesus Christ, which he endured for the human race, that you should recede from this servant of God, N. I conjure you, O Devil, by the holy cross on which our Lord [died for] the servant of God, N. [. . .] He commands you, accursed devil, who walked on the sea with dry feet. [. . .] He commands you, accursed devil, who commanded the winds and the sea and the storms. He commands you, accursed devil, who ordered that you be cast from the heights of heaven to the depths of Earth . . . .

This is an extremely abridged version of the exorcism; such texts can run to several pages in length. Yet, the same four elements can be seen in endless repetition throughout the above, as well as in even the most lengthy

Solomonic conjuration. For instance, we can apply what we've learned above to the First Conjuration found in the *Goetia*:

Declaration: I do invocate and conjure thee,

Address: O Spirit N.,

Invocation: and being with power armed from the Supreme Majesty, I do strongly command thee, by Beralanesis, Baldachiensis, Paumachia, and Apologiae Sedes; by the most Powerful Princes, Genii, Liachidae, and Ministers of the Tartarean Abode; and by the Chief Prince of the Seat of Apologia in the Ninth Legion,

Declaration/Invocation: I do invoke thee, and by invocating conjure thee. And being armed with power from the Supreme Majesty, I do strongly command thee, by Him Who spake and it was done, and unto whom all creatures be obedient. Also I, being made after the image of God, endued with power from God, and created according unto His will, do exorcise thee by that most mighty and powerful name of God, El, strong and wonderful;

Address: O thou Spirit N.

Declaration/Invocation: And I command thee by Him who spake the Word and His Fiat was accomplished, and by all the names of God. Also by the names Adonai, Elohim, Elohi, Ehyeh Asher Ehyeh, Zabaoth, Elion, Iah, Tetragrammaton, Shaddai, Lord God Most High, I do exorcise thee and do powerfully command thee,

Address/Instruction: O thou Spirit N., that thou dost forthwith appear unto me here before this Circle in a fair human shape, without any deformity or tortuosity.

Invocation/Declaration: And by this ineffable name, Tetragrammaton Iehovah, do I command thee, at the which being heard the elements are overthrown, the air is shaken, the sea runneth back, the fire is quenched, the earth trembleth, and all the hosts of the celestials, terrestrials, and infernals do tremble together, and are troubled and confounded.

Instruction/Address: Wherefore come thou, O Spirit N., forthwith, and without delay, from any or all parts of the world wherever thou mayest be, and make rational answers unto all things that I shall demand of thee. Come thou peaceably, visibly, and affably, now, and without delay, manifesting that which I shall desire.

Invocation/Instruction: For thou art conjured by the name of the Living and True God, Helioren, wherefore fulfil thou my commands, and persist thou therein unto the end, and according unto mine interest, visibly and affably speaking unto me with a voice clear and intelligible without any ambiguity.

The *Book of Abramelin*, which is now revealed as a rather accurate presentation of typical medieval exorcism, contains some solid practical information on the writing and execution of these conjurations in Book II, Chapter 14, "Concerning the Convocation of the Spirits." First of all, according to the text, the conjurations should be written in the language of one's birth, or at least a language that one understands. (In essence, this is a good instruction; though many of the grimoires do possess "Barbarous Words of Invocation" for which we no longer possess definitions. However, even an understanding of what "Barbarous Words" are is better than the blind recitation of conjurations written in an unfamiliar tongue.) *Abramelin* elsewhere states that the spirits will have no respect for someone who uses words in the rituals that they do not understand.[22]

Next, the instructions stress that the spirits must be conjured by "the authority of and their obedience to the Holy Patriarchs, rehearsing unto them examples of their ruin and fall, of the sentence which God hath pronounced against them, and of their obligation unto servitude; and how on one side and on another they have been vanquished by the Good Angels and by Wise Men . . ." Obviously, *Abramelin* is here instructing us in the "Invocation" portion of conjurations. Further, the aspirant is told to quite directly invoke the presence and aid the holy angels if the spirits refuse to obey.

The conjurations should be performed with modesty, but the operator must in no way appear timid. (The same vital instruction is given to those in Santeria and Palo who wish to work with Ngangas or Prendas.) Like the medieval exorcism manuals, *Abramelin* insists that the operator be "courageous," but should work "in moderation, however, without too overbearing hardiness and bravery." If a spirit shows itself utterly unwilling to obey, one must never give way to anger as it can only do injury to the operator himself, and it is exactly this for which the infernal spirits would be hoping. Instead, one must persevere in the work "with an intrepid heart, and putting your whole trust in God, with a tranquil heart you shall exhort them to yield, letting them see that you have put all your confidence in the Living and Only God, reminding them how powerful and potent He is; thus, therefore, govern yourself, using prudence towards them."

The element of instruction is covered next, where *Abramelin* reminds the operator to include the forms in which the spirits must be commanded to appear. Most grimoiric conjurations simply order the spirit to appear in an agreeable shape, or human form, etc. However, *Abramelin* instead has the operator insist upon shapes revealed by the holy guardian angel, who knows "better than you your nature and constitution, and who understandeth the forms which can terrify you, and those of which you can support the sight."

The *Abramelin* instructions for conjuration then ends with further exhortations to retain faith in the power and authority of God, and in the aid of the guardian angel to control the spirits and protect the operator. The elements of declaration and address are not mentioned, as they were perhaps elements that went without saying. The sixteenth chapter discusses the dismissal of the spirits, though it is much more relaxed about the subject than is common from the grimoiric texts. Usually a license to depart is included as a very important part of any summoning operation. We can see the general form for this in the *Goetia*:

> The License to Depart: O thou Spirit N., because thou has diligently answered unto my demands, and has been very ready and willing to come at my call, I do here license thee to depart unto thy proper place, without causing harm or danger unto man or beast. Depart, then, I say, and be thou very ready to come at my call, being duly exorcised and conjured by the sacred rites of magic. I charge thee to withdraw peaceably and quietly, and the peace of God be ever continued between thee and me. Amen!

Finally, the following two chapters of *Abramelin* (17 and 18) are titled "What We Should Answer Unto the Interrogations of the Spirits, and How We Should Resist Their Demands" and "How He Who Operateth Should Behave as Regardeth the Spirits." There is no need to outline all of the particulars here. Suffice it to say that the given pieces of advice are very good reflections of the instructions given to any official medieval exorcist, such as we saw above.

Constraints and Curses

If the grimoires truly deserve any part of their reputation for harsh treatment of spirits, it is due to the constraints and curses used by both the *Goetia* and the *Key of Solomon the King* to rein in disobedient spirits. These practices are adopted directly from medieval exorcisms, wherein a priest would use torment to drive an obstinate spirit from the body of a victim. The grimoiric techniques are reminiscent of some of the Voodoo-like processes employed in the darker arts of image magick (see chapter 10). The spirit's sigil or name might be threatened with flame, or sealed in a box of noxious fumes. Before we can continue, let's take a look at the process as it exists in the classical texts:

The *Goetia* contains two conjurations, each of which can be repeated ". . . as often as you please", and the text insists that the spirit will appear "without doubt." However, in the unlikely event that the spirit refuses to appear even after several recitations of the exorcisms, a further conjuration called a "Constraint" is read:

> I conjure thee spirit N., by all the most glorious and efficacious names of the most great and incomprehensible Lord God of Hosts, that you comest quickly without delay from all parts and places of the world; wherever thou may be, to make rational answers to my demands and that visible and affably speaking with a voice intelligible to my understanding as aforesaid, I conjure and constrain you spirit N., by all aforesaid and by these seven names by which wise Solomon bound thee and thy fellows in a vessel of Brass. Adonay, Prerai, Tetragrammaton, Anaphexeton, Inessenfatall, Pathatumon, & Itemon. That you appear here before this circle to fulfill my will in all things, that shall seem good unto me. If you be disobedient and refuse to come I will in the power and by the power of the name of the supreme and everliving God, who created both you and me and all the whole world in six days and what is contained in it. Eie, Saray, and by the power of his name Primeumaton which commandeth the whole host of heaven, curse you and deprive you, from ally or office, joy and place, and bind you in the depth of the bottomless pit. There to remain unto the day of the last judgement, and I will bind you into eternal fire & into the lake of fire and brimstone, unless you come forthwith and appear here before this circle to do my will in all things. Therefore come thou! In and by these holy names Adonai, Zabaoth, Adonai, Amiorem, come you, Adonai commandeth you.

This does not differ to any great extent from the standard conjurations we have already discussed, except that we can now see the first threats of discipline entering into the recitation. Actually, even this is a standard aspect of the art of exorcism. The admonition that the exorcist will deprive the demon of "ally or office, joy and place, and bind [it] in the depth of the bottomless pit" comes directly from ancient Middle Eastern sources. Remember the spirits in Babylon as well as the New Testament who feared being cast out "into the deep." The following is a short excerpt from a very long exorcism found in Thompson's *The Devils and Evil Spirits of Babylonia*:

> For the [victim], the son of his God,
>
> Thou shalt have no food to eat,
>
> Thou shalt have no water to drink,
>
> [. . .]
>
> If thou wouldst fly up to heaven
>
> Thou shalt have no wings,
>
> If thou wouldst lurk in ambush on earth
>
> Thou shalt secure no resting-place.

The similarity between this and the *Goetia*'s constraint is apparent: each demon being threatened with the loss of his foothold upon the physical plane and the starvation reserved for those departed spirits who have no human loved ones to feed and care for them.

The *Goetia* then continues with the possibility that the spirit will turn a deaf ear even to the above threats. It suggests that this could be due to the fact that the spirit's king has sent him elsewhere, and he therefore does not have the leave to heed the exorcist's call. An invocation of the king then follows, in which the king is commanded to dispatch the spirit. Other grimoires, such as *The Book of Abramelin*, state that the invocation of a spirit's king is intended as a disciplinary action. One invokes the king in order to establish the proper authority over the disobedient spirit. In any case, the Invocation of the King appears in the *Goetia* as follows:

O you great mighty and powerful King Amaymon,[23] who beareth rule by the power of thy supreme god El over all spirits both superior and inferior of the infernal order in the Dominion of the East, I invocate and command you by the especial and truest name of your god and by god that you worship and obey, and by the seal of thy creation & by the most mighty & powerful name of god Jehovah Tetragrammaton, who cast you out of heaven with all other of the infernal spirits and by all the most powerful and great names of god who created heaven, earth & hell, and all things contained in them, and by their power and virtue & by the name Primeumaton who commandeth the whole host of heaven, that you cause, enforce, & compel N. to come unto me here before this circle in a fair & comely form, without doing any harm to me or any other creature, and to answer truly & faithful to all my requests, that I may accomplish my will and desires, in knowing or obtaining any matter or thing which by office you know is proper for him to perform or to accomplish, through the power of God El who createth and disposeth of all things both celestial, aeriel, terrestrial, and infernal.

This seems to be the *Goetia's* answer to Solomon's invocation of the ruling angel of each spirit. The *Book of Abramelin* also works in this way, having the mage first bind the twelve princes of Hell, and then having those princes deliver the lesser spirits into the mage's bond. If a spirit is ever unwilling or unable to perform a task, one is to summon the spirit's prince to rectify the situation. However, *Abramelin* still places the holy guardian angel in authority over the princes, and it is through him that the mage binds the princes in the first place. If ever a command issued to a prince is not obeyed, the mage is instructed to invoke the angel. Perhaps this concept was originally part of the *Goetia*, but was lost somewhere along its trip from the *Testament of Solomon*. It is also possible that the latter books of the *Lemegeton*, focusing upon the invocation of angels, were intended to fill this gap.

After reading the Invocation of the King—perhaps two or three times—the goetic mage is instructed to return to the original two conjurations and read them several times again(!). It is inconceivable that the spirit would not have appeared by this point, unless the mistake is on the part of the operator. However, the *Goetia* acknowledges the possibility that the spirit might even be bound in chains in Hell, or otherwise not in the custody of his king. (Perhaps due to another exorcist who has bound it?) For this purpose, one is to recite "The general Curse, called the Spirit's Chain against all Spirits that Rebel." According to the text, this conjuration will force the spirit to come ". . . even if he be bound in chains, for the chains will break off from him and he will be set at liberty."

O thou wicked and disobedient spirit, because thou has rebelled and not obeyed nor regarded my words which I have rehearsed; they being all most glorious and incomprehensible names of the true God, maker and creator of you and me and all the world. I do by the power of hose names which no creature is able to resist do curse you into the depths of the bottomless pit, there to remain until the day of doom in chains of fire and brimstone unquenchable, unless you dost forthwith appear before this circle, in this triangle, to do my will. And therefore come peaceably and quickly in & by these names—Adonai, Zabaoth, Adonai, Amioram; come thou! come thou! why stay you for it is the King of Kings, even Adonai commandeth you.

Then, unless the spirit should appear at this point, one continues by writing its name and seal with a consecrated pen upon consecrated virgin parchment. (Remember that wherever the name and seal of a spiritual entity is present, so, too, is the entity itself.) Therefore, when the parchment is placed in a black box full of all manner of stinking fumes, and the box bound with metal wire, it is the essence of the spirit itself that is so entrapped. Though the *Goetia* does not mention a proper material for the box, I have seen lead suggested several times. It is the metal of Saturn, and would heat up quite nicely without burning away.

Before continuing, the *Goetia* instructs the exorcist to take a censer of coals (not the one used to burn the incense), place it in the quarter of the magickal circle from which the spirit is to appear, kindle the flame therein, and recite this Conjuration of the Fire:

> I conjure thee, O fire, by him that made thee and all other good creatures in the world, that you torment, burn and consume this spirit N. for everlasting. I condemn thee, thou spirit N. into fire everlasting, because thou art disobedient and obeyest not my command, nor kept the precepts of the lord thy god, neither wilt thou appear to me nor obey me nor my invocations, having thereby called you forth, who am the servant of the most high and imperial Lord, God of hosts Jehovah, and dignified and fortified by his celestial power and permission, neither comest thou to answer to these my proposals here made unto you, for which your averseness and contempt you are guilty of grand disobedience and rebellion, and therefore I shall excommunicate you and destroy thy name and seal which I have here enclosed in this black box, and shall burn thee in immortal fire and bury thee in immortal oblivion, unless thou immediately comest & appearest visibly, affably, friendly, & courteously here unto me before this circle in this triangle, in a fair and comely form and in no wise terrible, hurtful or frightful to me or any other creatures whatever upon the face of the earth and make rational answers to my requests and perform all my desires in all things that I shall make unto you, &tc.

I find it fascinating that this process, so widely regarded as sadistic and torturous, in fact grants the spirit opportunity after opportunity to appear before the real discipline is brought to bear. The *Goetia* suggests that the spirit might just appear after this Conjuration of the Fire. If not, then the black box should be hung from the tip of the magickal sword, dangled over the hot coals, and the following curse recited:

> Now O thou spirit N., since thou art still pernicious and disobedient and will not appear unto me to answer to such things as I should have desired of you or would have been satisfied in &tc. I do in the name and by the power and dignity of the omnipotent immortal Lord God of hosts Jehovah Tetragrammaton, the only creator of heaven, earth, and hell and all that is in them. Who is the marvelous disposer of al things both visible and invisible curse you and deprive you from all your offices, joy and place and do bind thee in the depths of the bottomless pit, there to remain until the day of the last judgment. I say into the lake of fire & brimstone which is prepared for all rebellious, disobedient, obstinate & pernicious spirits, let all the Holy company of heaven curse thee. The Sun, Moon, and Stars, the light and all the hosts of heaven curse thee. I curse thee into the fire unquenchable & torments unspeakable, and as thy name and seal is contained in this box, chained and bound up and shall be choked in sulphurous & stinking substance and burnt in this material fire, so I in the name Jehovah, and by the power and dignity of these three names Tetragrammaton, Anaphexeton, & Primeumaton, cast thee, O thou disobedient spirit N., into the lake of fire which is prepared for the damned and cursed spirits and there to remain until the day of doom and never more to be remembered of before the face of god which shall come to judge the quick and the dead and the world by fire.

After which, the exorcist should place the black box into the fire, and the spirit is sure to eventually manifest. Once it does, the fire must be quenched, sweet perfume must be offered (on the regular censer), and the welcoming and address to the spirit can continue.

The *Key of Solomon the King* offers a very similar version of this process. It is difficult to determine which one might have come first, and which borrowed the procedure. The extended length of the Key's procedure (eight pages!) suggests it may be the original, though it makes no mention of a black box.

The *Key* first attempts to summon the spirits with a conjuration, followed by a stronger and more potent conjuration. If these fail, then a short address to the angels is made for help, followed by an extremely powerful conjuration, the latter of which should conjure the spirits even if they are "bound with chains of iron and fire, or shut up in some strong place, or retained by an Oath." (Similar to the *Goetia's* constraint.) If these fail, the *Key* suggests (Book I, Chapter 7) that the spirits may be summoned to some other place by another exorcist by the same conjurations. Therefore, the exorcist should request that "they should at least send him some Messengers, or some individual to declare unto him where they are, how employed, and the reason why they cannot come and obey him."

It is only if these attempts fail that one is to employ the full curse. In this case one is to write the names of the spirits on consecrated virgin paper. The paper is then smeared with mud, dust, or clay. Then, the exorcist is to kindle a fire with dry rue, powdered assafoetida and "other things of evil odour." A very short Conjuration of the Fire is recited, and then the paper is cast directly into the flame while the curse (similar in content to the *Goetia's*) is read. Once the spirits finally agree to appear and obey the exorcist, their names must be written again on fresh paper, and perfumed with gum benjamin, olybdanum (frankincense), and storax.

For the stinking fumes, both the *Key* and *Goetia* suggest the use of asafetida,[24] otherwise known as *Ferula assafoetida*, an Asian herb that has a truly offensive smell when burned. This herb is used in small quantities in food to aid digestion, so it can be found in delis, health food stores, the Asian spice rack at your local supermarket, etc. I have also seen it suggested that paprika can be substituted, as it has the same color and a "rancid hot taste." The *Goetia* also has one use brimstone (sulfur), and both texts suggest utilizing even more things of an "evil odour."

Where it comes to the sweet odors offered when the spirits finally appear, the *Goetia* makes no suggestion. However, the ingredients listed in the *Key* seem to mimic the recipe for the sacred perfume given in Exodus, much like the incense used in *The Book of Abramelin* (see chapter 6.)

Thus are the curses and punishments employed by the medieval exorcist to constrain rebellious spirits. In chapter 10, we discussed one particular magickal image that seemed similarly sadistic, involving the jabbing of needles into the wax, melting upon hot coals, etc. And the spell was to gain the physical love of a woman! Yet, deeper investigation revealed the possibility that the spell was not intended to inflict pain on a hapless victim—but instead to sympathetically induce the sharp and burning passions of lust.

In this chapter, we also encountered a rather similar technique used by Santeros and Paleros to excite their own Familiars into action. Their use of spices and peppers in their Ngangas are not intended to burn or torture the inhabiting spirit, but merely to create a mystical vibration of heat and activity within which the spirit cannot lapse into inactivity.

I find the comparison with the grimoiric constraints and curses very intriguing. There we also find noxious and hot materials used to "excite" an unwilling or unable spirit. The *Goetia's* Conjuration of the Fire even threatens to bury the black box containing the demon's sigil, reminding me of the Palo Mayombe practice of cementing a rebellious Prenda into its pot and burying the entire thing under a tree. The similarities and differences between the two traditions suggest one of at least two things: on one hand, we may have two parallel, yet unconnected, magickal techniques in different cultures. These kinds of similarities between shamanic systems is quite common. On the other hand, we might have a further hint of connection between Africa and medieval European magick. In that case, the examples in the grimoires would illustrate a practice having mutated over time and distance.

Perhaps there is some relation in all of this to the "spiritual heat" mastered by the shaman (see chapter 2). It was considered necessary for the master to gain a state of spiritual agitation through which he ascended beyond the physical, and, interestingly enough, could not be harmed by injuries similar to those inflicted upon our goetic spirits and magickal images. The shaman could walk across or even swallow hot coals, apply heated metal to his skin, pierce himself with needles, or cut himself with blades. None of it could cause him harm because his own spirit already vibrated at the intense (ecstatic) pitch of heat and pain. Even more importantly, the physical afflictions were often a part of *how* the shaman reached such a vibration in the first place.

It might be safe to assume, then, that these same principles are at work in the techniques of agitating or "stirring up" earthbound spirits. Being that they are themselves beyond the physical, they should also be beyond physical concepts of injury or pain. Of course, by the time of the grimoiric constraints, we see such inclusions as threats of being thrown into hell, and the stinking substances which seem more geared toward nausea than spiritual heat. It is certainly understandable if one assumes that some amount of the Christian bitterness toward "demons" has crept into and corrupted the practice.

On the other hand, such stinking perfumes are sometimes prescribed by the grimoires to *attract*, rather than punish, infernal spirits. Agrippa advises the use of pungent smells in the summoning of the spirits of Saturn, and "in every evil matter, as hatred, anger, misery, and the like . . ."[25] The *Key of Solomon the King* instructs in Book II, Chapter 10, the use of sweet incenses for summoning good spirits and those of "evil savour" for the evil spirits. Therefore, it is even possible that the noxious fumes are themselves a kind of sympathetic magick meant to connect with and "stir up" the spirit who otherwise refuses (or is unable) to manifest.

Of course, the use of these curses will have to be left to the discretion of each exorcist. In all honesty, I know of few practicing mages who find much use for them at all. The lengthy conjurations repeated several times are generally more than enough to induce the necessary trance to make contact. (The concept of the spirit being unwilling or unable to appear hardly plays into it, since the spirit is supposed to reside anywhere its sigil is inscribed. Thus, failure to perceive the spirit is generally placed in the fault of the operator, and not the spirits.) Plus, there exist systems such as *Abramelin* that instruct against any harsh treatment of spirits, and instead rely upon the invocation of angels to do the chastising of disobedient spirits for us.

"Historical Turning-Point": The Testament of Solomon

Joseph Peterson, on his *Esoteric Archives* CD, explains the *Testament of Solomon* as an Old Testament pseudepigraphic "catalog of demons." It is pseudepigraphic in that it claims to have been written by King Solomon himself, while the text probably originates somewhere during the first through third centuries CE. As such, it is still one of the oldest known magickal texts attributed to Solomon, and is generally considered the father of the Solomonic tradition.

We have already discussed the overall plot of this apocryphal book in this chapter. In short, it depicts the ancient king performing a series of exorcisms in which he binds various demons of social ills and physical diseases. Most notably, he makes contact with the demons of the zodiacal decanates, and thus launches the pattern upon which grimoires such as the *Goetia* would later be based. In that same light, the *Testament* also depicts Solomon putting each bound demon to good practical use:

> 107. [. . .] And I commanded [the Spirits] to fetch water in the Temple of God. And I furthermore prayed to the Lord God to cause the demons without, that hamper humanity, to be bound and made to approach the Temple of God. Some of these demons I condemned to do the heavy work of the construction of the Temple of God. Others I shut up in prisons. Others I ordered to wrestle with fire in (the making of) gold and silver, sitting down by lead and spoon. And to make ready places for the other demons in which they should be confined.

It is obvious that this document was of Christian origin, as several of the spirits reveal prophesies that clearly indicate the coming of Jesus Christ as the Messiah. Plus, the story itself (as an Old Testament mythos) places the work into the trend of the day for Christian mystics to adopt aspects of Judaic mysticism.

In *Ritual Magic* (p. 33), Elizabeth Butler outlines more of the diverse cultural influences at work in the *Testament of Solomon*. She points out the Assyrian and Babylonian origins of the zodiacal demons of disease (though she is certain they entered the *Testament* through Egypt), and the similarities between some of Solomon's entities and the Chaldean and Akkadian gods. I also believe that much of the *Testament's* structure and ritual procedure can be ultimately traced to these Mesopotamian sources.

Professor Butler also includes several biblical sources for the *Testament's* content—from the book of Tobit (contained in the Catholic Bible), to the apocrypha (especially the *Book of Enoch*, which lists dozens of angelic names), and even the Talmud from which the story of the demon Ornias was derived. (In this latter we see a direct Jewish influence on the text.) We must also remember the *Testament's* (and *Goetia's*) relationship to Arabic mythologies, including the Quran and *The Arabian Thousand and One Nights*. The very fact that the story centers upon King Solomon betrays such Arabian influence.

Professor Butler also indicates the Egypto-Hellenic and Gnostic influences in the text, especially in the names attributed to various entities (especially angels). Looking into the Testament, we can see the twenty-seventh spirit of the zodiac (Pheth) mentions the word "aeon," which is a Gnostic reference to a supercelestial force of time. The ninth zodiacal spirit is constrained by an angel with the Gnostic divine name "Iaoth." The eleventh spirit of this same group is countered by "Iae, Ieô, sons of Sabaôth," which are all Gnostic divine names found in the Greek magickal papyri. There are even several references in the text to Solomon commanding all of the spirits "upon the earth, and under the earth, on dry land and in the water . . ." as we see in the Gnostic ritual of the headless (or bornless) one. And these are merely a few examples of the many Gnostic elements within in the *Testament*.

One can also take note of the heavily shamanic nature of Solomon's methods, besides the fact that he is constraining infernal spirits to perform work for the living. It is actually quite akin to what we would later see in Book I of Agrippa's *Occult Philosophy* concerning natural magick. After discovering from Asmodeus that the demon's sacred animal is a certain kind of fish, Solomon demonstrates the power that simple knowledge (and a little shamanic know-how) grants him over the spirit:

> 25. [. . .] And I Solomon glorified God, who gave wisdom to me Solomon his servant. And the liver of the fish and its gall I hung on the spike of a reed, and burned it over Asmodeus because of his being so strong, and his unbearable malice was thus frustrated.

Or this verse where Solomon makes use of his own spittle in an act to subdue a ferocious spirit:

> 32. [. . .] And one came before me who carried his face high up in the air, but the rest of the spirit curled away like a snail. And it broke through the few soldiers, and raised also a terrible dust on the ground, and carried it upwards; and then again hurled it back to frighten us, and asked what questions I could ask as a rule. And I stood up, and spat on the ground in that spot, and sealed with the ring of God.[26]

The use of saliva in magick has an extremely ancient heritage. In the most primitive of tribal magicks, the spittle of the local holy man was itself considered a kind of magickal elixir (remember that shamans were specifically more-than-human. See chapter 2.). Saliva was used in Babylonian healing rites, wherein the priest would spit into his patient's mouth as part of the cure. We can see echoes of this in the invocations used during rites of exorcism, where the priest proclaims, "The great Lord Ia hath sent me! He hath added His pure spell to mine, He hath added His pure voice to mine, *He hath added His pure spittle to mine*, He hath added His pure prayer to mine!"[27]

Joseph Peterson, in his version of the *Testament of Solomon*,[28] references several biblical instances of the magickal use of spittle; such as Mark 7:33 and 8:23 wherein Jesus heals a deaf-mute and a blind man by administering his own saliva. In John 9:6, we encounter a scene in which Jesus makes use of his spittle in a fashion very similar to Solomon in the *Testament*. This time it is in order to cure a man of blindness: "As he said this, he spat on the ground and made clay of the spittle, and anointed the man's eyes with the clay."

There are other shamanic elements within the *Testament* as well. Such as toward the end of the account, where the world pillar we discussed in chapter 2 seems evident. In this case, two demons are tricked by Solomon—on the pretense of proving their mighty strength—into lifting a massive pillar of stone into the air. Once there, the king sealed them with his ring and commanded them, "Watch." Being forced to sustain the weight between them, neither demon is free to cause mischief in the world at large. According to the legend, "the spirits have remained upholding it until this day." But, just as with the world pillar of the ancient shaman, "on whatever day this stone fall, then shall be the end of the world."

Finally, we cannot forget the principal thread of exorcism and the healing of disease that runs from the ancient Middle East through the *Testament of Solomon* and into the medieval grimoires. Plus, if the *Testament* is not the first exorcist's manual to suggest putting the beasties to work, it is certainly the door through which that idea entered into such literature as the *Key of Solomon the King* and (especially) the *Goetia*.

The self-descriptions given by the spirits to Solomon in the *Testament* do indeed remind us of the entries recorded in the *Goetia*. Such as the first spirit, Ornias:

> 10. And Solomon said to him: "Tell me, O demon, to what Zodiacal sign thou art subject." And he answered: "To the Water-pourer. And those who are consumed with desire for the noble virgins upon earth [. . .], these I strangle. But in case there is no disposition to sleep, I am changed into three forms. Whenever men come to be enamoured of women, I metamorphose myself into a comely female; and I take hold of the men in their sleep, and play with them. And after a while I again take to my wings, and hie me to the heavenly regions. I also appear as a lion, and I am commanded by all the demons. I am offspring of the Archangel Uriel, the power of God."

Although, we can see here that the focus is still not upon what the spirit can do for Solomon. Instead, he inquires into the natural function of the demon, and is interested in how to bind him from performing it. (Of course, this does not stop Solomon from putting Ornias and most of the other demons to work in the construction of the temple. Others, such as Obizuth were imprisoned in goetic fashion.) Notice, too, that the spirit Ornias claims to be the *offspring* of Uriel. This suggests the same kind of intimate relationship between the demons and the gods as was observed in Babylonian and other Middle Eastern religions.

In the *Testament*, King Solomon first summons a succession of fifteen demonic spirits (or twenty-one, as one conjuration resulted in seven female spirits of the Pleiades.) Among them were Beelzeboul (the Prince of Demons), Asmodeus, Obizuth (apparently a form of Lilith), and even one Rath, the "Lion-bearer," who represents the legion of spirits exorcised into the swine by Jesus in the New Testament. Others are given names such as Envy, Strife, Deception, and Jealousy. Each of these spirits embodies various illnesses, sins, or calamities that may be inflicted upon mankind, from destroying families to torching fields, and from violent physical illnesses to the sinking of ships. One spirit even describes itself as drifting on the sound of children crying in the night.

After these otherwise random entities, Solomon demands one more demonic power brought before him, and is greeted with the sight of thirty-six individual spirits at once. The king describes them as possessing many differing faces, such as those of asses, oxen, and birds. They introduced themselves in the following manner, all speaking as with a single voice:

> We are the thirty-six elements, the world-rulers of this darkness. . . . we also present ourselves before thee like the other spirits, from ram and bull, from both twin and crab, lion and virgin, scales and scorpion, archer, goat-horned, water-pourer, and fish.

Of course, these are the malign spirits of the thirty-six zodiacal decanates. Here, finally, is the true point of contact in the *Testament of Solomon* between the ancient traditions of zodiacal magick and the medieval grimoires such as the *Goetia* (see chapter 10, section "Image Magick").

Once they were all constrained before him, Solomon demanded the same information from them as he had for the other demons, but also seems to have asked these thirty-six for their proper characters. From there, the general arrangement and operations of these spirits should be familiar to the grimoiric student. The first spirit came forward on behalf of the first group of three and addressed Solomon:

> I am the first decans of the Zodiacal circle, and I am called the ram, and with me are these two.

These, then, are the demons of the three decanates (or faces) of Aries, and should therefore be governed by the planets Mars, Sol, and Venus respectively. No further clues are given to the proper arrangement of these spirits, but Solomon continues to interrogate each of the thirty-six on an individual basis. They reveal their names, their functions (sicknesses), and short incantations (including the names of their opposing angels) that will drive them away.

Spirit	Zodiacal Sign	Function	Incantation
1. Ruax	Aries	Causes the heads of men to be idle, and pillages their brows. "[29]	Michael, imprison Ruax!"
2. Barsafael	Aries	Causes migraines.	"Gabriel, imprison Barsafael!"
3. Arôtosael	Aries	Harms the eyes.	"Uriel, imprison Aratosael!"
4. ? Spirit missing in text	Taurus	?	?
5. Iudal	Taurus	Causes deafness.	"Uruel Iudal!"
6. Sphendonaêl	Taurus	Causes tumours of the parotid gland, inflammation of the tonsils, and tetanic recurvation.[30]	"Sabrael, imprison Sphendonaêl!"
7. Sphandôr	Gemini	Weakens the strength of the shoulders, causing them to tremble; paralyzes the nerves of the hands, and breaks and bruises the bones of the neck and sucks out the marrow.	"Araêl, imprison Sphandôr!"
8. Belbel	Gemini	Distorts the hearts and minds of men.	"Araêl, imprison Belbel!"
9. Kurtaêl	Gemini	Sends colics in the bowels, induces pains.	"Iaôth, imprison Kurtaêl!"

Spirit	Zodiacal Sign	Function	Incantation
10. Metathiax	Cancer	Causes the reins to ache	"Adônaêl, imprison Metathiax!"
11. Katanikotaêl	Cancer	Creates strife and wrongs in men's homes, and sends on them hard temper.	Iae, Ieô, sons of Sabaôth, in the name of the great God let him shut up Katanikotaêl.[31]
12. Saphathoraél	Cancer	Inspires drunkenness in men, and delights, causing them to stumble.	Iacô, Iealô, Iôelet, Sabaôth, Ithoth, Bae[32]
13. Bobêl	Leo	Causes nervous illness.	"Adonaêl, imprison Bothothêl!"
14. Kumeatêl	Leo	Inflicts shivering fits and torpor.	"Zôrôêl, imprison Kumentaêl!"
15. Roêlêd	Leo	Causes cold and frost and pain in the stomach.	"Iax, bide not, be not warmed, for Solomon is fairer than eleven fathers."
16. Atrax	Virgo	Inflicts fevers, irremediable and harmful.	"The fever which is from dirt. I exorcise thee by the throne of the most high God, retreat from dirt and retreat from the creature fashioned by God."[33]
17. Ieropaêl	Virgo	Sits upon the stomach, and causes convulsions in the bath and in the road, throws down men.	"Iudarizê, Sabunê, Denôê"[34]
18. Buldumêch	Virgo	Separates wife from husband and brings about a grudge between them.	"The God of Abram, and the God of Isaac, and the God of Jacob commands thee—retire from this house in peace."[35]
19. Naôth	Libra	Attacks the knees.	"Phnunoboêol, depart Nathath!"[36]
20. Marderô	Libra	Sends on men an incurable fever.	"Sphênêr, Rafael, retire, drag me not about, flay me not"[37]
21. Alath	Libra	Causes asthma in children.	"Rorêx, do thou pursue Alath"[38]
22. ? Spirit missing in text	Scorpius	?	?
23. Nefthada	Scorpius	Causes the reins to ache, and brings about dysury.	Iathôth, Uruêl, Nephthada[39]
24. Akton	Scorpius	Causes ribs and lumbic muscles to ache.	Marmaraôth, Sabaôth, pursue Akton[40]
25. Anatreth	Sagittarius	Rends burnings and fevers into the entrails.	"Arara, Charara!"
26. Enenuth	Sagittarius	Steals away men's minds, and changes their hearts, and makes a man toothless.[41]	"Allazoôl, pursue Enenuth!"[42]

Spirit	Zodiacal Sign	Function	Incantation
27. Phêth	Sagittarius	Makes men consumptive and causes hemorrhagia.	"I exorcise thee by the eleventh aeon to stop, I demand, Phêth (Axiôphêth)!"[43]
28. Harpax	Capricornus	Sends sleeplessness on men.	Kokphnêdismos[44]
29. Anostêr	Capricornus	Engenders uterine mania and pains in the bladder.	I exorcise thee, Anostêr. Stop by Marmaraô[45]
30. Alleborith	Capricornus	Associated with swallowing fish bones.	See footnote 46
31. Hephesimireth	Aquarius	Causes lingering disease.	"Seraphim, Cherubim, help me!"[47]
32. Ichthion	Aquarius	Paralyzes muscles and confuses them.	"Adonaêth, help!"
33. Agchoniôn	Aquarius	Lurks among swaddling-clothes[48] and in the precipice.	Lycurgos, ycurgos, kurgos, yrgos, gos, os[49]
34. Autothith	Pisces	Causes grudges and fighting.	Alpha and Omega[50]
35. Phthenoth	Pisces	Casts the evil eye on every man.	See footnote 51
36 Bianakith	Pisces	Has a grudge against the human. body. Lays waste to houses, causes flesh to decay, etc.	Mêltô, Ardu, Anaath[52]

To properly complete this information, I should add that the *Testament* ends with King Solomon conjuring two final demons: Ephippas and Abezithibod. The latter demon was conjured from the Red Sea and claimed to be the spirit who hardened pharaoh's heart before the Exodus, and aided the Egyptian army in their pursuit of the Israelites across the Red Sea. When the Egyptians were drowned in the waters, Abezithibod was imprisoned there as well, entrapped beneath the massive pillar discussed earlier in this section. Solomon had these final two demons carry that pillar into the air and bound them to hold it there until the destruction of this world.

Of all the elements of the *Testament* and earlier mysticisms that were adopted into the *Goetia*, it is extremely unfortunate that one of the most important was missed: the angelic powers necessary to control the spirits. (It seems highly unlikely that the angels contacted in the *Pauline Art* or *Almadel* would have much relation to the goetic demons. Although, the *Ars Nova*, which is connected with the *Goetia*, does invoke all of the standard angelic hosts.) Other texts did not bypass this vital aspect of the magick, such as the *Key of Solomon the King*: first, we see their invocation in the prayers spoken upon entering the magickal circle:

> Let all demons fly from this place, especially those who are opposed unto this work, and let the Angels of Peace assist and protect this Circle, from which let discord and strife fly and depart.

Then, if the first two long conjurations are not successful, the angels are called upon again in an "Address to the Angels":

> I conjure and pray ye, O ye Angels of God, and ye Celestial Spirits, to come unto mine aid; come and behold the Signs of Heaven, and be my witness before the Sovereign Lord, of the disobedience of these evil and fallen Spirits who were at one time your companions.

Agrippa also assures us in his Book III, chapter 32 ("How . . . evil spirits may be overcome by us"), that ". . . whosoever shall intellectually work in evil spirits, shall by the power of good spirits bind them; but he that shall work only worldily, shall work to himself judgement and damnation." In *The Magus*, Book II (p. 102), we find that "Likewise we are often to make orations and prayers to God and the good Angels before we invocate any evil spirit, conjuring him by Divine Power."

In order to address this lack in the *Goetia*, some modern practitioners choose to incorporate the seventy-two angels of the Shem haMephoresh, who are also associated with the zodiacal decans. The only problem is that these angels have their own lists of demons, and have no historical relation to the *Testament* or the *Goetia*. Perhaps we might look into the apocrypha (such as the *Book of Enoch* or the *Testament* itself), the Talmud, the Greek magickal papyri and Gnostic material,[53] and even the Arabic magickal texts for the angelic names best suited to the *Goetia*. Such a project would mean researching each and every demonic name in the grimoire individually, to discover any celestial powers associated with them. Of course, one could also follow King Solomon's example and simply demand of each spirit the name of the angel who opposes him.

What is important to our discussion here is the understanding that the angels are, in fact, necessary to spirit conjuration. Consider this exchange between Solomon and the spirit Tephras:

> 33 . . . And I said to him: "I am Solomon; when therefore thou wouldst do harm, by whose aid dost thou do it?" But he said to me: "By the Angel's, by whom also the third day's fever is lulled to rest." So I questioned him, and said: "And by what name?" And he answered: "That of the Archangel Azael." And I summoned the Archangel Azael, and set a seal on the demon, and commanded him . . .

Note how the demon is said here to act only when Azael allows him, similar to the Mesopotamian demons we discussed earlier in this chapter. The spirit is not evil in and of himself, but is simply an agent of disease used by the archangel Azael, who in turn serves only divine will (or natural law, etc.). Once the angel's name is known, Solomon immediately summons that angel and sets the celestial being's seal upon the spirit. The spirit is bound by the consent and under the authority of the ruling angel.

Thus, in any goetic working, the mage will not have mastery over the disease unless he can first gain the alliance of the necessary healing angel. This is not done rashly or hastily in the moments before attempting to treat the sickness. It is a process the shaman-mage must dedicate to months in advance, with the sole intention of mastering the ailment in general. The angel's name and information can be added to the mage's *Sepher Malachim*, and invoked according to the processes described in chapter 8 of this work. Once contact is established, one needs only ask the angel how to properly exorcise the demon, making sure to ask for any necessary words of power, etc.

Spirit-Taming in the Grimoires

And so from the *Testament of Solomon* descends the infamous *Goetia*. While the plot differs between the two texts, the foundational mythology upon which they are based does not. In both cases King Solomon is said to have summoned and bound all of the listed entities, and that it was through their agency that King Solomon gained his fame and power. Both texts also indicate that holy men can, by right, domesticate the infernal spirits to perform servile work. It is also true that both texts concern the demonic forces of the zodiacal decans, even if the attributions for the *Goetia* have been corrupted.

The "Magical Requisites" of the *Goetia* seem to be simplified versions of those found in the *Key of Solomon the King*. They appear in the *Goetia* in one short section, not including the pentagram, hexagram, secret seal, and brass vessel. Their brevity indicates the "notebook" form of this grimoire, assuming the operator already knows enough about these tools to collect them and prepare them properly:

The other magickal requisites are: a scepter, a sword, a mitre, a cap, a long white robe of linen, and other garments for the purpose; also a girdle of lion's skin three inches broad, with all the names written about it which be round the outmost part of the Magical Circle. Also perfumes, and a chafing-dish of charcoal kindled to put the fumes on, to smoke or perfume the place appointed for action; also anointing oil to anoint thy temples and thine eyes with; and fair water to wash thyself in.

This is followed with very simplified prayers intended for use with a kind of abbreviated Solomonic ritual bath:

The Adoration at the Bath: "Thou shalt purge me with hyssop, O Lord! And I shall be clean: Thou shalt wash me, and I shall be whiter than snow." And at the putting on of thy garments thou shalt say:
The Adoration at the Induing of the Vestments: "By the figurative mystery of these holy vestures I will clothe me with the armour of salvation in the strength of the Most High, Ancor, Amacor, Amides, Theodonias, Anitor; that my desired end may be effected through Thy strength, O Adonai! Unto Whom the praise and glory will for ever and ever belong! Amen!" After thou hast so done, make prayers unto God according unto thy work, as Solomon hath commanded.

More than likely, the last line of the above is in reference to the prayers for the circle and tools outlined in the *Ars Nova*. We will cover the preparation of the sacred space for this work in the section on magickal circles below.

Once the place of working is established, and all is prepared for the work, the *Goetia* then instructs one to utilize exorcist-style conjurations to summon the entity and bind it within the triangle of art (explained with magickal circles below); and, thanks to the *Ars Nova*, into the brass vessel as well. In particular, this operation makes use of a series of metallic talismans bearing the seal of the demon summoned. I have already covered this in depth in chapter 10, suggesting that the seal should be placed either in the triangle or within the vessel in the triangle (and *not* worn around the neck of the operator). The idea is to summon the demon with all of the conjurations and "requisites" outlined in the *Goetia*, but to never have to repeat those ceremonies twice for any one spirit. Once summoned, bound to the talisman, and sealed in the vessel, the spirit should always be conveniently on hand as a Familiar—in the same manner as the Santerian Nganga. It should only be necessary to open the vessel and speak the demon's name to stir it into action. Perhaps one should even rub the vessel while speaking the name in the tradition of the *Thousand and One Nights*—it should serve nicely to agitate the vessel and stir up the spirit.

I also discussed in chapter 10 the corruption of the astrological attributions in the *Goetia* from its Arabic source material. Technically, the seventy-two infernal spirits should relate directly to the thirty-six decans of the zodiac—a daytime and nighttime demon for each of the thirty-six faces. They should ultimately possess attributions similar to those hinted at in the *Testament of Solomon*, but this is sadly not the case. I have seen various attempts to "correct" the material, but have been largely unimpressed with them. The same goes for my own meager attempt at the same:

Of the seventy-two listed spirits, a full forty-six of them are described with absolutely no clue as to their proper zodiacal or directional attributes.[54] If any solution is to be found, it will have to come through the twenty-six remaining spirits that are given such hints as to astrological and directional association. I took the time to list and categorize the goetic demons based on these.

First we must consider the four cardinal directions and their demonic rulers as listed in the *Goetia*, which are the usual rabbinical and *Testament of Solomon* demon kings:

These 72 Kings be under the Power of Amaymon, Corson, Zimimay (or Ziminiar), and Goap, who are the Four Great Kings ruling in the Four Quarters or Cardinal Points, viz.: East, West, North, and South
. . .

Thus, as we look through the *Goetia*, we can keep our eyes open not only for directional references, but also for any spirits said to be under the authority of one of the above-listed great kings. There happen to be only six such references in the text, and all of them relate to the eastern direction or to the rulership of Amaymon.

1) Bael: *". . . a King ruling in the East."*

2) Agares: *"He is under the power of the East."*

3) Vassago: *". . . being of the same nature as Agares."*

32) Asmoday: *"He is first and choicest under the Power of Amaymon. . ."*

33) Gaap: *". . . things that belong to the Dominion of Amaymon his King."*[55]

70) Seere: *"He is a mighty Prince, and powerful under Amaymon, King of the East."*

Unless we count Gaap's apparent dual-rulership (east and south—see footnote with Gaap above), none of the other great kings or cardinal directions are given reference in the text. It would seem plausible that the first three spirits of the *Goetia*—all listed as demons of the east—should relate to the first three faces of Aries (Mars, Sol, and Venus). However, the planets actually associated with these spirits are Sol (king), Venus (duke), and Jupiter (prince) respectively. Plus, following the successive order of decans through the rest of the list of spirits shows no better result.

There are two further spirits who are at least given a directional reference, though they seem to live in the cross-quarters rather than the cardinal points. Perhaps they are under the dual rulership of two great kings:

9) Paimon: *"He is to be observed toward the North West."*

13) Beleth: *"[The Exorcist] must hold a hazel stick in his hand, stretched forth towards the South and East quarters making a Triangle . . ."*

Finally, there are three spirits that are granted direct references to the signs of the zodiac:

8) Barbatos: *". . . appeareth when the Sun is in Virgo."*

10) Buer: *"A great President and appeareth in Sagittary."*

14) Lerayou: *"This belongeth to Sagittary."*

If we assume that the *Goetia* makes use of the zodiacal attribution of Element to cardinal direction (Fire = east, Earth = south, Air = west, and Water = north), then these three spirits would be under the command of Gaap, Amaymon, and Amaymon respectively. On the other hand, perhaps we are supposed to consider the zodiac signs as placed around the circle in proper order (just like on a horoscope chart). If this were the case, the kings ruling these three spirits would be Corson (of the west), Gaap (of the south), and Gaap respectively. However, these are both merely speculation, and in neither case do they illuminate a logical pattern of attribution for the entire list of seventy-two demons.

There is also a single spirit in the *Goetia*—**66) Cimeies**—who is given a geographical location. It is said that he "ruleth over all spirits in the parts of Africa." To decipher this, we might need to research the classical texts of magick (like Agrippa's *Three Books*) that describe various parts of the world as governed by different astrological forces. Any zodiacal sign that governs Africa is potentially the clue to the proper rulership and attribution of the marquis Cimeies.

Finally, as I pointed out in chapter 10, the magickal images associated with the *Goetia* are sometimes of a zodiacal nature, betraying their origins in the Babylonian systems of decan magick. However, out of the full set of seventy-two, a mere fifteen are described with (seemingly) obvious references to zodiacal imagery:

5) **Marbas:** ". . . appears at first in the form of a great lion. . ." (Leo?)

6) **Valefar:** ". . . appeareth in the form of a lion with a man's head . . ." (Leo?)

20) **Purson:** "He appeareth commonly like a man with a lion's face, carrying a cruel viper in his hand, and riding on a Bear." (Many possibilities, including Leo and Ursa Major or Minor?)

21) **Morax:** "He appeareth like a great bull with a man's face." (Taurus?)

22) **Ipos:** ". . . and appeareth in the form of an Angel with a lion's head. . ." (Leo and/or Aquarius?)[56]

32) **Asmoday:** "He appears with three heads, whereof the first is like a bull, the second like a man, and the third like a ram." (I would bet on Aries, Taurus, and Gemini.)[57]

43) **Sabnach:** ". . . appearing in the form of an armed soldier with a lion's head, riding on a pale colored horse." (Leo? Perhaps Mars?[58])

45) **Vine:** ". . . and appeareth in the form of a lion riding on a black horse with a viper in his hand." (Mars? Saturn[59])

48) **Haagenti:** ". . . the form of a mighty bull with griffins wings at first. . ." (Taurus?)

51) **Balam:** ". . . appearing with three heads, the first is like a bull's, the second like a man's, and the third like a ram's head . . ." (Aries, Taurus, and Gemini—again!)[60]

52) **Alloces:** ". . . appearing in the form of a soldier riding on a great horse. His face is like a lion's, very red, having eyes flaming." (Leo? Mars?[61])

55) **Orobas:** ". . . appearing at first like a horse . . ." (Could, perhaps, be Sagittarius?)

59) **Orias:** ". . . appears in the form of a lion . . ." (Leo?)

60) **Vapula:** ". . . appearing in the form of a lion with griffin's wings." (Leo?)

61) **Zagan:** ". . . appears at first in the form of a bull with griffin's wings." (Taurus?)

Personally, I can find no rhyme nor reason in all of this material. I only hope that the data offered above will aid other scholars in their pursuits of the mysteries—or the restoration—of this text.

The problem with this flaw in the *Goetia* is that the text explicitly calls for one to inscribe the triangle, and thus evoke the spirit, in the quarter in which the spirit resides (under the great king who rules him). If we restrict ourselves to only those spirits of whom we can be (relatively) sure, we are limited to the six or seven spirits with solid directional references—most of them eastern. For all of the rest, it is usually suggested that one inscribe the triangle in the east anyway, since we cannot know their proper directions.

On the other hand, the text refers to three spirits who appear in relation to zodiacal signs, usually when the Sun enters that sign. This indicates the kind of astrological magickal timing we have grown accustomed to in these texts. Yet, it has broken down in the *Goetia*; if we attempt to apply such timing to the spirits of which we can be certain, we again limit ourselves; this time to only three spirits, and for none of whom we know the necessary great king! Several more have vague and irregular zodiacal imagery. However, any attempt to decide exactly where any sign should lay around the circle is speculation at best.

At least the *Goetia* remains a workable system if we forgo the directional associations of the great kings, and if we forget the origins of these spirits in the decans. Apparently, so far as the author of the *Goetia* was concerned, these were merely a group of infernal spirits who were governed by the seven planets. A fairly elaborate system of magickal timing is outlined in the text, perhaps added by the ancient transcriber who hadn't yet learned his astrology(?):

Observations: Thou art to observe first the Moon's age for the working. The best days are when the Moon is 2, 4, 6, 8, 10, 12, or 14 days old, as Solomon sayeth, and no other days are profitable etc.

The Chief Kings may be bound from 9 to 12 of the clock at noon, and from 3 until sunset. Marquises may be bound from 3 of the clock in the afternoon until nine at night and from 9 at night until sunrising.[62] Dukes may be bound from sunrising until noonday in clear weather; Prelates may be bound in any hour of the day. Knights may be bound from the dawning of the day until sunrising[63] or from four of the clock until sunset. Presidents may be bound in any hour of the day, except twilight, at night, if the King whom he is under is being also invoked, etc.[64] Counts or Earls may be bound in any hour of the day if it be in the woods or any other place where men resort not, or where no noise is, etc.

Of course, this does not show much more rhyme or reason than most anything else in the *Goetia*. We will simply have to wait for some intrepid scholar to translate the Arabic magickal texts into English, beginning with the *Picatrix*.

Astrology is not the only point of bad transition between the older demonologies and the *Goetia*. The medieval grimoire also suffers from a conflict between Christian dualism and the more shamanic cosmologies of earlier sources. There are several instances in the texts where the spirits—who should by all rights be earthbound jinni—claim to have once been angels in Heaven, and sometimes even express wishes to return to such grace again:

2) **Agares**: "He was of the Order of Virtues."

35) **Marchosias**: "He was of the Order of Dominations. . . .after 1200 years he had hopes to return to the 7th Throne."

37) **Phoenix**: "He hath hopes to return to the 7th Throne after 1200 years more."

41) **Focalor**: "He hath hopes to return to the 7th Throne after 1000 years."

To the Christian, all spiritual entities in the universe could be simplified into either angel or demon. Any celestial being that was either a member of the Christian pantheon, or adopted into it, was classed as an angel (or saint). Everything else in the universe—all elementals, jinni, faery, daemons, etc.—were swept into the same category as the infernal spirit. The entire bulk of them were believed to be under the direct authority of Lucifer or Satan.

Perhaps this in and of itself would not have been much of a conflict. In Christian cosmology, Satan is the very earthy power that governs the natural and physical world. (Much of his character, after all, was adopted from the Greek god of nature and sex named Pan.) Therefore, it might follow that Satan could be held accountable for the entire kingdom of life existing in the lowest shamanic worlds, both earthly and infernal.[65]

However, the problem arises from the further Christian dogma that states all demons were originally angels who rebelled in the heavens under the leadership of Lucifer. Having lost their war, they were cast upon and under the earth as punishment for their pride and treason. As a further humiliation, they were doomed to serve humankind as slaves for so long as our race exists.[66] This, at least, was the grimoiric mage's rationale for conjuring and binding spirits in a religious atmosphere that otherwise forbade it.

The problem with this view is simply that goetic spirits do not fit into the mold of the Christian fallen angel. Lucifer's "Rebel Angels" are more akin to the Judaic "Angels of Destruction," still celestial creatures, even if set over disasters and hurtful things. Yet, the jinni of the Arabic, *Testament*, and grimoiric traditions are obviously creatures of the earth, with nothing like the power ascribed to angels and gods.

The *Testament of Solomon*—a focal point of Christian, Gnostic, Arabic, and Jewish lore—makes itself very clear on the earthbound nature of goetic spirits. After the spirit Ornias delivers a bit of prophecy, King Solomon demands of him how he, an earthbound creature, could know such hidden things. Ornias replies:

113. [. . .] "We demons ascend into the firmament of heaven, and fly about among the stars. And we hear the sentences which go forth upon the souls of men, and forthwith we come . . .

If we were to assume that these demons were essentially of a celestial nature, then this statement should not be surprising. Yet, Solomon finds the statement odd enough to warrant further interrogation:

> 114. I therefore, having heard this, glorified the Lord God, and again I questioned the demon, saying: "Tell me how ye can ascend into heaven, being demons, and amidst the stars and holy Angels intermingle."

Apparently the king sees the natures of demons and angels as directly opposed (of course), and does not understand how a demon can ascend into the heavens. Ornias finally reveals that such ascension is not natural for the spirits, nor does it last very long in any given instance:

> And [Ornias] answered: "Just as things are fulfilled in heaven, so also on earth (are fulfilled) the types of all of them. For there are principalities, authorities, world-rulers, and we demons fly about in the air; and we hear the voices of the heavenly beings, and survey all the powers. And as having no ground on which to alight and rest, we lose strength and fall off like leaves from trees. And men seeing us imagine that the stars are falling from heaven. But it is not really so, O king; but we fall because of our weakness, and because we have nowhere anything to lay hold of; and so we fall down like lightnings in the depth of night and suddenly. And we set cities in flames and fire the fields. For the stars have firm foundations in the heavens like the sun and the moon."

The main conflict with the Christian worldview is that it rules out any possibility of benign or indifferent spirits upon the earth's landscape. Meanwhile, such grimoires as the *Goetia* and *Theurgia-Goetia* contain long lists of spirits both good and bad, hostile and indifferent just like the Arabic jinni. Richard Kieckhefer covers this subject somewhat in his *Forbidden Rites*, Chapter 7 (Demons and Daimons: The Spirits Conjured). The demons of the grimoires, he states, follow a more Graeco-Roman model wherein the spirits are ultimately attached to the natural hierarchies of nature. (Much as I mentioned earlier in this chapter, concerning the spirits and Leary's second circuit of evolutionary consciousness.)

The Magickal Circle

The magickal circle has become such a standard of our post-Victorian systems of magick—from the Golden Dawn to Wicca—that the reader may be surprised to see the subject saved until late in the final chapter of this work. Today, the circle tends to represent a focus of energy and a means of consecrating ceremonial space. Yet, the concept of the circle was mainly absent from the grimoiric operations of angel work and consecration.[67] Instead, they are associated principally with the conjuring of spirits. Agrippa discusses it in his Book II, Chapter 23:

> A circle is called an infinite line in which there is no *terminus a quo nor terminus ad quem*,[68] whose beginning and end is in every point, whence also circular motion is called infinite . . . [It is] judged to be most fit for bindings and conjurations; whence they who adjure evil spirits are wont to environ themselves about with a circle.

And the *Key of Solomon the King* states in a couple of different places:

> Verily, since no experiments for converse with Spirits can be done without a Circle being prepared, whatsoever experiments therefore thou wishest to undertake for conversing with Spirits, therein thou must learn to construct a certain particular Circle; that being done surround that Circle with a Circle of Art for better caution and efficacy.[69]

Now the Master of the Art, every time that he shall have occasion for some particular purpose to speak with the Spirits, must endeavor to form certain Circles which shall differ somewhat, and shall have some particular reference to the particular experiment under consideration.[70]

Historically, the concept of the magickal circle likely evolved from the circle of light cast by a campfire at night. In a primitive society, small children would certainly have been warned about crossing the boundary of that circle. Predatory creatures may fear drawing near the fire, but might grab children foolish enough to cross into the darkness beyond. An ancient exorcist would likely have had this in mind as he symbolically traced a circle around his infected patient.

After the agricultural revolution and the creation of urban life, the magickal circle developed an alternate usage as a focus of power. It appears in traditions outside the grimoires as such, even in grimoiric source material like the Greek magickal papyri.[71] There are, of course, some grimoiric magickal circles that retain this, such as the circle given in the *Key of Solomon the King* for the consecration of talismans. However, even by the time the circle reached the medieval exorcists, it retained its principal protective role. In many cases it is described as protecting the exorcist from certain harm or death by the infernal spirits. In others, it is described as being for the protection of any witnesses to the exorcist's work, assuming that the exorcist himself had long since risen above any vulnerability to the spirits.

Richard Kieckhefer suggests that this dynamic is also due to the Christian moralism of the day. The circles used in older magickal traditions and literature may have been for consecration and power, but the Church was more interested in citing them as proof that occult practice was unnecessarily dangerous. Why else, they asked, would the conjuror need the heavy protection of the magickal circle? This attitude seems to have slipped into the grimoiric traditions of exorcism, especially through the *Key* and *Goetia*.

We have already discussed, in chapter 7, something about the selection of the place where one will perform the evocations of spiritual beings. Those same sections of the grimoires also suggest locations in which infernal spirits will likely be found. They are, in fact, the very same places avoided by the Babylonians, who feared possession by evil spirits there. Naturally, these are places only the exorcist would have had to tread:

> Wherefore desolate and uninhabited regions are most appropriate, such as the borders of lakes, forests, dark and obscure places, old and deserted houses, wither rarely and scarce ever men do come . . . but best of all are cross-roads, and where four roads meet, during the depth and silence of the night (*Key of Solomon the King*, Book II, Chapter 7).

A relationship between magick and crossroads is fairly widespread. The Afro-Cuban faiths also involve crossroads in their magick, assigning to them gods and spirits who walk between the worlds. An intersection of roads is a kind of path node of humanity, where human wills cross paths regularly. These meeting places are naturally focuses of activity and creation. Then, each path from the crossroads links to other such nodes, where more human wills intersect on a daily basis, which are then connected to yet further nodes. Today, the pathways of human life, from paved roads to the internet, span the globe.

Especially in the grimoiric literature, crossroads have a special relationship to the religious symbol of the cross, which itself is understood as a glyph of the meeting of forces. The cross inscribed in the center of many circles marks off the four cardinal directions, and establishes the circle as the center-point where the four Elements meet.[72] This puts the exorcist at the center of his relative universe.

The *Goetia's* magickal circle is rather straightforward. The grimoire describes it in a fairly short section, accompanied by an illustration:

The Magic Circle: The Circle of Solomon is to be made nine feet across & the divine names are to be written around it from Ehayou to Levanah. A figure of the Circle of Solomon, that he made for to preserve himself from the malice of those evil Spirits, etc.

The Triangle: The form of the triangle that Solomon commanded the disobedient spirits into; it is to be made two feet out from the circle and three feet across. Note; this triangle is to be placed towards the quarter that the spirit belongeth to &c. Observe the moon in working, &c.

The goetic circle most commonly presented is that found in Crowley's edition of the *Goetia* as shown above. It is based upon the Qabalistic Tree of Life, beginning with the name of the highest Sephirah of Kether (Crown) and

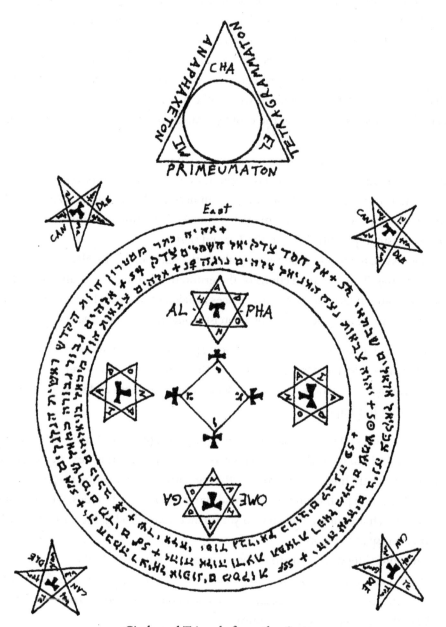

Circle and Triangle from the *Goetia*.

descending to the ninth Sephirah of Yesod (Foundation). This excludes the tenth and final Sephirah called Malkuth (Kingdom). Each section of the circle consists of a group of names in Hebrew associated with one of the nine Qabalistic Sephiroth, separated from the following section by a Greek cross. Included in each group are the divine name, the name of the Sephirah, archangel, angelic choir, and the name of the celestial sphere.[73] At the very end of the group of Hebrew names is appended a few English characters and planetary sigils. For instance, the group associated with Kether has appended "S.P.M." for "Sphere of the Premium Mobile."

In English transliteration, the Hebrew names are as follows:

	Divine Name	Sephirah	Archangel	Angelic Choir	Celestial Sphere
1.	Eheieh	Kether	Mettatron	Chaioth haQodesh	Rashith haGilgalim (Premium Mobile)
2.	Yah	Chockmah	Raziel	Auphanim	Mazloth (Zodiac)
3.	YHVH Elohim	Binah	Zaphkiel	Aralim	Shabathai (Saturn)
4.	El	Chesed	Zadkiel	Chashmalim	Zedek (Jupiter)
5.	Elohim Gibor	Gevurah	Khamael	Seraphim	Madim (Mars)
6.	YHVH Eloah v'Daath	Tiphareth	Raphael	Malachim	Shemesh (Sol)
7.	YHVH Zabaoth	Netzach	Haniel	Elohim	Nogah (Venus)
8.	Elohim Zabaoth	Hod	Michael	Beni Elohim	Kokab (Mercury)
9.	Shaddai El Chai	Yesod	Gabriel	Kherubim	Levanah (Luna)

The practicing mage may wish to copy the Hebrew, or utilize the English transliterations above. Either choice should be sufficient. It is also likely that the serpent is not necessary, as other manuscripts of the *Goetia* do not illustrate it. When drawing or consecrating the circle, begin at the head of the serpent with Eheieh and continue counterclockwise[74] to Levanah and the serpent's tail.

I also wish to include one goetic vestment here, because it relates so directly to the magickal circle itself. Some of my readers may be familiar with the existence of a pelt of lion's skin that is used within the goetic tradition. It is actually a kind of "girdle" (or belt) tied about the white robe during the donning of the other vestments. Upon this lion's pelt must be drawn the same names, and in the same manner, as shown in the circle. In fact, the pelt appears to be a kind of miniature magickal circle in itself, designed to further protect the aura of the operator. The *Key of Solomon the King* accomplishes this same thing with a simple paper crown inscribed with four divine names, explained in chapter 6 with the robe and other vestments.

There has been quite a bit of speculation concerning the triangle of Solomon. A common theory today is that the circle in the heart of the triangle was in fact a magick mirror. That is, a piece of glass painted black on the backside, providing a deep black surface for skrying.[75] It is true that magick mirrors as well as several other mediums were in common use by medieval skryers. Crystal balls, consecrated ink, holy oil, and chalices of wine are only a few of the devices that have seen the spirits of the *Goetia*. Remember that grimoiric magick was shamanism, and it tended to be extremely fluid. The magick was worked with what was available. Instructions and methods could change from one manuscript to the next, and eclecticism seemed to be the general rule.

However, as the triangle is depicted in the text of the *Goetia*, there does not seem to be any skrying device suggested at all. We are told where and how large to make the triangle in the "Observations" section, and further important information is hidden elsewhere:

13) Beleth: [. . .] He is very furious at his first appearance, that is, whilest the Exorcist allays his courage, for to do that, he must hold a hazel stick in his hand, stretched forth towards the South and East quarters making a triangle, without the circle, commanding him into it by the virtue of the bonds & charges of spirits hereafter following[76] & if he does not come into the Triangle by your threats, rehearse the bonds & charms before him, and then he will yield obedience and come into it and do what he is commanded by the Exorcist.

As we can see, the triangle is inscribed on the ground with a stick of hazel. Oddly enough, Beleth is one of only four spirits with whom a triangle is mentioned. The others are **34) Furfur, 44) Shax** and **64) Flauros**. In each of these last three cases, the triangle is specifically intended to keep the spirit from lying to the exorcist. It is interesting to note that many similar medieval texts, even the *Key of Solomon the King* make no mention of such a triangle. Most often, spirits are simply called to appear before the circle. In the case of the *Book of Abramelin*, the infernal spirits are constrained upon pure river sand on a terrace.

Therefore, it is difficult to be sure whether the triangle is for general use, or only for the four listed spirits. Admittedly, the illustration and description of the triangle in the "Observations" suggests it is for all the spirits. We then have to question whether or not the hazel stick is also intended for general use. It is not mentioned in the "Observations," though I would personally suggest adopting the practice in any case. If the exorcism is not performed on a dirt surface, a suitable triangle could be constructed or drawn upon the floor, and a hazel stick used in its consecration.

The use of a triangle for the purpose of summoning is philosophically profound. It extends from the Greek systems of magick, wherein geometric figures were considered of highest importance. The magickal circle itself is an example, as it also derives its power from the philosophy about its shape. Sometimes spiritual entities are summoned into circles,[77] and sometimes into pentagrams or pentagons. It is even an acceptable practice to use the proper geometric figure for each planetary spirit one summons. Those of Mars would manifest within pentagrams, those of Sol within hexagrams, spirits of Jupiter in Squares, etc. (See chapter 10 for some discussion of sacred geometry associated with talismanic magick.)

However, as acceptable as these may be, there is good reason why the triangle rose to a position of prominence in the literature of magickal conjuration, both in the medieval era and today. The triangle is the figure of Saturn—the planet of restriction—and is therefore a prime candidate for the containment of hostile spirits. At the same time, we know that the medieval mages were also the mathematicians and architects, and they knew the triangle to be the strongest structural shape known to man, thus strengthening the case for its use in containment.

Meanwhile, notice that the point of the triangle faces away from the circle and toward the quarter of the universe from which the spirit is called, while the base rests closest to the circle. It thus represents the spirit being pulled from the geometrical nondimension of potential (the point), and expanding outward to the first dimension (the line, or base of the triangle). The complete triangle itself represents the geometric plane (second dimension).[78] Likewise, upon banishing, the entity is sent backward from the triangle's base to dwindle away into the nonexistent point beyond the dimensions conceivable by man.

All of the consecrations for the *Goetia's* circle are contained in a "fifth book" (which some have called an appendix) of the *Lemegeton* called the *Ars Nova*. It is an extremely obscure fact that these prayers of consecration even exist, and they are certainly not included with any of the modern instructions for goetic experiments I have seen. Aleister Crowley did include a copy of the prayers in Mathers' translation of the text. However, the section appears only as an appendix itself, and is titled "Explanation of Certain Names Used in this Book Lemegeton." This refers to the fact that each section of the invocations it presents is associated with a divine name found somewhere upon the goetic circle or talismans. There is no mention of the fact that these are from a book of the *Lemegeton* at all; therefore, they have not generally been accepted as an important aspect of the goetic operation.

The *Ars Nova* itself does not offer any explanation, title, or instruction. It launches directly into the prayers, the first line of which is associated with "**Eheie, Kether,**" the first names one was instructed to inscribe in the circle itself (names of the Premium Mobile). The names then follow in successive order as they appear around the circle. We might take this to mean that one is to recite the invocations while inscribing the names.[79] However, as usual, this is probably only an option. Most grimoires seem content to allow the exorcist to draw the circle beforehand, and then recite the prayers over it. In this case, one would simply hold the sword or wand in hand, point it toward the first names of the circle, and follow round while invoking:[80]

Eheie. Kether: Almighty God, whose dwelling is in the highest Heavens:

Haioth: The great King of Heaven, and of all the powers therein:

Methratton: And of all the holy hosts of Angels and Archangels:

Reschith: Hear the prayers of Thy servant who putteth his trust in Thee:

Hagalgalim: Let thy Holy Angels be commanded to assist me at this time and at all times.

P.M. [Premium Mobile]

Iehovah: God Almighty, God Omnipotent, hear my prayer:

Hadonat: Command Thy Holy Angels above the fixed stars:

Ophanim: To be assisting and aiding Thy servant:

Iophiel: That I may command all spirits of air, water, fire, earth, and hell:

Masloth: So that it may tend unto Thy glory and unto the good of man.

S.Z. [Sphere of the Zodiac]

Iehovah: God Almighty, God Omnipotent, hear my prayer:

Elohim: God with us, God be always present with us:

Binah: Strengthen us and support us, both now and for ever:

Aralim: In these our undertakings, which we perform but as instruments in Thy hands:

Zabbathai: In the hands of Thee, the great God of Sabaoth.

S.H. [Sphere of Saturn][81]

Hesel: Thou great God, governor and creator of the planets, and of the Host of Heaven:

Hasmalim: Command them by Thine almighty power:

Zelez: To be now present and assisting to us Thy poor servants, both now and for ever.

K.S. [Sphere of Jupiter][82]

Elohim Geber: Most Almighty and eternal and ever living Lord God:

Seraphim: Command Thy *Seraphim*:

Camael, Madim: To attend on us now at this time, to assist us, and to defend us from all perils and dangers.

S. [Sphere of Mars]

Eloha: O Almighty God! be present with us both now and for ever:

Tetragrammaton: And let thine Almighty power and presence ever guard and protect us now and for ever:

Raphael: Let thy holy Angel *Raphael* wait upon us at this present and for ever:

Schemes: To assist us in these our undertakings.

S. [Sphere of Sol]

Iehovah: God Almighty, God Omnipotent, hear my prayer:

Sabaoth: Thou great God of *Sabaoth*:

Netzah: All-seeing God:

Elohim: God be present with us, and let thy presence be now and always present with us:

Haniel: Let thy holy Angel *Haniel* come and minister unto us at this present.

S. [Sphere of Venus]

Elohim: O God! be present with us, and let thy presence be now and always present with us:

Sabaoth: O thou great God of *Sabaoth*, be present with us at this time and for ever:

Hodben: Let Thine Almighty power defend us and protect us, both now and for ever:

Michael: Let *Michael*, who is, under Thee, general of thy heavenly host:

Cochab: Come and expel all evil and danger from us both now and for ever.

S. [Sphere of Mercury]

Sadai: Thou great God of all wisdom and knowledge:

Jesal: Instruct Thy poor and most humble servant:

Cherubim: Thy holy *Cherubim*:

Gabriel: By Thy Holy Angel *Gabriel*, who is the Author and Messenger of good tidings:

Levanah: Direct and support us at this present and for ever.

S. [Sphere of Luna]

The next invocation is called "The Explanation of the Two Triangles in the Parchment." Evidently, the exorcist is supposed to don the pentagram and hexagram of Solomon at this point, reciting the prayer for each one while doing so:

[For the Hexagram]

Alpha & Omega: Thou, O great God, Who art the beginning and the end:

Tetragrammaton: Thou God of Almighty power, be ever present with us to guard and protect us, and let Thy Holy Spirit and presence be now and always with us:

[For the Pentagram]

Tetragrammaton: Thou God of Almighty power, be ever present with us to guard and protect us, and let Thy Holy Spirit and presence be now and always with us:

Soluzen: I command thee, thou Spirit, of whatsoever region thou art, to come unto this circle:

Halliza: And appear in human shape:

Bellator: And speak unto us audibly in our mother-tongue:

Bellonoy (or **Bellony**): And show, and discover unto us all treasure that thou knowest of, or that is in thy keeping, and deliver it unto us quietly:

Hally Fra: And answer all such questions as we may demand without any defect now at this time.

Then follows the recitations for the triangle of Solomon titled "An Explanation Of Solomon's Triangle." I find it interesting that this invocation is performed only *after* the protective talismans have been placed on the person of the exorcist. I would also suggest that one have the brass vessel in place, opened, and with the metal seal of the spirit inside.[83] Then invoke:

Anephezeton: Thou great God of all the Heavenly Host:

Tetragrammaton: Thou God of Almighty power, be ever present with us to guard and protect us, and let Thy Holy Spirit and presence be now and always with us:

Primeumaton: Thou Who art the First and Last, let all spirits be subject unto us, and let the Spirit be bound in this triangle, that disturbs this place:

Michael: By Thy Holy Angel *Michael*, until I shall discharge him.

At this point one would begin the exorcism itself, starting with the first conjuration and progressing to the constraints and curses if necessary.

Once the spirit has been conjured, and if one wishes to bind the entity into a brass vessel, the *Ars Nova* provides a final necessary invocation. Unfortunately, it seems a bit garbled and is likely incomplete in some manner. To begin with, fifteen odd names of power are written along with something that appears to be an attempt at the Hebrew lettering for the names. Then the prayer is written with these names interspersed throughout:

> Jodgea, I humbly implore thee Rosen Emolack thou everlasting god Roson Subbartha thou omnipotent & everlasting Creator Roson Eloham thou god with us Skimoy Abomoth to bind & keep fast Rosen Elemoth [. . .] Mackhamasmack by thy divine power those evil & airy spirits Baseh Zadon of the spirit of flyes & spirit of the air Hinnon & spirit of Hinnon Molock Ehaddon with all the spirits of hidden treasure & the disturbers of mankind Molack with the spirits of Molack Johinnon in chains in thy brazen urn Michael with thy Arch Angel Michael . . . .

I have indicated missing text between the words "Rosen Elemoth" and "Mackhamasmack," though the prayer itself does not seem to suffer a break. What is missing are three of the names depicted above the prayer: Zadon, Behoma Reson, and Gamaliall.

It is unclear what the author intended with this invocation. It seems quite unlikely that one should break the prayer to intone these names in so many places. Removing the names gives us an almost sensible recitation. I also notice that the names Hinnon and Michael appear along with lines of the sensible part of the prayer that also mention those names. Thus, it seems likely that this section of the *Ars Nova* is intended as the rest of the text, where the names are associated with the invocation, but not necessarily read aloud as one goes along. (Perhaps the copyist merely became lazy by this point, or wished to conserve extra space at the end of the book.) If this is true, then we might assume that these names should be inscribed upon the brass vessel, obviously in Hebrew lettering.

The prayer itself would have to be completed so that it makes sense. It appears to be a very straightforward exorcism, even mentioning the "spirits that disturb mankind." I would assume, also, that one should present the secret seal of Solomon (see chapter 11) while reciting the invocation. Finally, the vessel can be capped and sealed, and the spirit will remain as the exorcist's own "Solomonic Nganga."[84]

The *Key of Solomon the King* offers two different circles for goetic conjuration, both of which are quite a bit more elaborate (or, at least, much larger) than the circle given in the *Goetia*. The first circle—apparently the "official" (or at least older) version—appears in Book I of the manuscript, while the instructions for using it seem to be scattered liberally through both books of the text. The second example only appears in a single manuscript,[85] and then in a single chapter of Book II. I see no practical reason why one should be more useful than the other. It would appear that the intention was to allow the mage to choose.

The instructions for example number one begin even before the master and his disciples reach the selected place of working. In Book II, Chapter 3, we find that the number of people involved in the ceremony is important. Besides the master, there should only be three companions in the circle, one person for each of the four quarters,[86] and I would suggest the master stands in the east. The *Key* also allows for five, seven, or nine people; obviously intending a sacred number in any case.

In Book II, Chapter 7, we find the instructions for the selection of the place and the preparation of the area for magickal work. (Return to chapter 7 for these instructions.) All of this is done previous to the time of working, and before the circle is drawn. Later on, the master and his companions are instructed to journey to the designated place in a particularly ceremonial (and frankly Catholic) manner. The master must lead the party while sprinkling holy water upon the ground before them with the aspergillum. At the same time, he must recite the following prayer in a "low and distinct voice":

> Zazaii, Zamaii, Puidamon Most Powerful, Sedon Most Strong, El, Yod Heh Vau Heh, Iah, Agla, assist me an unworthy sinner who have had the boldness to pronounce these Holy Names which no man should name and invoke save in very great danger. Therefore have I recourse unto these Most Holy Names, being in great peril both of soul and of body. Pardon me if I have sinned in any manner, for I trust in Thy protection alone, especially on this journey.

Meanwhile, the companions should be reciting to themselves the same prayers that were instructed for the days of fasting and preparation.

As I have mentioned elsewhere, each companion is intended to carry certain items, just as we see in the Catholic Church. The first should carry the censer, the fire, and the incense. The second should carry the book, the consecrated paper, pens, ink, and various perfumes. The third carries the knife and sickle. Finally, the master carries the staff and wand. All involved are also supposed to bear swords.[87]

Book I, Chapter 3—where the instructions for the first circle begin—gives the same instructions, though intended for five companions rather than three. Apparently, the "various perfumes" carried by the second companion are intended to be the stinking fumes used for the constraints and curses. The third companion is also intended to carry the holy lamp (or lantern) and the candles. The fourth companion, in this case, carries the crucible or chafing dish (the censer) along with the charcoal or fuel. Once the place of working is reached, the master must light and exorcise the holy lamp. He can then give it over to a companion, who will hold it for him to read the conjurations.

Then, the circle itself can be inscribed upon the ground with the knife, sword, or sickle of the art. No size is given for the diameter or radius of this circle (as it is for example two), but we know it must be large enough to allow at least four, and maybe as many as nine, people. The master should have enough room to circumambulate the circle around his companions. Also beware that the entire circle, once complete, is going to be extremely huge. Around the first circle, with a space of one foot between them, another circle must be drawn. This second circle is then surrounded by a third circle in the same manner. Both of these larger circles have various holy names, letters, and characters inscribed in the quarters and cross-quarters.

Next, a large diamond must be inscribed around the circles so that its sides touch the edges of the outermost circle and its points rest in the four quarters. Then, yet another diamond must be inscribed around the first one, at a distance of *half* a foot, with its corners also placed in the four quarters. The text states that the name "Tetragrammaton" is written in the space between these two diamonds "in the same way as is shown in the plate." Unfortunately, the plate does not show the name inscribed there at all. I would assume that one is meant to inscribe one Hebrew letter of the name "YHVH" along each side of the double-diamond.

Finally, four double-circles of only one foot in diameter are drawn in the four quarters so that their centers rest upon the four corners of the larger diamond. Within each small circle is written a divine name, and apparently censors are placed upon the center points. The *Key* does give an illustration of this circle, though it is extremely out of scale.

As this circle is inscribed, or at least before it is inscribed, the master is to recite Psalms 2, 54, 113, 57, 47, and 68. After it is complete, it is perfumed and sprinkled[88] as we discussed in chapter 7 of this work. Then, all can enter the circle; the companions placed in the four quarters with their swords drawn. The master should then recite an Exhortation of the Companions, as found in Book II, Chapter 13:

> Fear ye not, me beloved Companions, seeing that we draw near unto the desired end; therefore, all things being rightly done and the Conjurations and Exorcisms diligently performed, ye shall behold the Kings of Kings, and Emperors of Emperors, and other Kings, Princes, Majesties with them, and a great crowd of followers, together with all sorts of musical instruments, yet nothing should either the Magus or his Disciples fear.
>
> I exhort you by these Holy Names of God, Ehohim, Adonai, Agla, that none of you now presume to move or cross over from your appointed stations.

After this, the master can leave the circle and light the censers in the four quarters. Then, the *Key* instructs him to take a consecrated taper candle, light it (with exorcism, I would assume), and place it in some secret and hidden place. (I am not sure of the meaning behind this practice, but it seems obvious that this is not intended to be the holy lamp, which must remain in the circle to provide the necessary light for the work.) Then, he can reenter the circle, instruct his companions in any necessary information, and then continue with this Prayer of Consecration:

> When we enter herein with all humility, let God the Almighty One enter into this Circle, by the entrance of an eternal happiness, of a Divine prosperity, of a perfect joy, of an abundant charity, and of an eternal salutation. Let all the demons fly from this place, especially those who are opposed unto this work, and let the Angels of Peace assist and protect this Circle, from which let discord and strife fly and depart. Magnify and extend upon us, O Lord, Thy most Holy Name, and bless our conversation and our assembly. Sanctify, O Lord our God, our humble entry herein, Thou the Blessed and Holy One of the Eternal Ages. Amen!
>
> [After this, let the Master say upon his knees as follows:]
>
> O Lord God, All Powerful and All Merciful, Thou Who desirest not the death of a sinner, but rather that he may turn from his wickedness and live; give and grant unto us Thy grace, by blessing and consecrating this earth and this circle, which is here marked out with the most powerful and holy names of God. And thee, I conjure, O Earth, by the Most Holy Name of Asher Eheieh entering within this Circle, composed and made with mine hand. And may God, even Adonai, bless this place with all the virtues of Heaven, so that no obscene or unclean spirit may have the power to enter into this Circle, or to annoy

any person who is therein; through the Lord God Adonai, Who liveth eternally unto the Ages of the Ages. Amen.

I beseech Thee, O Lord God, the All Powerful and the All Merciful, that Thou wilt deign to bless this Circle, and all this place, and all those who are therein, and that Thou wilt grant unto us, who serve Thee, and rehearse nothing but the wonders of Thy law, a good Angel for our Guardian;[89] remove from us ever adverse power; preserve us from evil and from trouble; grant, O Lord, Who livest and reignest unto the Ages of the Ages. Amen.

Afterwards, the master rises and places upon his head a paper crown (really a circlet, or bandana) upon which is written the names Agla, Aglai, Aglata, and Aglatai. These names should rest on the front, back, and either side of the crown so that they form a kind of miniature magickal circle around the master's head, with the names in the four quarters.[90] This strikes me as somewhat similar to the *Goetia*'s use of the lion-skin girdle.

The instructions then continue in Book II, Chapter 7, from which we have already drawn some information. After all of the above is completed, the master must bring out a wooden trumpet inscribed upon one side with magickal characters and upon the other side with two names of God: Elohim Gibor and Elohim Tzabaoth:

The trumpet is sounded toward the four quarters of the universe, starting in the east. (This is likely adopted from the Revelation of St. John, where the angels of the Apocalypse bring about major changes upon the earth by blowing trumpets. There is also a probable relation between the Solomonic trumpet and Gabriel's horn, which the archangel is supposed to sound at the end of time to call the faithful home.)

We then have to return to Book II, Chapter 13, for the rest of the instructions. The magickal pentacles necessary for the operation should then be uncovered and shown to the four quarters. (This should perhaps be done *as* the master sounds his trumpet in each place.) The text claims that this will result in "noises and rushings." Regardless of whether or not anything is heard at this point, the conjurations can continue as we have previously discussed, starting with the simplest exorcism and moving on toward the curses if necessary.

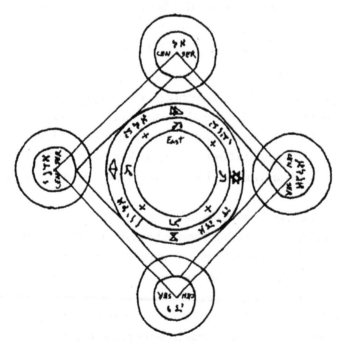

Solomonic Circle 1.

Once they have taken effect, Chapter 13 states that the "Emperor of the Spirits" will arrive and say, "From the time of the Great Addus until now, there hath not been an Exorcist who could behold my person, and unless those things which ye have showed unto us had been made, ye would not now have seen me. But seeing that ye have powerfully called us, as I believe, by the rites derived from Solomon, and which but few of your comrades, or Exorcists, posses, also they compel us against our will, and I therefore say unto thee that we wish to be obedient in all matters." I highly doubt that the spirit will recite this speech exactly, though the point is clearly made here that the entity must appear and swear its oath of loyalty to the mage.

Once the spirit has been received and welcomed, the master must produce small pieces of virgin card or paper, upon which are written the petitions of himself and his companions. These are placed outside the circle (surely with the tip of the sword) in the quarter from which the spirit king arrived. After the king confers with his own superiors, he is supposed to return and say, "That which thou desirest is accomplished, be thy will performed, and all they demands fulfilled."

The second example of a Solomonic circle is contained in a single chapter, found in Book II, Chapter 9, "Of the Formation of the Circle." In this case, one is to make the circle with the magickal sword or knife, a nine-foot cord, and the sickle. First, the master is to thrust the sickle into the ground in the center of the working area. One end of the cord is tied to this, and the other end is tied to the knife or sword. This forms a kind of compass, which allows one to inscribe a large circle upon the ground—eighteen feet across! The text also instructs one to leave a break in the circle toward the north, by which everyone may enter the circle before it is completely closed.[91]

Then, a large cross (really an *X*) is traced within the circle, so that it marks out four wedge-shaped regions toward the four quarters. The instructions say that "Symbols" are to be placed in these regions, though the illustration gives no examples. Next, two more circles are traced around the first one, with one foot's distance between each of them, just as we saw in example one. The illustrated names and figures are inscribed between these circles. In both cases, the open space is left in the north.

Around the largest circle, four pentagrams are inscribed in the cross-quarters "with the Symbols and Names of the Creator therein . . ." This is also not shown in the illustration, though I note a particular similarity between this and the four pentagrams around the goetic circle. Each pentagram in that grimoire possesses a Tau cross in its center, Tetragrammaton written within the angles, and a candle placed upon it.

Around all of this, a large square is traced so that its sides rest on the outer edges of the largest circle. Unlike the diamond of the previous example, the points of this square must rest in the cross-quarters. Then, more like our previous example, another diamond is inscribed so that *its* points rest directly in the four quarters. Finally, a small circle must be drawn at each point of the two squares—for a total of eight—and censers placed in each one.

Once all is complete, all present can enter the circle and the disciples place themselves in the four regions in the quarters. As before, each disciple is to have a naked sword in hand, and the master is to recite the exhortations, etc. Then the master leaves the circle, kindles the eight censers, returns to the circle and closes off the northern openings with the Sword or knife. The circle is perfumed, and the trumpet is sounded in the four directions as previously described. Finally, the master thrusts his sword, knife, or sickle upright into the ground at his feet, and the spirits can be safely exorcised.

As we can see, the focus of these circles from the *Lemegeton* and *Key of Solomon the King* is upon the protection they offer from hostile spirits. However, this is not to say that the talismanic aspect of magickal circles did not find a home in the grimoiric tradition.

We might take for example the *Munich Handbook of Necromancy*,[92] which displays several magickal circles, similar to that found in the *Goetia*, apparently intended for use as talismans *or* for inscription upon the ground.

אלהים גבור   אלהים צבאות

Trumpet Sigils.

Many of the magickal circles in that text are drawn to illustrate the circle itself, the proper arrangement of tools, furniture, and/or people within the circle, and sometimes even the invocations that must be read to consecrate the space. These are actually full-fledged diagrams of the working space (similar to those we see in magickal texts of today). One would not, of course, include the sword and other tools—as pictured in the image—when inscribing the circle upon the ground. In a similar vein, it could be that the verses often written around the circumferences of the circles are meant to be spoken as the circle is traced, rather than inscribed letter by letter.[93]

Kieckhefer also suggests that, instead of inscribing these circles on the ground, they can be used as magickal talismans in their own right.[94] Once inscribed upon parchment or tablets, the images of the circles can be used to constrain and command the spirits, exactly like the talismans from the *Key of Solomon the King*:

> When you see [the spirits], show them at once this circle, which has great power to terrify those fifteen demons; they will see it and say, 'Ask whatever you wish in safety, and it will all come to pass for you through us.' You should then tell them to consecrate their circle so that whenever you gaze on it and invoke them they must come to you quickly and do that which is natural to them . . . (*Munich Handbook*, Experiment no. 7).[95]

In fact, the magickal circles of the *Munich Handbook of Necromancy* bear a very striking resemblance to the Solomonic talismans of the *Key*.

At the same time, their association with the written conjurations of the *Handbook* remind me of the mnemonic illustrations of the *Notary Arts* (see chapter 10). When used in this manner, I would assume that the tools and prayers should be inscribed upon the circles, so as to visually represent the mystical, even sigil-like, configurations.

There are also further grimoiric circles that bear a relation to talismanic magick. For example, take the circle as described by Barrett's *The Magus*, Book II, Part III, "Of the Particular Composition of the Magical Circle." This is most definitely my favorite method of circle construction. It is not only designed to protect the mage, but is also intended to invoke the natural forces ruling at any given magickal time. The method is fairly simple and straightforward, but is also an elaborate system of magickal timing in and of itself. This includes not only the angels and ministers who govern the day and hour, but goes so far as to include even the names of the season, Earth, Sun, and Moon at the time of operation:

> The forms of circles are not always one and the same, but are changed according to the order of spirits that are to be called, their places, times, days, and hours; for in making a circle it ought to be considered in what time of the year, what day, and what hour, what spirits you would call and to what star or region they belong, and what functions they have.

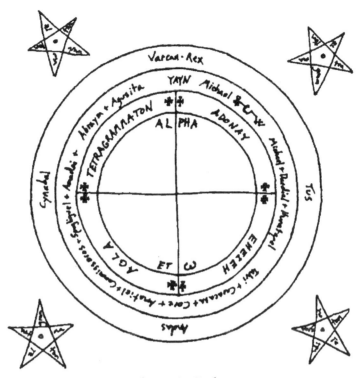

Solomonic Circle 2.

The *Magus'* circle is composed of four concentric rings, the largest of which is nine feet across. The spaces between the rings are only a hand's breadth. The four lines of the circles result in three bands (the spaces in between) that will be filled in with specific angelic and divine names and characters.

First, starting in the east and moving clockwise, the middle band must contain the name of the magickal hour in which one will do the work, followed by the name of the archangel of that hour and his seal. All of these names are found in chapter 5 of this work, and their sigils can be found in chapter 8. Then, following the seal, one must inscribe the names of the angelic ruler of the day and his ministers:

Day	Ruling Angel	Ministers
Sunday	Michael	Dariel, Huratapel
Monday	Gabriel	Michael, Samael
Tuesday	Samael	Satabel, Amabiel
Wednesday	Raphael	Meil, Seraphiel
Thursday	Sachiel	Cassiel, Asasiel
Friday	Anael	Rachiel, Sachiel
Saturday	Cassiel	Machatan, Uriel

Next, still in the middle band, follow various names associated with the yearly season in which the work is performed. Beginning with the mystical name of the season itself, the instructions also include the ruling angels of that season, the name of the "head of the sign" in that season,[96] and, finally, the names of the Earth, Sun, and Moon during that season:

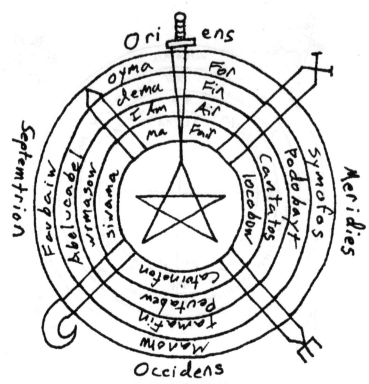

Circle from *Munich Handbook*.

The spring, Talvi; the summer, Casmaran; autumn, Adarcel; winter, Farlas.

The Angels of the Spring—Caracasa, Core, Amatiel, Commissoros.
    The head of the sign of spring is called Spugliguel.
    The name of the earth in spring, Amadai
    The names of the sun and moon in spring: sun, Abraym; moon, Agusita

The Angels of the Summer—Gargatel, Tariel, Gaviel.
    The head of the sign of summer, Tubiel.
    The name of the earth in summer, Festativi.
    The names of the sun and moon in summer: sun, Athemay; moon, Armatus.

The Angels of the Autumn—Tarquam, Guabarel.
    The head of the sign of autumn, Torquaret
    The name of the earth in autmn, Rabinnara.
    The names of the sun and moon in autumn: the sun, Abragini; the moon, Marasignais.

The Angels of the Winter—Amabael, Cetarari
    The head of the sign of winter, Attarib.
    The name of the earth in winter, Geremiah.
    The names of the sun and moon in winter: the sun, Commutoff; the moon, Affaterim.

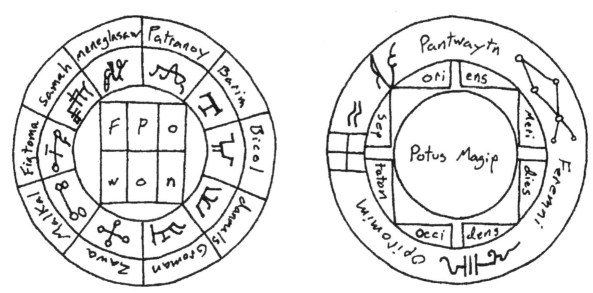

Solomonic Talisman-style Magickal Circles, from *Munich Handbook*.

This completes the names intended for the middle band of the magickal circle. In the outermost band of the circle, one is to inscribe the names of the "great presidential spirits of the air": an angelic king and (in most cases) three ministers. The king's name should rest in the east, and the ministers at the other three quarters:

Day	King	Ministers
Sunday	Varcan	Tus, Andas, Cynabal
Monday	Arcan	Bilet, Missabu, Abuhaza
Tuesday	Samax	Carmax, Ismoli, Paffran
Wednesday	Mediat	Suquinos, Sallales, (?)
Thursday	Suth	Maguth, Gutrix, (?)
Friday	Sarabotes	Amahiel, Aba, Abalidoth, Blaef(?)
Saturday	Maymon	Abumalith, Assaibi, Balidet

The inner band of the circle must include four divine names separated by crosses; though the text does not indicate which names one should use. More than likely, they are intended to be names appropriate to the operation. The illustration, however, shows three names (one seems to be missing) that are commonly associated with magickal circles: Tetragrammaton, Adonay, and AGLA. A common fourth is Eheieh, or perhaps Elyon.

In the center of the magickal circle, one must inscribe the word Alpha in the east and Omega in the west. The area is then divided by a large cross, not an X as we saw in the Key of Solomon the King. Finally (though the illustration does not include them), one is instructed by the text to inscribe four pentagons (I would assume pentagrams are intended) in the "four angles" around the outside of the circle. Whether this means in the four quarters or the cross-quarters is not clear.

Once the magickal circle is complete, a heavily Christian prayer of consecration is provided:

> In the name of the holy, blessed, and glorious Trinity, proceed we to our work in these mysteries to accomplish that which we desire; we, therefore, in the names aforesaid, consecrate this piece of ground

Circle of Sunday, *The Magus*.

for our defense, so that no spirit whatsoever shall be able to break these boundaries, neither be able to cause injury nor detriment to any of us here assembled; but that they may be compelled to stand before this circle, and answer truly our demands, so far as it pleaseth Him who liveth for ever and ever; and who says, I am Alpha and Omega, the Beginning and the End, which is, and which was, and which is to come, the Almighty; I am the First and the Last, who am living and was dead; and behold I live for ever and ever; and I have the keys of death and hell. Bless, O Lord! this creature of earth wherein we stand; confirm, O God! thy strength in us, so that neither the adversary nor any evil thing may cause us to fail, through the merits of Jesus Christ. Amen.

Then the circle is sprinkled with holy water, as we have seen elsewhere, while reciting the Psalm verse usually reserved for ritual baths:

Thou shalt purge me with hyssop, I Lord, and I shall be clean: thou shalt wash me and I shall be whiter than snow.

Raising . . . Familiar Spirits by a Circle, from The Magus

The Magus ends its Book II, Part II with generalized instructions for goety and necromancy, and then begins Part III with a full conjuration procedure. Thanks to the knowledge we have accumulated throughout this book, we can easily make sense of even the generalized instructions:

Now if anyone would call any evil spirit to the circle, he must first consider and know [the spirit's] nature, and to which of the planets it agrees, and what offices are distributed unto him from the planet. This being known, let there be sought out a place fit and convenient, and proper for his invocation, according to the nature of the planet and the quality of the offices of the same spirit, as near as it can be done; as if their power be over the sea, rivers or floods, then let the place be the sea-shore, and so of the rest. Then chuse a convenient time . . . [for] the quality of and nature of the planet and the spirit, as on his day and time in which he rules; he may be fortunate or unfortunate sometimes of the day, and sometimes of the night, as the stars and spirits to require.

In the above we see the selection of the place and the magickal timing (especially hoarary astrology) with which we have become quite familiar. The text then continues with guidelines for constructing the circle, which fore-shadow the fuller instructions given in Part III, and which we saw above in the section on magickal circles. *The Magus* here states the circle is made "as well for the defense of the invocant as the confirmation of the spirit," meaning that it is both defensive and talismanic.

Next, the instructions indicate the tools necessary to the work: such as lights, perfumes, ungents (holy oils), medicines, and lamens, images, pentacles, swords, scepters, and garments; all constructed, compounded, and / or consecrated "according to the nature of the spirit and planet." These are all subjects we have covered in depth in several previous chapters.

Having entered the circle, the instructions continue in a manner similar to our own chapter 7:

> . . . let him begin to pray with a loud voice after the manner following. First, by making an oration or prayer to God, and then intreating the good spirits; but we should read some prayer, or psalm, or gos-pel, for our defense in the first place. (*The Magus*, p. 100)

After which one can begin to conjure the spirit(s). The instructions for this, though brief, are reminiscent of the exorcism manuals we have already discussed:

> . . . let him begin to invocate the spirit which he disireth, with a gentle and loving enchantment to all the coasts of the world, with a commemoration of his own authority and power. Then rest and look round to see if any spirit does appear; which if he delays, then let him repeat his invocation, as above said, until he hath done it three times; and if the spirit is obstinate and will not appear, then let the invo-cator begin to conjure him with divine power; but so that all his conjurations and commemorations do agree with the nature and office of the spirit, and reiterate the same three times, from stronger to stronger, using contumelies, cursings, punishments, suspension from his power and office, and the like.

After which the spirit is to be received with courtesy. Its name is obtained and recorded, and the mage's commands or interrogations can proceed.

If the spirit should prove obstinate, ambiguous, or untruthful, *The Magus* suggests using the sword to inscribe a triangle or pentagon[97] outside the circle and to compel the spirit into it. Apparently, this is the influence of the *Goe-tia* and its triangle of the art. Further, the sword is extended beyond the circle for the spirit to touch while swearing any oath. (This is similar to *Abramelin*'s use of the wand for the same purpose.)

Once the mage has attained his desire from the spirit or is otherwise satisfied:

> License him to depart with courteous words, giving command that he do no hurt; and if he will not depart, compel him by powerful conjurations; and if need require expel him by exorcisms and by mak-ing contrary suffumigations. And when he is departed, go not out of the circle, but make a stay, and use some prayer giving thanks to God and the good angels; and also praying for your future defense and conservation, which being orderly performed you may depart.

If the experiment comes to naught, and no spirit will appear, *The Magus* insists that *the license to depart must be recited anyway.* Then, one can consider any necessary corrections to the procedure and try again at another appropriate time. In any case, one should never be defeated by failed attempts, "for constancy of repetition encreases your authority and power, and strikes a terror into the spirits, and compels them to obey."

Finally, the instructions end with an explanation that the spirits will not necessarily appear visibly. (Remember the *Key of Solomon* said the same concerning the appearance of angels.) In fact, says *The Magus*, infernal spirits should not be *allowed* to appear visibly without a dispensation from the mage to render themselves obedient. If the operation is one that does not specifically require an apparition, the text suggests focusing upon the physical instrument of the spell instead: an image, ring, character, etc. (The physical base which will serve as the body of the spirit.) One merely needs to inscribe the spirit's name and character upon the instrument.[98] And, of course, a final warning to always invoke divine and angelic aid in subduing the spirits.

Part III of this portion of *The Magus* begins with the elaborate circle we saw previously in the section on magickal circles. It then continues with several elements we have encountered in previous chapters: a Benediction of Perfumes, an Exorcism of Fire, the Habit of the Exorcist (complete with oration for the donning of the vestments), and its own version of the pentacle of Solomon.

> Of the Pentacle of Solomon: It is always necessary to have this pentacle in readiness to bind with, In case the spirits should refuse to be obedient, as they can have no power over the exorcist while provided with and fortified by the pentacle, the virtue of the holy names therein written presiding with wonderful influence over the spirits.
>
> It should be made in the day and hour of Mercury upon parchment made of a kidskin, or virgin, or pure, clean, white paper; and the figures and letters wrote in pure gold; and it ought to be consecrated and sprinkled (as before often spoken) with holy water.

The relation between this "Pentacle" and the hexagram of Solomon from the *Goetia* is obvious when we see the provided illustration. Unfortunately, it has degenerated quite a bit by the time it reaches *The Magus*.

The following section, titled "The Manner of Working," is an elaboration of the general instructions already given. It includes specific lunar magickal timing, a nine-day purification (increasing in intensity for the final three days), and further reminders to gather and consecrate the proper tools. Then, various angelic invocations are prescribed:

> . . . let him enter the circle, and call the Angels from the four parts of the world which do rule the seven planets, the seven days of the week, colours, and metals, whose names you will see in their places; and, with bended knees, first let him say the Paternoster or Lord's Prayer, and then let him invocate the said Angels, saying:
>
> *O Angelil supradicti estote adurtores mihi petitioni & in adjutorum mihi, in meis rebus et petitionibus.*
>
> Then call the Angels from the four parts of the world that rule the air the same day which he makes the experiment; and, having employed especially all the names and spirites within the circle, say,
>
> *O vos omnes, adjutore alque contestor per sodem Adonai, per Hagios, Theos, Ischyros, Athanatos, Paracletos, Alpha & Omega, & per haec tria nomina secreta, Agla, On, Tetragrammaton, quod hodie debeatis adimplere quod cupio.*

These are then followed by a conjuration specific to the day of the week one has chosen to work. These conjurations are given over twelve pages, each including the conjuration itself, the various angelic rulers of the day, the proper incense, and which spirits will answer the conjuration (including their forms, offices, and natures). While there is not space enough to provide all seven daily considerations, I have decided to offer one example as an illustration. The student may wish to obtain a copy of *The Magus* for the full set.

The Considerations of Saturday

-The Angels of Saturday: *Cassiel, Machatan, Uriel*

-The Angels of the Air ruling this day: King, *Maymon*; Ministers, *Abumalith, Assaibi, Balidet*. The wind They are subject to, the *south wind*.

-The fumigation of Saturday is *Sulfur*.

-There are no Angels ruling in the Air on Saturday above the fifth heaven, therefore in the four corners of the world, in the Circle, use those orations which are applied to Thursday.

(Thursday: Say the prayers following in the four parts of the world: At the East—*O Deus magne et excelse et honorate, per infinita secula*; or O great and most high God, honored by Thy Name, world without end.

At the West—O wise, pure, and just God, of divine clemency, I beseech thee, most holy Father, that this day I may perfectly undestand and accomplish my petition, work, and labor; for the honour and glory of thy holy name, who livest and reignest, world without end. *Amen.*

At the North—O God, strong, mighty, and wonderful, from everlasting to everlasting, grant that this day I bring to effect that which I desire, through our blessed Lord. *Amen.*

At the South—O mighty and most merciful God, hear my prayers and grant my petition.)

The Conjuration of Saturday

I conjure and confirm upon you, Caphriel, or Cassiel, Machator, and Seraquiel, strong and powerful Angels; and by the name Adonai, Adonai, Adonai; Eie, Eie, Eie; Acim, Acim, Acim; Cados, Cados, Ima, Ima, Ima; Salay, Ja, Sar, Lord and Maker of the World, who rested on the seventh day; and by him who of his good pleasure gave the same to be observed by the children of Israel throughout their generations, that they should keep and sanctify the same, to have thereby a good reward in the world to come; and by the names of the *Angels* serving in the seventh host, before Booel, a great Angel, and powerful prince; and by the name of His star, which is Saturn; and by his Holy Seal, and by the names before spoken, I conjure upon thee, Caphriel, who are chief ruler of the seventh day, which is the Sabbath, that for me thou labor, etc, etc.[99]

The spirits of the Air on Saturday are subject to the south-west wind: the nature of them is to sow discords, hatred, evil thoughts and cogitations, to give leave to kill and murder, and to lame or main every member.[100]

Their Familiar Shapes

They generally appear with a tall, lean, slender body, with an angry countenance, having four faces, one on the back of the head, on in the front, and one on each side, nosed or beaked, likewise there appears a face on each knee of a black shining color; their motion is the moving of the wind, which a kind of earthquake; their sign is white earth, whiter than snow.

Their Particular Shapes Are [101]

-A King, bearded, riding on a dragon.

-An old man with a beard.

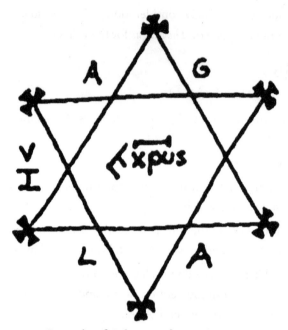

Pentacle of Solomon, from *The Magus*.

-An old woman leaning on a crutch.

-A god; a dragon; an owl.

-A black garment; a hook or sickle.

-A juniper tree.

Those are the figures that these spirits usually assume, which are generally terrible at the first coming of the visions, but as they have only a limited power, beyond which they cannot pass . . .

There might at first appear to be confusion in the text concerning this method of summoning. On one hand, it might appear to be a celestial evocation because the given conjurations are addressed to the angels of the days. For instance, the conjuration of Saturday is aimed at Cassiel. On the plate facing page 105 (as well as in chapter 8 of this book), we see the example of the angelic book with Cassiel on the left-hand page. The conjuration written opposite him proves to be the very same conjuration of Saturday we see above.

However, each day's conjuration given by *The Magus* is followed by descriptions of Familiar spirits who are active on that day. Their offices are described (typical goety, such as gaining material possessions, aiding in alchemical experiments, destroying enemies, etc.), along with their common shapes and warnings/instructions for the conjuror. The system itself makes use of the common goetic instruments: the wand, the seal of Solomon, a heavily fortified circle, etc. Therefore we must assume that the process is not supposed to result in celestial communication, but rather the conjuration of earth spirits.

I would assume *The Magus* is indicating a cross-semination between its angelic system (using the book and shewstone as we saw in chapter 8) and its goetic system. Perhaps one is to first create the angelic book, and then that book is used for the conjuration of the spirits. (Therefore, the mage does not attempt to command these spirits by his own power, but instead invokes the angelic princes directly to bring the spirits to the circle and superintend them.) However, this is only speculation on my part.

Meanwhile, *The Magus* continues its instruction along the more recognizable lines of the exorcism manual. If the conjuration is not successful, one should continue with stronger exorcisms; just as with the other grimoires, but no curses or harsh punishments for obstate spirits is mentioned at this point. First, one is to recite a general exorcism of the spirits of the Air, which is very similar to the *Goetia*'s constraint or the *Key of Solomon the King's* extremely powerful conjuration. If this is not successful, a prayer to God is given—to be said in the four parts of the world[102] in the circle. This prayer appears to be based on similar prayers in the *Key*. Finally, the text provides a further oration (really a conjuration) which is taken wholly from the first conjuration of the *Goetia* (quoted in full earlier in this chapter).

To end with, a section on the appearance of the spirits is given that also seems to be taken largely from the *Goetia*.

> Then let the exorcist, stretching out his hand with the pentacle [of Solomon], say, "Behold the pentacle of Solomon, which I have brought into your presence; behold the person of the exorcist in the midst of the exorcism, who is armed by God, without fear, and well provided, who potently invocateth and calleth you by exorcising; come, therefore, with speed, by the virtue of these names; Aye Saraye, Aye Saraye; defer not to come, by the eternal names of the living and true God, Eloy, Archima, Rabur, and by the pentacle of Solomon here present, which powerfully reigns over you; and by the virtue of the celestial spirits, your lords; and by the person of the exorcist, in the midst of the exorcism: being conjured, make haste and come, and yield obedience to your master, who is called Octinomos." This being performed, immediately there will be hissings in the four parts of the world, and then immediately you shall see great motions; which when you see, say, "Why stay you? Wherefore do you delay? What do you? Prepare yourselves to be obedient to your master in the name of the Lord, Bathat or Vachat rushing upon Abrac, Abeor coming upon Aberer."
>
> Then they will immediately come in their proper forms; and when you see them before the circle, shew them the pentacle covered with fine linen; uncover it, and say, "Behold your confusion if you refuse to be obedient!"

A formal welcoming to the spirit follows, complete with admonitions for the spirit to remain before the circle until such time as the exorcist is satisfied. Then "let the exorcist mention what he would have done." After all is accomplished, a simple license to depart is recited:

> In the name of the Father, and of the Son, and of the Holy Ghost, go in peace unto your places; peace between us and you; be ye ready to come when you are called.

The Book of Spirits (Liber Spiritus)

The *Book of Spirits* is the general model upon which the *Goetia* and all similar grimoires were based. It is simply a natural product of a literate culture of exorcists and physicians, who decided to create and pass down lists of the demons they had defeated. In this way, newly initiated mages could inherit the spirits of their forefathers, mirroring the older tribal inheritance of spirits from shamanic master to apprentice. Both the *Testament of Solomon* and the *Goetia* stand as two perfect examples of the *Book of Spirits*: with the demons' names in the form of litanies (lists), along with their seals, descriptions, and all necessary prayers and conjurations.

Of course, as we learned in chapter 8, magickal books of the medieval era were generally regarded as living beings in their own right. If the grimoire itself was not a living intelligence, then it was certainly home to all of the entities whose names and seals were inscribed within its pages. Little more needs to be said in this chapter about the origins and mystical nature of the medieval magickal book. The information given in chapter 8 applies to the books of both angels and spirits.

The *Key of Solomon the King* describes its spirit book at the end of Book I, Chapter 7, and it is clearly distinct from the angelic book described later in the text:

> Thou shouldest further make a Book of virgin paper, and therein write the foregoing conjurations, and constrain the Demons to swear upon the same Book that they will come whenever they be called, and present themselves before thee, whenever thou shalt wish to consult them. Afterwards thou canst cover this Book with sacred Sigils on a plate of silver,[103] and therein write or engrave the Holy Pentacles. Thou mayest open this Book either on Sundays or Thursdays, rather at night than by day, and the Spirits will come.

There is also an earlier reference in the *Key* to the book of spirits:

> . . . one of the Disciples shall hold open before him the Book wherein are written the prayers and conjurations proper for conquering, subduing, and reproving the Spirits.

So, the spirit book is intended to contain the conjurations and ceremonies that will exorcise the entities. Written in the Book, they serve a talismanic function similar to their intent when actively performed by the mage. The *Key* further suggests one inscribe all of the Solomonic talismans into the text, as they also serve the function of commanding and subduing the spirits who will be connected to the pages.

Binding the demons to the spirit book is no different here than it was for the celestial beings in the angelic Book. It is necessary to summon each entity to the circle through the proscribed ceremonies, and have them touch the book in swearing an oath of loyalty. This brings to mind *The Book of Abramelin*, which has the aspirant summon large numbers of spirits and conjure them to swear upon a set of talismans. Interestingly enough, Abramelin suggests that these talismans be kept together in book form and always carried on the person of the mage.

The only thing the *Key* does not mention in the above is the listing of the spirits in the book "in the form of litanies" such as we see with the *Goetia*. It should be necessary to record the name, seal, and functions of each spirit summoned and bound to the book.

The Magus contains a much better description of the spirit book and its consecration in Book II, Part II, "Of the Invocation of Evil Spirits, and the binding of, and constraining of them to appear." It does not omit any of the details passed over by the *Key*:

> Now, if thou art desirous of binding any spirit to a ready obedience to thee, we will shew you how a certain book may be made by which they may be invoked; and this book is to be consecrated a book of Evil Spirits, ceremoniously to be composed in their name and order, whereunto they bind with a certain holy oath, the ready and present obedience of the spirit. This book is therefore to be made of the most pure and clean paper, which is generally called virgin paper; and this book must be inscribed after this manner, viz. Let there be drawn on the left side of the book the image of the spirit, and on the right side thereof his character, with the oath above it, containing the name of the spirit, his dignity and place, with his office and power.
> [. . .]
> Which book being so written, is to be well bound, adorned, garnished, embellished and kept secure, with registers and seals, lest it should happen after the consecration to open in some part not designed,[104] and

endanger the operator. And, above all, let this book be kept as pure and reverent as possible; for irreverence of mind causes it to lose its virtue by pollution and prophanation.

We can see little difference here, in fact, between the spirit and angelic books. Their general construction, consecration, and care seem to be about the same.

The Magus continues with two different sets of instructions for the formal consecration of the spirit book. The first example is familiar enough, with the exorcist summoning each spirit listed in the book individually, by the conjurations contained within it. The book itself is placed outside of the circle in a triangle inscribed upon the ground, and each spirit is to lay his hand upon his own name and seal within it to swear both a "special and common oath." This means that all of the spirits should swear one common oath to the exorcist, as well as an individual oath tailored to each spirit as necessary. Once complete, the spirit(s) are licensed to depart, and the book is preserved as described above.

Of course, like the consecration of the angelic book, this process is not something that can be done in a day, or even several months. Each spirit has to be summoned individually, and that includes all considerations of magickal timing and the like:

> There is likewise to be observed the circumstances of places, times, hours, according to the stars which these spirits are under, and are seen to agree to; with their site, rite, and order being applied.

However, *The Magus* continues with a second option for the consecration of the book of spirits. This one is intended to sidestep the involvement necessary for the above procedure:

> There is another method extant among us of consecrating a general book of spirits which is more easy, and of as much efficacy to produce every effect, except that in opening this book, the spirits do not always appear visible.

One is first to compose the book as has already been described, with every spirit one wishes to contact along with their seals, information, and the common exorcisms that will be used to conjure them. The whole thing should be bound between two covers upon which are inscribed magickal images. These images have already been described and illustrated in chapter 10, section "Image Magick." They are the two images taken from the biblical book of the Revelation of St. John—the first of God (or Jesus) sitting upon his throne, and the second of the Lamb of God standing upon the Book of Seven Seals. The first image is placed at the beginning of the spirit book, and the second at the end.

Once the book is complete, the master must take it on a clear and fair night to a crossroads and prepare a magickal circle. The book is then opened and consecrated in a general manner (i.e., prepare an invocation, perfume and sprinkle the book, etc.). Then, all of the spirits listed within the text are summoned together by repeating the conjurations three times, and commanding them to come to that place within the space of three days to assure and confirm their obedience.

Apparently, no visible appearance of the spirits is necessary for this procedure. Even still, after the conjurations are accomplished, the license to depart is not omitted. Then:

> Then let the book be wrapped up in a clean linen cloth, and bury it in the midst of the circle, and stop the hole so as it may not be perceived or discovered: the circle being destroyed after you have licensed the spirits, depart before sunrise; and on the third day, about the middle of the night, return and make the circle anew and on thy knees make prayer unto God, and give thanks to him; and let a precious perfume be made,[105] open the hole in which you buried your book and take it out, and so let it be kept,

not opening the same. Then after licensing the spirits in their order and destroying the circle, depart before sunrise.

Finally, the general instructions for the use of this book of spirits are related:

> But when the operator would work by the book thus consecrated he should do it in a fair and clear season, when the spirits are least troubled; and let him turn himself towards the region of the spirits;[106] then let him open the book under a due register, and likewise invoke the spirits by their oaths there described and confirmed, and by the name of their character and image, to whatever purpose you desire, and if there be need conjure them by the bonds placed in the end of the book. And having attained thy desired effect license them to depart.

For our own book of spirits, I have decided to include the seven spirits associated with the planetary intelligences we met in chapter 8. The intelligences were the angels set over the seven planets, and whose names were drawn from seven planetary magickal squares. The names of the spirits of the planets are drawn from the same squares.

We can find information about these squares in Agrippa's Book II, Chapter 22, "Of the tables of the planets, their virtues, forms, and what divine names, intelligences, and spirits are set over them." Agrippa here persists in the Christian concept that the angels are set over the positive aspects of the planets, while the spirits are set over the evil. Therefore, it is intended for the mage to summon and bind these entities in order to remove negative planetary influences and dangers from his life. One and the same, in fact, with the exorcism concept of summoning and binding the demons of sickness.

Following is a list of the seven planetary spirits and their seals. Unfortunately, I am not aware of any known images for these entities. Space for these should be left in the book of spirits to be filled in as each demon is contacted:

Sigil of Zazel.

Zazel (ל ז א ז)

Spirit of Saturn. Ruled by Agiel, who governs especially when Saturn enters the zodiacal signs of Capricorn and Aquarius.

Sigil of Hismael.

Hismael (ל א מ ס ה)

Spirit of Jupiter. Ruled by Iophiel, who governs especially when Jupiter enters the signs of Sagittarius and Pisces.

Sigil of Bartzabel.

Bartzabel (ל א ב צ ר ב)

Spirit of Mars. Ruled by Graphiel, who governs especially when Mars enters the signs of Aries and Scorpio.

Sigil of Sorath.

Sorath (ה ר ו ס)

Spirit of Sol. Ruled by Nakhiel, who governs especially when Sol enters the sign of Leo.

Sigil of Qedemel.

Qedemel (ל א מ ד ק)

Spirit of Venus. Ruled by Hagiel, who governs especially when Venus enters the signs of Libra and Taurus.

Sigil of Taphthartharath.

Taph-Thar-Thar-Ath (ת פ ת ר ת ר ח)

Spirit of Mercury. Ruled by Tiriel, who governs especially when Mercury enters the signs of Gemini and Virgo.

Sigil of Chashmodai.

Chashmodai (ח ש מ ו ד א י)

The spirit of Luna. Ruled by Malkah, who governs especially when the Moon enters the sign of Cancer.

---

1. See chapter 1, the section dedicated to the *Goetia,* for a detailed explanation of the word "goety."
2. See *The Devils and Evil Spirits of Babylonia.* The occult student may see a similarity between this invocation and the last invocation in the modern "Lesser Banishing Ritual of the Pentagram" ("Before me Raphael, Behind me Gabriel, to my right hand Michael, and to my left hand Auriel"). The Golden Dawn adopted this invocation from a Jewish bedtime prayer—and I feel it is safe to assume that prayer was adopted from Babylon.
3. See *The Devils and Evil Spirits of Babylonia.*
4. However, this theory must contrast with the ancient origins of the spirits' appearances in religious iconography and image magick. See chapter 10.
5. See chapter 3.
6. See chapter 4 for more on the heavenly court.
7. Again, see chapter 4 concerning the heavenly court.
8. See *Ritual Magic,* by Elizabeth M. Butler (pp. 35–6).
9. East = Fire, south = Earth, west = Air, Water = north. See chapter 2, section "Three Worlds, Four Pillars."
10. It is the spirit which "disturbs this place" and not the triangle.
11. *Horkos* = oath.
12. An early form of what would someday become Lilith.
13. From Tablet XII of the Gilgamesh epic.
14. In certain cases, abbots and prelates were known to confer these offices.
15. Today, the pontifical, or missal, is put into the hands of the candidate instead.
16. The laying on of hands is demonstrated throughout the book of Acts in the New Testament.
17. See the exorcism and consecration of incense in chapter 6, taken from the *Key of Solomon the King.* The procedure given there is derived from this particular bit of Church procedure, with the incense being treated as a *catechumen.*
18. VIII, 26; P.G., I, 1122. The Apostolic Constitutions are a collection of eight volumes of treatises on Christian discipline, worship, and doctrine originating in the fourth century. It was intended to serve as a manual of guidance for living—especially for the clergy.
19. Though the Inquisitions began to ferret out heresy in the Church, they were eventually co-opted by this newly developing "medical profession." It was here that the Inquisitions gained their true reputation for witch-hunting, as it was mainly healers, midwives, and Pagan wisepersons that were targeted for extermination.
20. *Forbidden Rites,* p.146.

21. When such crosses appear in the midst of prayers and invocations, it indicates an instruction to form a cross either over yourself (from forehead to chest, and from shoulder to shoulder) or toward the object or person being addressed.

22. The author of *Abramelin* included many such instructions meant to separate his work from the other grimoires of the day.

23. This, and any directional reference to the east, should change depending on the spirit and the king one is attempting to conjure. Of course, the *Goetia* is so corrupt as to make the use of this invocation nearly impossible. We don't know which kings rule most of the spirits.

24. Thanks to those on the Ritual Magick e-mail list who provided the following information on the herb.

25. *Three Books of Occult Philosophy*, Book I, Chapter 44.

26. I take this to mean that he spit upon the ground, mixed it with the dirt to form a clay, and impressed the image of the seal ring into the spot. This secret bit of magick might be a strong argument in favor of fashioning our Solomonic rings in mirror image, so that they can be impressed into clay and wax.

27. See *The Devils and Evil Spirits of Babylonia*, p. 13. Emphasis mine.

28. Twilit Grotto, Esoteric Archives CD.

29. "Pillages their brows." Ignorance? Or writer's (and other artists') block?

30. Joseph Peterson points out that these are Greek medical terms found in Hippocrates, Galen, etc.

31. The demon continues with a grimoire-style spell: "If any one would be at peace in his home, let him write on seven leaves of laurel the name of the angel that frustrates me, along with these names: Iae, Ieô, sons of Sabaôth, in the name of the great God let him shut up Katanikotaêl. Then let him wash the laurel-leaves in water, and sprinkle his house with the water, from within to the outside. And at once I retreat." (The opposing angel seems to be Sabaoth.)

32. "If any one will write on paper these names of angels, [. . .] and having folded it up, wear it round his neck or against his ear, I at once retreat and dissipate the drunken fit."

33. "If you would imprison me, chop up coriander and smear it on the lips, reciting the following charm . . . And at once I retreat."

34. But if any one will say to the afflicted into their ear these names, three times over, into the right ear: 'Iudarizê, Sabunê, Denôê,' I at once retreat."

35. "If any one write down the names of thy sires, Solomon, on paper and place it in the ante-chamber of his house, I retreat thence. And the legend written shall be as follows . . . And I at once retire."

36. "If any one write on paper: 'Phnunoboêol, depart Nathath, and touch thou not the neck,' I at once retreat."

37. "If any one write on the leaf of a book: 'Sphênêr, Rafael, retire, drag me not about, flay me not,' and tie it round his neck, I at once retreat."

38. "If any one write on paper: 'Rorêx, do thou pursue Alath,' and fasten it round his neck, I at once retire."

39. "If any one write on a plate of tin the words . . . and fasten it round the loins, I at once retreat."

40. "If one engrave on copper material, taken from a ship which has missed its anchorage, [these words] . . . and fasten it round the loin, I at once retreat."

41. Apparently a demon of the ravages of old age.

42. "If one write: 'Allazoôl, pursue Enenuth,' and tie the paper round him, I at once retreat."

43. "If one exorcise me in wine, sweet-smelling and unmixed by the eleventh aeon, and say . . . , then give it to the patient to drink, and I at once retreat."

44. "If one write 'Kokphnêdismos,' and bind it round the temples, I at once retire."

45. "If one powder into pure oil three seeds of laurel and smear it on, saying . . . , at once I retreat."

46. "If in eating fish one has swallowed a bone, then he must take a bone from the fish and cough, and at once I retreat."

47. "If you throw salt, rubbed in the hand, into oil and smear it on the patient, saying . . . , I at once retire."

48. Perhaps associated with crib death other infant illness? It could also indicate something akin to colds or pneumonia.

49. "And if any one write on fig-leaves 'Lycurgos,' taking away one letter at a time, and write it, reversing the letters, I retire at once. 'Lycurgos, ycurgos, kurgos, yrgos, gos, os.'" This is just like the old "Abracadabra" formula, which was used in the same way to banish sickness and fevers.

50. "Therefore I am frustrated by Alpha and Omega, if written down."

51. "Therefore, the eye much-suffering, if it be drawn, frustrates me."

52. "If a man write on the front-door of his house: 'Mêltô, Ardu, Anaath,' I flee from that place." This seems similar to the concept of the Passover as described in Exodus.

53. Aleister Crowley, instead, chose to add the bornless invocation as a preliminary to the goetic operation. The Greek/Gnostic origins of the invocation certainly bring it closer to the goetic tradition, if we count the similar influence on the *Testament of Solomon*. Plus, the invocation itself is a preliminary to a Gnostic exorcism rite, thus associating it even closer to the essence of *Goetia*.

54. We do know their planets, but these do not seem to help establish which zodiacal signs are involved. The planets listed (in the form of the feudal rank of each spirit) simply do not align properly with the thirty-six faces.

55. However, there is a conflict here. Amaymon may be Gaap's king, but Gaap is also said to ". . . appeareth when the Sun is in some of the Southern Signs . . ." which would also put him under the rulership of the southern king Goap.

56. Actually, the full description is: ". . . and appeareth in the form of an Angel with a lion's head, goose's feet and a hare's tail." This sounds suspiciously like various Gnostic images of the Demiurgos IAO often found on seal rings.

57. Just above, I asked the question of how the zodiacal signs should be assigned to the directions of the circle. Perhaps here, with Asmoday, we have a clue. His three heads seem to encompass the first three signs of the zodiac (even though they are misarranged in the description), and we know that he rules in the east. Therefore, if any attribution of signs to the circle can be assumed for the *Goetia*, it may be to place Aries in the east and continue counterclockwise to Pisces, as with an astrological chart.

58. This magickal image does appear similar to those for Mars, and the functions of the spirit: ". . . to build high towers, castles and cities, and to furnish them with armour and to afflict men for several days with wounds . . ." seem very Martial as well. At the same time, there is a hint of Saturn in the pale-colored horse. Yet, Sabnach is a marquis, making him a Lunar spirit.

59. See previous note. This also strikes me as a very Martial—or perhaps even Saturnine—image. The description of Vine's powers tends toward Saturn: ". . . to discover things hidden, witches, and things present, past, and to come . . . will build towers, throw down great stone walls, make waters rough with storms, etc." Yet Vine is a king or earl—meaning Sol or Mars.

60. See note 57. Here is a repeat of the same imagery. While it is exciting to see the pattern repeated and confirmed, this also posses a further problem. We now have two demons claiming influence from the *same* three signs, even further throwing off any possibility of a clean match between these seventy-two demons and the decans.

61. Alloces is a duke, making him a creature of Venus. Yet, this is a magickal image of Mars if I've ever seen one.

62. A rather odd way to say "from 3 pm until dawn the next day."

63. Could the "dawning of the day" here be a reference to midnight? If so, it would be a rare example of magickal timing.

64. Perhaps this should be, ". . . and at night, if the King. . ."

65. This seems to be a large part of the assumptions behind the *Abramelin* operation, which summons and binds Satan and the other infernal powers in order to grant the aspirant power over the world of nature.

66. Interestingly, as in the previous note, this is also the logic followed by *Abramelin*.

67. One notable exception is the simple circle described by the *Key of Solomon the King* to consecrate talismans. See chapter 10.

68. In other words, a line in which there is no starting point nor ending point.

69. *Key of Solomon the King*, Book I, Chapter 2.

70. *Key of Solomon the King,*, Book I, Chapter 3.

71. *Forbidden Rites*, pp. 175–6.

72. According to Orthodox Christian tradition, this meeting-point of the four Elements is where creation is possible. Hebrew Midrashim depicts Yahweh forming Adam from dust gathered from the four parts of the world. (See Ginzberg's *Legends of the Bible*.)

73. These are not the names of the Seven Heavens.

74. Counterclockwise, that is, if one uses the Hebrew characters, which are written right to left. If one chooses the English transliterations, it would allow the circle to flow clockwise. That may rest easier in the mind of the typical modern mage, who generally tries to cast circles sunwise.

75. See Donald Kraig's *Modern Magick* for instructions on making a magick mirror for goetic evocation.

76. In our case, previously given.

77. Consider the Sigillum Dei Ameth of the Enochian system, over which the angels promised no evil influence could cross. The crystal ball rested at the heart of this circular talisman.

78. It is perhaps significant that this does not symbolize bringing the entity to our own third dimension. This is a big clue to us that no physical manifestation was ever expected by the grimoiric masters. The spirits are skryed instead.

79. I doubt that the names themselves are intended to be spoken along with the prayers.

80. Much thanks to Ben Rowe for making this material available to all on the World Wide Web. (In Memory) http://www.hermetic.com/browe_mem/ .

81. The *H* does not make any sense here. Perhaps it is a corruption from the Hebrew for Saturn: *Shabathai*.

82. The *K* makes no sense in this case. The Hebrew for Jupiter is Zadek, or Tzedek.

83. See chapter 10 concerning this method of using the goetic talismans.

84. It occurs to me that the Afro-Cuban use of Omiero might have an application here, as I described in chapter 4 concerning sacrifice.

85. Add. MS 10862.

86. Book I, Chapter 3.

87. Ibid.

88. Book II, Chapter 7.

89. I note that this very line appears in several Babylonian exorcisms, one of which I quoted previously. The Chaldean descent of the magick that the grimoires claim appears to be true.

90. When the master faces east.

91. Practitioners of traditional Wicca will be familiar with this practice, and this text is its origin.

92. CLM 849.

93. *Forbidden Rites*, p. 174.

94. Ibid., p. 171.

95. Ibid., p. 51.

96. I assume this is related to the four zodiac signs that mark the changes of the seasons.

97. This is likely intended to be a pentagram, though it is hard to be sure either way.

98. Though the text suggests inscribing the name and seal with blood or "using a perfume agreeable to the spirit." This latter is probably a reference to making ink of lampblack collected from incense smoke.

99. Interestingly, the same seven conjurations are given in the *Munich Handbook of Necromancy* in Latin, and are reproduced as such in Kiekhefer's *Forbidden Rites*, pp. 296–301.

100. Note that the spirits of the days of the week do not generally possess such negative characteristics. These are the spirits of Saturn, the planet associated with restriction and death. Compare these functions with other functions of Saturn in this book.

101. See chapter 10 concerning magickal images.

102. The four cardinal directions.

103. *The Book of Abramelin* also makes use of a plate of silver, though not in relation to a magickal book.

104. Or, "not intended."

105. Typical procedure. See chapter 7.

106. Similar to the *Goetia*.

Afterword

Since the time of their creation 400+ years ago, the grimoires have been viewed as dauntingly complex systems of ritual magick. That was due in large part to the manner in which the medieval authors chose to write; scattering instructions throughout the manuscripts, leaving out important information that was considered "given," using alchemical, astrological, and occult jargon (not to mention writing in Latin, Hebrew, and other languages), and similar tactics to confuse the curious. Mystical seekers of the modern age tend to feel that these rites are impractical for the typical urban occultist.

In fact, most grimoires only dedicate a single short chapter, if not two or three, to explain how the mage should strive to live day to day. They do insist that one live as an upstanding, honest, humane individual. To do otherwise would turn away the celestial beings with whom one is attempting to communicate. (See chapter 7 concerning this subject.) Medieval and Renaissance magickal literature is noted for its insistence on right living, owing very largely to its Judaic and Christian origins.

However, once the grimoires are reorganized and explained in modern English, much of the confusion associated with the medieval texts falls away. They are manuals intended to lead Westerners experiencing the shamanic vocation into contact with the angels and spirits of nature. As I have stated previously, the rites presented are generally intended solely to establish initial contact with the entities. After the basic tools and vestments have been made, the books and talismans consecrated, and the various entities contacted, the standard use of the magick is much less complicated. It is my hope that this simplicity has been communicated in the preceding chapters. Yet, at the same time, I hope I have communicated the dedication it takes to achieve the magick in the first place.

In this light, the complexity and involvement of the rites suddenly become less frightening. It may take months to prepare a single evocation, but having done it once, it need never be performed for that spirit again. For example, the rite of Abramelin is a one-shot deal. The Enochian system instructs one to perform a nineteen-day summoning of *all* of the Watchtower angels, after which (apparently) one must put away the linen robe and book of invocations, never to use them again. Even the *Goetia* is based upon the principle of binding the spirits to brass vessels so that they will be easily at hand.

The information given in chapter 12 on practical spirit summoning has not been as complete as that given for contacting angels in chapter 8. This has not been done to "protect" the reader by withholding information. Quite the contrary; this book contains, dispersed throughout its pages, all of the information one might need for goetic conjuration. If the student has followed the procedures outlined in this book from beginning to end, and made proper contact with his angelic guardians, then the art of spirit conjuration should present little problem.

I have also left the information sketchy in chapter 12 because chapter 8 contains more than enough information on its own. Like King Solomon in the *Testament*, one should not attempt to exorcise the spirits without first gaining contact with the angels whom govern them. The secrets of how to summon and bind infernal spirits are an aspect of the sacred magick, the mysteries taught to the mage-shaman directly by the angels and from no other source. As *The Book of Abramelin* states:

> [Further] advice may be scarcely necessary for the most part, since I have already explained unto you all things necessary to be done; and also seeing that your Guardian Angel will have sufficiently instructed you in all that you should do. [. . .] But your Angel will already have instructed you how to convoke them, and will have sufficiently impressed it on your heart. (Book II, Chapter 14, "Concerning the Convocation of the Spirits)

While this refers specifically to the guardian angel, the concept also applies in our case. One must first make contact with the angels who govern the spirits and ask them how to go about constraining the creatures of the infernal and natural realms. If necessary, one should follow the example of King Solomon and invoke the ruling angel set over each conjured spirit, to set his seal upon the demon and enforce the taking of the oath of loyalty.

This book has focused primarily upon the shamanic nature and roots of the grimoiric traditions. We have discussed shamanism as far back as the tribes of Siberia (the originators of the term "shaman"), into the biblical prophets, Arabic and Sufi traditions, and even some surprising insights into Afro-Cuban practice. All of these subjects bear some relationship to a study of the magickal processes outlined by the medieval grimoires.

We have also covered the basics of astrology, without which the grimoires simply do not exist. *Merkavah* mysticism (*Heckaloth*) was discussed, and we have touched upon many important Gnostic and Neoplatonic concepts. Finally, I have attempted to present the priestly (or temple) tradition that is so important to the literature, including its particularly Christian spin, while highlighting the fact that these texts are *not* a product of the political body we call the "medieval Holy Roman Empire." (Quite the contrary, the Solomonic and other manuscripts of this genre were in direct opposition to that empire. They, and the clerical and intellectual cultures who gave them birth, were the reason for the institution of the early Inquisitions, and they were its first targets.)

However, there are also other important lines of study which we didn't cover such as alchemy, Qabalah, gematria, geomancy; and we merely touched upon aspects of Neoplatonism. It has not been my intention to minimize their influence upon the Solomonic and other grimoiric literature. They were set aside only temporarily in order to focus upon what I considered to be a neglected area of the grimoires' mystical foundation. Taking the information contained in these pages as a starting point, further study into *all* of the above-mentioned areas will open the medieval texts to even further understanding.

Bibliography

Albright, William. *Yahweh and the Gods of Canaan: An Historical Analysis of Two Contrasting Faiths.* n.p.: Eisenbrauns, 1990.

Allegro, John Marco. *The Sacred Mushroom and the Cross: a Study of the Nature and Origins of Christianity Within the Fertility Cults of the Ancient Near East.* Garden City, NY: Doubleday & Co., 1970.

Armstrong, Karen. *A History of God: The 4000-Year Quest of Judaism, Christianity and Islam.* New York: Ballantine Books, 1994.

Barrett, Francis. *The Magus: A Complete System of Occult Philosophy.* New York: Citadel Press, 1995 (1801).

Bennet, Chris. "When Smoke Gets In My I." *Cannabis Canada,* April 1995.

———. "The Scythians, High Planes Drifters." *Cannabis Canada,* July 1995.

———. "Kaneh Bosm: The Hidden Story of Cannabis in the Old Testament." *Cannabis Canada,* May/June 1996.

———. *Green Gold the Tree of Life: Marijuana in Magic & Religion,* (with Lynn Osburn. Judy Osburn), 1995

Betz, Hans Deiter (ed.). *The Greek Magical Papyri in Translation: Including the Demotic Spells: Texts.* Chicago: University of Chicago Press, 1996.

Budge, E. A. Wallis. *The Egyptian Book of the Dead: (The Papyrus of Ani) Egyptian Text Transliteration and Translation.* New York: Dover Publications, Inc., 1967 (1895).

———. *Egyptian Magic,* Citadel Pr, (Reissue Edition October 2000).

Burton, Richard Francis (trans.), A. S. Byatt (Introduction). *The Arabian Nights: Tales from a Thousand and One Nights (Modern Library Classics).* Modern Library, 2001.

Butler, Elizabeth M. *Ritual Magic.* University Park, PA: Pennsylvania State University Press, 1998.

———.-*The Fortunes of Faust (Magic in History Series).* University Park, PA: Pennsylvania State University Press, 1998.

Casaubon, Meric (ed.). *A True and Faithful Relation of What Passed for Many Years Between Dr. John Dee and Some Spirits*. New York: Magickal Childe Publishing, Inc., 1992 (1659).

Cicero, Chic and Sandra Tabatha. *Self Initiation Into the Golden Dawn Tradition: A Complete Curriculum of Study for Both the Solitary Magician and the Working Magical Group*. St. Paul, MN: Llewellyn Publications, 1998.

———. *Secrets of a Golden Dawn Temple*. St. Paul, MN: Llewellyn Publications, 1995.

Crowley, Aleister (ed.). *The Goetia: The Lesser Key of Solomon the King, Clavicula Salomonis Regis. Translated by Samuel Liddel MacGregor Mathers*. York Beach, ME: Samuel Weiser Inc., 1995.

Cunningham, Scott. *The Complete Book of Incense, Oils and Brews*. St. Paul, MN: Llewellyn Publications, 1997.

Dalley, Stephanie (ed.). *Myths from Mesopotamia: Creation, the Flood, Gilgamesh, and Others*. Oxford, UK: Oxford University Press, 1998.

Davidson, Gustav. *A Dictionary of Angels: Including the Fallen Angels*. New York: The Free Press (division of Macmillan, Inc.), 1967.

Davila, James R. "Heckalot Literature and Shamanism." World Wide Web, *Mediator Figures in the Biblical World at the Divinity School of the University of St. Andrews*, (http://www.st-andrews.ac.uk/~www_sd/mediators.html), 1998. (First published in the *Society of Biblical Literature 1994 Seminar Papers* Atlanta, Ga.: Scholars Press, 1994, 767–89.)

DeKorne, Jim. *Psychedelic Shamanism: The Cultivation, Preparation, and Use of Psychotropic Plants*. Port Townsend, WA: Loompanics Unlimited, 1994.

Eliade, Mircea. *Shamanism: Archaic Techniques of Ecstasy*. Bollingen Series LXXVI, n.p.: Princeton University Press, 1972.

Fanger, Claire (ed.). *Conjuring Spirits: Texts and Traditions of Medieval Ritual Magic*. University Park, PA: Pennsylvania State University Press, 1998.

Farber, Phil. *FutureRitual: Magick for the 21st Century*. Chicago: Eschaton Books, 1997.

Ginzberg, Louis. *Legends of the Bible*. Philadelphia—Jerusalem: The Jewish Publication Society, 1992.

Green, Miranda J. *Dictionary of Celtic Myth and Legend*. New York: Thames and Hudson, 1992.

Gunkel, Hermann. *The Legends of Genesis: The Biblical Saga and History*. New York: Schocken Books, 1964.

Hamilton, Edith. *Mythology, Timeless Tales of Gods and Heroes*. Boston: Mentor Publishing, 1953.

Heidel, Alexander. *The Babylonian Genesis; The Story of the Creation*. Chicago: University of Chicago Press, 1963

———. *The Gilgamesh Epic and Old Testament Parallels*. Chicago: University of Chicago Press, 1963.

Henson, Mitch (ed.). *Lemegeton: The Complete Lesser Key of Solomon*. Jacksonville, FL: Metatron Books, 1999.

Isolation Tank Experiment, The. World Wide Web, (http://www.garage.co.jp/lilly/experimentx.html).

James, Geoffrey. *The Enochian Magick of Dr. John Dee: The Most Powerful System of Magick in Its Original Unexpurgated Form*. St. Paul, Minnesota: Llewellyn Publications, 1994.

Jewish Storytelling Coalition. *There is a Story Told . . .* World Wide Web, (http://www.ultranet.com/~jewish/story.html), 63 Gould Road, Waban, MA, 02168, 1996.

Kaplan, Aryeh. *Meditation and Kabbalah*. n.p.: Red Wheel/Weiser, 1989.

Kieckhefer, Richard. *Forbidden Rites: A Necromancer's Manual of the Fifteenth Century*. University Park, PA: Pennsylvania State University Press, 1998.

Kraig, Donald Michael. *Modern Magick: Thirteen Lessons in the High Magickal Arts.* St. Paul, MN: Llewellyn Publications, 1993 (1988).

Laurence, Richard (trans.) *The Book of Enoch the Prophet: Translated from an Ethiopic MS. In the Bodleian Library . . .* San Diego: Wizards Bookshelf, 1995.

Laycock, Donald C. *The Complete Enochian Dictionary: A Dictionary of the Angelic Language as Revealed to Dr. John Dee and Edward Kelley.* York Beach, ME: Samuel Weiser Inc., 1994.

Layton, Bentley. *The Gnostic Scriptures.* Garden City, NY: Doubleday, 1995.

Leary, Timothy. *The Psychedelic Experience: A Manual Based on the Tibetan Book of the Dead.* New York: Citadel Press, 1995.

Leitch, Aaron. "The Ancient Gods and Neopaganism." World Wide Web: *Paradigm Shift Magazine,* (http://members.aol.com/para93/), Fall 1998.

———. "A Discourse on the Enochian Watchtowers." Chicago, IL: *The Terminal Journal,* Eschaton Productions, Inc., Spring 1998.

———. "Lilith: From Demoness to Dark Goddess." London: *Pagan Dawn: The Journal of the Pagan Federation,* (Samhain) Winter 2000.

———. "The Modern Western Occult Tradition." World Wide Web: *Paradigm Shift Magazine,* (http:// members. aol.com/para93/), Spring 1999.

Mathers, S. L. MacGregor (trans.). *The Book of the Sacred Magic of Abramelin the Mage.* New York: Dover Publications, Inc., 1975 (1900).

———. (trans.) *The Key of Solomon the King (Clavicula Solomonis).* York Beach, ME: Samuel Weiser Inc., 1972.

——— (trans.) *The Grimoire of Armadel.* York Beach, ME: Samuel Weiser Inc., 1995.

Myers, Stewart. *Between the Worlds.* St. Paul, MN: Llewellyn Publications, 1995.

Patai, Raphael. *The Hebrew Goddess.* n.p.: Wayne State University Press, 1990.

Peterson, Joseph (ed.). *Twilit Grotto: Esoteric Archives.* CD-ROM, (www.avesta.org). P.O. Box 384, Kasson, MN, 55944.

——— .(ed.). *Mysteriorum Libri Quinti: or, Five Books of Mystical Exercises of Dr. John Dee.* Dyfed, Wales: Magnum Opus Hermetic Sourceworks, 1985

Pritchard, James. B. (ed.). *Ancient Near Eastern Texts: Relating to the Old Testament.* n.p.: Princeton University Press, 1969.

Regardie, Israel. *The Middle Pillar: Edited and Annotated with New Material by Chic Cicero and Sandra Tabatha Cicero.* St. Paul, MN: Llewellyn Publications, 1998.

Rowe, Ben. "Classics of Magick." World Wide Web, *Norton's Imperium,* (http://w3.one.net/~browe/index.htm), 2001.

Schwartz, Howard (editor), Uri Shulevitz (Illustrator). *Lilith's Cave: Jewish Tales of the Supernatural.* Reprint edition, Oxford Univ Pr (Trade), 1991.

Smith, Mark S. *The Early History of God: Yahweh and the Other Deities in Ancient Israel.* HarperCollins College Division.

"Stories of the Baal Shem Tav." World Wide Web, *The Hasidic Stories Homepage,* (http://www.storypower.com/hasidic/stories1.html), 2001.

Thompson, R. Campbell. *The Devils and Evil Spirits of Babylonia*. New York: AMS Press, 1973.

———. *Semitic Magic : Its Origins and Development*. York Beach, ME: Samuel Weiser, 2000.

Tyson, Donald. *Enochian Magic for Beginners: The Original System of Angel Magic*. St. Paul, MN: Llewellyn Publications, 1997.

———. (ed.). *Three Books of Occult Philosophy: Written by Henry Conelius Agrippa of Nettesheim, Completely Annotated, with Modern Commentary*. St. Paul, MN: Llewellyn Publications, 1995.

———. *New Millennium Magic : A Complete System of Self-Realization* (Llewellyn's High Magick series). St. Paul, MN: Llewellyn Publications.

Waite, Arthur Edward. *The Book of Black Magic*. (or: *The Book of Ceremonial Magic*). York Beach, ME: Samuel Weiser Inc., 1972.

Wilson, Robert Anton. *Prometheus Rising (Introduced by Israel Regardie)*. Tempe, AZ: New Falcon Publications, 1983.

Ishtar Rising (or, Why the Goddess Went to Hell and What to Expect Now That She's Returning). Santa Monica, CA: New Falcon Publications, 1994 (1989).

Sex and Drugs. Phoenix, AZ: New Falcon Publications, 1987 (1973).

Woolfolk, Joanna Martine. *The Only Astrology Book You'll Ever Need*. Lanhan, MD: Scarborough House/Publishers, 1990 (1982).

Yates, Frances. *The Rosicrucian Enlightenment*. London: Routledge, 1993.

www.google.com. *Google*. Internet search engine.

Illustration Bibliography

The bulk of sigils and talismans used throughout this text were hand drawn by Aaron Leitch. They were also edited in digital format by Aaron Leitch and Steve Kinney.

The photos of the Sigillum Emeth, burin, and aspergillum were provided by Aaron Leitch, and scanned/edited by Steve Kinney. The photo of the *Pauline Art* table of practice was provided by Carrie Mikell, and scanned/edited by Steve Kinney.

The photos of pages from the Notary Arts are from an unfinished manuscript by Carrie Mikell, "The Ars Notoria." They are digitally enhanced versions of original pencil sketches. These pages are intended to have text included, but this is missing from the photos. The photos were provided by Carrie Mikell, and scanned/edited by Steve Kinney.

The icons from the book of Revelation (the Conquering Christ and the Lamb with the Book of Seven Seals) were created by Carrie Mikell for use in *Secrets of the Magickal Grimoires*. They were scanned and digitally edited by Steve Kinney.

All public domain images (the Vision of Ezekiel, Gabriel and Zachariah, the Fiery Furnace, Soul of the World, Mage in Oratory, Enochian Holy Table, Mighty Angel, Sigils and Plates from *The Magus*, Mage Summoning, Solomon and Belial, Asmodee Contract, Ashtaroth, and the Kircher Tree of Life) are provided by the owner/moderator of the Solomonic Mailing List. See http://groups.yahoo.com/group/solomonic/ for files, photos, links and discussion related to Solomonic magick and anything else covered in *Secrets of the Magickal Grimoires*.